K.A. SILVA

Theo smiled thinly at the older woman giving her the stink-eye. The woman squinted at Theo's dolls, then frowned at the shock of Theo's orange hair falling into her eyes. Or maybe the biddy disapproved of her nose piercing. Or her multiple tiny silver and copper pentagram earrings.

"What are these supposed to be?" the woman asked, jerking her chin toward Theo's dolls.

"Dark and pretty things," Theo replied.

The woman frowned, then turned her attention to a different artist's table filled with traditional ceramic-headed dolls in ball gowns. Theo liked the gowns but felt the expressionless faces of the figures, with glassy eyes and stitched-up mouths, were far creepier than her own tiny faelings. Those dolls were frozen, silenced, soulless. She'd been given similar dolls as a young girl. Each one ended up crammed in the back of her closet, and she swore she could hear them whispering in the middle of the night. The first stuffie she'd made, a fierce hippo, was intended to guard against those sinister things.

This wasn't her first art doll show, or even the largest she'd ever attended, but this one had a reputation for attracting wealthy collectors, and the judges were also well-regarded pros. Theo posted her dolls online, of course, but even her best work tended to get lost among the thousands of Etsy dealers and doll sites. Nothing beat appealing to a potential buyer in person. Even if the average collector preferred traditional baby dolls or sock monkeys, there would always be a few people attracted to more offbeat designs. She could ensure the odd looks she received while waiting for the one or two people who would appreciate her art. Right now people would be thinking ahead to the winter holidays, looking for gifts, so she'd presented in a smaller gallery last weekend in Milwaukee; this weekend here in Spring Green. Nearly mixed up the two and would've headed the wrong way last Saturday had she not double-checked her emails. Organized, tidy life was not her forte. These dolls, delicate, unique, and carefully crafted, represented the sum of her skills.

She'd give anything to be more widely recognized on her own merits, for her art to find its own niche. Her parents' toy company didn't want her weird little fae. Which was absolutely the point—shaking the birthright she didn't want.

Dorothea Theodora Van Baum had money in the bank from licensing some dress designs to Van Baum Dollmakers back in her teens. Theo, as she preferred to be known, designed and crafted strange little dolls unlikely to ever be mass-marketed.

She sighed, sitting down again, and offered up a quick prayer. Holding her goddess pendant in her left hand, she closed her eyes. *Goddess, let your beauty shine through my art in all your names. I ask Circe to help me transform base things into beautiful creatures. I ask Maab for a dose of laughter and grace, no matter what happens today.*

Her table held an entire landscape of oddities. She'd crafted tiny autumnal trees from driftwood and moss, arranging them on a tattered bit of old carpet resembling the brown, dry grass of October. Rough-edged rocks, sandstone and slate, created a mountain and a cave. The shoreline of a tray of sand met molded hard silicone ocean waves. Theo's delicate, carefully crafted dolls inhabited every nook and cranny.

The mermaids with their bony-ridged tails and seaweed hair beckoned from the sea toward sleek otters in fisherman's garb on the beach. Trolls crouched in the mountain cave. Cloven-hooved satyrs with the curling horns of mountain goats pranced upon the rocks. All these were under six inches tall, made of felt and fabrics, hair, beads, and molded baked clay. The forest folk, however, were the most detailed. Theo spent countless hours on each of these, and she hoped they'd win her an influential patron or two, if not the grand prize.

Theo's inspiration for the Fair Folk came from Arthur Rackham's drawings and her own nightmares. Spindly arms ended in thorny fingers, autumn leaves for hair, misshapen noses or coldly beautiful china masks hiding their true faces. She'd brought seven of her best faery dolls. Not one of them gave a damn whether humans believed in them or not. They were separate from humanity, coldly grinning or utterly expressionless. Theo's friend Cassie declared them "evil, alien little things," and refused to accept one when offered. Theo made a witch doll for Cassie instead, but her own preference was for these.

In the oldest tales, faeries were not kindly or interested at all in the welfare of humans. Theo didn't much like humanity either. People could be real assholes. Like that judgey woman just now. No, Theo didn't make cute felted fluffy things or the folksy primitives that were all the rage.

Hers were detailed enough they might even possess souls.

She'd whispered spells over each and every one of them, asking for the guise of life to shine from every beaded eye. Prayed for some spark of magic to inhabit each. Whether they attracted or repulsed people wasn't important, as long as she was confident each was as unique and amazing as she could make them.

An elderly woman with immaculately styled long gray hair approached Theo's table. Her ID badge was pinned to her burnt-orange blazer with an ornate, bejeweled brooch in the shape of a bee. Close behind her followed a middle-aged lady with dark curly hair, wearing a floral-patterned skirt and blazer a bit too tight for her generous midsection. The lady would've been lovely if she'd worn something more flowing, less constrictive. As it was, her style mimicked the severe, close-tailored older woman's. The way she hovered just behind the elderly one immediately made Theo sad.

Theo smiled at the floral lady, standing and smoothing down her wispy, layered skirts. These didn't look like the patrons she hoped to attract, but you never could tell.

"What have we here? Goblins?" Severe Lady asked.

"The Fair Folk," Theo corrected.

Severe Lady bent to study the woodland folk frozen in mid-dance. "Faeries? I've never seen any like these."

"Tinkerbell was a myth used to sell kids' toys," Theo said.

Floral Lady darted a nervous glance between them. "They're very unique, aren't they?" She reached for one of the dolls. "May I?"

At least this woman seemed more genuinely interested than her companion. "Gently, okay?" Theo requested.

Floral Lady nodded, and carefully plucked one of the fae dolls, a courtier with glittering beetle carapaces for armor, from the forest scene. "Are those made of plastic or metal?" she asked.

"Japanese beetles."

Floral Lady recoiled, and quickly set the doll back down.

Theo grinned. "They're invasive. Doing my part to eradicate them."

Severe Lady picked the fae courtier up, turning it to see all sides. Theo stood straighter, crossing her arms. She included something unique in every doll design, and insects or bits of taxidermy worked well for creepy little faeries. *Wait 'til these pantsuit-wearing chicks notice the bird skull on the Queen of the Dance.*

"It's certainly unusual," Severe Lady said finally, setting the doll down, "but I'm not sure how broad its appeal would be." She fixed cold blue eyes on Theo.

Theo brushed her hair off her face. "Yeah, I don't make mass-market crap. Takes a certain kind of person to appreciate my art."

Severe Lady's sharply-defined lips curled upwards. "I'm sure it does. Well. Good luck to you." She strolled to the next table, exclaiming in pleasure at a grouping of primitive Raggedy Anns. Floral Lady scurried after the older woman without so much as an apologetic wince.

"Joyless prole," Theo muttered, adjusting the position of the courtier.

The exhibitor at the other end of the table, who'd silently watched the whole exchange, shook her head. Her dolls were all felted animals, displayed on shiny green fabric. They were fairly cute, if traditional. She came closer and asked quietly, "You know those two are judges, right?"

"Shit." Theo's hope sank, watching the ladies coo over the yarn-haired dolls. "Seriously?"

"Yep. I think they're wanting dolls that fit the show theme more."

Theo gestured at her tiny trees. "Uh, yeah. 'Autumn Nostalgia.'"

"Maybe they're thinking more along the lines of childhood favorites," the felt-animal crafter said. She smiled. "I think yours are really creative, though. I've never seen any like them."

Theo sighed. "People want country primitive. Not weird."

"Well, clearly you put a lot of work into these. I hope you do well anyway, no matter what Mrs. Brecken or Molly Gunter think." The felter nodded at the judges, who were now several tables away, examining a display of restored antique baby dolls with staring glass eyes. Now *those* were the creepiest things here. The felter offered her hand to Theo. "I'm Jennifer, by the way."

"Hi. Theo." They smiled. Theo indicated the little animals. "Those are pretty cute. I really like the armadillo."

"He rolls!" Jennifer demonstrated how the doll could be curled into a ball with its glued-on clay plates jointed like a real armadillo's, and gave it a roll across the table.

"Awww. Super cute."

"I think yours are amazing. But I have to tell ya, I wouldn't want one in my house. Is that a real bug head?"

"Wasp. Yep. I call her Clarisse." Theo stroked the silken gown of that particular fae lady, who clutched a wand tipped with amethyst in her insectoid arms. "Faeries were never meant to be friendly, or like humans at all. In the oldest stories they have their own agenda, their own politics."

"Like Grimm's faery tales? Darker than what you'd find in a children's book."

Theo nodded. "Exactly. Anyway, yours are adorable, and I hope you do well. Be nice if one of us gets a chance at the grand prize."

As the day wore on, a couple garbed in Neo-Victorian clothes stopped and exclaimed over Theo's creatures, but were plainly dismayed at the prices. Theo offered to sell them one of the satyrs at a discount, and after some discussion they agreed. She smiled after them, happy at least one doll found a good home.

Maybe if she'd finished making the Oz character dolls in time to bring them, those would've sold better. Or maybe not. Theo had reread most of the L. Frank Baum books over the past month, both her own well-worn favorites and a few she'd borrowed from her friend Cassie. She planned a whole line of dolls based on the characters, but with a dark and original twist to make them creepier for Halloween. With back-to-back shows the past couple weeks, no time for crafting.

She snorted, watching the judges exclaim over a cutesy felt teddy bear. Yeah, this was the wrong crowd for her designs.

When the contest results were announced that afternoon, Theo didn't even get an honorable mention. A couple of other makers looked as disgruntled as Theo felt. They'd brought dolls with abstract faces, odd shapes, art glass and found objects. Interesting enough as artworks, but they had no soul. Nothing leapt from their eyes and begged Theo to touch them, talk to them. Still, she nodded to the artists as they all wandered from the prize table back to their own displays to pack up. Clearly these judges didn't care for anything nontraditional. The two-thousand in cash first prize would've ensured a comfy, happy Yule this year. Oh, well, she still had some in savings.

Theo wrote the judges' names down in a spiral notebook. Damned if she'd enter anything anywhere these snobs judged again.

Jennifer gave her a sympathetic smile. "It sucks you didn't win anything."

"No big deal," Theo said. "Hey, how much for the armadillo?"

Once all her dolls were carefully wrapped in tissue and packed in sturdy plastic storage containers, with the new armadillo tucked among them, Theo borrowed a hand truck to lug everything back to her car. Jennifer stopped her. "Hey, some of us are going out to a supper club, you want to come with?"

"Nah, thanks though."

"Are you sure?" Jennifer gestured over at one of the stuffed animal artists. One of their critters—a squirrel, if Theo recalled right—took third place. "Martina offered to buy a round of drinks."

"Thanks, but I have a ticket for the Darkside tour at the House on the Rock tonight."

"Oh. That's the place with the suspended room, right?" Jennifer shivered. "I can't do heights."

"Yeah, but that room isn't part of this tour. They do the place up real creepy for Halloween and it's even better than the standard daytime tour. I go every year," Theo explained.

She'd first visited this odd roadside attraction as a child. Her older brother Danny made fun of six-year-old Theo when the giant whale in the Heritage of the Sea hall frightened her, but it was so *big*. The leviathan reared up from the frozen fiberglass waves over two hundred feet, and no matter at what point she viewed it along the gallery circling the fierce display, it always seemed on the verge of coming to life to swallow her up as a snack. The rowboat splintered between its massive jaws didn't help. She'd never been to the ocean and never wanted to. Legends of slimy beasts under the choppy waves of Lake Superior made for great inspiration, not so much for a happy time out on a boat with family determined to teach her how to catch a fish. She didn't even like eating fish.

All the rest of the House, however, was fair game. She loved the orchestra of mannequins in rubber masks, the Victorian musical dioramas playing awful morality tales for the price of a token, the excess and overwhelming presence of the amassed collections. Props beside genuine antiques, with neither labeled. A winding labyrinth of dollhouses, and another, larger one of entire church pipe organs taller than her parents' house.

And, of course, the carousel. Hundreds of hand-carved animals on parade with nary a horse to be found. She loved that well before she read the tales written about it. Easy to believe it was possible to climb aboard a snarling chimera of elegant mermaid and ride until she wound up somewhere Else. Some dark and magical land.

If, that is, riding the beasts was ever allowed. She'd tried once and been kicked out, as a rebellious, none-too-cautious teen. Tonight she'd simply stand and watch the wonderful spectacle.

Who needs a prize from a clique of old biddies, anyway? I'll stand right next to the carousel and enjoy it, that's prize enough. And maybe, if the tour guides aren't watching, I can sneak on board.

Cheered by this plan, Theo carted her unwanted dolls out to her car. The sun was nearing the horizon, red-orange light bathing the trees in an autumn conflagration. She'd grab dinner somewhere, something fast and greasy, then head up the highway to the House. The carousel waited, as did the self-playing instruments and the laughable taxidermied badgers. Everything dusty, everything the same as it had been for years. Everything over the top and too much. She loved all of its wonders, real or fake.

Her family understood her affection for the bizarre roadside attraction about as well as they did Theo herself. In past years, she'd visited with a friend or two, and her ex-boyfriend Mark came with her once, before they broke up. In fact, his snide running commentary throughout the entire tour of the place cemented doubts she was already having about their relationship. Anyone who couldn't just absorb the wonders of the House on the Rock and cheerfully accept all of its kitsch and quirks couldn't accept hers, either.

If she'd planned ahead, she could've asked some of her witchy friends to come along. By the time she thought to ask them, Gwyn and Adam had plans this weekend. Her friends had offered sympathy and given her the space she asked for, following her breakup with Mark. Her fault that she hadn't let them know she was ready to socialize again.

So, alone this year. Fine. She'd have a blast all by herself. Just her and a house full of bizarre artifacts. No crotchety judges, no sneering older brother or bewildered, fussy mother. The House was weirder than she was, and she could get happily lost among its over-the-top exhibits. Especially with the place in full Halloween drag, sporting skeletons everywhere, fake ghosts lurking in the shadows. It would be weird and wonderful, and she didn't need anyone with her to enjoy it.

Better to go alone than to suffer the company of anyone who didn't accept her.

Vowing to have a good time, she cranked up some horror surf rock and peeled out of the hotel parking lot. After all, Halloween was right around the corner. She wouldn't be much of a witch if she didn't go find some fun.

2

The Scarecrow never slept, but this night in particular weighed on him heavily. He paced his room hour after hour, watching the constellations traverse the silent sky, feeling as though some massive monster were crushing his chest. Over and over he checked his best court tunic for any straw poking through its forest-green weave. Made sure the new soft suede gloves which served for his hands were spotless. Adjusted his peaked hat of deepest indigo blue atop the molded burlap of his head, trying to decide the most pleasant angle.

Would she approve of the changes he'd made to his appearance? No more ragged straw sticking out of his sleeves or falling ungracefully out of his tunic when he stumbled. He'd even added sweetgrass to the straw stuffing his clothing, for a lovelier scent.

No more painted mouth incapable of bestowing a kiss. The finest tanners and tailors in Oz made his new head with a true nose and ears, eyes which could shut, lips and a tongue. Though still incapable of tasting anything, at least now he could appear less comical when engaged in deep conversation.

He'd cautiously asked Glinda for other enhancements as well. Anything, everything he could think of to be more like a living man for his heart's desire.

He'd considered all of it a great deal. Three years of unhappy yearning. A month ago, the Scarecrow sought the counsel of his dearest friend the Tin Woodman, Nick Chopper. In the second year of his advisory to the throne of Oz, Scarecrow was more miserable than when last the light of his life vanished in a swirl of magic.

"Are you not content with your lot, my friend?" Nick asked. "Your reputation as a wise and caring advisor to our Queen has spread to every corner of the land. You're much to be envied."

"I know," Scarecrow sighed.

Nick frowned mildly. "I heard you commanded an expansion to the Royal Library. Books procured from far and wide. Surely spending so much time improving your knowledge pleases you."

"To a point."

The nickel-plated woodsman, now Emperor of his own domain, cocked his head to one side and studied his friend so long, steam began creeping out of his head. Finally, he leaned back. "Ah."

"Ah?"

"Ah. I know what troubles you."

"Then please enlighten me, old friend! It's taken me so long to realize something is wrong with me, and yet longer to understand I don't know precisely what."

The plated man gave him a wistful smile. "You're heartsick."

"Me?" Scarecrow laughed, startled. "But I don't have a—"

Nick grabbed Scarecrow's shoulder in one firm hand and thrust his other inside the royal tunic the straw man wore. Scarecrow was too shocked to mount a protest. Nick yanked out a small, compacted ball of straw, peered at it closely, then shoved it back into the Scarecrow's chest.

"That was rude. If you weren't my friend—" Scarecrow began, but Nick cut him off.

"A heart. I suspected as much years ago when we first met." The metal man smiled. "You've never thought it of much consequence, but yes, you have one. And it's all knotted up in pain."

Scarecrow sighed. "I considered applying to the royal physician for help, but I'd assumed since I'm not a meat creature he would be of no use."

"This isn't a pain of meat or even of straw. Your spirit is sick."

The Scarecrow gave him a sharp glare. "Now that's insulting."

Nick sighed, shaking his head. "Would you listen? You came to me because deep down you know this has to do with your feelings. For *her*."

Scarecrow hadn't admitted this to anyone, especially himself, but as soon as Nick spoke the words, he felt their truth. He slumped. "I'm a fool. She's not coming back."

"She might."

"Why would she? She had to tend to her family. She's of marrying age. No doubt time for her to start a family of her own. I don't begrudge her that."

"Yes, you do."

Scarecrow stared at his friend in growing anger. "I understood perfectly well why she had to leave us! How could I possibly hold that against her? Twice she was thrown here by accident, and twice she went home, to people who need her more than we do."

"Would you stop saying *us* and *we* as if all the rest of us were walking around all gloomy, letting our straw fall out?" Nick scolded.

Scarecrow glared at him, self-consciously tucking a few loose strands of straw up under his hat.

Nick spoke softly. "You wish she would have stayed. For you."

Scarecrow wanted to deny it. Wanted to say something rude to his friend and stomp out as heavily as his straw feet were able. The sympathy in Nick's eyes stopped him. "What if I do," he grumbled. He stared at his hands. He'd taken to wearing old garden gloves again. Just as he had when he first met her.

"It would've been selfish of me to ask her to stay."

"But you're in pain."

"What of it?" Scarecrow snapped. "Being made of straw doesn't exempt me from the struggle of life."

Nick shook his head again. "You came here for advice, didn't you? So shut up and let me advise you for once. This is my territory and you damned well know it."

Morose, Scarecrow nodded. "Yes. Fine. Tell me how to destroy this longing well and good so I can be free of—"

"Go to her."

Scarecrow gaped. "I—go? How could I—but that doesn't—but how even—" Hearing the words tumbling out of him shamed him into shutting up. He took a deep, slow breath, letting the cool autumn air inside his straw-filled chest. "How?"

Nick shrugged. "Do you love her?"

Scarecrow clasped his hands together, squeezing his fingers all out of shape. After a long silence, he nodded. "She is my heart's desire," he whispered. "Foolish though I know that sounds."

Nick rose, clapping him on the shoulder. "The *how* is your problem, my friend. But I'm telling you, if you want this healed or killed, the only way to do it is to find her and tell her how you feel."

Impossible. How could he travel to her world, the Outside World that she called Kansas, so far beyond the desert no cartographer had ever mapped it? No talking scarecrows where she came from. No magic. Very likely even daring to set one boot in her world would render him insensible and mute.

She'd been seventeen when last in Oz. Time moved differently in her world. What if she'd found a husband already?

And yet.

What if she still thought of him?

Her embrace, after they'd survived some terrible danger. Her smile when he brought her sunflowers, nuts, apples. Anything and everything he could find which he hoped might please her, delight her, nourish her.

She'd let him carry her basket. Asked him to serve as her bed when they passed a cold night outside. Even though she wanted to sleep by the fire, and Lion was just as soft and warm, she'd taken Scarecrow's arm as her pillow, snuggled against his straw body. "Lion snores," she'd said, but he'd been so happy. Even though their little campfire terrified him.

She slept curled against him, and he was happy. All night spent awake and watchful, for her. Every crackle and pop of sap in the fire frightening him. He'd forced himself to remain as still as possible so as not to interrupt her sleep.

Anything for her.

So here he paced, in the longest night he could recall, a month after Nick gave him the advice which would forever change his life.

He kept checking out the open window. Dawn lagged. Mere hours now between himself and the woman who'd stolen his heart before he realized he possessed one.

Had he thought of absolutely everything? He patted his pockets. Yes.

Needle and thread in case his clothing ripped, so his straw wouldn't spill out. The small wooden box cleverly crafted by his friend Nick, with the emerald ring tucked securely inside. Just in case. His finest clothing and fresh straw.

When the sky at last lightened to pink, Scarecrow checked his appearance one last time in the mirror. The crisp peak of his new hat, the sleekness of new gloves and boots, the stylish long lines of his tunic and trousers. Blue eyes freshly painted in oils. Yes. This was as handsome as he could make himself. He hoped it would be good enough for her.

He gazed out over the glittering city as it awoke. Birds began timidly to chirp. He'd never see this again. Yet it didn't move him in the least.

All he could feel was hope and terror.

He hurried through the palace to a private reception parlor where the young ruler of Oz sometimes entertained important dignitaries. He wouldn't see Queen Ozma Tip today. A letter sat on her desk, waiting for her to find it later. Scarecrow torturously considered every single word in it before committing to ink, with his signature at the end. This wasn't fair to his Queen, nor to the many citizens who considered him a friend. The thought of having to stand through endless speeches of farewell, however, sounded likely to prey on his fears. His doubts.

No one should get the chance to talk him out of this.

Glinda the Good and Nick waited in the parlor, talking quietly. Both rose when Scarecrow came in. Nick smiled sadly at him.

"Are you ready, old friend?"

"I am," Scarecrow choked out.

He shouldn't be so frightened. Going forth into the Outside World was worrisome, to be sure, but *she* would be there. Somewhere.

If the Good Witch's spell worked.

If his love wanted him.

If he didn't collapse into an inanimate husk upon arrival, all magic sucked from his body by whatever terrible powers ruled that world.

He straightened his shoulders as much as he could. Cursed straw, always difficult to stand at his full lanky height. He should've asked for a wooden frame. Nick could've made him joints or something. Too late now. There hadn't really been time, anyway. Glinda sent a summons last night for him to be here at dawn, ready to leave.

Glinda glided daintily around the low table and plush chairs, her dress floating as if moved by a light wind no one else could feel. Scarecrow glanced into her eyes and immediately wished he hadn't.

The fae have old, old eyes. You didn't want to meet their gaze if you could help it. Her eyes burned like ancient coals that reached the smoking stage a few hundred years ago but weren't even close to dying out yet.

Her hair fluttered around her face, individual auburn tresses like vipers. One stroked his cheek. He flinched.

Glinda chuckled, low and musical. Scarecrow shivered. Nick took a careful step back, out of her direct line of sight. Scarecrow saw the woodman's hand slide down his hip and pause upon failing to find his axe hanging there.

Nobody liked doing business with Glinda. And she was relatively benevolent, as Oz witches went.

"Are you truly certain you wish to leave us, Scarecrow?" She smiled. "We will miss your singing. Such a lovely voice from a straw chest."

Eyes downcast, he nodded. "I haven't been at my best for some time. It would be foolish to continue on, pretending to be interested in court business, when I can't devote my brains fully to the work."

"He's heartsick," Nick spoke up. "This is something he needs to do."

Delicate, chilly fingers touched Scarecrow's chin and tilted his head up. He held still, feeling the prickle of her power all down his straw spine.

"And you accept that you may never return here? Once I have sent you away to the Outside Countries, we have no way of retrieving you, and they have no magic you could use to get back to us. With or without your delightful girl." Glinda stared into Scarecrow's eyes.

His throat had never felt dry before. Suddenly he understood the expression.

"I accept," he said. She gave a slow nod, and he dared add, "But are you sure this will work? This will take me to my heart's desire, prevent me from—unbeing?"

She smiled. "My spell is crafted and ready. You will arrive safely, near to your heart's desire. What happens then is up to you. Be warned, straw man." Her brow wrinkled briefly. "The spell will last until the next full moon, when the veils are thinnest between worlds. Were matters not so chaotic I would send you then, but the dark of the moon will serve now."

Confused, Scarecrow asked, "Chaotic? What do you mean?"

Glinda giggled. "Fine things are coming. Fae things." Her eyes glittered. Rubies, not coals, encompassed his soul entire in their stare. "Do you still want a detailed explanation, or would you rather go find your true love?"

"No, that's fine," Scarecrow replied hastily. The one thing he knew about fae business was that it was no place for anyone not born of their dark blood. Their politics and court intrigue nearly destroyed him before, when he'd dared stand in the way of the feuding and ever-shifting factions. This was the only sphere of knowledge he'd come across that the less he knew about, the better. "What happens at the full moon, to me?"

"If your heart's desire accepts you truly, you will remain with her. Love will sustain you." Glinda brushed back the excited tresses writhing over her shoulders as if seeking to detach themselves. "If she does not, at the full moon your magic will fail. You will be as all other scarecrows in that world. Hay and old clothes without a word more to say to anyone."

"Oh," Scarecrow said softly. *Dead. She means I'll be dead.*

Nick's eyebrows shot up. "Maybe this wasn't such a good idea, Scarecrow. Perhaps you ought to think about this some more."

A flash of disappointment crossed Glinda's sharp features. Scarecrow looked from her to Nick and back.

Well, if his beloved didn't feel the same, he might as well be a stuffed thing on a pole in a cornfield anyway.

Scarecrow nodded. "Send me there. Please."

"Are you sure?" the witch asked once more. Her eyes glittered.

"I'm sure." To Nick, he added with a smile, "You always insisted a heart was a better thing to have than brains. I'm about to prove which of us is right."

"Take this." Nick held out a small pendant of polished, swirling Evstone.

Scarecrow accepted, peering at the stone. Nick indicated an identical one linked to a pocket-watch chain. "Glinda enchanted them, in return for me clearing stumps from her garden. I'll be able to talk to you. To find out how your journey goes."

Touched, Scarecrow tucked away the gem in a pocket and hugged his oldest friend. Well, oldest barring *her*. "Thank you. I'll keep it safe."

"The sun rises," Glinda warned. "Step away, Tin Man, lest you want to journey with him."

Nick retreated. Tears at the corners of his eyes shone in the dawn light spilling through the stained glass window. "Stop that, you'll rust,"

Scarecrow said, and Nick managed a grin at the old refrain. "Goodbye, Nick. Thank you."

"Close your eyes, and focus your every thought on this: *I am seeking my heart's desire,*" commanded Glinda.

Scarecrow inhaled, smelling the emerald dust and the faint flowery perfume of the Emerald City one last time. He shut his eyes and repeated the spell, tense, feeling the magic creeping into his straw as Glinda wove her enchantment on him. *I am seeking my heart's desire. I am seeking my heart's desire.*

A whirlwind kicked up around him, dust blowing in his face. Scarecrow clutched one hand to his hat. He kept his eyes tightly closed, feeling his feet leave the floor. Did she conjure a tornado? Was this what his love felt like when she was blown so far away from her homeland?

A horrible wrenching sensation made him double over in surprising pain.

Oh, this was bad. This was worse than having his straw yanked out. That was merely uncomfortable and inconvenient. This must be what actual agony felt like. He gasped. The howl of the wind deafened his ears. His body compressed tighter and tighter until he couldn't even scream.

The sudden release of everything dropped him to the ground. Scarecrow lay there, wheezing as though he had lungs, trying to aerate his straw. Pain prickled through his whole frame as he slowly uncurled. Blinking back tears, he tried to focus. Everything was a blur, deafening, hot. Hard yellow bricks underneath him, bright red lights above, things zooming past. A number of people stood around, pointing and exclaiming at him. Pounding, aggressively cheery music assaulted his ears.

With effort, he braced his knees and struggled to his feet. Dizziness threatened to send him tumbling to the floor again. No, wait, the floor itself tilted to one side. Looking around, he saw wooden, gaily painted horses mounted in regiments upon the walls, fighting for space with enormous kettle-drums and an army of bird-winged faeries carved with their arms outstretched. The high ceiling bore thousands of tiny red fireflies between the hanging statues and, weirdly, a carriage, and more suspended drums.

People near him smiled, murmuring to each other. The hot air swirled with constant movement. He cringed from the thousands of candles above until he realized they weren't burning, but lit with some sort of internal magic.

No sign of his love. He spun. A parade of creatures gallivanted past in tiers, those strange red fireflies illuminating their march. Their feet didn't move. How were they sweeping by so quickly? Were any of them even alive? Unicorns, merpeople, odd centaurs. Many others he couldn't name but which wouldn't have been out of place in the Emerald City.

Were these travelers who'd come before, their magic lost, now frozen as statues for all time in this horrible, deafening parade?

Disoriented and ill, Scarecrow staggered to a velvet-padded bench. A young woman already sitting there squealed and leapt to her feet, running to grab a young man. They stared at Scarecrow, laughing. Their strange clothing was nothing like the fashions of any region of Oz. None of the women here wore a dress of white and blue. Panic rose. Did he botch the spell somehow? Did Glinda overstate her powers?

"Great makeup," someone said to him. "Isn't the hay scratchy though?" The accent was strange, but at least he understood the words. Part of the spell, no doubt.

"Straw, not hay," Scarecrow muttered. His head hurt. *She's not here. I have to get out of here, can't think, that noise!* He stood too quickly, took a step too hastily, lost his balance and tumbled down the sloped brick floor toward a yawning doorway in the shape of a great beast's mouth.

Gasps and cries went up around him. His limbs sprawled every which way, his gloves slipped across the smooth bricks. He struggled to right himself. Tears trickled down his cheeks as he flopped, ungraceful, aware he looked ridiculous. This was as bad as learning to walk, fresh off the cornfield pole.

Worse than his humiliation, everything *hurt*. If this was what humans called pain, he wanted no part of it. His straw body had never experienced anything like it before.

"Oh crap, don't move, your leg looks broken," said a sharp, feminine voice just behind him.

Was that her? Had she found him? It sounded like—and somehow not like—his love. "Dorothy?" he asked, hope wavering in his chest. He stared up into an unfamiliar face.

The pale young woman pushed her pumpkin-orange hair from her hazel-green eyes, frowning at him. One eyebrow quirked upward. Tiny silver beads there and at her nose gleamed pink in the reddish lights.

"*Nobody* calls me that. Do I know you?"

3

The performer costumed as a scarecrow stared dazedly at her. Theo's first aid training kicked in. She felt the back of his head gently, checked for blood on her fingers. Only bits of straw came away. Good, though he might still be concussed.

"Don't move," she told him again, pulling her hoodie off and bundling it to cradle his head. She checked his left leg, bent at a horrible angle. *Oooh, that's definitely broken.*

Theo glared at a couple standing nearby, staring. "Maybe make yourself useful? Get some help?" she snapped. The boy fumbled out his cell phone.

Theo placed her hands gently just above and below the unhappy angle of the performer's shin. "Okay, this is probably going to hurt, but we need to straighten this out."

Wide, frightened blue eyes met hers. "We do?"

"Yep. Take a deep breath and let it out slowly," she ordered. His leg felt oddly squishy. Her fingers couldn't even find the bone. This couldn't be good. As he exhaled, she grasped his leg and jerked to reset the bones—and damned near bent it too far the other way. There was no resistance at all. "What the fuck?" she muttered.

"Is that all right?" the man asked.

"I—I don't know," Theo admitted. "Does it hurt?"

"It did at first. It's better now, I think." The performer's voice was a soft tenor, with an accent Theo couldn't place. New England maybe? The end-of-word Rs were *ahs,* but without a Southern drawl. *Bettah.* "Thank you. You're very kind."

Theo eyed him uncertainly. He should be in so much pain. Having broken a bone or two, Theo remembered crying a lot.

He sat up, adjusting his hat with a wry smile. "I never was very graceful."

"Don't move, you could have a concussion. Do you know if you hit your head?"

"I don't think so, just clumsy as usual. What's a concussion?" he asked. Before Theo could answer, he handed her back her hoodie. "Thank you. I don't suppose you could help me? It's so loud in here." He braced his hands on the floor, trying to rise, gloves slipping.

"Here, let me help." Theo put her shoulder under his left arm, bracing her knees. The performer was surprisingly light. As she stood, helping him up, fearing this was a mistake, he must've been able to put weight on the leg after all. It felt like he wasn't leaning on her in the least. "Are you sure you're okay?"

He nodded. "Can we just—is there someplace else? I can't even hear myself think."

"Can you walk?" She noticed his right foot turning sideways, and tightened her grip on his ribs, bracing him with her shoulder. "Maybe we should wait for the paramedics to get here and check you out."

"Oh, my feet? No, they always do that, I'm used to it." Awkwardly, he corrected his steps.

Maybe he has a disability. She shouldn't embarrass him. Theo walked him down the sloping floor toward the gaping monster's mouth, the doorway into the Organ Room. He stopped abruptly a few feet inside, and Theo instinctively tensed her thighs, ready to support him.

But he still seemed to weigh nothing.

He stared up at the immense red-globed chandeliers, the light gleaming off organ pipes reaching twenty feet to the darkened ceiling. Ahead, an entire brewery's tanks loomed. Clockwork right out of a nineteen-twenties silent film rose on the far wall. And everywhere, organ pipes of every length splayed in wide fans, jutted at odd angles, or rose like crowns from their massive keyboards. The vast, dark room was decorated with spiderwebs and skeletons. Some of them might even have been fake.

Theo quirked an eyebrow at the costumed man. "You haven't been in here yet?" Maybe each hired spook had to remain in one specific area of the attraction. Though she thought she recalled others roaming the grounds freely in search of visitors to frighten.

"No, I just arrived, right before I saw you."

"Okay, there's a bench up ahead. I still don't think you should even be walking. You sure your leg isn't hurt?" Theo squinted at his face in the dim red light. He still seemed dazed. In shock, maybe. *Dammit, getting him up was a bad idea.* Though it was cooler and quieter in here, less crowded.

She helped him to the padded bench and sat next to him. He continued to gawp at the room, overwhelmed. "Maybe we should let your boss know you were hurt." She nodded at his boots, soft black suede with upturned toes. Cute but definitely not safe. "Didn't they tell you to wear good sneakers? Something with non-slip treads?"

The performer's dark brows creased. His makeup was really good, reminding her a little of the movie version of the character, though his long tunic with fancy gold trim looked like the formalwear of two centuries ago. "I don't understand. Maybe the spell didn't work after all. I think we might need an interpreter."

"An interpreter?" She checked his pupils, but in the gloomy room it was hard to tell anything. His gaze did track hers. "Are you dizzy? Ringing in your ears, or any difficulty focusing on me?"

"Why, should I have?" He blinked at her. "I was a little dizzy at first. It's better in here. Thank you for helping me." He shook his head. "How thoughtless of me, I haven't even asked your name. I'm Scarecrow."

"I see that. I'm Theo."

"Pleased to make your acquaintance. So people call you Theo, but never Dorothy." He studied her. "Do you know Dorothy?"

Theo laughed uncertainly. "Uh, not personally, no."

"Oh." He turned glum. "Thank you for helping me, but I need to find my friend. She should be here somewhere."

Things clicked. "So...you're Scarecrow and you're looking for Dorothy?"

He nodded. "Yes. I came here to find her." He sighed. "A very long way. I'm not even sure where *here* is."

"This is the Organ Room. Back there is the Carousel Room." Theo remembered she had a visitor's brochure from the ticket desk. Pulling it from her purse, she uncrumpled it. "Short tour for the Darkside, as I'm sure you know." She shared the map. "Your costume's kinda tame for a haunted house event, don't you think?"

"Pardon?"

Theo giggled. "Wait. Are you searching for Dorothy so you can eat her braaaaaiiiiinnnss? Because this I have to see."

His eyes widened. "Why would I want to eat her brains? And why would you want to see such a horrible thing?"

Theo threw both hands up. "Come on, you are totally missing a great visual joke here. You're not Zombie Scarecrow?"

"No." He drew back with a worried frown. "I think maybe you have me confused with some other scarecrow."

"Aren't you with the House?"

"What house?"

"Aren't you here to scare people," Theo amended. Maybe he did hit his head. Or else he just wasn't the brightest.

"Certainly not!" He paused. "Wait, did I scare you?"

Theo rolled her eyes. "Only because I thought you'd bashed your brains on the bricks. Which it kind of sounds like you may have. I should've made you wait for the paramedics."

He removed his tall, peaked hat and patted the top of his head. A stitched seam ran across it, behind his ears, with straw sticking out of it. "No, everything's in order. Though I'll admit," he said, replacing his hat and scrunching the brim down over his ears, "they may be a little jumbled, because I'm not understanding everything you say. Of course, the spell may not be translating everything properly. You sound like you're speaking common Ozian, but with a strange accent."

She'd give him props for digging deep into the character, anyway. And his voice was interesting, smooth and warm, the accent creeping around the edges of it. What *was* that, Bostonian? Maine?

Just then, a performer in a bloody skeleton outfit approached, long bony claws outstretched, breathing harsh and slow. The Scarecrow's eyes widened. He stumbled up from the bench, grabbing Theo's hand. She squeaked, startled, then laughed. The skeleton hissed.

The Scarecrow tugged her hand. "Run! Come on!"

Theo let herself be pulled along, catching up to him in a few strides. The carpet in here offered more traction than the bricks in the previous room. The Scarecrow's foot triggered a pop-up ghoul, shrieking at them from behind one of the organ benches. With a yelp Scarecrow jerked backward, then quickly hauled Theo in a different direction. "This way!"

Normally she wouldn't let some random stranger touch her at all, but he seemed harmless enough. She wanted to see what story he was trying to build. If he wasn't a zombie denizen of the cornfield out for brains, she was curious what the actual joke was.

His fright was contagious. Theo giggled, her heavy boots pounding after his lighter steps, excitement bubbling up her spine. "Look out, another one!" she shouted, pointing at a werewolf who leaped over an exhibit railing, snarling.

Scarecrow's limbs pinwheeled, nearly falling over as he tried to change direction. Theo caught his shoulder, shoving him upright, but clearly it was a masterful dance move on his part, as she felt none of his weight, and he immediately took off running another way, his gloved fingers secure around hers.

Okay, this was fun. Someone was absolutely going to yell at them any second for tearing through the attraction like crazed bats on crack. She hadn't just run for the hell of it in forever. This guy was crazy fast, too, despite stumbling every few steps. It was all she could do to keep up. Breathless, exhilarated, she tugged at his fingers. "Wait! Slow down, I don't run for anything!"

He slowed. Theo heaved for breath. "Oh my Goddess, chill a minute, I think we lost 'em."

He wasn't even breathing hard. "What was that?" he asked, looking fearfully behind them.

"Last one was a werewolf, I think. Saw its snout."

"A what wolf?"

"Graaaahhhhh!" snarled the werewolf, sharp teeth glistening in its rubber muzzle. It must've gone through one of the hidden employee doors and cut across to the top of the Doll Carousel stairs above them. It slowly descended, backlit in crimson. Scarecrow backed away alongside Theo.

"Oh no," Theo gasped, helpless laughter taking over. "No, okay, stop, I really can't run anymore."

The Scarecrow pushed her behind him, raising both fists to the were-wolf. "Stay back, you! Or I'll knock those teeth into the next kingdom!"

The wolf growled, shaking its head, advancing step by step. Its furry paws made raking motions toward them. Giddy, Theo grabbed the Scarecrow's leather belt to keep from collapsing in a giggle fit on the carpet. "Oh save me," she managed to say between hitching breaths.

"Don't worry Theo, I've faced worse creatures than this mangy mutt." Scarecrow's voice trembled. He made a halfhearted jab at the werewolf. "Here you, go away! Leave the lady alone!" Over his shoulder he hissed at her, "I'll distract him, you run. On three. One, two—" He lunged at the werewolf. "Three!"

"Oh Goddess," Theo exclaimed. She let go of his belt and Scarecrow flew at the werewolf.

The werewolf was more surprised when Scarecrow tackled him without effect. The startled performer shoved the straw man aside.

"Hey! What the hell!" yelled the werewolf, deep voice partly muffled by the mask.

"Run, Theo! I've got him," shouted Scarecrow, launching himself at the werewolf again.

"Get off me," the werewolf growled. He slapped away the Scarecrow's swinging fists, grabbed his tunic in both paws, and flung him bodily several feet away. Straw spilled across the carpet.

"Oh," gasped Theo.

Scarecrow staggered to his feet, bringing his hands up in a defensive pose again. "That all you got?"

"Jesus, dude, knock it off," the werewolf protested, backing away. "Rule number one, don't touch anybody!" He shook his head. "You're done, man. I'm reporting you." The werewolf stomped past Theo.

Alarmed, Scarecrow stumbled to her, a trail of straw following him. The grappling had popped two buttons off his tunic, and the padding for his costume was spilling out.

Theo stopped him, one hand on his chest. Loose straw shifted underneath her fingers. "Hey, that was fun, but maybe you took it too far, huh?"

His eyebrows almost touched the underside of his floppy hat. "Too far? Didn't you see those teeth?" He glared after the retreating wolf. "Don't know what rules he's citing. Are there rules here about *not* fighting off attacking wolves?"

"Okay, I think you're going to get in trouble. Maybe we should get lost before Teen Wolf comes back with some pissed-off authority figure," Theo suggested. "Besides, you're leaking."

"Oh, crows," Scarecrow sighed. "Pardon me, thought I had everything buttoned down perfectly. I wasn't expecting to be attacked today. Nobody told me anything about wolves." He shot another glare the way the other actor had gone.

"Yeah, okay, come on. Let's get your straw back in."

Theo bent to pick up a wadded handful of surprisingly soft, sleek straw. The Scarecrow held his tunic open, nodding thanks at her. A red lamp shone down directly behind him. It cast his shoulders and hat into stark shadows, and shone muted through his back. Theo paused, frowning. That must be a trick.

Scarecrow took the wad of straw from her hand. "Thank you. I think my clothes will need mending now to be strawtight again. Did you happen to see where my buttons went?"

She took in the lines of burlap etched across his cheeks, the brick-red paint on his nose. If that was makeup on his face, it was extremely well done. Even his stance, one boot turned sideways without a hint of discomfort, made him look more actual scarecrow than costumed human. Fluff littered the carpet. Straw spilled from his tunic even as he tried to shove handfuls of it back in, as though they were in a horror movie and his guts had been slashed out of his stomach. Theo saw the hole where she should've seen his chest, or at least a tee shirt or something under the costume.

He wasn't wearing anything under the tunic and the straw. And he wasn't extremely skinny.

He wasn't *there*. She could see all the way through him to the backside of his tunic.

4

"**I**'m glad you weren't hurt." Scarecrow smiled wryly. "Nick always says I fall apart in a crisis too easily. Guess there's some truth to that." He tucked more of his stuffing back inside, but with the buttons missing it was likely to all tumble out again. So far, the two-legged wolf hadn't returned.

Theo stared at him, motionless. Perhaps the shock of the attack was just now setting in. He'd read some people could have delayed reactions to such unexpected trauma. Her giggling throughout it was surely a symptom. Everyone experienced fear in different ways.

If that thing came back, they'd need to move in a hurry, though. Scarecrow placed one hand gently on the young woman's shoulder. "Are you all right?"

She swallowed hard, eyes searching his. "How did you do that?"

"Oh, the fisticuffs? Well, after the run-in with the flying monkeys, I took some boxing classes. Didn't want to be caught helpless ever again." He chuckled. "Sometimes just the threat is enough to make an opponent reconsider."

"No, the—Your costume makes it seem like you don't even have a body."

He frowned. "See, I really think we need an interpreter. I understand the words you're saying but your meaning escapes me."

She yanked open the front of his tunic, spilling clumps of straw. "This! How are you doing this? It looks like you don't—" Her fingers shoved into the middle of his chest.

Startled, he clutched her wrist. "Please don't. I'm trying to get it back in, not lose more of it." That was rather rude, but clearly they did things differently around here. Carefully, he pulled her hand out of his chest and tried to pat back into place the stuffing falling out. "You don't have to help, but I'd appreciate if you wouldn't make it worse. That thing could be back here any second."

Her eyes were wide and fearful.

With a sigh, he bent to scoop up more straw, his other arm clasped around himself to hold it all in.

"You're stuffed," she whispered.

Scarecrow laughed. "Barely, until I can find those buttons and sew them on again. Aha!" His clumsy fingers plucked one of the large buttons from the carpet. "Well, now we're getting somewhere."

She was still standing there, staring at him.

"Does your map show a place where we might be safe from that mutt?" he asked. She continued to gape at him. Scarecrow came closer, noticing how she drew up her shoulders, though she didn't yield a step back. Poor girl must be in shock. He tapped the odd map she clutched. "Please. I could use your help." The way she'd begged him to save her, she must be terrified of the thing. Little wonder, with those big teeth it had.

Slowly she nodded, turning back the way they'd come through the room full of disembodied organ pipes. "This way. They probably won't check the café since it's closed."

He scooped up the last of the fallen straw, shoved it inside himself and held his tunic closed the best he could.

Checking fearfully behind her every minute, Theo led him back through the cavernous dark room, full of gleaming trees of drums and ominous red chandeliers, up to a doorway with a velvet rope across it.

Scarecrow gave her a reassuring smile.

"In here. And stay quiet," she said, ducking under the rope.

He followed, his straw shifting around inside him uncomfortably. He hoped all his belongings had remained in his pockets. Remembering the stone Nick gave him, he patted his trousers pocket, reassured by the small lump.

It was very dark in here, though he could see a wall of windows with trees beyond. Tables and chairs crowded the floor. He'd no sooner crept around a large circular fountain burbling up from a pile of stacked rocks, keeping right behind Theo, when she whirled on him and dropped into a cross-legged seat on the cold floor.

"Okay," she hissed. "Talk."

He blinked. "What should I say?"

She scowled. "Come on. Are you really that Scarecrow? From...Oz?"

"You've heard of Oz?" Hope rising, he dropped to the floor next to her, scooting closer to whisper. The bubbling fountain provided noise and cover. This should prove a fairly safe hiding spot, unless the wolf-thing was able to smell them. "You know who I am?"

"Yeah, of course, everyone does."

Dorothy must have told of her adventures when she returned here. Or perhaps the Wizard had trumpeted his own exploits far and wide. "Wonderful! Tell me then, where can I find Dorothy?"

"You came here looking for Dorothy," Theo repeated. "From Oz. Like, the actual land of Oz, from the stories."

"Well, I don't know what you've heard, but yes, I asked Glinda, the Witch of the South, to send me here. If this is the world Dorothy calls home, she didn't paint a picture half-accurate for us with her descriptions of Kansas."

Theo kept frowning. "You're really a living scarecrow. Full of straw."

He quirked a brow at her. Didn't she just see all the stuffing falling out? He fluffed his tunic at her. "Yes. And since we seem to have a rel-atively safe retreat here for the moment, I need to sew this button back on or else I'll have a hard time doing anything else." He pulled the small sewing kit from his pocket and unrolled it, choosing a large needle his fingers could grasp more easily. Trying to thread it proved trickier than he'd anticipated.

To his relief, Theo took the needle and thread from him and thread-ed the eye deftly even in the dark room. She bit her lip, studying his tunic. "Um. You want some help?" she asked.

"Would you? That's extremely kind."

She pulled out a slender object like a playing card, black on both sides. Its purpose was a mystery until she touched something on it and light sprang forth. She handed it to him. Scarecrow blinked at it, seeing a picture truer than any portrait painter could make. It depicted Theo with a carved pumpkin. Its grin reminded him of the gangly creature Ozma Tip had made, Jack Pumpkinhead.

"Don't flash it around, you'll draw attention. Point it here," Theo hissed.

He held his straw in and aimed the lighted portrait at his tunic. She crouched forward, sewing the button back in place swiftly. She tugged his tunic closed and rebuttoned it. He whispered thanks, trading the lit portrait for his sewing gear, tucking that safely in a pocket again.

"Here I took so much trouble to appear well-turned-out, and I'm already a mess," he chuckled.

Theo slipped the odd thin portrait into her handbag. "Okay, I'm still trying to accept you're real. That Oz is real. Not just a place in kids' books and movies."

Maybe Glinda's spell was tripping over words with no equivalent in Ozian. That would explain the jarring nonsense which kept interrupting her speech. "I'm not sure what you mean. I know I'm unusual." He smiled. "Dorothy told me scarecrows don't move around in this land, either, so I expect I'll get some strange looks."

It was all he could do to remain polite. If his love was here somewhere in this dark and unnerving place, he shouldn't be sitting here chatting. He should be searching for her, protecting her if necessary from the creatures roaming around.

Scarecrow grasped Theo's hand in his, but she flinched and he released her, shaking his head. "I'm sorry to be any trouble, and thank you again for helping me, but I can't stay here. I need to find Dorothy. She should be around here somewhere."

"You're searching for Dorothy Gale. As in the real Dorothy? She was real?"

He sighed. "Maybe you should explain to me what you mean by *real* because I think I'm not understanding any of this very well." He scratched his head. "Perhaps my brains did get shaken up by the whirlwind. Glinda didn't warn me about any side effects. Maybe she assumed my brains are so wonderful they wouldn't be affected."

Theo took a deep breath. "I mean, you're supposed to be just a character in a book. Oz is a fairytale. Hell, I just re-read a bunch of the series last week." She paused. "Shit. Maybe I'm dreaming."

"I don't think so. Unless we're both dreaming. I've never been able to dream, so you'll have to do the deciding for us both, I suppose."

She stared at him. "Promise you're not messing with me. I'm serious."

"So am I," he replied. Did everyone here make so little sense?

"Oz is real," she whispered. She raised a hand as if wanting to touch him, but held back.

Scarecrow closed his fingers gently around hers. "Yes, of course it is. Just as real as you are." She looked at his hand, but didn't pull away. "I'm glad you know who Dorothy is. I need to find her. She's supposed to be here." He grimaced. "I hope. If I didn't do something wrong and throw the spell off. Do you think that wolf will be back?"

Theo rubbed her thumb over his, staring at it. The straw crackled inside his glove. "That was just a guy in a mask. You didn't need to attack him."

"A mask?" The Midsummer Ball sprang to mind. Nothing the fae loved more than a masquerade, and they'd flocked to the palace when young Ozma announced the rejuvenation of the ages-old tradition. Scarecrow was sure it had been Glinda's idea. There seemed to be more of the slender, beautiful Fair Folk among the dancers than anyone he recognized. He'd felt awkward, his own fierce owl mask no real disguise. His floppy steps gave him away immediately. Most of the ball he'd sat off to the side, engaging with Nick in a contest to guess the identity of the maskers.

The wolf-thing was a masker! No wonder it protested instead of tearing him limb from limb. Now that he thought over what actually happened, the creature never laid a paw on him before he jumped it.

He frowned at Theo. "Then why did you ask me to save you?"

"I thought you were an actor! All the spooks here are just actors, hired to frighten the guests for fun."

"I wondered why you were laughing. Thought you were frightened out of your wits."

"No. Goofballs in bad masks and jump scares don't frighten me."

Her eyes were dark brown in the dim light, and for a moment he was unable to gather his thoughts at all, so much did the color remind him of *her.*

"Do you understand?" she continued. "Nothing here is real. Even half the artifacts in the House are fakes."

"So you assumed..." This made sense finally.

"Okay." She brushed her hair back, though it immediately flopped over her forehead again. "You're the Scarecrow of Oz. Not what I expected."

Back to not making sense. "You were expecting me?"

"No. Definitely not at all." She flashed a smile. He smiled back, puzzled. "In the books, Baum described you as having a painted smile on a burlap sack for a face, and here you are instead dressed like a really dedicated cosplayer." He raised a brow at her, and she amended, "You look human, just really well costumed."

"Ah, well, I had some changes made. So as to be a bit more like a meat person for—well. Just wanted a change. Still burlap, since it's the best material to ensure my brains stay where they ought to be." Books. Wait a minute. "I'm in a book?"

"A whole series of books, written for children."

"Oh." Should he be flattered? "Is it the custom here for children to read tales of murder, court intrigue, or carnal pursuits?"

She stared at him. "Not put so bluntly, at least."

"Ah." Those books must be fairly watered-down, then. Professor Wogglebug taught the true history of Oz in his classes. Scarecrow sat in on a few as part of his duty to oversee an educational overhaul for the Kingdom, which had sadly dwindled under the Wizard's neglect. Though the Wogglebug presented the grim timeline of wars, beheadings, and usurpers to the royal lineage truthfully, Scarecrow felt the need to caution him. Not all children were sturdy enough to take in the lessons with the obvious relish the Wogglebug gave to the bloody events.

"So you came here by magic, hunting for Dorothy."

How many times did he have to repeat this? Maybe Theo was having as hard a time comprehending his words as he did hers. Counseling himself to be patient, Scarecrow nodded again. If all the frights here were merely parlor tricks, then his beloved was in no danger. He still itched to find her, but the tension in his chest eased.

"What makes you think she's at the House on the Rock?"

"I have no idea what particular house she's in. Glinda told me to focus on specific words to take me to my—to Dorothy."

"What words?"

"That's a bit personal. It was a spell to send me here. I appreciate your help with this," he touched his chest, where only a bit of straw poked out, "but I'd really like to find her now. Would you lend me your map, or come with me and help?"

"Um."

"Something wrong?"

"Well, I always assumed Dorothy was made up. Not a real person."

Things were beginning to add up unpleasantly. She kept saying *was*. Time moved differently here than in any of the fae lands. Would Glinda have neglected to account for that?

Unhappy memories rose of the Midsummer Ball. He'd accidentally bumped into some of the guests before he retreated from the ballroom floor. A tipsy Langwidere, one of Oz's lesser witches, threatened to transform Scarecrow into a weevil and let him loose among the dancers, to see whether he'd be less clumsy in that form and evade everyone, or be crushed. Glinda intervened at the last second, but he'd seen the glitter in her eyes, her amusement. Had he not been one of Ozma's most favored advisers... He shivered just recalling it.

Would Glinda have allowed her spell to send him to a time in Dorothy's world where she was already married? Glinda never particularly liked the young woman. Scarecrow had neither forgotten, nor forgiven the Good Witch who'd simply watched their arduous trials through her magic painting, no doubt enjoying every horrible bit of it. Glinda was fae, a powerful sorceress. Little he could do or say about any of it. He knew he still existed only because he was moderately useful to the crown.

He was honestly shocked when Glinda agreed to craft a spell to push him through the magical barriers keeping the worlds apart. Perhaps the witch had some vestigial sympathy after all. Or what if she'd seen the opportunity both to rid the court of its wisest advisor and to amuse herself at his expense?

What if he'd been sent here to disrupt Dorothy's family? If she was partnered happily, with children of her own...

He slumped against the rock wall of the fountain. Oh no. Please, no. He couldn't do that to her, come hat in hand asking to be hers, much less for her to be his. Not if she'd moved on without him.

"Hang on," Theo said, rousing him from these awful thoughts. "Dorothy was a kid. Like nine or ten. Please don't tell me you're—"

"Crows on a stick, no! Those books of yours must get a lot wrong if they don't even have that part right." He scowled. "She was seventeen when she helped me off my pole in the cornfield. I was a few days old. And she was only a few months older when I last saw her. Three years ago. When she rescued all of us from the Nome King's gallery of victims." He studied Theo's face. "You keep referring to her as though she's been famous for some time. How long has it been since she returned home?"

Theo bit her lip. Her eyes glistened.

He'd been played for a fool. Again. He should've foreseen this, should've known the witch would grant him the letter of his wish but not the spirit of it. "How long?" he asked again, grasping Theo's hand.

Her slender fingers closed over his and squeezed. "If she was real—"

"Absolutely."

"Then if the author of the books heard her story somehow and wrote it all down right after she came back home…" Theo paused, slowly shaking her head.

He closed his eyes. "Tell me. Please. Is she married?" He tensed, bracing himself for the worst.

"Scarecrow, the first Oz book was published a hundred and twenty years ago."

It felt like every spark of magic fled his body. He may as well be a senseless bundle of straw in cast-off clothes. An invisible hand closed around his chest, crushing all hope. He blinked back tears, unable to meet Theo's gaze, his hand frozen in hers.

"Is—is that—" He forced himself to push his voice out. He could barely form words. "How long do people live here, without magic?"

Theo didn't answer. She squeezed his hand.

Scarecrow felt ice spreading from his center all through his limbs. There was no point in him moving ever again.

5

Theo thought it best to make themselves scarce when she heard sirens. No way could she let the paramedics examine the straw man. Explanations or apologies to the staff for the attempted fight with the werewolf bro would be guaranteed awkward and preferably avoided.

She tugged and hissed at Scarecrow until he glumly followed her out of the empty café, through the Organ Room again, skirting around the creepy doll carousels and out into the chilly, damp night.

Scarecrow barely reacted when the breeze whistled through the open rails of the covered wooden walkway, though it buffeted him sideways. He took hold of the floppy brim of his hat but otherwise ignored it. They were at least twenty feet above the ground here. If he was made of straw, a really strong gust might blow him over. Theo hooked her arm around his.

He didn't seem to register her presence, though when she pulled at his arm he fell into step beside her easily enough. No one else nearby. Glimmering jack-o'lanterns provided just enough light to see the next turn ahead in the walkway, where a secluded bench gave protection from the elements.

She sat down on the sheltered bench and patted the spot next to her. "Come on. We should be okay here for a few minutes."

He sat, long legs splayed before him, feet turned sideways. With his head down in shadows, he was a sad puppet bereft of its guiding strings.

"So did Glinda say why Dorothy would be in this specific location, or this year?" she prompted.

"No."

"She didn't say where exactly she'd be?"

"She did not."

"Do you know if—"

"I don't know anything!" he snapped.

Theo flinched.

He cradled his head in his hands. "She said the spell would set me down near to her, but nothing about the exact spot, or the year, or whether she'd still be alive when I got here!" His voice was sharp, bitter, and sounded on the verge of breaking.

"I thought Glinda was a good witch?"

He laughed unhappily. "Ha! The titles the fae invent to amuse each other in front of us lesser creatures. If by *good* you mean *not as malicious as the rest of them,* sure."

"So you think she tricked you? Why?"

"Why?" He met her gaze briefly. "For a laugh, most likely." He frowned. "Though I thought her magic picture could only show her what happens in Oz, not outside of it. I'll admit it's a bit of a stretch for her to take this much trouble for a joke if she couldn't witness the effects."

Wow. So much for goodness and light. Was everything in the stories candy-coated? A jaded Scarecrow and a sadistic Good Witch definitely didn't fit in the Oz she knew.

Theo sat back, silent as a giggling couple tromped past, heading for the gift shop exit.

The exit.

Where everyone would be funneled back out of the grounds. She grabbed Scarecrow's hand.

"Hold up. You're not just the actual Scarecrow of Oz. You're a time-traveling Scarecrow."

He frowned. The lantern at the corner of this fenced-off cubby reflected in his eyes strangely. She really wanted a good look at him in better lighting.

"Time-traveling?"

"You said it was three years ago you last saw her, right? So maybe around Nineteen-hundred, Nineteen-oh-one in our world."

He shook his head. Straw rustled and crackled. "Oz is under the dominion of the fae. All the books say time flows at different speeds between different lands. When Dorothy was—" He halted, pulling his fingers free of hers. She let go. His face tilted into full shadow. After a long moment, he continued, in a quieter voice, "The last time she visited, it had been only a few months for her since she first was in Oz. Three years had passed for us. Three very long, terrible years." He shook his head again with a soft laugh. "I thought I'd worked out the formula for it. Figured out her time relative to ours. I never considered a spell could shove me forward so far."

"What if it didn't?" Theo asked. "I mean, what if there is no formula, no way to predict how fast or slow the years go between this world and Oz? It could be random. The same thing might've happened to Dorothy."

He froze, silent. If she took his hat off, would she see the pins and needles which he supposedly had for brains poking through his head while he was thinking hard? Tempting to remove it just to see. He jerked upright so fast she startled.

"You're right." His eyes were wide and hopeful. "What if she returned here? Now?"

"Who says you're the only time traveler?" Theo asked, grinning.

"She could be here!"

"She could be. Shoved forward in time in this world." Suddenly that didn't seem like such an exciting idea. A girl from the turn of the last century, from the gray frontier of flat Kansas, thrust into the twenty-first century and the extravagant madness of the House on the Rock during Halloween season? Goddess help her.

The same thought clearly occurred to Scarecrow. "Has a lot changed in that time?"

Theo choked on a laugh. "Uh, serious understatement. Yeah."

"She must feel lost," he said, frowning the way they'd come. "We need to find her!"

Theo grabbed his hand before he could go charging back in. There had to be some disgruntled paramedics and even less gruntled staff searching for them. "Not that way. You only saw a couple rooms of the House. The place is a maze, and even weirder right now with all the Halloween stuff." He frowned, and she explained, "All the masks and play-acting and creepy decorations. Last thing we need is to be hunting through all that in the dark."

"Then as soon as it's light, back we go," Scarecrow declared, resettling his hat firmly atop his head. The determined expression on his face made her smile.

Yeah, this was more like it. This was the Scarecrow who stepped off the throne he'd just gained to make sure his friend Dorothy was able to get home safely.

"Or," Theo offered, "since they'll be kicking everyone out in about an hour, we could just go wait at the front door and see if she's here."

He frowned, one dark eyebrow quirked upward.

"If she's still in the House, all we have to do is get to the exit and wait there. The staff will turn her out at some point." She grinned. "You up for a stakeout?"

He gave her a pained grimace. "Interpreter?"

"Never mind. Just come on." Theo jumped to her feet.

He didn't need any prompting this time, bouncing upright and hurrying after her. They ran along the walkway, Theo's bug-stompers thumping, Scarecrow's soft boots making no sound, although she could hear a lot of rustling and crinkling. He staggered and stumbled. Theo again hooked her elbow through his and helped him along. Her eyes met his when they careered around the next corner, and they both grinned.

They burst into the florescent lights of the gift shop. Theo halted to avoid slamming into some tourists browsing the nearest tee shirt rack. Scarecrow almost toppled onto them before Theo flung a hand across his chest, surprised for a second at the yielding feel of him. She tried to catch her breath, be less obvious.

The woman at the cash register frowned at her, then noticed Scarecrow and smiled. "Did ya have a good time then?" she asked.

Scarecrow stared at the merchandise depicting the Infinity Room, the Carousel, and grinning skeletons for the Darkside event. Theo was struck immediately by the weave of the burlap fabric of his face under the bright lights, how his eyes tracked across the myriad items in the gift shop but still seemed a bit *off*, as if they weren't quite wet enough. He wasn't breathing hard after their dash, and his wrists were bent at awkward angles. Straight out of the uncanny valley.

The cashier was still watching them, smile becoming a little puzzled. Before any prying questions could be asked, Theo smiled. "Yeah, it was great. Thank you, Happy Halloween!"

Theo pulled Scarecrow toward the exit. The last thing they needed was to stand around until the staff thought to radio the cashier. Clearly she hadn't heard about the short-lived Battle of Dudebro Werewolf. Yet.

"Wait," Scarecrow protested, his heels skidding on the low-nap carpet. "Why are we leaving? I was reading that." He gestured at the rack of magnets.

Theo hissed into his ear, "I'll get you a souvenir when we don't have the staff pissed off at us and annoyed paramedics probably coming through here any second. Come on."

He followed, head still turned toward the items. "Theo, wait, listen. I was *reading* those things. The lettering style is unfamiliar but I can read your language. Don't you think that's strange?"

"What? Yeah, maybe, I don't know." She hurried out into the main entry hall, tugging him along, though after a few steps he caught up. Once they'd pushed open the main doors and the cool night slapped her in the face again, she slowed, heart hammering. A quick glance back showed no signs of pursuit. "Okay. I think we're all clear. Car's this way." She set off into the parking lot.

"Wait, wait," Scarecrow insisted. He pulled back on her hand. Theo stumbled, surprised at his sudden strength. He'd wrapped his other arm, bonelessly but effectively, around a lamp post. He let go when he saw he had her attention. "Not fun to be yanked around, is it?"

"Sorry," Theo said, "but we do need to get out of sight. My car's right over there. We can wait there and watch the door."

"But this is all very strange. How is it—"

"Seriously, we need to move. Now," Theo interrupted, seeing the ambulance parked a few feet away. Its lights were off and no one was inside the vehicle, but that only meant the paramedics were liable to emerge from the House any second. The guy who called them almost certainly mentioned a scarecrow. And Scarecrow was damned hard to miss.

He glanced at the main doors. "This is the exit you mentioned?"

"Yes. And we have a clear line of sight." Theo unlocked the passenger door of her old Civic. "Hop in."

Scarecrow paused, finally noticing the cars scattered around the lot, the wet asphalt, the bulging ten-foot urns planted with succulents adorning the median. "In that?"

"That's the idea. We can sit here out of the wind and watch the front, see if she comes out."

He watched her dive into the driver's side and shut the door before reluctantly folding his lanky frame into the car. He shut the passenger door and Theo stifled a laugh. The seat was cranked forward and Scarecrow's arms and legs were cramped in front of him, bent every which way.

"Here, let me help." Theo reached down to adjust the latch. "You look really uncomfortable."

He resettled his feet and his elbow found the arm rest on the door. "I don't mind. I've been jumped on, thrown down, ripped apart."

"That doesn't hurt?"

"Not really. It's inconvenient and a little embarrassing, but I've never felt pain until today." His eyes met hers in the darkened car, and again she wished she could determine what about them bothered her. "At least, I assume that's what's meant by pain. It felt like I was being crushed and burned at the same time."

In the enclosed car, she was aware of his scent. Sweet straw and sunlight on open fields. A few strands of straw stuck out of the gap in his tunic where the other button was missing, as well as poking out of the ends of his gloves where they met the tunic sleeves. Seated now in a more or less normal position, Theo had a hard time accepting she'd even seen his limbs bending in abnormal ways a minute ago.

"So you don't feel pain?" she prompted. He shook his head. "How much do you feel, then? I mean, if you don't have nerves..."

"Since I've never been a meat person, I'm not sure how to describe it. I sense enough to know when I'm touching something, when it's hot or cold, though those don't really bother me. Nick and I have had numerous conversations about this. He used to be a meat person so he recalls a little of it."

"Nick. The Tin Woodman?"

Scarecrow's dark brows arched. "You've heard of him?"

"He's in the books."

"I think I'll need to read these books. If I ever have time."

Theo noticed a family leaving the building. A mom and dad and a couple of sleepy kids, the littlest of three carried dozing in the father's arms. Scarecrow peered at them, leaning forward, then relaxed again.

What did Dorothy actually look like? Some artists depicted her as a blonde, cherubic Gibson Girl of the turn of the last century. Or as a child; but he'd dashed that notion. Would she have the gingham dress and pigtails? Scarecrow's gaze remained on the entry doors to the House. Presumably he'd recognize her.

"What's she like?"

His voice softened. "Dorothy? Why, she's—she's brave. Resourceful. Catches on very quick no matter how strange the situation may be to her. Loyal and honest."

"She sounds perfect."

"I think so, yes."

Well, nobody was perfect, but for his sake she hoped Dorothy was as close to his glowing description as he thought. Pretty brave of him to come all this way, into a world far less interesting than Oz, seeking a young woman who might or might not be all that.

He'd returned to watching the front door, the straw poking from under his hat trembling, as though he was barely holding excitement in check. Might be a long wait. The House on the Rock would be open for another half hour. Sighing, she tugged her jacket closer over her chest and shoved her hands into the pockets.

"Are you cold?" he asked.

His clothing appeared to be all brushed cotton, with tailored shoulders and a leather belt on the tunic. More suited for standing at court than being out on a cold fall night. He wasn't shivering at all.

"A little," Theo replied. "I'll turn the heat on if I get too chilly."

"You have a fireplace in this contraption?" He shook his head at the confines of the car. The back seat was piled with books, fabric grocery bags, soda cans on the floor and brochures for roadside attractions. "You know I'm flammable, right?"

"There's no fire. Just an electric heater that comes out the vents." She indicated the dusty vents in the dash.

"Electric?"

"You have a lot to learn," Theo said. "Tell you what, after you find your girl, I can set you up with a phone or something."

"If this means you can direct me to a library where I can study your world, thank you. I'd still like to know how it is I can read your language. I hadn't thought Glinda's spell would cover that."

"Aren't you speaking English right now?"

"I'm speaking common Ozian. As are you."

"I can see your lips forming the words," Theo pointed out. "If we were really speaking different languages, wouldn't it look more like you were being dubbed?"

He pinched the bridge of his prominent nose. "Again, an interpreter would be helpful."

Theo leaned closer, enunciating very clearly. "Watch my lips. Do I seem to be speaking different words to you than what you're hearing?"

Uneasily, his eyes flicked from her mouth to her gaze. "No."

"Well, then we're both speaking English, or we're both speaking Ozian."

Scarecrow tapped one finger to his lips. "Apparently so. I need to think about this. It's very strange."

Theo sighed. "No, strange is a man stuffed with straw who can move around and think and speak." She rubbed a hand through her hair. "We need to come up with some kinda cover story for you. I think enthusiastic cosplayer should do it at least until November."

"Yes, a library would be nice. Or at least a dictionary, if we can't have an interpreter for all these odd words you keep using." He chuckled. "I know I'm a curiosity, however. The one and only talking Scarecrow of Oz. As I said, it's a fae realm, so anything's possible."

"What are the fae like?" Theo asked. Faeries. Real ones! If a living Scarecrow could walk around in this world, then the stories of changelings and pooka, silkies and banshees could be real.

Now she considered it, the idea held less appeal. Those things were not friendly to humans. Cute as dolls, as art, as stories. She'd read old legends and modern fantasies all her life, creating faeries in her head, making dolls of them, wishing them to life the best she could. At least a couple times a year, she went walking in the woods, listening carefully, watching for any sign of the spirits which surely watched over the trees and animals. What if the old legends were true? The oldest stories did not paint the Fair Folk as benevolent. An actual wailing spirit haunting the misty moors, determined to carry off a soul? She shivered.

"The Fair Ones?" He looked around cautiously. Other than a couple of guys laughing and talking as they walked to their car, the parking area was deserted. "Well, not to be trusted. They can—"

"Shit. Down!" Theo yelped, clutching his shoulder and pulling his head down with hers below the dashboard level.

"I knew it, I knew talking about them was a bad idea," Scarecrow groaned.

"No, it's the paramedics. We can't let them see us."

Theo waited, tense, listening to the indistinct grumbling and the sounds of a stretcher being loaded back into the ambulance. She kept a tight grip on Scarecrow's shoulder until she heard the engine rumble and the low scrape of tires moving past them. When all was quiet, she dared a peek. Gone. Good. "Okay. All clear."

He immediately checked the front door of the House. Another family exited the attraction, but Dorothy must not have been among them. He frowned and leaned back in the seat.

"You were saying?"

Scarecrow shook his head. "I'm not sure talking about them is wise. If you've heard of them, you must know that, don't you?"

"Old British Isle tradition referred to them as the Fair Folk or the Goodly Ones, so they wouldn't overhear."

"Don't be too sure. Some of them are so powerful we don't even know all they can do."

Well, that definitely fit with myths here. "I've always been fascinated by faery stories. I make dolls of them."

"Dolls? For children?"

"For adults, mostly." She leaned closer, confiding, "Maybe it's silly, but I put spells into them. I feel like it makes them more alive."

He stared at her. "Dolls for spells? Magic poppets?"

"Sort of," she admitted. "I cast spells on them as I make them."

He shrank away from her. "You're a witch," he whispered. His gloves fumbled at the door.

Theo frowned. "Well, yeah, I thought the pentagrams kinda gave that away." She gestured at her jewelry. "Chill, I don't have flying monkeys or anything."

"Glinda sent me to you deliberately," Scarecrow groaned, now actively scrabbling at the door seeking escape.

Crap. If he ran out, he was fast enough she might not catch him, and Goddess only knew what trouble he'd get into unsupervised. Theo locked the doors. "Wait, calm down," she pleaded.

He found the handle and yanked it but the door didn't budge. His eyes widened. "Stop playing with me! I'm not a mouse!" he yelled, raising a trembling finger.

"I'm not messing with you, calm down." Theo reached for his shoulder. He jerked away, cringing against the door.

"Stop, please!" he gasped. Tears glimmered in his eyes. "Whatever you intend, just let me find her. Let me find Dorothy. Please. Whatever Glinda told you, I swear I'm loyal to the Seelie Court. Please, don't rip me up, don't burn me, I'll do whatever you ask, but please just let me find her and tell her how I feel before you destroy me!"

witch. Glinda sent him straight to another witch. A witch who made magic poppets. Who asked a lot of questions about Oz and the fae. This was a test, and she was prying so much he must've failed it already. She was toying with him. She yanked him around by the hand or arm as though he were a rag doll. Maybe that's how she saw him—another poppet to be controlled.

"Before you kill me," he begged, "please just let me find Dorothy. That's all I ask."

Theo stared at him, eyes wide and dark in the confines of this strange metal room on wheels. He'd seen another like it pull away without benefit of horse or oxen. That should've driven home the point he was in a magic realm. This wasn't Kansas at all. He'd been sent to another land controlled by the Fair Ones as some sort of punishment. How had he offended the crown? Or Glinda?

Ozma Tippetarius liked his company, listened to his sage advice. Of course. With Scarecrow out of the way, the Queen would fall more and more under the influence of the Seelie Court. Within a year Glinda would have the young ruler wrapped around her pinkie finger. This was a mistake. A terrible, selfish mistake.

Tears trickled down his cheeks. He bowed his head. What a fool to think he might find *her* again. He'd played right into Glinda's hands. No wonder she agreed so easily to send him through the veil between worlds.

He flinched at a light touch on his shoulder. No way out of this. Might as well face it like a man. He raised his head.

Theo's expression radiated concern. "Why would you think I'm going to hurt you?"

"Lady Theo, please do me the courtesy of not tormenting me. Just do whatever you intend and get it over with."

"I'm not going to hurt you," she protested. "I don't want to tear you up or burn you or whatever it is you're afraid of. Until an hour ago I thought you were just a character in a book."

"But you're a witch! You make poppets and cast spells!"

"Yes, I'm a witch, but not that kind. I cast spells for strength and protection, and to try to make my little dolls seem more alive. Not to hurt people." She shook her head. "Come on, haven't I been helping you since I found you on the floor? I thought you'd broken a leg and I just wanted to help. Have I done anything at all to hurt you? Because if I have, I'm sorry."

The customs of the fae were an impenetrable mystery to Scarecrow, as to anyone not of their blood. However, one thing was absolutely certain. They never apologized. Ever. Not to each other as far as he'd witnessed, and absolutely not to any lesser creature.

"You're not one of them?" he asked cautiously.

She choked out a laugh. "Scarecrow, as far as I know, faeries don't exist in this world. Old stories say they did centuries ago, but left for some underground realm when mankind defeated them in battle. Ancient myth." She fell silent a moment. "I guess you're proof there's some truth to the stories. I don't know what to think now. But I won't hurt you. Promise."

He nodded slowly, fishing out his kerchief to wipe the moisture from his face. Good thing his paint was in oils or he'd have been unable to see at all now.

"How can you cry? Isn't your head full of bran and pins?"

"Certainly not." He tapped a finger to his temple. "Magic brains. Though I don't know what the Wizard made them out of." He blinked to clear his vision, dabbing at his cheeks. "I don't know what makes the tears. A useful way to clear out any moisture, I suppose."

"I didn't mean to scare you." Theo offered him her hand. "Friends?"

He hesitated. She seemed sincere. And no fae would ever apologize to the likes of him. Even Glinda laughed at him, called him Straw-Bale.

Scarecrow laid his glove in Theo's palm. Her skin was warm and soft. She squeezed his fingers gently, and he returned the gesture. "Friends." What an idiot he was. Superior brains, indeed. "I suppose you must think me a fool now." He sighed. "I feel just as foolish here as I did tripping over holes in the road of yellow brick. Back then I didn't know enough to walk around them."

"Hang on, tell me something. You never actually met the Wicked Witch of the West, did you? That part was only in the movie, I thought."

He bit back another comment about an interpreter. "No. Dorothy melted her while I was stranded in a tall tree, just empty clothes and a sad head getting rained on 'til I could barely think." Horrible, endless days then, the wind rushing past his ears, certain his straw head would eventually rot and that he'd still be conscious as it happened. He shivered. "Once the witch was dead, Dorothy came back with Nick and they saved me. I thought I'd be stranded forever."

"So then, if the witch didn't burn you, why are you so scared of witches?"

Yes, he'd definitely need to read these books she kept talking about. "Haven't you heard about the war?"

"What war?"

"When the Wizard left. Before we recovered the lost Ozma and secured her on the throne."

"The books say the Wizard appointed *you* ruler of Oz."

He laughed, startled. "Ruler! He appointed me Regent Awaiting the Wizard's Return. Which did not suit the Seelie Court one little bit. And half the ordinary people of Oz didn't care for a stuffed man sitting on the throne, even though I did my best for the whole nation, not just the court. Several of the witches and minor lords had been itching to steal the throne when the Pastorian line of rulers died out, but they were too afraid of the Wizard. How he managed to keep them at bay as long as he did is beyond me. With two of the most powerful witches dead and the Wizard gone who knows where, a lot of the lesser sorcerers, dukes and ladies of the Fae, and so forth, saw a great opportunity."

Realization dawned in her eyes. "A civil war."

Scarecrow nodded. "The witches Mombi and Maab partnered to take the throne. But a whole host of lords formed a coalition under the Witch of the North, Locasta, and demanded *she* rule." How naive he'd been, hoping to unite the factions. "Since none of them had any rightful claim, I insisted they lay down arms. That didn't go over too well."

Theo scrunched around in her seat, eyes wide. "So what happened?"

"Three years of bloodshed. Magic running wild over the innocent populace."

"Oh damn." She squeezed his hand. "What stopped it?"

"Tip did. Well, more accurately, finding out Tip was the lost Pastoria princess stopped it, because Glinda suddenly stepped in and declared him the sovereign Queen. Made him change his sex to a girl. Glinda's powerful enough none of the others dared to defy her. At least not openly."

"Okay, the books do mention that." Theo leaned closer. As the light from the lamp-posts outside caught her eyes, they turned more green then brown.

He reminded himself she wasn't fae. At least, she didn't think she was. Best not to mention the eye color to her.

"But what did they do to you personally?"

"Locasta wanted to control me. She—she did things to me, to figure out how."

"What things?"

He looked into those worried eyes again, so like and yet not like his love's. Dorothy's were deepest brown, the color of warm earth. In shadow, Theo's eyes appeared the same hue, though green in the light. Enchanted eyes.

She spoke quietly. "I'm sorry. Didn't mean to dig up bad memories for you."

"It's all right." In truth, he'd reacted shamefully a few minutes ago. She should at least hear why. "Everyone knew the Wizard chose me for my brains, which he himself put in my head. So, in case I was a sorcerer and just didn't know it yet, Locasta decided it was too risky to simply throw me onto a bonfire. Instead she spent a year taking me apart, over and over again, to see if she could break the spell animating me or make me her puppet."

He didn't feel pain, not how people of flesh described it, but he could feel loss. Discomfort. And fear. Horror, when Locasta conjured a swarm of locusts burrowing into him, tiny mandibles gnawing his straw. The feel of them moving inside his belly, his chest, the maddening clicking of their jaws as they worked up into his head until he shrieked, limbs torn off, helpless—

He took a long, steadying breath. Theo's spicy, floral scent filled his chest in the small spaces between clumps of straw. Calmer, he continued, "She painted over my eyes so I couldn't see what she was doing, opened my head to poke around in my brains. Pulled me apart and scattered my straw for her goats to eat. Clothes too. Which is how I learned the magic giving me life wasn't centered in my clothing."

"Oh dear Goddess, how awful," Theo whispered.

"It was. She tried rebuilding me with evil spells, but I still wouldn't be her slave. Whatever magic made me was stronger than hers." The next part was the worst. Best to skim over it. "I felt I had a duty to Oz. I'd been set to protect the throne until the Wizard returned, but he never did. I wouldn't yield to Locasta. So she dragged the Lion and Nick to the palace and did horrible things to them. Forced me to watch."

"No," Theo said. Tears trickled from her eyes. Scarecrow was about to offer her his kerchief, then saw it was damp and covered in straw fluff. Probably wouldn't be comfortable for her tender skin. Gently, he brushed a finger across her cheek, allowing his glove to soak up her tears. He'd have to dry it later, but that was all right.

She sniffled, smiling weakly at him.

"I couldn't do anything. I pleaded with her to leave them alone." He needed a moment to blot out the images in his head. "The funny thing was, by then word had gotten around Locasta was keeping me prisoner and that I told her I'd never yield. Everyone knew I was friends with the strange young sorceress who'd dropped a house on the Witch of the West and melted the Witch of the East. The commoners feared the lords and ladies of the Seelie Court, and thought I must be their champion after all, if I wouldn't give in to the Witch of the North." He snorted. "As if I had a heart like Nick, or bravery like Lion. He went down fighting. By that point I was begging the witch to stop." His friends never conversed about that dark time, once they were through it. None of them wanted to revisit those memories.

One of Scarecrow's first requests to the new Queen, which Ozma granted, was to seal the palace dungeons off forever. He'd overseen the bricking-up himself to be sure.

"Did she..." Theo paused, her face pale. "Are they dead?"

"No." He forced cheer into his voice. "Since the people were rumbling about all this, Locasta gave them a very pretty public speech. How impressed she was with my fortitude under duress. How my immense wisdom finally persuaded her to release me and her claim on the throne."

"All bullshit." Theo scowled fiercely, her petite nose wrinkling.

He smiled. "Correct. She installed me again as Regent. Of course I had to promise to obey any order she gave me, on pain of my friends suffering. As it turned out, she ended up too busy fighting with Mombi and Maab to pay me much mind. And then Jinjur's uprising threw everything to the wind again."

"Jinjur was real?"

"Of course. And very foolhardy for leading an army of women against the Palace Guards, but her coup was briefly successful." The woman general Jinjur had taken advantage of Locasta's divided attention to overrun the Palace with her revolutionaries. Pity all she wanted was to plunder the Royal Treasury, not to actually overthrow the rule of the fae. Her uprising had only sown more chaos into an already fractured Empire.

Theo shook her head. "Scarecrow, I'm so sorry. The books don't talk about any of that horrible stuff. They say you ruled peacefully until Jinjur's army took the Emerald City."

"You said these books are for children," he pointed out. "Not surprised they leave out a few things."

"So Ozma is on the throne now? The girl who used to be Tip?"

"She was when I left." Which felt more and more like a terrible mistake. "She trusted me, and I left her. I thought she'd be safe enough. She has Nick, and the Lion and Tiger to protect her. The mechanical guardian TikTok, if she's remembered to keep him wound up. Glinda seems to like Ozma." As much as any fae could, at least. Ozma Tip was in awe of the ancient fae witch. Now she'd turn to her more often, instead of asking Scarecrow to help.

He felt suddenly as if those locusts were back in his belly. Resisting an urge to check, he rubbed one hand across his forehead. "What have I done," he murmured.

"You came here searching for Dorothy."

"Yes. Which was a very selfish thing."

"Are you taking her back to Oz?"

She didn't understand. "I can't. I can't go back."

Theo frowned, shaking her head.

"This was a one-way journey. I have no way to go home." He shuddered. "I'm a fool. I thought if only I could see her again, tell her... But what does that matter? I've left Ozma Tip unguarded. Not that I could protect her physically, I mean, but Glinda seemed cautious around me. Amused, but cautious. Perhaps she's only been waiting for me to leave."

Theo sat back, chewing her lower lip. "Has Glinda ever tried to hurt you or Ozma?"

"No," he admitted.

"Has she said she wants to rule Oz?"

"No. But she's one of the Fair Folk. Very high in the Seelie Court, respected by all the factions. Well, feared by them, at least."

"Maybe that's a good thing. She'll keep everyone in line. And she said Ozma should rule, right?"

"Yes." No way of knowing what the Good Witch thought or wanted, not really. She was an enigma behind her flowing dress and tolerant smile. He shook his head. "I just can't help fearing I've played right into whatever she's planning. All because I'm foolish enough to hope..."

Theo touched his arm. "Hey. You came here for love, right?"

Unhappily, he nodded.

"Well, if the old stories about faeries are real, maybe the ones about true love are too. How love has the power to heal."

"Glinda said something like that. If I can find Dorothy, and if she wants me, then love will sustain me in this world." The instant the words left his mouth he wanted to take them back. He had no guarantee his beloved felt the same.

She liked him well enough, as much as she liked the others, at least. She'd hugged him several times. And they'd spent one incredible night, on their way to petition the so-called Good Witch of the South. All of them full of hope after Dorothy's triumph over the Wicked Witch. Buoyed by their success. They'd stayed a night at a farm along the way. Scarecrow went to the barn, accepting the farmer's offer to replenish his stuffing with some fresh straw. In the cold hours before dawn, Dorothy came to him, shivering, eyes gleaming in the moonlight.

"Wait," Theo said, dragging him out of the memory. "What happens if you can't go home, and when you find Dorothy she—well, what's the worst case?"

"The worst would be if she doesn't regard me the same way," he replied softly.

"And then you're stuck here?"

"Then the magic which animates me fades." Which hadn't sounded as horrible as the possibility she wouldn't feel the same. They'd never been alone when she returned to Oz, when they went with Ozma to the Nome Kingdom. A brief adventure, and then she left again. Never had a chance to really talk. Knowing now he might've endangered the Queen by abandoning her for this risky quest would eat at him all the more if he ended up rejected, alone.

At least he'd spend his last hours of existence knowing he was a fool in two worlds instead of just one.

Theo wrapped her delicate fingers around his hand. "So, what, you'll just..."

He shrugged. "I don't know. Collapse into a senseless, brainless heap of straw, I imagine."

"No." Theo's tone and expression turned fierce. "Nope. Not gonna happen. Not if I have anything to say about it."

What could she do to prevent it? Well, she *was* a witch. Maybe she knew some helpful spell.

Maybe there was such a thing as a good witch, here.

"Thank you," he said. "You're very kind to a fool."

"They're locking up."

Crows and blight, he should've been watching more carefully. Could Dorothy have slipped past while he was cowering inside this metal room?

"You didn't miss anyone," Theo assured him. "I've kept an eyeball on it. Any of them her?" She nodded at the people dispersing through the grounds in twos and threes.

He checked each face as they moved into pools of light. He slumped. "She's not here."

They watched one of the attendants lock the front door and walk into the paved grounds. "Okay." Theo brushed back her pumpkin-orange hair. "So if she was here at all, she must've left while we were still inside. Don't worry, I'll help you track her down."

"Should we just knock on doors? Do people stay up all night here, or should we wait until morning?"

"Neither. I bet if she just showed up here tonight, same as you, she's pretty confused. Would she ask for help?"

"Naturally."

Theo pulled the miniature, illuminated portrait from a pocket and pressed a button. How could that help? He watched her swipe across the glass and then tap her fingertips on it as letters formed beneath them.

"We can start by checking local hospitals. Maybe the cops. Who knows, maybe they're actually good for something." She frowned, tapping something on the glass, then lifted the device to her left ear.

"Can the portrait tell you where we should look?" Scarecrow wondered.

"Kind of." She held up one finger to him, then spoke in a more pleasant voice, "Hi, I'm trying to find a friend of ours who's, uh, missing. Her name's Dorothy Gale."

To whom was she speaking? Scarecrow opened his mouth and Theo quickly pressed her forefinger to his lips. He took the hint.

"Yes. Just like *that* Dorothy. She might be a little confused. Has anyone been admitted who—right. I know. I get it, I do, but we're really worried about her. She hasn't taken her meds and we can't find her. Could you just tell me if anyone fitting her description has shown up in the past couple of days?"

Theo smiled and thrust the lit glass toward Scarecrow. Baffled, he blinked at her.

"Describe Dorothy," she hissed at him, indicating the magic device.

"Oh. Well, she's a beautiful young woman, wearing a blue checked dress," he began, but Theo rolled her eyes. She tugged at her hair and pointed at her face. "Er. She has long dark brown hair and deep brown eyes. Tanned skin. Freckles across her nose," he added.

Theo put the glass to her ear once more. "She's seventeen. She might be talking a lot about Oz or Kansas. Right, yeah, like I said, she stopped taking her meds." Her hopeful expression sagged. "Okay. Thank you."

She lowered the glass, tapping at it. "The admitting nurse hasn't seen anyone like that. Which, I guess, yay, she's not in the hospital."

"Your magic glass lets you hear and speak to other people?" he guessed. Theo nodded. He peered closely at the artifact. "Why, that's wonderful! Perhaps I was lucky to run into a witch, after all. There's a first time for everything."

She snickered. "Everyone has a phone now. It's not a witch thing."

How handy such a thing would be in Oz. And everyone here carried such a useful artifact? Maybe Theo didn't consider herself unusual because everyone here was a witch. Little wonder the fae gave up on this world long ago. The wonders he'd seen thus far certainly gave Glinda competition.

Theo tried another conversation with the local sheriff's office, repeating Dorothy's description. "Nope, they haven't run into her either. I gave them my number in case they find her. I don't give my phone number to *anyone*. Hope you appreciate the sacrifice I'm making here."

"I very much appreciate your help," Scarecrow said gravely. "I'll repay you however I can."

She laughed. "No, I was joking. You don't have to pay me back for this. It's fine." She smiled at him.

He returned a smile uncertainly. Well, no matter how strange her words or mercurial her moods, she seemed an ally. He was likely to need all the assistance he could muster. This was turning into more of a trial than he'd anticipated.

"Maybe she didn't just arrive tonight. Maybe she's been here a while. Days, months. She could've settled in, found a place to live, who knows?" Theo suggested.

Scarecrow nodded. His love was resourceful. If she'd suddenly found herself in this place, so far from the Kansas she knew, no doubt she'd find friends and secure a place for herself somehow.

What if she'd made a new friend who was now as dear to her as he had been, when she first came to Oz?

"Here, let's try any Dorothies in this county." Theo's finger danced across the glass. She handed it to him.

Amazed, he quickly read the first few entries in a list of them. None of the Dorothies were named Gale, and his chest tightened. Different surnames. Perhaps she'd been here some time. Perhaps she'd married. Then he noticed a word showing in nearly every entry.

Obituary.

Trembling, he sat there, eyes fixed upon the glass.

"What?" Theo asked, taking it back from him. "Oh."

Scarecrow stared out the window. There could be a simple reason why he hadn't seen his love here. A very cold, very simple reason. She *was* a meat person. Mortal.

It was probably only due to the vagaries of difficult magic Glinda didn't plunk him down directly before her grave.

Theo placed a hand on his arm. "Scarecrow, we don't know that any of these are her."

"They're all dead. Every name you have conjured there."

Theo moved her fingertip up the glass, bringing more names into the frame. "Not all of them. Here's an article about one who won a garden contest just this year! Here, look, she's..." She paused. "Eighty-two."

Scarecrow closed his eyes.

"There's a picture," Theo offered.

If she was aged, his time with her would be cut short. Did that matter, if she loved him? He dared a look. The white-haired lady in the magic portrait screen had kind blue eyes and apple cheeks. "It's not her," he muttered.

"Well, we'll keep searching."

"This is a fool's errand, and more the fool I to have undertaken it." He shook his head, unable to keep his anxiety inside any longer. "Even if she is here somewhere, why would she want me? I'm just a scarecrow. Just a suit stuffed with straw."

"I thought you were known as the wisest man in Oz."

"We're not in Oz," he snapped. "Everything here is strange and I'm stumbling over my own feet again, lost and just as brainless as I was when she found me in the cornfield."

"Okay, you'll figure stuff out the longer you're here, right? Give it a couple months and you'll be—"

"I don't have a couple of months! I have until the next full moon before my magic runs out."

Theo's eyes widened. "The next full moon?"

"How long have I got?"

"'Til Halloween," she said. Scarecrow glared, frustrated. She swallowed. "One week."

He felt everything slipping away from him again. Even with all these wonderful items at his disposal, how would he find her? Maybe doing things the hard way was best after all. At first light, he'd start knocking on doors. Hopefully this town wasn't a large one, and someone had seen his beloved.

"She has to be near here, right? Maybe—" Suddenly music startled them both. Theo frowned at the magic glass, swiped a finger across it and put it to her ear. "Hello?"

Could the sheriff have located Dorothy so quickly? Who knew what fine tools the man possessed, in a land like this. Scarecrow tensed, watching Theo, but her expression turned from puzzled to stony. She stared past him.

"Is she okay?" Theo asked, her voice thick.

This couldn't be good.

"Okay. I'll be home soon as I can." She lowered the glass. Her eyes remained fixed on it in her palm.

"What's wrong?"

Her gaze finally raised to his. "It's my grandma."

She seemed unwilling to say anything more. Scarecrow laid a gentle hand on her arm. After a moment she took a deep breath.

"She fell. Broke her hip. She's been admitted to the hospital."

Clearly a hospital wasn't someplace anyone wanted to go. "Theo, that's terrible. What can we do?"

"We—you don't have to come with me. I know you need to find Dorothy." Theo blinked back tears. "But I need to go. Gramma is the only person in my family who understands me. She's getting really old and fragile." She patted his hand and gave him a weak smile. "I'll come back as soon as I can. I'll help you find her. But—"

"Will it take many days to travel to see her?"

"No, about three hours to drive home. I just need to check on her, make sure she's okay. Then I can come back for you."

Perhaps he could repay his new friend for her assistance after all. "Is she in pain?"

"Probably. Broken bones hurt like hell, and I've heard hips are pretty bad."

Scarecrow nodded firmly. "I'll come with you, if that's all right. I can sing for her."

"You can what now?"

"I'll sing," he explained. "I've been told it's a comfort. Perhaps it'll make your grandmother feel better."

Theo laughed, sounding as though she didn't believe him. "Not sure warbling about not having a brain is going to do much, but that's nice of you."

"Hmm. I don't know any songs about brains or the lack of them, but if this is a favorite of your grandmother's I'm willing to learn."

Theo stared at him. "Right. Okay. The book Scarecrow, not the movie one. But you sing?"

"I have an excellent voice," he protested. "Here, let me—"

They both jumped at a rap on the window. One of the staff stood next to Scarecrow's door. He hadn't noticed their approach. Theo shoved a key into a hidden spot below the large gear-handle in front of her. Scarecrow clutched at the seat when everything shivered and rumbled. The window next to him slid down.

"Hi, sorry," Theo called to the man frowning in at them.

"You can't stay here," the man said.

"Yep, got it, we're leaving. Have a nice night," Theo said. The man kept frowning, but moved away.

Scarecrow placed his hand on the edge of the window, trying to ascertain how it moved, startled again when it slid upward. He didn't jerk his fingers back quite in time. "Ah, Theo?"

"We have to go. Last thing we need is them calling the cops on us." She blew out a breath. "If you're coming with me, I promise this won't take too long, and we can keep searching online. Maybe make a few calls before we come back, get a better idea where to look."

"Theo..."

"Oh Goddess, sorry!" The glass lowered again. "That didn't hurt?"

He massaged his fingers back into shape. "I don't feel pain." He frowned, remembering the terrible pressure of the whirlwind sweeping him between worlds like so much bundled cloth. "Usually."

She closed her fingers around his, worry plain in her eyes. "I'll help you. We'll figure everything out. Okay?"

He nodded. The gloves were fine new ones, the fingers precisely shaped. He could almost pretend they weren't full of straw until something like this happened to twist them out of joint.

New head, new face. Other adjustments he'd asked a very embarrassed Nick about. Things to make him more of a man, less of a floppy, graceless heap of straw. Who was he fooling? Even if his love were still alive, even if he succeeded in locating her, she'd laugh at him, surely. A straw man hoping to please a mortal woman.

Theo rubbed her eyes. "It's going to be a long drive, and I need coffee. If I didn't have to do this I'd say screw it and get us a hotel room here, but I can't do anything else until I'm sure Gramma Hildy's going to be okay. I'm sorry."

"No need to apologize. I understand."

He didn't, not wholly, having never had an actual family. Unless one counted Nick and Lion and the young woman they all followed into the depths of the earth and back. He was fond of Ozma Tippetarius as well, despite the young ruler's attachment to that ridiculous Pumpkinhead and the snide Sawhorse. Meat people tended to be more connected to each other. Probably due to the fact they would have to part one day, when their organs stopped and their bodies decayed.

He never truly considered before that the same would happen to his love. Perhaps already she was in the earth, nourishing flowers.

Theo roused him again. "You do that a lot, don't you?"

"Do what?"

"Give up your time with someone when they need to go be with their family."

He met her gaze, finding only sympathy. "What right do I have to demand anything?" he asked.

To his surprise, Theo snorted. She buckled a strap across her front and yanked on a lever between the seats. "Promise me one thing."

"What's that?" he asked warily.

"When we find Dorothy, you won't wuss out. You have to tell her how you feel." She shook her head. "I can deal with the fact Oz is real and way different than I thought, but I am *not* going to put up with an emo Scarecrow. You're gonna get your emotional shit together and man up. All right?"

Scarecrow opened his mouth, had no idea what to reply, closed it. He nodded.

"Good." Theo grinned. "Buckle in so you don't end up on the dash-board."

"What?"

With a snarl, the entire room lurched forward. It wasn't a room, it was a carriage. Hastily he found a strap and buckled it, mimicking her movements. Theo grinned wider and slammed her hand over the lever. The carriage picked up speed, trees along a dark drive zipping past. It was worse than riding the Sawhorse when he had a notion to race. Scarecrow shut his eyes, clinging to the strap across his chest.

Theo laughed, patting his leg. "Hang on. Coffee first. You want coffee? Or can you drink anything?"

"No," he gulped, feeling an unpleasant sense of motion as the carriage leaned into a curve in the road.

"Seriously, why are you hanging on for dear life? You're straw. If we crash I'm the one who'll be hurt, not you."

He dared to open his eyes. "I won't let you get hurt, Theo."

She smiled. "Yeah, I know. Same goes for me, right back at ya."

His brains must have been too shaken by the sudden movement. It took him a minute to catch her meaning.

Feeling warm, he grasped her hand in his and smiled back.

7

The drive back to Appleton took forever on the dark highways. Nothing more isolated than a rural road on an autumn night, and Theo was glad to have company. Especially since her traveling companion was unique. After an hour or so of steady travel, Scarecrow finally relaxed enough to peer out the windshield at the stars. Theo slid open the cover to the moon roof for him and directed him to lean the seat back. He stared up at the constellations in the clear night with wondering eyes, his face illuminated in brief flashes by passing cars.

Theo chose a playlist full of Massive Attack, Bjork, and Eurosynth to start the drive home. Scarecrow jumped at the first note of "Human Behavior."

"How are you making that music?"

Theo tapped her phone. "I have a bunch stored on here. I hate driving in silence. You mind?"

"I don't mind." He listened raptly, tapping his fingers in time.

She sang along, though she couldn't match the high girlish range of the Icelandic artist. Scarecrow tilted his hat back to expose more of his burlap ears to the music.

At least he'd stopped freaking out. She had the definite impression he didn't tell her everything about being tortured by the witch. Certainly traveling with her now would be less scary than *that*.

A quiet track came on, instrumental and moody. Theo watched the dark trees whisking past, barely seen at the edges of the headlights.

How badly was Gramma Hildy hurt? Tough old woman had lived through the drawn-out death by cancer of her husband of forty-five years, as well as decades of social upheaval. She'd marched for equal rights in Milwaukee, protested the Vietnam War, remained outspoken and cheerful. She was Theo's hero. The fact that her son, Theo's dad, was embarrassed by her only added to Theo's appreciation.

Gramma lived by herself still in the beautiful old house where she and Grampa Horace raised their three children. Theo dropped by every week to play gin rummy with her. Gramma Hildy always baked something, rhubarb pie or coffee cake or fabulous oatmeal chocolate chip cookies. At Mom's insistence, Gramma agreed to allow a cleaning service to come in twice a month. She cleaned the house beforehand, because she couldn't bear the thought of anyone dropping by and finding her home dirty. This past year, Theo did a little cleaning herself every visit. Gramma wasn't as energetic as she used to be. And now this.

Crap, Dad would probably press his argument to put Gramma in an assisted living facility. Those places were total grifts. He'd use this as an excuse to demand she pick one, argue she couldn't look after herself anymore.

Maybe he had a point. What a depressing thought.

Rumble strips at the side of the lane startled Theo fully awake. "Dammit," she muttered, adjusting the steering.

"Are you all right?"

"Yeah, I'm good."

"Perhaps you should rest," Scarecrow suggested.

Theo shook her head. "Can't. We still have a ways to go."

"You could show me how to operate your carriage," he offered.

Theo laughed. "Teaching you to drive is gonna take way more time than we have. Thanks, though," she added at his crestfallen expression. She swigged more coffee. An hour and a half to go. Madison was behind them now, with nothing but dark, empty fields and small-town traffic lights for miles before they'd meet up with the interstate's gaudy billboard lights. "Help me keep an eye out for deer."

"You have deer here?"

"Of course. And they wander onto the roads and get hit. Last thing we need is to slam into one tonight."

Scarecrow nodded. "I don't imagine they'd care for that. I'll watch." He raised his seat-back to better watch out the front windshield. His eyes narrowed, peering ahead, where the bright headlights picked out grasses and the occasional road sign.

In profile, his aquiline nose stuck out well past the rest of his face. It reminded her a bit of the actor who'd famously portrayed him in the best-known Oz film, but also that in the books his features were all painted and flat on a flour-sack head. "So why did you change your face?" she asked.

He winced. "Oh. Well, there are disadvantages to wearing a painted smile all the time. I was also tired of people remarking how one of my eyes was a bit larger than the other. The farmer who painted my features was no great artist, though I think he did the best he could. Meat people can show their emotions on their faces. It took me some time to memorize every possible expression."

"You're very good at them."

He smiled. "Thank you, that's nice to hear."

"What about the nose, though?"

He touched its prominent curve. "What about it?"

Theo chuckled. "Well, it's just kind of a big leap from a painted-on triangle to that."

"I wanted to be more like a true man. You don't think it suits me?"

He seemed so worried that she patted his arm. "It's very handsome. I'm sure Dorothy will think so too." It was actually kind of adorkable. She hoped Dorothy didn't go for the conventionally handsome type with chiseled features, because Scarecrow didn't fit that category. "You look fine. Totally fine. Uh, manly." She flashed a smile, and he nodded, mumbling thanks. "Why keep it painted red, though?"

He slumped further down in his seat, fidgeting with his gloves. "I didn't want to appear so different she wouldn't recognize me."

No chance of that. Straw stuck out of his tunic where the missing second button left a gap.

"She told me once she liked me as I was, before I received my brains," he continued softly, "but she also said she wished I were a real man. So I've tried to be both."

He'd changed himself just to please a girl he hadn't seen in three years? Yikes.

Mark, her last boyfriend, sprang to mind. Theo thought at first he appreciated her witchy aesthetic, her flowing skirts and tight bodices, swooping cloaks and heavy boots suitable for tromping around the forest in style. Then he'd made comments about her wearing the same stuff all the time. About her top showing off her boobs too much to other guys, or how if they were attending one of his friends' indoor LARPing sessions she could at least put on some more feminine footgear. Theo reluctantly gave in, worn more modest blouses and flats.

Except then his treatment of her changed. He'd talk over her around his friends. Get petulant when she didn't coo over every single rose he presented her. The same single red rose, every time he saw her, each given to her with a flourish which he probably thought was elegant. He frowned at her when she'd curse in public. Hush her when she spoke during coven ceremonies. Turned out Mark didn't want Theo as she was. He wanted a femme girl in flowing skirts who demurred to her vampire-wannabe, coven-leader lover.

Yeah, fuck that noise. She'd thrown him out after a shouting match that ended in him trying to force himself onto her. She hadn't put her boots on before kicking him in the family jewels, and it hurt her foot. Inconsiderate asshole.

"Have I upset you?" Scarecrow asked.

"No, no. Just thinking about the creep I used to date."

"Oh," Scarecrow said, brows arching. "I hope I don't remind you of him."

"Not unless you're going to insist I act more feminine."

He blinked. "Why would I?"

She shrugged. "I didn't mean you would. Just that some men don't know what to do with a woman who doesn't want to suck up to them every minute."

"Hmf. There were a few of those in the Emerald City. Even after Ozma ascended to the throne." He gazed into the night with a faint smile. "I remember one braggart who was dragged in by the city watch for boasting he'd beat the new Queen like a stubborn goat until she learned some manners."

In the books, the descriptions of the young ruler ranged from brave to annoyingly wallflowery. "What did she do?" Theo asked.

He snorted a laugh. "Tip took off her robe and crown and challenged the lazy drunkard to a fist-fight right there in the throne room! It took three rounds, but she knocked him cold. Lion refereed." He shook his head, grinning. "Tiny, skinny Ozma standing there, out of breath, one eye turning all puffy but pleased as anything she'd won fair and square. I don't think any man in Oz said a rude word about her after that."

Theo laughed with him, picturing it. "Oh dear Goddess. Didn't Glinda object?"

Scarecrow leaned closer with a conspiratorial grin. "She wasn't there. Off on some business at the Seelie Court. So Ozma Tip waded into the fight like a teenage street rat. Oh, it was beautiful."

In the books, Ozma was turned into a boy as a baby and never knew her true identity, until Glinda forced Mombi the witch to confess the enchantment and reverse the transformation spell. "Guess she still kinda was a teenage street rat."

He laughed. "I suppose so! Hadn't thought of it that way." They quieted, listening to the music. "Ozma is still Tip," he said, with a thoughtful nod. "They just wear royal gowns now."

Maybe there was good reason Oz symbolized a more tolerant, open society for many people. Scarecrow didn't seem to have any prejudices about gender roles. Maybe that was the fae influence? Just how like the faeries of old myth were these people? "Hey, do you know if—"

"Look out!"

Something huge, shaggy, and pale streaked across the road. Theo stomped the brakes and swerved. Scarecrow flailed, startled. Theo grunted, righting their course, slowing. A quick glance in the rearview showed no other headlights anywhere close, and no sign of the beast. Deer. Had to be a deer.

Shaking, she eased the gas back down. "Telling me there's a deer two seconds before we hit one is not helpful," she growled.

"But there wasn't a deer," he protested.

"So what the hell just ran across the road?"

He leaned away from her, eyes wide. "Well, I only caught a glimpse, but it looked more like a khalidah. You didn't tell me to watch out for those."

No. No fucking way. "It was a goddamn albino deer," she snapped. "And I really need you to keep a sharper eye out, okay?"

"Of course, you're right," he said softly.

Aware her heart was thudding, she adjusted her death grip on the wheel. Well, she was awake now for sure. She blew out a shaky breath.

Scarecrow faced straight ahead, watching carefully as black trees swept past, silent.

"Sorry, I didn't mean to yell at you."

His eyes flicked to her, then ahead again. "I understand."

Wow, now she felt even worse. "I'm sorry," she repeated, this time taking hold of his hand. "That scared the hell out of me. Not your fault. It jumped out so fast."

To her relief, he squeezed her fingers back. "It's all right. I'm thankful your carriage can outrun a khalidah."

"Scarecrow, that wasn't a khalidah." She vaguely remembered the term from the first book. Some kind of composite monster bigger and fiercer than the Cowardly Lion. She couldn't recall how the party escaped an attack. "Those aren't—" *Real.* Yeah. She was about to tell a talking scarecrow that a tiger-bear creature wasn't real because she'd only read about it in a children's book.

She swallowed, trying to sound more convincing than she felt. "Those don't exist here."

"They don't?"

"No. No such thing. Just a deer. Either an albino one or just really pale. They try to cross in front of cars all the time and end up dead on the side of the road."

"Oh." He twisted around. Only blackness and very distant headlights back there. "Maybe I was mistaken." He perked. "Maybe you mean something different by a deer than I do. Do yours have antlers and four skinny legs and very short tails?"

"Yeah." Sourness swirled in her stomach. She swallowed it down. Should've bought water as well as coffee. Drinking anything acidic now was a bad idea.

"Oh," he said again, eyebrows knit. "Well. It didn't look like that at all."

"You didn't bring other Oz creatures here with you, did you?"

He shook his head. "Nothing flesh can cross through the veil from Oz to the Outside World. All the books say so." Frowning, he added,

"I must have been mistaken. Perhaps my brains haven't adjusted to this world yet."

"Do you see anything back there now?"

"No, do you?"

She checked the mirror again. "Nope."

The animal had been far too massive for a deer. Bear, maybe, though that would be extremely rare.

Especially not a huge white polar bear. With stripes.

Whatever it was, she sure as hell wasn't about to turn around for a closer look. Tonight was weird enough without adding Ozian monsters. She turned up the music and put the pedal down.

8

D ays passed with no word from the Scarecrow.

Nick Chopper spent the first day consoling young Ozma Tip-petarius, who was understandably upset. Running off without even say-ing a proper goodbye seemed a little cowardly. Even Lion growled and lashed his tail when he heard their friend left Oz for good. Nick nodded and listened while each of them went on at some length about how thoughtless and worrying their straw friend's actions were. He em-pathized, but didn't offer his own thoughts.

Alone on the third day since Scarecrow left, Nick took out the Evs-tone on its delicate chain. The swirling inclusions in the pink rock were still and silent. Though tempted to use it, each time Nick hesitated and then tucked it away in his pocket again. If Scarecrow had found Dorothy, and she welcomed him, interrupting them would be rude. If the straw man hadn't survived the terrible whirlwind Glinda had called up...

Well. He wasn't going to think about that.

He'd begun wearing a sleek, rose-patterned silk waistcoat just to keep careful hold of the stone, afraid it would be damaged banging against his nickel-plated side, or damage him.

Walking with his head down through the echoing corridors of the Emerald Palace, he didn't see Lion until the beast snorted. Nick jerked upright with a clatter.

Lion smirked. "Since when did you get so interested in rocks?"

"Would you stop sneaking up on people?" Nick complained, putting a hand over his heart. He could feel the velvet shudder as it slowed its frantic pace. So odd that an organ of sawdust and velvet could beat, but he'd ceased to wonder about it until something happened to remind him—such as an enormous cat scaring him after a stealthy approach on padded paws.

Lion regarded his claws on one forepaw, radiating smug satisfaction. "Still got it."

"I thought you were off gallivanting around the forest with Tiger."

"Nah, decided not to go." Lion nodded at Nick's waistcoat. "You've been acting strange since the straw man left. What's all this stuff?"

"The rock is a linked Evstone. Glinda enchanted a pair of them."

"Who's got the other one?"

"Scarecrow," Nick said.

"You mean he took it with him to Dorothy's world? What's it do?" Lion growled before Nick could reply. "Hold on. Are you gonna use it to pull him back? Pull both of them back? Is that why you aren't upset about him leaving?"

Upset wasn't the word. Resigned, perhaps. Nick had known for years his attraction to the ridiculous, clumsy, oblivious Scarecrow was not only unrequited, but also his friend hadn't the faintest clue those feelings existed. Now the shred of a chance Nick half-hoped might one day blossom was utterly crushed.

He shook his head. "There's no way to get him back. He's gone."

Lion scowled. "So what's the rock for? Just a lover's souvenir?"

Nick froze, jaw agape.

Lion snickered. "Don't act like you weren't obvious. Calling him your bosom friend, asking him to be your treasurer. As if you didn't simply want him to be with you night and day."

"I wish it had been obvious," Nick sighed. "Maybe then..." Who was he kidding? Scarecrow had been infatuated with Dorothy from the moment she helped him off the pole in the cornfield.

Lion put a paw on Nick's shoulder. "I don't know how miserable I'd be without Tiger. I understand, my friend. Now, what's the rock for?"

"It should allow me to talk to him, even in her world."

"So is he all right? Did he find her?"

"I don't know. I haven't tried to use it yet."

Lion scoffed. "And they called me cowardly."

"I'm trying to be considerate." Nick felt heated. "It would be rude to interrupt them."

Lion glanced around, stepping cautiously closer. His rumbly voice dropped to a whisper. "You think the Good Witch really sent him to her?"

"She said her spell would take him to his heart's desire." Nick shrugged, shoulders clacking. "You know she likes dancing around the truth, but she never outright *lies*. I have to assume he's with Dorothy, wherever she is. And since he hasn't contacted me yet..."

"Ah. Well, good for him, I guess. All that talk about getting a brain when it was blindingly obvious what he really wanted." Lion's muzzle wrinkled. "Took him long enough to figure it out."

"He didn't," Nick admitted wearily. "I had to tell him."

"You—" Lion's turn to gawp. He shook his head, and what might have been respect shone in his amber eyes. "Well."

Nick sighed again. "Yeah."

Lion clapped him on the shoulder hard enough to jostle him sideways a step. "You need a drink, I bet. Why don't you come out with me and Tiger tonight? We're going over to Madam Jinjur's, let the girls comb our fur. You know she keeps a couple of boys on staff too." He winked, whiskers twitching.

Wallowing in flesh was pointless. Nick shook his head. "No thanks."

"We'll save you a seat in case you change your mind." Lion paused, his pupils slitted against the bright green light of the hallway.

"What?" Nick demanded.

"Nothing." Lion turned to go. "You're a good man, Nick. Let me know when you hear from him."

He padded away silently. Nick watched him disappear between the massive marble columns.

Much as Nick would like a distraction, pretending he was having a good time with some young meaty man wasn't going to heal his heartache. Funny, how gaining a stuffed heart gave him sudden clarity after years of considering himself unable to love. Back when he was made of flesh, he'd courted Nimmee Amee, a witch's servant girl who lived at the edge of the forest, because she gave the first spark of affection he'd received since he'd left home. Deep down, under his efforts to be a caring suitor for her, he knew he didn't love her. Just didn't want to accept it. As his body was replaced piece by piece with tin parts, it was easy to tell himself his transformation was why he felt only friendship with the girl, not the passion she displayed for him.

Over and over he told himself it was his lack of a meat heart in his tin chest which caused him to abandon the relationship. Guilt dogged him. When Dorothy and Scarecrow rescued him from a rusty fate, the prospect of regaining a heart, one which might love Nimmee, carried him through their terrible adventures.

When the Scarecrow became stranded in a river along their journey, Nick was distraught. A kindly stork rescued the straw man, bringing him back to the party, and Scarecrow was so overjoyed he hugged them all. When he flung his soft arms around Nick's neck, pressed himself to Nick's hollow tin chest, Nick experienced a jolt of soaring happiness. The feeling so confused him that he kept repeating he needed a heart in order to love the girl he'd left behind. Repeated it so often to himself he almost believed it.

The heart the Wizard installed in his chest did give him a moment of joy. Then followed nights upon nights of dismay and self-disparagement. How could he have left the girl who loved him, even though he was no longer flesh and bone? Who desired him still, when he was all cold metal?

The truth didn't dawn on him until the night the party spent on a farm on their way to find Glinda. Dorothy was invited to sleep in the farmer's home. Scarecrow went to the barn to refresh his straw. Lion found a sturdy fir tree and fell solidly asleep in the safety of its low, concealing branches. Nick paced outside for hours.

Surely his friend couldn't restuff himself. How would he manage his hands and arms? He was adorably clumsy as it was. Definitely lacking the expert touch required to put himself back together, even if he managed to take all the old straw out. Nick should offer to help. Just as any friend should do.

Nick was three paces away from the barn when he heard a low moan.

And then a hushed, hesitant voice, though he couldn't make out the words.

A softer, higher sound, wordless and keening with pleasure, set Nick's entire body afire with jealousy.

Scarecrow was in there with Dorothy. Making her make those sounds.

Nick suddenly realized his axe was in his hand, gripping it so tightly his fingers were stiff, locked in place. Frightened, he backed away, out of range of those quiet, intimate voices. He strode to the far fence marking the farmer's property and stood there shaking. His joints rattled. Leaning on the fence, he tried to blot out the sounds echoing inside his metal skull.

It wasn't until that moment he understood he was in love with Scarecrow.

Scarecrow, who only ever gazed in rapt affection at the young woman journeying with them. And she kept saying over and over, to everyone they met, how badly she wanted to return home.

She did, with Glinda's help. Sure, she'd cried, hugged them all, and smiled sadly at Scarecrow for an extra second or two. And then she'd vanished.

Nick dared to hope then. Hoped perhaps his friend would notice. Nick wasn't like Dorothy. Nick wasn't about to leave.

He didn't want to remember the torment which followed. The war between the fae factions over the throne. How many people his axe struck down, blood gushing from arms or necks. The horrible time in the dungeon. The acid eating away his legs hadn't truly hurt Nick. Hearing his friend pleading for Nick's life and Lion's, abasing himself to beg the Witch of the North to stop the torture, broke his heart.

Hope grew back when they were released, like a sapling after a forest fire. Slowly. Cautiously. General Jinjur's invasion of the Emerald City and the Palace itself drove Scarecrow back to Nick. What a giddy delight, knowing his friend regarded him as a safe haven, a sturdy ally. They'd managed together to save the boy Tip, enlisted the help of the Good Witch of the South even though she'd cared nothing for the struggles of the Kingdom before. Scarecrow agreed to return to the western land of the Winkies by Nick's side.

He'd seemed content enough, if still absolutely oblivious to the overtures Nick gently made. So hard to be patient with him some days. But as they were straw and tin, they had time, Nick consoled himself. Eventually Scarecrow would realize how loyal this friendship truly was.

Eventually never came. Instead, Dorothy returned.

Ozma Tip asked them all to come with her on a mission to liberate the royal family of Ev from imprisonment in the Nome Kingdom. At first, Nick was happy to be journeying side by side with Scarecrow, proud that the new young Queen chose them both to help her. What none of them knew was that Dorothy had returned, ending up in Ev, an unwilling guest to the witch Langwidere.

The instant Nick and Scarecrow both looked up to see Dorothy leaning out of a tower window, waving at them, her long dark hair whipping in the wind, Nick's heart turned cold. A glance at Scarecrow's face confirmed the worst. Those painted blue eyes were dazed again.

Dorothy was too caught up in their dangerous adventure to spend any time alone with Scarecrow, but he still hovered at her elbow, anxious to please her. Nick's annoyance softened after the girl from Kansas managed to save the rest of the party from a dreadful fate. The Nome King transformed nearly all of them into ornaments for his underground palace. Dorothy and her pet chicken survived and used the Nome King's own Magic Belt to revert them all to their proper forms.

Nick was sorely tempted to ask his Queen to use the belt, to open Scarecrow's eyes and heart to the person who adored him more than Dorothy ever could. Instead, he held his tin tongue as Dorothy was magicked back to the Outside World, and did his best to comfort Scarecrow's bewildered grief at her leaving them a second time.

When she left, again, they all went with Ozma Tip back to the palace. Tip, unused to being a girl after growing up male, clung to Nick's hand on one side and Scarecrow's on the other while she addressed her subjects. Told them the land of Ev was again under the rule of its rightful fae Queen, and an ally of Oz.

It had taken Nick so long to comprehend who he really was. He saw the same fear, confusion and panic, in the eyes of the young ruler.

How could he deny her whatever strength he possessed? He remained at the palace.

Months marched past. Scarecrow mooned about the grounds, listless, grave. Nick did his best to stifle his own feelings, to encourage Ozma Tippetarius to be mindful of her subjects' needs, their hopes and fears.

Sometimes he wondered how he'd feel if she'd remained male. Grown up to be King rather than Queen. No use wondering about it now, no more than there was any point in wishing he hadn't told Scarecrow to go after his one love.

As if she heard his unhappy thoughts, footsteps sounded along the corridor. He recognized the tread. She couldn't be dainty to save her life.

Ozma Tip swung around a pillar into the main hallway, startled when she saw Nick. "Oh! General. I didn't hear you."

He smiled. "I was just standing here, thinking."

She laughed, curling a long lock of black hair behind the poppy over her left ear. "You don't make any noise while thinking. Not like Scarecrow."

The ridiculous *pop* when the straw man concentrated so hard he pushed one of the pins he had for brains right through his burlap head never failed to make Nick chuckle. He didn't want to recall that sound now.

"How are you today, Your Highness?"

Tip cast a furtive glance up and down the corridor. "Come on, you don't need to call me that when it's just me and you."

Nick offered his arm. She took it and they strolled together. "What's on your mind?" she asked.

"Not much. I was just thinking about when we accompanied you here with the Good Witch, actually."

Tip made a sour face. "That stupid gown. Ugh."

"I thought you looked very pretty."

"I hate dresses. They don't have pockets. I can't carry anything."

"You could ask the royal seamstress to make you gowns with pockets."

"Why didn't I think of that? Yes. I will."

"So what business occupies you today?"

Tip steered them out to a balcony overlooking the rose gardens. Below, the gardening staff packed their tools into wheelbarrows, toil completed for the evening. One noticed the Queen, and Tip waved. The man gave a low bow in return before continuing on his way.

"Galloping goblins, I'm so sick of people bowing and curtseying," Tip growled.

Nick laughed. "You could make it a law that no one could bow to you."

"The Pink Witch wouldn't let me. 'The dignity of the crown, respect due the monarchy something something.'"

He laughed again. Yes, it was a pity Ozma Tip was too young. She was enjoyable company. "Too bad. So, what have you been up to today?"

Tip gazed out over the garden as the sky turned golden-pink. "I wish he'd said goodbye."

Nick swallowed. Old habits persisted, even with a metal throat. "Me too."

"Do you think we'll ever see him again?"

"No."

Ozma Tip scowled. She turned back to the garden view. After a moment, she kicked the stone balustrade with a bejeweled slipper. "*Why?* Why did he have to go?"

"He loves Dorothy." Nick forced the words out. He wanted to see them hanging in the air, wanted their coldness and clarity.

Tip didn't give him time to wallow. "Well, duh! We all do. And we love him. What's so special about her that he had to leave us?" She snorted. "Kansas. It sounds horrible. Why would anyone want to live such a stupid place anyway? No magic? I mean, what the actual dirty Nome bollocks."

Much though he agreed, Nick wrapped an arm around Tip's shoulders and hugged gently. "Don't let the Pink Lady hear you cursing."

She leaned against him. At least somebody found his cold touch a comfort.

"Screw the Pink Lady. Screw this whole Queen thing! I'm so tired of it." She wrenched away, spinning around to glare at Nick. Tears glimmered in her eyes. "What good is being Queen of all Oz if I can't even keep my friends around?" She took hold of his arm. "Promise me you won't leave too."

His heart caught, then resumed beating. The poor child. "I won't."

They stayed like for some time, her leaning on him, hugging his arm to her chest until the metal warmed.

Finally, she spoke again, her voice back under control. "What's with the waistcoat, anyway? Never seen you wear clothes before."

"Does it look bad?"

"No, it's great. Very," she paused, frowning, "elegant."

"Really?"

Tip nodded. "Yes. I think I'd like Jack to wear something similar. Can you have your tailor make him one too?"

Nick bit his tin tongue. The gangly Jack Pumpkinhead, a creation of wood, old clothes, and a carved gourd for a face whom Tip had made years ago, would appear extra silly with formalwear hanging off his stick-figure frame. Next thing you know, the Queen would want her Sawhorse outfitted with a satin saddle blanket. "I'll ask."

She tugged his arm. Obediently he walked with her back through the echoing halls, escorting her to the royal chambers. She hesitated at the door. "Hey Nick?"

"Yes?"

"Thank you, for not," she chewed her lip, blinking up at him, and a warm feeling kindled in his chest. "For not treating me any differently. I know you must understand how weird all this is."

"I can only imagine how difficult the past years have been for you."

She stepped closer, voice dropping. "I wanted you to know, if you ever want to talk, you can come to me."

Surprised, he stared at her.

She blushed. "I mean, you've always been here when I needed you. All of you guys. And the past couple days you've been upset. About him. I'm upset too, but I know he was more than a friend to you."

Where did all this insight come from? Tip was growing up faster than he'd thought. Nick nodded, dumbstruck.

Tip patted his hand awkwardly. "I'm really glad you didn't go with him. I'm glad you stayed. So, um, thank you."

"Of course," Nick murmured.

She stretched on tiptoe. He leaned over so she could whisper in his ear.

"I think Dorothy better be damned grateful. I know she probably doesn't even think about the fact he left all of us for her, but still, she better be grateful. Or I'll go after her and give her something worse to think about," Tip hissed.

Nick barely smothered a hearty guffaw, turning it into a choking cough. "You know what I think?"

"What?"

"I think Oz has the best Queen on the throne, if she's willing to go thrash anyone who doesn't appreciate her friends."

Tip gave him a curious frown. "Well, yeah. I wouldn't deserve any friends if I didn't."

Nick nodded, still smiling.

"Thanks, Nick. Good night." He murmured the same back, and was about to leave when she asked, "Hey, would you keep the Good Witch busy tomorrow?"

He raised a brow. "Why, what are you scheming?"

"Nothing. Just wanted to try to find the library again."

"Which library?" He thought with a pang of Scarecrow's vast rooms of ceiling-high bookshelves.

"The magic one," Tip whispered. "I'm gonna see if I can make the magic painting show us lands outside of Oz."

He studied the determined set of her jaw. "To find Scarecrow?"

She nodded. "I just want to be sure he's all right."

Well, it wasn't as though the Evstone was a state secret. He'd just wanted to keep it to himself. If Glinda caught her young charge perusing forbidden tomes again, the punishment this time might be worse than locking her up for a week in her rooms. With a sigh, Nick drew out the stone and showed it to Tip. "We can use this to talk to him."

Her eyes widened. "This? How? Have you spoken to him? Where is he?"

"No, no I haven't. I don't know."

"Well, use it! What are you waiting for?"

Pained, Nick gently pried her fingers from the stone and tucked it safely in his pocket again. "He'll contact us when he's ready."

If Scarecrow survived the dangerous trip, which no one ever had before from this land to the realm beyond. No one in recorded history, at least, save Dorothy, but she was from the Outside World in the first place.

Ozma Tippetarius glared at her tin general. "I command you to get hold of him. Now."

"No, I'm sorry, Your Highness. It wouldn't be right."

"I don't see why not."

She'd only voiced what he himself felt, every hour, every minute since Scarecrow left. "If he found Dorothy right away, one of two things has happened." He held up a finger. "One, and for his sake I hope this isn't the case, she might have married someone else, or doesn't feel about him the way he feels about her."

"Then she's an idiot," Tip snorted.

Well, agreed, but not the point he was trying to make. "Two, they're reunited at last. And people in love tend to, well, not pay attention to anything or anyone else. Even their friends."

"You think they're too busy kissing?"

There was an image he didn't need. Nick winced. "Something like that."

"But what if it isn't either of those? What if he didn't make it?" Her expression mirrored his fear.

"We just have to hope that's not the case. After all, the Good Witch is the most powerful sorceress in all of Oz. I'm sure her spell worked."

"Has she said that Scarecrow made it to the other world safely?"

The fae witch was, in fact, notably absent since the morning of Scarecrow's departure. Nick hadn't heard she'd gone anywhere, but neither had he run into her anywhere on the palace grounds, which was a bit unusual. "I haven't spoken to her."

"Then use the damned stone!"

Nick closed his eyes, struggling for calm. "Let's give it another day. I just don't want to interrupt him if—if things are going well."

When he opened his eyes again, Tip stood there forlorn, staring up at him with a worried pout. "You don't want to find out if he didn't make it," she accused.

"Don't say that," Nick pleaded.

"What if he's dead? I heard a whirlwind carried him off. What if it ripped him apart? He's just straw!"

"Don't say things like that!"

"But what if—"

"Tip, be quiet!" Nick snapped.

Startled, the young Queen gaped at him a second, then shut her mouth, backed into her room with a wounded look, and shut the door silently.

Regret filled him immediately. She was barely fourteen, for Oz' sakes. Not to mention his lawful ruler. He was about to knock on her door, apologize, when the heavy footsteps of the night watch sounded at the end of the corridor. Nick gulped down his remorse, straightened his shoulders, and turned to face the man on patrol.

Glinda had appointed the Royal Guards to patrol outside Ozma's door all night, every night. Nick volunteered himself for the duty when he heard about it, but the way Glinda sweetly demurred made it clear she wanted one of her own men here.

"For safety's sake. One never knows when the Nomes will try something," she'd explained. "Besides, General, don't you have more important tasks, like training our army?"

If he lingered, it would be reported to the Good Witch. Who insisted Tip must be a regal Queen at all times. And who'd sent the Scarecrow to fates unknown without seeming concerned about him.

Nick held himself stiff and formal as he inclined his head to the guard. "Soldier."

The guard bowed the precise three seconds required by court propriety. "General. Is the Queen abed?"

"Yes. I just escorted her here a minute ago."

"Very good, sir."

Nick couldn't think of a way to get the man to leave. His heart thumped unhappily in its tin cage. With another nod, Nick left. The faint clink of metal behind him made him turn. The guard slipped a key from the lock on Ozma's chamber door and gave the handle a firm shake to be sure it was shut tight.

They locked her in at night? She was the ruler of all Oz and the owner of this palace! Who would— Nick slowed, then made himself resume a calm, confident stride so as not to attract the guard's further notice.

Had to be Glinda. But why?

He suddenly remembered her face as she'd caressed Scarecrow's jaw, right before conjuring a small tornado. Nick had been too preoccupied with his own grief to really consider the witch's motives. Stupid of him. The fae always had some hidden agenda, and none more than the so-called "Good Witch" of the South. Tip was on the throne through her vocal support and hers alone. Just as Scarecrow served as Regent only with the sufferance of the witch Locasta, once she'd ensured his loyalty through fear.

Damnation and rust. Why hadn't he thought about the parallels before now?

He needed to speak with Glinda. Express his very real concern for Scarecrow, and gauge her reaction. She didn't feel love, couldn't possibly sympathize with the yearning heart of a straw man, much less any feeling creature of flesh. So why did she craft a spell to do what he wanted? More than one spell, if the hints Scarecrow dropped about improving his body to be "more like a true man" had actually been satisfied by the witch's magic.

And why keep Tip locked up at night, under guard?

Nick strained to remember every detail of the morning Scarecrow left as he walked to his own quarters. What were the fine, fae things set to come at the full moon?

Why hadn't Scarecrow contacted him yet?

Cold inside, Nick Chopper locked his door behind him. He'd never felt the need for such security before. Not in the safest building in all of Oz.

The half-moon shone through his window, rising over the black shadows of trees.

Nick closed the shutters and bolted them. He set the Evstone on his table, sat in front of it, and stared at it all night, a million fears swirling in his chest.

9

Theo pulled into the hospital parking lot in the early morning. She was fairly certain visiting hours didn't start until eight. She also wasn't about to let that stop her.

Grimly she kicked open the creaky driver's-side door, stood and stretched. She waited for Scarecrow to join her, fidgeting with her jacket in the chilly night air. He fell in behind her as Theo stomped across the lot to the emergency room door. A security guard hastily rose from a desk in the entry area to block her way.

"Hi, are you hurt?"

Crap. Maybe they wouldn't let her in unless... "My friend's not feeling well," she announced, gesturing back at Scarecrow.

The guard looked at him dubiously. "Oh yah?"

Theo glared a warning at Scarecrow. "He's—it's his stomach. He hasn't been able to eat a thing and I'm worried about him. Where's the admitting desk?"

The guard frowned at Scarecrow. "Can't eat a thing, huh?"

"No. Not a thing," Scarecrow replied, shaking his head.

Smart man. Theo gave him a quick nod before the guard turned back to her.

"All right then, just go straight ahead there. Should be a nurse at the desk on your left, right before the main lobby. Hope it's nothing serious," he said.

Theo grabbed Scarecrow's hand, flashed a smile at the guard, and marched in. "Thanks," she muttered at her accomplice.

"Why are you lying your way in?" he whispered, matching her stride, though he stumbled once on his floppy feet.

"Because the guard probably wouldn't let us in at this hour otherwise. Anyways you went along with it, so you're in it now too."

"I didn't lie," he pointed out. "What happens when they find out you—"

"Goodness, what's the matter?" asked a white-haired woman in a crisp uniform. The night admitting nurse, Theo guessed.

Theo took a deep breath. "I need to see my grandmother right away. Hilda Van Baum. She was brought in tonight."

The nurse frowned. "It's after visiting hours. I'm sorry, but you'll need to come back when—"

"No. I need to see her now. I need to be sure she's all right," Theo insisted.

"Hon, it's two in the morning. She'll be asleep. Now you're more than welcome to check on her once the hospital opens at—"

"Do you see that plaque on the wall?" Theo snapped, pointing at a large plaque etched in brass on the two-story wall of the main lobby. Though the room was dark, a few amber lights picked out the donor plaques and the staircase next to them. Water burbled down a series of plant-filled levels. Theo's voice was too loud in all this peaceful hush. Fine. All the better to make a nuisance of herself.

The nurse kept frowning. "I really have to ask you to calm down. This is a hospital. People are sleeping."

"Perhaps we should come back," Scarecrow suggested.

"No." Theo's arm remained raised, black-painted index fingernail thrust toward the wall of honorariums. "See that biggest brass plate there? Let me tell you what it says. It was donated by the Van Baum family in memory of *my* grandfather Horace. He died in this hospital. I am Dorothea Theodora Van Baum and I need to make damned sure my gramma doesn't die here too. Now tell me what room she's in or I'll call the hospital director right this second."

She didn't know who the hell the director was, much less have them on speed dial, but the brass plaque did have her family name on it. Grampa Horace left a generous donation in his will, in appreciation for the nursing staff who'd tended him for months here as his organs stuttered and failed. Theo's dad also contributed to the hospital's fundraisers every year. If she had to be part of this disgustingly wealthy family, the least they could do was loan her their power when it really counted.

The nurse met her fierce glare without flinching. Well, crap. Should she pull out her phone? Stomp out in a huff, or run for the stairs?

The nurse relented, shaking her head. "Fine. As long as you promise to be quiet from here on out. Young lady, you ought to learn better manners, no matter how much money your family has." She tapped on a keyboard. "What's your grandmother's name?"

"Hilda Van Baum." Theo's shoulders sagged in relief. "Thank you," she mumbled.

The nurse gave her another frown, but checked the records. "She's in room two-twelve. Upstairs, south wing."

"Thank you. I'll be quiet. Sorry," Theo said, and the nurse's expression softened a bit.

"I certainly hope so. You too," she told Scarecrow. He straightened up, touching one finger to his chest in surprise. "Whatever this little circus is, it can wait until morning. Are we clear?"

"Not really," Scarecrow said.

Theo grabbed his hand and tugged him along. "Yep. Got it. We'll be quiet. I just really need to see her." She hurried to the elevator, giving him a light push into it when he hesitated. "Come on. We're going up."

"We are?"

"Yep." Theo brushed her hair out of her eyes, waiting as the interminably slow elevator took them up a floor. Vaguely upbeat classical music was matched in volume by the hum of the motor.

Scarecrow ventured, "I thought you didn't allow anyone to call you Dorothea."

"I don't. But it comes in handy sometimes. Well, my family name does, anyway, and it sounds more stuffy if I say my whole name. Every stupid, stuck-up syllable of it."

"So your family has power in this world, I take it? Are you royalty?"

"What? No. My family runs a toy company. I'm sure no one outside of the industry knows they exist." She rolled her eyes. "No matter how important Dad thinks they are. Come on." With a *ding,* the world's slowest elevator stopped, disgorging them. Theo checked the door numbers and determined which way they should go. She started off at a brisk pace.

He fell into step beside her again. "Why did that woman seem to think I might be as noisy as you are? And what's a circus?"

A confused frown creased his brow. In the silent hallway of the hospital, he rustled with every step. His straw poked out of his tunic. The brick-red triangle of his nose made her think of an odd clown from some exclusively rural troupe.

"She probably assumed I brought you to entertain the entire ward or something. You do sort of look like you're here to perform a singing telegram."

He muttered something again about an interpreter.

It was actually a relief to have someone with her. Hospitals creeped her out. All silent, sterile-smelling, dimly lit hallways. "Hey, thank you for playing along to get past the guard. Thanks for coming with me in the first place."

Scarecrow nodded. "Thanks for helping me find Dorothy. If I'm able to ease your grandmother's pain, reason enough to journey here."

His appearance might at least make Gramma Hildy smile. Maybe Scarecrow could help her sneak Gramma Hildy out of the building. No way would she want to be in here, given a choice. Now Theo could give her the option of running away if she wanted to go. Hospital patient heist for the win.

Theo found the correct room and paused, stilling her nerves. Gently she opened the door and peeked inside. The room was dark, save for a thin band of amber light above the head of the bed. She could barely see a small face among the white sea of pillows and blankets. Theo took a tentative step into the room. "Gramma?"

The occupant of the bed didn't stir. Theo tiptoed to the side of the bed.

Scarecrow lingered just inside the doorway.

Up close, Theo barely recognized her grandmother. Since when was she so small and helpless? Pale and crumpled, like someone wadded her up and tossed her aside?

"Gramma Hildy? It's me, Theo," she whispered. She patted the mound of blankets carefully to find Gramma's hand. The old woman's fingers felt knobbly and cool. Why was she so cold? Oh no, Goddess no please—

The elderly woman made a small sound, turning her head. Theo let out the breath she'd been holding. She gently sat on the edge of the bed, squeezing Gramma Hildy's hand between hers. "Hey. It's Theo. Sorry, I didn't mean to wake you," she said, suddenly aware a sound sleep at two a.m. might have been the better option for the old lady. She'd charged in here because she needed to see Gramma for herself. Hadn't even thought about whether that was the best thing for her grandmother. "Go back to sleep. Everything's okay," she whispered.

"Theo?" Gramma Hildy peered at her. "Why are you here?" She blinked at the dark room. "What time is it?"

Goddess, how stupid this had been. Stupid and selfish. Heat spread across Theo's face. "Uh, around two-fifteen, I think."

"Uff da," said Gramma Hildy.

Theo winced. "I'm sorry. Just needed to see how you were. I can come back in the morning."

Gramma chuckled, her head sinking back into the pillow. "Don't tell me you raced over here just for me, you silly goose."

"I kinda did."

"Well, as long as you're here, you may as well stay." Gramma raised her left eyebrow. "Thought your big doll show was this weekend?"

"Sort of. I mean yes, it was, but it didn't go very well."

"Is that your brother with you?"

Theo turned. Scarecrow hovered at the door. He'd silently shut it, but seemed uncertain what he should do. "Um, no. Just a friend. I kinda dragged him along."

"Well come over and say hello, young man," Gramma said, regaining a little strength in her voice.

Of course. Leave it to Gramma Hildy to show hospitality even when in the hospital. "It's okay, come on over," Theo sighed.

Scarecrow approached the bed, doffing his hat. When he stepped into the faint light by the bed, Theo noticed long strands of straw sticking out of the stitched seam on his head like uncombed hair. He made a low bow. "Lady Van Baum. Apologies for our untimely visit."

Gramma Hildy laughed. "Well! What a charmer. You're not untimely at all. My favorite granddaughter always visits on Sunday." She smiled at Theo. "Not exactly the front parlor with coffee and krumkake, but I'm still glad to see you, hon. And any friend of Theo's is welcome. What's your name, you well-mannered boy?"

"He goes by Scarecrow," Theo interjected quickly. "He's an actor."

"Well, I can certainly guess what show you're doing," Gramma Hildy chuckled. "Theo, help me sit up and we can chat awhile."

"Oh, no, you should be sleeping."

"Well, I'm awake now and you'll just have to deal with me." She tried to shift position grimacing. "Oh! Ohhh."

"Stop moving," Theo begged. "Let me get the nurse."

"Gosh and buckets, we don't need a nurse. You can push that button to raise the bed just as well, can't you? I'm sure they have worse patients than me to look after. Help me up."

Theo slowly raised the upper part of the bed. Hildy fussed while Theo carefully helped her rearrange the pillows under and around her until she declared she was comfortable as a pillbug in a wool rug.

"That's better," she sighed. "Theo, hand me some water. Is there any coffee?"

"I could see if they have any at the nurse's station." Doubtful there was anything other than burnt vending-machine sludge to be found at this hour. "You won't be able to get any more sleep if you drink coffee, Gramma."

"I wasn't sleeping much anyway. Never mind, never mind. Tell me all about the doll show. Why didn't you win?"

"Judges didn't like my dolls, I guess."

"Well, phooey on them! Did you get their names?"

"Gramma," Theo groaned.

"Did you?"

"You are not going to blog about the judges, Gramma. Not this time."

Hildy gave Scarecrow a self-satisfied smile. "You better believe I ratted out the last stick-in-the-mud who put down my granddaughter. Everyone on my subscriber's list knows not to buy any copies of that woman's doll magazine, I can tell you."

Theo put a hand over her eyes. "She writes very opinionated reviews. Of everything," she explained for Scarecrow's benefit.

"A critic?" he asked.

"Something like that," Theo agreed. Her grandmother cheerfully ran right over her.

"Oh yah, you better believe it! But if you'll tell me when your show premieres, I'll come see it and write you a nice review." She beamed at Scarecrow.

"My show..." Scarecrow repeated slowly.

Goddess, how could she explain any of this? "He's mainly just researching right now," she tried, rubbing Gramma Hildy's hand. "I'm helping."

"Oh that's right, you told me you were rereading the Oz books." Gramma Hildy nodded. "I thought that was for your dolls. Didn't realize you were assisting a performer friend." Her sharp eyes raked the Scarecrow from head to boot. "Come closer. Let me see your makeup."

Scarecrow obeyed, and Gramma Hildy reached her other hand toward him. He accepted it, his eyes darting uncertainly toward Theo.

Theo shrugged helplessly.

"Hmmm. Not bad. But you know looking the part isn't enough," Gramma Hildy said. "Let's hear your singing voice."

"Certainly," Scarecrow agreed. "What sort of a song would you like?"

Theo put a hand over her face, knowing what the answer would be. Dragging him along was a mistake. Of course Gramma Hildy would want to put an actor through his paces. She loved theatre and musicals. She'd taken Theo to the touring Broadway shows in Appleton, after the performing arts center was completed downtown. Calling Scarecrow a cosplayer and spending half an hour explaining the concept to her grandmother would've been easier than implying he was performing in a show. Especially as he didn't know the words to any song Gramma would demand.

"Why don't you pick one?" Gramma beamed. "Surprise me."

Oh, no. If his singing voice turned out to be terrible, Gramma would insist on teaching him. Right now. From her damned hospital bed at way-past-dark-o-clock. With other patients presumably fast asleep in the rooms around them. This was a bad idea. She should've just waited for visiting hours.

"Are you in any pain?" Scarecrow asked, his voice gentle.

Gramma Hildy stared at him a moment. She never admitted any discomfort past the occasional remark that her bones felt a storm coming. Theo expected a curt denial and a subject change.

Surprising her, Gramma nodded. "I believe I will need to call the nurse in a minute or two. Old bones not what they used to be. But let's hear a song first."

"All right." Scarecrow sank into a chair next to the bed, though he didn't release Hildy's hand. He smiled at her. "This is a very old song. I hope it brings some relief and comfort to you, Lady Van Baum."

"I'm no lady," Gramma Hildy chuckled. "Let's hear it."

The straw man took a deep breath, chest expanding, though Theo had seen for herself he didn't have lungs. She didn't get more than a second to wonder about it. The language flowing from his mouth next sent a shiver down her entire spine. The tune was in a minor key, mournful but somehow light. What was that, Gaelic? Old English? She caught bits of words, half-familiar sounds, in his warm, soothing, strong tenor. Strange consonants tripped from his tongue like a patter of rain. A refrain rolled up and down like waves on the lakeshore.

She perched on the bed, entranced. The air warmed. Gramma's eyes drifted shut and she relaxed. When the last note faded from Scarecrow's lips, Theo shivered.

She thought Gramma Hildy had fallen asleep, but felt strength in the old woman's fingers as she gave Theo's hand a squeeze. "Lovely," she whispered. "Thank you, dear. I think I'd like to hear it once more while I rest my eyes. Would you mind?"

Scarecrow nodded, and took another deep breath.

"Can you sing it in English?" Theo asked.

"I think so," he murmured, brows knit a moment in concentration.

Theo waited. The air felt oddly charged. Her face prickled as if she'd fallen asleep on a particularly rough carpet.

Scarecrow lifted his eyes to her and began singing again, and the short-cropped hair on the back of Theo's neck stood up. What the hell?

"Long you have fought all the powers
Long you have strained to no end

Don't you know you can't stop the nightfall?
Can't you see your death coming, my friend?

"Winter will cover you in snow
The dark will envelop your shame
Can't you welcome the end of this struggle?
You must welcome the end to your pain."

Theo shuddered. She gripped Gramma Hildy's hand tightly. What the hell was he thinking, singing that to her? No, how could he be telling her to give up, it was just a broken hip, her grandmother wasn't going to die! Theo tried to open her mouth, to protest, make him stop. Her muscles were all tensed, frozen. The tune changed.

"Death may be sweet, but I'll stay a bit longer
Night may be dark but my spirit is stronger
So go away, Death, you'll not take me today
Though broken my body, you still will not break me
And I won't go along with you, old crow, not today
I won't go to the dark, not today."

Relief rushed through her. Scarecrow's eyes closed. He returned to the sweetly sad melody.

"Come now, I see how your bones all do break,
I see how you long for the pain soon to end.
I'll wrap all your woe in my chilling embrace
And comfort the troubles no mortal can mend."

Theo found herself shaking her head. Scarecrow's eyes opened and met hers. In the amber light, the blue appeared dark as a midnight sky, but his voice strengthened, lightened.

"My bones may be broken, but they'll grow a bit stronger
Night may be long but my heart will beat longer
So go away, Death, you'll not take me today

Though tired my spirit, you still will not break me
And I won't go along with you, old crow, not today
I won't go to the dark, not today.
And I won't go along with you, old crow, not today
I won't go to the dark, not today."

Gramma Hildy sighed deeply. Her eyes were shut and her body relaxed.

Shaking herself out of the eerie impression that electricity filled the entire room, Theo rubbed Gramma's hand. "Gramma Hildy?" she squeaked, her own voice weak and strained.

Her grandmother sighed again, deeply asleep.

Theo stood up, wobbling, oddly heavy. What just happened? She rubbed her arms. Goosebumps all over.

"I'm not certain if the rhymes worked," Scarecrow said, startling Theo. His voice was back to his normal tenor, his odd accent distinct even though he spoke quietly so as not to wake Gramma Hildy. "I've never tried it in modern Ozian before, and I'm not much of a poet. Nick is much better at this kind of thing."

"What did you do?"

He blinked at her in apparent confusion. "She asked for a song. She was in pain. I chose a song to help her heal. Was I supposed to sing something different?"

Theo came around the end of the bed, glancing worriedly at Gramma Hildy. "That was for healing? Sounded like you were telling her to give up and die."

He shook his head, frowning. "Did I not translate the refrain well enough? It's a dialogue between Death and a man in prison. Despite what he's suffered, he's not giving up. I thought that was evident."

"Yeah, I got that, but what did you *do*?" Theo demanded. She stopped a few inches away from him, staring.

His burlap features and painted arched eyebrows gave him an air of bemused harmlessness, but the air still rippled with some kind of energy. Like being out in a thunderstorm, lightning crackling all around, the raw power of nature poised to smack down on her any second.

She shivered again and tugged her jacket closer. "You did something. I can feel it." She didn't quite dare touch him.

Scarecrow blinked, and suddenly everything was quiet. Normal. Calm.

"I'm sorry," he said. "Was that not what you wanted?"

Theo's legs felt weak. Too many hours driving. She clutched the bedrail. "Did you," she began, but too many words, too many questions flooded her brain. "The air felt weird. While you were singing. Did you do something?"

"Oh." He brightened. "Yes, there's a lot of magic in Old Ozian songs. I wasn't sure it would affect anything here, in your world, but I thought it was worth a try."

"Magic. You cast a spell?"

"No. I sang magic," he corrected, smiling.

"You. Sang. Magic."

"Well, yes," he said, quirking one eyebrow. "I mean, you didn't expect me to wave my hands around and chant nonsense, did you? I'm not a witch. I only know a few songs."

The books definitely did not mention this. Magic songs, nope, not something she'd read about in any of the Oz tales. Magic powder, magic potions, silly chants with made-up words, sure, but nothing about an ancient language which the Scarecrow could sing a spell in. "I didn't know you could do that." Damn, this was all just too much. She wavered. Her knees didn't want to support her.

Somehow their positions reversed and she was sitting in a chair next to the bed all of a sudden. "How," Theo mumbled, "How did..."

"Oh. Oh, I see. I'm sorry, Theo, I didn't realize it would affect you too. Here, there's an extra blanket," Scarecrow said.

His voice, she realized, was very kind. Warm. Warm as the soft fuzzy thing around her shoulders. She sank. "What'd you do?" she mumbled. Her own voice sounded very far away.

"I didn't realize you were in pain as well. Just rest. I'll be right here." She felt a gentle touch on her shoulder.

"'M not hurt," she muttered.

"Apparently you are. I didn't realize it would affect pain of the spirit as well as pain of the body," Scarecrow sighed. "I'll remember that next time. Rest, Theo."

She wanted to argue, but this chair was so nice. The blanket on her so warm. His voice the calmest, most soothing sound she'd ever heard. Was this what Gramma Hildy felt right now too? Soft and warm and like nothing in the world could ever hurt her. It felt weird not having her body tensed. Weird but good.

A healing spell. He'd sung a healing spell. Actual magic.

She hadn't realized how tired she was. Theo sighed, smiling. "Night night, Scarecrow."

His hand squeezed her shoulder gently. "Good night, Theo."

Warm and safe and for the first time she could remember, utterly relaxed, Theo forgot to be surprised at the sensation. She slept.

10

Within a few hours, the hospital was full of light and commotion. Scarecrow did his best to stay out of the way as people in pale green or pink tunics bustled in and out of the room, prodding Lady Van Baum to sit up, checking cuffs they put on and took off of her arm, waking Theo. The elderly lady declared herself bright-eyed and bushy-tailed, though he had to assume this merely an expression, unless her tail was quite small and hidden. Theo had dark circles beneath her eyes and was plainly disgruntled at being woken.

They sat and chatted with Lady Van Baum while she ate oatmeal and juice, toast and an egg. "Your singing is lovely," she told Scarecrow. "I can't wait to see your production. Promise me you'll drop by once I'm back home and treat me again to a performance."

"Thank you," said Scarecrow. "I can't promise yet. First I need to find Dorothy."

"Oho." Lady Van Baum smiled. "Of course. Off you go then, down the Yellow Brick Road. Although you know you'll probably find what you were looking for right at home after all."

"The road of yellow brick?" Scarecrow frowned. "I didn't know it continued on this side as well."

"What now, dear? These old ears aren't what they used to be. This side of what now?"

Scarecrow opened his mouth to explain. Theo stepped between him and her grandmother.

"Are you feeling any better, Gramma?" Theo asked.

"Much better," Lady Van Baum assured her. "Seeing my favorite granddaughter always cheers me right up."

Another woman walked into the room, checking something on a flat pad of paper. "Good morning, Mrs. Van Baum. I'm Britta, your physical therapist. Are you all done with breakfast?"

"No rest for the wicked," Lady Van Baum grumbled, though she flashed a smile at Theo and Scarecrow. "Seems I'm being shanghaied. Off you go, you two. Why don't you stop by soon as I'm back home in a couple days?"

"You'll be home that fast? That's great," Theo said.

Britta turned her sunny smile to Theo. "Yep. We've ordered home nursing for the first week, and regular visits to therapy, but she can go home in a couple days."

"I won't need any home nurses," Lady Van Baum declared, swinging her legs over the side of the bed with a grunt. "Doing just fine. I feel much better today. But as long as you're here, be a dear and help me to the commode."

Britta seemed surprised. "Careful! We don't want you making the injury worse right away."

"I'm fine, quit your fussing, I can do it myself," Lady Van Baum grumbled, waving away any assistance. Britta hovered at her side nonetheless, wrapping an arm around the old woman's midsection to steady her. As she limped past, Lady Van Baum smiled at Scarecrow and patted his arm. "You go have fun. Careful my Theo doesn't drag you off on an adventure. At least, not an adventure that'll require us to bail her out of jail."

"Jail?" Scarecrow repeated.

Theo rolled her eyes. "Gramma Hildy, it was *one time*. I was fifteen. And it didn't require any bail, it was just a warning."

Lady Van Baum winked at Scarecrow. "Watch out for her. And don't forget to send me an invitation to your show! I'll bring all my friends. We all just adore the Wizard of Oz."

Now this was a happy coincidence. "You know the Wizard?"

Theo grabbed Scarecrow's arm. "Come on, she's fine, let's go home. Love you Gramma Hildy! Be nice to the nurses."

"Oh, I'm always nice," Lady Van Baum singsonged. She waggled her fingers and smiled.

"Your grandmother knows the Wizard?" Scarecrow asked, reluctant to leave. Why was Theo ignoring what sounded like an important connection?

"She doesn't mean your Wizard." Theo ushered him from the room. "Not the real one."

Oh. "This is about the books again?"

"The stage show, probably. Never mind." Theo rubbed one hand across her face. "She's not hurt as bad as Mom made it sound on the phone. Thanks for coming along anyway."

"Glad I could help."

They walked down a corridor bustling with people in uniforms. He nodded politely at everyone, receiving smiles or chuckles in return. When the door slid open for the small room which conveyed people upstairs or down, a young child within it, holding her mother's hand, stared up at Scarecrow with wide eyes. He smiled at her and tipped his hat to the mother. Theo didn't pay them any attention, stepping past them as they exited, to stand in the up-and-down room. It felt rude not to at least say good morning, so Scarecrow murmured a greeting as he passed.

"Mom, that was the Scarecrow," the child said, just before the door slid shut.

Scarecrow asked Theo, "How is it everyone seems to recognize me?"

She sighed. "I keep telling you, everyone knows the story of the Wizard of Oz. Though probably most of them have only seen the movie."

"Explain to me what a movie is, please?"

She scratched her black fingernails through her hair roughly. "I will sit you down and show it to you at some point, I promise. Let's find your Dorothy first."

"Of course." Here he was letting his attention wander from his most important mission. No matter how strange this world or how oddly people stared at him, finding his beloved was absolutely paramount.

"Soon as we get home, I'll make some coffee and start searching the web for her. Bet we can track her down in an hour or two." Theo yawned widely. A ding signaled the end of the ride and the door slid open.

"I'm assuming you don't mean an actual spider's web." Colloquialisms continued to be annoying.

She shook her head. "No. No spiders. I'll explain later." She trudged into the soaring main lobby. He followed, gazing around.

Though sunlight shone through the tall windows, numerous lamps in the ceiling and walls illuminated every corner and panel, eliminating all shadows. He'd noticed last night the building seemed to be made of glass and metal, with no obvious barred doors or fortifications. Perhaps this city had no fear of wild monsters. He hadn't noticed passing through a city gate at any point, only that the trees along the high road gave way to buildings and street-lamps and finally a city laid out with orderly buildings lining slick paved streets.

Theo said khalidahs didn't exist here. Perhaps it was safe to assume giant spiders, Wheelers, or worse didn't roam the forests. Still, the abundance of light everywhere was reassuring.

Once again he climbed into her metal carriage and endured unnerving speeds while she whipped the steering wheel around turns. She drove them along hilly streets hemmed in by neat, white-sided houses. The trees gleamed golden and orange in the bright day. *Autumn here as well,* he thought, *though the air is chillier than in Oz for this season.*

If the seasons corresponded right now, yet time didn't flow at the same rate in both worlds, how many days had passed for his friends back home? He patted his pockets, reassured to find everything in place including the Evstone Nick gave him. He shouldn't allow too much time to pass before letting Nick know he'd arrived safely. For all he knew, a month could've gone by in Oz by now. *Perhaps I should wait until I have actual news to report, though.* He glanced at Theo, intending to ask her how they could find Dorothy while not even in the same town where he'd arrived.

Her eyelids drooped. She stared wearily ahead, seeming to take turns more by memory than with any sense of alertness. They stopped at an intersection where a red lamp hung overhead. Theo rubbed her eyes.

"You're still tired," he observed. "It doesn't seem my song did you much good."

She chuckled. "I crashed hard, but that damned nurse woke me at six when she came in to take vitals on Gramma Hildy."

Scarecrow hadn't noticed anything being taken from the old woman, but the attendants fussing over her at dawn were indeed noisy enough to startle him from his silent thoughts as well.

A loud honk behind them made him jump and turn. A woman in another carriage impatiently gestured at him.

Theo held up one finger in a returning salute and started the carriage moving again. "Yeah, screw you, Karen, not all of us are awake at this unholy hour."

"Perhaps you should rest more," Scarecrow suggested.

"Story of my life. Look at you. Traveled from another world, sat up all night, and here you are way too chipper at morning-thirty," she laughed. Suddenly she leaned closer, eyebrows going up. "Oh Goddess. That's why your eyes look so weird. Are those painted on?"

He placed one hand on the wheel to correct their course since her leaning over was accompanied by a veer to the right. "Well, yes, of course."

"I knew there was something strange but I couldn't figure out what it was last night. You can actually see with those?"

Scarecrow frowned. "Jellia Jamb practiced over and over before painting these for me." Though it was odd not to have his big round eyes anymore, one larger than the other, he'd wanted every detail to be as close to a meat person as possible. Well-molded ears and nose, an actual chin, a tongue of pink felt. Lion roared with laughter upon catching Scarecrow practicing licking his lips in one of the palace's tall, mirrored walls. He merely wanted every expression to appear correct. Scarecrow failed to see anything comical about it. His new eyes were of a deep Munchkin blue, and he'd found to his relief they could see in the dark just as well as his original ones.

"They move." Theo kept stealing glances at him. "How are you even doing that if they're painted on?"

"Yours move," he pointed out. "What's strange about that?"

She stared at him a full five seconds before shaking her head and returning her attention out the front sloped window of the carriage.

"This is gonna be harder than I thought," she muttered.

"What is?"

"Passing you off as a cosplayer in broad daylight. Maybe we should only go places at night. Less noticeable then."

"Are you implying I don't look enough like a meat man?"

She choked on a laugh. "You—" She met his stare and shut up. After a moment she said, "You look fine."

He'd studied faces for years. Read books on anatomy. Paid careful attention to every thoughtless expression all the citizens of the Emerald City displayed when in conversation with one another, and when they thought no one was observing them. He kept a notebook dedicated to every emotion and its corresponding facial expression, what a pout of the lips could mean, what a raised eyebrow might imply. And now his first friend in this bewildering world found his eyes strange? All his careful attention to detail for naught? How would Dorothy regard him?

Eyes. How Dorothy's gleamed, wide in the faint moonlight. How her chest heaved as she slowly unbuttoned the top of her blouse. Scarecrow's pleasure at unexpectedly seeing her that night in the barn turned swiftly to confusion as she approached hesitantly.

"Dorothy?" he asked. "Is something wrong?"

"I couldn't sleep," she said.

"Oh. Well, perhaps you should ask the farmer's wife for some warm milk," he suggested. "I've heard it can help."

She shook her head. Her hair was free of its ribbons, spilling over her shoulders in a dark cloud. "I thought maybe you could—I was cold." She came closer.

Obligingly Scarecrow shifted over on the straw bales where he sat to make room for her. "Shall I fetch you a blanket?"

She laid her hands on his tunic, rubbing the patched fabric. "No, I—I was hoping maybe..." She trailed off. He was at a loss to help her. She stroked his face, from the brim of his hat down to where the rope at his neck kept his head stuffing from coming out. "You're really good at warming me up."

"Oh. Well, here." He snagged a saddle blanket from the top of the nearest stall and spread it over the bales.

She stretched out atop the blanket, still breathing harshly. Why was she unbuttoning her blouse if she was cold? When he moved to cover her up with the edge of the blanket, she placed his hand inside her blouse, staring up into his face with wide eyes. Her skin was incredibly soft.

"Here," she whispered. "Here, Scarecrow, please. You're so warm."

Her arms went around him. Awkwardly he lowered himself over her, hoping his straw would help, feeling the heat of her body spreading from his chest to his legs. "Is this better?"

"Yes. Touch me."

She moved his hand over the firm, rounded curves of her chest. He hadn't done so before when he'd served as her bed, nights when they'd camped along the roadside on their way to the Emerald City. He'd been polite about touching her at all, except to wrap an arm around her when she pulled his hand across her stomach, curled around and behind her to keep her warm in the cool night air.

She resettled her legs, and suddenly he found his between hers. "Wouldn't you be warmer if—"

"Kiss me," she whispered, an intensity in her eyes he couldn't comprehend. When he hesitated, she pressed her lips to his painted ones. Such softness, and how sweet her breath! Her scent suffused his straw, creeping through the weave of his burlap face, dizzying. Her hips pushed up against him. The wave of heat pulsing through her, warming him immediately, was wonderful and confusing.

"Dorothy, I don't know what—"

She gave a frustrated laugh. "I really wish you were a real man. I know you're sweet on me."

"I'm sorry I'm not a meat person, but tell me what to do. I just want you to be happy," he whispered.

"Kiss me," she said again.

He pressed his painted mouth to hers. She moved against him. He remembered to stroke his hand inside her blouse. A small, hard bead formed on the softness under his palm. When he gently rubbed it, Dorothy moaned, her hips lifting against his, and he felt a dampness which wasn't there before. "Are you all right?"

She nodded, eyes closed, and twined her slim, warm fingers between his clumsy gloved ones. She guided his hand down her stomach. When he touched between her legs she made an eager sound, her muscles tensing against him everywhere.

Whatever this was, he'd never heard such noises from her. "Does this help make you sleepy?"

She laughed. "Oh Scarecrow."

Her breath was hot across his face, her eyes tightly shut, her body undulating beneath him. She was certainly much warmer than before, warmer even than he'd felt when they lay together a few dangerous feet from a small campfire. She moved his fingers against her, tugging her skirt upward, and when he cautiously pressed his hand into the yielding softness there she cried out, her body jerking. Alarmed, he would've pulled back, but she grabbed his hand tightly and pressed his fingers against her, biting her lip, her legs wrapping around his.

He followed her lead, astonished as he slowly realized those squeaks, cries, and stifled groans were sounds of pleasure, not pain. She kissed his painted mouth, gasped when he explored the amazingly soft curves of her body without further prompting. His gloves traced the twin swells of her chest. He sought and discovered which gentle movements made her tense and gasp, which strokes of his fingers brought her to tears as she wrapped her arms tight around him. She squeezed his straw so hard it compacted in his chest. Scarecrow didn't care.

Whatever this was, Dorothy was soaringly happy and he'd given her this. His touch made her happy! If only he could know what sensations she felt. Did men of flesh experience this same overwhelming wonder?

"Please," she whimpered, "Oh please." Her hips ground up against his. "Ugh! Why am I stuck here with things that aren't even real men!"

Dismayed, he begged, "Dorothy, tell me what you need."

She smacked his chest. "Dang it! I wish you were a real man. This won't work." She shoved him off her, wiping moisture from her cheeks with the back of her hand. "This was stupid."

"I'll do whatever you want," he pleaded.

She gave a curt laugh, breathless, and tugged her dress down as she stood. "You can't. You're just straw."

He wished he knew some magic. Some words he could say or potion he could drink, if only he had a mouth capable of swallowing. Some spell which would grant her wish so he might please her better.

It took him months of study, many probing questions asked of Nick and Lion and even the Wogglebug to tease out the facts of physical love. So much time spent just to glean a few hidden truths from reams of sly misdirection and coy double meanings in terrible novels. To locate actual, documented anatomy among dusty tomes, many of which oddly skipped over that portion of a female meat person's body. The first time he'd asked Nick for more information and used the proper names for the organs of love, the Tin Woodman choked and coughed and turned red.

Scarecrow had gone to great lengths to change his form. Worried he might seem too different to his love. Vacillated between changing everything and keeping the features she'd seemed to favor. And now the first friend he'd met here thought his new eyes looked strange. He'd anxiously waited in blind fright while the head maid of the Emerald Palace, trustworthy Jellia Jamb, slowly painted new eyes on his freshly-stuffed head. If even that detail didn't pass muster here, how could he hope the other adjustments he'd made would be enough? How foolish to think for a minute his love would view him as anything other than the simple creature of straw he'd been when she helped him down from his lonely cornfield post.

Theo turned the carriage into a drive next to a cottage with a high peaked roof. "Here we are. Home sweet home."

The cottage boasted a sturdy stone foundation, wooden shingles covering its outer walls. A brick chimney rose above the roofline. Sheaves of dried cornstalks and fat pumpkins decorated a cozy front porch. "It's very nice," he said.

Theo smiled. She pulled the key from its socket and the growl of the carriage stopped. "Thought you might like it. Okay, just need to lug all my doll show stuff inside and get settled, and then we can keep searching for Dorothy."

He unkinked his frame from the seat, relieved to be able to stretch. Though he didn't have muscles to become sore, he much preferred the open air. Theo opened a hatch at the rear of the carriage and lifted out a large box of what appeared to be translucent wax. "Quick orientation for ya. Next door on that side are the Reeves. Mrs. Reeve thinks I'm going to Hell and keeps leaving those hideous propaganda tract cartoons on my porch. On the other side are the Singers, who are pretty nice people. Once in a while we trade cookies."

Scarecrow nodded as she gestured vaguely at the houses to the left and right of her own, noting her tone of voice as she described her neighbors even though her words wandered off into some local terms he didn't know yet again. He gathered hell and cartoons irked her, cookies were a good thing. Seeing another large box in the carriage storage area, he lifted it out, knees buckling when it proved heavier than he'd anticipated.

Theo smiled at him, taking the box from his arms. "And over there, as you can see, are the dead folks." She nodded across the road, where a low gray stone wall stretched. On the other side, he could see numerous trees shading a plentitude of stone markers. Many were carved into tree stumps, tall urns, or posts with crossbeams. "They're pretty quiet neighbors." Theo grinned. She carried the box up the porch stairs, set it down, and unlocked the front door. "Just leave that, I'll get it," she said when he struggled to lift the other box up the stairs.

How useless he was. Yes, really should've asked Nick to build him wooden limbs for better strength. He followed her inside the house, waiting while she retrieved the second box. "Is there anything I can do to help?"

"Nah, not yet anyway. Just need to put this stuff in the studio and then I'll get some coffee started."

Her movements were sluggish, her eyes half-shut. Meat people needed so much more care just to function. He'd always felt superior for not needing sleep or sustenance, but Theo pushing herself just so she could help him felt wrong. He'd been the one to insist the party stop to rest whenever Dorothy's feet started to drag, after their very first night when she'd explained to him she needed to sleep.

"Why don't you rest awhile first? You seem weary."

Theo shook her head. "No, wasted too much time already, driving back here to check on Gramma Hildy when obviously she's fine. Well, she will be, anyway. I bet she didn't actually break her hip, probably just sprained something, the way she was hopping around this morning."

He followed her into a sunny room crowded with tables. The tables were covered in scraps of fabric, beads, and numerous other small things he couldn't immediately identify. "No, it was broken. The song magic went right to her hip and worked better than I'd hoped."

She paused, frowning at him. "How do you know?"

"I could feel the magic concentrating itself around her. It was certainly more charged right over her hips and legs. Just as it was around your head and chest, though it seemed more diffuse for you, which is why I guessed your pain was one of spirit," he explained.

She crossed her arms, tossing the sheaf of orange hair out of her eyes. In the sunny room they gleamed emerald green. "What the hell would you know about that?"

"I'm sorry," he said, taken aback.

Theo sighed, shoulders dropping. "No, you're just trying to be helpful. You don't know anything about me."

"I know you're a generous person," he ventured.

"Hah. Certainly not acting like one." Theo touched his shoulder. He kept still, unsure how to react. She shook her head. "Painted eyes. Magic. This is all a lot."

He nodded. "Dorothy told us there was no magic in Kansas. She didn't mention there were witches here, however."

Theo laughed. "No. This is Wisconsin. A few hundred miles east and north of Kansas. Goddess bless, there is so much you're gonna need to learn."

"I'm a dedicated student," he promised. Lion's jeers at him for always having his eyes fixed upon a book came unpleasantly to mind. All his devoted study, seeking out every book he could find which even mentioned the Outside World, now seemed horribly inadequate preparation for all this. He dragged his brains back to the present moment. "But I believe a good teacher is most effective when well-rested and content. I can see you're still tired. Please rest." Theo pouted, so he added, "You did say we should confine our search to the night hours, to avoid too much attention."

She snorted. "You're going to attract attention no matter what."

Embarrassed, he lowered his gaze. "I suppose trying to become more like a true man was doomed to fail. I'll always be straw and cloth and paint."

"Is that what you want? To become flesh and blood?"

"I want whatever she wants me to be." He shrugged. Ridiculous, thinking all these alterations would be enough. Why hadn't he instead asked for a spell to turn his straw to meat, his burlap to soft skin? It never even occurred to him.

Theo snorted again, this time sounding angry rather than amused. "You're fine just like you are. You're the goddamn Scarecrow of Oz, for crying out loud."

He had no idea how to take that.

Theo shook her head. "Fine. You win. I'll get a nap first. I am really tired."

He nodded, relieved. "Thank you."

"You're thanking me for crapping out on you? I know you're worried about Dorothy."

"She's resourceful, and there seem to be no monsters here. I'm thanking you for helping me, when you clearly have other obligations."

He didn't allow his doubt to tint his voice. For all his troubles in improving himself, all his dedication to advancing his intellect, he was still just a scarecrow. Stuffed with straw, incapable of lifting anything weighty, a fool for hoping anything he could accomplish would make his love regard him as a true man. As *real,* a word he was coming to detest.

"Your song really did heal Gramma Hildy?"

Scarecrow immediately smiled for her. "It did. I'm sorry it didn't work as well on you."

"You could..." she began, paused, bit her lip. "You could try it again. I wouldn't mind."

"Really?"

"Yeah." Theo stifled another yawn, her cheeks turning pink. "Um. Okay. I'll just lie down on the sofa, and maybe you could try singing magic at me again?"

He nodded and followed her across a wood-paneled hallway into a parlor with a small fireplace, happily not in use right now. A brass screen in front of it bore a five-pointed star in a circle, and more pumpkins in orange and white, grayish-blue and rosy-yellow were piled on either side of the hearth. A long sofa, topped with several small pillows and a purple fur, took up most of the space in front of the fireplace. Bookshelves were built into two walls, which right away lightened his mood. He could read while she slept and perhaps learn something useful about this world. Hanging plants soaked up the sunlight at a row of windows. The entire ambiance was warm and welcoming.

Theo unhooked the drapes, letting them fall over the windows. She kicked off her boots and shrugged out of her jacket, tossing it on a chair. She sank onto the sofa, plumping the largest pillow under her head and drawing the purple fur over her body.

Scarecrow stood in the center of the room, unsure how to proceed. He'd been asked to sing before for friends, and sometimes at the university for scholars interested in Old Ozian. He'd not realized, when he first found the old scrolls full of the archaic language, that the songs possessed any value other than as curiosities, but he'd memorized many of them all the same. A lot of the old history could only be found inscribed in that dusty tongue. He'd learned the songs were magic by accident, in the palace dungeons when Locasta imprisoned them, singing the Prisoner's Lament to cheer the Lion. To give some meager sliver of hope to his friend after another day of torment, when the great beast seemed on his last breath.

Scarecrow sang, and Lion kept breathing. He slept. The guards were amazed to find some of his injuries healed the next morning.

He sang the mournful tune every night from then on. Every night, to keep his friend alive, though life meant yet another day of howling pain. It even worked to keep Nick's heart beating, though it couldn't repair the acid burns.

Seeing Lady Van Baum in pain, lost in a sea of white sheets and blankets and nearly as pale as the bedclothes, that song was the first thing which came to mind. He hadn't ever thought he'd sing it again, after the time in the dungeons finally ended.

As if hearing his thoughts, Theo asked, "Can you sing something more cheerful, though? The Death-versus-the-prisoner one is kind of creepy."

"Yes," he replied at once. She waved at a chair, and he sat, composing himself. The chair was turned toward the open doorway to the hall. Through a studio window he could see leaves of scarlet and yellow fluttering in the morning sunlight. Autumn colors. Pumpkins and dried cornsheaves demonstrating some sort of reverence for the harvest, even here. A suitable song sprang from his memory, and he took a minute to translate it into more modern words.

This tune was brighter, paced at a walk instead of a dirge. He inhaled, smelling the sweet flowers and dark spices permeating the air of Theo's home, as well as her skin and clothing. Some of his worry faded. He might or might not yet be what his love wanted, but he was here in this strange world, and he'd found a friend, and right now that friend needed healing sleep.

Scarecrow sang.

> *"Bright is the sun on the field, o my girl,*
> *Light is the wind on your face,*
> *Merry the morrow when all will return*
> *And fast as the wind we will race.*
>
> *"Red are your lips when you laugh, o my girl,*
> *Gold is the wheat and the corn.*
> *We'll all go a-racing and chasing afield*
> *Rejoicing, in autumn reborn.*
>
> *"Will you race with me, chase with me, dance with me?*
> *Will you run down the moon and welcome the sun?*
> *Oh yes, I will race you and chase you and dance with you*
> *From morrow at noon til midnight has come,*
> *Forever in autumn til winter has come."*

Theo sighed. Her eyes closed, the fur covering her, though a sock-covered foot poked out. The sock had a colorful woven pattern of pumpkins and corn stalks. A young witch with hair the shade of a ripe pie pumpkin, buried contentedly under a cover the hue of midnight over the mountains, who seemed amazed such things as a living scarecrow or a magic song could exist in her world.

Softening his voice as much as he could, he continued,

"Light is the wind in your hair, o my girl,
Fast are your feet 'cross the hills.
And when autumn comes round once again we shall go
Racing the sun sinking into the dells.

"O will you race with me, chase with me, dance with me?
Will you harvest the light and keep safe the sun?
Oh yes, I will race you and chase you and dance with you
From the rise of the moon to the set of the sun,
Forever in autumn til winter has come."

He watched Theo carefully. At the last note, she stirred slightly, and disappointment rose. Perhaps this song wouldn't work on witches. Then she snored, shifted around, and dropped into steady, restful breathing.

Good. So he was useful for something, at least.

He wanted to go stand among the golden trees swaying in the wind outside. Nodding to himself, he rose and left the room quietly. The song stirred a sense of homesickness. He'd sung it last only a week ago, at a fall feast after the traditional harvest race the Munchkins had held every year since time immemorial, probably earlier even than that song was written.

The sheaves of corn and pumpkins in Theo's home reminded him of the abundant fields where he'd stood watch. The original purpose for which he'd been created, though he'd yet to discover how or why he'd been given consciousness. He'd failed to keep the crows from eating all the farmer's corn. That was before he'd gained his superlative brains from the Wizard.

Dorothy's wistful voice rose in his memory. "I liked you just as you were," she said, right before he went to claim his reward from the enigmatic Wizard.

"It's very kind of you to like a scarecrow," he replied, "but I'm sure you'll like me even better once I have brains."

She smiled, turning away.

Her frustrated exclamation, that night in the barn. "I wish you were a real man."

Fine stitches on his glove-fingers held in his straw, let him direct the movements of what otherwise would be no more than scratchy, bristly stalks of oat-grass. His head was full of magic brains and he'd memorized so many things, ancient songs and the nuances of human expressions alike, but his body was still just straw and cloth.

Nick was right. He should've given this more thought. Funny, how his friend who valued romance above all should be the sensible one, when all Scarecrow could think of was seeing his heart's desire one more time.

Nick! With a surge of guilt, Scarecrow brought out the Evstone. Thus far he'd accomplished nothing he'd hoped to do in this land, but as the flow of time between worlds was yet uncertain, he shouldn't delay contacting his friend any longer.

He went outside. The porch felt too exposed. Recalling Theo's statement that he would draw attention no matter what, he hurried down to the side of the cottage. There was a shed in the back, surrounded by several trees. A worn wooden bench waited beneath the shelter of a tree with sweeping, gold-leaved branches. It seemed a safe enough spot, hidden from the neighboring houses by red-branched shrubs.

He cupped the stone in one hand, touching it with the other, concentrating on his friend. "Nick? Nick, can you hear me?"

Silence. He was about to try again when a tinny voice came through the stone. "Scarecrow?"

"Yes! Can you hear me?"

There was a scrabbling, metallic sound. The pink inclusions in the stone swirled and dissolved, and then the hopeful face of the Tin Woodman peered from a haze above the stone. "Scarecrow! You're alive!"

Relief and chagrin filled his chest. Nick sounded about to cry. It must've been too long there since Scarecrow left. He managed a smile for his metal friend. "Did we ever conclude that debate? I thought there was some argument still that *living* does not necessarily mean *alive*."

Nick laughed, dabbing a handkerchief to his eyes before the moisture could track down his face and mar the polished cheeks. "You're still walking and talking, I see, so good enough for me. How are you? Did you find Dorothy?"

"No, not yet." He did his best to keep his tone cheerful. "I'm all right."

"I'm so glad," Nick sighed, tucking the kerchief in a waistcoat pocket.

"How long have I been gone? When did you start dressing up?"

Nick chuckled. "Five days. And this is just to keep the Evstone safe. Wouldn't want it to get all banged up. Or scratch me."

"Five days? It hasn't even been a full day here," Scarecrow said.

"So you have a little time left."

"A week."

Not that a time limit would matter if he wasn't manly enough for his love.

"So she wasn't where you ended up?"

"No. Everything was confusing." He tried to emphasize what little had gone right. "I met a new friend, though, and she's been helping me. She thinks it won't be too difficult to find Dorothy."

Nick's flexible throat contracted. How simple a movement, how like a meat person, and he was all metal. Why didn't Scarecrow ask for more adjustments to his own form? If only he'd had more time to prepare, surely he'd have thought of more he could change, commissioned more work from the tailors. Magic, though, was notoriously fickle about cycles of the moon and positions of the stars. Glinda firmly let him know to make his preparations swift, and barely a month passed between his humble petition to her to craft a spell, and her sending him through the veil between Oz and this place. Far too late now.

"That's great," Nick said. "I'm happy for you, my friend. I'm sure you'll find her."

"What if..." Scarecrow began, but stopped. He forced himself to meet Nick's worried gaze. The image wavered. Surely it took a great deal of power to keep open this small bridge across the veil. He shouldn't waste it bemoaning his own failures.

"What if what?"

"Nothing. It's very strange here. You should see the magic everyone uses. They have carriages which steer like ships, with no beasts to pull them, and tiny portraits they use to talk to each other at a distance." Realizing one particular detail would surprise Nick, he added, "Oh, and by the way, the woman who's been helping me? She's a witch."

"A witch? Helping you find Dorothy?"

Scarecrow nodded.

Nick frowned. "What's she getting out of this?"

"I don't know," he admitted. "She isn't like Oz witches. She seemed surprised I could sing magic."

"Well, you are one of only two or three people who still knows those stuffy old songs."

"True, but her amazement seems more regarding the fact magic actually exists."

"What? That makes no sense. What kind of a witch is she?"

"She makes dolls, yet she insists she doesn't use them to control people. She lives in a charming cottage, worries about her grandmother's health, and she just asked me to sing her to sleep a few minutes ago."

Nick cocked both brows up in disbelief. "Are you sure she's really a witch?"

Scarecrow shrugged uncomfortably. "You have a point."

"Be careful," Nick advised.

"I am." The image flickered, vanished, then returned, though Nick's features appeared fuzzy. "Oh dear. How much magic do these stones have?"

"Not sure, the Pink Lady didn't say. Scarecrow, I know you had her cast some other spell on you, before you left," Nick said quickly. "Do you feel any different?"

Now Scarecrow felt even more foolish for having asked for any special additions to his form whatsoever. "Not really."

"Fine, good, I guess."

"I thought discussing this made you uncomfortable?"

Nick cringed. "No! I mean yes, it does, but I'm not talking about that. Things have been strange since you left. And," he looked around, then continued in a quieter voice, "I'm worried something bad is coming. Worried you're part of it somehow."

"What sort of bad? You know I'd never—"

"Did the Good Witch do anything else to you? Any hint of magic other than what you asked her for?"

Accepting the alterations he'd had specially crafted felt odd, yes. Especially the one which he'd needed Glinda to weave into his straw. That part seemed to amuse the witch. Her hand setting it in place, when the spell took hold and he felt his form altered, had been decidedly terrifying. The magic disoriented him for a minute or two. It had taken all his will to keep perfectly still so as not to mar the spell. How would he even know if she'd added anything else? He wasn't in the habit of having magic touch him at all, nor had he been a creature of meat as Nick once was. The sensation of that particular alteration was strange and new enough. No way he could tell if she'd done more than he requested.

"I don't know," he admitted. "Nick, what's happened? Is Ozma safe?"

"I've been keeping close by her, don't worry. And I'm keeping TikTok wound daily as well. Lion and the Tiger are still—" The sound faded, though Nick's mouth kept moving.

"Nick? Nick, what was that?"

"Try to find out," Nick said, frowning. "Scarecrow, you're fading in and out. Try to recharge the stone if you can. I'll do—" More distortions. "Careful." The stone swirled pink and white, opaque.

"Nick? Nick, can you hear me?"

No answer. The Evstone was mute, a lump of rock.

Nick would find a way to recharge the stone on his side. Scarecrow had no idea what might work, if anything, in this world. He doubted he could stroll down to the nearest stonesmith's here and have them immerse it in a charged bath of wyvern blood. He cursed himself with renewed vigor for having abandoned his post as Royal Advisor to the Queen. What if Nick's fears weren't just healthy paranoia regarding the fae? Why indeed would any witch help anyone without receiving something they valued in return? Crows and blight, he'd been so eager to find his beloved, he'd brushed right past any doubts about why Glinda agreed without asking for anything from him.

Was Theo any different? Well, true, she'd accepted his help for her grandmother, for whom she genuinely seemed to care. That alone marked her as not the sort of witch he was used to, not the sort molded by the ancient magics of Oz. Yet her moods were puzzling, her speech full of words he didn't know, her eyes changing in the light as fae eyes did.

Something buzzed his ear. He swatted it, at first thinking a bee was attracted to the scent of sweetgrass in his clothing. A tiny pixie tumbled to the brown grass at his feet. He barely had time to blink before it launched itself at his face. He flinched as it sank its claws into his left ear. He felt its teeth tugging at the burlap threads, its wings buzzing loudly.

"Little thief!" he exclaimed, swatting again. It squealed, trying to rip loose a thread for its nest. A nest where it would lay hundreds of eggs, and spring would hatch swarms of the nasty little faelings. Scarecrow grabbed the pixie around its waist. It shrieked, squirming, biting, clawing. He pried it from his ear, disgusted. It struggled in his grip, spitting noxious green juice. He jerked his head back. Their spittle could dissolve straw, at worst, and would stain his face at best.

Theo said khalidahs didn't exist here. That the fae left this world ages past. She'd failed to mention these nasty little pests infested her yard.

The pixie tried to yank itself free, intent on attacking him again. Scarecrow hurled it to the ground and stomped his boot down on it. His foot wasn't heavy enough to kill it, and he had to twist it, standing, rubbing his boot into the hard ground under the dying grass. When the nasty thing finally stopped moving completely, he wiped his sole on another patch of grass and slunk back to the porch, head down, hoping no one noticed him. He should recommend Theo hire an exterminator. An unchecked pixie infestation could destroy all these lovely trees and shrubs.

Not wanting to remain outside any longer despite the warm sun, he opened the front door and quietly shut it behind him. Investigating Theo's library while she napped was the better plan after all.

As he passed the open door to the studio, the array of odd objects on the tables drew his attention. Curious, he investigated them more closely. Dolls in various stages of completion lay or stood on every surface: a ball-gowned creature with no head and the wings of a huge moth. A knight armored in reflective beetle parts. A mermaid with the head of a dried seahorse. Perhaps Theo was aware of the pixies after all, as a few of the poppets showed clear similarities. Spotting one of the large boxes she'd carried in, he opened the top, unwrapped one of the dolls inside.

His fingers fumbled it. Hastily he set it on a table so he wouldn't drop it. All his practice at fine motor skills hadn't completely overcome his innate clumsiness. Turning the tiny figure to face him, he froze.

Wild, wiry hair like snakes haloed its head. The doll's thin arm held a mask on a stick up before its face. The mask was of a rose-cheeked girl, brightly smiling. A pink ballgown, sparkling with tiny jewels, clothed the doll. The arm was made of delicate wire, and trying to move it might snap it. He really wanted to see behind the mask.

It reminded him far too much of Glinda.

Suddenly, he didn't want to examine the other dolls.

Large sheets of paper, drawings and watercolors, were scattered on the tables under the half-finished dolls and bits of ribbons, fabric, and jeweler's tools. The word OZ sprang immediately to view on one sheet. He gently tugged it from under the detritus for a better look.

The drawings made his fingers curl. A chill settled in his chest. A monster with tangled mane and far too many teeth was labeled *Lion*. Next to it was a sketch he peered at for a moment before the tin funnel hat became clear, nearly obscured by a multitude of gears and cogs, pipes and wires. Theo had drawn the Tin Woodman as some sort of mechanical horror, with five arms ending in pincers or needles. With a shudder he dropped his eyes to the bottom of the paper.

Was that supposed to be him? Ragged clothing barely concealed open ribs, ribbons of straw falling out of the chest. Vinelike arms ended in wicked claws. The face had two different sizes of black button eyes over a stitched mouth stretched into a horrible wide grin. *Scarecrow*.

How could she think of him, of his friends, as such horrors? Her question about him eating Dorothy's brains came to mind. This was perverse, appalling, grotesque! He dropped the paper, wiping his gloves against one another almost unconsciously to rid them of the feel of something horrid. It didn't appear she'd constructed any dolls based on these drawings yet, thank the sweet sunlight. He wouldn't be able to bear remaining in the same house as such little abominations.

Unless they were in the boxes still. Waiting to be unwrapped. Frozen grins and sharp claws hidden by tissue paper.

Raising his gaze, he noticed now the repeated motif of five-pointed stars within circles all around the room. A stained glass star in a circle hung in a large window facing the front porch. The table with the jeweler's tools upon it had a padded high stool beside it, also displaying the pattern in woven dark wool, and a rug beneath it boasted the same arcane design, surrounded by glyphs he didn't recognize.

This was where she cast her spells. This was the witch's studio, where poppets were built and incantations chanted to whatever powers she gave fealty. Nick was right. He should be more careful. What was Theo intending to do with hideous dolls of himself and his friends?

She'd said she hadn't been expecting him. This seemed to tell a different story.

"Scarecrow?"

He jumped, a chill shooting through him at her voice. If he'd possessed a beating heart it would've stuttered.

"Scarecrow? Where'd you go?"

How was she awake already? He located his voice after a couple of faint tries. "In here."

As her steps sounded in the hall, he screwed up his courage and picked up the distasteful sheet of drawings again. Turning to face her, he summoned his sternest tone. "What exactly is this?" He held out the drawings.

She blinked at him, eyes wide. "Oh. Um. I can explain—"

"What spell were you intending to cast with this? I'm nothing like this hideous monster! My friends aren't monsters!" he shouted, anger rising.

"No, of course not, I..." She gulped. "Scarecrow, look, they're just dolls. This is what I do. I make dolls and sell them. It's my art."

"Art?" he demanded, flapping the paper at her. "These are horrible!"

Theo flinched. "Wow, thanks. I worked really hard on those. And they're not supposed to be like how you and your friends are in the books. I deliberately twisted the characters, did my own take on a dark Oz. You don't have to like it. Goddess knows most people don't get it so

I don't expect you to either, but this is my art and I did my best on those sketches, okay?"

He hesitated. "Your art?" Reluctantly he studied the drawings again. Forcing himself to look past the hideousness of their appearance, he saw now the care put into the strokes of ink, the brushes of color.

She folded her arms across her breasts, shoulders hunched. "Yeah. I know it's not what most people would find pretty. It's not supposed to be pretty. I know I'm not all that awesome a dollmaker." She huffed a laugh. "As you could tell if you saw my sales figures. But I promise you I wasn't setting out to hurt you with those. I haven't even made any of them yet."

Her frown and her withdrawn pose sowed doubt, but this made no sense. A witch dabbling in art? "You said you weren't expecting me, you thought I was just a character in a book, but you're planning to make poppets like this? To what end? What spell were you casting?"

Her brows furrowed. She shook her head, gaze jerking up to meet his. "No, no it's not like that. Not at all. These were supposed to be stupid little creepy dolls for Halloween. I had no idea you were real."

He didn't want to ever hear that word again. "I am real! And if you're planning on casting some magic on me to change me into this—this horrible thing—then be warned, I know some songs which aren't so nice! I'll sing them if I have to!"

She snatched the drawings from him, crumpled up the paper, then roughly tore it into pieces. They fluttered to the carpet. "There. Done. Okay?" she demanded.

"I," he said, then could think of nothing else.

"For the last time, I'm not that kind of witch. Hell, I don't even have the kind of magic you do. I can't heal broken bones. I don't know any old languages, just a little bit of German and Norwegian from my family." She stared up at him, just a step away. "I am not going to hurt you. If you don't understand that yet, then I don't know what else I can do to prove it to you."

Scarecrow's anger melted into guilt.

Her eyes gleamed with moisture. "If you don't want my help, I won't stop you. You can leave. But there's something you need to see first."

"Theo, I'm sorry." The words felt thick in his mouth. "I'm too used to Oz witches. I didn't mean to..." Yes. Yes, he did. He'd allowed his fear to master him. Theo hadn't hidden anything from him, hadn't tried to discourage him. She'd mentioned the dolls before, had made no real secret of them. Twice now she'd fallen asleep in his presence. She trusted him. And he'd just insulted her handiwork to boot.

She glared out the window. "It's fine. No big deal."

Scarecrow took her right hand in his gently. "I shouldn't allow my past to color my dealings with you. This is a different world. You're a different kind of witch. An actual good witch. I've never known a witch to make art. Your—your drawings were very detailed. It's not my place to judge them." He took a deep breath, inhaling her scent of sweet spices. As if she'd spent all day baking with honey and cardamom, roses and orange blossoms. "I don't know why I'm jumping to conclusions rather than thinking everything through. I used to be much better at unraveling riddles."

She sighed. "For any individdle?"

He cocked an eyebrow.

"Never mind. I'll show you later." She shook her head. "Apology accepted. You seem like you've been through a lot of bad shit with witches."

"Yes, well, that's an understatement." He fell silent a moment, wanting to turn the uncomfortable conversation elsewhere. "It seems my song didn't do its job."

"What? No, are you kidding? I crashed hard. Great nap. Woke up a few minutes ago, felt great, dove right into—" she halted, eyes dimming as if her volatile energy had suddenly failed.

"You came in here to show me something," he remembered. "What was it?"

Her eyebrows knit together. "Oh, Scarecrow. It's—I woke up and realized we're going about it all wrong. Our first step should be to find out more about Dorothy. The actual Dorothy, not the one from the books."

"That makes sense," he agreed.

She swallowed, turning her phone towards him and swiping a finger across the screen. "I did some digging and found this."

The black-and-white picture made the ball of straw in his chest jump. "That's her! That's Dorothy!" He was surprised to see Theo on the verge of tears once more.

Oh no.

Theo took the phone back. "Wait. You need to read the whole thing." She cleared a slew of papers away from a white placard on a desk, bearing letters of the alphabet in an odd, unadorned script. A large black mirror he'd taken for some sort of magical scrying-glass lit up. Theo's fingers tapped swiftly across the letterboard, and suddenly Dorothy's picture filled the glass. Scarecrow took a step toward the image, heart in his throat, dismayed at his beloved's wan appearance. She clutched a dog collar in one hand and wore a shapeless white shift. She didn't look well.

"Where is she?" he asked.

Theo's eyes were dark and shaded. "She's dead, Scarecrow. She died over a hundred years ago, imprisoned in a lunatic asylum, raving about Oz. No one believed her. They locked her up because she wouldn't shut up about it." Tears rolled down her face. "I'm so sorry, Scarecrow. Dorothy's dead."

11

He stared at her, motionless. Goddess, she hated having to be the one to tell him.

"No," he said finally. "That can't be right."

Theo gestured at the desktop screen. "Read it."

Scarecrow bent to read the small text aloud. "'*The Wizard of Oz,*' *beloved by young readers for over a hundred years, has inspired countless films, plays, shows and spin-offs. L. Frank Baum's original characters the Scarecrow, the Cowardly Lion, and the Tin Woodman are instantly recognizable, as is the little girl in a gingham-checked dress, Dorothy Gale of Kansas. What most people don't know is there was indeed a real Dorothy, who Baum met and whose wild delusions inspired the Oz stories. Her own story is far more tragic and often glossed over by historians. The discovery of her patient records earlier this year has inspired a new exhibit at the Museum of Oz.*"

Theo hugged her arms across her chest, biting her lower lip. She'd skimmed through the webpage from a self-proclaimed Oz researcher. Didn't bother to read the whole thing, just far enough to see the death date recorded by the asylum doctor, and the researcher's assumption that the forgotten young woman's final resting place was likely in a potter's field of unmarked graves.

"What's a patient record?" Scarecrow asked.

Theo sniffled, wiping her face roughly with the back of her hand. "Just keep reading."

His voice was quiet and halting as he continued. "*Dorothea Gale was the only survivor of a tornado strike in her tiny hamlet of Persistence, Kansas in 1897. Her family was killed and their farm destroyed. Rather than going over the rainbow, the teenaged girl was found by a rescue committee from Lawrence, Kansas, a few days later, wandering barefoot and delirious. According to the town doctor, she was severely dehydrated and malnourished, suffering from brain fever. She was treated for several days and then taken in by a nearby farming couple who had known her family. They hoped to give her a normal life after her tragedy, but Dorothy's insis-*

tence that she'd traveled to another land populated by witches, fairies, and talking animals eventually led her new aunt and uncle to leave her in the care of the Thompson Asylum. Treatment with hydrotherapy (plunging the girl into freezing baths), and the very new and primitive science of electroshock therapy, made Dorothy subdued and obedient."'

Subdued and obedient. Yeah, probably a vegetable. Horrible.

Scarecrow blinked. Tears glistened on his fabric cheeks, starting to soak in. "But she did travel to Oz," he whispered. "Why would they do these terrible things to her?"

"No one believed her. She was too old to believe in magic and faeries. People assumed she was going crazy. Sick in the brain."

He shook his head. "This is horrible."

"Yeah. Yeah, it is. I'm so sorry, Scarecrow."

He closed his eyes a moment, bracing himself as if against a stiff wind. "You said she died."

Theo scrolled down the page, showing him how to work the mouse for himself. "Here. Next to last paragraph."

He hesitated, then leaned close to the screen again. This time he read silently.

This was awful. He'd come so far to find a woman he clearly loved, and landed in the wrong century and hundreds of miles off course.

His story couldn't end like this. His being here at all proved Oz was real. Magic was real.

What if I could find a spell to send him back in time, so he could find Dorothy before she was committed to a cold, gray asylum?

Yeah. Sure. Just whip out a cauldron and some frog eyeballs, no problem.

Where the hell would she even start looking? She'd joined a coven at twenty, then last year was seduced into a different one, headed by her then-lover, charismatic vampire-wannabe Mark. Theo left their group of pretenders when she kicked that asshole out of her life. Her mentor Gwyn and their mutual friends had been hinting that Theo should rejoin the nicer coven, when she felt ready to be social again. None of them, as far as she knew, ever attempted magic more strenuous than blessings or thanks-givings. Her friend Cassandra practiced a more crop-centered spellcraft, but as lovely and generous as she was, Cassie didn't have much luck making her fields grow, outside of a bounty of pumpkins. No way would any of them know how to send anyone back in time.

Scarecrow turned. Tears ran down his face, leaving damp trails on the burlap. "Tell me you have some magic to stop this." His voice sounded raspy, desperate, like dried corn sheaves scraping together.

Theo shook her head, her throat tight. "I don't—there isn't anything," she stammered. "Not that I know of."

"I thought you said you're a witch."

"I don't know any serious magic. Not unless a protection charm or dowsing for water can help." His grimace, blinking back more tears, made her own eyes blurry. "I'm so sorry. It's already happened. There's no way to go back in time." She grasped his arm, feeling the straw yield and rustle inside his sleeve. "Maybe we can get you back home. Maybe Glinda or someone—"

"Glinda sent me here," he snapped, voice rising in pitch. "She knew what she was doing, I guarantee you. She sent me here to torment me. Shunted me out of the palace very happily, knowing perfectly well I'd find out this," he gestured at the computer screen with its terrible words in cold black and white, "and then die once my magic runs out! Crows and blight, I've already run out of power for the one link I had to home. How can you be a witch without any magic? Can't you just harvest some from the damned pixies infesting your yard? I have to at least recharge the stone."

His words filtered past the anguish in her brain finally. "Wait, what are you talking about? Pixies? What stone? What link to home?"

He tugged a smooth lump of rhodochrosite from a pants pocket, thrusting it at her. "My Evstone only lasted long enough for a few minutes' conversation with Nick, and I wasted it chatting about unimportant things! Tell me you can recharge this, at least?"

"Wait. You used this to talk to Nick? When?"

He made an impatient gesture at the window. "A little while ago. It's been five days for him. Something bad is going on around Ozma. I never should've left." He curled his hand around the stone, thumping both fists on the desk. "I'm such a fool. Glinda's probably been scheming to get rid of me for ages, and then I just walk right up and beg her to send me to Dorothy's world. No wonder she didn't ask for anything in return. I was already handing her exactly what she wanted."

"Back up." Theo wiped her eyes and held out a hand. "Let me see that. Please."

He dropped the stone into her palm. It felt oddly warm. Theo peered closely at it. Nothing unusual she could see. "So this is a magic rock?"

"Evstone," he repeated. "From the Kingdom of Ev. Very common in magical crafting. It retains whatever spell one puts on it. It must've taken an enormous amount of power to break through the veil between worlds just for those few minutes we talked." He drew in a haggard breath. "Nick can have his stone recharged, but I don't know what could do that here, if you don't have a spell or any spare charges laying around." He scowled. "If we ground down enough pixies it might provide a minute or two of magic, at least."

"Okay hold up, what the hell do you mean pixies? Like tiny faeries?"

He looked at her as if she'd just asked him if air was breathable. "Yes, what else would I mean? Pixies. Nasty little faelings. I killed one in your back garden earlier."

She gaped at him. "You what?"

"Do you truly not know what I'm talking about?" He strode to a crafting table and picked up one of the unfinished dolls. "This! Four wings, nasty teeth, vicious little claws, absolutely no regard for personal space. You're making poppets of them. Don't tell me you've never seen one."

That particular design was from one of her nightmares. She dreamed she was picking flowers in a lush field when suddenly biting insects swarmed, which turned into tiny, grotesque little people. She'd run and run, swatting at them, unable to find any cover or make them stop.

It took her a second to find her voice. "Not in real life."

A deep grimace wrinkled his face. "I am starting to detest that word."

"I just—these don't exist," she insisted, taking the doll from him and waving it around the room. "None of these do! Not here anyway. Not mermaids or dragons or faeries of any kind."

"Just creatures in stories?" he asked, his voice cutting.

Right. Just like a talking scarecrow. If Gramma Hildy hadn't seen and spoken with him too, Theo might've doubted everything that happened the past twenty-four hours. This was getting too weird and too serious.

Swallowing down a retort, she looked at the pink stone again. For just an instant, she thought she saw a glow coming off it. When she raised it closer to her face it was simply a rock. "How would you usually recharge this?"

Scarecrow shook his head. "Drop it off at the stonecrafter's guild. Or I suppose, if we had some wyvern's blood or fermented faery mushrooms we could soak it in that. Guessing you don't have those tucked away in your cabinets somewhere. What difference does it make now? I'm stuck here with no magic, something foul is afoot in Oz and I'm not there to help, and Dorothy is—" He broke off, covering his face with one spread-gloved hand. "What a useless fool. Useless, pointless bale of straw. She saved my life three times and I can't even stop her from..." He fell silent, shaking.

His grief sparked something red and stubborn inside her.

No. No, fuck this. Amazing things couldn't just drop into her life for no reason.

Theo always wanted to believe in magic. In faeries. Unseen courts and mysterious creatures lurking just out of mortals' perceptions. She hadn't spent countless hours whispering her hopes to legendary goddesses, seeking out hidden forest glens where nature spirits might still dwell, believing there must be more to this world, to give up now. Not when the legit Scarecrow of Oz landed right at her feet and needed her help. He was proof, damn it! Proof she wasn't a silly child at twenty-six. Proof her dolls weren't just her own wild nightmares made tangible, if he insisted they looked like actual fae. And she'd been right where and when he arrived in this world.

"Things happen for a reason," she muttered. "There has to be more to this."

"I'm sure all the reasons are back in Oz," Scarecrow rasped, "and Glinda or someone else on the Seelie Court is plotting to overthrow the throne." He gave a sharp laugh. "Though why they'd fear my brains enough to want me out of the way, I have no clue. Clearly I wasn't too bright after all, if the mere hope of something I'll never have was enough to cloud my judgement."

"That is fucking *enough*," Theo snapped. She slapped the stone down on her desk, grabbing his arms. He flinched. "You are brilliant, and loyal, and you can *sing magic* for Goddess' sake, and—"

Wait.

He could sing magic. Magic strong enough to heal broken bones. To make her feel at peace, something she couldn't recall ever having felt before.

Scarecrow stared wide-eyed at her, frozen, his arms caught in her grip, the straw inside crimped narrowly where she held tight. "Theo?"

"Magic," she whispered. Hell yes. That could work, couldn't it? "You can sing magic."

He blinked. "I...yes."

"Know any songs about time travel?"

He shook his head slowly, his gaze unfocused. Theo realized she was squeezing his arms tighter than a human would've found comfortable and let go. He remained stock-still, silent.

"You must know some kind of song that would help," she prodded. "Some old tune about finding a lost love. Or traveling to meet her."

Again he shook his head, but she heard an odd sound, like small bits of metal jostling against each other or sorghum grains being crumpled in a small sack. He stared at nothing.

Come on, Scarecrow. Use those magnificent brains I know you have.

A popping sound came from his hat, though she didn't see anything different, then another and another, like strong fabric forcibly punctured. His head jerked up, eyes wide, refocusing on her. "Not for traveling in time, but I know a song about stones. Ozian stones. I don't know what it actually does." He pursed his lips, frowning. "I don't really know what most of the songs do. I learned they were magic by accident. Haven't had the time to research more than a handful of them."

"So maybe you can recharge your phone-stone here. Find out what's going on at home. Maybe your friends can find a way to bring you back."

"Glinda said there was no way back."

Theo snorted. "Yeah, and that bitch lied to you. Didn't she say she was sending you to Dorothy?"

"Well, no. Not as such."

Theo brushed back her hair and crossed her arms. "In the books, spells in Oz needed specific words to make them work. Is that part true?"

"Hm." He rubbed his chin. "Yes. I think so, at least. The Wishing Pills and the Powder of Life needed incantations to make them take effect."

Man, she really, really wanted to know how much in the books was true and how much was invented by Baum. "You actually did go on an adventure with Tip and the Saw-horse and Jack Pumpkinhead and the Wogglebug? That whole thing with the Gump falling into the jackdaws' nest and—"

"Don't remind me. Being stuffed with money was embarrassing."

In the second Oz book, a horde of jackdaws took all the Scarecrow's straw when he and his friends were stranded in a cliffside aerie. His friends repaired him by stuffing him with the paper money littering the nest. It must've smelled like bird poop.

"So what words exactly did Glinda say to send you here?"

"I don't know if she said anything. I was too intent on repeating what she told me to concentrate on."

Theo raised an eyebrow at him. Scarecrow avoided her stare.

"So what was it?"

He sighed. "'I am seeking my heart's desire.'"

"Which would be Dorothy."

"Obviously," he muttered.

"Did she actually promise her spell would send you to Dorothy?"

"No." He scowled. "The fae never lie outright. They're experts at twisting words around so you think you're gaining a pot of gold but instead find you've agreed to a century of serving as their scullery-maid. Worse than the Nomes if you ask me." He shook his head, his gaze falling on the web page about Dorothy's sad imprisonment and death for only an instant before he turned away. "She didn't directly promise to send me to her. But she talked about love sustaining me in this world. Probably to distract me. If I'd just taken the time to think this through— Mold and ruin! She was counting on my foolish hopes." He swept his hat off with one hand, slapping down the pins sticking up through the burlap of his head. "Foolish, gullible, brainless!" He looked absolutely miserable.

Theo caught his arm. "Stop that! Quit beating yourself up, or I'll turn you into a pumpkin. No, not really," she added when he flinched.

"You witches have an unpleasant sense of humor," he muttered.

Theo waved her arms. "Just chill out and let's think about this! There has to be something we can do. If you can sing a spell to recharge your rock, so you can talk to Nick again, maybe he can find the spell Glinda used to send you here. I bet there's a way to reverse it." She stared hard into his eyes. Despite being painted, they tracked her movements like any human's. Shed tears. She could see tiny holes at the centers of his pupils, spaces in the weave of the fabric forming his face and head. Tiny windows into a soul formed of straw and bran, pins, and yearning.

Gulping, she drew back a step. He was speechless. Gently, Theo took his gloved hands in hers. Such soft suede. "Even if I can't get you to your love, I'll do my damnedest to get you home," she said quietly.

After a long moment, his gaze dropped. He nodded. "Thank you, Theo."

"We'll figure it out." She glanced at the screen, dimming while they'd been arguing. "There has to be a way."

His eyes followed hers, but he didn't turn around to see the terrible words again.

"I would like to sit quietly and turn my brains to this problem for awhile." He frowned slightly. "If the Old Ozian songs work better here when translated into common Ozian, I should think carefully about the words to the stone song. Words have their own power, so I must be very specific. Also, there might be other songs I haven't thought of in a long time which could also be helpful. I need to think."

She blurted out before she could stop herself, "Do pins pop out of your head every time you concentrate?"

He grimaced.

"Just curious," Theo mumbled.

"They're not pins," he said firmly, "They're magic brains. The Wizard himself put them in my head. I wouldn't expect you to understand, since you're not accustomed to proper magic."

Theo bit back a grin. "Right. Got it." She picked up the pink rock, swinging its chain from her fingers. "I'll see if I can find any spells for imbuing minerals with magical intent. Never paid much attention to crystal stuff before, but there's a ton of books and websites." He shifted out of her way as she plunked her ass down in front of the computer. She pulled up a playlist of old Goth tunes and cranked the volume.

At the first choral howl of "This Corrosion," Scarecrow grabbed his hat and jerked a step away from her. "Must that be so loud?" he exclaimed over the noise.

"Yeah," Theo yelled back. "Gotta have the right music to research heavy magic shit."

He winced. "I can't think! I need quiet!"

Well, crap. Sitting in silence while he concentrated and popped more tiny pins out of his head, magic brains or not, sounded guaranteed to make her fidgety and irritable very quickly. "I need music," she returned.

He gripped the back of his neck and stalked across the room. Past him, Theo saw the graveyard through the front window. "Hey," she called, "Why don't you go over there? Totally quiet. You can pace and ponder to your heart's content and I can work on this stuff in the environment I need to focus."

"How can you possibly focus on anything?"

She shrugged. "This is how I work. You go over there and do your thing and I'll do mine. Meet back here in like an hour?"

Scarecrow gave her an exasperated glare, but nodded and wiped the remaining moisture from his face with the back of a glove. He straightened his tunic and hat, smoothing everything down, tucking some loose straw back inside his chest. Hm, she should find another button for him too. Keep him from coming apart.

Watching him as he patted his arms back into shape, she sang along out of habit. *Too bad I can't sing magic. There must be a dozen songs about time and lost love.*

With his straw tucked in, from a distance, she could almost pretend he was just a regular guy with a tan. In pseudo-courtly clothing like he'd just come from LARPing. With a beak-nose that was actually kind of adorkable, and dark blue eyes which conveyed sharp intelligence despite being painted on. They didn't bother her so much now.

"Do I look common enough?" he asked, voice raised over the music.

Not in the slightest. Theo nodded, giving him a thumbs-up.

Scarecrow nodded back and left. Theo watched him walk across the deserted street to the cemetery. At least he wasn't likely to run into anyone else over there. No one who'd care what he looked like, anyway. He could stand among the quiet dead and think about a song for his dearly departed love.

"Dammit. Focus, Theo," she muttered, quickly wiping fresh tears welling up. Crystals. Maybe the New Agey stuff was actually helpful here. She turned the Evstone over in her palm. No glow, no heat. Just a mildly pretty rock. With a sigh, she brought the browser back up.

The Oz researcher's web page drew her in again before she could start a new search. *"Dorothy died in the Thompson Home for the Mentally Ill in 1907, aged twenty-five years. Dr. Thompson's notes for the day the young woman died seem especially stark: 'Patient Gale, Dorothea, found expired in room this a.m. Hydrotherapy prior day failed to revive flagging vivacity. Body tendered to undertaker H. Ness for burial in town potter's field. Fam. notified.'*

"It was not uncommon," the researcher continued, *"for patients to be shut into their unheated rooms on cold nights even after a full eight hours of being dunked into icy tubs of water, which was thought to shock the heart and brain into healthy circulation. The probability that Dorothy died of hypothermia, alone, in this cruel and primitive hospital feels all the more heartbreaking after her failed escape attempt."*

She'd tried to escape? Theo scrolled back. Dorothy managed to slip away from the asylum once during a thunderstorm. Hail and a tornado sighting created a disturbance among the patients. While the attendants were wildly trying to round up patients running around the building in terror, somehow Dorothy made her way as far as the Kansas River. A search party the next day found her on the bank not far downstream from the asylum, nearly drowned, babbling about her magical fairyland and gnomes, even less aware of her surroundings than before.

"Goddess bless," Theo breathed, "She did go back to Oz again." That matched up pretty well with the storm which whisked Dorothy to the edge of the Deadly Desert in the third Oz book, even though in the book it was a storm at sea.

The researcher stated the actor, playwright, and failed businessman L. Frank Baum visited the asylum several times during his stint as a traveling chinaware salesman, intrigued by the tale of the young woman who'd ridden a cyclone and survived but lost her sanity. Possibly he'd intended to write a play based on the real life events, but then became more interested in the wild rantings she spouted. Witches and little faery people and men made of tin.

Dr. Thompson, who in the grainy old photographs appeared every bit as dour and heartless as Theo expected, had briefly noted the visits in the logs he kept for each patient. After Dorothy was brought back to the chilly old asylum, she was allowed only one more visitation from Baum before Thompson decreed the young woman was far too agitated by the playwright, and shut her away from the world completely for years before she died there.

Son of a bitch. Dorothy might not've been sane, but she wasn't making up stories. She'd have been better off never returning from Oz. Maybe she'd hoped her family would somehow be alive again if she returned from a place full of magic. "But she came back and it killed her," Theo growled. She glared at the photo of the asylum director. "You better hope I don't find a way to time travel. I'll kick your smug patriarchal balls so far up your throat you'll choke on 'em."

She studied the group photo of women in plain white shifts, their hair all cut painfully short, haunted eyes in pale, undernourished faces. Like the gloomiest yearbook photo ever. Thompson Asylum, Class of 1900. "Dorothea Gale, voted Most Likely to Melt a Witch," Theo muttered. One younger woman in the group picture was circled, tentatively identified as Dorothy. Scarecrow's reaction confirmed it.

Why didn't anyone talk about this? This was far worse than the original bloody versions of Grimm's faery tales. This actually *happened*. She'd read annotated editions of a couple of the Oz books, watched the classic movie a dozen times, but none of this bleak history was ever mentioned.

Well, at least a museum was doing an exhibit on the true background of the girl who went to Oz, even if they didn't believe the fabled land really existed. Disgusted, she scrolled through the rest of the article. If this information had been out there for years she would be well and goodly pissed off. None of this was hinted at in any of the research she'd done on the books, tracing back origins of the strange creatures Baum wrote, to see how they descended from older faery tales. How could anyone sing about going over the rainbow, knowing what horrible things happened to the real—

"Her asylum diary has been carefully restored and will be on display for this exhibit, courtesy of the Thompson family. 'The Real Dorothy Gale: Tragedy and Madness' runs through October 31st at the Museum of Oz," the article concluded.

A diary. Dorothy kept a diary inside that awful place. Theo checked the article date: two months ago.

So her diary was sitting right now in a museum in Kansas.

Would any Oz fans read it? Not likely. Many of the ones she'd come across on fan forums seemed cheerfully centered around the classic film, not at all enthused about Theo's ideas for a series of dark and scary dolls based on the characters.

She winced. Scarecrow had every right to be indignant at those drawings. Even though she never thought he or Oz were real. If someone drew *her* as an evil hag with warts and claws, she might not react very well either.

Should she tell him about the diary? Had he read that part at all?

She was surprised to see Scarecrow hurrying back toward the house. It hadn't been an hour already, had it? The sky was dark, with leaves blowing past. She couldn't remember what time she'd sent him over to the cemetery to do his deep, silent thinking.

The front door opened and slammed shut.

"Hey," Theo called, "Go easy on my house, it's old and—"

He stumbled into the studio, eyes wide, one hand clasping his hat on his head. His straw poked out of his tunic, disheveled. Maybe the wind drove him back here for safety. Instead of greeting her, he immediately went to the window and peered out worriedly.

Theo turned off the music. "Crap. Did someone see you? What's wrong?"

"Theo, is it normal in your world for dead people to get out of their graves and walk around again, even when they have parts falling off?"

"Uh, no." She reluctantly came to the window. "What happened?"

A decaying face smashed into the glass. Theo shrieked, jumping back, slamming into a table. Scarecrow flinched, raising both hands to ward it off. The corpse pressed its head against the window, one bulging eyeball rolling crazily. Its lower jaw hung askew. A tattered, dirt-smudged suit barely clung to its body. One skeletal hand slowly raised and smacked the glass. The window rattled.

"So, this is not typical." Scarecrow's voice shook.

Theo gaped at the undead man. The one eyeball rolled and fixed her in a goopy stare.

"Fuck," she said.

12

T*his was supposed to be a simple, quiet talk with Professor Wogglebug,* Nick Chopper thought, *not a traveling circus on a mission.*

Nick's first mistake was tromping loudly through the palace. It had seemed like a good plan, getting himself noticed by all and sundry, in case any of Glinda's lackeys were around. His mistake was going anywhere near the grand throne room. Normally Tip wouldn't be there so early in the morning, as Glinda insisted on tutoring sessions for her first thing each day. Lessons in etiquette and posture, how to walk regally in one of the Queen's many traditional trailing gowns, how to give a toast appropriate for each High Feast Day. However, Glinda had been strangely absent from the palace the past few days, and today young Ozma Tippetarius played hooky from her lesson.

The Lion and the Hungry Tiger bounded into the hallway right as Nick walked past the throne room, startling him. Both were intent on chasing a large green soap bubble. It popped against Nick, splattering him with luminescent magical plasm and the odor of fresh-cut grass. Nick shushed the cats. Tip's laughter, however, signified the jig was up.

Great. Now he'd been caught by one of the people he hadn't wanted to involve in all this, and he looked as though he'd had a run-in with a seasick goat to boot.

"Aren't you supposed to be with your tutor?" Nick asked.

Tip hiked up her skirts to run across the throne room, a huge grin lighting up her face. "Nick! You're an emerald man instead of a tin one." Her face was flushed from whatever game she'd been playing with her two overgrown house cats. "Hm. Maybe we should have the royal jeweler make you an emerald body. I kind of like you green."

"That would be too heavy, and a waste of emeralds." Nick lifted his right knee, feeling the gunk trying to seep into his joints. "This isn't very nice, Your Highness."

"Sorry." She waved her scepter in a seemingly random pattern. The green liquid vanished from his body. She grinned. "Getting better at this magic stuff. So what are you doing today?"

"He's up to no good," Lion declared. "I can smell it."

"Smells like oil to me," the Tiger snorted. "Yuck. Not appetizing at all."

Nick gently pushed the Tiger's enormous muzzle away from his midsection. "Just making the rounds, tending to my responsibilities."

Tip glanced up and down the corridor, but no one else was around. "Did you use the stone yet?" she whispered.

Nick's hand instinctively closed over his vest pocket. "We shouldn't be talking about this here."

The Queen crossed her arms and frowned. Lion and Tiger, taking their cue from her, plumped down on their haunches on either side of Nick, staring at him with enormous slitted eyes. He knew Lion was kidding around, and wouldn't hurt him after all they'd been through together. The Tiger, on the other hand, was a bit of a wild card. Impossible to predict what went through that stripey brain at any given moment.

Tip's eyes widened. "You did, didn't you? You spoke to him! How is he? Did he find her? Is he coming back?"

"Shhhh," Nick begged, leaning closer to her. "Yes, but not so loud."

"Well? Tell me!" demanded Tip.

Tiger poked Nick's leg, jostling him back a step. "Tell us!"

Nick glared at the Tiger. "You don't even know what this is about."

"Do too. 'Bout the straw man. The one who always smells like hay without any tasty mice."

"We're not allowed to eat mice," Lion reminded him, "on account of the Mouse Queen saving my butt from the poppy field."

"No mice," agreed Tip, giving the Tiger a scratch on his head. "Come on, spill it, Nick! Is Scarecrow all right? Did he find Dorothy?"

Not the secret mission he'd hoped for at all, but no helping it now. Nick sighed. "We can't talk here."

"Why not?" Tip frowned. "Just tell us already!"

"Something is going on, and I don't know what yet, or who is involved," Nick said softly. "I need to talk to Professor Wogglebug and see if—"

"Ooo, a secret mission," the Tiger rumbled, loud enough anyone on either end of the echoing corridor could have overheard.

"Will you shut up?" Nick hissed.

"Now I'm interested," Lion said.

"General," Tip said, smirking, "I order you to involve us in whatever mission you're on."

Nick sighed, putting a hand over his face. "Your Highness—"

"*Orrrrrderrrrr* you," Tip repeated, slowly and emphatically.

"All right, fine, but we can't let anyone see you trooping over to the Wogglebug's when it's not a lesson day. It could raise suspicions."

Tip looked at the Tiger. "You remember where that secret passageway is?"

Tiger's muzzle wrinkled. "The one that smelled like chicken, or the one that smelled like dust?"

"Dust, I think."

"Ugh. Yes, I remember."

"Secret passage?" Nick asked. Scarecrow had found one in the Emerald Palace, though it only went behind the servants' quarters. Probably some past monarch wanted to be able to spy on them to prevent schemes of uprising. Ozian rulers hadn't always been kind and benevolent. He'd explained at length to Scarecrow why lingering in the dank, cramped passageway while people were occupying those rooms was rude, over Scarecrow's point it might provide invaluable, uncensored information about human interactions. The concept of *privacy,* at least, made sense to the straw man and he'd agreed to leave the passage alone.

"There are some good things about being Queen." Tip smiled. "Go on over to the University. We'll meet you in the cellar."

No getting out of it now. If he didn't show up where asked soon enough, Nick knew the young Queen would absolutely have her cats search every room of the old building until they found him. Making a racket as they went. Unlike the Lion, the Hungry Tiger couldn't be quiet. His stomach would rumble like clockwork every few minutes. If one could call a wall-shaking, dish-rattling tremor a rumble.

Nick relented. "Just please, don't tell anyone, and don't let anyone see you. Any of you," he cautioned.

Tip's grin faded. "You're really serious about this. Nick, what exactly is going on? Does this have to do with you-know-who-in-pink-frills not being around for days?"

"I don't know. Possibly. Just please, be discreet," Nick whispered.

"We will," Tip promised. She frowned at her scepter. The royal insignia, an emerald-encrusted Z within a golden O at the top of the slender staff, glowed faintly green. She swished it through the air and mumbled something. "Nobody's listening," she declared. "Just us."

Nick nodded. "Good. Let's keep it that way."

He sketched a bow and hurried off, remembering just as he burst into the inner courtyard that he was supposed to be merely making his usual rounds. He slowed to a stroll, though itching to race to the tall spires of the University not far past the Palace walls. He greeted gardeners and servants as he went. Normally he'd linger for some time in the flower gardens, sampling the perfumes of any new roses in bloom. It was a chore to do so today, but upon spotting one of the guards watching from a balcony, Nick paused to sniff deeply of a fine pink climbing rose on one of the garden path's many arbors. He picked up his pace once the guard went back inside.

He did visit the Wogglebug every so often to chat with the very chatty insect professor, so walking sedately over to the University shouldn't draw any attention. Nick made a point of stopping at the main door to exchange pleasantries with the docent, who gave tours of the older wings when class wasn't in session. As the Wogglebug was often too engrossed in his own research to remember he had a class to teach, the docent was usually hanging around.

Not too many Ozians wanted a tour. Frankly, the whole building gave Nick the creeps. The University had only been converted to a school the last few years. Centuries before, it served as a temple to the fae, who'd been worshipped as gods. Some parts of it predated even the Pastorian royal line of Oz, and there were rumors of deeper caverns below it where strange altars yet stood, unseen for hundreds of years.

The docent's eyes lit up on seeing Nick. The Tin Woodman politely brushed off the younger man's invitation yet again to go see the paintings in the original chapel. The docent's clear disappointment made Nick sigh inwardly. The crush was obvious. Under different circumstances he might've taken the time to have more than a passing conversation with him, but definitely not today. Nick murmured a few words of encouragement about how much tidier the place was when the docent was around, then hurried through the echoing great antechamber.

The interior was cool and damp. Nick tried to avoid the place on rainy days in particular, as parts of the roof leaked. The Wogglebug, however, was sure to have a fire lit in his chambers. Nick took a side stairway up as swiftly as his joints could manage. He was supposed to meet Tip in the basement. The chilly, very damp basement, a crypt really, though all the funeral urns were long since cleared out to a deeper level so they wouldn't be disturbed further.

He rapped lightly on the door, hearing muttering and clicking sounds on the other side. No answer. With any luck no one would be keeping tabs on the Wogglebug, as Glinda certainly made no secret of how distasteful and ridiculous she found him. Nick knocked louder, and this time heard the bug call out, *"Entré!"*

Nick opened the door. The room was chaos not even his straw friend would be able to disentangle. Books and papers cluttered every flat surface and some of the round ones. A stack of tomes perched precariously atop a marble bust of a previous King Pastoria, possibly Colin the Third. Scrolls stuck up out of a copper kindling bin. Nick hoped the professor wasn't using those to start his cheery little hearth fires, whether by accident or not.

What Nick took at first for a new table suddenly stood upright, proving to be the rounded beetle back of Professor H.M. Wogglebug, T.E. The land of Oz had plenty of insect species, including several kinds of wogglebugs, but only one individual was Highly Magnified and Thoroughly Educated, as the Wogglebug was quite fond of pointing out.

The Wogglebug's antennae were curled like grand mustachios. They twitched upward when he spied Nick. "Goodness! My old comrade, the shining knight of tin! You are looking most splendid today, sir." His four hands all held objects: an unlit pipe. A pocket-watch. A wind-up beetle toy. A scroll. He dropped the scroll carelessly to the floor among a sea of papers, tucked the other things into his waistcoat pockets, and threw out all four arms in warm welcome at Nick.

As if Nick didn't drop by every so often just to make sure the building hadn't burned down yet and the students were still actually being taught something. He clasped hands with the Professor, very gently, mindful of the bug's delicate fingers. "Thank you. I see you're trying a new antennae pomade."

The Wogglebug toyed with one antenna, smiling. "Indeed. I rather think it suits me. Come in, pull up a chair, or chop up one if you'd rather. I don't use them, and the nights are turning chilly again." He gestured at the fireplace, a clacking, chittering sound coming from his mandibles. Though Nick knew this was how the Professor chuckled, the sound still set his tin teeth on edge.

"Actually," Nick said, "I need you to come downstairs with me. Just for a few minutes."

"Whatever for?"

"I was hoping to get your help on something. A dangerous intrigue," Nick said, remembering the professor enjoyed reading mysteries and fancied himself a sharper mind even than the Scarecrow.

"Oh? What sort of intrigue?" The Wogglebug leaned closer. "Would this happen to involve a certain debonair young tour guide? The one with the adorable little mole on his left cheek?"

"No," Nick replied quickly, one hand pushing the insect's shoulder back a few inches. Was the Wogglebug interested in the docent's crush on Nick? The faceted black eyes staring curiously at him made him uneasy. The bug was a known gossip, so most likely he'd already bandied about rumors of lingering glances and yearning sighs. Sternly Nick continued, "This is a matter of royal security."

The insect's eyes popped even more, if that were possible. "Oho! How very spicy!" He drew upright, quivering. "You don't mean to say you and our illustrious Queen—"

Nick groaned. "No, and would you get all these ideas about secret trysts out of your beetle-brain? Something is going on. I think it has to do with the Good Witch, or the Seelie Court. Something involving Ozma. Have you heard anything strange lately?"

The Wogglebug tittered and click-clacked, folding his first set of arms smugly over his spotless silk waistcoat. "Oh, well if it's court gossip you want, I heard Duke Thingrass has rather a *tendre* for the Nome ambassador, Count Oglaff."

"Not that kind of information." By now Tip might be in the basement waiting for them. Though it was clearly not a class day, there were still students milling about in the dormitory level and servants on the main floor of the University. The last thing he needed was anyone spotting the unmistakable feline entourage of the Queen. "Please. Come downstairs so we can discuss this. Act casual."

"My dear Nicholas, my acting has never been anything less than formally acclaimed."

"And no puns," Nick warned, tugging the bug's ornate jacket sleeve. "Come on."

"My study is perfectly secure," the Wogglebug protested as Nick dragged him into the upper hall.

"Not for Her Majesty it isn't. She can't be seen mixed up in this. The Good Witch has armed guards locking her into her chambers at night."

"Locking Her Majesty in?"

"Yes," Nick said, "Now do you see?"

"I'm beginning to," the bug mumbled, sobering, and followed Nick quietly enough down the back stairs.

They entered the cellar just as the Tiger emerged from behind a heavy stone shield carved on a wall. Tip was close behind, bearing a lantern, and the Lion padded cautiously after, eyes darting around the low-ceilinged room.

"That was fun," the Queen declared. "Professor! How have you been?"

The Wogglebug executed a low bow with florid gestures from all four hands. "Your Majesty, I am well, thank you ever so much for asking. How does Your Highness this rather gloomy day?"

Nick suppressed an urge to roll his eyes. Ever since the boy Tip became the Queen Ozma, the bug had been unnecessarily courtly. Although this was preferable to his attempts at wit.

"We're all here." Tip's eyes gleamed bright green in her excitement. "So what's all the secrecy for, Nick?"

He didn't really have any kind of a plan, or even any hard evidence besides the suspicious guard on the Queen. Blast and rust, this sort of thing was Scarecrow's department, not his. "Have any of you seen the Good Witch lately?" Nick asked. Best not to speak her name out loud when trying to avoid her attention.

They all glanced at each other.

"She told me she had duties at the Seelie Court, and she'd be back in a day or two," Tip said, "but that was four days ago."

"She didn't leave you any special instructions?"

Tip frowned, readjusting her gold circlet with its enchanted poppy blossoms over her forehead. "Just the usual 'listen to your tutors and don't go running in the garden when it rains.'"

"Why don't you elaborate upon your concerns for us, Nick?" the Wogglebug asked. "I don't much care for the damp down here, and I'll wager neither do you. Let's out with it, and then Her Majesty can scamper back down the secret tunnel to the Palace and we can get back to my nice warm study."

Nick paused. "You already knew there was a tunnel down here?"

The Wogglebug preened his antennae. "More than one."

Tip perked. "Really? Where?"

"Can we get back to the matter at hand?" Nick sighed.

"You haven't told us what it is," Tip argued.

Should he tell her she was being locked in, treated with extra scrutiny? Was she aware of it already and simply assuming it was part of Glinda's overbearing care? He brought out the Evstone. "I spoke with Scarecrow yesterday."

Immediately he was interrupted. "So what's happened?"

"How fares our straw comrade?"

"Surprised he didn't have all his straw shaken out. Heard a whirlwind grabbed him."

"Are we getting snacks with this meeting?"

Nick glared at the Tiger. "No. Scarecrow seems all right, though he hasn't found Dorothy. He'd been in her world less than a day when we spoke. And a witch is helping him."

Tip cocked her head to the side. "Who? I thought he hates witches."

"None of the ones here. He met one over there. I warned him to be cautious."

"One moment, friend Nick," the Wogglebug said, "Did Glin—" Nick immediately shushed him. With a sober nod, the professor continued, "Did the Good Witch not say her spell would set our straw friend down near to Dorothy? What went wrong?"

Nick shook his head. "I don't know. I keep thinking about it. I don't recall either of them actually using Dorothy's name. I fear the Good Witch may have misled him."

"Surely such a spell would have cost an enormous amount of magic," the bug mused. "What favor did he perform to garner such largesse?"

"That's just it," Nick said. "Nothing. The witch sent him to Dorothy's world without asking a thing in return. Does that sound like the fae we all know?"

They all stood silently a long moment. Tiger's stomach rumbled.

"So," the Wogglebug spoke up, "the Scarecrow was sent where he asked to go, but hasn't found whom he sought. No one has seen our pink-gowned mistress in some days. And the Seelie Court is holding a secret meeting tonight."

"Secret meeting?" Lion growled.

"How do you know?" Nick demanded.

The Wogglebug shrugged. "I have friends everywhere, you know. I'm quite popular among some of the court in particular."

Given how some of the fae appeared to be part butterfly, dragonfly, or beetle, this made perfect sense. "Wait. The Seelie Court is meeting without Gl—our pink-loving witch?"

Tip scowled. "When do I start getting invited to the Court meetings? Aren't they supposed to include me?"

"Well, per the ancient Charter of Oz," the Wogglebug began, taking up a stance he was known to favor for teaching class.

Tip stomped a foot. "Hang the Charter! I'm the Queen, and part-fae! They should let me in. How dare they hold meetings in my city, anywhere in my Empire even, without so much as telling me about it?"

Lion's furry brows raised. "You want to rub creepy elbows with those things? You know they tortured us, right?"

"They smell too sweet," Tiger added. "Like candy coating something spoiled."

"Per the Charter, Your Highness, you do have the option of attending any full meeting of the Seelie High Court. However the Charter is a bit muddier where it concerns only the lesser dukes and ladies meeting in private chambers." The Wogglebug adjusted his spectacles, frowning up at the green-splotched stone ceiling as if worried it might suddenly give way and crush him. His voice lowered to a hush. "I gathered this particular meeting was taking place in the full knowledge that the Pink Lady would not be able to attend."

Glinda boasted so many honorifics in the Court that Nick had no idea what her actual position was, but he'd always assumed she held a post of great and ancient power among the fae. Certainly the war ground to a very abrupt halt when she'd placed Ozma upon the Emerald City throne. Locasta, the Witch of the North, grudgingly knelt on the marble floor in a puddle of rich velvet robes before the newfound young Queen. Vicious Maab and the crooked Mombi pledged fealty. They never would've stopped fighting over the seat of Ozian power for Ozma Tippetarius alone. Glinda cowed them all.

Could they really be plotting treason?

"Maybe they're getting tired of her being around," Tip offered. Her voice shook a bit, and she sank her fingers into Lion's thick mane.

Maybe the Seelie Court was tired of Tip being on the throne and planning something to undermine her, which also meant undermining Glinda. Nick swallowed dryly. "Whatever they intend, you know I'll stand by you, Your Highness."

Empty niches surrounded them, which once held funeral urns for ancient Ozian royalty. The history of the Empire was one long sequence of overthrows and battles between kingdoms after another. Just because Tip's mortal ancestors, the line of Pastorian kings and queens, held the throne for two centuries before the Wizard arrived, didn't mean it would continue now without assistance.

Tip had barely begun to explore her faery powers, and Glinda was stingy about training her in them. Nick felt sick. If some of the powerful Seelie Court, fae nobility all, wanted to wrench back the reins of power, there'd be little he or anyone in this room could do about it. Scarecrow might've been able to anticipate their plot, and advise the Queen to avoid a terrible end. How convenient for the fae that Scarecrow wasn't here.

Glinda sent him through the veil to Dorothy's world merely because he asked her to. Ominous and ugly as that was, why do so at all if she wasn't part of the faction planning to usurp the throne?

Nick's head hurt. *Blast and rust, Scarecrow. I could really use your advice right about now.*

"I wish Scarecrow was here," he muttered. "He'd figure it all out." He held out the Evstone. "I've recharged it today, but I can't reach him. He must still need to charge his stone for them both to work."

Tip hugged the Lion. Tiger rubbed against her other side. "I wish I could hear what's going on at the secret meeting."

Nick shook his head. "No way any of us could sneak in. They always use magic wards to warn them of any spies or intruders. I tried to walk in as if by accident once. Didn't get ten feet from the door before their monkeys set upon me." Even the threat of flung excrement was enough to send him hurrying away. Not to mention, if angered, a pack of flying monkeys could absolutely hoist the Tin Woodman into the air. During their first adventure with Dorothy, monkeys dropped him into a chasm, where he dented horribly upon the rocks and rusted in the rain, unable to climb out. He shivered just remembering it. He'd still be there if Dorothy hadn't melted the Witch of the West and sent the witch's freed slaves, the Winkies, to rescue him.

"So we cannot approach in person, nor may we use any magic to spy on their meeting," the Wogglebug said, ticking these options off on his spindly fingers, "but I propose we use neither. That way they may not have prepared any countermeasures."

Nick glared at the bug. "You're talking in riddles again."

"Not at all." The Wogglebug tugged a metal beetle from a waistcoat pocket. "Observe!" He stuck a tiny key into its belly, wound it several times, then ordered it, "Climb into the niche third down from the top, and listen for one minute. Return here without being seen."

"What flavor is that?" Tiger wondered, eyeing the beetle as the Wogglebug set it on the cold floor.

"I don't think you can eat it," Tip said.

"Really?" Nick scoffed, watching the clicking little toy waddle across to the wall and begin clumsily climbing it. "A wind-up toy. That's your great plan to penetrate the Seelie Court."

The Wogglebug preened. "Observe and learn, my nickel-plated friend."

The beetle settled itself in the niche and went still and silent. They all stared at it.

"This is stupid," Tip fumed. "How is a toy supposed to help? So what if it sneaks past the magic wards and the guards?"

The Wogglebug tipped out a bit of snuff onto one delicate hand. "I'm told patience is a virtue. I wouldn't know, having very little of the stuff myself, but it is something a Queen should learn." He snorted the mix of ground green mushroom, antennae curling tightly.

Nick wanted to knock the mother-of-pearl snuffbox to the floor and stomp it to bits. How was showing off mechanical twaddles going to help? The Seelie Court were almost certainly planning treason, Glinda was off on some mission of her own which might or might not have anything to do with the fae lordlings, Scarecrow was unavailable to assist them and Tip might very well be close to the end of her reign. They should leave tonight. Just grab what they needed and go hide out somewhere, let the fae go to war without Nick or any of his friends getting trapped in the middle of it all over again.

He took Tip's hand. "I think we should go. Whatever's going on, it isn't good, and I don't want you caught up in it."

Her eyes widened. "You think the Seelie Court is really plotting against me? Won't Glinda protect me?"

Nick glanced around, chilled at the mention of her name. Hopefully they were deep enough underground the word couldn't carry to the witch, wherever she was. He shook his head. "I think the fae don't care about any of us, no matter how nicely they curtsey to you."

"Tsk," said the Wogglebug. "And nobody paid attention. I should flunk you all." He held out the mechanical beetle, smirking.

Lion blinked. "How did that..."

Nick followed his stare to the wall niche. The mechanical toy had snuck past all of them.

"I shall now prove the old maxim that a bug in the hand is worth two in the niche," the Wogglebug said smugly.

"So your toy might be able to sneak in and out of the meeting," Nick argued. "So what? How does this help us? What we need is to be able to hear what they're saying, and if you've put some enchantment on that, the fae will know it in a hot second and smash it to pieces."

"And then they'll come hunting for the person who made it," Lion growled.

The Wogglebug sighed, shaking his head, casting his round black gaze to the ceiling. "Lo, I toil among common minds. One day you'll all acknowledge me as the brightest creature in the room. Observe." He pried the back wings open. Inside the mechanical beetle, a thin ribbon wound around a metal spool. The professor twirled it with his fingers, then pressed a lever inside the beetle. The ribbon began turning on its own, threading between two small shiny stones.

The Tiger bared his teeth, Lion's ears flattened, and Tip and Nick stared dumbly when their own voices, sounding strange and distorted, issued from the mechanical beetle's mandibles. *This is stupid. How is a toy supposed to help. So what if it sneaks past the magic wards and the guards.*

"I'm told patience is a virtue. I wouldn't know, having very little of the stuff myself, but it is something a Queen should learn."

"Magic," snarled the Lion. "What did we just say? The fae will sense that immediately, you bugbrain!"

"Not magic!" The Wogglebug retorted. "My own invention. I call it a lodeo-audiometric device. By use of two tiny lodestones, I can capture sounds on a strand of Quadling eelskin coated in powdered iron. The whole thing is powered by wound springs and gears."

"Like TikTok." Tip examined the beetle.

"I may have studied our gear-brained friend once or twice when he was wound down," admitted the Wogglebug.

Though the mechanical guardian TikTok wasn't alive, it still seemed rude for the Professor to have poked through his innards. Even Scarecrow had agreed not to take apart TikTok, as he wasn't certain he could properly put him back together. The copper mechanical man saved Dorothy from an attack by vicious Wheelers once, and deserved more respect than that.

Setting aside for the moment the idea the Wogglebug had possibly screwed up anything in TikTok's gears and wires, Nick peered at the wind-up beetle. Its flat voice conveyed no emotion, but it repeated their words exactly.

"How long can it listen before it runs down?" Tip asked, one finger wiggling the metal mandibles of the toy.

The Wogglebug closed its wings, brushing the moist dirt of the old crypt from its metal feet. "If wound tightly, assuming it doesn't have too far to go inside before it can sit and listen, perhaps half an hour."

Maybe the professor was good for more than gossip after all. "Do you know where this secret meeting is?" asked Nick.

"I do, as it so happens. A certain courtier asked me to join him for drinks later, and he let slip he'd be attending some dreary fae hobnob tonight, upstairs at the Last Twitch." Professor Wogglebug smiled broadly, black eyes gleaming in the light from Tip's lantern. "So I propose to arrive early and dine in the common room, surreptitiously sending this little marvel upstairs to eavesdrop, and then once my companion is suitably in his cups and the rest of them gone, I may sneak up and retrieve it."

Though it seemed a good enough plan, the mere mention of the pub sent a shiver down Nick's metal spine. He'd gone in exactly once, to view the reputed broomstick of the dead Wicked Witch of the West for himself. How that cursed thing ended up over the bar of a seedy pub was anyone's guess. He'd asked, and received seven or eight conflicting stories, each more unlikely than the last. The bartender insisted Dorothy herself gave him the broomstick when the Wizard left Oz. Nick had expected the broomstick to be a fake. One look at it turned him cold on a summer's day. It was real.

The fae who patronized the pub seemed amused by its ghoulish decor, with the skulls of defeated monkeys and various other props from the war mounted on its dark walls. No thank you. Nick had seen enough actual bloodshed. Drinking in a pub full of grim trophies, no matter if most of them were fakes, held absolutely no appeal. "You go there often?" he asked the Wogglebug.

The Professor shrugged. "It's perhaps rather *outré*, but one does meet the most interesting people."

"I want to see it," Tip said.

Lion shook his great mane. "You're way too young for that."

"I'm the Queen. A Queen is never too young to go anywhere in her Empire."

Tiger sighed. "They banned me after I ate a waiter by mistake."

Nick stared. "You ate a waiter?"

"It was a talking pig!" the Tiger groused. "How was I to know? Anyway I spit him back out and he only needed eighteen stitches."

"Perhaps, Your Majesty, undertaking this particular task requires a bit more subterfuge," the Wogglebug suggested. "I'd be happy to accompany you there some other time, if you have your lovely heart set on seeing the dreary inside of that particular establishment, but tonight I propose I alone patronize them."

Well, if the mechanical beetle really could capture everything said in the secret conference, it was worth a try. With any luck, the fae lordlings didn't plan to rush straight out and topple the throne after discussing it in private. Nick patted the Wogglebug's shoulder. "Very well. You go to the Last Twitch and set your little crawling friend loose in the upstairs meeting room. Send it up there before the actual meeting so no one catches it sneaking in." He held out a hand to Tip. "Your Highness, I would like you to stay in some other room tonight than your usual bedchambers. Lion, Tiger, you stay close to her."

Tip swallowed, nodded, and stroked Lion's mane.

Lion growled, eyes narrowing at Nick. "You think they intend to try something tonight."

"I hope not," Nick said. "Just a precaution."

The seriousness of what could occur tonight sunk in for all of them. Even the Tiger was silent.

"I'll sleep in the library," Tip announced. "I can build a little fire in there and Lion can push one of the sofas by it."

She meant Scarecrow's library. The hearth in that vast room was dusty and always empty, for obvious reasons. The library did have several plush reading chairs and one of the sofas which, once upon a time, served as half of the body of a cobbled-together creature called the Gump.

Nick agreed. "I'll ask Jellia to bring you some kindling. Be sure not to tell anyone else where you'll be, and go there before your usual bedtime. Lock yourself in and don't admit anyone except us." The Palace's head chambermaid Jellia Jamb was loyal and could keep a secret. The rest of the staff, doubtful.

Ozma Tip stared up at him with fearful, wide eyes. "You think I'm in real danger?"

"I think we should be very careful," Nick replied. "Speaking of, time for you to get back to the palace. I'm sure your tutor must be looking for you by now."

Tip turned to the Wogglebug. "Promise you'll bring your beetle to me as soon as you can. I'll—I'll request you come help me with my Ixian grammar. There's supposed to be a delegation coming next week and I'll have to give a toast in Ixian." She scowled. "All those rolling *Rs.*"

The professor made a trilling sound with his mandibles, then smiled. "All in the tongue, my dear. I'll be happy to tutor you. Shall we say tomorrow afternoon?"

"If the Pink Lady isn't around," Lion said.

He had a point. It would be extremely difficult for them to meet if Glinda was in the Palace, whenever she returned. Fingers crossed she'd stay gone another day at least. "We might have to meet separately, to avoid suspicion. Go on, Tip, please, and don't get caught anywhere you're not supposed to be." Nick squeezed her shoulder gently. "Be quiet as a mouse."

She nodded, then poked Tiger's muscular shoulder. "Let's go. See you tonight, Nick?"

"Count on it." Nick touched his chest over the welded panel where his velvet heart beat. Before the Lion followed Tiger and Tip back into the tunnel, Nick stopped the great cat. "Stay close to her, my friend. If worse comes to worst..."

Lion gave one firm nod, though his eyes shone with worry. "I'll be there no matter what."

Nick watched them disappear down a gray, dank tunnel. The wall section closed behind them with a grind and a thud.

The Wogglebug clapped Nick's hollow back. Nickel-plated tin rang dully in the moldy crypt, and Nick shivered.

"Well!" said the bug. "Quite an adventure, hey my friend? I'm all a-quiver to find out what the Fair Ones are planning. Intrigue really gets the ichor pumping, doesn't it?"

Nick glared at him. "You do understand, if you're caught, they'll do horrible things to you. If you're very lucky, they'll kill you first."

The professor's cheery tone dropped. "I know, good Nicholas, I know. But the only way I can go through with this is to pretend it's all some grand lark, like in one of those terribly awful novels by Madam Plumly."

"I thought you liked those books."

"Yes, well. There's rather a stark difference between a bloody good tale and my good tail bloody, and I'm trying not to think about the latter." The Wogglebug wiped his fingers on a silken scarf, glaring at the clammy walls with obvious distaste. "Do let's go upstairs and partake of some courage like friend Lion does on occasion."

"Some other time." Nick couldn't get away from this gloomy basement fast enough.

The Wogglebug paused as he started up the stairs. "I am struck by a fabulous notion."

"What?"

"This invention of mine. An inconspicuous insect which can listen in on the most private conversations. It needs a name suitable for skulduggery." He tapped his chin thoughtfully. "I have it! I will call it—"

"Let's go," Nick prodded him. "If you make us stand here one moment longer I'm bound to rust."

They hurried up the stone steps. Even once back out in the sunlight, a chill lingered in Nick's empty guts. Secret plots, secret passages, strange inventions and a meeting in a freakish pub. He feared only Scarecrow's brains could hope to unravel this tangled web. At least he could take comfort in knowing his straw-stuffed friend was safe, enjoying a world far less dangerous, no matter how new and bewildering it might be.

13

"This can't be happening." Theo stared at the decomposing figure outside the window. "Zombies aren't real."

The thing smeared its cheek against the glass, back and forth, as if trying to press its face through the barrier. Bits of wet flesh came loose and clung to the window.

Scarecrow backed away from it. Of course he'd read tales of spooks, hauntings, restless spirits without bodies which floated endlessly through the dark sublevels of the crypt beneath the old temple in the Emerald City. A body without a spirit was another thing entirely. "You keep using that word," he pointed out sharply. "I don't think—"

"It does mean what you think it means," Theo said, eyes fixed on the hideous thing wiping its face against the glass.

"Well, I was going to say, I don't believe that word applies anymore."

She seemed too shocked to take her eyes off it.

"I was just sitting on a bench, thinking, when I heard a noise behind me. I turned around and it lurched at me," he explained. Disturbing though the sound was of the corpse's face against the window—*squueeer-rrrchh, squeeeeeccchh*, slowly back and forth—at least it didn't seem to be able to get inside. "I saw a grave a few steps away, where the earth was churned up. This hasn't happened before?"

Theo choked on a laugh, never taking her eyes off the thing making a mess all over her wide front window. "No. Not outside of a movie."

If a "movie" only referred to untruths, and unpleasant ones at that, he might be better off if she never fully explained it to him.

She looked at him finally, gulping. Her skin was paler than normal. "How the hell is it walking around in broad daylight? Didn't anyone notice? Unless this is the start of the undead apocalypse. Were there more of them?"

The corpse raised both hands and began slowly thumping on the glass. The window rattled.

Scarecrow peered across the road, unnerved by the way the thing's one eyeball rolled to follow his movement. It slapped a bony hand against the window and he jumped. The cemetery across the street was deserted, not a single sign of movement save for the wind in the trees. "No, just the one, I think." He forced himself to calmly take stock. "I think we're safe for the moment, since it doesn't appear intelligent enough to get in."

The next blow of the corpse's hands sent fractures crackling to the edges of the glass.

"Did you really have to say that?" Theo groaned.

Scarecrow backed away. This seemed to make the corpse angrier. It raised both hands again and smashed against the glass. Shards exploded over the nearest table and the wood floor. The thing gurgled wetly, reaching in.

"Fucking hell," Theo gasped. "A weapon. We need a weapon." She ran for the hallway.

Scarecrow found nothing more vicious in the near vicinity than a large pair of scissors. Better than nothing. Determinedly he shoved his fingers and thumb through the handle-loops. Perhaps putting out the thing's eye would render it helpless and more easily dispatched.

Theo hurried back in, brandishing a fireplace poker. "Goddess, this is insane," she breathed. She advanced with obvious reluctance, the iron poker held well in front of her.

Scarecrow moved closer to her, forming a unified, terrified front.

The corpse stretched its neck. A glop of something gray fell out of its collar onto the table by the window. Its bony fingers found the edge of a sturdy table and latched on. It began hauling itself over the windowsill.

"Oh fuck no," Theo shouted, "you're not coming in here, you dead bitch!" She thrust the poker at its shoulder. It pierced the thing's rotting jacket, sinking straight through.

The corpse grasped the poker and pulled. Theo was too startled to let go, stumbling and then planting her feet. The thing hauled itself inside the room farther, undeterred by the metal stick embedded in its body.

Scarecrow rushed forward, jabbing the scissors into its eye. The thing let go of the poker to wave wildly at its own face, gurgling louder. *"Skkkkkkaaaaagggh."* Its bony jaw tried to form words, tongue rotted. It grabbed Scarecrow's hand. With a yelp he staggered back, jerking his glove out of its grasp, feeling stitches ripping. The corpse's flailing hand located the scissors and yanked them out, bringing the eyeball with it. The scissors clattered to the floor, trailing goo. The blind corpse resumed dragging itself over the window ledge, one kneecap sticking out of its trousers as it brought a leg up to climb inside.

"Are you fucking kidding me?" Theo yelled. "Those were my good fabric scissors!"

"Can't you cast a spell?" he shouted back, retreating. "A protection bubble or a blast of wind? What kind of witch are you?"

"Not that kind!" she protested. Her back bumped a table, sending small jars of tiny gems and buttons rolling. One smashed on the floor.

The thing now had both knees over the ledge, pulling itself onto the nearest table.

"Scarecrow, I don't have any magic! Why don't you sing something? One of those not-so-nice songs you mentioned would be really great right about now!"

"I don't know any songs about making undead things dead again!" He looked around frantically for anything else to defend himself.

The corpse tumbled to the floor with a sickening squelch and crack. It made a scratchy, rasping sound, clawing slowly upright again though it was now missing its left arm at the elbow. *"Ssskkkkkaaaaagggrrrrrrruuu-uhh."*

There had to be something else they could throw at it, something to stop it. Maybe shove a table at it and trap it? He set both hands against the nearest table and pushed. His straw yielded, crumpling, and the table didn't budge an inch. Crows and blight, why did he have to be so useless? He snatched up the nearest thing on the table, one of Theo's unfinished dolls, about to hurl it at the monster.

He blinked. His brains were working today after all. "Theo, your poppets! Command them to attack!"

She stared at him. "What?"

"Your dolls! You made them, you put spells on them. Tell them to fight!"

"It doesn't work like that!"

"Well have you ever tried?"

"No!"

The corpse took a swipe at him but missed. "I think this would be a good time to try!" Scarecrow scrambled away, suddenly noticing he'd backed into a corner. Theo was near the door to the hallway so had an open escape route. The corpse ignored her, coming for him.

He feinted to the right, dodged left. The corpse mirrored him even though it had no eyes, blocking his escape. Its remaining hand reached for him again. Scarecrow ducked aside. Something grabbed his foot, tugging it sideways. Bracing one arm on the table behind him, he glanced down.

The missing forearm was crawling up his leg!

Crying out in terror, he slapped at it but couldn't dislodge its bony grip. Rationally he knew the worst it could do would be rip him apart, but such an overpowering sense of *wrongness* emanated from the decaying thing, his straw wanted to tumble out of his body and run for the hills.

"Theo, please! Tell them to fight!"

The corpse swayed forward, reaching for him blindly.

"Goddess bless and keep us, give me your power!" Theo shouted, raising her arms toward the ceiling.

The crawling arm curled its fingers over Scarecrow's belt. He grabbed it in both hands, struggling to pull it off. The corpse reached for him again. The smell of old meat left in an open midden pile on a hot day wafted over him.

"Just command them, they're your spell-poppets, for corn's sake!" he yelled, voice rising to a shriek as he saw larvae and beetles writhing and crawling in the corpse's clothing. Its fingers latched onto his tunic. He struggled, desperate to shake it loose. Bugs, disgusting bugs covered in its smelly decaying ooze were going to crawl inside him, dig into his straw and lay eggs, and he would feel them doing all of it. *"Theo!"* he screamed, unable to free himself from those clutching claws.

"Faeries, attack!" Theo cried, pointing at the corpse. "Kill that dead bitch! I command you, if there's any magic in you, kill the zombie!"

Nothing happened.

Scarecrow moaned, gloves gripped around the thing's reaching arm. A pillbug scurried onto his hand. He yelped, swatting it away.

The corpse leaned closer, insects swarming up out of its yawning, jawless mouth. *"Ssshhkaaaaawww,"* it rasped, pushing its face closer to his.

Suddenly the air around him exploded with buzzing wings. He shut his eyes, clamped his mouth shut, managed to pull away, lost his balance and fell sideways to the floor. *Not bugs, not in me, no!* His fingers scrabbled for purchase on the floor. His right arm rustled, a sense of loss sweeping up his shoulder. The corpse clutched his right glove in its own dead hand. It turned, reorienting on him. Scarecrow's boots found a table leg and shoved, shooting him across the wooden floor away from the monstrous thing.

Tiny figures in armor charged past him. Shocked, he froze, then relief burst throughout his chest. The dolls. The dolls were attacking!

Miniature knights with wolf-heads on steeds of painted clay galloped past his nose. A dull *thunk* at his chest drew his attention. One of the knights whacked with a sword at the decayed arm still clinging to his tunic, jostling a finger loose. Scarecrow grabbed the arm firmly in his one good hand and yanked it free, though it tugged straw out with it. Another knight thrust a spear through the armbones, pinning it to the floor. Scarecrow scrambled away as fast as he could, regaining his footing.

Knights and tiny dragons jabbed at the corpse's feet. Flying faelings swooped into its head, knocking it off balance. The thing swung Scarecrow's captured hand at them, but it was slow and clumsy.

"Oh dear Goddess," Theo muttered, staring at the battle from a safe distance near the door.

"It's still coming," Scarecrow gasped, joining her. He brushed his tunic off frantically to clear it of any bits of dead thing.

The dolls battered, stabbed, and pummeled the corpse. More of them hoisted themselves from the open box on the floor, ripping their coverings away. They charged into the fray. Unfortunately the festering thing was only mildly inconvenienced, landing a blow that sent a winged poppet spiraling hard into the wall. It turned and lumbered slowly toward Scarecrow again, stopped by a table in its way.

"They're alive," Theo said, eyes wide.

"No, they're your magic," he corrected. She had to understand this, had to accept it and direct the dolls, keep the spell going. "Theo, you created them. You gave them form and purpose. Tell them exactly what to do and how to do it!"

She stared at the tiny homunculi all battling the corpse. "I can do magic," she whispered.

He grasped her shoulder, willing her to focus. "Of course you can, you're a witch!"

Something sparked in her eyes, gleaming green a moment even in the dull light. Her shoulders drew up, her gaze hardened into a scowl, and she braced her legs in a fighting stance. "Hell yeah I am. Hey! You little knights, get in front of its feet! You flying guys, get behind its head and all of you hit it at once!"

The corpse bumped along the side of the table, seeking an opening. *"Brrrrrnnnng,"* it gurgled. *"Ssskkkkaaaaaghrrrrrruuuuhhh..."*

Theo shoved Scarecrow's shoulder, startling him. "Get a shovel," she ordered. "Should be one in the back yard. Through the kitchen, that way, go!" She called to the dolls, "On three! One, two, three!"

A swarm of flying poppets dove toward the corpse's head right as dozens of dolls hit its bony legs. Its knees buckled. With a hiss it flailed at the table, trying to right itself as it fell.

This could work.

Scarecrow ran in the direction Theo pointed, stumbling down the hallway and through a swinging wooden door. His soft boots slid on a tiled floor and he crashed into a counter, spilling straw. A sink and a rack overhead full of pots and pans confirmed this must be the kitchen, though it lacked a cooking hearth. Spying a door with a window inset, he lurched for it, turned the bolt and yanked it open. He tripped on the unexpectedly low stair and tumbled into the back garden.

Blasted locusts, he'd be lucky to have any straw left to heft a shovel once he found it at this rate. No time to gather up the puffs of it falling out of his sleeve or his tunic. It took another few frantic seconds for him to spot a rusty shovel standing against the back shed. He grabbed it and ran back inside, managing not to trip on the steps this time.

When he burst into the studio, Theo was standing on a table, shouting commands at her poppets. She was a fierce queen directing her troops in battle, eyes emerald-bright, sock-feet planted apart on the tabletop, heedless of her own crafts underfoot. Glowing threads waved wildly in the air, connecting her fingers and the dolls. For a moment all he could do was stare at her, astonished. Her glare was savage as the Nome King's, her skirt swirling around her exposed shins as she gestured at her tiny shock troops. "Stab the fucker! Yes! Don't let it get up!"

"Shovel." Scarecrow offered his prize to her. She grabbed it, still waving one hand at her dolls, threads of light streaming from her fingers to their frantic bodies.

The crazed corpse was a couple of feet away, trying to regain its footing. Marauding dolls buzzed around it, a bejeweled swarm of shining wings and swirling gauze.

Theo gripped the shaft of the shovel tightly in both hands. "Yaaaaah! Die, you smelly bitch!" she screamed, leaping off the table and slamming down the sharp edge of the shovel into the corpse's neck as she landed. A loud crack and ripping noise was followed by a tiny cheer.

Scarecrow leaned over the table. The dead thing's head rolled to a stop. Its arm flopped, its legs twitched. The dolls swarmed the head, stabbing it.

Theo wasn't done. She raised the shovel and jabbed it into the corpse's back again and again. "Die, you walking cesspit! This is my house and you do not," —crack!—"get"—runnnch—"to come inside!" Shhhrumpf. Snap.

The dolls withdrew to a respectful distance. Scarecrow's gloved hand was still clutched in the corpse's claw. As Theo pounded the shovel sharply into the body, breaking it into smaller and smaller pieces, the bits all shuddered at once and then lay still. The head deflated as if only some force of will had been keeping it intact. What was left of its tendons liquefied on the floor, dripping into the cracks between the wooden boards.

Whatever had animated the corpse, it was just a rotting body now. One too far gone to withstand the beating Theo continued to administer.

"How dare you," Theo snarled, smashing the sharp edge of the shovel down on the thing's legs and back. "How dare you attack my friend! How dare you set foot in my house! You nasty, vicious, stupid—"

"Theo?"

Theo kept smashing. "And look what you did to my studio, you slimy," —*chunk*—"smelly," —*runnch*—"idiot fucking maggot-muncher!" *Crack snap crrrrunnnnch.*

"I think it's dead," Scarecrow offered. "Again."

Panting, she slowed. She stared wildly at him, then poked one of the bits with the shovel. It made a wet noise as she turned it over, but didn't stir. "Oh goddamn it," she growled. "Look what it did to my floor." She tossed the shovel aside.

Cautiously he came around the end of the table, keeping a wary eye on the corpse. The bugs had all fled under the witch's savage onslaught. "Oh dear," he murmured, seeing the harsh marks and chips in the previously polished boards. Between the gouges and the fluids, the floor was ruined. He was about to say something to that effect, then noticed Theo was trembling. When his tentative fingers touched her shoulder, she flinched.

"Theo, are you injured?"

She shook her head, staring down at the rotting mess and shattered bones. Her blouse, skirt, and shins were spattered with gray ooze. Bits of it clung wetly to her bare hands. "I'm gonna be sick." She pushed past him, stumbling down the hall. He heard retching noises, followed by a flush of water.

As if in response to some silent agreement, the dolls trooped back to the open boxes. One by one they climbed or boosted each other into the boxes and rustled down into the delicate papers within. The winged poppets, disdaining to return to confinement after enjoying flight, perched on a collection of display stands, folded or tucked their wings, and went motionless.

Theo was still coughing somewhere. At the far end of the hallway, tucked under a staircase next to the swinging door to the kitchen, he discovered a water closet occupied by a fine porcelain commode, a pedestal sink, and Theo.

She leaned on the sink, scrubbing her hands and arms with a lump of soap, water running from a tap. When at last no trace of goo remained and her skin was rubbed red, she dropped to her knees on the floor, pale and shivering. She'd stripped off her outer clothing, spattered with bits of dead thing, all piled in the corner of the water closet.

Unsure whether she wanted privacy or sympathy, he waited a few steps away. "Are you all right, my friend?" he asked softly.

Her shoulders barely lifted in a shrug.

Scarecrow fell into a cross-legged seat on the hallway carpet. He spoke quietly. "Thank you for fighting that thing. You're far braver than I."

She shook her head, eyes closing, leaning back against the door-frame. She panted harshly, displaying a fair amount of cleavage barely contained by the brassiere she wore. Her shoulders trembled with every breath. She was all round curves and pink softness and he could practically see the wild energy simmering just under her skin. A powerful witch for sure. Realizing he was staring at her exposed flesh, he averted his gaze.

"What the hell, Scarecrow." Her voice was full of fear. "What the fucking hell just happened in my house?"

"Well, you just used your magic to fend off an attacking bug-infested corpse and hacked it to death. Second death, I suppose."

She stared at the floor.

"Also, you're going to need a carpenter, I'm afraid."

"What the hell, Scarecrow," she repeated, her head jerking up to glare at him. "I hacked a walking dead thing to pieces in my own craft room!"

He nodded.

"And my dolls, which have never shown the least sign of life before, suddenly all turned into soldiers just because I asked them to?"

"Well, that is how witchcraft works, I believe. You made them and enchanted them, so—"

"You don't get it," she interrupted. "I could never do real magic before. Not before you showed up." Her tone was angry, but fright shone clear in her eyes.

"Theo," he said softly, "I can't explain any of this. I have no idea why a corpse would invade your home, or why you never were able before to bring your magic poppets to life, but I'm very glad you did. That thing might've—well, perhaps not killed me, but it was full of crawling pests, and I'm relieved they didn't crawl into me." He gestured at himself, forgetting his right hand was still back in the studio in a dead thing's bony fingers. He shuddered.

Theo stared at the straw jutting out of his wrist, then at his chest. He looked down. Oh. Well. There actually was quite a lot of him missing. The tunic gaped open, and as he watched, another loose clump of straw tumbled out. What a mess. At least he didn't see or feel any bugs. He sighed, but upon turning back to Theo saw absolute horror in her eyes.

"Oh. No, Theo, I'm all right. Well, I mean, I will be," he assured her.

She gagged, whipping her head back to the commode. She clutched the sides and heaved.

Oh dear. Embarrassed, he tried to scoop the loose straw back inside his tunic. Something heavy and wet peeled off his hat and fell with it to the carpet. He stared at the glop of decaying flesh. A small, white squirming thing slowly pushed its way out of the slime.

Scarecrow shuddered, kicking the hat away from him. Good thing he didn't have a stomach. If he had, it contents would be joining hers in that porcelain bowl. If the glop actually touched any of his exposed straw...

"That was too close," he gulped. "Much, much too close. Theo, is there any on me? Did it get into me anywhere? Oh no. Please, help me."

He scrambled closer to her, shaking. Theo immediately examined his chest, his exposed straw, his face. He turned around so she could check his back. She stretched out his arms to examine every inch, poked tentatively inside his torn wrist, checked his legs. He felt her light touch on his head, tracing the seam protecting his brains from the harsh and sometimes truly repulsive outside world.

Finally she relaxed, hugging him from behind. "You're good. No more nasty slime anywhere."

"Oh thank the sweet sunlight," he sighed. "Thank you. That was horrible." He turned around.

Her pale pink skin was free of any trace of dead thing, although he spotted a bit in her hair. Ugh. He tugged his handkerchief out and used it to carefully snag the little globule, flicking it toward his hat.

"Do I have any more on me?" she whispered.

She eased out of her crouch so he could view her belly, her bare thighs, her delicate toes. A blush crept over her skin from her chest up to her cheeks. Meat people usually didn't like revealing so much of themselves. Such smooth skin, with freckles in the hollow of her thighs right next to—

He felt heated, turning away quickly. How had she received sun-kisses there?

"You're fine." He felt a bit exposed himself. "I don't see any more of it."

"I am going to shower for days," she groaned. Suddenly she threw her arms around his shoulders. "Thank you for helping me fight that thing."

"I didn't do anything," he protested. Truly, he'd been next to useless. Any idiot could fetch a gardening tool. If only he possessed claws like Lion or an axe like Nick, he could've stopped the thing before it reached Theo's house, and they wouldn't be sitting on the floor bemoaning the mess.

He'd led it right to her home! Might as well have laid out a welcome mat for the blasted thing.

Theo's arms tightened around him. He felt her shivering against his back. "If you hadn't insisted I order the dolls to fight—dear Goddess, that thing would've killed us both." Her breath warmed his ear.

He'd been almost useless. She'd been magnificent. "I—you're a witch. Of course you have the power to control your dolls."

"No. This is because of you. I think you brought Oz's magic with you." She laid her head on his shoulder. "Thank you, Scarecrow."

Awkwardly, he patted her bare arm with his left hand. She was warm and trembling. Suddenly he was both acutely aware of the shape of her body pressed against him, and of the implication that if he'd actually brought magic to her world with him, he might be responsible for the darker things too.

He stayed silent and very still, his glove on her arm, her head on his shoulder. Scarecrow listened to Theo's breath, felt her heart beating against him. He felt warm but vulnerable, and increasingly as though all sunlight was slipping away into shadows.

14

ven after scrubbing until her skin hurt in the shower, Theo felt contaminated. She avoided thinking about what had just happened, focused on all that needed to be done. Her house was tainted. Her safety
violated.

Though she wasn't sure how she could explain any of this, she texted
her friend Gwyn, who agreed to come over and to bring some friends.
Theo avoided answering her questions about what had happened, saying
only someone had broken in and she was safe for now, but could use
some help.

She used rubber gloves to bag up her discarded clothing and poor
Scarecrow's beslimed hat, tossing it all into the trash. He'd lost a ton of
straw at the back stoop, and the wind scattered it across her yard and into
the Reeves' next door. One more thing for her bitchy neighbor to complain about. Theo gathered up as much of the straw as she could. He'd
need it back.

Scarecrow had volunteered to keep watch for any more hideous dead
things while she cleaned up. She found him in the studio, peering out
the broken window, the shovel in his left hand. He nodded at her as she
dumped his recovered straw on the table.

"All quiet so far. If you have a glove I may borrow, could you
please...?" He held up his right wrist, straw sticking out of the open
sleeve.

Still hard to believe that didn't hurt. She eyed the glove on the floor,
stained and glistening with slime. Ugh. "Guessing that's trash."

He grimaced. "I'm not touching it, and I wouldn't recommend you
do either."

"Not sure any of my gloves would fit you."

He laughed. "Theo, I don't have hands like a meat person. They'll be
whatever size the gloves are. I'd just like to be able to use them both."

"So I just need to stuff a glove with your straw and, what, jam it back
on your wrist?"

"I prefer to sew them to the sleeves. Less chance of them being ripped off accidentally. You wouldn't believe how often that happens. Jellia started using strong twine."

Theo nodded, gazing at the mess on what used to be her lovely studio floor. Gouges, slime, broken glass, and the decrepit remains marred the old boards.

Scarecrow's eyes followed hers. "Once you've sewn a new hand on for me, I'll help clean all this up. I would've started already, except I worried something might sneak up if my attention were elsewhere."

"No," Theo said. "We need backup. We need help boarding the windows, at least. First let's get you fixed up, though."

"You could set your dolls to stand guard," he suggested.

Could she? All her tiny fae dolls animating to defend them must have been a fluke. Had to be. She'd talked to the dolls before, when creating them or posing them. Never the slightest sign they *heard* or *thought*.

In those few minutes when the zombie cornered Scarecrow, Theo was furious and charged with bright fire. Commanding her dolls felt right, felt amazing. Had she really seen golden threads running from her fingertips to the dolls? A delicate web of magic connecting them all. She squinted but saw no shimmering threads in the air now. No connection at all to the lifeless bits of wire and clay. Whatever force had coursed through her, she felt only numbness now.

Two of the dolls lay crushed and twisted on the floor, spattered in gray slime. Theo shivered. Not bringing those to life again if she had anything to say about it. Zombie faeries.

She blew out a breath, swiping her hair out of her face. "I have no goddamn idea how I even did that."

He blinked. "Theo. You're a witch." As if this were obvious and he was being extremely patient in telling her again.

"I've been practicing magic for years and I've never been able to animate dolls before! No. This has to be because you're here."

He shook his head, frowning. "Theo, your ability is your own. I didn't give you the skill to command your poppets because I *can't*. Maybe my arrival here awoke something sleeping inside you. Your natural gift for magic."

She'd prayed for a spark in every doll she'd carefully molded and stitched, glued and crafted. For a bit of the Goddess' spirit to reside in them and bring happiness to their future owners. The host of winged faeries perched now on display stands, their wire legs bent as if she'd posed them sitting on the bars, motionless. Lifeless. Soulless.

The man standing in front of her had a hand missing, but he was clearly alive. With straw still poking from his open tunic. *Focus, girl. Worry about magic stuff later.* She found a pair of tan suede gloves, thread, buttons, and a pair of sewing scissors not coated in goop. She held up the gloves. "Will these work?"

He nodded. "Perfect. Thank you, Theo."

"Don't thank me. If I'd been faster, your hand wouldn't have been torn off."

"If I'd been able to keep it from coming into your home in the first place..." He sighed, shaking his head.

"Not your fault."

"Maybe it is," he mused, staring out at the graveyard. "If you never saw pixies or used your magic before you met me, maybe I am affecting your world. Glinda didn't mention any side effects of me coming here, only that I have a limited amount of time to find—" He stopped abruptly, blinked, and became very still.

Oh, Goddess. Dorothy. Theo had damned near forgotten the shock which sent him over to the cemetery to do some deep thinking. "Scarecrow, I'm so sorry about Dorothy."

"You don't have to apologize for things you didn't cause, Theo." He straightened his shoulders, smiling faintly. "We should focus on what needs doing right now. Let's fortify your house and get this mess cleaned up."

She curbed her impulse to go hug him. Right after the attack, she'd been so overwhelmed, she'd simply wrapped her arms around him, relieved. Relieved she had someone to turn to after such a hideous experience. He'd been a perfect gentleman despite her sitting there in only her bra and undies. His touch was soft, his straw crinkling gently when she embraced him.

It didn't mean he wanted or welcomed her impulsive hugs. *For crying out loud, I can't keep treating him like one of my dolls. He's a living person and he just found out the woman he loves died ages ago. Ease up, girl.*

While she stuffed both gloves, Scarecrow tucked handfuls of straw back into his tunic. Clearly, he'd done this before.

What did that feel like? Did he become aware of the straw only when it was inside his clothing, or did he sense it no matter where it was outside of him, once it had been part of him?

"Let me sew these on for you. Um. Do I need to say a spell or anything?"

"I don't think so." He raised one eyebrow. "Two? The left hand didn't get torn."

"You should have matching gloves. Hands," Theo corrected herself, holding out the right one.

He laid his right arm along the table. Theo lined up the right glove with his open sleeve and tried to tuck all the loose straw into it, wedging it against his wrist. She jumped when the fingers wiggled.

"That's you doing that, right?"

"Yes. That's me." He shivered. "I can see why you'd ask, though. Nasty crawling arm."

Deftly she stitched the glove over the open sleeve, tucking strands of straw in as she went. "This feel okay?"

He flexed the fingers and thumb one by one. "Perfect. Thank you."

"Give me the other one."

Theo carefully clipped the rough thread holding the existing glove on and swapped it for the new one, sewing swiftly but carefully. "How's that?"

He wiggled the fingers and closed them briefly into a fist. "Good. Thank you, Theo." He nodded as she sewed a replacement button tightly to his tunic. "Much better." He plumped and patted his midsection, rearranging the stuffing. He was a bunch of straw in clothing. Losing his hand didn't hurt him, and she could fix it simply by sewing on a new glove. Yet he clearly had his own mind, unlike her dolls.

"What brought you to life?" she asked. "Was it witchcraft?"

He shook his head. "I really don't know. I've never been able to find out."

"One of the Oz authors wrote that you were the reincarnation of some psuedo-Chinese emperor who got his soul stuck in you through a beanpole. Even past the obvious racism in that particular book, I've always felt that origin story was bullshit. You were awake before you were hung on the pole in the cornfield."

His brow wrinkled. "I understood some of that. I don't know anything about a beanpole or an emperor. And yes, as soon as the farmer began painting my face, I could hear and see, before he put my body together."

"What's your earliest memory? Did you think anything before then?"

Scarecrow frowned. "What's this all about?"

Heat spread across her cheeks. She took a deep breath. "Do you have a soul?"

"I don't know," he said quietly. "I think. I feel. Nick says I experience some things as meat people do, and some not at all the same way." He shrugged, eyes downcast. "As far as I know, I'm the only living scarecrow. Not even Locasta's experiments on me could determine how I came to be. I'm sorry, Theo. I don't know how to answer you."

How rude, asking him all this stuff, after he'd expressed his frustration at being just a scarecrow. Called himself a fool when obviously that wasn't the case. Thoughtless of her, reminding him of whatever torture a witch put him through.

He resumed patting and plumping the straw, evening out his chest stuffing. He seemed skinnier than when they'd first met, with some of his straw scattered to the wind from her backyard.

She'd need to get more straw from somewhere. Maybe Cassie could spare a bale.

When Theo last saw her lovely greenwitch friend, Cassandra was embroiled in a lawsuit with her bigoted neighbors, who objected to her Farming While Black, and their shady bus-bench lawyer. Theo sighed. Cassie was dealing with her own problems right now. Theo shouldn't dump this on her friend.

Not on any friends, really, but she'd feel safer as soon as the front window was boarded over. "I have no idea how the hell to explain this crap to anyone," she muttered, surveying the goop on the floor again.

"I take it no one would believe a corpse attacked us."

"Maybe we could say someone threw it through the window. Some kind of sick, awful prank." She snorted. "I could blame it on my creepy ex."

"That would be a lie," he argued, "and possibly get someone in trouble, wouldn't it?"

Theo stared at him. His dark blue eyes gazed steadily back at her without judgement, but clearly waiting for her to agree.

Great. A walking conscience. Just what she needed when everything was turning batshit crazy.

"Fine, Jiminy Cricket, no blaming this on my ex."

He opened his mouth, raising a finger.

"Don't. Don't even say it," Theo sighed. "I don't guess you know any songs for fixing broken glass?"

He frowned. A pin popped up through the top of his head, in between the long strands of straw sticking from the seams. A hat, she should get him a new hat. With Halloween nearly here, any costume shop ought to have a suitable peaked felt hat to replace the beslimed one.

"None that I can think of," he replied. "You don't have a spell for that?"

"What?" She snorted. "Uh, no. I'm not that kind of witch."

"Perhaps not, but," he hesitated, "you obviously have some fae in you."

"What?"

"You clearly have some fae blood. I can see it in your eyes. You did say they used to be here in your world. And, well, they're not the most chaste of creatures."

After a second she caught his meaning. "You're saying centuries ago, some faery fucked one of my ancestors?"

He winced. "There are certain bloodlines in Oz. Ozma Tip, for instance. Royal blood can only be from the Fair Folk. That's the only reason the Pastorian line held the throne for as many generations as they have. Blood alliances. Magic passed down through the lineage."

"What exactly about my eyes makes you think I'm fae?"

"Well, they shift color. And all witches are Fair Ones. Though not all fae practice witchcraft. Plenty of them seem content to spend their time drinking, dancing, and indulging in carnal pleasures when they're not scheming against each other." He wouldn't meet her stare.

Seriously? Did he just compare her to a magical nympho? She folded her arms under her breasts. She'd grabbed an old Hexxennacht tee and plain heather-gray sweats from her closet after showering, comfort over style, but now the sinister deer skull on the shirt felt appropriate. She boosted her boobs up with her arms so the ominous logo was facing Scarecrow more prominently. "You do realize you just insulted me."

His eyes widened. "What? Oh no. Dear me no. That wasn't what I meant at all."

"So in Oz, faeries are backstabbing party bitches, and all witches are fae, and I must be one of them because I have hazel eyes and did something with my dolls I can't even understand now?" she demanded.

He took a step away from her. "I'm sorry, Theo. I didn't mean to offend you at all."

Well, he'd been tortured by a witch, and she still didn't know the details. And it wasn't as though he'd accused her directly of being slutty, not like her ex-boyfriend Mark. She stilled her temper, brushed her fingers through her mop of hair. "I'm not some loose party girl. And I never saw a spell work right away 'til today. I have no idea how I did any of that. I'm not magical. I'm not fae. This has to be because you're here."

"If you say so," he murmured.

Deep breath. Her nerves were still on edge. Would be until that gaping open window was covered so nothing else could climb in.

"Like you said, let's get this place straightened up and fortified. And then we can figure out what to do about..." How was she supposed to help him get back to Oz? Though if real magic were anything like in old legends, every spell had a counterspell. A remedy. "We'll get you home. Somehow."

He nodded slowly. "Thank you, Theo. I seem to keep making mistakes. Not thinking very clearly, I suppose. Perhaps coming into your world has affected my brains." His shoulders slumped, eyes downcast.

Goddess bless, now it was really difficult not to hug him. She shouldn't've gone off on him. As weird as all this was, it must be doubly weird for him and heartbreaking to boot.

Screw it.

She embraced him, feeling him startle, straw rustling all over. "You have nothing to apologize for. I'm the one being bitchy. I get bitchy when I'm scared. Sorry, Scarecrow."

"I—it's all right," he murmured in her ear. Gently, his arms went around her.

He smelled of open fields and sunlight, of warmth stored in golden sheaves. His body crackled and crinkled as she held him. He carefully patted her shoulders with the hands she'd given him. A little thread and stuffing was all it took to repair his wounds.

If only she could fix his heart as easily.

15

Chimes at the front door alarmed Scarecrow. Theo startled as well, then blew out a breathy laugh.

"No worries, that's probably Gwyn. I asked her to round up some friends, to help patch up the house."

Resourceful. Scarecrow nodded approval, trailing after her to the door.

Theo paused before she opened it. "Oh, hey, um. Just so you know. My friends are all witches. Good ones. Not scary, okay?" She flashed a smile at him and yanked the door open before he could react. "Hey, thanks for coming!"

"Holy shit, Theo, you got some weird energies going on in here," exclaimed a broad-framed woman with long silvery-blue hair. Her stare fell on Scarecrow. "Aha! This must be for you." She handed him a hat of patched felt, with bits of straw glued under the brim.

The hat lacked the bits of ribbon his very first one had sported, and it was black rather than blue. However, the patches immediately reminded him of his original sad, cast-off clothing. The outfit he'd worn, hanging from that lonely cornfield pole, when a young woman in a blue and white dress found and rescued him.

A gift from a witch? Should he accept this at all?

Theo touched his arm. "Is this okay?"

He forced a smile. "Of course. It'll do nicely. Thank you," he said to the older woman.

"Oh, Scarecrow, this is Gwyn. She kinda mentored me. Gwyn, this is a new friend. He just goes by Scarecrow," Theo said.

Gwyn smiled at him, her sharp blue eyes behind delicate spectacles raking him from crown to foot. Now this woman surely was a witch. Her hair spilled almost to her generous hips. She wore a multicolored woven shawl over a loose, red flowing dress, belted at the waist with several scarves knotted together. Various pouches hung from the belt.

"Wow, you really look the part," Gwyn said to Scarecrow, echoing his thoughts about her. "So is the costume for a convention, or Halloween, or what?"

Scarecrow raised an eyebrow. "I always dress like this."

Gwyn laughed, a full, warm sound right from her belly. "Love it. Nice to meet you."

"A pleasure," he replied, sketching a nervous bow. If all Theo's friends were witches, he couldn't rule out any of them also having the blood of the Fair Folk. Best not to offend any of them. He settled the hat on his head.

Gwyn raised an eyebrow at him, but turned to Theo. "Show me the damage. Some asshole broke in? You see who it was?" Encountering the mess in the studio, she stopped and stared. "What the actual hell."

"Yeah, um, someone threw a Halloween prop through the window. Scared the crap outta me," Theo said. She cast a pleading look at Scarecrow.

He frowned, but kept his mouth shut. If this woman was a witch, why wouldn't she understand dark magic was at work here? Theo's insistence that she wasn't the same sort of witch as he was used to in Oz came to mind. Perhaps this Lady Gwyn also didn't realize she could cast spells.

Witches who didn't know rudimentary magic. What a strange world this was.

Theo spent the next half-hour darting between the studio and the front door as more people arrived. Young men with strong arms brought in a large wooden panel to cover the broken window. They set up a saw in the back garden which cut through boards faster than even Nick Chopper could've managed. A chest appeared on the kitchen floor, filled with ice and bottles. Commotion arose throughout the house.

Theo embraced every person who entered, even a couple of people whom she didn't previously know. Over and over she repeated a story: they'd been working in the studio when what appeared to be a dead body crashed through the front window and attacked.

One of the men, Arturo, braved the stench and goo long enough to poke at the remains, muttering about "radio-control wires or a transmitter," finding nothing. He stroked his black mustache and goatee and *hm-mmed* a lot, reminding Scarecrow of Professor H.M. Wogglebug, T.E.

Arturo straightened up finally. "How exactly did it 'attack'?"

"It—I don't know, it lurched around and grabbed Scarecrow," Theo said.

All eyes in the room turned to him.

Lying was not Scarecrow's habit. "It seemed very animated."

"Very," Theo agreed.

"So you beat it to death with a shovel." Arturo sounded dubious.

The man who'd arrived with him, Adam, huffed and gestured at Theo. "Can't you see it was real enough to freak her out?" Adam demanded.

"Well, yeah, a well-made fake corpse smashing through your window is enough to scare anyone. I just don't see how anyone could've made it seem like it was attacking, though, unless they were right in the room. You're positive no one else was here?" Arturo asked, looking from Theo to Scarecrow.

"I didn't see anyone else," Scarecrow said.

Theo shook her head, arms clasped around herself.

"That's a really sick joke," said a younger woman, Juniper. "Who would do this?"

"Oh, I can think of someone," growled Gwyn. "I bet I know just the psychotic creep who did this, and I may have to pay him a visit on Halloween."

Theo rubbed her nose. "I didn't actually see anyone, Gwyn. I don't know who it was."

Arturo prodded the corpse's head with his boot. It squelched. He grimaced. "Looks like they made the claws sharp enough to hook onto stuff easily. I see it nabbed one of your craft projects." Scarecrow's old right hand was still snagged in the bony arm on the floor.

Scarecrow thought of crawling insects, and shuddered. He smoothed down his tunic and trouser legs, unable to dismiss the notion something might have invaded his clothing.

"Well, whoever it was, this will come back on them threefold," Gwyn stated. She pointed at the broken window. "Arturo, Adam, Vince. You guys clear out the glass, please, and nail up the panel. It'll do until Theo can get the window replaced. Juniper, if you and Sue can mop up this mess, the rest of us will clear space. We're gonna need to clean and reconsecrate this room. A house blessing sounds like a good idea as well. Too much negative energy in here." She turned to Theo. "Where's your mop bucket and cleaning stuff, sweetie?"

More than once, Scarecrow found himself accepting orders from the older witch, who clearly was accustomed to her commands being obeyed. As they were all orders which helped Theo, however, he didn't mind. Quietly he swept up broken glass, held long boards in place so they could be nailed over the remaining windows in the studio. When the room was clean and smelled of lemons instead of rotten flesh, the party spread throughout the house. What began as a mission to clean and fortify Theo's home now felt like a boisterous celebration. He'd never been comfortable at parties, especially when he didn't know the guests.

A party full of loud Outside World witches was a bit more than he felt able to handle. Too reminiscent of one of Glinda's Emerald Palace balls. At every one of those, it was clear the suggestion for Scarecrow to be stuffed into his finest court clothing and be present all night to amuse the guests was really more of a command. Having to remain still while some minor lady of the Seelie Court opened his tunic to pet the packed straw, giggling, or a couple of drunken dukes used him for sword practice, ruining yet another fine jacket by running it through with rapiers, was all humiliating. Glinda watching with a smile on her heavily made-up baby-doll face only made it worse.

There were far more horrible things they could've done to him. He'd held his tongue and held still.

Nobody commanded him to stand around and be an object of curiosity here. Yet at every turn, someone asked him about his costume, or where his show was performing, or how he'd met Theo. He murmured vague replies, retreated to a different room, tried to stay out of the way. Which is how he ended up in the closeted pantry just off the kitchen.

He took in a slow breath, the scents of oats, apples, and the dark beans Theo called coffee filling his nose. It was a comforting smell, even if the last item was unfamiliar. He could feel the loose straw rustling in his chest. No idea where to procure more fresh stuffing. At least the pantry was dark and quiet. He left the door open a crack and tried to calm himself. Alone, silent, the terror from earlier banished, his mind went places he had no wish to explore.

Dorothy was dead. A century dead, after terrible imprisonment. From all he could gather, her stories of adventures in Oz spread far and wide in this world, and yet no one believed they were true. She'd been locked away simply for insisting she'd met faeries and a talking scarecrow.

He closed his eyes, pressing his thumbs against his temples. His brains shifted a bit. If only he knew some magic to rescue her now, to prevent her tragic end, whether or not she wanted him still. There must to be some way to get to her. A song, perhaps, if only he could divine which one.

In the cemetery, before the corpse lunged at him, he'd run through every old Ozian song he could recall, but not a single one seemed relevant to this terrible situation. No songs about time. A few about returning to a longed-for home, but as he'd never been to Kansas, they probably wouldn't transport him to Dorothy.

His brave, irrepressible, amazing Dorothy. Who'd died trapped in a cold, harsh prison far from family and friends. What must've gone through her mind, night after dark night in such a terrible place?

Did she think of him? Call out to him, or their friends, in her torment?

And Ozma Tip. She was Scarecrow's responsibility as well. His friend, who when she was a boy, bravely went with Scarecrow to try and regain the throne of Oz for him. They hadn't known then that Tip was actually the lost Ozma. Scarecrow never craved the power of the Empire, only wanting to improve life for all the commoners who'd suffered under the Wizard's negligent rule. All those whom the deaths of the witches of east and west had freed. Ozma's ascension to the crown surprised everyone, but Scarecrow knew her. Knew she'd be fair and just. Being asked to live in the palace as an advisor to the Queen was more of a duty than an honor, but he'd accepted. Used his brains in service to Tip because she genuinely wanted people to be free and well. Even though a royal life meant enduring the numerous balls he dreaded, feasts at which he couldn't eat, boring ceremonies meant to instill respect in visiting dignitaries.

All the court nonsense made him withdraw into memories of a bright, brave young woman with braided dark hair, her smile warm as the sunlight. How his clumsiness along the road of yellow brick made her laugh, how pleased she was when he foraged for anything she could eat along the way. How it felt to embrace her. She'd saved him from an existence of utter boredom in the cornfield, again when he was nearly lost in a fast-running river they needed to cross, again when the flying monkeys ripped him apart and left him to die atop a great dead tree. Yet again when he'd suffered transformation into a gold ornament in the Nome King's hideous salons. If not for her persistence, he'd never have received his magic brains, either.

Dorothy had rescued him so many times.

Right now he felt as stupid and helpless as if he were stuck on a pole again. Dorothy was dead. He was lost, far from home. And the one friend he'd made here now needed to guard against dark magic which he must've brought with him. He slumped against the pantry shelves, pinching the bridge of his nose, and massaged his temples as he'd seen meat people do. No bright ideas sparked in his head.

He brought out the Evstone. He should try singing the Stone Song, try to recharge the stone's magic, contact Nick. At the very least, Ozma Tip deserved a report.

How could he break the terrible news to Nick? He'd failed to find Dorothy. Failed to save her. He stood there holding the Evstone, unable to work up the courage to try a song.

"Lemme help you set the table," a voice said loudly, startling Scarecrow. He peeked out the crack of the door. The older witch, Gwyn, followed Theo into the kitchen.

Theo opened a cupboard and took down an armload of plates. "Thanks. And thanks for picking up the hat, too. Oh, what do I owe you?"

Gwyn chuckled, taking silverware from a kitchen drawer. "Nothing, sweetie. So. Your friend seems very polite."

"He is."

"Ya know, I can't help but think of the last guy who came off all well-mannered around us but was a dick to you in private."

Theo scowled. "He's nothing like Mark."

"I sure hope not. The night you kicked him out—I still wish you'd let me take you to the hospital for a rape kit. I hope our cutting-off spell gave him hives. And if he's not responsible for this latest nasty prank, I'll eat my scarves."

Theo suffered that kind of attack? Heat rose in Scarecrow's chest. He hadn't known such a terrible act existed, until stories started coming out of Quadling country during the war. Stories of the Winkie Guard terrorizing housewives and maidens, and then a surge of babies born in villages bereft of their menfolk. After Scarecrow read what exactly congress between a man and woman consisted of, he'd been doubly horrified by the crime.

Gwyn put a hand on Theo's shoulder. "Sweetie, seriously, although you're not at all responsible for Mark being an asshole, you don't have the best judgement where it comes to men. Remember Alex? All the drunken phone calls?"

"Scarecrow doesn't drink," said Theo.

Couldn't. Even when sometimes a scent intrigued him.

"Didn't Mark always dress up as his Masquerading Vampire character or whatever? Just absolutely obsessed with playing a role?"

Theo shook her head. "Gwyn, I get it. It's not the same at all, so stop worrying."

"There was some really bad juju in your studio, Theo. I felt it even before I stepped inside. He seems nice, but I gotta ask: are you absolutely positive your new boyfriend didn't set you up for the dead body thing? Because if it wasn't Mark, this was someone with a very twisted sense of humor."

"No, Scarecrow's not like that!"

"Whoever threw that through your window went to a lot of trouble to terrify you. I don't blame you for freaking out."

"Scarecrow had nothing to do with it. And he's not my boyfriend. We just met like a day ago."

Gwyn's eyebrows arched. "Oh, honey, you just met him and already invited him home? What do you know about him?"

Scarecrow remained absolutely still and silent in the pantry. This was decidedly awkward.

"He's a good guy. I promise. He defended me when that thing came through the window." Theo's face was bright pink. "We both thought it was real for a minute."

"Yeah, I didn't think you'd whack the hell outta your floor with a shovel if you weren't terrified. But back to my point. Mark would enjoy this shit, and he was all courtly and sweet to my face. All those goddamn red roses he gave you."

"Are we talking about Mark?" asked Arturo, strolling into the kitchen.

Scarecrow groaned inwardly. If the whole party moved into the kitchen he'd be trapped in the pantry all night.

"That guy was an asshole. If he did this, you should sue him for the cost of replacing the floor and the window."

Theo sighed again. "I can't prove anything. I just want to feel safe in my own home again."

Gwyn enveloped Theo in a bear hug. "You will. After dinner we'll do a circle, and bless the whole house. Clear out all the negative vibes."

Theo returned the hug. "Thanks, Gwyn. I really appreciate all you guys coming over to help."

Arturo adjusted his thick spectacles. "So, your new beau. Does he stuff actual hay in the costume? Isn't that itchy? 'Cause if it's real hay, Adam is allergic, so it'd be nice to know."

Straw, not hay. Hay bunched up in bulky clumps. Very uncomfortable. Only the finest oat-straw filled Scarecrow's clothing ever since he'd moved into the Palace as Tip's advisor.

"Yes, it is real, and we already swept and mopped and vacuumed everything. If there's any left laying around, please tell Adam to steer clear. Also, Scarecrow is just a friend," Theo repeated.

"What does he practice? Faery magic?" Arturo persisted. "I haven't heard before of anyone basing their worship on the Wizard of Oz, but—"

The door chime sounded. Theo pushed Arturo out of the kitchen. "He's not actually a witch. Food's here. Move."

"I hope you're right about this one, sweetie," Gwyn said. She left the room as well.

Theo stood alone, her brows knit, mouth set in an angry line.

Scarecrow was certain he'd made no sound, but suddenly Theo looked right at the pantry, walked over and opened the door. He jerked his eyes to the floor. "Oh. Um. I didn't mean to—I came in here to think. It was quiet."

"Oh Goddess. You heard all that, didn't you."

"I take it your former partner was not a good person."

"Understatement of the year. Arturo had it right. Mark was an ass-hole. Probably still is." Theo put a hand over her face. "Can we just pretend this never happened?"

"I truly didn't mean to eavesdrop."

"I know. I know you didn't." Theo gestured toward the door to the hallway. "Do me a favor. Go pretend you were just now coming out of the bathroom, and let's all have dinner."

He nodded, relieved she wasn't angry with him. Wait. Dinner? "I can't eat. Will this be an issue for your friends?"

"Can you pretend to eat?"

"How? I don't want to dirty my tongue. It's practically brand new."

Theo stared at him. After a moment she broke into giggles.

He smiled hesitantly, not sure what was funny. "How should I pretend?"

"You know what, never mind. You be you. We can tell everyone you have a special diet or something." She took his hand and gently tugged him out of the pantry. "Go sit. I have to pay the delivery guy. Be there in a minute."

"Very well," he said, bemused. He waited after she left the kitchen, thinking.

Theo's last lover mistreated her. No wonder her friends looked askance at him, pestered him with questions, if they were worried about her. Though why everyone seemed to assume he was her new love baffled him. He'd keep quiet during the meal and observe everyone else.

As usual.

He sighed.

He walked into the dining room and claimed the only empty seat, right next to Theo. The happy chatter around the table ceased only long enough for Gwyn to ask their goddess for a blessing on the meal. Scarecrow lowered his head and followed their custom of holding hands a moment. A plate laden with food was thumped in front of him.

"Oh, thank you, but no." He offered the food to the person to his right, Vince, who'd lugged wood inside after cutting it to the correct size to barricade the windows. Seemed a cheerful enough fellow.

Vince asked, "You sure?"

"Yes. Please go ahead, don't worry about me."

Gwyn stared at him. Everyone else was passing food around the table, sauces, a pitcher of water and bottles of beer.

Scarecrow didn't know how to deflect the witch's suspicions. "I don't eat—"

"Much," Theo finished, flashing a smile at Gwyn. "He barely eats anything. Hey, anyone want some wine? I think I have a couple bottles of red."

Theo's friends, apart from Gwyn, didn't seem witchy at all. They teased each other about construction skills or lack thereof, or tried to make light of the disgusting ooze they'd cleaned from the studio, hallway, and powder room floors. Not sniping and insulting each other. Nobody threw a lightning bolt at anyone else. Their easy conviviality reminded him more of dinners at Ozma's table than of any gathering of witches.

He'd been forced to attend a dinner at the Seelie Court at last year's formal Winter's Eve party. Glinda insisted he come along, promising he wouldn't be injured. He'd ended up stretched at length along the great dining hall table, with pumpkins, gourds, and fall flowers surrounding him, several trays of food balanced atop his body or held up in his hands. As he never physically tired, this didn't strain him for hours on end, but the experience was mortifying. Two young duchesses found it enormously funny to force him to "drink" dandelion wine. The bitter liquid soaked his head, the fumes dizzying him. Jellia Jamb had needed to wash his poor brains and launder the sack of his head.

"Wine?" asked Juniper, holding a glass out to Scarecrow.

"No thank you," he said. "Never had a taste for it."

"Thank you, all of you," Theo said. "I really appreciate everyone running over to help."

"Hey, Adam said free beer, so that sealed it for me," Vince laughed.

Arturo nodded. "You know we're always available if you need us, Theo." He cast a mild glance at Scarecrow.

For fields' sake, what did Scarecrow need to do or say to prove his good intentions? "Thank you for securing the house," he told them. "I'm not much use when it comes to carpentry."

"I'm sure you have other skills." Gwyn's tone was bright, but reminded him far too much of Glinda.

The first time he'd met the so-called Good Witch of the South was when they'd gone to her castle with Dorothy, to petition for some way to return their friend home to Kansas. Glinda asked what the rest of the party intended to do once Dorothy left them. She'd seemed merely curious at the time, but afterwards he realized she'd most likely wanted to know if any of the young witchkiller's friends intended to seek power for themselves.

"What will you do when Dorothy leaves us?" Glinda asked him.

"I'll return to the Emerald City," Scarecrow replied, "since the Wizard left me in charge as Regent until he returns. I'll do my best to rule wisely." In truth he was terrified of the responsibility, but more worried the Wizard might punish him if he returned and found the city in an uproar.

Glinda frowned an instant, then smiled brightly. "I'll deliver you safely back to the Emerald City. The people shouldn't be deprived of so wonderful a ruler."

"Am I really wonderful?" asked Scarecrow, surprised.

Glinda's smile stretched wider and her eyes glittered. "You are unusual."

He still wasn't sure if she saw him as a threat or merely inconveniently in her way. She hadn't lifted a finger throughout the war to help him or his friends.

Gwyn viewed him as potentially dangerous to Theo. He frowned at her, trying to come up with a retort to persuade her he would never harm anyone.

Theo came to his defense. "He has amazing skills."

"Oh ho." Adam grinned.

Theo turned pink. "Oh my Goddess, not like that." Everyone laughed. "You guys are the *worst*."

"Not like what?" Scarecrow whispered to her.

"Never mind."

"Everyone feel up to participating in a circle?" Gwyn asked. "We've done the physical cleaning and protecting, now let's make sure all negative energy is banished."

With a general murmur of agreement, the other witches stood, stretched, began wandering from the room. As Gwyn glided from the table, Scarecrow muttered in Theo's ear, "What does she have against me, anyway?"

Theo sighed. "You heard some of it. My last ex liked dressing in costume too. And was overly polite."

"Am I supposed to treat her rudely, then? And this is my best clothing, not a costume."

"I know. I know. Just put up with her a little while longer tonight, okay? She means well. She's always been like the witchy aunt I never had." Theo smoothed down her tunic, dashing some crumbs from her trousers. "My folks never understood why I went pagan. Gwyn took me under her wing. Taught me it was okay to believe and do what feels right for me." Her brow creased. "We're going to do a circle ceremony now, to clear the air and ask for protection. I'd really like it if you joined in too, but I understand if you'd rather not."

"Magic, but not Oz magic?"

"Yep."

He nodded warily. "That sounds all right."

Whatever this ceremony was, it better not involve a blood sacrifice. Or a straw one.

He paused at the entry to the studio. Candles! Red pillars flickered on every table. The carpet with the five-pointed star lay in the center of the scrubbed floor, covering some of the damaged boards. Five short white candles in glass holders gleamed at the points of the star. One clumsy stumble here, and Scarecrow would be ablaze.

As he hesitated, Theo grabbed his right hand, tugging him into the center with her. Fear shot up his back as he passed a candle, but Theo smiled at him and clasped his fingers securely in hers.

He managed a nervous grimace in return, shuffling his feet farther from the nearest flame. Even a tiny spark could prove fatal. She hadn't said anything about candles. Why hadn't anyone mentioned there'd be candles involved?

"All ready then?" Gwyn asked.

"Ready," Theo replied. The others murmured agreement.

Gwyn closed her eyes. "We are here together for our friend, Theo, who has suffered a vicious attack. We ask the Goddess to bless and protect her and her home. Let no evil thoughts or deeds disturb her in this safe place."

They were all silent a long moment. The candlelight cast flickering shadows on the walls. The ceiling and the darkness of the boarded-over window pressed into the room. Scarecrow felt surrounded by more than just the seven witches gathered for this strange consecration. His straw prickled. He stared at the nearest candle on the carpet. It looked hungry. Why had he agreed to any of this?

Gwyn raised her voice. "Bless and keep safe our dear friend, now all fear is at an end."

The others echoed the words, beginning to sway left and right. "Bless and keep safe our dear friend, now all fear is at an end. Bless and keep safe our dear friend, now all fear is at an end."

Theo murmured the words as well, eyes closed, holding Scarecrow's hands. The witches, all facing Theo, clearly directed their prayer at her. She gave his fingers another squeeze and opened her eyes to gaze up at Scarecrow. With a start, he realized she was asking for protection for him as well.

The chant continued. Gwyn's strong voice increased in pace, and she began thumping her left foot to keep time. The glass holders at the points of the carpet star jittered. Scarecrow edged closer to Theo.

This wasn't like any ritual he'd ever heard of. No begging incomprehensible powers. No beseeching in fear, no blood sacrifice as the Ozians performed in less enlightened ages, no offering up children to the fae for their playthings or worse purposes. These witches all radiated kindness, friendship, acceptance. They didn't want to placate evil. They intended to simply banish it with their own warm hearts. If only they didn't use candles, he thought he might enjoy observing this.

As the chant grew faster, the witches began dancing widdershins with arms raised, hands clasped, feet pounding the floor with each beat of the rhyme. Despite his anxiousness, Scarecrow found himself murmuring the words along with them. Theo smiled at him, her eyes shifting from the brown of chestnut to the green of moss as the shadows and light played across her face.

Words bubbled into his brain. An ancient tune about safety in a storm, an enemy defeated. Caught up in the tangible energy buffeting him from all sides, he raised his voice in song. Theo held his hands tightly, keeping him in the center of the circle with her. Gwyn chanted louder and the witches raised their voices as well, a counterpoint to his.

He flew through the rhymes in Old Ozian, feeling dizzy. Theo gave his fingers a squeeze and he blinked at her. The chant continued. Some of the witches smiled at him. Gwyn's eyes widened, but she continued stomping her feet, tugging the circle of witches around them. The room grew warmer, brighter.

None of them could've understood a word of that. It took Scarecrow only a few seconds to begin translating in his head, and he threw all his energy into the song again:

> "Come in, ye travelers, in from the cold
> The wind is blowing out fierce and bold
> I've iron and ale and I'll tell you a tale
> Of a wicked fae queen and a maiden of old.
>
> "Irene had a cow and a sheep and a man,
> The fae grabbed them all and off she ran.
> Irene cursed the night, and wished a mean blight

On the crooked old faery who ruled all the land.

"Away to dark fortress Irene had to go
She took only her salt and her iron hoe
To fetch back her man was her desperate plan
As she walked alone in the bitter snow.

"Now the queen was a crafty old fae, it is true
The chill in her hands would turn a man blue
Her gate was unlocked, all mortals she mocked
For killing her was a feat no mortal could do.

"Irene caught her sleeping and struck her a blow
Straight over the head with her iron hoe.
With husband she fled back to their homestead
And the queen chased them screaming of blood and woe.

"Now Irene knew well no fae could she kill,
She hoed swiftly round them and with it salt filled.
The queen struck in all might but to her great fright
The iron and salt her very blood chilled.

"So gather ye close by the fire, my dears,
Drink to Irene and forget all your fears.
That snowy cold howl is the old faery's yowl—
Let her scream all she likes, she won't get in here!"

Juniper and Adam laughed merrily, breathless, dancing. Gwyn's stare was fixed upon Scarecrow, but she didn't break the dance or the chant, all of them shouting now.

Turning back to Theo, he faltered.

She was glowing. Heat flowed from her as though a fire burned within her chest, waves of it crashing outward.

He suffered an instant of terror before the shock of it hit him, making him stumble, the witches around them a blur. Before he could fall, Theo clasped him in a tight embrace.

All the flickering flames burst into showers of sparks. Gwyn and the other witches cried out and fell to the floor as the rolling wave of light slammed into them.

Scarecrow clutched Theo's arms, cringing. *No, oh no, not fire magic, I'll burn to ashes!* Her arms, her breasts were fiery, heat leaping into him, no, no please— He struggled but she held him tight. "Stop," he gasped, "Theo!"

"Scarecrow, don't move!"

His ears were ringing, vision blurred, panic sweeping through him. He tried to pull away but her embrace only tightened. She was saying something over and over into his ear, what spell was this, why was she doing this, he'd only wanted to help—

"Stop," she begged, "you're safe! Stop fighting, you're safe. Scarecrow, stop, you're safe."

He blinked and the world slowed, the fire faded. Her eyes were dark and worried, staring into his. He wasn't burning. He was fine. Bewildered, he saw the candles glowing steadily, calmly.

The witches sat on the floor, panting, smiling at each other and Theo. Smiling at Scarecrow.

"That was awesome," Vince announced.

"Was that Gaelic?" Juniper asked.

He wasn't on fire. How? What just happened?

Theo slowly released her hold, watching him carefully. Her hair was a shock of orange flame above her warm, bright eyes, her lips parted, breathing hard. How had he not noticed before she was fire incarnate? Yet the wave of heat left him unharmed. "Are you okay?" she asked.

"I—I think so." He checked again for any sign of a burn, any scent of smoke in his clothing. Nothing.

"Sorry," Theo laughed gently. "Didn't want you to fall on a candle." She let go.

He nodded, glancing down to be certain his legs were nowhere near the once again deceptively tiny flames.

"Hey Gwyn, very cool effect with the candles," Arturo said, adjusting his glasses. "Where'd you get those?"

Gwyn didn't take her eyes off Scarecrow. "Let's close the circle." Everyone slowly stood, out of breath, delighted. Again they joined hands. "We thank the Goddess for this blessing. We thank each other for this loving act done for our friends. This house is safe. So mote it be."

"So mote it be," all repeated.

They all stood in silence a moment. Only the sound of their breath filled the room. Then hands dropped, a sigh swept the gathering, and happy chatter bubbled up again.

"That was so cool. Did you feel it?"

"I definitely felt it. Beautiful."

"What just happened?" Scarecrow whispered to Theo.

She blinked at him. "I thought that was you. Your song."

"Oh." He hadn't considered the lines about fire before singing it. Which clearly was a serious mistake on his part. Theo keeping him exactly in the center of the circle probably just saved his life. "Thank you, my friend."

She gave him a puzzled smile. "For what? You're the one who just called up a wave of protection."

"Is that what that was?" he muttered.

"Thank you," Theo said to the rest. "Thank you so much. I really appreciate it, Gwyn. All you guys rock," she called to the others, as they drifted from the room, talking and laughing.

Gwyn walked around the room, snuffing the candles. She stopped in front of Scarecrow. "You didn't mention you practice magic."

"I don't," he protested weakly.

Her eyes narrowed, spectacles glinting.

"Really, I don't," Scarecrow said.

"I know some old Gaelic songs. Never heard that one before. What region is it from?" Gwyn asked.

"From the Quadling country, I think," he mumbled.

Theo patted his chest. "He's a scholar of old folksongs."

"Hm." Gwyn picked up a small bundle of pale green leafy twigs tied together. "I was gonna do a sage smudge too, but I feel like we don't need it now."

"Yeah, no, I feel great. The house is clean. Thank you. Hey, you know what, I feel like another glass of wine." Theo shot a pleading look at Scarecrow.

He followed her back to the dining room. Theo poured herself a tall goblet and quaffed a third of it at a gulp before she even dropped into her chair. Scarecrow sat next to her, shaken by how close he'd just come to a fiery death.

Gwyn joined them, to his dismay. She plucked an unused glass from the center of the table and emptied the bottle into it, but spoke not a word. She sank into a chair and propped her feet up on another.

"Hey, thanks for having us over, but we both have work in the morning, so we gotta split," Arturo announced. Adam stood next to him, smiling. Arturo nodded at Scarecrow. "Good to meet you, man. Sometime we should sit down and discuss folklore, since you dig old folk songs. My master's thesis was actually on gender roles and patriarchal norms in old Spanish fairy tales."

Scarecrow tried to parse that, frowned, gave up. "Nice to meet you as well," he replied.

Adam grinned. "Ignore him. He'll go on for hours if you give him an opening. You going to be okay, Theo?"

She waved, swallowing more wine. "Yep. Perfect. Thanks for coming over, guys. Thanks for bringing Juniper and Sue too."

The girls waved back from the hallway, and all of them departed. Vince wandered into the dining room. "So hey, do you still need the saw for anything?"

"All the downstairs windows barricaded?" Gwyn asked.

"Yep, all but the small ones in the kitchen. Man, I hate to see the nails in all this great old wood. I hope the asshole who's harassing you gets caught. You filed a police report, right?"

"No," said Theo.

Vince's eyes widened. "What, really? Look, Theo, I think maybe you should. Any dude who's sick enough to smash your window with a fake dead body could, you know, escalate."

"I think things will calm down now," Gwyn said. "Thanks for coming along and doing so much work, Vince. You're the best."

He blushed. "Nah, just happy to help out. You, uh, coming?"

Gwyn smiled at him. "I'll be home soon. Theo and I need to chat for a few minutes."

Vince nodded, bade them a good night, and departed.

Theo raised her eyebrows at Gwyn. "Wait. You and Vince?"

Gwyn shrugged. "He's a sweetheart. Definitely cuter than my ex-husband."

"That he is." Theo clinked her glass against Gwyn's and they both drank.

In the following silence, Scarecrow could hear the wind rustling through branches. Full dark outside. Golden light emanated from a lamp above the table. A warm energy filled the room. Light within, keeping the darkness outside at bay.

Gwyn removed her spectacles and wiped them with a scarf. "Okay, you two. Let's hear it."

Scarecrow exchanged a wary glance with Theo. "Hear what?" they both asked.

Gwyn snorted. "Remember when you and I first started talking about magic, I told you I'd seen two absolutely amazing spells performed that convinced me there really are more things in Heaven and earth than most people dream of?"

Theo nodded.

"Well, now I've seen three." She frowned at Scarecrow. "Where did you learn that song?"

Blast and blight.

Theo kept her expression neutral. She gulped more wine.

"I happened upon a collection of very old songs in a library," Scarecrow replied.

"Uh huh. Where was this library?"

"Back in my home country. I was making a study of ancient history, and discovered a trove of old music. No one had disturbed it for ages. I believe many of the songs were forgotten completely until I found them." The scrolls were dusty, fragile, dry. It took him all of an afternoon to patiently unroll one of them without damaging it further. "It seemed to me someone ought to learn them again. They held stories barely recalled by any modern scholars."

"Your home country?"

He nodded.

"That was definitely Gaelic. Your accent isn't Irish in the least, unless it's Boston Irish."

Scarecrow looked to Theo for help. She put both hands over her face. Gwyn stared intently at him and he didn't know how to answer. "Where exactly are you from?" she asked.

"Okay," Theo said loudly, startling Scarecrow. "Fine. Knock it off, Gwyn."

"Knock what off? Your friend here cast some powerful protection magic just now and I'd very much like to know where he learned it."

"I'm not a witch," he protested. "I only know a few songs. And I have no idea what you mean by Gaelic."

"It's hard to explain," Theo sighed. "Just let it go, Gwyn, please?"

Scarecrow wished suddenly he could drink. It was very unfair that meat people could use a simple fermented liquid to escape things they'd rather not face, and he couldn't.

"Where'd the dead body come from?" Gwyn asked.

"Told you, someone threw it through the window. Probably bought it at a Halloween store." Theo shrugged.

"Where is it now?"

"I believe it was tossed in the midden can out back," Scarecrow said.

"The midden can," Gwyn repeated, her expression thoughtful. "You are definitely a history student." She took another sip of wine. "That wasn't a prop body. I took a good look at it. Goddess, what a stench."

Theo exchanged a glance with Scarecrow. "You think it was actually a real dead body?"

"I didn't want to say anything with everyone else here. Dismembering a corpse is illegal, I think."

"Oh." Theo downed more wine.

"Come on." Gwyn rose from the table slowly, cracking her knuckles. "Whatever is going on here, whoever that used to be deserves more respect than to be shoveled into a trash can. Last thing you need is an unhappy spirit hanging around."

Scarecrow hadn't even considered a spook bothering Theo on top of everything else. Not good.

Theo's laugh sounded forced. "A real dead body? You think so? Damn, that's gross."

"I'm willing to bet someone dug it up from across the street. Grab a flashlight. You, fetch the body," Gwyn ordered Scarecrow.

He frowned. "Why me?"

"I don't want to go over there." Theo crossed her arms over her chest, glaring at Gwyn. "I'm safe in here now. Tromping into the cemetery at night is stupid. Cops might see us."

"Leaving the body here 'til trash day is guaranteed to invite more negative things into your personal space. No arguments. Either of you. I can see there's more going on here than you're willing to tell me. Fine, keep your secrets if it makes you feel safer. But we are absolutely laying that spirit to rest right the hell now." Gwyn came around the table and grasped Theo's shoulder.

Scarecrow was up and in the way immediately. "She said she doesn't want to go out." He kept his tone mild and calm, but stared down the older woman. Whether Gwyn was a witch or not, the least he could do here was stand up for Theo.

Gwyn frowned at him. "Not asking. This needs to be done."

"Then go do it yourself," he argued, removing her hand from Theo's shoulder.

Gwyn twisted out of his grip and suddenly crushed his fingers in hers. Straw crinkled. Scarecrow jerked away. She clutched his shoulder, squeezing hard. Angrily he shrugged her off.

"Gwyn!" Theo shot to her feet with a glare. "Leave him alone. He's just trying to protect me."

Scarecrow tried to tuck Theo behind him. She wouldn't have it, shouldering him out of the way to thrust her petite nose up to Gwyn's.

"You are being very pushy," Theo growled. "I don't appreciate this shit."

Gwyn narrowed her eyes at Scarecrow. "Where exactly are you from and what are you doing in my friend's home?" Her voice carried a definite undercurrent of threat.

"I told you, he's—"

With a sharp gesture, Gwyn dismissed Theo's interruption. "Let him answer."

Crows and blight. Scarecrow raised his shoulders higher. "I think you've already guessed the answer to the first question. I'm here because Theo needed to visit her grandmother and permitted me to come along."

"Did you have anything to do with the dead body?"

He huffed. "Certainly not. It attacked me."

"You don't belong in this world. Goddess knows what effect you'll have on it. On her," Gwyn snapped, indicating Theo.

"I'm sorry, what the actual fuck?" Theo demanded, hands on her hips. "Did you not just hear him sing a protection spell for me? Everyone heard it. Everyone felt it!"

"Theo, this man is not natural, and having him around you could be causing a lot of disturbance. Magical disturbance. You know this. Remember the night we talked about summoning spirits and—"

"Does he look like a spirit?" Theo yelled, smacking Scarecrow's chest. He staggered back a step, straw crunched. She threw him an apologetic glance, then scowled at Gwyn again. "I didn't summon a damned thing. I found him at the House on the Rock. I'm helping him and he's helping me. I'm not gonna sit here and let you come into my house and insult one of my friends!"

Gwyn's ample bosom expanded with a deep breath. "I'm only saying this because I'm worried about you. And if you really were attacked by an animate corpse, then this is already dangerous."

"Scarecrow isn't unnatural, and he won't hurt me." Theo poked a finger at Gwyn. "You need to leave now."

"Think about what you're doing," Gwyn argued.

"I've thought about it. He stays. You can go. Now."

Though the witch's words stung, this woman had mentored Theo, and did seem to harbor genuine care for her. "I give you my word, Lady

Gwyn, I will do everything in my power to keep Theo safe," Scarecrow promised.

Gwyn's expression softened somewhat. "I believe you mean that. But this house had some very disturbing energy in it when I came in, and the one thing new in her life is you. Whoever and whatever you are, your intentions may not matter. Keeping spirits around that aren't meant to be in this world is a recipe for disaster."

"Out," Theo snapped, pointing at the doorway.

Gwyn's lips pursed, but she nodded and walked out of the room.

Theo stood there, trembling.

This wasn't right. "Theo," Scarecrow began, but she shook her head.

"If you need my help, please call me," Gwyn said from the front hall. The front door opened and closed.

Theo was silent, fuming.

Scarecrow had been here less than a full day, and already he'd caused a rift between witches. In his experience, this was never a good thing. This was not the world he'd expected. Not from anything Dorothy had said, not from the books the Wizard had left behind. Despite his magic brains, he felt, yet again, lost and inadequate.

16

Theo gulped another glass of wine. Scarecrow hesitated. Broaching an uncomfortable subject to an angry witch wasn't wise, but he couldn't ignore Gwyn's warning, either. "Theo, I'm not happy about what she said, but there may be some truth to it. I can't be certain I didn't bring Oz magic with me. You claim things like this never happened to you before. Not even pixies in your garden."

Her eyes gleamed in the golden lamplight. "I know you *did* bring magic here. You must've. And I'm glad."

"But we don't know if the corpse attacked because I'm here. What if—"

"I don't care," she declared. "Anyway, you fixed it. The protection song you sang—that was amazing. I could already feel the circle helping and you made it even stronger."

While nearly setting himself on fire in the process. "Yes, but still," he continued.

Theo threw both arms around him and hugged tight. Startled, he stumbled back a step. "No. She's wrong. You didn't reanimate a corpse. You didn't make the zombie attack. You aren't dangerous." His straw crackled, compacting. She released him. "Oh, Goddess. I keep hugging you without even asking. Sorry about that."

He could feel warmth slowly evaporating from his straw. "I don't mind."

Theo nodded. Her hair fell over her eyes again. She brushed it to one side. "I'm sorry about Gwyn, too. I had no idea she'd be such a bitch."

"She's just concerned for your safety."

Theo's shoulders dropped and she sighed deeply. "She's kinda right, though."

"Excuse me?"

"About the dead thing. Dead guy. Whoever he was. Last thing I want is an unhappy ghost hanging around." She bit her lip, raising her eyes to his again. "Would you show me what grave he came from? If we're lucky, the caretakers haven't noticed yet and we can sneak over there and rebury him."

"You're sure you want to do this?"

"Yeah. Well, no. I don't want to at all. But we should."

He couldn't refuse the plea in her dark eyes. "Perhaps we'd better bring more weapons, though, just in case."

"Good call. Score one for the famous brains."

He accompanied her outside, picking up a rake with wicked tines as well as the trusty shovel. Though he was loath to touch the bag with the remains, Theo snapped colorful stretchy gloves over his hands to prevent his fabric from becoming contaminated. He held the sack in one outstretched arm and hurried across the street with her.

The branches overhead creaked and rustled. The half-moon glimmered high above. Dead leaves swirled past. Being able to see in the dark didn't comfort him at all tonight, with uncertain movement glimpsed between tall marble memorials. He led Theo to the bench where he'd been fruitlessly mired in thought and pointed to the churned-up earth nearby. They tiptoed to a marker at the head of the disturbed grave.

Scarecrow set down the bag of remains and leaned over, trying to read the weathered gravestone. The engraving had worn away, lichens and cracks in the stone further obscuring the name of the dearly departed. He brushed at the lichens, gloved fingers rasping against the stone.

Theo nudged him. "Don't get the ghost's attention. Keep watch while I dig." She handed him the rake.

"This doesn't seem very safe," he murmured. "Are there guards patrolling the grounds?"

"Probably not, but keep your voice down."

The trees swayed overhead. Grave markers and massive tree trunks nearly hid Theo's comfortable house from view. There were, in fact, a lot of graves here. He'd been preoccupied in the daylight, intent only on finding some spot far enough from the street where he wouldn't be easily seen or interrupted while he strained to think of a solution. Now he realized there were dozens of graves between them and safety.

Dozens. Each with a moldering body under the ground.

He gripped the rake tightly, head turning at each half-heard whisper of dry leaves, each skittering movement which was probably just the wind. "We shouldn't be out here," he whispered.

The crunch and hiss of the soil under Theo's shovel made him wince. Surely everyone would hear that.

Those with any sort of ears left, at least.

Did the bag just move? He poked it with the rake. A gurgle came from the wet sack.

"Theo," he hissed.

"Shhh," she hissed back. "Holy crap, check it out." She fumbled a thin black stick from a pocket and clicked a button. A beam of light shone down into the hole. "Freaking zombie motherfucker. I can see the busted-up coffin. It climbed right out through the ground."

"Theo, I think it moved."

"What?" She turned to look right as he poked it again.

Suddenly the outline of a skull shoved against the bag, stretching it. The jaw moved. *"Sssskkkkkaaaaggghhhgggrrrooooww,"* the skull said.

"Holy shit!" Theo swung the shovel up, her eyes wide and wild. She stumbled on the loose earth, fell against the gravestone, scrambled back to her feet before Scarecrow could reach her.

"Waaaaaarrrrrrre," the skull said. Its voice was liquid, burbling, the bag wet and trembling with its effort to speak. The sound made all his straw prickle. It hadn't said anything coherent during its attack. This was different. What danger could a beheaded, mostly-dissolved corpse in a sack truly do?

"Wait!" Scarecrow cried, lifting a hand toward Theo before she could swing the shovel. "It didn't say that before, wait, what if it's trying to tell us something?"

"Like what?" Theo demanded.

"I don't know." Summoning what courage he could, he prodded the skull through the bag with the pole end of the rake. "Here, you, what do you mean by speaking when you ought to be dead?"

"Nnnnnoott...deeeaaaddhh," the skull gurgled, its cheekbones straining against the bag.

"You most certainly are," Scarecrow insisted.

Theo braced to whack the corpse again, trembling. Scarecrow edged closer to her, keeping his makeshift polearm aimed at the quivering bag of talking sludge.

"*Waaarrrreee deemm...nnnoott deeeaaaddddhhhh,*" the skull groaned. "*Sssskaaarrrkrrrrooowww...wwwaaarrre   nnnoottt   ddeeeaaad- ddhhh...uufff Ozzzzz...*" The voice faded to a hiss, and the bag crumpled. The skull remained pressed into its side, jaw open, motionless.

Scarecrow and Theo stared at each other. Straightening his back, he poked cautiously at the bag again. It didn't move or speak.

"Did it say Oz?" Theo whispered.

"Sounded like it."

"Who the fuck was this guy?" Theo shone her lightstick upon the gravestone. "Oh no. No way."

Scarecrow crouched to read the lettering. Still couldn't make out the first name, but the surname might be BRIGHT. That looked like a BR and a T, at least. Underneath the name and strange symbols Scarecrow couldn't decipher were the words, OUR DEAR BUTTON.

"Button Bright," Theo whispered. "Are you fucking kidding me?" She looked at Scarecrow. "Another person who went to Oz, buried right across the street from my house?"

"Who is this?"

"Seriously. You never met Button Bright? He's in the books. A boy who keeps getting lost."

Scarecrow shook his head. "No one I've met."

Theo clasped her arms around herself with a shiver. "This is too weird."

Whether this person had visited Oz or not, this couldn't be coincidence. The bagged bits of corpse offered no further answers. Scarecrow nudged the bag toward the open grave. "We should let him rest, whoever he was."

"Are there zombies in Oz?"

"Not that I ever encountered," he mused, "though there were rumors, during the war. Wild tales of bones coming up from the ground in parts of the Forbidden Forest."

"If it was trying to warn us, why did it attack you?"

"I don't know."

They stared at the motionless sack.

Theo swallowed visibly, gesturing at it. "Toss it in."

Gladly he did so, hoping he was just imagining the contents shifting around still. The liquid sound of them, and the stench, he definitely did not imagine. Theo poked it down into the shattered coffin with the shovel and immediately began throwing chunks of dirt after it, while he nervously raked loose soil into the hole. Somewhere nearby an owl hooted, making him jump and stare around wildly.

"Okay, good enough. Let's get the fuck out of here."

He stayed close by Theo, turning around every few steps to make sure nothing was creeping up on them from behind. The third time he stumbled into her back she stopped, setting a hand on his chest.

"Would you quit that, Scarecrow? You're making me skittish now."

Though her eyes were wide and she held tight to the shovel, its spade end ready to hit anything if needed, she wasn't shivering as badly as he was. "Aren't you scared?" he whispered.

"Goddess yes. If anything else pops up, I'm gonna whack it to kingdom come." She laughed nervously. "I'll whack the zombies, you scare the crows."

"You expect us to be attacked by crows? I should warn you, I couldn't frighten them at all."

She took his free hand in hers. "But you lured the witch's crows down and twisted their necks. You're stronger than you look. Come on, let's get out of here."

Startled, he suffered her dragging him a few steps until he could regain his footing on the uneven ground. *She knew about the crows?*

Killing them one by one as they flew at him, shrieking and cawing, was one of the more distasteful things he'd ever done. He'd had no choice. The Witch of the West very much objected to their mission to capture her broomstick, and sent wave after wave of her underlings to stop them. Nick slaughtered the wolves. Scarecrow the crows. Lion and Nick together killed the Winkie guards. When a swarm of stinging insects descended, a buzzing black cloud with the promise of a painful death for the young woman and the lion, Scarecrow offered up all his straw. They pulled it bodily from him to cover Dorothy and the big cat, hiding them from the swarm. The hornets stung Nick over and over until they wore themselves out, crushing themselves against his shining tin.

In those few minutes, with his awareness dulled down to the noise of the swarm and Dorothy's heated breathing under his straw as she clutched his sack-head tight, he silently begged for her to live. Whether he survived being unstuffed or not, she should live.

Discovering that being unstuffed would not in fact kill him was a happy surprise. However, the flush on Dorothy's skin, the broad smile on her face as she helped tuck all his straw back inside his clothing, was lovelier by far. He'd saved her from the vicious flock and the stinging swarm. He couldn't save her from the terrors of the Outside World.

And now dark magic brought a dead thing out of its grave to menace his only friend here. A dead thing which knew about Oz. Had this Button Bright wanted to kill them, or had it been under someone's control? How did it know where he was?

He needed to figure out how to recharge the Evstone. Call Nick as soon as possible. Something terrible was afoot.

Theo tugged him by the hand through the creepy, chilly graveyard. Nothing jumped out at them. She helped him to his feet when he stumbled on the curb, though she wasn't too steady herself.

On the porch, she paused, breathless. Her eyes in the amber lamplight from above were mossy green. "Screw the living dead, I can't deal with cryptic warnings on top of everything else. Let's go inside and have another glass of wine."

"Maybe you should rest instead," he suggested.

She shook her head, opening the door. "Too wound up. Keep me company? Tell me a story? An Oz story. But only nice stuff, okay?"

"If you like," he said, puzzled. He cast one more glance over his shoulder at the cemetery as they went inside. Must be his imagination. Those weren't eyes flickering in the shadows, gone now. Anyway, spooks didn't have eyes.

Had to be just the wind.

He kept hold of the rake.

17

Red and gold leaves swirled along the tall, green marble colonnades as Nick did his best to step quickly but quietly. The sun was just rising. He'd paced in his quarters all night, but no word had come from Professor Wogglebug. Nick considered stopping by the Last Twitch pub in the late, dark hours before dawn, but since he didn't frequent the place, showing up would only draw attention.

The Emerald Palace was peaceful. An autumn mist hung over the gardens, the damp making Nick's knees ache dully. The day would undoubtedly be sunny, the fog chased away with the light, but right now all sound was muffled. Unpleasant as it was for a man of metal, at least it helped conceal the noise of his feet. The smell of woodsmoke faintly mingled with the fog. No doubt Jellia Jamb and the rest of the staff had been up an hour or more already, building fires in at least one of the vast kitchen hearths to cook breakfast.

Someone by now must've noticed Ozma Tip wasn't in her chambers.

Sneaking around like this brought back memories of the time they'd been trapped in the palace by General Jinjur and her all-girl army. She'd ousted Scarecrow as Regent, taking advantage of a temporary absence by Locasta, the Witch of the North, to overrun the Emerald City. Scarecrow at first was grudgingly willing to relinquish the throne, saying he'd never wanted the job in the first place, but Jinjur's announcement that she'd throw the straw man into a bonfire once she'd breached the Palace changed his outlook. Nick, Tip, Jack Pumpkinhead, and the Wogglebug helped Scarecrow with a desperate plan. They built a flying machine to escape the surrounded palace by air. To gather supplies to build it, they explored the many passageways in the Emerald Palace, indoors and out, obvious and partly hidden. Good thing Nick still remembered a few routes.

He found the narrow outdoor stairway, concealed between two giant pillars, which took him to the second floor, bypassing the halls and inner staircases used by the staff and residents of the grand, cold building. Easing open the aged oak door at the top, he squinted into the dim hallway nearest to the Scarecrow's former quarters. They were located in the farthest wing from the lavish royal chambers and guest rooms. Scarecrow, like Nick, didn't need a soft bed or a marble bathtub. The room he'd chosen as his own had served as the royal library for ages. It withstood castle sieges during the Old Kingdom years. There was only one door, of heavy oak banded in iron, and iron bars were worked into the walls when the room was constructed. It was rumored to be fae-proof. Nick had never heard of any of the Seelie Court, Glinda included, willingly setting foot inside even when the door was open.

Scarecrow was positive there was a secret passage in the library, but so far Nick hadn't located it. It was the safest possible room for Tip to wait out whatever was coming—assuming anywhere in the Palace could be considered safe, if there truly was a coup afoot.

Nick checked the corridor before tiptoeing across to the library door. His ankles creaked. Blasted mist getting in all his joints. He knocked quietly.

Silence.

Knocking again a bit louder, he whispered, "Tip? Lion? You in there?"

A low growl came from the other side of the door. "Who wants to know?"

Nick sighed. "Who do you think, Tiger? Open up."

"How do I know it's really you?" the Tiger asked.

"Use your nose, you big furball," Nick said, exasperated.

He heard loud sniffing noises. Another deep voice spoke up. "What is it, Tiger?"

"Can't tell. Might be an oil salesman."

"An oil—oh for all the evil trees in the forest. Move, Tiger."

The bolt clunked and the door swung open. Lion nodded at him. "All quiet here. Any news?"

Nick slipped inside and shut the door quickly behind him, easing the bolt closed. "Nothing. The Wogglebug hasn't been by?"

Lion shook his head, curly mane brushing over his broad shoulders. "Haven't seen, heard, or smelled him. Been quiet all night." He nodded at the enormous stone hearth where a fire crackled, the logs dwarfed by the huge andirons in the shapes of coy fire-nymphs. One of the long sofas was pushed close to the hearth.

Nick could see a small lump buried in quilts and furs. "How is she?" he asked.

Tiger returned to the sofa, stretching out between the furniture and the fireplace. "Asleep. We really should get her up soon. Isn't it breakfast time?" He yawned, licking his wide jaws.

Lion shrugged. "She stayed up for hours. Finally crashed just a little while ago, worn out and worried."

Tip was curled up on the sofa, something black and pointed sticking out of her grasp from under the covers. Nick leaned over to peer at it. One of Scarecrow's old hats. A few strands of oat-straw were still caught in the band.

Lion shook his head, his gruff voice unusually quiet. "She must've searched through every shelf in here. Climbed up half of 'em, convinced she should try to find the secret exit, just in case the door got broken down. Did Scarecrow ever find it?"

"Not that he told me," Nick said. The fire chased the damp from his legs. He stood near it, grateful for the heat. "I think this room is pretty safe, as long as the fae side of her isn't bothered too much by the iron. But she can't stay in here forever. The Good Witch is sure to notice."

"Well, if push comes to shove, this feels pretty defensible to me," Lion growled.

Tiger huffed. "But it's so far from the kitchen!"

A rap at the door startled them all, stirring Tip. Nick's axe was in hand without a thought. He strode to the door. "Who goes there?"

"Is there some sort of secret knock or code word? You didn't tell me," complained the Wogglebug from outside.

Nick let him in, glancing up and down the silent corridor before re-bolting the door. "I guess we should have one. So? What happened?"

"Is the Queen not awake yet? Oh. I am terribly early." The Professor clasped two of his hands together. He undid a woolen scarf from around his thin neck. "Quite the chill out there this morning. I fear this winter will be a dreadful one."

"I'm awake," Tip mumbled, sluggishly throwing off covers. She rubbed her eyes. "What happened? Professor, how long have you been here? You guys didn't start without me, did you?" she protested. Dark circles ringed her bright green eyes.

"He just came in. Your Highness, sure you're ready to wake up yet? You don't look well," Nick observed.

"I'm fine. So let's hear it," Tip ordered, sitting up on the sofa. She kept hold of the hat, clutching it to her side like a favorite stuffed toy.

"Well, it's still quite early. Are you sure you wouldn't care for tea first?" asked the Wogglebug. "I know I'm famished after such a long night."

The Tiger rose to his feet, licking his lips. "Ooo. Tea! And can we have pie and bacon and eggs and—"

Tip patted his head. "Later. First I want to hear what happened at the secret meeting." She turned expectantly to the Wogglebug. "Did your beetle work?"

"I only just retrieved it this morning." The Professor withdrew the metallic insect from a pocket of his voluminous coat. "Unfortunately, my fae friend wanted to drink the night away and then—well. It was some time before I could extricate myself."

"So you haven't heard yet what your wind-up toy—lode-aural thingy learned?" Nick asked, correcting himself when the Wogglebug scowled.

"No, I came straight here as soon as I was able to sneak the instrument from the conference room."

"Well let's hear it!" Tip exclaimed, padding over to them.

Nick echoed the sentiment. "We're all here and who knows how long it'll be before someone misses the Queen and comes looking. Play that thing, Professor."

Even the Tiger came closer, saucer-eyes wide, as the Wogglebug wound up his invention tightly. He opened the back wings and rewound the long sliver of eelskin around a spool. When he paused, Nick made an impatient gesture.

"Enough with the drama. Play it, now."

"It merely occurred to me there could be spells uttered on here," the Wogglebug said, a tremor in his voice. "Things which may not have affected my instrument could still cause havoc for us when it speaks them aloud again. We don't know what sort of ceremony the Seelie Court engages in. What if there's a curse? For instance, in *The Flutterbudget of High Street,* there's a curse pronounced at the start of a secret ceremony, which poor Mabel overhears from her hiding-place under the table, and it—"

"Are you seriously claiming the Seelie Court works the same as in those stupid romances?" the Lion growled, baring his teeth.

"That one's good," the Tiger argued. "I've read it."

Lion pawed Tiger's muzzle. "You have not, you can't even read."

"One of Madam Jinjur's girls read it to me. Same thing."

Tip pointed her staff at the flagstones before the hearth. "If any spell comes out, I can force it into the fireplace and contain it there."

The Wogglebug hesitated. "Are you quite certain, Your Majesty?"

Tip chewed her lip. For a moment she looked like the scared, beaten boy she'd been when Nick first met her years ago, instead of the royal, part-fae girl she'd become when Glinda forced her to resume her original sex. He wondered sometimes, if Tip could choose, whether she'd stay Queen or prefer to be a King instead. It wasn't up to her, though. Glinda insisted due to the particular position of the constellations, Oz needed a Queen, and Ozma Tip had to be it. Male or female, she was still so young. So unsure of her faery powers. And trembling in the chilly room. Nick draped a quilt over her shoulders. Wouldn't do for the ruler of Oz to catch a cold.

She nodded thanks. "Do it. Wait!" She hurried to the sofa, rooting among the covers for a moment until she found her golden circlet and jammed it on her head.

Tip returned to the group, scepter firmly in hand and her delicate crown perched over her ears. She still looked tired and frightened, but at least she was reaffirming her role as their ruler. Poor child.

At her nod, the Wogglebug clicked the latch to make the metallic insect replay what it heard. Setting the bug on the hearthstone, he scuttled behind the Lion.

The canned, emotionless voice of the machine sent a chill through Nick. The entire party hushed, all of them craning forward to listen.

"Well met cousin did anyone follow you. No I was not seen. I came on the night wind. Excellent. And we are certain the barkeep will say nothing. No he has been charmed. He knows only that some business is being conducted and not to open the door."

It was hard to distinguish how many speakers there were. The mechanical insect repeated everything in the same continuous monotone, without inflection or significant pause.

"Then everyone has wine. Good. Let us begin. Wait I have not checked the room for unfriendly magic. Why who do you think would disturb us. Mombi. Ha ha ha ha."

The laugh, repeated in that same emotionless, tinny voice, sent shivers through Nick.

"That dried-up old prune. The only thing she was ever good for was turning a baby fae into a silly boy-child. Too bad she beat him 'til he ran away. If she had just eaten the child we would not have Ozma on the throne now."

Tip's nostrils flared, eyes narrowing. Her fingers tightened on her scepter.

What the fae said was true. If the old witch Mombi hadn't treated the boy Tip as a bond-slave, he might not've determined to run away from her. His flight led him to then-Regent Scarecrow, soliciting aid from Nick, meeting the Wogglebug, and having a wild adventure with them all. So many things nearly went badly wrong on that whole journey. Surely if Ozma Tip hadn't been made Queen, the lordlings of the Seelie Court would still be squabbling for control of all the Empire. Wrecking the countryside as they did.

"I feel no magic here cousins. Let us begin. Has anyone heard from Glinda. No she was supposed to be at her palace but my sister called there yesterday and her servants had no word from her."

Nick winced. Please, please, let the pink-robed witch be far from here, too far to hear her name mentioned by this metallic thing. The next words it repeated made him freeze.

"I told you. We know where she is. She has gone to speak with the lords of the Unseelie Court."

The Wogglebug gasped. Lion's head rose, whiskers trembling. Tiger's muzzle set in a scowl, showing his enormous fangs. Tip shivered, pointing the head of the scepter at the mechanical bug. A green glow from the scepter made her face appear more unhealthy.

The Unseelie Court! What business would Glinda have with those monsters? To even call it a Court was a joke. The Unseelies were vicious, chaotic, malevolent creatures. Ancient and powerful fae, formed of the elements themselves, aeons before the more civilized Fair Folk came to Oz with their human servants and pets. It was rumored that even the Nome King refused to treat with them, and they were unwelcome within the legal boundaries of Oz.

"Is it true then. She actually speaks with those disgusting things. Seriously Ansel you don't know. Know what. That the Unseelies will be our vanguard. They will push through the veil in the steps of the anchor."

"What in the name of all that's holy is this?" murmured the Wogglebug.

"Do we trust them. Of course not. But better they get ripped apart going through the veil than us. When will be our turn. When Glinda says so. I thought the whole point of this meeting was to decide if we are with her or not. This is a dangerous venture."

Very dangerous. Dangerous for all of them here to be listening to whatever terrible plot this was. Nick felt cold despite standing near the fire.

"She has assured us of victory. All we need do is follow her plan. The mortals have all forgotten our power. They will kneel and we will reclaim what is our rightful land."

So it was true. Members of the Seelie Court were plotting treason.

"I don't care what the rest of you do. I'm not a fool. We have no assurance at all the Unseelies will respect our authority. They are too wild. Glinda will control them. How can you be sure. They are so old. They cannot even agree which of them should rule in the Shadowlands. How can anyone form an alliance with such as they."

Was Glinda seriously planning to unleash the Unseelie Court back into Oz? A powerful spell kept them in the Shadowlands since the start of modern Ozian history. Scarecrow had been fascinated by a book he'd found detailing the Unseelie things of darkness, pointing out excitedly to Nick that the khalidahs and Wheelers were direct descendants of the Elementals roaming the forbidden sands of the Cold Desert. He'd tried to figure out whether the Shadowlands were an actual place or merely a nickname for the darker parts of the Empire, the uncertain spaces one naturally avoided, such as a deep, spooky forest thick with dead and twisted trees.

Nick asked Scarecrow, at the time, to find some more pleasant topic of conversation. He still suffered horrible flashbacks of their time in the dungeons. Now he wished he'd listened. If the Unseelie Court were coming here, he needed to know how to fight them off.

How to kill them, if need be.

The insect spy continued to spit forth what it had overheard in its tinny, unnerving voice. *"We do not need to ally with them. Only to send them forth to clear the way. And do you trust them even with that. No but I believe Glinda has a vision. A vision that will benefit all of us. Pah. You are as feeble-minded as that sack of straw she gave to the mewling babe who sits on the throne. Glinda deals in dark magic too dangerous even for her and I for one will not be her puppet. Oh that's where you are mistaken. Glinda. What are you doing back so soon."*

Nick startled. The Tiger growled, and Lion backed away a step, ears flattened into his mane. The Wogglebug gave an audible gulp. Tip paled but didn't move an inch.

"Why hello my dears. It appears someone forgot to invite me to this little gathering. My how cozy you all are. All packed into this ridiculous box. Silly children. Lady Glinda Sovereign of the Shadows we meant no offense. Well it sounds to me as though you have some doubts. Doubts about my vision. Which I have pondered and planned for centuries well before you were whelped Ansel. You silly pup. Gzzzzrtt."

The professor stared at Nick, thin membranes blinking over his round black eyes, frightened into silence. Nick shook his head, tensed, gripping his axe in tightly. As if he could chop at the hideous thing which had already happened, or strike down what was coming.

"There you will never have to doubt me again Ansel. Does anyone else have a question they wish to ask. No my lady. We are your humble vassals.

Yes you are and you'd best not forget it ever again. Bark bark. Not you Ansel. Sit. Stay."

Nick shuddered. Tip had gone past pale into snow-white, her emerald eyes dulled to moss green, hanging onto her scepter as if only whatever magic resided in it could keep her safe.

Damn Glinda. No love lost for any of the smirking lords of the Seelie Court, but damn her cruelty all the same.

"Most Elegant and Charming Mistress may we know one thing. Speak and I shall do my best to lay your silly fears to rest my dear. How will we safely cross the barrier. Fear not the anchor is in place. I will ensure it is at the correct location when the moon is right. Sowwain approaches. Again the old doors will open. You say you have no love for the Unseelie Court but I promise you they have their uses. You will see. Trust and follow me. We are with you Lady. Good my dears. Now I believe you all should go your ways. Philemon I saw a disgusting bug in the bar waiting for you. How you can pursue such perversion is beyond me but even you will be rewarded once we have retaken our lands. Lady Glinda I assure you I do so in order to learn the mood of the Queen whom the bug adores. When I am balls-deep in him he tells me everything and his noises of pleasure are most amusing. How does this differ from your dalliance with the dried-up old witches before the Girl Warrior came."

The Wogglebug clutched his scarf to his face. Nick was embarrassed for him. Having such things repeated in front of Tip must be absolutely mortifying.

"I don't, I wouldn't, never, Your Highness," the professor cried aloud.

Tip's eyes were as wide as they could open, but she accepted his protest with a jerk of her head.

"Shut up, Bug," Lion muttered. His claws flexed as he glared at the metal insect on the hearth.

Its mechanical voice slowed, which made its repeated words all the more sinister-sounding. *"Ha ha ha. Philemon you continue to surprise me. Very well enjoy your amusements. You will tell me at once if you learn the Queen suspects anything. Of course my Lady. Thus far she is as ignorant as that striped housecat she keeps by her side. Good. Then I think we are done...here...you are all...*" With a clacking sound, the mechanical bug stopped.

Lion snarled. "Those smug bastards."

"Where are they? I'll eat all of 'em," Tiger declared so loudly his deep voice echoed back from the fireplace.

"Shut up, both of you, please," Nick said. "We need to think."

Rust and ruin, how he wished Scarecrow was here. He yanked the Evstone from his pocket, cupping it in one hand and trying to focus his whirling thoughts upon it. The stone glowed but then faded. Scarecrow must not have recharged his stone yet. Despair rising, Nick shoved the rock back in his waistcoat.

"Never." The Wogglebug's voice wavered. He held up two trembling hands, beseeching Tip. "I never tell any of them anything of note, I swear, I give them silly gossip and prattle and they think I am an idiot, they boast of things they think I won't understand when we are—Phil talks in his sleep," the professor said. He sank to the floor, wrapping his fingers over his eyes. "Your Highness, I promise, I only—"

Tip knelt and embraced him. "It's all right, Professor, I know you'd never betray me. Not after all we went through."

She hugged the sobbing Professor, rocking with him back and forth gently. She turned worried eyes to Nick. Lion and even the Tiger were staring at Nick as well. Waiting for him to decide what they should do.

"Your Highness, it does sound like your life could be in danger," Nick said. His voice sounded squeaky. Fog must've got into it. "And obviously the Good Witch is behind it. Whatever they're planning, it doesn't sound like they intend to let you stay on the throne."

Tip stood, shaking, the brightness returning to her eyes. "Well—good. I didn't want to be Queen anyway."

"But you're the best Queen of Oz ever," argued the Tiger.

"If the Seelie Court starts running things again, the entire Empire will suffer," Nick said. He gazed at the dying fire, recalling his life before a witch's curse caused him to lop off one limb after another. "You're too young to know what that was like. The faeries in charge of every hamlet, every city. Every mortal person subject to their twisted law. I ran away from my village as soon as I was tall enough to swing an axe. Ran and hid in the forest where nobody cared if I lived or who I served, and the damned fae caught up to me anyway."

"They've always run the Empire." The Wogglebug slowly rose. He wiped the tears from his face, smoothed out his antennae repeatedly. "They still are, it just doesn't appear so to anyone not well-versed in the Court politics. Forgive my bluntness, Your Highness."

Ozma Tip shook her head. She glared at the motionless mechanical insect on the floor. "They don't run me. They never will. I don't care how much of my blood is fae. I'm not with them and I never will be." She spat into the fire. "And I'm not Glinda's princess doll no matter how much she tries to make me into one!"

"Tip," Nick cautioned, taking a step toward her. If the witch over-heard—

"Knock knock," trilled a voice from the other side of the door.

Lion and Tiger immediately crouched in front of Tip, ears back, fangs bared. With a clicking of his mandibles, the Wogglebug skittered behind the sofa.

Nick's heart pounded. Blasted bogtrolls! The bitch was back.

"Yoo hoo," Glinda trilled. "Come now, I hear voices, Ozma dearie, is that you?"

"Everyone calm down," Nick muttered. "Professor, get out here and act casual, damn it."

The Wogglebug timidly emerged from behind the sofa, keeping hold of his scarf like a protective amulet. "Please do not open the door," he whispered. "We're safe in here. This room is witch-proof! Scarecrow chose it specifically for that reason as much as he did for the books, you know."

"All of you be quiet," Tip hissed. She took a deep breath, resettled her circlet over her forehead, and walked to the door. "And smile even if it kills you, got it?"

Nick forced himself to lower his axe and refasten its loop to his hip. Lion nudged Tiger, retracting his claws, and the stripey cat growled but then sat down. Once Tip saw they all were attempting a more casual stance, she slid back the bolt and opened the door.

"Glinda," she said simply, "you're back."

The witch's coal-black gaze flicked over the room. She smiled. "Well, my goodness. What an early hour for a court gathering, and you aren't even dressed, my dear! What is all this?" Her tone was light and fluttery.

Nick reminded himself not to grind his teeth at the sound.

"Oh, I was trying to read up on the history of Ix." Tip gestured at the walls of bookshelves.

Glinda's gaze darted to some books laid out on a reading table, then back to Tip. Her smile never faltered.

"You know," Tip persisted, shuffling her feet a bit, "seeing as how they're coming to see us next week. You keep telling me I have to know all this ceremonial stuff, even for the other countries of the Empire."

"Of course," Glinda said. "Did you fall asleep studying, you sweet child? How devoted. I'm glad to see it. But it really is unseemly for you to be receiving visitors in such a state of undress." Her gaze settled on Nick.

He made a low bow. "Apologies, Lady Glinda. The Queen mentioned she'd be studying Ixian this morning with the Professor here, and I asked to join in. I hear Ix has wonderful timber and I wanted to be able to talk to the ambassador about it. I thought maybe doing so in his own tongue might win us some favors." He forced a chuckle. "I didn't expect Her Highness to not be quite ready for us yet, since she agreed to the time."

"I totally forgot it was supposed to be at seven," Tip said immediately. "Thought for sure we'd said nine o'clock."

The Wogglebug trembled but also made a low bow with his usual elaborate flourishes. "I humbly beg forgiveness, the error was mine. I shouldn't have expected Her Highness to recall such a silly appointment when she has so much on her mind."

"I see," Glinda murmured.

"We should get breakfast first." Tiger's stomach rumbled.

Glinda's shoulders relaxed. Ever so slightly, but they did, and Nick let out the habitual breath he'd been holding, even though he didn't need to breathe.

"What a practical idea," Glinda announced. "Ozma dear, come with me and let's get you presentable. Your Ixian lesson may take place after morning court." She held out one hand.

Tip stiffened, but nodded. Still wrapped in her quilt, she turned and gestured at the rest of them. "You guys, I have to go do court stuff. See you back here afterward?"

"Okay," said Tiger. "I'm famished. Breakfast first?"

"Breakfast first," Tip agreed.

Tiger and Lion at least would stick close by Tip, and watch every move Glinda made around the young Queen.

"Oh, surely we can find some less gloomy study room. The Professor may bring books to you. It's so dreary in this older part of the palace. What's that?" Glinda asked, frowning. Her gaze was fixed on the mechanical bug.

Nick's mouth opened but he didn't have a ready reply. The Wogglebug swooped to the hearth and retrieved his creation.

"My newest invention," he proclaimed, his voice not shaking a bit. Nick was proud of him. "You see, by means of a spring and gears, if I wind it so, it can crawl wherever I tell it to go. Took me weeks to design. Here, let me—"

"Ozma dear, we really should get you out of such a chilly room and into your proper dress," Glinda interrupted, turning away in obvious disinterest.

Nick exchanged a relieved glance with the Wogglebug.

"I like it in here," Tip announced, her chin lifting. "I'll go have breakfast and do court stuff, but if I have to study that stupid language just for a stupid ambassador's visit, I'm gonna do it in here. In Scarecrow's room."

Glinda's brow creased mildly, though she continued to smile. She still hadn't crossed the threshold of the door.

Tip crossed her arms, pouting. "I will study in here. I'll get the servants to bring up more firewood. I like it here." She looked around at the cluttered shelves, the books about the Outside World stacked on a table next to Scarecrow's favorite reading chair just as if he was going to walk back in any minute to resume his studies.

Glinda noticed the hat laying on the sofa. Her eyes glittered. "You miss your old advisor. Of course. Has he not contacted you yet?" she asked Nick suddenly.

His throat felt dry as a rusted can in the desert. "No."

Glinda smiled wider. "Well. I'm sure he will soon. Once he remembers you. He's probably having the time of his life with Dorothy." She tittered. "Ah, young love." She held a hand out to Tip again. "Come along, my sweet, let's get you cleaned up." Glinda settled an arm lightly over the Queen's shoulders, guiding her toward the far wing of the palace and the royal chambers. "And do let's have that old blanket washed, it smells of musty straw. You gentlemen have other things to do, I'm sure."

"That we do," Nick said, forcing a cheery smile to his metal lips.

As soon as the witch was well out of sight, Nick shut the door. His limbs quivered with restrained anger.

The Wogglebug set all four arms on his nonexistent waist and huffed. "And she dares refer to me as a perversion, that sickeningly sweet hag! What, and pardon my Nomish, an utter bitch."

Nick nodded agreement. "I don't think she suspects anything. Good job there, Professor." The bug's antennae quivered. "Are you all right?" Nick asked softly.

The Wogglebug tutted, smoothing down his rose-patterned waistcoat. "It does not befit a Thoroughly Educated gentleman to be anything less than courtly in the presence of such absolute trash." His expression was always a little hard to read to Nick, but the uncertainty in his round eyes was plain right now. "You—you won't say anything to anyone about—"

"You haven't done anything wrong." Nick grasped the Wogglebug's outstretched hand very gently. "Not my place to judge you."

"I believe I shall reconsider some of my acquaintances," the Professor said quietly. He tucked the mechanical insect into a coat pocket. "Now if you'll excuse me, I should brush up on my Ixian. Wouldn't surprise me if a servant wait on us the whole time we're studying from here on out, in order to report back to the Pink Lady. However it is comforting to confirm," he glanced around at the bookshelves and high walls, "the Scarecrow's determination that this room is the safest in the Palace, likely the safest in all Oz."

With his head held high, he left. Nick stood alone a few minutes more, staring at the iron bands on the door. He suspected the room affected Tip more than she admitted, but if the human side of her was stronger, the library was the best place she could be.

They'd need all the defense they could muster against the Seelie Court. No idea how to fend off any action by the Unseelie. The shadowy creatures were frightening even to the civilized fae. Why were they risking letting them loose here? Did Glinda have some plan to control them? All this talk of the fae regaining their lands was as confusing as it was worrisome. They still controlled Oz, and Ev, and Ix, and every other nation of the Empire. Not openly in some cases, but only a fool would think they weren't the real power behind every kingdom. Still, Tip improved things immeasurably.

Because Glinda tolerated her.

Glinda just effectively squashed any dissent in the Seelie Court's ranks. She wasn't merely aware of whatever the secret plot was, she was running it.

Why all this shadowy planning? She already knew more magic than any of the rest of the witches, probably more than most of them combined. Tip was no threat to her. Why was the Seelie Court talking about regaining control of lands they already ruled? He knew little of the ceremonies of the fae, but whatever this Sowwain was, it sounded important.

None of this made any sense. Nick's head hurt. He pulled out the Evstone again, but no matter how hard he concentrated, when he spoke his friend's name aloud, the stone was silent.

Damn it, Scarecrow. We need you. I need you. Please hear this, somehow. Please talk to me. I need your brains here.

The Evstone was cold and quiet. With a sigh, Nick tucked it securely in his waistcoat. Maybe his friend could point him to something here which would help.

If, that is, he ever heard from the straw man again.

18

Birds twittered. Sunlight warmed her eyelids. Theo grunted and tried to tug the blanket over her head. Suddenly her feet were cold. Head pounding, she squinted up at the cross-beamed ceiling. Daylight spilled through the front window. A man wearing a pointed hat stood silhouetted there, his back to her.

The prior night percolated back into her remaining brain cells. She lay on the rug of the living room. Empty bottles towered over her on the low table nearby. She remembered the zombie. Yelling at Gwyn. A spell cast in the circle, rushing through her like searing joy, making ordinary candles explode into fireworks. And Scarecrow humoring her repeated requests for stories, one after another through at least one more bottle of dry Tempranillo, while she hung on his every word. Though she could barely recall any of them now.

Theo winced. Pretty sure she'd hung on his shoulder all night, too, as she sank further into intoxication. She had a vague memory of playing with the straw sticking out of his collar. Maybe two bottles after Gwyn left. After the trek to the cemetery to rebury what was left of a dead body. Still no idea what to make of its bizarre warning. Or the fact that she'd bought a house right across the street from a dead Oz character.

Her groan made Scarecrow turn from the window. At once he came over and knelt next to her. "How do you feel?" he asked.

She could tell he was trying to speak quietly. The sound still reverberated through her skull. She groaned again.

Offering her a glass of cool water, he said, "Drink this. I'll bring you some tea."

She forced herself to sit up, drawing the furry purple blanket around her shoulders with a growl, and accepted the glass in both hands, closing her eyes, drinking deeply. Everything tasted like sour wine.

Wait. Tea? How did he know how to make tea?

Theo set the empty glass down and rubbed her face. Her vision improved somewhat though her mood didn't. Scarecrow had vanished.

She'd crashed on the floor, apparently too drunk to go up to her bedroom. Or make it the few steps to the comfy sofa. She glared at the two empty wine bottles on the coffee table. What the hell time was it? Her phone wasn't here. Based on the amount of light coming in from the windows, well after sunrise. Why were the curtains open?

She scowled at the front window. "Fucker, how dare you wake me up," she muttered at the sun.

It did not seem perturbed. The untrimmed shrubs just past the porch railing waved their flaming-red leaves like cheerleaders with pom-poms. She'd always hated cheerleaders. She grunted, sinking back into the throw blanket. Trying to pull it completely over her head left her feet uncovered.

"I never have understood what prompts meat people to drink things which only make them surly the next morning," Scarecrow said. She hadn't even heard him return. Those suede boots were near-silent, without any real weight on them.

Theo grumbled, "Not my fault wine tastes good and eats brain cells."

"I did warn you after the first bottle." He handed her a steaming pottery mug. "I found your pain tea in the cupboard. I hope this will ease your suffering."

Oooh, pain tea. Yes. Theo's greenwitch friend Cassie made a special brew just for her. It eased the occasional flareups from her demon pancreas, an inherited condition which killed one of her great-aunts. She wasn't supposed to drink alcohol at all, but last night had been a lot to cope with. The tea might help her head, and definitely her guts. Theo drank deeply.

Scarecrow tapped the side of his hat. "My brains are working exceptionally well today. I saw your kettle on the big metal square, and the knobs labeled burners." He fiddled with his gloves. "Although I wasn't prepared for invisible fire. Singed myself checking to see if the magic burner was actually working." Two of his suede fingers were dark brown and crusted.

She was fairly sure there were more gloves in the house somewhere. Might need to keep some around all the time, if he continued to have issues with zombies and stovetops.

"Magic burner. Right." She rubbed her eyes and gulped more of the bitter tisane. "I should show you how to use the kitchen. Thank you, Scarecrow."

"You're welcome. Is that any better?"

Theo grunted, wrapping the blanket tighter around her shoulders. The floor was not particularly comfortable. How dare it not be as plush and comfy as her bed?

"I'm sorry I wasn't able to lift you onto the sofa. You seemed unable to stand up. I did try."

Instead he'd covered her with the throw blanket, set a pillow under her head, and apparently kept her company all night. And figured out how to use an unfamiliar appliance just to make her some tea.

Yeah, Dorothy better have appreciated Scarecrow. Theo would stomp over a hundred annoying cheerleaders to win a boyfriend this thoughtful.

"You stayed up all night?" she asked, then realized it was a stupid question. In the books, he'd told Dorothy he didn't require sleep the very first night they were trekking the yellow brick road together. He had, in fact, not really comprehended her need for basic things like sleep and water at first.

He gestured at a pile of books by her reading chair, frowning. "I hoped I might find some useful spell in your grimoires here, but they all seem more focused on centering one's energy or making little charms. Do you keep your secret spell books somewhere else?"

"My secret..." She broke into a chuckle that turned into a cough, and finished off the mug of tea. "Scarecrow, that's it. That's all I know, right there. Those two shelves full of magical books. I keep telling you, witches here aren't like Oz witches." Shaking her head, Theo threw off the blanket and stretched. Cold. Grungy. Tongue all bleh. She needed a shower and something in her stomach, now that her queasiness was quelled. She braced one hand on the coffee table, levering herself up. Scarecrow rose as well, his expression concerned. "I am completely unable to deal right now, okay? Let me get a shower first. Then we can figure out what to do."

"Very well." He extended a hand toward her when she wobbled.

Waving him off, she lurched for the hallway, pulled herself upstairs, and managed to climb into the tub shower without knocking her shin on the side of it for once. Hot water felt wonderful. Scrubbing her hair and skin with her favorite patchouli soap, she began to feel more awake.

The past day felt surreal. She hadn't dreamed the zombie attack, or commanding a legion of tiny creatures of felt and wire to attack the disgusting corpse as best they could. When she'd abandoned them, the battle finished, they'd simply returned to a dormant state. For a few wondrous minutes there, her fingertips tingled with energy. Like touching the ends of a battery with wet hands. Thin golden strings extending from her fingers to each tiny doll. Scarecrow insisted that was all her own magic.

Could she really do that again?

Would she be able to ever again, once Scarecrow returned to Oz?

Her stomach rolled over. She leaned against the shower wall.

A full moon for Halloween excited her only a few days ago. Just the thought of it shining over the black, spindly trees, round and orange as a pumpkin, made her giddy with anticipation. She'd planned to attend Gwyn's Samhain party.

Fucking Gwyn and her ridiculous warning. Dangerous spirits, my fat ass. Scarecrow was about as dangerous as a stalk of dry corn, and he was stuck, if Theo couldn't help him. Once the gorgeous full Halloween moon arrived, he'd fall apart like bunched straw in old clothes. His intelligent blue eyes would go flat and motionless, just paint on burlap. What difference did it make if she could command dolls to fight, if she couldn't save him from that?

Theo shivered, wrapping her arms over her breasts. *No. I can't let that happen. There must be some way we can get him home.*

Of course, if he went home, she'd never see him again. Probably never be able to invoke whatever magic animated her dolls without him here. Definitely never be able again to hug a soft straw body and feel his crinkling, crunkling arms hugging her back.

She wiped water out of her eyes and turned up the heat. Two days' worth of stubble bristled on her legs. Grabbing her razor, she focused on not cutting herself in sheer tired clumsiness.

Half an hour later, dried, dressed, and determined, she chose a rich pumpkin coffee from the pantry and started a pot brewing. The telltale rustle of straw behind her made her smile.

"I'm fixing breakfast. You don't want anything, right?"

Scarecrow shook his head, looking curiously at the gurgling coffeepot. "So you don't actually eat the beans?"

Did they not have coffee in Oz? "No, we grind 'em up and strain boiling water through them. Though you can eat the beans too if you want a rush of caffeine." Theo fixed herself some granola and gestured at the small breakfast counter. "Sit if you want. I need to eat first. Then we can decide what to do next."

Scarecrow sat on one of the two wooden stools at the counter, hands clasped together. "You seem to be feeling better."

"I will be once I've had coffee." She poured pumpkin spice creamer into her favorite Halloween mug. The steam off the coffee made her close her eyes, inhaling deeply. "Hell yes. I love this season."

"This is a special drink for autumn?"

"Coffee is a year-round pleasure. Here." Theo poured a second, smaller mug and set it in front of him.

"Oh, no, thank you, I can't—"

"You don't have to drink it. Just smell it." She raised an eyebrow at him. "You can smell things, right?" If he couldn't with a nose like that, there was a serious design flaw somewhere.

He nodded, leaned over and sniffed. His eyes widened. "Oh. Very nice."

"Right?" Theo plopped her butt onto the seat next to him, wrapping her hands around her mug. Her fingers warmed immediately, and she inhaled the sweet rich fumes again before taking a long gulp of it. The spices made her tongue very happy.

Scarecrow copied her, wrapping long gloved fingers around his mug and sniffing the lovely aromas of pumpkin, cinnamon, allspice, and Costa Rican beans. He smiled.

Theo grinned back. "Let the fumes get into your brains. Maybe the caffeine will spark some brilliance."

"Magic brains don't need enhancement," he said, but kept inhaling the steam anyway.

"Uh huh."

She munched her cereal, studying him. In the sunlight through the kitchen windows, his painted features looked both unrealistic and comfortingly familiar. His eyes didn't bother her anymore. Strands of straw poked out of his hat and the buttoned breast of his tunic. No way anyone would take a long look at him and mistake him for human, but his face conveyed intelligence and curiosity. Dangerous? Absolutely not. Hard to believe he could hurt anyone, ever.

"You ever sing a spell that did some damage?" she asked.

His brows lifted. "Damage?"

"You said you knew some songs that weren't very nice. Like they could be used to attack."

"Oh. Well, in theory."

Theo set down her bowl, staring at him. "In theory? Were you totally bluffing me?"

"It seemed prudent, in case you intended to use dark magic on me," he mumbled.

Theo laughed. "So you *are* capable of lying when you have to!"

"I didn't lie," he argued. "I said I knew some not-so-nice songs. Which I do. They're battle songs, so possibly they could do some damage, as you put it."

"But you haven't tested them."

"I haven't tested most of them," he admitted. "I found out the Prisoner's Lament could heal by accident." He fell silent, gazing at the steam rising from his cup.

Theo waited, but he seemed lost in memory. Didn't seem like it was a good memory, either. His lips flattened in a thin line and his gaze was far away, making him look serious and old.

"How old are you?" she asked. He blinked at her, and she felt heat across her face. "If you don't mind me asking."

"I don't mind. Let me think. I was created in late summer, between First Harvest and Fall Harvest, so if we're going by Oz years, I'm six."

Her jaw dropped. "You look way older than that. Like, thirtyish."

"Is that good or bad?"

"Uh, just really weird. I'm twenty years older than you."

"Is that considered old or young here? I've never met a witch under two hundred before. Surely Lady Gwyn is at least a hundred."

Theo choked on her cereal. She coughed and laughed for so long Scarecrow rose from his seat in obvious alarm. She waved him away, tears running down her face. Grabbing a napkin, she wiped her eyes and mouth and took several deep breaths.

"Older?" he guessed.

She shook her head, still giggling. "No. I don't even know if she'd be pissed or flattered if she heard you say that. She's like fifty."

"Oh." He sat back down, lips pursed. "Time moves differently here. How many moons long is your year?"

"Depends. Lunar calendar doesn't match solar calendar very well. Thirteen or so."

"And how many nights in a moon cycle?"

"Twenty-eight or twenty-nine."

"Comparable," he murmured, nodding. "Yet I don't recognize any of your stars. Very odd. I thought Oz was separated from the Outside lands merely by the deserts."

"The fae rule Oz and the lands around it, right? Ev and Ix and stuff? Are those real?"

"Very real. I've only been to Ev once. Most of my life has been spent in Oz itself. Until now." His voice was quiet.

In some of the Oz books, L. Frank Baum had described Oz as a faery land. Maybe that was closer to the truth than he knew. Theo dredged up what she could recall of old British folklore. "We have stories about how the fae left this world for some underground realm ages ago. The stories say time moves differently there. This one knight was captured by faeries and lived at their court for a while, but when he finally escaped and returned home, a hundred years passed in this world."

"No, it's the other way around. Dorothy went only a few months between her first trip to Oz and her return, yet three and a half years passed for us."

Theo shook her head. "Maybe there's no formula for it. Maybe it's random."

"The two realms must align sometimes. The seasons match right now, at least." He frowned deeply. Theo heard a small pop from under his hat. "It was the dark of the moon when Glinda sent me here, but I noticed it's half-full already in this world."

Theo got up to pour more coffee, taking Scarecrow's mug as well. She brought back a fresh cup for him. If just inhaling the steam was actually helping him think, she'd gladly brew pot after pot of it. "Witches generally don't want to cast anything light and airy during the dark of the moon. That's for hidden things. Secrets."

"She said she would've preferred to send me at the full moon, but some sort of fae event was happening then. Chaotic things."

"Well, Samhain is when the veil between our world and the fae realm is thinnest," Theo explained. "Halloween has always felt magical to me. A night when anything can happen."

Ever since she was a tiny child, Halloween fascinated her. Scary costumes made her wary but not afraid, curious to see where the monsters roaming from house to house were headed. She'd always known some of them must be real, not just other kids in costumes. Convinced if she picked the right one and followed it all night, eventually it would lead her to a magic house in the deep woods, or a fairy door to another world. "Or to your certain death," her brother Danny scoffed when she told him her not-every-costume-is-a-costume theory.

Some of them surely must've been real. Sort of like an actual living scarecrow sitting at her kitchen counter, sniffing pumpkin spice coffee with a nose made of painted, molded burlap.

"Interpreter, please," Scarecrow grumbled.

"Halloween, All Hallows' Eve, Samhain? So in Oz you don't have some kind of end-of-autumn celebration or holy day?"

"Oh. Winter's Eve. Yes. The country folk build enormous bonfires after the last harvest is gathered in." He shuddered. "I can barely stand to see them from the palace. They light up the hills all over Munchkinland and the Quadling country. Ordinary scarecrows are burned on them as offerings for the Fair Ones." He shivered again, clutching his coffee mug tighter. "In the old times, living people were offered up to the fire. At some point that changed to effigies."

Theo reached over and gave his arm a gentle squeeze. "You're a person, not an effigy. No bonfire sacrifices here." Didn't feel like the right time to mention Midwesterners loved bonfires and many houses boasted backyard fire pits, used throughout summer and fall into winter.

He gave her a half-smile. "Thank you."

"So chaos at the full moon at Winter's Eve? Is that normal?" She went back to her granola, head full of cackling witches, faery mounds, and now leaping flames with people dancing around them.

He shook his head. "I know the moon cycle has some significance to spellcasting, but the fae have their own ceremonies which ordinary people aren't allowed to attend. They aren't written down, either. Best not to get mixed up in the Seelie Court affairs." He stared gloomily at his coffee cup. "I've had enough of them, never wanted to get involved in the first place."

"Well, if the border between our world and Oz really is thinnest at Samhain, maybe you can cross back over then?" She grabbed his arm. "Just like in the stories. There has to be some truth to them!"

"Old stories," he said, his voice strengthening. More pins popped under his hat. "Yes. The veil between worlds. Easier to cross from this side to Oz. How did people enter the fae lands from here?"

"Usually carried off by faeries."

He snorted. "Small chance of that. Glinda wanted me gone. I'm sure of it."

"Or what if..." Faery mounds, old Celtic burial mounds. There were ceremonial mounds not far from here, at High Cliff, made centuries ago by ancient tribes. She'd never heard of them opening as doorways to another world, but who knows? "We could try opening a mound! If we can do it on Samhain, maybe there actually will be a door and we can send you home."

"This Samhain occurs on the night of the full moon?"

"This year it does, yeah. Pretty special."

"The night my magic ends."

Theo huffed. "There has to be some way! Some truth to the old legends. Something we can use to help you."

He sat in silence a long moment. Finally he sighed, and turned a smile to her. "You're right. It's worth a try."

"We still have nearly a week. We should explore every option, right?"

"Yes. Yes we should." His smile widened. "Thank you, Theo. I shouldn't give up *all* hope just because I'll never..." He sighed again. "Perhaps it's for the best. I'm only a scarecrow, and she's—was—a meat person. I just wish I'd been able to see her again. To help her. Thinking of her trapped in that terrible place the rest of her days...."

"I know," Theo said. "I know. I'm so sorry, Scarecrow. I'm sure she thought about you too. All she talked about was Oz. She told your stories to the author L. Frank Baum, who wrote a ton of books about the place. Even if he made up half of it, they're wonderful. I bet her diary is full of stories about you and Nick and everyone."

He stared at her. "What?"

So much for cheering him up. As usual she'd simply blabbered out the first thing on her mind and made things worse instead of better. "I shouldn't even be talking about her. Goddess bless, you must be hurting so bad, and I wasn't even thinking, Scarecrow."

"No, you said a diary. Dorothy kept a diary? Why didn't you mention this before?"

"The article I showed you mentioned it. Apparently it was just rediscovered this year."

His shoulders tensed, his body motionless.

She explained, "It's sitting in a museum in Kansas right now. On display through the end of the month. I didn't know if you'd read that far on the web page."

"I did not," he whispered. Tears glistened in his eyes. "Dorothy's diary. Her last recorded words."

"Would you like to read it?"

He hesitated, wiping a glove across his cheeks, eyes focused on nothing.

"Nobody's going to judge you for not wanting to," Theo promised. "I won't. I can only imagine how much it would hurt you to—"

"Can you take me there. To Kansas." His voice was so quiet it wasn't even a question, as if he were preparing himself to be denied this.

"Yes," Theo replied. "Fuck yes. If that's what you want. Of course."

He looked at her with such obvious pain and gratitude she wanted to crush him in a hug and cast a spell to make all the pain go away. Maybe sing that creepy prison song for him, if she could remember the words right.

"Thank you, Theo. You are a true friend. I'm grateful I met you."

"Oh Scarecrow." She threw both arms around him, careful not to squish him too badly. His straw crinkled and rustled and he was so goddamn soft. His arms went around her and hugged back strongly, surprising her. Dammit, now she was crying too. "Of course we'll go see it, if you really want to."

"Can we get there and come back in time for the full moon?"

How far was Kansas, anyway? Geography wasn't her strong suit. "I think so. Come on."

They hurried to the studio. The web page about Dorothy's sad ending was still on her desktop when Theo woke up the computer. She tapped the screen. "There's where they talk about the diary. Hey, maybe some Oz fan already posted it online. Let's see." She tried a search for *Dorothy Gale diary,* but the only relevant result was the same article. "Of course it wouldn't be that easy. All right. Road trip it is."

Scarecrow watched her type and scroll. "You simply put in the words for anything you wish to know and this scrying-glass shows you?" At her shrug, he shook his head with a wry smile. "And you say your world has no magic in it."

"Advanced tech the same thing as magic, famous sci fi quote something something," Theo laughed.

He raised a brow at her.

"Don't look at me like that. It's just science and computers and stuff. Not magic like Oz magic."

"This is useful magic. Why do you keep paper books at all when you have such a library as this?"

Theo shrugged. "I actually prefer real books. I like touching them while I read. I like the smell of old pages."

He was standing right at her shoulder, leaning over to read with her. Close up, his scent filled her nose. Straw, she realized, smelled a lot like old books.

Very pleasantly like.

I'm looking up the diary of his dead lost love and suddenly noticing again how nice he smells. Goddess, get a grip, girl.

Shaking off her embarrassment, she pointed at the map on the screen. "Hey, it's not too far. One day's drive to this museum. Wamego, Kansas. We can drive there overnight, see the diary tomorrow." She tapped her fingers on the desk. "I'm sure it's locked up behind glass. Maybe we can say we're scholars writing a paper or something. Get you access. I should probably get us a hotel room. Rooms. You figure we'll be there a couple days, so you can read all of it, right?"

"How many volumes is this diary? My excellent brains enable me to read faster than many meat people."

Theo smiled. "Of course they do. The point isn't how fast you can read it, the point is you're going to want time to absorb it. Trust me on this."

"Oh. Yes, I see." He appeared to mull this over.

Theo found her phone on one of the studio tables. At least it still had a decent charge despite being unplugged all night. She pulled up Wamego hotels. Wamego was a fairly small town, smaller than Appleton for sure. Not many listings. She picked the motel with the most star ratings and called it. "Hi, can I get a reservation for tomorrow night, please?"

The front desk clerk informed her they were booked solid through the next weekend. Theo glanced at Scarecrow. He was studying the map on the computer. Bet this wasn't at all how he'd envisioned a trip to Kansas. Wrong century, wrong state. She tried the next listed motel only to be told they too were full up.

"It's the festival, of course," the clerk said brightly. "We have rooms available next week, though."

"What festival?"

"Oztoberfest. You know, with the Oz Museum. People book rooms a year ahead of time," the clerk offered unhelpfully.

Great. Delaying the trip was impossible. If the High Cliff ceremonial mounds could be used as doorways, they'd need to be here in time to try on Samhain, not three or four states away. Assuming she could keep Scarecrow from falling apart before the faery doors opened. Just her stupid luck all the rooms in Tiny Museum Town, Kansas, would be taken right now because of some stupid—

Oz festival.

Totally focused on all things Oz.

Probably with plenty of cosplayers. Dorothies, Wicked Witches, and Scarecrows filling the streets.

"Oh my Goddess, this is perfect."

"What is?"

"There's a festival going on. Right now, where the diary is. An Oz festival."

He blinked. "People here pay tribute to Oz? To the Court, or the Fair Ones in general? I thought you said your people regarded all that as imaginary."

"No no no, a *'Wizard of Oz'* festival."

"So he did make it back to Kansas," Scarecrow mused. "How old is he now?"

Theo resisted the urge to smack him. "No! I'm talking about a festival celebrating the books and the movies. Here." Her fingers danced across the keyboard. On the festival's home page up she scrolled though photographs, lists of performances, and craft vendors. "Check it out. You'll blend right in. We won't have to worry about awkward cover stories or anything."

"That's supposed to be me?" he demanded, pointing to an actor in one of the photos from the previous year's costume contest. "I'm nowhere near so stuffed."

"Totally missing the point. I just need to find us someplace to stay. Maybe we could sleep in the car. If the cops don't bust us for vagrancy." She called the other two listed motels, which also had no vacancies. The only thing left was an RV campground.

Her family's old RV was parked in a storage yard. Possibly. It'd been years since they went on any kind of a camping trip together. Theo was seventeen on the last summer trip. Her brother Danny enjoyed the vacations way more than Theo, collecting souvenirs at the various parks and campgrounds. Per her dad, the whole point was to "get out in Nature," but they'd barely paused at any of the natural wonders which they traveled for days to see. Dad only wanted a photo op at each, maybe a quick browse of the gift shop, and they were back on the road to cram in as many tourist attractions as possible in a week's time. At every gift shop he checked to see what toys they were selling, and whether Van Baum Toys made any of them. Pathetic.

Danny had asked to keep the camper when her parents decided its family vacation days were over. Last she heard, he intended to renovate it. Replace the perpetually-troublesome radiator. Install better plumbing. No idea what kind of shape it was in, or if it was still running.

"I don't sleep," Scarecrow reminded her. "You don't have to worry about my comfort. I'm fine just standing in a corner."

"That is the saddest thing you've said yet," Theo sighed. "Quiet a sec, lemme think."

She'd never driven the RV, but she'd driven Arturo's old pickup truck once, when he and Adam helped her move into this house. How hard could it be? There must be videos online she could watch. The tricky part would be asking Danny to borrow it.

She rubbed her nose and sighed. "Well, shit. I guess you're gonna have to meet my brother."

"This is a bad thing?"

"Maybe, maybe not. Let me call him. The sooner I get this over with, the sooner we can get on the road."

Scarecrow nodded and went back to the map. His gaze seemed unfocused, one hand knuckled at his lips, deep in thought. No doubt pondering Dorothy's sad fate. Well, she couldn't time travel, but at least she could get him to Kansas.

Mood sinking, she called Danny, forcing cheer into her voice. "Hey, bro, how's it going?"

"Not bad. I'm driving, Theo. What do you need?" Danny immediately sounded wary.

"Is the RV drivable?"

"Yes, I used it for a softball game two weeks ago. Why?"

"I need it. Can you bring me the keys?"

"What do you need it for?"

"Road trip, duh." Theo thought fast. "There's a big craft fair going on in Kansas and I wanted to go with some friends."

"Kansas? Which friends?" Danny asked.

"Sue and Gwyn," Theo lied. "And a new friend."

"Sounds crowded."

"The camper sleeps four."

Danny sighed. Theo could picture his frown. "Theo, you've never even driven the RV. Why aren't you asking Mom and Dad about this? I'm sure Dad could loan you money for a plane ticket."

"Because they'll say no, or make excuses why I shouldn't go. I am twenty-goddamn-six, Danny. I am old enough to travel to promote my art. Dad goes on road trips for work all the time. He just doesn't see my dolls as an actual career, and I'm really tired of him dismissing what I want to do with my life just because it doesn't fit with what he wanted for me, and—"

"Oh my God, enough, Theo. Okay, I get it, fine."

"So you'll bring the keys over today?"

Danny hemmed and hawed. "Does it have to be today? I'm kinda busy. Margie has a church group dinner here tonight. I just picked up a cheese tray and I'm getting ice for the sodas."

Danny was insufferable enough. His wife Margie was always bright, cheerful, and perfectly made-up. As if no deeper emotion ever penetrated her brain and everything was always sunny no matter what the circumstances. She had to be an alien.

"Oh, no, sure, I get it. You have a life. Which doesn't include your little sister."

Scarecrow raised one eyebrow. Theo ignored him.

"I mean it's not like you can just drop everything to run over here on a moment's notice. It's cool. How about I swing by, then?"

"You're coming by? Today?"

"Sure, why not? You always say I don't spend any time with Margie." Theo grinned. "Hey, I have a fabulous idea! Why don't I bring my friends over to this church supper thing? You know, foster friendship between religions and all that. We can even bring stuff for a house blessing. I bet your place really needs one by now."

"No. Theo, no. Are you home right now?"

"Well, yeah, but if I need to pick up some food to bring by your place, I'll have to get out to the store quick."

"Stay there. I'll bring you the keys."

"Oh." Theo tried to sound surprised. "Okay. You sure? I don't want to be a bother."

There was a pause, then Danny muttered, "Very funny. I'm already at the Kwik-Trip. I'll see you in a few minutes."

"Okay, buh-bye!" Theo hung up and burst into laughter.

Scarecrow stared at her.

She shook her head. "Consider that lesson one in manipulating your family. There's absolutely no way Danny wants my witchy friends at his perfect wife's church supper. Even if we brought Jell-O salad." She grabbed his hands. "We're going on an Oz road trip! Woo hoo!"

"It has been some time since I went on any happy adventures," he admitted. His pronunciation of the word as *advenchuhs* made her smile. "Ones that didn't end up endangering me or my friends, at least."

His friends. "Did you use the song about rocks to recharge your phone-stone yet?"

"Not yet. Last night I didn't want to wake you, and I didn't wish to leave you alone and unguarded." His face drooped. "I've been negligent. If it's all right with you, I'd very much like to try to reach Nick."

So he stayed near her the whole time she slept. Feeling warm, she clasped his hands in hers. "Thank you. Yeah, please, go for it."

"I don't know how he'll take the news about Dorothy," Scarecrow said, picking up the pink Evstone from Theo's desk. "He enjoyed our journeys with her almost as much as I did, and his heart's always been more attuned to emotion than mine. How can I tell him I've failed, and our Dorothy is gone?"

The moisture beading in his eyes made it clear his heart was every bit as affected as the Tin Woodman's would be. Theo rubbed his shoulder, unsure if he'd accept a hug right now. He looked lost. "You didn't fail. Nothing you could've done."

"And what of my abandoning my post as Royal Advisor?" he demanded. "How can I atone for that?"

Theo took a deep breath. "I'm sure Nick will forgive you, right? Look, we'll find a way." She handed him a tissue. He nodded thanks, wiping his eyes. "Make with the singing. You can do this."

He cupped the Evstone in one hand, frowning. "I don't know if this will work. You might want to cast a protection spell or something, just in case there are unexpected effects."

Theo rolled her eyes. "Not that—"

"—kind of witch," he finished with her.

She did take a few steps away from him. Just in case.

Hesitantly at first, Scarecrow began singing. The melody was wistful but light. Theo could easily imagine an Irish fiddle accompanying him, and wished she knew how to play an instrument at all. Before he'd finished the first verse, the Evstone started glowing. Encouraged, his voice gained strength and volume. He paused, took a breath, and sang in English:

> *"The stones of my land lie still and cold*
> *Over the bones of my clan.*
> *Seven miles deep they mined the gold*
> *Through the ages of faery and man.*
>
> *Built they a tower of stone and blood*
> *High up on the highest hill,*
> *Miners and masons did best they could*
> *And stony they lie there still."*

The Evstone gleamed brightly. Theo shielded her eyes. Scarecrow gazed at it, unaffected by the light, a smile spreading across his face at last. "It worked! I can contact Nick!"

"Awesome!" Theo suddenly remembered, "Wait, Danny'll be here any minute."

On cue, a knock sounded at the front door.

"Shit. Hide the glowy stone, please. And just be chill."

"I don't really experience cold or heat," he said, clearly puzzled. He tucked the stone away in a pocket.

"Just…" Theo raised both hands to him, pleading, then hurried to answer the door.

Her brother stood on the porch, arms crossed in his sweater-vest. Theo smiled. "Hey, Danny. I see you're stylin' as ever." His khakis had crisp creases and his loafers were barely worn. "Rocking the suburban dad look even without a kid. Nice."

Danny came in, scowling. Theo was glad her friends had cleaned the entire first floor. No dust or clutter for her brother to gripe about.

"You sure you can drive the RV? Have you ever practiced at all?" he asked.

"Yeah, sure. No big deal. You bring the keys?"

He tugged a ring of them from a pants pocket. Theo did her best not to make grabby hands at him while he carefully unhooked the RV keys from his ring. "Wow, you have the key to every prison cell. How does it even fit in your pocket?"

Danny frowned. "I have keys to the boat and to Mom and Dad's house in case of an emergency. They count on me to be responsible for things."

Ouch. Theo scowled. "Can I just have the keys, please? Promise I'll gas it up before I bring it back."

"Kansas, huh?" Danny shook his head. "I remember us going through there once when we were kids. Lots of boring prairie and corn fields. Do you remember?"

"Not really." Theo's eyes remained on the keys, impatient. "Thanks so much for bringing them by, Danny, I really appreciate it."

"So who're you going with?" He walked toward the open studio doorway, then froze.

"Hello," said Scarecrow, coming forward. He smiled mildly at Danny. "You must be Theo's brother."

"Yeah. I'm Danny. And you are?"

"Scarecrow. Very pleased to make your acquaintance." Scarecrow bowed.

Great. So much for the rest of her family remaining ignorant of his presence at all.

Danny eyed Scarecrow. "You're going on this road trip?"

The straw man nodded. "There's a festival. An Oz festival." He shot a questioning glance at Theo.

"Yep. The craft fair is part of it. Lots of fantasy fans with disposable income, perfect market for some art dolls, right?" Unable to contain her impatience any longer, she nabbed the keys from Danny's fingers. "Thanks again, bro. Tell Margie I said blessed be." She gave her brother her widest, sunniest smile, grabbed his elbow, and propelled him toward the front door.

He stopped with one hand on the doorknob, leaning down to whisper heatedly to Theo, "Who the hell is this guy and what are you up to?"

"He's my friend, and he's coming along. To, uh, help me sell my dolls. I'm doing a whole Land of Oz line." Never mind that her drawings were toast.

"Oh. So the costume is a publicity thing to sell dolls for you?"

"Yep," Theo said brightly.

"Huh. I didn't think you'd ever go for more conventional toy designs. Listen, I know you think I don't like your art, and there's some truth to that. But Theo, I've always thought you had talent, if only you'd put it to better use. I hope you know that."

Theo felt heat in her cheeks. *Better use? You didn't see my dolls holding a damned zombie at bay, bro.*

"You know, if your Oz dolls do well at this festival, you should talk to Dad about producing a whole line of them. He might go for it."

There it was. The periodic reminder that Dad wanted her to make dolls only if they were suitable for a ready-made market of happy consumers. That he'd only accept Theo's art as a proper career if she actually made steady money at it. "Hey, thanks, bro. Tell Dad I really appreciate his vote of semi-confidence now that I'm doing something more conventionally acceptable."

Danny scowled. "Theo—"

"No, it's cool. I'll be sure to let him know what kinds of toys the vendors are selling, too, so maybe next year he can wheedle the local stores into taking a shipment of his mass-produced bean-bags or cheap plastic crap." Theo flung open the front door. "Thanks for the keys. I'll bring it back in one piece. Better get back to your church supper. I'm sure Margie's already talking to her friends about her husband's needy little sister. Wouldn't want you to keep her waiting and speculating what I did wrong this time."

"Theo, wait." Danny raised his hands, then frowned. "No. Forget it. I'm not getting pulled into your drama with Dad again. Go do your 'art.'" He made air quotes with his fingers. "Have fun at your craft fair." He shot a scowl back down the hall at Scarecrow. "And be safe."

He stomped out. Theo shut the door.

Scarecrow shook his head. "Theo, I have only limited experience with family quarrels, but—"

"That's right," she snapped. "Just stay out of it, Scarecrow." She stormed upstairs to pack.

All her life, Danny was upheld as a model for Theo. How she should behave. How she should dress. How she should think in order to gain the approval of her very traditional parents. Dad especially.

Her dolls were valuable, damn it. Unique. She put all her heart and dark dreams into each of them. She'd won juried exhibitions in college. She'd sold a few to collectors around the world. Her art mattered. Her art was *good*. But no, Dad couldn't comprehend anything which wasn't gobbled up by masses of children with parents willing to buy them the latest toy fad. Bet the Van Baum Toy Company's latest silicone, realistic infant dolls couldn't stop an attacking chipmunk, much less an undead corpse.

Theo took a deep breath. Another. Forced herself to calm down.

Silence downstairs. She'd snapped at Scarecrow, and he'd done nothing wrong. He believed in her talents more than her own family did.

Guilt flooded her stomach in the wake of anger. Her mouth tasted sour again and her throat burned. Great. Getting all worked up by the same stupid argument all over again with Danny.

Screw Danny. She had a road trip to pack for. She chewed a couple of antacids and tossed clothes into a duffel bag. She grabbed a couple of blankets from the hall closet just in case she'd need them in the RV. Once satisfied she had all necessary items from her closet and the bathroom, she stomped downstairs, forcing cheer. Not every day she could go on a road trip with a walking straw man.

At the foot of the stairs, she heard voices down the hall. Couldn't make out the words, but that was definitely Scarecrow talking to someone with a smoother, milder voice. Melodic, like some old crooner. Bing Crosby maybe. Curious, she went to the studio.

Scarecrow stood near her desk, his cupped hands holding a pink glow from which the voice emanated. As Theo came closer, she saw the flickering image of a man with a steely jaw and a funnel-like hat cocked at an angle, hovering just above the bright surface of the Evstone.

Not a steely jaw, she realized. A tin jaw. The man's silvery eyes rolled like ball bearings in her direction. Holy crap. Was that the Tin Woodman?

"Oh. Good day," the metal man said. He dabbed at his eyes with a handkerchief. Scarecrow must've broken the sad news to him.

Scarecrow turned, surprised. "Oh! Theo. Ah. This is my friend Nick Chopper. Nick, this is Theo, the witch I was telling you about. She's taking me to Kansas."

The Tin Woodman made a very courtly bow, his silvery body flashing in reflected light. "Very gracious of you, Lady Theo. Scarecrow tells me you've been an enormous help to him. Thank you for taking such good care of my friend." Nick Chopper's voice had an accent like some New England aristocrat's. Theo suddenly envisioned him strolling the boardwalk at a turn-of-the-century coastal summer resort, clad in a striped linen suit.

"Well, he's been taking care of me," Theo replied, coming closer. The hologram image above the stone smiled at her. She looked from Nick to Scarecrow. "You tell him everything?"

Scarecrow nodded.

"So Dorothy left a diary." Nick shook his head. "I am so very, very sorry, my friend. I hope when you read it..." he trailed off. "Well. At any rate, I wish you both a safe journey."

"Thank you, Nick," Scarecrow said. "I'll get back if I'm able. Please tell Ozma Tip I am sincerely sorry."

"We'll get Scarecrow home," Theo spoke up. "We're researching old legends about burial-mound doorways on Sa—Winter's Eve," she corrected herself, recalling Scarecrow's term for the late harvest festival. "And whatever songs he might know that could help. Anything you can find out on your side would be great."

Nick Chopper nodded gravely. "I'll do whatever I can. But Scarecrow, things here have taken a very bad turn. The Seelie Court is plotting to remove Ozma from the throne, and worse," his voice quieted, "it seems our Lady in Pink has been recruiting members of the Unseelie Court as well."

"The Unseelie Court? Aren't those, like, monsters?" Theo recalled tales about the dark members of the fae, creatures who actively hated and even hunted humans. Things that would do much worse than capture a baby to raise it as a pet, or make a strapping young lad dance in magic slippers until he dropped dead.

"We don't talk about them," Scarecrow murmured, eyes wide. "Nick, are you certain?"

"Professor Wogglebug was able to capture what was said at a secret meeting of the Seelie Court with a new gadget of his. What we heard was absolutely chilling." Nick grimaced. "Tip heard it too. They have some plot underway to regain control of the lands they've lost. And the Pink Witch is at the head of it all."

The Pink Witch. Our Lady in Pink. Of course. They were talking about Glinda, the so-called Good Witch. In the books she dressed all in red, but who else could it be? "I never trusted that bitch," Theo growled. "Stringing Dorothy along when all the time she could've just tapped her heels and wished herself home."

"You've told her about that?" Nick asked.

Scarecrow shrugged. "They have books here, Nick. Someone wrote children's tales out of our adventures, it seems."

"I wouldn't tell those stories to my own children," Nick exclaimed.

Theo crossed her arms, scowling. "Glinda's a bitch, the fae are twisted, and I'm gonna get Scarecrow back safe to Oz if it kills me."

Scarecrow smiled at her.

Nick nodded. "Thank you, Lady Theo. I can see he's found a true friend there. I'm grateful." Strength returned to his voice. "We don't know much yet, only that they're planning to move at some faerie ceremony called Sowing." He frowned. "Sowham. I don't know, but we need—"

A chill went down Theo's back. "Samhain?"

Nick perked. "Yes, that's it. Do you know the ceremonies of the fae, Lady Theo?"

"Samhain is also Halloween. Your Winter's Eve. The night when the doorway between worlds can open. There might be a way then to send Scarecrow home."

Nick's heavy brows rose. "No wonder she talked about chaos at the full moon. That's when they're going to attempt a coup!"

Scarecrow closed his eyes, pinching the bridge of his nose. "Everything all at once. Of course that's why she sent me here, so I'd be out of the way when it happens. Nick, did they say anything else? Who else is involved? Is it the entire Court?"

"It's safe to say we don't trust any fae at this point. We have to assume every witch and courtier is part of the plot." Nick looked at Theo. "Present company excepted."

"Is Ozma safe?" Scarecrow asked.

"For the time being. Lion and Tiger are stuck to her like furry glue. The Wogglebug is trying to coax more information out of the courtiers he's friendly with, although I wouldn't blame him for never speaking to any of them ever again. So far the Pink Witch is acting like everything's perfectly normal."

Scarecrow frowned. "Why would she treat with the Unseelie Court? Everyone knows they're savage and untrustworthy. And she has enough magic herself to make Ozma disappear." He rubbed his chin, then asked in a hopeful tone, "Unless Ozma Tip is finally employing her own faery powers?"

Nick shook his head. "Not really. She's not allowed to learn much. If we could only get into the forbidden library, she might—"

"Oh," Scarecrow said brightly. "There's a tunnel to it from my room."

Theo would give anything to have a room with a secret tunnel to a forbidden library.

This was clearly news to the Woodman. "What? Why didn't you tell me?"

"Well, I only went through it once. It's through the fireplace, and unfortunately it comes out in the fireplace in the forbidden library as well. So I avoided it after nearly blundering right into the flames." He shivered. "I could see the bookshelves, though."

Nick pressed articulated metal cylinder-fingers to his forehead. "How do I open the secret passage?" he asked, his voice tight.

"You just—" The image flickered out over the Evstone. Scarecrow clasped the rock tightly. "Nick? Can you still hear me?"

Abruptly the Tin Woodman's face loomed close in the magic transmission. "Can't talk. I'll call to you later," Nick whispered harshly.

"Why my dear Woodman, how are you today?" a voice trilled. The sound immediately put Theo's teeth on edge. The Evstone went dark, inert. A lump of rhodochrosite on a small chain.

"Was that—?"

"Glinda," Scarecrow confirmed.

"I'll pull her eyelashes out if she so much as sneers at your friends," Theo snarled, fingers curling into fists.

Scarecrow shuddered. "Theo, you don't know how powerful she is. She could burn me alive with a flick of her wrist. All the other witches of Oz live in terror of her. Ozma is only on the throne because Glinda said she should be. She's what stopped the war."

Fresh chills went down Theo's arms. "She's really that powerful?"

"She truly is. I have no idea what the limits of her magic are." He shuddered all over, rustling loudly. "I'm pretty sure she only kept me around because I amused her."

Theo stared at him. Fear was plain in his eyes, his stuffed body trembling.

Glinda *did* things to him.

How dare that fucking bitch.

"You're saying she could overthrow Ozma all by herself? Kill your friends and not break a sweat doing it?"

Scarecrow winced. "Very likely. I don't know why she even allows Ozma Tip to sit on the throne."

"Hold up. If she's really all that, and she's plotting to take over Oz, what does she need the Unseelie Court for? Why go to a bunch of untrustworthy creeps if she could get the job done all by herself?"

"I—" He blinked, stammered, sat down on the stool by her desk. "I don't know. You're right, Theo. It makes no sense."

"Why does she have to wait for Samhain? Why not just take control, if she's such a badass?"

He shook his head helplessly.

He wasn't scared for himself, she realized, no matter how much the witch terrified him. He was afraid for Nick. For the girl, Queen Ozma. His friends back in Oz.

She closed her hands over his. "We'll figure it out. We'll get you home."

If Oz was even a safe place for him anymore.

He took a deep breath, cupping the Evstone tightly in his palm a moment, then tucked it back in his trouser pocket. "Maybe there's a reason Glinda didn't send me to Dorothy, but calculated a time when she'd already be—gone. Perhaps Dorothy knew something which threatens the Seelie Court."

"Maybe there's something in the diary to help you get home. What if Dorothy left some clue we can use?"

"Dorothy did say she wished terribly hard to return to Oz," Scarecrow said slowly, blinking. "Perhaps she unwittingly called upon some magic she didn't know she possessed, to conjure a storm to reach us the second time."

Theo grinned. "I bet that pink bitch didn't count on your girl leaving behind some notes."

"Perhaps not," he murmured, his eyes searching her face.

Goddess bless, she'd do anything to fix this. To give him some hope.

She quieted. "Do you still want to read it?"

"Very much so," Scarecrow said. "Of course, to see if she wrote down how she managed to get back to Oz. More than that...I feel strangely about it. As though it would hurt me not to read it, now I know it exists." He rubbed his chin, frowning. "It makes no sense. She's—she's gone. Why would I need so badly to see it?"

"Because you love her."

"Is this what love is?" He sighed. "This is more Nick's area of expertise. I'm not really sure how to do any of it."

If he was as obsessed with his brains as the fictional Scarecrow of Oz was in the books, she was honestly shocked he'd come all this way. "Why didn't you just ask Glinda or someone to magic away your feelings so you could get back to doing your research or whatever?"

His head jerked up, staring at her. "I—I never thought of that."

"Would you, if you could? Would it be better if you didn't feel any of this?"

There were parts of her life Theo would much rather not feel anything about. Not remember. Sneering mean girls in middle school, mocking Theo for her thick thighs and shyness. High school classmates laughing at her black dresses and dark eyeliner. College boys who assumed she was getting drunk because she wanted them to do sweaty, fleeting things to her body, rather than because she was nervous at parties and the alcohol helped remove the fear. And of course, every disappointed, disapproving look or word her parents had ever given her.

Scarecrow frowned. "No," he replied at last. "Nick told me once he was grateful for the suffering his heart endured, because it meant he could still feel. Perhaps there's truth in that. I feel loss. Emptiness. But when I was with her, I was happy." He shrugged. "Nick says I do have a heart, I've just never thought it of much consequence. He must be right, and my neglecting it has made me defenseless against this—whatever this is. This love-pain."

"Well, if it helps, meat people all have hearts and we're still pretty stupid when it comes to love."

"You've experienced this," he noted, his eyes locked on hers.

She swallowed, ducking her head. Those dark blue eyes saw too much, despite being painted on. She smacked Scarecrow's shoulder, nearly knocking him off the stool. Whoops. He was so ridiculously light. "Come on, you. There's a diary waiting for us in Kansas."

"Yes," he said hesitantly, then gave her a firm nod, smiling at last. "Yes. Absolutely. There must be something we're meant to find."

"Soooo...road trip?"

He smiled. "Road trip!"

19

L oading up and backing the RV out of its parking spot in the storage lot took a lot longer than Theo expected, and by the time she steered the lumbering camper onto the interstate, traffic was crazy. She'd completely forgotten it was Monday. Should've waited until later to even start out, but she wasn't turning around at this point. Turning the damned whale at all was difficult enough. Pretty sure she'd scraped the paint getting the thing through the storage yard gates.

Scarecrow explored the interior of the RV while she foraged for road snacks at a convenience store. He was curious about everything. While she could understand that, given how different Oz must be, she'd flatly insisted he stay in the camper while she went to buy salt-and sugar-laden noms. When she returned to the RV, she found the trundle bed pulled out, cabinets open, and Scarecrow rummaging through the bedroom area.

"Remarkably clever." He nodded at the various pulled-out drawers. "This is almost as good as a magic tent, and a far sight better than our cramped accommodations aboard the flying Gump."

Theo dumped the bags of snacks next to the driver's seat and started closing everything he'd opened. "Glad you approve, but all this needs to be stowed before we can get on the highway."

"It truly has everything! I'll be able to make your tea right there." He pointed at the mini stove in the kitchenette. "I can sit over here," the banquette bench, "and read while you sleep, there's room for other travelers we might meet along the way, and it even has an armory."

"We are *not* picking up hitchhikers," Theo said firmly. "No extra guests on this trip."

"I've found every journey tends to accumulate travelers as one goes."

"Scarecrow, we're more likely to run into axe murderers than friendly Munchkins." Something else he'd said finally hit her. "Wait. What armory?"

He held up an aluminum baseball bat. "Admittedly a very small armory, but this should be capable of defending us. If I'm able to wield it."

He let the batting end drop to the floor with a half-smile. "I really wish some days I possessed Nick's strength. Although I can't imagine being made of anything but straw. Being all metal would be terribly hard and uncomfortable."

Theo took the bat. It had Danny's initials on it. A mitt and knee pads lay on the closet floor. "This is Danny's softball gear. Guess he left it in here after his last game with the guys." She hefted the bat and tried a swing, checking it before she whacked the wall in the cramped bedroom nook. A decade had passed since she'd bothered with sports at all, but she could boast a handful of home runs in middle school games. Dad encouraged her to try sports throughout school, buying ridiculous amounts of gear in an effort to keep Theo active. Theo enjoyed softball and hockey pick-up games, but not enough to compete for a varsity team spot. Mom remarked hockey wasn't the most feminine sport. Dad asked her why she didn't take up tennis or swimming instead.

As if she'd ever display her generous ass and thighs in a skimpy skort or a swimsuit in public. She endured enough peer mockery throughout school, almost always assigned the part of the class weirdo. She didn't need more body-shaming on top of that.

Theo shoved the bat back into the closet. As she slapped the door hard to fasten it closed, she noticed the open bathroom was missing a toilet. *Really, Danny? Could've warned me you were nowhere near done renovating this piece of crap. Well, whatever, that's what fast food places are for.*

"Come on, help me close everything up. As slow as this monster goes it'll be over twelve hours driving. I just want to get on the road."

Scarecrow nodded and shut the rest of the things he'd opened. "Thank you, Theo."

She smiled. "All good."

Once at cruising speed, she tweaked the side mirror angles. The RV chugged along reasonably well, though it was sluggish to respond to her foot on the gas pedal. This wasn't so bad, on the interstate at least. "Think I'm getting the hang of it."

"What animal moves the wheels?" he asked. "It sounds big, whatever it is. I can hear it growling."

"Combustion engine."

He frowned. "Combustion?"

"It burns gasoline to turn the whatevers. Not really my area of expertise."

"I wish I were staying long enough to finally learn all the words you use." He tapped his fingers together, studying the hood warily. "It burns? I assume safely contained well away from this cabin?"

"In there, under the hood. You're safe."

He nodded, clearly not wholly reassured.

The famous film had invented the scene where the witch threw a fireball at Scarecrow. That wasn't in the book. The only time he'd come close to being burned in the literary Oz series was when he'd been tied to a stake and a fire lit under him by King Krewl of Jinxland, in the book *The Scarecrow of Oz*. He'd been saved only by the intervention of a flock of giant friendly birds, the Orks.

If any of that even happened. "Were you ever almost burned at the stake?"

"Crows and blight, no! How horrible."

"Really wish I knew how much of the books was true. You had all kinds of wild adventures in them."

He shrugged. "It sounds as though many of the stories were spun from thin air." He turned quiet and thoughtful. "I wonder how much Dorothy told this children's author of yours. How much she left out. The part about me killing the witch's crows was left in?"

"Yeah. You guys were on your way to get the witch's broom. She saw you coming with her one good eye and sent forty wolves, forty crows, a swarm of hornets, and a bunch of Winkie soldiers to stop you."

Scarecrow nodded slowly, gazing out at the sunny sky. "That's true. We slaughtered them all. They'd have killed us otherwise. If she hadn't sent the flying monkeys, we might've made it to her tower unharmed."

"Wait. You slaughtered them all? I thought the Winkie soldiers were frightened off by the Lion's roar."

He raised an eyebrow. "The Winkie Elite Guard were the toughest of the tough. It took Lion and Nick fighting together to kill the brigade she sent to attack us."

"Oh." Baum definitely left that part out. "What did Dorothy do?"

"I protected her." Scarecrow's expression was grave. "Their spears couldn't hurt me. I kept between them and her. It was frightening, but over fairly quickly once Lion was able to maneuver." He sighed. "I don't know if they were too afraid of the witch to give up the fight, or if they were only concerned about their reputation. Everyone hears stories of the atrocities the Winkie Elites committed during the war."

In the book, the Winkie people were timid by nature and only obeyed the Wicked Witch of the West through fear. The stories were definitely whitewashed. What about the sweeter elements in the series, though?

"Did you ever meet Scraps, the Patchwork Girl?"

"Who?"

"So that would be a no. Damn. I liked her."

"This is another character in the books?"

"Yes. She was a girl made of a patchwork quilting and cotton stuffing. She was made to be a servant but was really more of a free spirit. Created by Dr. Pipt's wife—the guy who made the Powder of Life."

"Ah. Dr. Pipt I haven't heard of, but the Powder of Life was real. A Dr. Nikidikt made it and some amazing Wishing Pills as well." His mouth quirked into a half-smile. "When I learned of this sorcerer, I wondered if perhaps his magic was what animated me, but after the war it was difficult to track people down. So many died, or fled, or changed their names if they were wanted by the fae for alleged crimes. I never did locate him, and the farmer who constructed me swore he used no magic. Swore it under torture. Perhaps the feed-sack which he used for my head had some sort of magic spilled on it by accident. Impossible to know now."

"Wait. The farmer who built you was tortured?"

"Locasta brought him in to interrogate him. Once she was sure he was just an ignorant peasant, not secretly practicing magic—which of course the commoners aren't allowed to do—she tossed him out instead of killing him. He was lucky." He frowned. "When I returned to the Palace as Ozma Tip's advisor, I asked her to compensate the poor man from the royal treasury. She did." He regarded Theo directly. "What's this about a girl made of a patchwork quilt? Is she significant? Mind you, it's entirely possible such a creature exists in Oz. The one constant is that Oz is always wilder and more surprising than you think."

"Yeah, she's significant to you, anyway. You both had an immediate crush when you met," Theo explained. She felt heat in her cheeks, and tried to focus on the road ahead.

Scarecrow laughed. "Oh, I see. So your children's author decided I could only be suited for romance with another stuffed being."

Well damn. It did seem pretty insulting when he put it like that. "Um. Yeah, I guess. Up 'til that point you didn't seem interested in anyone."

"Not even Dorothy?" he asked, mirth vanishing.

"No. Remember, in the books, she's a child."

He fell silent, clasping his hands together in his lap and staring at his gloves.

"Come on, the books were intended for kids. Kids don't care about romance, they want adventure and thrills." The implication was ugly-clear. Since Baum hadn't mentioned any hint of romance between Dorothy and Scarecrow, and portrayed Dorothy as a preteen child instead of a young woman, either that had been simply another alteration to make the book acceptable for children, or—

"Perhaps she didn't feel the same," Scarecrow murmured. "I never understood my feelings for her, was never smart enough to tell her she meant everything to me in so many words. If she didn't speak of this it's my own fault."

"Scarecrow, I'm sorry."

He shook his head. "You needn't be. Over and done now."

Theo's hands began to cramp. The RV kept drifting a bit right, and hitting the rumble strips along the side of the road set her teeth on edge. She asked Scarecrow to fetch her wrist braces from her bag, and then to hold the wheel steady while she strapped each of them on. She slowed down, and traffic passed them.

She might've underestimated the hours using this monster was adding on to the trip. They'd hit Madison at the tail end of rush hour. Great.

"I didn't see your dolls," Scarecrow remarked. "Didn't you bring them?"

"No, why would I?"

"You told your brother you were going to sell some of them at the fair in Kansas." He paused. "That was a lie. I see."

"Thought about it, actually. But it didn't seem right."

"Why not? As I understand it, you make the poppets in order to sell them. If this is your livelihood as well as your magic, I'd think you'd want to sell your wares whenever you could. I know I'm taking time away from your life, Theo. Please forgive me."

He was apologizing for taking her on the wildest adventure she'd ever had? "Don't be silly. This is great. I mean, I'm traveling with the actual Scarecrow of Oz, how cool is that?"

Wait. He understood she needed to earn a living? The trust her grandparents set up covered the mortgage on her house, but for other expenses she needed to pay her own way. Working for Dad's toy company, churning out bland designs to be mass-produced in overseas factories, was not an option she'd ever accept. "I thought you didn't use money in Oz? Like everyone just gave away their stuff, or bartered it or something."

He laughed. "What? No. You said you'd read about the mishap in the jackdaws' nest. Those birds accumulated quite a hoard of jewelry and money. When the birds took all my straw, my friends used what they could find to save me. I was forced to walk around for days crinkling with dirty paper money before we could find fresh straw. It was disgusting."

"Oh. So I should've brought a tub full of little faery dolls to hawk them at the fair, while you're reconnecting with your lost love through her diary?" She shook her head. "That's just not right. This trip is about you, not me."

Scarecrow was quiet for a long time.

"Thank you, Theo."

"Yeah, of course." She smiled, and he returned it. Theo relaxed a bit despite the traffic.

They passed fields of dry cornstalks, small lakes, roadside produce stands with painted wooden signs advertising pumpkins for sale. Scarecrow watched the scenery rolling past. The way Baum described it, Oz sounded pretty much like the Midwest. Munchkinland was supposed to look just like the view they passed right now, except all blue. Blue grass, blue-painted houses, blue corn. Blue cast-off clothing stuffed with straw and hung on a pole in the cornfield to keep the crows away.

"Do you ever think about what your life would've been like, if you stayed in the cornfield?" she asked.

Scarecrow nodded. "Often. I would've been such a simpleton, knowing only the sun, the fields, the rain and the crows. No one to talk to, nothing interesting to learn." He shuddered. "And probably tossed on the bonfire come Winter's Eve."

"Didn't the farmer who made you know you could talk? That you were a person and not just some stuffed mannikin?"

"I don't think he had the faintest clue. Not until the war, probably, when Locasta's soldiers dragged him to the Emerald City. He and his neighbor put my body together, painted on my face, and hung me in the field. I didn't know enough to even call after them as they walked away."

"How long were you there before—" Wait. Bringing up Dorothy over and over couldn't be helping him.

"A few days. I don't know. I didn't understand time at that point. I remember being rained on once, which was extremely unpleasant. It took a full day of sun to dry me out, and I recall being very distressed I had no way of stopping it from happening again."

Being stuck on a pole, unable to get down, helpless against the weather, all sounded like the scarecrow equivalent of a crappy childhood. "So you pretty much would've asked the first person who came by to get you down."

He nodded. "I'm glad it wasn't just anybody. If I'd never met Dorothy, I'd never have gained my brains."

"You know, you were just as smart before the Wizard put magic brains in your head." In the book, his brains consisted of pins, needles, and grains of dry bran. She'd seen the pins, so it seemed likely the rest of the cobbled-together placebo currently filled Scarecrow's head. Thinking without actual brain cells. Well, he could talk and sing without lungs.

He shook his head. "No, I was a fool before I won my brains." He sank into his seat, limp and listless. "Dorothy told me she liked me as I was before. Perhaps if I'd foregone brains, she would've stayed in Oz. Or taken me back to Kansas with her. She said they had fields and crops in Kansas."

Theo tried to picture him standing day after day, season after season in the dusty prairie, just a stuffed man with a smile painted on his sack-face. "You couldn't have gone to Kansas, could you? I mean, there's no magic. What if you'd gone there and ended up just a brainless scarecrow on a pole in a cornfield?"

"At least I would've been able to see her every day," he said softly.

Theo didn't have a reply.

Traffic around Madison was hellish. Theo inched the camper along, irritated. At this rate they wouldn't reach Kansas 'til well into morning. The RV groaned and chugged through the turns as they headed away from the capitol under a darkening sky.

Scarecrow proved a good travel companion, fetching her fresh sodas from the fridge whenever she asked and making no comment about her music choices. Miles swept by. Theo turned the headlights on, and the camper bumped along country highways. As the hours passed, Scarecrow became more and more withdrawn, curled up in his seat, gaze distant.

She filled the silence with words. "Nick looks different than I expected. I guess all of Oz is pretty different from the books."

Scarecrow nodded.

"What about Ozma?" Theo prodded. "Please tell me she's not evil."

"Oh, no, she's wonderful! Her edicts have reversed some of the terrible laws the fae enacted in their individual provinces. None of the witches dare to break the law now. Glinda's magic picture would see them, or else her book of records would note the crimes. Granted, that depends on someone watching or reading, but I think Glinda checks fairly often." He sobered, shaking his head. "I hope Nick's taken that into account. She could be watching any of my friends. If Glinda is fomenting treason, who knows what the rest of the fae are up to."

Torture and war. Violent coups. In the books, faery magic stopped all aging and death in the land of Oz. Every book had a happy ending. More alterations to make the stories kid-friendly.

To dispel her unease, she changed tracks. Thumping darkwave blasted from the speakers. Scarecrow jerked upright, one brow raised at her.

"Too moody," she explained. "Need something with energy now."

He nodded, though he pulled his hat down over his ears.

Undeterred, Theo sang along at the top of her lungs. When the camper swerved too much and someone honked at her she stopped bouncing to the beat and concentrated on getting through the traffic. They traveled west toward the last glow of sunset.

Just past Dodgeville, the sodas caught up with her. A check of the GPS showed an isolated gas station coming up where she could pee. "Getting off this exit," she announced. "I need a rest stop."

"Your legs are tired? You haven't been walking."

"No, to—I need to, um—"

"Oh. Meat people need to expel waste," he said brightly. He fluffed the straw in his chest. "Happily I need never do that. When my straw becomes musty, I only have to replace it with fresh material. And the old straw isn't wasted. I've been donating it to Jack Pumpkinhead to use for mulch in his pumpkin patch."

"Good for you," Theo muttered.

"It really is a shame you meat creatures must consume food and expel what your bodies don't use. Very inconvenient."

"Says the man who's never had the pleasure of eating chocolate, pizza pretzels, or really good wine." Theo smirked. "You don't know what you're missing."

"Perhaps not."

She eased the RV off the highway, thankful the off-ramp was long and straight enough she didn't have to brake hard or turn sharply. The gas station's bright florescent lamps drew the last straggling moths of autumn. Theo parked by one of the pumps. Might as well top up so she didn't have to stop again for awhile.

She took out her credit card out but grimaced at the shabby duct tape over the reader indicating it didn't work. Sticking the nozzle in the tank, she stretched and looked around. No other cars here. She shivered, tugging her jacket closed and buttoning it. Not even any music playing overhead. The occasional *zzzt* of a moth blundering into a bug zapper and the clunking chug of the gas going into the RV tank were the only sounds.

A glimpse of movement made her turn. Thought she saw something shiny just around the corner of the building, a wheel or a hubcap maybe. Nothing there when she squinted past the spill of the lights. The silence was wrong somehow. Unnerving.

"Hey Scarecrow? Wanna come out here?"

He popped out of the passenger door eagerly. "I won't draw too much attention?"

"There's no one here." She glanced around uneasily again. No sign of whatever she thought she saw. Hard to tell if anyone was even inside, but the store was lit up, with neon beer signs flickering in the windows. This place was the only light source visible in the dark night. Not even any street-lamps along the off ramp back there.

She usually had no fear of traveling alone. Not around town, not on road trips for art doll shows. Certainly never afraid in the company of friends. A brisk breeze made her hunch her shoulders.

Now she really needed to pee, and had to go inside to pay anyway.

"Will you come in with me?" she asked.

"Of course."

Theo locked the RV and headed for the store. "Thanks. Let's make this fast."

Inside, no sign of a clerk. Racks of chips and beef jerky stood high enough she couldn't see over them. A small beer cooler was well-stocked with national brands and cheap local favorites. The restroom door was locked. Goddess, she hated having to ask, but so be it. She grabbed some Cheezy-Korn, cinnamon donuts, a couple more sodas and energy drinks, and headed for the counter.

Scarecrow wandered the two cramped aisles while she acquired snacks. He rejoined her, eyes fixed upon a rack of maps. "Midwest Road Atlas?" he read aloud.

He'd been interested in the route, amazed at the expanse of territory just in this part of the country, and his straw-stuffed gloves couldn't operate her smartphone. "Grab one if you want." Theo dumped her purchases on the counter. "Hello? Anyone home?"

A squeaking noise and low voices came from behind a door adorned with faded sale flyers. The door opened and a young man in a Stihl ball-cap emerged, eyes too wide, smile strained.

Theo took a step back.

"Hey, evenin'," the clerk said. "Got any gas out there?"

"Yeah," Theo replied. She took another step back from the counter before checking out the window. "Pump three." As if any other customers were crowding the pumps.

Goosebumps prickled over her arms. Suddenly she didn't want to ask for the restroom key.

The clerk nodded. A thin smile stretched his cheeks. "Headin' up to House on the Rock?"

"Uh, no," Theo replied. That was oddly specific. Then again, Dodgeville marked the highway turnoff to go north to the tourist attraction. Probably the only non-locals who stopped here were headed that way. "Going west. How much?"

The clerk stared at her.

"How much do I owe you?" Theo repeated, taking her wallet out of her purse.

"Oh. Uh. With the gas, let's see..." The clerk rang up their items. "Thirty-four seventy-two."

Theo laid a couple of twenties on the counter. As the clerk made change, she checked outside again. The camper was undisturbed. Nothing moved under the flickering lights. Still no other cars. Maybe the locals bought their beer and smokes elsewhere.

"So west, huh? Taking a vacation? Ya know, the Dells are just as much fun this time of year. Lotta color on the trees," the clerk said, handing back her change. He began bagging her snacks and drinks.

His hands were shaking.

Another squeak came from the tiny office behind the door. The clerk froze, then continued loudly, "So where ya headed to then?"

"Kansas," Scarecrow said.

The clerk barely glanced at him. "Ya don't say! So what's in Kansas that ya can't find right here?" The clerk didn't comment on Scarecrow's costume or burlap skin. He'd barely acknowledged him. As if he were trying not to look at him at all. He fumbled the donuts, fingers shaking, missing the bag. They bounced on the floor.

Theo scooped up her stuff. "Don't need a bag. Thanks!" She hurried to the door.

"Hey, uh, you need tires checked? There's an air pump right around the—"

"I'm good thanks!" Theo shouted. She broke into a run.

Scarecrow was at her heels fast enough. She shoved the snacks at him when they reached the RV, unlocked the door, and pushed him in before dumping the gas nozzle back in its holder. Staring around while she screwed the gas cap back on, she swore she saw something moving just beyond the reach of the lights. *Shit. Whatever the hell this is, I am out of here. Pee later.* She clambered across Scarecrow to the driver's seat, cranking the engine. The sound of the beast roaring to life was a relief.

As they pulled out of the lot, Theo checked the side mirrors. She caught a glimpse of wheels near the pumps, before darkness swallowed all behind them as the station lights abruptly went out.

Theo floored the gas and the camper snarled, accelerating way too slowly for her taste. She headed for the highway.

"What just happened?" Scarecrow asked.

"No idea. Not sure I want to know."

He peered into the passenger side mirror, blocking her view. "I don't see anyone following us."

"Scarecrow, I need to see!"

"Sorry." He moved out of the way, looking worriedly from her to the road ahead.

Theo almost missed the turn back onto the highway. She braked hard not to overshoot the on-ramp, sending the RV creaking and swaying. Scarecrow grabbed the armrests and Theo clung to the wheel, desperately braking and fighting her instinct to spin the wheel hard. This tank didn't steer like her car.

Nothing behind them, not even headlights, as they climbed the ramp to the highway. She kept checking the mirrors as she slowly brought the beast up to sixty-five again. No sign of anything back there.

She relaxed her death grip on the wheel.

"Are you all right?"

Theo nodded. "Yeah. Yeah, I'm good. We're good. Could you put those drinks in the fridge for me?" Buying energy drinks had been a waste of money. Whatever was going on back at the gas station, she was wide awake now.

And still needed to pee. She'd hold it. Somewhere soon there should be a state rest stop, before they crossed the Mississippi. With other travelers pausing as well. People around, and better lighting. Safer. If she had to ask Scarecrow to stand guard, that would still be better than whatever the hell just happened.

She squeezed her thighs together and tightened her grip on the wheel.

20

Scarecrow checked the mirrors, but other than the occasional carriage lamps creeping up and then passing them he saw nothing unusual as they drove on through the night. No meat people in Oz ever traveled at night. Even under Ozma's rule, not every road was safe. The road of yellow bricks had dangerous spots, and only a great fool would dare walk along it after darkness fell.

He'd been that fool once. Luckily nothing happened while he and Dorothy were traveling at night. He could see in the dark about as well as day, and didn't know enough then to be wary. At her insistence that they needed to find shelter for her to sleep, he'd found an abandoned cabin, which later proved to belong to Nick Chopper. That night, while she slept in a pile of leaves in the corner, Scarecrow watched out the single window of the cabin, listening to the hooting of an owl. He'd had no concept of danger then. Fortunately that part of the woods was quiet and relatively safe.

As their trip seemed again now. When after some time nothing out of the ordinary occurred, he opened the road atlas and checked Theo's magic phone to judge where along the route they might be. How vast this land was! This wagon sped along the smooth gray road far faster than the Sawhorse could gallop.

Lights up ahead. The highway funneled through a rock bluff, its edges carved flat more expertly than the Nomes themselves could've managed. The wagon's lamps illuminated a green sign just ahead of a tall structure of open metalwork: MISSISSIPPI RIVER. He leaned against the window and peered down. The metal bridge crossed a broad stretch of darkness. Though a few lights picked out the peaks of the bridge itself, the water below was black. Impossible to guess how swift or deep it might be.

Much like the river in Oz where he'd been stranded while crossing on a raft with his friends. The bottom was deeper than he thought, and one good shove with his pole dropped it nearly under the surface. Stupidly he'd hung on, his feet left the raft, and before anyone could help he was clinging to a wooden pole just above the roiling water while the raft surged downstream. On a different journey, with Tip, when they crossed a river he'd become so waterlogged it took hours for his straw and clothing to dry, spread out in the sun, helpless. None of his experiences with rivers were pleasant.

This bridge proved sturdy despite the unnerving sound the carriage wheels made crossing it, and his shoulders slowly relaxed.

A sign read THE PEOPLE OF IOWA WELCOME YOU, although he saw no people. Iowa. He flipped through the atlas and found it. The listed population was over three million. Some quick calculations awed him at the vastness of the number. That couldn't possibly be right. He pointed it out to Theo.

"Yeah, I guess," she responded. "Though why the hell anyone would want to live here is beyond me. Nothing in Iowa but corn fields."

They passed numerous buildings, a town of some kind, glaringly lit and full of ugly, obtrusive signs. "This isn't a corn field."

"Okay, so nothing here but corn fields and river port towns. Hog farms maybe." She glanced at him. "Though I guess the fields and farms are familiar enough to you. Any of this look like Oz?"

"Some," he agreed. "Although all the buildings here are so strangely made. All tall and square. How does anyone relax in those?"

She laughed. "I don't think relaxing is high on the list. For most people, you go to work, you go home to eat and sleep, you go back to work. The grind of daily existence."

He shook his head. The ugly towers and huge rectangular monstrosities belching smoke were not at all inviting. Nothing like the domed, cozy homes of the Munchkins or the beautiful, gleaming towers of the Emerald Palace. Doubtful these even had wonderful libraries, much less secret passages. What a sad life these otherworlders must lead.

Then again, they didn't have to worry about roaming, murderous khalidahs or giant spiders. An especially rusty chimney ahead belched smoke into the night sky. Small wonder the great beasts kept clear of places such as this.

Theo squirmed.

"Do you still need to relieve yourself?"

She laughed. "Well, I'm not gonna pee on the seat, so yeah. Kinda wish I could just go in a soda bottle like you guys do." She coughed. "Um. Well, meat guys, I mean."

It took him a moment to follow. "Oh. You mean the dual purpose of a man's sex organ, to expel urine. One of the few bits of good design on a meat person, when so many other organs seem redundant. No, mine doesn't do that, I have no need of it since I don't eat or drink." His smile faltered. Why was she staring at him?

"You—you have a—"

"Not originally," he admitted. "I designed one. In the hope it would..." he paused, sinking.

"To make Dorothy happy?"

"Yes." Such a fool he was. It hadn't even occurred to him to instead ask for a spell to turn him into a meat person. If such magic existed. "Perhaps if I was made of meat, I wouldn't be constrained by Glinda's spell to perish at the full moon."

Theo slid her fingers between his and held tight. "Not gonna happen. We'll figure it out."

He nodded, though he'd thought of no song yet which might help. Too many of them were untested, words he'd never sung.

The music playing changed to a quiet song, full of rising and falling sighs. Lovely and strange as some of these were, he'd noticed no magical effects. People here must treat music much like the commoners of Oz, as something merely for enjoyment. His own initial pleasure in song or dance was tempered by learning how dangerous some tunes could be. Still not sure whether singing them in old Ozian or the common tongue here was most effective. This would require more study and experiment, time he didn't have. Everything about this fool's venture was frustrating and depressing.

Theo let go of his hand to rub her eyes. She was pushing the limits of her fragile flesh body's endurance, all for his desire to read Dorothy's diary.

Well, not *everything* here was bad.

"Do what you need to," he urged her. "You're clearly unhappy. I can keep watch. Can you just use the corn field? It should be fairly private."

"Oh hell no. Anyways I can't pull over here, there's a ditch." Theo growled, "Just have to get to the next decent rest stop."

Scarecrow checked the map. "There isn't one for miles."

A sign on the right side of the road pointed to something called a golf course. Theo slowed the wagon. "Bet they have a big parking lot and it'll be deserted at this hour. Good enough."

"What's a golf?"

"A boring waste of time for rich people." She sniffed. "My dad loves it."

"If it's a waste of time, why would—"

"Scarecrow, I just really need to go, okay?"

He nodded. Meat people were so cranky when their flesh demanded something. Just as well he'd never experience it.

The wagon pulled into a bumpy drive and came to a reluctant stop in a gravel lot. A building with dark windows sat to the east, a lone lamppost casting poor light upon the structure. The place appeared deserted. A fleet of smaller carriages with white roofs and open sides waited in rows near the building.

"This'll work," said Theo. "Okay. Would you keep an eye out, please? I might be a few minutes." She grabbed a packet of tissues.

"Of course."

Theo unbuckled herself, shoved the door open, and jumped from the wagon. She hurried to the building and tried the door, but it was locked. He followed until she cursed and ran into a clump of bushes. He heard her groan with relief.

Dorothy had wanted privacy at such times. He paced a few steps away.

Strange stars filled the night sky. A chill wind rustled the straw poking from under his hat and the branches of a nearby oak. It creaked and swayed ominously. Just in case trees here could grab and throw, he stayed well clear of it. He'd been bodily hurled once by the trees of the Forbidden Forest and had no desire to experience that again.

He walked to the edge of the lot to investigate the herd of silent carriages. Beyond them a brown lawn swept down into a hollow. Thin, tall pennants on sticks waved in the wind. They dotted the open ground below for some distance. Here and there a tree seemed to have been deliberately ignored in the clearing of land. If this was pasturage, it was clipped nearly to the roots of the grass by whatever grazed here. Goats, probably. He shuddered, checking in all directions. No sign of the nasty, straw-eating beasts.

A squeak made him turn and peer into the darkness. All color was washed out beyond the area lit by the wagon's lamps. Nothing out of the ordinary by the squat building labeled *Clubhouse*. Nothing stirred by the wagon. He'd left the door open. Theo must still be occupied.

Squeeeeaaak. Eeek.

Scarecrow whirled. Something moved in between the rows of parked carriages.

A lot of somethings.

He took a step back. A song, he needed a song, something for battle. Untested. No time.

One of the moving things skittered forward. Its wheels slipped and sent gravel flying, but it quickly regained balance. A low-slung muzzle on a stout neck lifted and nostrils flared. It cackled, a hideous high laugh.

"Wheelers," he gasped.

More cackling rose from all around as an entire hunting pack rolled into the gravel lot. The ragged ribbons decorating their scarred, lean bodies fluttered in the wind. Long legs ended in sharp-bladed metal wheels. Their tiny ears lay low against their bony heads, adapted for the harsh desert winds. Their eyes were unblinking black stones. Multiple rows of jagged fangs showed in their open muzzles.

"Scarecrow?" Theo called.

He spun toward the wagon. Theo walked around the front of it, squinting in the bright lamps. She couldn't see in the dark. "Scarecrow? What's wrong?"

"Go back," he shouted, as more squeaking, creaking, cackling Wheelers circled them. "Now!" He broke into a run toward her.

Theo's eyes widened. She backed toward the wagon's door. A Wheeler skidded around the front. Before Theo could react the beast slammed head-on into her, knocking her down. It lunged at her, jaws snapping air when she flung herself to the side and scrambled under the wagon. The

Wheeler snarled, stretching one long forelimb after her, slashing its sharp wheel into the edge of the wagon. Sparks flew and metal screeched.

Scarecrow cringed at the sparks. The creature pawed at Theo, bent down and snapped its powerful jaws at her, but she scooted further under the massive wagon where it couldn't reach. The Wheelers hooted and laughed, closing in. Two of them raced around to the other side of the vehicle. He could only hope Theo would be safe in the exact center of its underbelly.

"Scarecrow!" she yelled.

"Get away," he shouted at the monsters, "I'm warning you!"

"Hay man warnzzz," one of the Wheelers chortled. It darted toward him. Scarecrow jerked back. Another lunged from his left. Quickly they surrounded him. He could see his frightened reflection in their dead, black eyes, orbs of stone polished smooth by the desert winds. He'd never run into them before, but Dorothy had. The mechanical man TikTok saved her by whacking the Wheelers with a lunch-pail. Scarecrow had nothing to swing at them.

One of them lunged and grabbed a mouthful of his tunic. Scarecrow yelped, swatting at its nose. It tore free a length of fabric and straw in savage teeth, then spit it out and giggled wildly.

"Not tazzty," it said.

"Girl will be tazzty," another hissed, and they all cackled, high scratchy voices filling the night.

"Leave her alone!" Scarecrow yelled. He didn't get two steps toward the wagon before another Wheeler skidded in between him and it.

"Hay man can't eat," it said. Its dead eyes fixed directly upon him. It grinned all the way back to its small, ragged ears. "Too bad. More for uzzzz."

"Fuck off!" Theo shouted from under the wagon. "Leave him alone or I will fuck all of you up so bad!"

Another round of giggles and high, freakish cackling went up. The worst they could do to Scarecrow was rip him apart, which would be extremely inconvenient. If they reached Theo they'd bite and tear and rend, the whole pack of them slashing at her.

No carriage lamps showed on the highway mere yards away. Nobody here to help.

Scarecrow picked a song and took a breath. "Theo, cover your ears!" he shouted.

The Wheelers were still laughing at him when the first notes hit their ears. He raised his voice over their cries and put all his strength into the forceful words of the War Song of Red Top Mountain. He sang of axes cleaving skulls in twain, of sturdy men climbing the mountain to slaughter anything in their path.

The Wheelers' cackles turned to howls of anguish.

One of the larger Wheelers reached for him, hissing. Inspired by the next verse, he thrust forth one hand as though wielding a sword. He sang as loud as he could of the ancient warrior Iowyn, how his sword cut off the head of the mightiest Hammerhead on the mountain, how the rocks ran red with blood.

The attacking Wheeler screeched, clapped its forewheels to its ears, and collapsed onto the gravel. Blood flowed from its ears and mouth. It spasmed, gurgling.

Scarecrow turned, still singing. Every Wheeler wailed, clapping their hard sharp wheels to their own heads in a futile attempt to block their ears. Limbs jittered as they fell, unable to stand on two wheels. The nearest ones flopped like dying fish, teeth exposed in snarls. Blood ran freely from their nostrils and ears and their black cold eyes stared at nothing. As he finished the verse, two more fell and did not rise again. His path was clear.

Theo, oh no, please tell me she covered her ears! He ran to the wagon, dropped to the ground, afraid what he'd find underneath.

Theo stared back at him, crunched into a ball with her fingers stuck in her ears. Another Wheeler howled and dropped right next to Scarecrow. Theo flinched. He extended a hand to her. "Come on, let's get out of here!"

She wriggled closer, eyes wide. He could hear movement behind him, pained and angry screeches, the harsh rattle of gravel kicked in the air by the writhing beasts. Scarecrow stretched until he could tug at Theo's arm. "Come on, come on!"

"Can I take my fingers out?" she yelled, too loud in the close confines of the wagon's underside.

He winced and nodded. She grabbed his hand and crawled out. Scarecrow helped her to her feet, bracing himself against the wagon.

"Bad hay man," a Wheeler howled. It shook blood from its face, fury staggering it forward even as it tried to hold one forewheel to a crimson-drenched ear. "Tear you to piecezzz!"

"Run!" Scarecrow shoved Theo toward the open wagon door.

She leaped in, reached back and hauled him up by the collar of his tunic, slamming the door the instant he was inside. Her shaking hands fumbled the key. The wagon sputtered, then growled to life and jolted forward. A Wheeler screamed, jumping with a clang onto the metal nose of the wagon. Scarecrow yelped and flung himself back against his seat. The monster's wheels slipped on the slick metal. Theo chunked a lever on the steering column and the wagon roared forward. The Wheeler screeched, scrabbled, and abruptly dropped.

The wagon bumped hard over it. Bones crunched.

Theo's face was chalk-white. She spun the steering wheel and the wagon tipped, groaned, righted itself. Scarecrow stumbled to the rear of the wagon and pushed aside the curtains in the small bedchamber. Three Wheelers pursued them, but they wobbled, tripped and fell, four limbs sprawling. The battle song hurt them badly, and even the ones still alive were too unsteady to give chase. As the wagon roared and lurched, gaining speed, one Wheeler raised itself and shook a threatening forewheel at him.

He crouched on the bed, staring out the window for some minutes, panic slowly fading as the monsters were left behind. Night closed around them once more, the darkness only occasionally broken by the lamps of enormous wagons heading the other direction. Surely the other travelers were going too fast for the wounded Wheelers to catch them.

He made his way to the front of the wagon again and dropped into his seat.

Theo's fingers clenched the steering wheel. She gave him a frightened glance and then immediately checked the mirrors. "We lose 'em?"

"They're far behind. At this speed they'll never catch us." He shook his head. "I wonder if they ate the golfs or if there's a symbiotic relationship between them."

Theo stared at him. "What?"

"The Wheelers," he explained. "Just wondering if they took over the native range of the golfs back there, or if—"

"Those were Wheelers?"

"Well, yes. Obviously."

"They didn't look like that in the book. Not even that scary in the 'Return to Oz' movie." She shivered, gripping the wheel more tightly.

It took a moment for his rattled brains to catch her implication. "You don't have Wheelers here?"

"No." Her eyes were wide. "Not until now."

They were quiet for the next few miles. Theo turned up a gage marked *HEAT*. She was pale and shivering.

"Are you all right?" he asked.

She nodded sharply.

He realized no music was playing. Recalling she'd turned a particular dial to adjust the sound, he reached for it. She stopped him, her hand upon his.

"What was that song you sang?"

He felt chilled suddenly. She had a small reddish-brown smudge under her left nostril. Blood. "Theo! Oh no. How much of it did you hear?"

"Like two seconds before I jammed my fingers in so hard it hurt."

Pained, he plucked a paper tissue from a box of them and carefully dabbed her nose and upper lip. "I'm so horribly sorry. I tried to warn you, I didn't know what else to do, if they caught you they'd kill you for sure, Theo I am so deeply sorry," he babbled. He felt as though his insides were contaminated with pond water. Should've made certain she was prepared before he sang. He'd never sung it before, only guessed at the effects. All the more reason he should've been positive she was safe before he opened his stupid mouth.

Theo's fingers wrapped around his, halting his ineffective daubing at the dried blood. She took a deep breath, shuddering. "It's fine. I'm fine. You did great. You destroyed them, Scarecrow."

"You were hurt too," he protested. "It was too great a risk. I should've tried to lead them away from you. Shoved straw up their noses or something."

She shook her head firmly. "No. You saved my life. Those things," she inhaled, shivering again, "those Wheelers. First one got my arm. Goddamn sharp wheels." She pushed up the left sleeve of her jacket. He hadn't noticed she'd been cut. Her jacket was torn. A scratch ran across her flesh. "It's okay. The jacket took most of the damage."

"Oh no. No, that's not good. We need a poultice right away, something to suck out any poison."

"First aid kit should be in the glove box there."

He opened the cupboard she'd pointed out. A white box with a red X on it displayed the same words on its lid. Opening it, he found a bewildering assortment of ointments and papers.

"Cleaning wipe, antibiotic, bandage," Theo directed.

Fortunately these items were clearly labeled. He handed them to her in that order, holding the steering wheel steady as she tended the wound. To his great relief, her skin wasn't deeply cut. The scratch was no worse than what a thornbush might have inflicted. Still, one book he'd read claimed the Wheelers were contaminated with the sand of the Deadly Desert, the edges of which they prowled. Best not to take any chances. He told her this while she rubbed ointment on the scratch and adhered a pink, flexible plaster over it.

"I think I'm good on my tetanus vaccinations. Should be okay."

He nodded uncertainly, tucking away the kit.

"You saved my life. Those fuckers had some scary sharp feet. Wheels. Whatever."

He nodded again. Straw was all bunched in his throat, and he could think of no reassuring thing to say.

"That was one hell of a song. Did you ever sing that one before?"

He shook his head, twisting his gloves together in his lap.

She was quiet for a time. Then she closed her fingers over his. He squeezed back gently.

"That..." she hesitated, taking a swallow of the canned drink in the holder before continuing. "That sound. Those squeaking wheels. Same sound back at the gas station. Behind the door. Did you hear it?"

Yes. Now he'd heard the terrible noise for himself, it was a sound he'd never forget. If those monsters had been waiting behind the door, that would explain the anxiousness of the clerk.

The lights of the station winked out when they left. He'd thought at the time perhaps the shop was closing since no other travelers were present. The clerk was almost certainly dead. Bloody chunks strewn on the slick floor. Wheelers were notoriously messy diners.

His throat crinkled, straw flexing in revulsion.

Theo shivered again, holding tight to his hand. "Could you maybe sing something?"

Helplessly he shook his head. "I don't think—I'm not really—I can't now." No soothing words would come. All he could think of was the Wheelers cackling. The screech of their hard wheel-paws on the metal of the wagon. The terrible notion that this world had no Wheelers in it before he arrived, and they'd been waiting at the station. Which meant they'd stalked him and Theo for miles since then, attacked them as soon as they'd stopped.

And they'd overheard him say where they were headed.

"How big is Kansas?" he asked.

"I dunno. Average sized state, I guess. Why?"

"How big is average?" He snatched up the road atlas from the floor. The shape of this kingdom—state—on the map reminded him of the borders of Oz. Hopefully it took as long to traverse as his more familiar land, and the Wheelers wouldn't find them. "Are we staying straight on this road?"

Theo plucked her magic phone from its holder and swiped a thumb across it a few times. She turned it so he could see. "We turn due south at Cedar Rapids onto eye-three-eighty. Then west at Iowa City."

He sank into the seat. "Good. That's good."

"You think they'll still try to follow us? You killed half of them!"

"I don't think they can track us, as fast as we're traveling." Wheelers couldn't read maps, either.

As far as he knew.

"Scarecrow, what the hell are Wheelers doing here?"

He had no answer.

Theo stared out at the gray road, the blackness beyond. "Next time we stop," she declared, "I'm buying some earplugs. And if we see those monsters again, you sing your goddamned heart out. You sing them all to Hell."

She tapped her phone, turned the music knob up, and took another swig of her drink before grasping his hand in hers and pressing it upon her right thigh. Her fingers entwined tightly with his. He could feel the tenseness in her body.

The Wheelers had hidden in the station. Waiting. Why didn't they burst into the shop instead of hiding behind a door? As small as that place was, with only one obvious exit, it would've been easy for the pack to ambush and kill the meat people inside. Rip Scarecrow to shreds, scatter his straw. Why let anyone leave at all, if they were only hunting for an easy kill?

The clerk seemed quite interested in their destination. Anxiously so. What if the Wheelers ordered him to question any travelers? Were they intelligent enough to plan ahead?

Scarecrow glanced at Theo. She hummed along to the music, something sweet and wistful this time instead of dark and thumping. She held his hand tight as if afraid of letting go.

He wouldn't let her out of his sight again. He curled his fingers around hers, feeling her warmth seeping into his straw.

Trying to ignore the music playing, he retreated into memories of a dusty library, scrolls no one had unwrapped in centuries. Songs in a tongue hardly anyone still spoke, some of which might make useful weapons. Possibly one of which could take him home.

Now he also needed to make sure he took the rest of Oz's monsters back with him.

21

Theo barreled past Cedar Rapids and Iowa City. After the third turn onto yet a different highway, she consciously relaxed her shoulders. They passed through Des Moines around eleven o'clock. Glaring billboards reflected from the moody clouds overhead. Nearly four hours and several interchanges since they'd left the screeching, hideous Wheelers behind, but she kept checking the mirrors.

Those squeaky-wheeled, dead-eyed hyenas had been hiding at the gas station. They were fast enough to follow them halfway across another state to catch them at the deserted rural golf course. She pushed the camper over the speed limit. The engine whined, floorboards shook and everything else rattled, gas mileage plunging. Even if the remaining Wheelers were too injured to pursue she'd make damned sure they had no chance to catch up again.

What became of the gas station clerk? She could try a web search when they stopped next, but probably no news reports would be posted until the morning. If anything was reported at all. Maybe the Wheelers dragged the clerk out into the fields. Maybe there'd be no news for months until some farmer found the remains come spring.

Scarecrow hunched into himself, chin in one hand. Theo tried a couple of times to engage him in lighter talk that had nothing to do with what just happened, but he barely replied.

Finally, slowing as she changed lanes, she asked, "Do you think the clerk is still alive?"

"No."

"Why didn't they attack us then? If they'd blocked the door while we were—"

Scarecrow shook his head. "I don't know." He removed his hat. Numerous pins and needles stuck up from his head. "I've been thinking hard about it but I don't have an answer." He patted the pins all down inside his head again. "I'll just have to keep trying."

"Can they still track us? How did they follow us as far as they did?" Reflexively she checked the mirrors again.

"They're excellent hunters. They can reach incredible speeds on flat terrain. However, I think we're safe. We've taken several sharp turns, and our scent should fade with distance. The survivors probably won't bother pursuing."

"Probably?"

His worried eyes met hers. He nodded up at the clouds. "In any case, if it rains, it'll wash away any trace they could follow."

Come on, rain.

She tried to hold off another bathroom break as long as possible, but the energy drinks and stress made another stop inevitable. Dark countryside spooled out on either side of the interstate. Miles to go yet before the Missouri state line, where there'd be a rest stop. Dammit. Again, ditches and fences off to the right, the shoulder all broken concrete badly needing repaving. Ahead, the bright logo of a truck stop beckoned.

Fear of stopping warred with her bladder. This did not improve the situation.

Theo flicked on the turn indicator and veered onto the exit ramp. The sight of numerous big rigs at the stop reassured her. If anyone could fight off a horde of creepy hyena-shark things on wheels, a bunch of cranked-up truckers with handguns sounded perfect. She stopped the camper in the parking lot near the trucks.

Goddess, she was so tired. The energy drink crash hit, and now the Demon Pancreas was starting to complain. Her stomach was sour. It would be so lovely to get some actual food in the diner—if they made anything not deep-fried twelve times over. Still at least five hours of driving to go. Her eyelids drooped.

Tempting to just crawl into bed. Scarecrow would let her know if the Wheelers came back or anything else tried to pounce on them.

No. Best to just get this trip over with, get to Kansas as quickly as possible. How exactly they'd get access to Dorothy's diary, how long Scarecrow would need to study it, and how he'd react were all still impenetrable mysteries. Her head hurt. The diner parking lot was dark, and no one moved. On second thought, maybe this wasn't the best idea. She could hold off a little longer, find somewhere else.

When she touched the gearshift a soft glove closed over her hand. Theo blinked at him, vision fuzzy.

"You need rest," Scarecrow said.

"No, I'm good."

"If by 'good' you mean 'desperately needing food and sleep,' then I concur."

Theo shook off his gentle touch. "I'd rather just push on."

"You're seconds from dropping. You need at least a nap. Please, Theo."

She could only glare at him for a second. His expression was so full of concern, she was almost ready to agree and simply drop into bed. Her stomach turned over and sent bile up her throat. She grimaced. "Ugh. Okay. Food and a bathroom break. You win this one. Half an hour here, tops, and then we need to get moving again."

He nodded, clearly relieved. Theo found her purse and locked the camper behind them. She tugged her jacket tighter, eyes darting as they crossed the parking lot to the painfully bright lights of the truck stop diner.

A couple of burly men with battered ballcaps sat inside and a waitress Theo's mother's age leaned on the long counter. Theo plopped into a vinyl booth seat. Scarecrow sat facing her, looking around curiously. The waitress laid a couple of plastic menus on the table.

"Hi there, what can I getcha, hon?"

"Coffee, please. A carafe. And do you have any healthy stuff? Like a chicken wrap maybe?"

"Well aren't you a delicate thing. Always too special for the rest of us."

"Excuse me?" Theo's head shot up. Her father sneered down at her.

"Over twenty-five and still playing with dolls. I don't know why we even sent you to college."

"It's not playing with dolls," Theo argued. "I sell them!"

"It's not enough you won't get a real job, but now you have to play with a life-sized doll." Dad jerked his chin at Scarecrow.

The straw doll smiled cheerfully, oblivious to the insult. His floppy limbs sprawled in the booth seat, eyes frozen in a painted stare.

"No, stop it," Theo said. She should get up, had to get away. Dad loomed over her.

"Why can't you just work in the company? You could be a secretary, some easy position, earn your living honestly instead of running around with your heathen friends and making trash like this." Dad shook Scarecrow's shoulder. The stuffed man toppled over.

"Stop it!" Theo yelled, trying to stand. "I'm an adult! I'll do what I want."

"You'll never grow up. All this nonsense about Oz and magic and fairies. You'll never make anything worth selling and you'll never make anything of yourself."

"Shut up! Just shut the fuck up for once!"

"Still just a scared little girl," Dad scoffed, brushing off his hands in disgust. "Why couldn't you have been a son like Danny? At least then I wouldn't have to explain why my grown child still runs around like a five-year-old playing at all this ridiculous, stupid—"

"Shut the fuck up!" Theo screamed, launching herself at him. Her fists slammed into his shoulders, shoving him back. She'd knock that sneer off his face, she'd show him she was strong enough to fight for herself, she'd—

"Theo!"

"Leave me alone! You don't know anything about me!"

"Theo, stop!"

"You never even wanted to learn what—"

A soft glove caught her fist, deflecting it. Wide blue eyes stared into hers. Straw dust clouded the air. Theo sneezed, wiped her eyes.

Scarecrow cautiously released her hand. "Are you all right?"

She was in the driver's seat. The engine idled. The parking lot was starkly lit and quiet beyond the warmth of the camper cabin.

Scarecrow nodded at her. "You're safe. Everything's fine." He readjusted his clothing, tucking straw back inside himself and rebuttoning the tunic. She'd pummeled the stuffing out of him.

"Ohhhhh fuck." Theo flopped back in the seat. "Did I seriously fall asleep right here at the wheel?"

"You're exhausted. Please, lie down for a while. We don't seem to be in any danger here."

Her hands felt weak even with the braces on. She took hold of the wheel again. "Still hours to go."

"All the more reason to rest."

"Sorry I hit you."

He smiled. "I'm fine. Takes more than a violent nightmare to hurt me."

Heat spread across her cheeks. "Thought you were someone else."

"Glad to hear it. Now please rest. You're in no condition to drive like this."

"How long was I out?"

"Only a few minutes before you started thrashing around."

Theo groaned, rubbed her eyes. "Okay. Get me another energy drink."

"You finished the last one a half-hour ago."

Which explained the sour stomach. She'd gulped down too much caffeine and junk food all night. "Okay, can you bring me some antacids? I think they're in my purse." Suddenly she recalled other, more personal things in her bag. "No, wait. I'll get them. And then maybe we'll go in there and see if they have something bland like soup." She nodded at the diner and killed the ignition.

She'd left the purse back on the bed, next to the bathroom door. The cabinets swayed and wavered as she moved toward the back of the RV. Stumbling, she grabbed the edge of the banquette, pushing off it to travel the next couple of steps. She gritted her teeth. *No. I am not weak. I am not small.*

When she sat on the bed, rooting in her purse, the rustle of straw made her look up. Before she could comment about getting a little privacy, he began singing the autumn song. The one that somehow filled her with immediate peace and sleepiness despite the lyrics about racing and chasing through the fields.

"Oh that's not fair," she growled, trying to get up.

Scarecrow took a step closer, his voice gentle but the melody insistent.

"Will you race with me, chase with me, dance with me?
Will you run down the moon and welcome the sun?
Oh yes, I will race you and chase you and dance with you
From morrow at noon 'til midnight has come,
Forever in autumn 'til winter has come."

"No," Theo yawned. "Stop it, Scarecrow."
He shook his head, still singing.

"Light is the wind in your hair, o my girl,
Fast are your feet 'cross the hills."

"I'll get you for this," Theo muttered, sinking into the bed. When did her eyes close? How dare he sneak attack a song at her.

"And when autumn comes round once again we shall go
Racing the sun sinking into the dells."

"Bastard," she sighed. A blanket drew over her. A crinkling hand patted her shoulder, and a warm voice continued singing words she was too tired to register.
She suffered no dreams this time.

• • • •

LIGHT AND MUFFLED NOISE filtered into her brain until she realized she was awake. Theo blinked, confused for a moment until she saw Scarecrow sitting at the banquette table, watching out the windows. He'd left the bedroom curtains open. She was fully clothed, and he'd draped a thick wool blanket over her. A growl in her stomach reminded her she hadn't eaten anything good for her in—what time was it, anyway?

Throwing the blanket off, she groaned and stretched. Immediately Scarecrow came to her, smiling. "Feel any better?"

She gave him her best Death Glare. "That was fucking evil."

He shrugged. "It was safer than allowing you to push on when your body clearly was done pushing for the night."

She wanted to snap at him. More than done with men trying to control what she did and when she did it. When she rubbed the sleep from her eyes and focused finally, his expression was all concern. Gentle, not smug. Her anger faded. "Don't do that again without asking me first," she mumbled.

"I won't. I was worried." Humbly he held out both hands to her. "Forgive me?"

Theo sighed. "Yeah, okay, fine." She grabbed his gloves and stood, wavering a bit. "Ooooh. Yuck."

"Perhaps I should've closed all the curtains so the sunlight didn't wake you."

"No, no. Should get up. What the hell time is it?"

"The sun's been up for some little while."

Not helpful. Theo staggered to the front of the RV and checked her phone. "Oh my Goddess, that was not a nap. That was seven hours wasted! We won't reach the Oz Museum 'til afternoon at this rate."

"Does the time particularly matter?"

"I just want you to have plenty of time to read the diary."

"Thank you, Theo. I'm very sorry to put you in such distress." His head drooped.

How the hell did he manage to be so nice about everything? She'd been on the receiving end of enough guilt trips from her mother to see he wasn't shoving one at her. He genuinely felt bad for causing her any trouble.

She brushed her hair out of her face. Bed head for sure. Have to tidy up before she set foot in the diner. Granted, the truckers were guaranteed to stare anyway.

Scarecrow didn't care that her hair glowed like a rabid pumpkin, or that her ears were pierced multiple times, or think the delicate silver stud in her left nostril was unladylike. Maybe the fae in Oz looked even wilder.

He was preoccupied right now with tucking stray bits of straw back inside his tunic where one of the Wheelers tore the fabric.

"Still have your sewing kit?" she asked.

"Yes." He fished it from a pants pocket and handed it over. "Very kind of you."

She unspooled a length of green thread and chose a needle. "Gonna need to get you more clothes at this rate."

"I always say, there are worse things than being a scarecrow. As long as I have friends around, nothing too terrible can happen to me." He smiled at her. "Thank you, Theo. I'm sorry to be so much trouble."

"Goddess' sake, stop apologizing."

"Is it not the custom to apologize here, when one has put someone else in danger?"

She huffed, finishing off the quick row of stitches. "Unless you summoned those creepy hyenas on roller skates, you haven't done anything wrong."

"What if I did, though? Inadvertently?" His brows furrowed. "Twice you've been attacked since I arrived. And your friend Gwyn said—"

"Screw Gwyn. She doesn't know shit about you. About Oz."

"She is a witch, though," he pointed out. "Perhaps she has a bit more experience in these matters. She did recognize I wasn't from your world."

Are you kidding me? Theo straightened up, scowling. "Scarecrow, anyone who takes one good look at you can figure that out. Never mind what Gwyn said. Far as I'm concerned you have every right to be here. You didn't deliberately call up the dead or ask the worst biker gang in Oz to come play a round of golf, right?"

"No, but—"

"Let's get some breakfast and get back on the road. If your girl left us any clues to send you home, let's read them."

"Home. Yes." His mouth twisted, but he raised his head and met her determined glare. "Thank—"

"Thank me when we have what we need. Come on."

Scarecrow followed her silently from the RV.

The diner's restroom was clean enough, the air warm, and the coffee strong. Theo ignored hostile truckers around them while she wolfed down a spinach and mushroom omelet. *Let 'em stare. Wild hair, don't care.* Tempting to turn around and ask if they'd never seen a wicked witch before. She sipped her coffee, making sure to extend her pinky finger. *That'll show 'em who's fucking dainty.*

Scarecrow bent over his coffee cup, inhaling the steam. He smiled at the waitress who dropped off the check although she eyeballed both of them as if wondering whether freaks tipped well.

He nodded at Theo. "I think you're right. This drink does seem to help my brains."

"Good."

"Who were you hitting?"

She paused mid-chew. "What?"

"Earlier. Your nightmare."

"Doesn't matter."

"Ah."

She pointed her fork at him. "Don't do that."

"Do what?"

"Lean back looking all wise, like you understand the secrets of the universe."

"I can't help it if my brains are especially sharp today. You're the one who suggested the coffee."

"Oh really. So tell me, straw sage, what's my problem?"

He cocked his head to one side. "If I had to guess, I'd say your family hasn't been supportive of your gifts. Your magic. Do they not accept your talents?"

"I keep telling you, not that kind of witch."

"But you are, Theo," he insisted. "You create astonishing dolls. You imbue them with life. The craftsmanship you put into even simple stitches demonstrates your heart as much as your skill. Once I realized your dolls weren't intended to cause harm, I noticed how detailed they all are. How much thought and care you spend on them. I'll take an army of those to conquer any evil sorcerer, any day."

"My dad thinks they're awful. Unmarketable." She shoved the last forkful of omelet into her mouth and mumbled around it. "I mean, hardly anyone buys them. It was precocious and promising when twelve-year-old me designed a line of doll clothes. Apparently when a grown woman makes tiny faeries it's a waste of time."

His dark brows drew sharply down. "Your father is mistaken."

Theo choked out a laugh. "Good luck telling him that. About anything."

"I fail to see how crafting marvelous beings, so detailed they can fight off a reanimated corpse, is a waste of time."

"Yeah, well. My family didn't see that, and if they had, they'd know I was even more of a freak than they think already." The other diners, mostly guys in padded vests with full beards, continued to frown at her. She'd had enough. Standing, she tossed her napkin on her empty plate and gulped the last of the coffee. "We're done here." She tucked a couple of fives under her plate. *Freaks and weirdos tip well, bitch.*

Standing beside her as they waited for a cashier to ring up the tab, Scarecrow's voice was low and full of puzzlement. "Theo, I've met witches who style themselves 'good.' Who pretend to care about other people. You're the first actual good witch I've ever seen. I would've been lost without your help. You do care, and I for one greatly appreciate you."

Theo wouldn't look at him. Where was the damned hostess, she just wanted to get back on the road, play some loud obnoxious music and not think about her father or the rest of her family for a day.

"I'm sorry your family doesn't value your magic. If I get back to Oz, I'll make sure everyone knows of your kindness and skill. Maybe I'll try writing some songs of my own."

What the hell was she supposed to say to that?

She mumbled thanks to the hostess who handed back her credit card. Cold air swirled in from the front door as another trucker came in for breakfast. He stopped upon seeing Theo and Scarecrow, then chuckled. "Thought Halloween was next week?"

"Out of my way or I'll turn you into a toad," Theo said. She grabbed Scarecrow's hand and marched out of the diner, head high.

They were back on the interstate at cruising speed before he asked. She knew he was going to. "Can you actually turn—"

"Not. That. Kind. Of witch." She pulled up the loudest playlist on her phone and cranked the speakers.

Scarecrow winced, tugged his hat down over his ears, and sat back to watch the miles fly by.

22

"Are you sure nobody saw you?" Tip asked, shutting the door. Nick lifted his feet, showing her the furs he'd carefully tied onto his metal shoe-plates to silence his steps. "I came up the outside stairs. No one around."

"Good." Tip hesitated, her hand on his arm.

Her face was wan and thin, limbs trembling, eyes red. Over Glinda's protests, the young Queen slept in Scarecrow's library the past two nights. Her partly-fae blood did not react well to the iron-enclosed room. Nick patted her hand. "How are you feeling, Your Highness?"

"I'm fine. Did you see the Professor anywhere?"

"No." Continuing to meet in secret was risky; not knowing what the Good Witch was up to was riskier. Court functions prevented Nick and the Wogglebug from slipping away to the library the past two days and nights. It seemed Glinda just coincidentally happened upon Nick more often. She'd interrupted his talk through the Evstones with Scarecrow yesterday. Nick didn't think she'd overheard anything, but he still checked over his shoulder more often.

If Tip hadn't used a spell to slip a note into his pocket tonight, he wouldn't have chanced it. She'd sent a summons to the Wogglebug as well. Nick wasn't in the library two minutes before a furtive knock sounded at the door: *tap, scritch scritch, tap scritch.* Same secret code Tip had given Nick. Happily he'd remembered it. The note itself turned into a sweet roll within a few minutes of his reading it.

He unbolted the door. A veil-shrouded figure in layers of gray Ixian priestly robes stood outside. Some of the delegation from the land of Ix had arrived early to consecrate rooms in the Emerald Palace, preparing for the upcoming visit of their witch-queen Zixi, which accounted for all the extra court business and ceremony. He hadn't expected one of the Ixians to show up in this disused wing of the palace. "Can I help you?"

"Stand aside, friend Nicholas," the muffled voice of the Wogglebug came from under the veils.

Nick let him in, sliding the heavy bolt shut behind him. Long, spindly arms unraveled the veils, scarves, and outer robes to reveal the Professor. Nick shook his head.

"That's some disguise."

The Wogglebug's faceted eyes twinkled, mandibles clicking merrily. "Clever, don't you think? I felt, with the foreign visitors wandering the palace, no one would look twice at a drab Ix sect."

Tip snorted. Lion growled and shook his mane. Tiger merely blinked huge eyes at the Professor. "I miss something?"

"No." Nick ignored the Wogglebug's self-satisfied smile. "All right, we're all here, and who knows how long it'll be before the Pink Lady checks up on any of us in her magic picture."

All of them sobered. The witch frequently employed magic artifacts to spy on her Quadling subjects. Her gilt-framed painted picture, now hidden somewhere in the Palace, could show any person or place in Oz if Glinda merely asked to view them. Her book of records had an enchanted quill which continually scribbled the actions of every person in Oz. A retinue of secretaries took turns reading it in case anything of note was recorded. The iron protection of this room should prevent both scrying objects from seeing anything inside its walls.

"I spoke to Scarecrow," Nick said. Briefly he told them of his conversation with their straw friend, and of meeting an actual good witch who was helping Scarecrow in the other world. "She must be very powerful. Her hair was as bright as a bonfire, and she wears several talismans in her ears and nose."

"She must be ancient," the Wogglebug exclaimed. "I've heard only the eldest fae have orange or red hair. Our Lady of Pink Dresses being, of course, the most obvious example."

Tip nodded. "I'm glad he has someone like that on his side. Are you sure she's truly good, though?"

Nick shrugged. "Scarecrow trusts her."

"He doesn't trust any witch," Lion said. "So either she really is good, or she has him under a terrible spell."

"Let's hope it's the first. She seemed determined to help." Nick braced himself for the awful words which needed to be spoken. "There's bad news as well. He arrived too late. Dorothy...is dead."

Lion's ears flattened, whiskers drooping. "No," he muttered, "oh, no."

Ozma Tip curled her thin fingers into Lion's mane, wavering on her feet.

Nick felt tears starting again. "She died a long time ago in the Outside World. Scarecrow is traveling to Kansas to read her diary."

Tiger was stunned. "She was such a sweet girl," he whined. "Even though she wouldn't let me eat her pet chicken."

The Wogglebug cleared his throat, voice raspy. "Although I only met her briefly the once, after your adventure in the terrible domain of the Nome King, she seemed a lovely young lady. My friends, I am deeply sorry for your loss."

Nick struggled not to let memories surface again. He'd cried his heart out to a thick, heavy silence after his last talk with Scarecrow. Once Glinda was out of earshot, of course. "She was lovely and brave, yes."

Lion blinked back tears. Now Nick couldn't hold his in either. He fished out a handkerchief to dab the moisture before he rusted. He'd never have gained his heart without Dorothy's help.

"What happened to her?" Tiger asked.

"I don't really know. Scarecrow mentioned something about her being locked up. They thought she wasn't right in the head." Nick chuckled weakly. "All her stories about men of tin and talking lions didn't impress her countrymen, apparently."

"Her countrymen must be horrible people," Tip burst out. She clutched Lion tightly, shaking. "How dare they. I should go there myself and teach them all a lesson."

"I understand how you feel." Nick laid a hand on her shoulder. "I do. But time moves differently there. She's been gone a long time in the Outside World. There's nothing we can do for her."

"What good is being fae at all if I can't save the people who matter?" Tip cried. "Scarecrow's trapped in that horrible world, Dorothy's dead, the stupid Seelie Court wants me off the throne, the horrible witch'll hurt all of you if you try to protect me, and I can't do any real magic! The only spells I know are all stupid!"

Nick let her pound her fists against his chest. He expected to hold her, comfort her, but to his surprise and pride, once she'd let out her anger, she straightened her back and glared at the barred door.

"*She* sent him away. She knew he wouldn't find Dorothy." Emerald eyes gleamed bright and furious. "I'll make her pay."

The big cats growled agreement. The Wogglebug adjusted his robes anxiously, eyes downcast.

"Let's not give up yet," Nick said. "The court doesn't seem to have caught on to our meetings. Scarecrow has a powerful ally in the other world, and she might be able to get him back to us. At least we can still talk to him. Most importantly, he told me where the secret passageway to the magical library is."

"The one with all the spellbooks?" Tip asked, brightening.

Nick nodded. "Through there." He pointed at the massive stone fireplace. A cheery flame burned upon a small pile of logs.

Tiger pounced on it. "Well what are we waiting for!" His enormous paw swatted the logs out of the way. Sparks scattered. The others shouted, but flames caught on a bookshelf and the hearthrug immediately.

The Wogglebug grabbed one of the buckets of water placed strategically around the room and doused the bookshelf. Good thing Scarecrow kept emergency water at hand, always terrified of both fire and witches. Nick stamped out the embers on the rug. His metal shoe warmed up, but the fire died. Burnt hair smell filled the room. Tip leaned on a chair, coughing.

"Idiot," Lion snarled, cuffing Tiger over the head.

"I didn't know it would do that!" Tiger protested. "I thought it would just go out if it wasn't in the fireplace."

"That's not how fire works," Lion sighed, nuzzling the abashed Tiger. "You could've been burned. Don't do it again."

"Sorry," Tiger mumbled.

The Wogglebug shook his head at the smoking, soaked books. "Good thing our straw friend isn't here to see this."

"We'll fix it before he gets back." Tip picked up her scepter. The jewels in its finial glowed green. She waved it in a complex pattern at the fireplace, muttering a charm under her breath. "I don't feel anyone on the other side. Let's go."

"I'm going first," Nick announced.

Ozma Tip's sharp eyes met his for a long moment, but finally she nodded and touched his arm. "Be careful. I don't want to lose you too."

Nick felt around the hot edges of the blackened iron shield which covered the back wall of the fireplace, reflecting heat back into the room. He pressed, pulled, got soot all over his metal fingers. He'd been in this library dozens of times and never really noticed the design. The shield was shaped like a huge book, a winding road carved into the wall leading to its open pages. He peered closer. Right where the road met the book, was that a tiny crack?

He pressed his fingertips hard against that spot and heard a click. With a push, the shield gave way. The outline of the book opened into the back of the fireplace, forming a small door. Blackness beyond.

The Wogglebug handed a lantern to Nick. The narrow, low-ceiling passageway full of cobwebs stretched off as far as he could see. He shifted the light to his left hand, took his axe in his right, and muttered an apology to any spider lurking in here as he hacked away the webs. He heard a scuffle briefly behind him, an argument over who should be next, and then Lion was at his back, sneezing.

"Quiet," Nick whispered.

"I hate spiders." After the Wizard granted their wishes, Lion overcame his cowardice by killing a monstrous arachnid which had terrorized the southern forest. The feat gained him dominion over the wild beasts there.

"At least these are tiny," Nick pointed out as one scuttled away.

"Did you guys say spiders?" Tiger called from behind them.

"Shhhh," Tip hissed.

"I like the way they crunch," Tiger mumbled.

"Can we not speak of crunching things?" the Wogglebug complained.

Trying to ignore them all, Nick kept moving, swinging his axe in short swipes. The tunnel walls and ceiling closed in around him. This better not become any narrower, or they'd be stuck.

Suddenly his axe hit stone ahead. He froze, listening to the echo in the passageway.

"What's wrong?" Lion whispered.

"I think we're at the end. Hold on."

He brought the lamp close to the wall blocking the passage. He pushed but couldn't budge it. His fingers explored the seams where the walls met, but nothing gave way.

Scarecrow had opened it at least once, enough to see a fire burning on the other side. Nick spread his fingers against the cold stone. No heat now, and no visible way to open the wall. How had Scarecrow managed it?

Shining the light in the upper corners and along the seams brought no answers. Nick set the lamp on the floor to wipe the spiderwebs from his hands and face. Blast and forge, he was no good at puzzles. He dug the Evstone out of his pocket. "Scarecrow? My friend, can you hear me?"

Nothing. The stone remained dark. Nick sighed.

"Move," Tip said, and Tiger grunted. Lion's claws scraped the stones as he tried to spread his feet farther apart. Tip wriggled up between his forepaws as Nick half-turned. She'd crawled under the cats. Her robe and hair were covered in cobwebs. She sneezed again, furiously wiping stray bits of spider silk from her face. "What's wrong?"

"I can't figure out how to get past this."

Tip squeezed between him and the wall to study it. The heat of her body pressing against Nick's metal was discomfiting. He edged back. Tip dropped to her knees. "Hey, there's something written on the floor."

Nick peered but couldn't see anything. "What is it?"

"It's in Old Ozian," Tip said. "I don't know all the words though. Something like: *seek things below your station*. Or maybe *rank*, or *power*. I haven't learned all the vocabulary yet."

"Can you read it aloud?" the Wogglebug called softly.

The strange, lilting language of the old fae rolled from Tip's tongue.

Nick grabbed her robe and yanked her back from the floor stone, which suddenly slid to the side. A sharply slanted drop ended in a roaring green fire.

"Bogtroll asses," Tip gasped.

Nick clasped her against him, bracing one arm against the wall, feet set firmly against the floor. Carefully he leaned to study the fire. "No wonder Scarecrow never actually went in this way."

Tip scoffed. "That's not a real fire! Do you feel any heat?"

"No," Nick admitted. Despite the crackling roar from below, the bright green flames emitted no smoke or warmth, nor did there seem to be an actual chimney flue. "Illusion?"

"Has to be. Probably Mombi's work. It's her specialty," Tip sniffed. She shook off Nick's grip and plunged down the drop.

Nick gasped, reaching for her too late, but Tip's head suddenly poked back out of the fire. "Yep. Illusion. Oh—you have to see this. Come down here."

Nick followed, with Lion edging down the slanted stone behind him. Stepping out of the fake fireplace, Nick's jaw dropped.

Shelves held tomes with ancient, cracked bindings, cubbies of scrolls, and rows upon rows of dark jars and sealed bottles full of archaic substances. An eye stared at Nick from one of the larger jars. He shivered. One wall was covered by a truly ugly tapestry depicting the bloody, legendary Battle of Red Top Mountain. Though the warriors of Iowyn's Brigade and the Hammerhead tribes they slaughtered were picked out in colored thread, the pools and rivulets of blood running between the mountain rocks appeared disturbingly wet. A single door shimmered in the opposite wall, as if not quite there.

In one corner, on a pedestal illuminated by magic lamps, a shining quill scratched away at an open book on its own.

"The secret library," Tip said in awe. She was staring at the shelves of books and scrolls, her back to the Book of Records. "The one Scarecrow found the old scrolls in. Before Glinda moved in and hid the door."

The Wogglebug stood beside Nick, staring at the scribbling scroll. "Is that—"

"I think so," Nick said. "This is a very bad idea. We need to leave. Now."

"Wait!" The Wogglebug hurried over to the book and adjusted his spectacles. "Nothing of our meeting in Scarecrow's library is here. It only just started noting our presence in this room."

"Well make it stop!" Nick snapped.

The Wogglebug shook his head. "I have a better idea. Your Highness, please gather whatever you need from here quickly, and let's be gone. I will rip the page out and move the ink farther from the pen to prevent it from recording our exit." He gestured at a bottle of dark emerald ink into which the quill periodically dipped.

No one here right now, but certainly one of Glinda's secretaries would come check on the book at some point. "I agree. Tip, we shouldn't be in here."

Tip stared at him wide-eyed. "Nick, this room—these books—do you know how badly I've wanted to get in here?" Spotting the tapestry, she recoiled. "Gross. Looks like the blood's actually flowing."

Tiger's huge nostrils flared. "It is. That's real blood."

"This is dark magic," Lion growled. "Unseelie Court stuff. No one should touch anything in here. Ozma dear, we should go."

"No, wait," Tip argued. She studied the awful tapestry a moment, then lifted it up. Behind it, a swirling whirlpool of paint moved slowly within a gilded frame. "The magic picture. I knew it!"

"Don't touch that," Nick begged.

Of course Tip stuck her hand right into it. Nick ran to her and pulled her back. Magic dripped from her fingertips. Tip wiped her hand on her robe. The lush fabric sizzled.

Nick shuddered. If she wasn't part fae, it would've killed her. "What did I just say!"

Tip scowled. "I'm fine. You guys, look! The magic picture. We should ask it stuff."

"Can it show us Scarecrow?" Lion wondered.

"Magic picture, show us Scarecrow," Tip ordered.

The swirling paint gave no sign it heard.

"Try it in Old Ozian," Professor Wogglebug suggested.

Tip spoke again. The paint shimmered, crackled as though on fire, and resolved into a dark cornfield. Nick gaped. The magic picture was rumored to only work if the desired subject were in Oz. The scene sputtered, blurred, resolved, blurred again, for an instant showed the silhouette of a man in a peaked hat among the tall waving cornstalks.

"It's working," Nick gasped.

The image's colors ran together as the paint sloshed around in the frame. With a crackle of magic sparks, it resolved for only a second into a long leg ending in a wheel. Ribbons fluttered, wrapped around the leg. A glimpse of yellow teeth in moonlight. The painting fizzled again. Nick jumped in front of Tip to shield her as sparks sprayed. Magic burned his upheld arm, sending shorts of pain along his metal frame.

"Nick! Nick, are you hurt?"

He fell back a step, panting, a wave of heat searing through him. Tip waved her wand above his sizzling arm, speaking words he didn't understand. The acidic pockmarks where the magic had spattered him slowly closed, nickel plating creeping back over his tin. He hadn't felt actual pain in years, not since his flesh was chopped off and replaced bit by bit with tin parts. Shaken, he mumbled thanks.

"This place is dangerous," the Wogglebug said. "Your Highness, we shouldn't be here. Not even you are safe, especially if Her Pinkness finds out you've been intruding."

"This is *my* palace. I am the rightful Queen. All of this belongs to me, not her," Tip growled.

"All right, but if she catches us here," Lion muttered, leaving the thought unfinished. Nick's frightened eyes met his. The witch Locasta tortured them for months, first to see whether they were magical enough to truly challenge her powers, and then just for her own amusement. If not for Scarecrow's singing, both of them would've died in the palace dungeon.

And Glinda was far more powerful than Locasta.

Tip addressed the painting again, but after a fitful whirl of paint, it returned to its featureless circling, as if the colors were caught in a slow, liquid cyclone.

"That thing at the end looked like a Wheeler," Tiger said.

Nick frowned. "Yes, it did."

"How could a Wheeler be in the Outside World?" Professor Wogglebug wondered.

This was bad. Nick reached for the Evstone only to find the sparks from the painting had burned through his waistcoat. After a panicked search he found the stone on the floor. He let out a deep breath upon determining it wasn't cracked. He held it in cupped hands, spoke his friend's name. Nothing. "Damn it, Scarecrow! Lightning and ruin!"

"We have no way to warn him," Lion muttered, whiskers twitching.

Tip slammed her hands against the wall. "Filthy Nome bollocks! Why can't magic just *work* when we need it to?"

"Perhaps the painting truly cannot see well beyond our borders," the Wogglebug suggested. "However, we have other worries. Your Highness, can you have it show us the Unseelie Court?"

Tip studied the painting with furrowed brows. She brushed a long lock of dark hair from her face. Her tiara was askew, littered with cobwebs, hair tugged free of its pins after the crawl through the secret passageway. Her robe of quilted silk and royal nightgown were stained, ripped, blackened with soot. Her expression was fierce and focused. At this moment, she was more regal than ever.

Nick had to smile, despite everything. She was going to make a fantastic ruler.

If Glinda let her live.

"Show us what each member of the Unseelie Court is doing right now," she ordered, then repeated the command in Old Ozian.

The paint swiftly gathered itself into a scene of darkness. It conveyed no sound. Nick squinted at shambling shapes in what might be a cave underground. He thought he saw stalactites, faintly glowing with patches of magic fungus. Suddenly a bright red light burst into the painting. Nick startled back, reaching for Tip's shoulder, but nothing came out of the frame this time. When his vision adjusted, he saw the fiery light came from a pair of wavering heads. Dark eyes flickered inside balls of flame atop blackened, spindly tree-limb forms. They looked as if Jack Pumpkinhead had been set afire and still lived.

"Fire-walkers," the Wogglebug gasped. "I thought those were a myth." He pointed at the darker, shambling stacks of rocks. "Those must be rock trolls."

Nick's mother told her misbehaving children tales of such monsters to keep them from roaming after dark, scare them into doing all their chores. "The rock trolls eat naughty children," he mumbled.

"Rock trolls eat anything," Tip corrected quietly. "I read it in one of the old books."

"Where are they going?" Lion asked.

Tip shivered. "They're coming here. Don't ask me how, I just *know*. They're coming here. Those awful things. Underground. To the Emerald City."

"Professor," Nick asked, "you said you've mapped the secret tunnels under the University?"

The Wogglebug clutched his disguise tightly around his head as if wanting to disappear into the robes for good. "Not all of them. And I never go to the deeper levels. Way down where the ancient altars still stand. Altars slick with blood..."

"Shut up," Lion snarled.

Tip stood straight, though pale. "Show us Locasta," she commanded the painting, repeating the words in the older tongue.

The paint flowed, resolving into the self-proclaimed Good Witch of the North. Her white hair stood out from her head, her wrinkled features drawn tight over her skull. She stirred a cauldron, lips moving, though they could hear nothing. She lifted something wrapped in a blanket. It wriggled. When a tiny fist stretched from the blanket, Tip gave a cry, raising her scepter.

Locasta let the blanket unroll, dropping the wailing infant into the cauldron. She grinned at the splash and erupting steam.

Nick's jaw dropped and tears sprang to his eyes. Tiger growled, starting forward. Recovering his wits, Nick grabbed the ruff of Tiger's neck, planting his feet to stop the beast from attacking the painting. "She's miles away, you can't get to her!"

Tiger bared his fangs, head swinging wildly from Nick to Tip to Lion. "A baby! She just *killed* a baby! I only ever *thought* about eating one, I never did it, and she just dumped one into her spell-pot and I bet it can't even swim!"

The Wogglebug gulped. "Friend Tiger, if it's any consolation, I am certain the infant perished quickly. Probably the moment it hit whatever vile magic is in that cauldron."

"She's evil," Tip cried. "Murderer! Evil witch!"

Nick agreed, but doubted they could do anything. "Can your spells reach through the painting?"

Tip raised her scepter. Emeralds and diamonds glowed. With a curse she thumped the butt of it against the floor. "No. I don't know how. Horrible old hag! I'll have her dragged here at once. I'll reopen the dungeon, I'll chain her and seal her up forever!"

The Wogglebug stepped in, grim. "Your Highness, you will do no such thing. Not now. Not yet," he amended when Tip whirled to glower at him. "We must learn exactly what they plan. When they will strike."

"Winter's Eve," Nick remembered, chagrined. In all the strain of the night, he'd forgotten what the witch Lady Theo said. "They're going to do it on Winter's Eve."

Tip's eyes widened. "There's a big party. Every lord and lady of the Seelie Court is invited. It's going to be the event of the century."

Why hadn't Nick heard about this? Court parties for the end of autumn were all the fashion, and the past two years he'd endured having kindling stuffed in his stomach, a fire lit inside him for the guests to roast soft-mallow fruits and chestnuts. He'd been relieved when nothing at all was mentioned as the celebration date grew closer this year.

"They're all coming here this time," Tip continued, shivering. "To the Emerald Palace. I saw one of the invitations. The Pink Witch told me she's throwing a big party for me, but it's supposed to be a surprise and so I should pretend not to know. I thought it was just her playing a stupid court game again. All the fae are coming. *All* of them." She clutched her scepter tightly. "She told me not to be frightened, because many of them aren't regular people at all. Lots of very old fae."

"We need to go," Lion repeated, eyes darting around the room.

In the silence, the scratching of the magic quill made Nick want to throw it into the fire. Any fire.

Tip spoke more Old Ozian words. "Show me Mombi," she repeated for the benefit of the rest of the group.

The image changed from Locasta stirring her terrible brew to a small cottage lit by black candles. Mombi hunched over a spellbook, mouthing something. She reached to the sky, withered hands shaking, then grabbed a fistful of sparkling dust from an open canister and sprinkled it onto a strange object. At first Nick thought it was a bundle of straw, bound with red ribbon. The old witch lifted both hands, still chanting, and the object rose into the air before her. The straw was bunched and tied roughly into the shape of a boat's anchor, though only a fraction of the usual size. The witch seemed careful not to touch it, turning her hands in the air several inches away to make it rotate in midair. Sharp green eyes examined the anchor from under her wild fringe of rust-red hair.

"What's that?" Lion asked.

Tip shook her head. "Don't know. Never seen anything like it. It's not an illusion as far as I can tell. The only other thing she does really well is transformation."

"Maybe she's trying to turn it into a real anchor," Tiger said.

The Wogglebug's mustaches twitched. "Why in Oz would she want to?"

Tiger shrugged. "Maybe she needs to go fishing?"

"I wish the Wizard were still here," growled Lion. "He kept all the witches from the city a good many years."

"Show me the Wizard," Tip commanded, repeating it in Old Ozian. She'd never met the man, unless one counted him stealing her from the palace and giving her to Mombi as an infant. Rather than eat the baby, Mombi changed her into a boy and raised her as a bound-slave. If Tip hadn't run away from her, she'd be a boy still.

If Mombi hadn't done something else to him.

The painting swirled. White streaks of paint circled within the frame. "I thought he left for the Other World." The Wogglebug frowned. "We won't be able to see him if he's not—" They saw a snowy mountain-top through swirling clouds. A large colorful blanket was snagged on the highest peak.

Not a blanket. The hot-air balloon the Wizard used to leave the Emerald City. Just below it on a jagged crag was a broken, brown thing. The basket. A skeleton in black rags hung over the side of it.

"Oh," said Lion. "Well. Guess we're not getting any help from him."

Nick's chest tightened. "The poor man."

They all stared in silence a moment. "We should go. This gains us nothing," muttered the Professor.

Tip took a deep breath. *"Taispeán dom Glindala."*

"No," Nick exclaimed, but the painting flowed, changed, resolved into the Good Witch of the South. Her red robes and long scarlet tresses billowed in a strong wind. Sand blew past. Under the waxing moon, she stood on a flat rock, facing away from them. Across the gray dunes, figures skated toward her. Their thick muzzles opened to show rows of gleaming teeth. Ragged bits of fabric streamed out from their muscular bodies, skin the color of the sand.

"Sharks of the Deadly Desert," the Professor whispered, the old nickname given the creatures by sand-faring pirates ages ago.

Lion spat. "Wheelers."

"She's in her red robes." Tip's voice shook. "Not pink. She's doing serious magic."

The Wheelers slid up to the rock in a spray of sand. Their dead, black eyes seemed to stare right at Nick. His axe was raised and his knees clanked. He forced himself to keep still. Those things couldn't see them. The magic picture was invisible to anyone being spied on. The Wheelers' heads lifted, jaws snapping open and shut. Dorothy had described the terrible laughter of those monsters. Though Nick never heard it himself, he could well imagine the horrible sound.

Glinda spoke to the Wheelers. They fidgeted, rolling this way and that, but their ears were turned to her. She gestured broadly, then turned and pointed right at Tip, speaking soundlessly in the moving painted image.

"She can't see us," Ozma Tip breathed. She backed up anyway. Nick put a protective arm around her. She leaned into him. "She can't see us, don't worry."

Suddenly, as one, every Wheeler head lifted in a silent howl, and they raced toward the painting. Nick flinched as each one blurred and vanished upon passing the edge of the frame.

"Wheelers aren't allowed in Oz," Lion rumbled uncertainly.

"I don't think she cares," Nick replied. "Professor, any idea which desert that is?"

Shifting sands surrounded Oz on every side. The Empire was only kept from sinking into the deserts by ancient spells laid down by the first fae, aeons ago. If the Wheelers were invading, it would be helpful to know from what direction.

The Wogglebug adjusted his spectacles, leaning forward. "The rocks are volcanic. See the strata running through the big jagged boulder there? You can see where a line of iron has been crushed by the enormous pressure of—"

"South." Nick remembered the dark, jagged rocks and high peaks they'd crossed on their way from the Emerald City to petition Glinda, years ago. Back then, despite the dangers he, Lion, and Scarecrow faced on their journey with Dorothy, none of them imagined the Good Witch they were walking toward was so full of deceit.

"She's sending them to her palace," Tip said. "The Ruby Palace."

It made a sick kind of sense. Glinda's domain as ruler of the Quadling country was isolated from the rest of Oz by the Red Mountains. She could have a whole battalion of monsters quartered there and the rest of the Kingdom would never know.

"She really is working with the Unseelies," the Wogglebug whispered. "Those creatures were formed of the desert itself, of ill winds and life-sucking sands. Old elements."

Glinda smiled, watching after the disappearing Wheelers. She looked up at the moon.

"Winter's Eve is in five days." Nick's grip tightened on Tip. "We need to get you out of here. Someplace safe."

"We could run to the Forbidden Forest," suggested Lion. "The beasts there are a match for any skinny Wheeler. We'll protect you, Your Highness."

"She'll check there first," Tip argued. She tapped Nick's hand. With an apology he released her. She shook her head, scowling at the painting. "I need to learn more spells, fast."

Glinda froze. Slowly her head turned toward them.

Her black eyes narrowed. She pushed her slithering hair away from them to stare right at Ozma Tip. Her lips lifted and her teeth, her real teeth, sharp as needles, caught the light.

Nick jumped forward and yanked the tapestry down. "That's it. Let's go!"

Tip gestured helplessly at the shelves of books. "I need these!"

"Let's go," Nick repeated forcefully, his eyes snapping to Lion. The great cat nodded and wrapped a paw around Tip's waist.

"He's right. I'm sorry. Move."

"No, I need these, I can't fight her without magic!" Tip cried. She leapt away from Lion, her hands scrabbling over the tomes, frantically checking the titles. "This one!" She snatched a slender volume off a low shelf.

"Move, move, move!" Nick ordered.

Lion unceremoniously took Tip's gown collar in his mouth and dragged her away from the bookshelf like an unruly cub. The Wogglebug quickly pushed the remaining volumes together so it wasn't obvious anything was missing, then hurried to the Book of Records where the quill continued to write, damning them as it recorded all their actions. Tiger faced the only door to the room, hackles raised, backing slowly toward the fireplace as Lion took a running leap up into it, carrying Tip with him.

"Rip the page and let's go," Nick hissed, one foot on the hearth. The emerald flames still roared, logs crackling but never consumed.

The Wogglebug bent over the book, reading carefully. As soon as the quill lifted to dip itself in the inkwell again, he plucked the well from the pedestal with one hand, moving it out of reach, while two more hands held the book firmly. The quill sought the ink, but the Professor kept moving it. He licked the fingers of his free hand, wiped them along the seam of the page, and tore two of them out neatly. The quill darted at the inkwell. Stepping back, the Wogglebug's rounded bottom hit another pedestal, causing the urn upon it to wobble. Nick winced, too far away to catch it, but the Wogglebug spun and grabbed the urn before it hit the floor. The quill lunged for the inkwell. The Wogglebug jerked it out of reach and the quill lanced his hand.

Yelping, he dropped the inkwell. Glass shattered. Thick green ink pooled on the floor, spreading out along the cracks in the stone.

Nick and the Wogglebug froze. Blast and rust! No way to conceal their intrusion now.

"Tiger, catch," the Wogglebug said. He wadded up the pages and lobbed them at Tiger.

Tiger caught the ball of paper in his jaws and swallowed with a grimace. "Ugh!"

"Go," the Wogglebug urged as the quill drifted down to the spilled ink and tried to refill itself. He pulled the priest robes over his head and tugged the sleeves down as he moved toward the door. The quill rose again.

Nick didn't need to be told twice. He shoved Tiger at the fireplace. The great cat bunched his muscles and leaped up. Nick scrambled up after him. He heard the secret library's door squeak open and shut as the Wogglebug escaped. Nick lifted his feet out of the hole over the green fire. "Close it," he begged Tip. "Quickly!"

Tip was white as snow, green eyes staring dully. Lion shook her by the arm. She startled, then waved her scepter at the stone floor panel. It slid shut.

"Hurry, back to Scarecrow's room," Nick urged. "That damned pen is probably writing about us already!"

Tip shook her head. Her eyelids fluttered. "Donn' think so," she slurred. "Iron." She pointed at the passageway floor. In the flickering light of their dying lamp, traceries in the stone Nick had taken for crumbling cracks were lines of powdery red rust.

"Thank the stars," Nick gasped.

Tip's eyes rolled up and she collapsed.

"Go. Go!"

They shouldered through the secret passage, Lion making frightened little growls as he tried to tug Tip along by her robes. Nick took her feet and they carried her back to Scarecrow's protected library. Nick lifted the young Queen onto the sofa and immediately ran back to the iron shield in the fireplace, pulling it shut until he heard a hollow *thunk*. He threw himself at it twice to be sure it was firmly closed, metal clanging on metal.

Tip breathed rapidly, unconscious. Her brow was cold and clammy to the touch.

Metal bars on the door, thick walls and bookcases shrouding a massive iron cage. What kept the witch's magic from penetrating here was making their part-fae Queen sick. "She can't stay in here any longer," Nick groaned. "It'll kill her."

"Let's take her to her bedchamber," Lion offered. "We'll stand guard." Though his voice was deep and determined, Nick saw fear in his old friend's amber eyes.

"I will eat anyone who tries to mess with her," Tiger snarled. He coughed. "No more paper though. That was nasty."

Nick once witnessed Tiger devour six whole hams, twenty roasted turkeys—bones and all—and a hundred peeled baked potatoes in the space of a few minutes, and then demand dessert. If any stomach was strong enough to withstand a couple pieces of paper, his surely could.

Fae of all kinds were converging on the Emerald Palace. Glinda was assembling an army of monsters. The most powerful witches in Oz were crafting spells of unknown purpose. Elemental spirits made flesh, the most ancient and undying Unseelie Court, were heading this way. The safest room in Oz from all these threats made Tip sick.

Nick rubbed his forehead. He had no magnificent magic brains. His stuffed velvet heart was useless. How could he defeat forces this powerful, this evil?

A gentle paw touched his leg. Lion's whiskers quivered. "Whatever it takes," he rumbled. "You have us."

"Whatever it takes," Tiger repeated, lashing his tail. "I'll kill anyone that touches her."

Nick took in a deep breath. He had no lungs anymore, but old habits died hard. "Whatever it takes," he agreed. "For Ozma. For Oz."

"For Oz," the cats echoed.

"Tiger, with me. Let's get her to my quarters. She can hide there at least a day, I hope. Lion, go find Jellia Jamb, tell her to bring willow-bark tea and a warm compress."

"On it," Lion growled. He rose on hindpaws to slide open the bolt of the library door and checked outside. With a nod back at Nick, he glided on silent feet into the hallway and vanished behind a pillar.

Tiger stayed close as Nick gently gathered Tip into his arms. "She can't die," Tiger muttered. "She just *can't*, Nick."

"She won't," Nick promised. He took a careful step into the gloomy, empty corridor. His metal foot rang on the marble floor. Walking slowly, he headed for the concealed exit. Just a few hundred feet out and down to his own chambers in the western wing. A few hundred feet, and probably several guards. "Do me a favor. Run ahead and distract anyone who might raise an alarm."

Tiger nodded. "Do you think the bug's safe?"

"I don't know. I hope so."

"Yeah. Me too. I kinda like that jerk." He flicked his tail and bounded out the door.

Tip muttered and struggled in his arms. Nick shifted his grip, trying not to cause her any discomfort while keeping his balance as he descended the outside stairs. "Shh, Tip. Everything's all right."

From below, a roar and a cry. Then a lot of men yelling and the clang of metal. Tiger's snarling laughter. "Aw come on, let's play! I'm bored!"

A wail made Nick freeze. The shouts of the guards turned angry. Nick dared a peek over the stone balustrade concealing him from the garden below. In the torchlight marking the edges of the formal rose garden, a striped orange streak shot across the grass. Bumping along, screaming, one arm clamped in the Tiger's jaws, was a Palace guard. A second later, the entire barracks pounded after them in full armor with halberds raised.

After he'd led them on a merry chase, they'd better not try to stick the big cat with those halberds. That would not go well for the guards.

Nick hurried to his quarters unopposed and laid Ozma Tip on the bed he never slept in. He tucked warm blankets over and around her. She sighed, sinking into the pillow.

He waited, pacing, axe at the ready, listening for any sound of trouble.

Five days. Five days 'til the party of a century, the convergence of far too many hostile and powerful fae upon the palace, and very likely the end of Ozma's reign. He watched her sleep, thin features sharp and faery-like, breath shallow, perspiration beading on her forehead like a feverish mortal child. She hadn't wanted to be Queen. Blast and rust, she hadn't even wanted to be a girl. This was all Glinda's doing. Glinda changed her sex, put her on the throne, stopped a civil war between the witches' factions.

All so she could now plot a coup the likes of which Oz had never seen. None of this made any sense.

Nick paced and waited and listened. It was all he knew how to do.

23

Kansas turned out to be both the flat, endless prairie which Dorothy had described to him, and yet livelier than he'd expected. Scarecrow watched the scrubby trees and gentle hills covered in brown fields pass for mile after mile. Farmhouses and tall red barns appeared more often than he'd envisioned. Then again, after a hundred years, there were bound to be a few changes.

They stopped midmorning at another station with a shop so Theo could refuel the wagon and procure more of the energy drinks and sugary snacks on which she seemed mainly to subsist. Scarecrow insisted on coming with her into the shop.

No terrible squeaking sounds, nothing more worrisome than a large dog barking at him from the seat of an enclosed carriage. People stared at them. Scarecrow smiled politely in return. Theo purchased a pair of bright orange capsules labeled "ear plugs" in addition to her usual canned drinks and bags of comestibles. She took a few minutes in the public water closet there, and then they were off again.

As they continued due west, the trees thinned and shrank to shrubs. Huge rolls of grass lined the edges of fences in vast fields, drying in the sun. A few drab brown cows with only two horns, if any, grazed in some of the fields.

Where a dirt road intersected with the paved one, a wooden stand displayed fat orange pumpkins, corn sheaves gathered with pretty ribbons, and short scarecrows with painted round faces. Above a stubbly field of sheared cornstalks, a gray farmhouse with a peaked roof sat patiently, enduring the gusting wind. The windmill near the house wobbled and spun. In this flat landscape, he could easily envision the house battered by a cyclone, sent whirling into the gray sky.

"You okay?" Theo asked.

"I'm fine. Just thinking."

More dry fields slipped past. One large stand of unharvested corn boasted a sign at the dirt road next to it: CORN MAZE - PUMPKIN PATCH. He glimpsed children disembarking from an open wagon. Perhaps the parents were initiating their offspring in a local harvest deity ceremony?

"You don't offer up children to the fae here, do you?"

"What? No. Definitely not."

"Oh. Good."

"Do people do that in Oz?"

"They did for centuries until fairly recently. Until Dorothy changed everything." All he could hear right now was Theo's music, but he knew exactly what those rustling leaves and rubbing, creaking stalks would sound like in the breeze. Even though he'd only heard the noise for a few days before a young woman with wonder-filled eyes paused at a fork in the road of yellow bricks.

Dorothy laughed when he first told her of his wish. "What does a scarecrow need with a brain?"

"The crows mock me. They aren't afraid of me at all. The Old Crow said it's because I have no brains," he explained. "They say I'm silly and stuffed. I don't know how to scare them. I'm sure if I only had a brain, they would respect me."

The young woman smiled, patting his shoulder. "You are silly and stuffed. I don't know how any brains would make you better." She studied him for a moment. Her eyes were dark and bright at once, and he found himself fascinated. Unlike his, her eyes were wet and moved and she had the most delicate, thick lashes to protect them. "I'm going to the Emerald City to ask the Wizard to send me home. It's a pretty long journey, I think."

Scarecrow bobbed his head and nearly fell over. Standing on his own was vastly different than hanging from a tall pole. "It is, so I hear. Days and days away." Suddenly he wanted more than anything to talk more with her, listen to her melodic voice. Couldn't do that if she left. "Would you like company?"

She hesitated. Perhaps he was being too forward. Another idea occurred to him, which was a lucky accident since he had no sense at all. "Do you think perhaps the Wizard might be able to give me some brains, so I wouldn't be such a fool?"

"He might," the young woman said. "I guess I could use someone to carry my basket."

"I'd be delighted to carry it for you. I never tire."

Her silky-furred animal growled at him, biting his leg. Curious, he bent over to examine it.

"Don't mind him, he just thinks you're strange," the young lady said.

"I don't mind. And I suppose I am strange compared to you meat creatures." He straightened his back as much as he could and smiled at her. He couldn't help but smile. It was painted on. "Though I'm only a stuffed thing, and a fool at that, I'd love to come with you. I'll make myself useful somehow."

"All right," she agreed. "You can come along." She handed him her basket. He nearly toppled again, unused to bearing any weight, but quickly righted himself. The young woman frowned at him with lips pursed as if already regretting her decision.

"Thank you. I hope the Wizard is as magnificent as you say, and can give me some brains. It's such a great disappointment to know one is a fool."

She chuckled, and they set off together. Not the most auspicious start to a friendship. Yet through the miles and days following, she relied on him to gather nuts and berries for her, to watch over her when she slept, and even to lie against her when the nights turned colder. He knew nothing of love. All he knew was she delighted him and he'd do anything to keep her safe.

It never really sank into his head all this was so she could leave. Until she did.

The wagon bumped hard, jarring him back to the present.

"Damned potholes," Theo griped. "Not like I can avoid 'em in this freaking whale."

Vast swaths of open fields ran to the far horizons, the paved road cutting between them. A bare sketch of a wire fence edged along a cornfield. No habitations of any kind. The croplands of corn, grass, and open fields full of stubble blended into each other as if the landscape was one enormous farm. Clouds drifted overhead, an endless herd of them plodding east. No other carriages passed for some time.

Scarecrow imagined Dorothy growing up in this land. How small she must have felt. How alone.

Theo announced, "Coming up to the turn for highway sixty-three, and then after that, another forty-five minutes or so." She glanced at the route on her phone. "Maybe an hour. We have to go through a couple of small towns."

He nodded. "Thank you, Theo. I'd never have managed any of this without you."

"Yeah. Of course. No problem."

They exchanged a hesitant smile. Neither of them spoke of the Wheelers, or the undoubtedly dead shop clerk.

No city gates or guards heralded the arrival at Wamego. The open, brown land simply yielded to blocky buildings. More carriages passed by, the road widened. Gravel lots filled with brightly painted, oddly shaped carriages and signs advertising farm equipment gave way to trees in red and brown autumn foliage. They passed a sign: OZ MUSEUM AHEAD TO THE LEFT. How very strange, that people who didn't even think his country was real would erect a museum for it.

Theo turned left, and the ugly stores and garish signs dominating the roadside were replaced by modest houses, yards with a bit of green grass under carpets of fallen golden leaves. Just as he began to think the city was rather pleasant, the homes ended at an intersection. Beyond, buildings of bricks all the color of dead cornstalks arose. The street ahead was blocked.

"Figures," Theo grumbled. "The last leg in requires actual legs."

She found a spot to park the wagon. Turning off the machine, she took a deep breath and looked at Scarecrow.

Trepidation prickled down his crackly spine. He straightened his tunic, made sure no loose straw poked out of any seams, and climbed down from the wagon into a crisp breeze. He tugged his hat more firmly over his ears.

Yellow bricks led along one side of the street. He stepped carefully over the cracks before he noticed Theo's boots strode firmly atop them. They were painted onto the larger squares of pavement, not real bricks at all. He'd tripped on the actual road so many times, lacking the sense to go around the holes where bricks were missing. Ahead, a family posed next to painted wooden likenesses of a little girl in a blue-checked dress, a lion standing on two legs, a bulky canister of a metal man, and a scarecrow in blue with a too-wide smile on a flat circle of a face.

Scarecrow stopped. The family laughed, pointed magic phones at each other, put their arms around the flat wooden characters. That's all he and his friends were to people here, lifeless characters in a child's tale.

Theo tugged gently at his fingers. "There's the museum. Check out the flying monkeys." She nodded upward. Above a deep-green store-front, OZ MUSEUM was prominently displayed in gold letters. Statues of gray winged monkeys were frozen in poses of mischief all around the sign. Paintings on the glass windows depicted the poppy field, a wooded glen, a green-skinned witch. And over and over, the child who was sup-posed to be Dorothy and the grinning stuffed idiot which must represent himself.

"Ooh! It's the Scarecrow! Can we get a photo with you?"

He blinked at the smiling people suddenly surrounding them. "I beg your pardon?"

"A pic. With you. Great costume," said the mother. She was dressed in pink, with large shimmering wings fastened to her back.

"Shit," Theo muttered. "Hi guys, sorry, we don't really have time to—"

"Who're you supposed to be?" a tiny child asked. She wore a blue-checked dress and her hair was tied into twin pigtails. She crossed her arms and frowned up at Theo.

"Pardon us, we just need to—" Scarecrow began, but the mother in pink grabbed her children, tugged them against her and threw one arm around Scarecrow's shoulders.

"Thanks, this is great," she said brightly. "Okay kids, say 'There's no place like home!'"

Theo glowered when the family shoved her aside. The father of the family pointed his phone at them, laughing. "Oh, that's great! Nice ex-pression there too, Scarecrow. I can tell you haven't gotten your brains from the Wizard yet."

"Sir, I don't think I like your intimation," Scarecrow snapped. Theo hooked her arm in his and yanked him toward the museum door.

"Gotta go, have fun, watch your step on the Yellow Brick Road," she called over her shoulder, then apologized in a growl. "Ignore them, Scarecrow. Tourists. They don't know any better."

"A complete stranger just called me brainless," he protested. "The very nerve!" Before he could complain further they were inside the building, surrounded by wooden shelves crammed full of toys, cups, loose printed tunics on mannequin displays, books, stuffed dolls. Everywhere the word OZ. He came to an abrupt halt, arm in arm with Theo.

She seemed as taken aback as he was, staring around the room. "Okay, I'm betting this is very weird for you. Take a breath and let's just find what we came here for."

"I don't breathe," he murmured. The vast quantity of *things* crowded in on him, all depicting some version of him or his friends, witches, or printed words of unfathomable significance. He shrank away, but there was nowhere to go except back outside where that obnoxious family would probably try nailing him on a pole for a more realistic pose.

No, wait. A door. A door made of thin silver threads. He went for it, his sudden movement jerking Theo forward a step.

"Welcome to the Oz Museum! Happy Oztoberfest!" chirped a woman, startling Scarecrow. He hadn't even noticed there was a counter over there, so covered in merchandise was every surface. "Oh, love your costume! You can purchase tickets to see the museum here."

Theo took the lead, digging in her bag and presenting a thin card to the shopkeeper. "Two, please. Where is the Dorothy Gale diary?"

"It's in a special display, just past the Wicked Witch. Are you two here as performers?"

Scarecrow frowned, but Theo told the woman yes, concluded her transaction and steered Scarecrow by the elbow toward the door of silver thread. She whispered, "Okay, I'm sure a lot of this is going to seem whack to you. Their website said they have a lot of stuff from the movie."

"Interpreter," he muttered, falling behind her to pass through the creaking door. Lights within were dimmer. Magic lamps focused on a cluster of mushroom-like tiny houses and a girl in a blue-checked dress.

Her dark auburn hair was gathered into twin pigtails. She clutched a wicker basket and held a black-furred animal in the crook of one arm.

Scarecrow stopped. Was that supposed to be—? A sign at her feet confirmed it.

Theo hovered at his side. "Anything like her for real?"

His gaze sharpened, taking in every detail. The statue's skin gleamed, unlike the flesh of actual meat people, and her smile was unnervingly frozen. And yet her expression of joy and wonder was not so different from his love's. At every new discovery along the road of yellow brick, she would exclaim, point, and investigate. Lush fields of blue corn, the glow of the Red Mountains in sunset, the unearthly glittering green spires of the Emerald City. All of it was as new to her as it was to him, that first journey, and his delight in sharing it all with her made even the dangers worthwhile.

Theo nudged him. His straw crackled loudly in the enclosed space. "You okay?"

"Yes, thank you," he murmured. "She was shorter, and her legs were strong from farm work. Her body was shaped more like yours than this statue's." He indicated Theo's generous curves, top and bottom, with a wave. "Her hair was more dark brown than red, her flesh tanned from the sun." He shut his eyes to block out the statue and better remember the real Dorothy. "She was strong and cheerful. Walked so far with me, day after day. She lost the ribbons from her hair after a few days. I tried tying strands of my straw to hold it back from her face, but my fingers were so clumsy. I was always clumsy. Every time I tripped or fell, though, she pulled me back to my feet with a laugh."

"Are you sure you still want to read all the details of what happened to her?"

"Yes."

"Come on then."

Leaving the statue behind, they passed a long glass case holding a multitude of books, all with the word OZ on the covers. Scarecrow slowed, reading the titles. One cover depicted a very floppy straw man in a crown seated opposite a metal man composed of cylinders and hard angles. Him and Nick? "Who drew these? That's nothing like Nick Chopper. And I hated wearing a crown. It was the symbol of a lie."

"Kids' books," Theo reminded him.

"Don't children deserve to know the truth?" he grumbled.

Around a corner, a wall displaying numerous illustrations made him pause again. One in particular gave him a chill. A lumpily-stuffed, floppy straw man, wearing a tunic and trousers not unlike his own and with a peaked hat, was bound to a pole. A crowd gathered at the foot of it and a fire licked just below the prisoner's boots. "Is that me?"

Theo shrugged. "Remember I asked if you'd ever been almost burned at the stake?"

"How horrible." He shivered. The straw figure's wide mouth and huge staring eyes expressed dawning unhappiness, as if he were only just comprehending his imminent destruction. Again, it was unlike and yet oddly like how he'd appeared before commissioning this new head, this more lifelike face. Staring at the illustration was like gazing into a mirror warped by fire.

Theo took his hand in hers. "Diary?"

He nodded, straightening his back and his resolve. "Lead on."

They passed more displays behind glass: portraits, large paper broadsheets, ceramics and shoes and clothing. None of it made any sense to him. None of it was what he'd come here to find. Proclamations that the Wizard was "wonderful" and "classic" and "a triumph." Theo explained in a low voice this was all from "the movie." What significance did any of this have? None of it spoke of the horrors they'd faced, the civil war, the cruelty of the fae.

Scarecrow halted in front of a fenced-off corner. A statue sat in front of a painted cornfield, dressed in a green tunic with a patched black hat, its burlap features deep in thought. Too many words fought for dominance in his brains to express a single one. Finally a complaint he'd heard Theo utter seemed best. *"Really?"*

Theo giggled.

He glared at her, chin lifting. "I do not look so—so foolishly pondering. Or so shabby."

She peered from the statue to him. She bit her lip but couldn't keep a smile off her face. "Actually, they got the nose pretty close. And the eyebrows."

"The sack is all wrong. And I haven't worn rope ties to keep my straw in for years!"

A girl standing nearby laughed. Scarecrow scowled. He dusted off his tunic, tugging it straighter. "I do not. Look. Like that."

"You kinda actually do, just cleaned up better."

"Hmf." He turned away from the insulting statue, grandly ignoring Theo's continued failure to hide her mirth.

Picking up his pace, he headed along a gallery lined with more glass cases. Lights within them illuminated more dolls, books, tea sets and framed portraits. Baffling, all of it. As if the artificers for the royal treasury had crafted things to commemorate his adventures with Nick, Dorothy, and Lion against the late Witch of the West, but deliberately avoided accurately depicting any of them. Rounding a corner, the strange statue of a cylindrical-bodied Tin Woodman startled him. The effigy was bulky where the real Nick was graceful, joints clunky instead of the delicately fitted slivers of plated tin which enabled Nick to move swiftly and decisively.

Had this Tin Woodman fought with the witch's forty wolves or the Winkie brigade, all of the party would've perished.

Shaking his head, Scarecrow strode on. At the end of this corridor, double doors stood open beneath a sign heralding the Wizard. Sound and flickering light came from the dark within. He slowed enough to glance inside, expecting some sort of altar to the Wizard, whom this world seemed to revere. Perhaps he'd returned here and never found a way back to the Emerald City. Certainly, Scarecrow noticed the man's name mentioned at nearly every step in this museum. A few people worshiped on simple benches, their faces entranced, all gazing up at a magic picture hanging on the opposite wall. Unlike Glinda's magic painting, this one had no elaborate frame, but cavorting inside it were the man garbed in green with straw falling out of his tunic, the girl in the blue-checked dress, and the clunky silver man meant to be Nick Chopper.

Scarecrow stared. How was this possible? Was this other version of himself real after all?

"That's the movie," Theo whispered in his ear. "Might be better for you to watch it with me, not here. I know you'll have a few things to say about it, but these people are here because they love it and just want to enjoy it. Please don't go in there."

"But how—where is this happening? You said there's no magic here, yet this—"

"It's not happening now. This was filmed a long time ago. Gramma Hildy saw it in the theatre as a kid."

"What do goats have to do with your grandmother? And how do you have a magic picture on public display which can show people the past? How is there a version of me in your world's past?" His head hurt. Pressing fingertips to his temples, he massaged his shifting brains, but it didn't help.

Theo caught his left hand in both of hers, worry in her dark eyes. "I'll explain all of it, okay? But not here, not now. Let's just find the diary and see if we can convince the staff to let you read it."

"This makes no sense."

"I get that." Theo tugged him away from the inexplicable temple with its magic painting. This one even produced sound. A cheery song floated from the darkened room. "Not here, not now, let's let these folks alone. Come on."

He followed, head down. He didn't want to see any more of this. A lion standing on hind paws beamed at them from another decorated alcove, more man than beast. They went through a pitch-black hallway, flanked by a sign pointing to a haunted castle and a menacing tree from which Scarecrow instinctively shrank. A green-skinned statue dressed in black raiment sneered at them. The winged monkey crouched beside her was far less foul than the real thing. Just the sight of this pale imitation reminded him of the stench of their fur, the filthy feathers brushing him as he struggled in the grip of the one who'd dropped him into the spiked branches of a tall, dead tree. The coarse feel of strong monkey fingers ripping his straw out, leaving him empty and cold. With a shudder, he turned away. A tall soldier in a gray uniform scowled at him, brandishing a halberd. Another statue. These people seemed infatuated with painted statues.

A wooden pedestal topped with a glass case stood before a wall on which his love's sad portrait was painted. Dorothy huddled with a group of women of various ages, all in simple white shifts, faces haggard, eyes distant.

The case on the pedestal held an open book.

"This must be it," whispered Theo.

He stared at the portrait, larger than life and so much more desperate than he remembered her. Sweet, laughing Dorothy. How had she become this downcast, miserable woman? Dorothy stood with shoulders hunched, her once-lovely hair chopped straight across her brow, shadows in her eyesockets as if all the life had left her body and only a shell remained.

They hadn't believed her tales of Oz. People in this world couldn't accept it was real. This woman went through dangers unheard-of to help save Oz *twice*. Instead of listening, they locked her up with deranged souls. Reduced her to this listless living doll in a drab white gown.

The book's pages were covered in a tiny scrawl which veered all over. He'd never seen her write anything down, but surely these couldn't be her words. Not his Dorothy. She spoke and moved with purpose, with determination. Always went straight after what she wanted. Always said what she thought.

His feet drew him closer to the book although dread rose with every step. No, this was a mistake, he didn't want to see her like this. Didn't want to read her words written in whatever prison she'd been caged. No happiness here. His eyes flicked to the wall. Below the giant, terrible portrait of the tormented women, a sheet of printing was fastened. THE REAL DOROTHY: TWISTER, TALES, AND TRAGEDY. A quick read told him only what Theo's scrying-screen had said. Sanitarium. Delirium. Electroshock. These words meant nothing, they didn't convey her spirit.

His gaze settled back on the book.

The pages were yellowed, the ink brown and faded. A dim magic lamp shone upon on it from overhead. It took him a moment to adjust his brains to the odd, jerky lettering.

The open pages of the diary read:

"—*when I am cured mebbe I kin see famly agin. I wish docter Thomson wud promise me this but he only shakes his head when I ask, he says only I must get Well first and then we shall see. I am so tired but I very much want to be Well. So I will keep riting my dreams down here like he has askd. They never feel like only dreams but docter Thomson says there is no Oz, it was never Real but only a dream and if I pick apart what was in the dream I will see it is so. Only I do not know yet how to do this and again last night I dreemd of Oz.*

"*I was back in the corn field, everything blue like the sky, blue grass blue corn and blue cloths on the Scare-crow. Nick the Tin Man was there to even tho this is not how it happend when I was in Oz the first time. I did not see the Lion but Billina the hen was there eating corn. Scare-crow and Nick said We are so glad you are home, come with us, but I knew this was Oz and not home. The Scare-crow smiled the whole time and I was so angry at him, I wanted to hit the smile off his face. It was all rong and so I hit him, I hit the Scare-crow over and over and yelled at him. I said Where were you, you said you would always protect me but you cud not even protect me in Oz when the Witch's soldiers took me, you are nothing but straw. And he kept smiling the whole time I was punching him and Nick said forget about him, I will protect you, but I said No you did not eether. You are neether one real Men and I was stupid to listen to you. More stupid than the Scare-crow who thought a bunch of pins and bran made him smarter. More foolish than the Tin Woodman who thought a heart would make him care about me like I wanted him—*"

Scarecrow drew back with a gasp, straw twisted in his throat. The words must continue on the next page. He tried to lift the glass case out of the way, only then seeing the small fasteners and lock which held it to the pedestal. "Theo, help me," he begged.

Her hands on his arm. "Stop, it's locked. Stop."

"No. I can't. I have to know. I have to," he choked. Angrily he shook the pedestal but it was too heavy for him to topple.

"Shh, stop, please," Theo hissed, forcing him back, pulling his hands away from it. "I'm sorry, Scarecrow. This was a terrible idea." She clasped his hands in hers, staring up into his face with worried eyes.

"Dorothy," he said, unable to pick any coherent thought from his reeling brains.

Theo embraced him. He felt moisture trickling down his cheeks. "I need to read the rest," he whispered.

She nodded, her cheek rubbing against his collar. "We'll find a way. Just take a breath. Calm down."

"It's very sad." A stranger's voice interrupted.

Scarecrow forced himself to contain the wild surge of pain in his chest, to face yet another stranger who never knew the young woman he'd come all this way to fail to save yet again.

A tall woman with long white hair nodded at the diary. "I'm honestly surprised they decided to exhibit it. Really depressing, what happened to the real Dorothy."

"Depressing isn't the word." Theo sounded angry. "More like absolutely horrible."

"Yes. Yes, it was. Mental illness was poorly understood in those days." The woman studied Scarecrow curiously. "Are you all right?"

"He, uh—reading this kind of hit close to home for him." Theo released Scarecrow but stood in front of him.

"Oh," the woman said. "Forgive me, I didn't mean to pry."

"A good friend of his went through some shit like this." Theo nodded at the black-and-white painting on the wall of the miserable prisoners. She took a deep breath and her tone lightened. "Anyway. We're, uh, working on a paper about mental illness and its connections to children's literature. Is there a way we could sign up to study the diary? Like maybe transcribe parts of it?"

The woman seemed uncertain. "Well, that sounds like a fascinating topic. Jim Thicke is writing a book about Dorothy's experience in the asylum and her conversations with L. Frank Baum." At Scarecrow's blank look, the woman explained, "Jim's a famous Oz historian. He's received permission from the Thompson family to borrow the diary, at the end of this exhibit next weekend, so he can study it for his book. I'm sure it'll be a very in-depth treatment of the whole story."

"Okay," Theo persisted, "so how can we get permission to have a closer look at it before he borrows it? I mean obviously we'll wear gloves or whatever. We just need to read it."

"You'd have to apply to the Thompson Foundation, as they own the diary. But if you're interested, you should come to the presentation tonight."

"What presentation?" Scarecrow asked. Some historian pawing through Dorothy's private diary didn't please him one bit. *The only person reading that should be me. I was her first friend in Oz. Her closest friend. And I must know what she meant, what she thought, why she would dream such terrible things.* There had to be some reasonable explanation for the awful things he'd just read. Perhaps this wasn't really Dorothy's writing at all. The only way to know would be to read the entire thing. See if there was some reminiscence in it he didn't recognize. Something in those children's books that matched, to confirm this to be another fiction. Theo would know, she'd read the books. She could help him determine if some detail he didn't recognize at all was in those children's stories. Yes. Excellent idea. His brains were in fine form today. Some unfamiliar detail would certainly prove this wasn't really Dorothy's diary, just the scribblings of a lunatic, of course his Dorothy would not have said such hurtful—

Theo elbowed his side.

He refocused on the older woman, who was smiling expectantly at him.

"Beg pardon?"

"I said, admission is free. Eight o'clock tonight, in the little theatre back there where the movie is showing. It should be a pretty small crowd, just a few of us academics and hard-core fans. Jim will read aloud a few pages of the diary and discuss Dorothy's real history."

Well, that sounded terrible. Scarecrow opened his mouth to say so. Theo hooked one arm around his waist and squeezed tight.

"Sounds great, thank you! We'll be there." She beamed at the woman. "Thanks for the invite. Have a good day."

"What," Scarecrow said.

Theo propelled him, stumbling, away from the diary, past another statue of a smiling woman in a ballooning pink dress, out a door marked EXIT. It took him several steps to get his boots under him and walk instead of being dragged. "Did we not have this discussion about you yanking me around? Just because I'm straw does not mean I enjoy this," he snapped.

"I know, I'm sorry, but we have to go to that reading."

They breezed through the shop again, out into the afternoon sunlight. "Why would I spend even a moment listening to some complete stranger violating Dorothy's privacy by reading her innermost thoughts aloud? Assuming she even wrote any of it." He stopped, shame creeping through him. All his straw felt compacted, matted, uncomfortable. Patting his chest and stomach into better shape, he tried to regain some dignity.

Theo watched him, chewing her lower lip. "You think she didn't?"

"No." Yet that rambling narrative did conjure her voice in his memory. He rubbed his forehead. "Maybe. I don't know. I have to read all of it to know for sure."

"Okay, well, our only shot at it is gonna be tonight."

He raised an eyebrow at her, frowning.

"The place has a lot of security cameras," Theo explained quietly. "A lot. And probably alarms to keep thieves from walking off with all the expensive collectible stuff they have. Bet you set off an alarm trying to shake the case, so that lady came to see what was up. There is no way in hell we can steal that book from the case."

"I wasn't implying we should..." He sighed. "Perhaps in a moment of excessive emotion I wanted to. A little."

She searched his eyes. "You still want to read more?"

Ah. So Theo read the open pages too. His face felt hot. He touched his nose, his cheek, just to be sure nothing was actually burning. "Yes. I have to."

"Then we just need to go to this presentation tonight, when they'll have the diary out of its case, and steal it."

He blinked.

Theo grinned. "You up for some crimes?"

He could feel his brains quivering. "Steal the diary?"

"Yep. Granted, we'll have to do it in front of a room full of people and then hightail it outta town in a whale of a crappy RV that'll be visible for miles on these stupid flat highways."

His mind ran through the layout of the museum, the size of the small room with the magic picture, calculated the number of people likely to fit in the space, the time needed to get back on the road before they could be sure no one would be able to pursue them. "I think I have an idea. My brains weren't so shocked by all this after all."

Theo grinned wider and offered her arm to him. "Fabulous. I saw a taco place up the street. I am starving. Wanna come smell a taco while I stuff my face?"

"Interpreter?" he sighed, but accepted her arm.

"Tacos are the universal language. Trust me. Come on, Brainy. You plot. I'll eat."

24

Tacos proved to be better than expected, the salsa wonderfully spicy. An hour later, Theo's tongue was still tingling. Since people in town kept asking for selfies with Scarecrow, Theo figured it was better to retreat to the RV park and lay low until the talk at the museum tonight.

The tiny camper resort was just a few parking spaces with hookups. It boasted only a narrow plot of withered shrubs, decorated with pumpkins and fall mums in pots. Just across the road, a cargo train chugged past. The view was one of spindly, struggling trees and a car-repair shop next door. Motor oil scented the breeze. The word "resort" was stretching things.

Scarecrow seemed oblivious to their surroundings, pacing in the limited garden, head down. He'd been clearly uncomfortable in the taco place. He'd barely spoken a word since they parked here.

Theo leaned against the side of the camper, watching him. Since he'd identified the bedraggled young woman in the asylum photographs as his Dorothy, the real Dorothy, the diary was likely legit. He'd put her on a pedestal. Reading how angry she'd been with her Oz friends must've been a big shock to him. He'd been pacing since they stopped, lost in his own head. Didn't seem like that was a good place to be right now.

"You okay?" she asked for the third time.

Scarecrow waved a hand vaguely at her, nodding, but continued walking between the scraggly bushes and potted purple mums.

Was this really a great idea? Now she had time to consider it, she realized the thrill of stealing candy from the convenience store as a kid did not actually compare to stealing a priceless book from a museum. No idea whether it'd be a felony, but she was definitely too old for a stern warning and a seat on a precinct bench until her parents came to collect her. Dad wouldn't bail her out if they got busted. Not to mention, the last thing she wanted was for Scarecrow to end his days in a dingy jail cell.

"You still sure you wanna read the rest?"

"I'm sure." He paused. "Theo, if you don't want to be involved, I completely understand. It's selfish of me to even ask you to participate. I only intend to borrow the diary, but perhaps the museum staff will still regard it as theft. Surely if I explain myself when I return it, they'll—"

"Oh hell no. You think you can just walk back in there and hand it to them after we've stolen it in the middle of a public event?" She snorted. "We can mail it back anonymously from Iowa or something."

"If it's that serious, you shouldn't be involved. I shouldn't have asked you along for this."

Theo laughed. "You taking credit for my idea now?"

His dark brows wrinkled. "Well, you suggested it, but my brains figured out the best strategy for acquiring the diary."

"Right. We go in, you sing everyone to sleep, we grab the book and run like hell. Super complicated." A pained expression crossed his face, and she regretted her words. "It's a great plan. If it works."

"I can't decide which song would be best. The Prisoner's Lament is mainly for easing pain, and if the listeners are quite well, it probably won't put them to sleep. I could try the Autumn Festival song, but I've no guarantee it would affect others as it does you. Perhaps it only makes witches sleepy." He shook his head. "I'm having a great deal of trouble concentrating. My brains seem muddled."

No mystery why. "Scarecrow, I'm sure Dorothy wasn't just angry at you. She probably felt like everyone abandoned her in that awful hospital."

"I should've come with her," he muttered. "Should've asked to, at least, when she left Oz the second time. A talking scarecrow would have proven to everyone Dorothy's stories were true. Prevented her from ending up a prisoner, doubted, tormented."

"Without magic, you'd just be stuffed clothes. That wouldn't have helped either of you."

His chin lifted, painted eyes glaring steadily into hers. "That's what I'll be in a few days in any case. I can't change what happened, but maybe I can vindicate her now. Speak up, insist on Dorothy being recognized as a hero in her world as well as mine."

Theo bit her lip. "Not sure that's—"

He gave a determined nod. "Yes. Yes, I owe her this much and more. She saved my life, Theo. I failed her."

Theo went to him. "No, you couldn't know what things were like here. No way you could've stopped any of it."

His voice raised in protest. "I could've persuaded her to stay in Oz! Kept her safe! Even if she didn't want me. Even if she thought me a fool."

She was getting sick of that word. Sick of him using it to describe himself. "She was the fool for coming back here," Theo scoffed. "She was lucky enough to return to Oz a second time, knowing nobody here believed her, and she still came back to Kansas *again?* I mean seriously, what the hell was she thinking? *That* was stupid."

"Don't you talk about her like that!" Scarecrow shouted. "You didn't know her!"

"Good thing I didn't," Theo retorted, "'cause I'd've told her she was stupid for leaving you! Most people would kill to have a boyfriend as good as you!"

He gaped at her.

Theo took a step back. Her hands were curled into fists, her shoulders tense. The wind blew her hair over her eyes. She ducked her head, heat spreading across her cheeks.

They stood there in silence a moment. *Well, shit. Way to make things weird.* She took a long, deep breath. "I'm going in for some tea."

He nodded, turning away. His voice was subdued. "I'll stay out here. I need to determine what song would be best."

Theo hesitated, but he was already pacing again, head down, rubbing his temples. She climbed back into the camper and started a kettle on the burner.

Hours passed. Theo surfed the web on her phone. No reports about a gas station clerk murdered or anything strange discovered at a rural golf course in Iowa. Did the Wheelers clean up after themselves? How could they, with no hands? They were worse than wild animals, they wouldn't even if they could.

She glanced out the window again. Scarecrow paced tirelessly, shaking his head, mumbling to himself. As the afternoon wore into evening, her guilt simmered into irritation.

Who the hell gave up the chance to stay in a faery land to come back to a flat, dull country devoid of imagination? Yeah, okay, so Oz wasn't all sweetness and light and the fae turned out to be pretty vicious. It was still a colorful, magical land where men could have limbs lopped off and replaced by tin, lions could talk, and a scarecrow could develop a heart as well as a brain. Spells could be cast and adventures enjoyed. Hell, if they did get caught tonight and Theo went to jail, this week would still be more exciting than anything else the past couple years. Why would Dorothy have wanted to come back to her drab farm life at all? Just for her aunt and uncle? Did they mean that much to her? *Screw that, I wouldn't leave Oz just for Mom and Dad and Danny.*

Gramma Hildy, though. Gramma was the one who taught her to search for faery rings, to leave dewy spiderwebs undisturbed, to listen for the number of times an owl called at midnight. Who told her stories of *nisse,* the Norwegian gnomes who would help with farm chores if provided a saucer of milk every night. Her first copy of *The Wizard of Oz* was a gift from Gramma Hildy. What if Theo were whisked to Oz, with no means to get back, and the sweet old woman never saw her again? She'd already lost her husband. Her only son, Theo's dad, hardly ever bothered to visit her. He'd be fine bundling her off to a rest home and visiting only at Christmas. The occasional five-minute phone call.

Theo was the only one who spent time with Gramma Hildy regularly now. They understood each other. Just the thought of abandoning her, even to go to Oz, made Theo feel horrible. Maybe that was what Dorothy felt for her adopted aunt and uncle.

Right. The people who put her into the asylum to cure her craziness, so she'd stop babbling about Oz all the time.

Theo looked out at the sad little garden plot again. Scarecrow wasn't in sight.

Alarmed, she threw open the door and jumped out. Relief washed through her when she spotted him on a bench a few feet away from the camper.

Goddess, she shouldn't have opened her mouth at all. Shoving her hands in her jacket pockets, Theo walked over slowly and sat down on the other end of the bench. She ran a hand through her hair. "So, what I said earlier. I was rude."

He nodded. "I'm sorry for raising my voice to you."

She dared a glance. He was studying her with a curious expression. She swallowed and forced a casual tone. "You figure out what you're going to sing?"

"I think perhaps the Prisoner's Lament may be the best choice." He shrugged. "Failing that, as long as the path is clear, I believe we can still get a running head start."

Theo snorted a laugh. Scarecrow smiled.

Yep. Not bringing up the other stupid thing she said. Just gonna pretend it never happened. It was a wonder she didn't have an infection from sticking her foot in her mouth all the damned time.

"The sun's going down," he observed. "Do you need to eat or rest before we attend this gathering?"

"Oh, sure, I can always eat."

He raised one eyebrow. "I've noticed. No doubt this is what fuels your constant drive to stay conscious. Although if you have bad dreams every night, I understand why you'd choose to remain awake as long as possible. Fighting your relations even while you sleep must be exhausting."

Theo cleared her throat. "We should focus on the plan. Drive the camper downtown as close as we can get to the museum. We stay near the exit door, you sing everyone but me to sleep, grab the book, we run back to the RV and get on the road immediately."

Twice now this man who wasn't even human figured out things about her she'd never told anyone. Not her friends, certainly not her family, not even the shrink she'd been forced to see after beating up Mindy Schoenberg on the playground in fifth grade. The shrink kept asking Theo whether she disliked the other children, which made her "act out" and "spend so much time off on her own" and "still believe in faery tales." As if hitting Mindy had anything to do with anything other than Mindy calling Theo fat, ugly, and a baby. The bitch had it coming.

Scarecrow frowned at her. She yanked herself out of the memory. "Right? That's the plan?"

He nodded. "The only thing I can't decide is how to handle anyone who doesn't fall asleep. Especially if they try to stop us."

She swung her legs back and forth under the bench. "I can always punch them."

"Theo!"

"What? This is a heist. Gotta plan for things going south, and be ready to kick some ass. Be fae, do crimes."

"Maybe we do need an interpreter," he grumbled.

"Maybe the Oz historian guy can do it. Come on, let's go find dinner."

Eventually they found a restaurant without too long of a wait for a table. Scarecrow wrapped his long, gloved fingers around a mug of coffee, alternately inhaling the steam from it and looking around the dining room. "Everyone seems to be enjoying their meal," he observed.

Theo wiped burger grease from her mouth. "Food's not bad."

"Does every meat person like the same things?"

"Every meat person has different tastes. Not just in food. In books, music, lots of stuff."

He studied her intently. "Can meat people have different tastes in love?"

"Of course, yeah. I mean that's a whole thing. Some people are wired to like girls, some to like guys, some for anybody, even some who prefer no sex at all." Dammit, she really wished she'd ordered a beer right about now. Drinking before a heist was probably a bad idea, but this conversation was a little too much. Theo stuffed more fries in her mouth so she wouldn't have to talk.

"I once overheard Dorothy say she found my friend Nick handsome," Scarecrow said.

Theo shrugged. She could see it. The Tin Woodman's remarkably expressive metal face was on the ruggedly handsome side: strong jaw, intense eyes and sharply defined brows. A little too conventionally gorgeous for her taste. She'd always been more attracted to guys who didn't fit the male-model mold. That was probably her first mistake with her last ex, Mark. He'd been conventionally handsome, carried himself with a cockiness she mistook for self-confidence. The day she caught him shirtless and flexing his chest in the mirror should've ended things. She'd laughed, which made him angry. *Goddess save us from men obsessed with their muscle groups.* Mark was too pretty for his own good. Didn't even have an interesting nose.

Come to think of it, maybe she did kinda have a thing for guys with interesting noses. As a kid, she'd seen Basil Rathbone in an old Sherlock Holmes movie and experienced a brief crush. Now *there* was a manly nose.

Her fatal mistake was glancing up right then at the blue eyes staring at her over a nose that could break icebergs. Heat flamed from her chest to her cheeks.

"Do you think Nick is handsome?" Scarecrow asked.

Theo choked on a fry. Coughing, she spat into her napkin, chugged her tepid glass of formerly iced tea. When she could breathe, she managed, "Sure, I guess."

Scarecrow slumped, his mouth curved sharply down. If he was just burlap and magic, she wished she could learn to enchant her sewing that well. He looked every inch a living scarecrow, more convincing even than the floppy-limbed actor who'd played him. Bulwar? Bolger? Something. Another fine nose there. *Oh my Goddess, get your mind out of this gutter of noses.*

"I suppose I shouldn't draw any conclusions until I've read the entire diary," Scarecrow mused. "On our first adventure together, I didn't have my brains yet. I didn't understand much at all. I was happy to just go along with her. When she returned to Oz, we were busy with the Nome King and Lady Langwidere, didn't get much of a chance to talk. Besides, for part of that I was turned into an ornament, so I missed a few things."

"You seriously were turned into an ornament?" In the third Oz book, *Ozma of Oz,* the evil Nome King delighted in forcing his prisoners to play a rigged guessing game. Almost all of them were transformed into tchotchkes in his palace, including the Tin Woodman and the Scarecrow, as well as Ozma herself.

"So I'm told. Dorothy said I became a gold card-tray." He shivered. "If she and the yellow hen hadn't rescued us all, I'd be there still, brainless as a post."

"Seems like there's a lot of transformations going on in Oz."

"Well, a number of witches specialize in it. Mombi. Langwidere, when she's not too busy admiring her collection of heads. Glinda has been known to dabble in it." He sighed. "Had I been thinking clearly, I'd've paid one of them to transform my straw into flesh. Perhaps then I'd be more appealing. Not that any of it matters now."

"You look fine," Theo insisted.

His eyes met hers and a wry smile quirked his lips. "Even the nose?"

Especially the nose. Theo ducked her head, hair falling over her face, and reached for her fries. "Yep. It's fine."

"I know it's vain of me to be concerned about my appearance. My one good quality has always been the brains the Wizard gave me, and I can't even take credit for those. Dorothy rightly called me a fool."

"She *what*?" Theo's head shot up. "Scarecrow, you can't let what she said in the diary get to you. She was angry. Hopeless. Feeling trapped." His expression turned gloomier with her every word. She struggled to find something more positive. "Her head was in a really bad place at that point. Try not to focus on that part. You two had some good times together, right? When she was in Oz?"

"Oh, she called me a fool then too. She was right. I didn't know how to do anything, couldn't think properly until I received my brains."

"You were barely days old," Theo argued. "You just hadn't experienced anything yet. Meat people have to learn stuff as they grow too. It's not like we pop out quoting Shakespeare and programming Mars missions."

He raised an eyebrow, but bit his lip instead of asking for an interpreter again.

Theo rubbed her hands over her face. She'd run out of both tea and water and it was too hot in here. "Never mind." She checked her phone. "Crap, almost time. We should go." She dug out her last ten-dollar bill and tucked it under her plate. Not the server's fault the place was jammed and she seemed to be the only waitress on duty.

As they walked up the street toward the Oz Museum, Theo's guts jittered. She checked to be sure she'd brought the earplugs in her purse. "Heist heist baby," she chanted under her breath.

"Is that a spell?"

"Yeah. Sure. Let's make a heist spell."

"What's a heist?"

"What we're about to pull off."

"Oh, you mean the theft," he said brightly.

Theo grabbed his arm, yanking him downward so she could hiss in his ear. "Not so loud. Act like we're here for the festival, not the diary."

"Should I flop around and grin like a fool? That seems to be what the other scarecrows are doing." His contempt was plain as he glared at a group of costumed people having an impromptu dance-off in the middle of the street. A Munchkin doing an Irish jig was holding his own against a Scarecrow and Tin Man duo engaged in a pop-and-lock. A small crowd laughed and cheered them on. This town took its Oz celebration seriously.

Theo suppressed a giggle. "They're probably only familiar with the movie Scarecrow, not you. Just act casual. Smile."

"Not easy anymore," he muttered. "Having a smile painted on would've been an advantage tonight."

Theo clasped his hand in hers. "Don't worry. We got this. You sing 'em all to sleep, I'll grab the book. We'll be long gone before they wake up." She poked his side. "Imagine their faces when they all come to and the book's gone and the last thing they remember is a scarecrow singing a weird song at them! Wish I knew a spell to turn all the security cameras off. Then they'd really be freaked out." Pretty sure she could get them out without passing the cameras again. If she recalled right, there was a fire exit right next to the museum theatre.

He chuckled. "Thank you, Theo. I'm glad you're along with me. Glad you're not that kind of witch."

She grinned. "Who knows? Maybe I am. Maybe this would be the perfect time to come into my full witchy powers. I do have them hazel fae eyes, right?" She wiggled her eyebrows.

"I've reconsidered," he murmured. "Perhaps you are fae even if you're not that kind of witch. They do tend to enjoy causing chaos."

She giggled. "Be fae, do crimes."

"Apt."

The same white-haired lady whom they'd met earlier in the day greet-ed them at the museum doorway. Tonight she wore an emerald-green dress with a silky scarf, printed with illustrations from the original *Wiz-ard of Oz* book, pinned with a brooch in the shape of silver slippers. Nice touch. Most people didn't know the original color of the magic slippers Dorothy took from the Wicked Witch of the East. This lady was defi-nitely the more scholarly type of fan.

"Glad you could join us," she said. "Just about to start. Please make your way back to the theatre."

"Thank you for the invitation." Scarecrow doffed his hat, bowing. The straw hair sticking out of the seams of his head fluttered with the movement.

"Goodness," the lady said, "Your costume is very thorough. Were you going more for the look of the Neill drawings?"

"Sorry?" Scarecrow frowned, resettling his hat on his head.

"Yep, thank you." Theo hooked her arm in Scarecrow's and tugged him away. "Way to draw more attention to us."

"I was only being polite," he protested.

"You don't need to be polite at a heist."

"Well that's just rude." He sniffed. "I'd think acting impolite would reveal us more readily as being interlopers here."

"Just act casual, please? The less these people remember about us, the better."

Theo checked for cameras as they hurried along the twisting path through the museum. Her spirits sank. At least one small camera was trained on each exhibit from the darkened rafters. She was pleased to have remembered correctly: an EXIT door was right next to the small theatre room. Hopefully it led to an alley with no cameras.

With the lights on in the theatre and the large screen blank, she could see just how tiny the space actually was. Her folks' basement family room, used mainly for having their friends over to watch Packers games, was bigger than this. And had a wet bar to boot. At a rough count, twen-ty people were crammed in here. A man with fluffy white eyebrows in a black polo shirt stood behind a small podium in the corner. He beamed as they walked in.

"Ah, nice to see the Scarecrow here! My favorite character," the man announced. All eyes turned to Scarecrow and Theo.

A few people wore Oz tee shirts or jewelry depicting rainbows, witch hats, or the familiar characters, but no one else was in costume. Great. Then again, with everyone staring at Scarecrow, maybe they wouldn't remember Theo as clearly.

Right. Sure.

Goddess, she just had to go with orange hair for Halloween. Couldn't stick with basic black. Well, when she was dyeing her friend Cassie's braids and decided to color her own hair, Theo hadn't planned on robbing a museum.

She elbowed Scarecrow. "Bow."

He cast a startled glance at her, but swooped his hat off and made a more courtly bow than at the front door. "A pleasure, sir."

The fans giggled and chuckled. "Great costume," one said. "But wasn't Scarecrow's clothing all blue in the book?"

"The Palace attire is officially green," Scarecrow replied. He whispered to Theo, "I thought we didn't want more attention?"

"Kinda have no choice at this point. Might as well lean hard into it."

There were no seats left, so they stood along the wall just inside the door. This suited Theo fine. Easier to make a break for it.

The white-haired lady came in, smiling, and stood right at the open door. Blocking a quick exit. Dammit. She seemed nice. Theo didn't want to have to punch her.

"All set then?" the man at the podium asked. At a nod from the white-haired lady, he cleared his throat and spoke up. "Welcome, everyone, to the Oz Museum at Oztoberfest! I'm Jim Thicke, and I've been an Oz fan all my life. It's wonderful to be back here at the museum for another celebration. This year we have a very rare item to share, although I'm not sure I'd exactly call it a treat." He held up the worn, brown cloth-bound diary. "This is the diary kept by the real-life Dorothea Gale. Author L. Frank Baum read a newspaper article about the girl who survived the tornado that wiped a Kansas settlement off the map, sought her out in the asylum where she was confined, and wrote down her fanciful tales of witches, talking scarecrows," he beamed at Scarecrow again, "and a road of yellow bricks. However, her own story didn't have a happy ending."

Scarecrow's hand found Theo's and gripped tightly. She gave him a supportive squeeze back.

"As those of you who've already viewed the exhibit here know, Dorothea was deeply affected by the tragedy which took her family from her. She retreated to a fantasy land in her mind. Understandable, given the horror she'd been through, but mental illness due to trauma was poorly understood in eighteen-ninety-nine. When she failed to fully return to reality, her adopted aunt and uncle sent her to the Thompson Sanitarium for a cure." The lecturer opened the diary. "I'm sure you've all seen the exhibit, so you know what sort of awful experiences Dorothea had in the asylum. Electroshock. Cold water immersion as 'therapy.' Her stay there was, unfortunately, typical of turn-of-the-century treatment for mental illness. Tonight, I'd like to focus less on what happened to her in the sanitarium, and read to you some of the amazing things she wrote down concerning her friends back in Oz. The stories which landed her in such a depressing place. Though imaginary, Oz was more important and real to her than anything in this world."

"Pardon me," Scarecrow interrupted. Every head turned.

Theo took a deep breath, bracing her feet. She fumbled the earplugs from her purse.

"We'll answer questions after the presentation," the lecturer said, his smile turning puzzled.

"I don't wish to ask a question, but to offer a remembrance," Scarecrow said. "A song to honor what Dorothy suffered in that horrible place. She saved Oz and none of you know the real story. She saved me."

The lecturer frowned. "Yes, actually, I'm sure everyone here tonight is familiar with—"

"You are not," Scarecrow interrupted, drawing his shoulders up straight.

"Goddess bless," Theo murmured, and stuck the earplugs in.

The white-haired lady moved toward them. Confusion and disapproval smeared the faces of every listener. Scarecrow's hand tensed in hers, he opened his mouth, and every other person in the room froze.

She could dimly hear the melody, not the words, but recognized it as the creepy-sad song about the prisoner and Death. She let go of him to put both hands over her ears for good measure.

He sang, and the white-haired lady wavered on her feet. The lecturer clung to the podium, sinking. A couple of seated people simply slumped over. Bizarre to see the effects without feeling them herself this time. Theo caught the white-haired lady before she collapsed and laid her out on the carpet. Her pretty scarf was going to be dirty when she woke up.

Scarecrow continued the song, eyes shut, putting all his heart into it. People leaned on each other, drifting into slumber. Good to know Oz fans were just as messed up as she was, with enough pain of some kind that the song knocked 'em right out. The lecturer alone struggled, letting go of the book to clutch at the podium. That was her cue. Theo stepped over the unconscious white-haired lady and grabbed the diary.

To her surprise, the lecturer latched onto a corner of it and wouldn't let go. He was saying something to her, eyes full of fear.

"I'm really sorry," Theo yelled. "He needs this. Let go!"

Scarecrow came closer, still singing. The man shook his head, staring at them, clinging to the diary for dear life.

Well, crap. She tried prying loose the man's fingers, but he pulled back, leveraging against the podium even as his knees wobbled. Scarecrow stopped, the song done. The lecturer tried to stand, gaining strength.

She really didn't want to punch him. He looked old and not unlike her Uncle Sven. He was bringing his other hand up, a couple of people in the front row stirred, Scarecrow reached for the diary but hesitated. Now or never. Theo swiftly plucked one of her earrings out and jabbed the back of the hook into the weathered flesh of the man's hand.

He yelped, letting go. Theo yanked the book against her boobs and grabbed Scarecrow's hand. "Time to go!" she shouted, dragging Scarecrow from the room. She kicked open the emergency exit next to the theatre entrance. A fire alarm blasted, loud enough to penetrate the earplugs. Wincing, Theo checked their surroundings quickly. An alley. No idea which way to the RV.

Scarecrow tugged her hand, yelling wildly at her, and took off for the left-hand end of the alleyway. Trusting he knew what he was doing, she broke into a run as well. He stumbled on the uneven pavement. She managed to haul him back upright without dropping the diary. They burst out of the alley into a street. A car honked at them, brakes squealing. Scarecrow faltered again but Theo pulled his arm against hers and ran harder. They crossed into another alley. *Goddess, please let this be the right direction, please guide us out of this mess!*

Breathless, they emerged into an open parking lot. The RV had never looked so welcoming. Theo's chest was about to explode. She unlocked the door, clambering in and across to the driver's seat, Scarecrow right behind her. She keyed the ignition, thrust the diary at Scarecrow, released the brake and chunked the monster camper into gear. Her head felt clouded. Pain shot through her side. Everything was too hot.

When Scarecrow tapped her arm she jumped. He mouthed something at her.

"What?" she yelled.

Frowning, he plucked the earplug from her right ear. "I said, that didn't go as well as I'd hoped. But we have the diary. Thank you, Theo."

She pulled the other earplug out. "You're welcome. We gotta go." The RV's engine guttered to a stop. Sirens wailed from back the way they'd come. "Shit."

Scarecrow clung to the diary, staring out the windshield. "Theo."

"Fuck, come on, come on," she snarled, pumping the gas, trying the key again.

"Theo—"

"Dammit, start, you bitch!" To her relief, the engine caught and rumbled. A sharp rapping on the driver's window sent her heart slamming against her ribs. "Holy fuck!"

The lecturer, panting, stared up at her. "Stop! Wait!" he shouted. "That's priceless!"

"Really sorry," Theo yelled back.

"We'll return it later," Scarecrow called, leaning over her. Theo floored the gas and Scarecrow toppled into her lap, wedged between her boobs and the steering wheel. "Oh! Pardon me."

She tossed him off her with one hand while trying to steer with the other. The lecturer ran alongside the RV for a few steps before Theo lurched the camper over the curb and swung it wildly into the street. They picked up speed, leaving the wild-eyed lecturer in the diner parking lot. Scarecrow climbed back into the passenger seat, hugging the diary tightly, as Theo oriented them eastward. A fire engine screamed by them, heading into town. A cop, lights flashing, zoomed past right after. Theo checked the side mirrors but nobody was pursuing them. Yet.

Her navigation app told her to turn north onto a narrow country road. She hesitated, then braked hard to make the turn. This might work in their favor. The cops probably would be searching the bigger highways. No streetlights at all in this direction. The RV bounced over the uneven pavement, picking up speed.

Scarecrow held onto the armrest, boots braced on the dash. "Theo! Would you put the safety restraint on, at least, please?"

Oh. Barreling down country roads in this beast at possibly unwise speeds, right. She fastened the seat belt over her chest, attention divided between the dark road ahead and the mirrors. Something leaped in front of the RV. With a shriek, Theo slammed the brakes. The wheels skidded. She struggled a few panicked seconds to right the groaning camper. A frightened deer bounded away.

She sat there shaking, breath hitching, hands clenched on the wheel. Dust from the road wafted in front of the headlights. With trembling fingers she clicked the brights on. The deer was gone, nothing else in sight but miles ahead of flat prairie and some fenceposts lining the fields on either side. Nothing in the rearview.

"Are you all right?" Scarecrow asked, placing a hand on her arm.

She nodded sharply. "Yeah. Yeah, all good."

He left his hand there, watching her with obvious concern. Theo swallowed dryly. Her stomach rolled over. She swallowed the bile down. "Could you," she began, heard how weak her voice sounded, and tried again. "Could you get my wrist braces for me, please?"

He fetched them at once. "Are you calm enough to operate this wagon safely?" His voice was quiet, without judgement.

"I'm okay."

He patted her shoulder. "Please don't put yourself at any risk for my sake."

She chuckled weakly. "Kinda late for that. At least this monster can run over just about anything trying to stop us." She resettled herself in the seat, adjusted the air, brought up a calming playlist of Euro synth. "Okay. Off we go. Tell me if you see any lights behind us."

"I see two lights off to the east. Possibly a farm."

"Car lights, I mean." She eased down on the gas, straightening the RV out in the narrow lane. Screw it, might as well ride the centerline unless they saw someone coming at them. "Or flashing lights. Especially if you see flashing lights."

"Flashing lights are a bad thing?"

"Yeah. That means we're screwed."

They traveled north only fifteen minutes before turning east again onto a rough county highway. This was actually a good idea, avoiding major interstates, at least until they were out of Kansas. Though she'd noticed a number of other RVs in town for the festival, none were as battered as this one. Not to mention, the bloodstains on the front bumper kinda stood out. They'd stick to back roads for a while.

"I feel rather guilty," said Scarecrow, studying the cover of the diary. He hadn't opened it yet.

After all that, he had second thoughts? She glared at him. "Really?"

He winced. His eyes dropped again to the diary.

After some miles passed, the RV's bright lamps cutting a path through the darkness ahead, her shoulders relaxed. The music of Röyksopp played quietly through the speakers, calming her heart rate and easing the stitch in her ribs. *So, guess I'm a nationally wanted criminal now, taking this priceless book across state lines. Uff da.* Fingers crossed the lecturer historian guy didn't note down their license plate. Or that the cops didn't recover fingerprints, or her DNA off the earring hook she'd left behind.

Scarecrow was still staring at the closed diary, silent.

"I think we're clear." She indicated the banquette behind her. "Why don't you go ahead and read it? You can turn the light on back there, it won't bother me."

He stood slowly, swaying as the RV bumped over the cracked asphalt. He held the diary against his chest as if only it could keep him warm. "Please let me know if you need anything," he murmured. He sat down at the table, placing the diary carefully in front of him. His expression in the rearview mirror was deadly serious.

"Same," Theo told him.

He opened the cover, took a deep breath, and bent over the pages. He didn't turn the lamp on. Guess he could read in the dark and the breath was symbolic. Such a weird blend of inhuman and very human.

Maybe whatever Dorothy had written would offer him a clue to return home. Theo's stomach clenched. She drank the last of her soda, but the pain didn't ease. She didn't want to interrupt him to ask for some pain tea or a water from the fridge. Digging a couple of antacids out of the bottle in her purse, she kept an eye on him in the mirror as he slowly turned the pages.

I hope whatever's in there doesn't hurt him more.

Miles and hours crawled by. No other cars traveled this road so late. She turned north to avoid going through Atchison as they had before. The tiny county highway was closely hemmed by harvested fields, a few trees serving as windbreaks. The RV stuttered as it climbed a hill, curves forcing Theo to slow more.

Scarecrow was suddenly beside her. Theo jumped. "Holy crap, Scarecrow! Don't do that. You're so damned quiet."

He stared out the front windshield, tears gleaming in his eyes.

She reached for his arm. He leaned away.

"What's wrong?"

"I'm wrong," he whispered. "I'm simply all wrong, somehow."

What did Dorothy say about him? Did she insult him? Break his heart? That bitch. "Scarecrow—"

"Stop," he groaned, "Please. Stop here. I can't—I need to get out."

"Scarecrow..." What the hell could she say?

"I need to be outside. Just for a minute. Please, Theo, stop, I need to be outside right now, I can't—it hurts." His voice was brittle, raspy.

Theo eased on the brake, pulling to the side as much as she could on the narrow road. The instant the RV shuddered to a halt, he flung open the door and fell out. Alarmed, she unbuckled and scrambled after him. He rose to his feet, straw knocked loose from his tunic, hat askew.

"Scarecrow?"

He waved her off. He strode unsteadily toward a broad field of un-harvested corn, climbing over a wire fence, falling again. Theo bit her lip to keep from calling after him. She watched his lanky figure disappear in-to the cornstalks. In the dim moonlight she could just make out the tip of his hat moving among the rows. Some yards in, he stopped. Theo squint-ed into the night, a chilling breeze blowing in. She buttoned her jacket, shivering.

He stood in the middle of the cornfield, alone. If he made any sound, it was swallowed by the crackling rustle of the dry corn in the night wind.

What the hell had Dorothy written?

Leaving the door open and the engine running, Theo went to the banquette table and turned on the light. The diary was cracked along the spine. Most likely no one had opened it in decades before it came to the museum. It lay open at an entry which stopped mid-page. She checked, but the remaining pages were blank. He'd read to the end. Easing into the seat, she pulled the diary closer and frowned at the messy cursive let-ters. "Thought they taught penmanship back then?" she grumbled.

The first lines which caught her eye read, *"asked not to have the lec-trikal agin but Nurse Livia said I had to. I always feel so sick and cant rite for days after that. I hope it is making me Well with all this sickness."*

Guess anyone's handwriting would suffer if they kept getting elec-troshocked in the name of therapy.

There was something before that about straw. She went back a page, then another, trying to find the start of the entry. The lack of any real separation between paragraphs made it difficult, but she noticed a slight difference in ink colors between one long blotch of words and another, and started in there.

"Nurse Livia very upset with me today when I complained of female pains. She examined me in my private area and asked had I been with a boy. I told her no I am a Christian girl. But when she told Dr Thomson my vir-gin seal was broke he said I must tell him who it was, I said it was no one at the saniturum but he made me rite it here or else it will be two more days of

cold water baths. I hate the baths, I am sure they made me sick with chills last spring, so here I will rite down what happend.

"I do not think I sinned since Hank said we wud marry. This was back on the farm, before. He said this was what a husband and wife do and he promised to come back for me after the harvest and we wud then wed. I let him touch me in my private area, it felt good, and since we were betrothed it cud not be a sin. I let him climb on top of me and that part hurt but after he said I was beautiful. He said I made him so happy. So you see this was all very nice but then the twister came.

"When I was in Oz I worried I wud never get Home agin. So I started thinking what cud I do if I had to stay in Oz which was beautiful but also very fritening. The Tin Woodman was very handsum and strong, and first I thot maybe I cud wed him and he wud protect me always. I held hands with him a lot and he was very nice to me, but when I asked if he wanted to kiss me he turned all tung tied. He said he didn't like me that way. I cried and he cried too and got all rusted and I had to oil him again. He said no I was not ugly but he did not want to be my husband. I guess he was still thinking about a girl he knew before he became all made of tin, for as I have told you he was a real man once.

"The Scare-crow always followed me around, always did what ever thing I asked. He was not handsome at all, in fact his face was all painted very badly, and he was floppy as a dead chicken, but I thought maybe it wudn't be so bad to have him for a husband since he didn't mind getting all torn up to save me. He fell down all the time and had to be picked up. And he was always asking me questions even about dumb things like What is the sky and Why did I need to eat and sleep? But he was soft to sleep on even tho the straw was terribly scratchy, but if I found a blanket to put over him it was just like a straw bed."

Theo turned the page, anger rising. This sweet, intelligent, devoted man was nothing but a bedroll to Dorothy. An ugly bedroll who might be a convenient shield to have between herself and the dangers of Oz.

"I realized he wudnt be able to give me children like Hank wud, but if I had to stay in Oz I needed someone to help me. There were always monsters and horrible critters around like the kallidas that tried to eat us. I know you dont think kallidas are real Dr Thomson but I assure you they are in

Oz and they are meaner than bears and twice as big. Nick Chopper the Tin Woodman saved us from a pair of them by chopping a log bridge so they went down into a great canyon but I have told you that part already. As to the Scare-crow I knew he wud never leave me, although he was a fool and only made of straw and old cloths, he always put himself between me and any Danger.

"But after that night in the barn I knew he cud never make a good husband. I was so lonely and still upset Nick Chopper didnt want to marry me so I went to the Scare-crow and asked him to lie with me like Hank and I done. But he was too stupid, he was too clumsy and his straw scratched me, and when I pulled him on top of me he didnt have a manhood at all."

Theo's hand was over her mouth, holding in the swirling sourness in her throat. She rubbed water from her eyes and checked outside. Scarecrow's hat still stuck up above the waving corn. The entry continued onto the next page. She turned it so viciously the paper ripped at the top.

"You may think this was a sin but I have thot about it a lot and decided no it was not, because we did not lie together as a man and wife do since the straw man had no sinful parts. And besides he was just a silly stuffed dolly without a brain, not a real man at all. After that night I knew there wud be no husband for me in Oz and Id better find a way to come Home. Then wen I did come Home, Hank did not beleeve me about Oz and he went away. All I wanted then was to go back to Oz where at least the land was green and full of magic. I went looking for storms and as you no I finally found one the night the river rose and it took me back to Oz like I asked it to. Exept when I returned there things were changed, there was a new Queen, I still had to stay with Nick Chopper to protect me even tho he did not want me as a wife, and another man all of copper called Tik-tok, and worst of all the Scare-crow followd me like a puppy everywere. I almost told him to leeve me alone, I was so tired of his ugly painted sack-head. But it was very dangerous agin and so I held my tongue and kept close by all these strange things pretending at being men. I had to or I wud have been hurt or killd. But I promise you I did not sin with any of them, not even the Scare-crow, because he is not a real man so what we did doesnt count."

Theo's chest hurt. She slammed the diary shut and leapt to her feet. "You fucking bitch. You heartless, shallow little bitch!"

Still cursing, she looked out at the dry cornfield. Clouds hid the moon. Beyond the headlights, she couldn't see a damned thing. "Scarecrow?" she called.

Corn rustled in the wind. Her eyes strained to pick out his hat among the tall stalks. Wrapping her arms around herself at the next gust, she dropped to the ground and walked toward the fence. How long had he been out here? *Oh Goddess, please don't let him have done anything stupid after reading that.* She couldn't see anything but the waving, creaking, creepily rustling corn right in front of her. The sound of it put her teeth on edge.

"Scarecrow, you all right? Where are you?" she shouted.

Under all the rustling and creaking she thought she heard a laugh. High and cackling.

Theo vaulted the fence, landed hard, and broke into a run between the stalks that swallowed the horizon.

25

Scarecrow stared up at the moon, tears beading in his eyes, trickling down his cheeks. Not a real man. Just a silly stuffed dolly. A fool so many times over. The Old Crow who'd taken pity on him in the cornfield in Oz was wrong. The crow told him, "You're not frightening because we can see you're not a real man. You don't act like one. Shows you haven't got a brain." So Scarecrow braved wild animals and witches and had even been torn to pieces in his quest to obtain some brains. Just so he could think himself the equal of a meat person.

Blight and ruin, what an absolute idiot.

None of it mattered. Not his magical brains. Not the changes he'd made to his form. Not this dangerous, doomed adventure he'd undertaken to find Dorothy. She felt nothing but contempt for him.

How did I not see it? Every grimace Dorothy made, quickly smoothed into a bland smile, when he bounced up to her ready for another day's long walk. Every time she'd found someone else to talk to during the expedition to the Nome Kingdom, turning away from him.

Yes, she'd saved his life more than once, but that only proved she felt obligated to do so. A passage within the first few pages of her diary read, *"I almost left him in that tree after we kilt the wicked witch, but he saved me from the crows and the wasps so I figgered I owed it to him to see if he could be put back together. Besides Nick said we had to go get him and I knew if I said No he would just cry."* She should've left him to die. Better if his head rotted away in the rain and wind than to be rescued and imagine Dorothy cared about him at all.

Tears ran down his face, soaking the burlap. Where in all fields' name did they even come from? Magic tears. Let them soak him, let mold grow in his straw, it didn't matter now. He was nothing to her. Let him return to the earth. Certainly he'd make good compost, right here in this corn field.

Some distance away he could see the lamps of the wagon where Theo waited. How could he possibly face her? She must think him pathetic. Especially if she'd read any of that. He cringed. *I'm not a man. I'll nev-*

er be a man. How foolish to think a few alterations to a straw body could change anything.

His first conversation with Dorothy came all too readily to mind. She'd asked him how he came to be, since in her world scarecrows couldn't speak or walk. He described to her in detail his very first conscious experience, how first he'd heard a Munchkin farmer talking with another, when they painted Scarecrow's ears on his sack of a head. He could see as soon as they painted his eyes. He'd curiously watched them stuff his body, and then felt complete when they sewed his head on.

The Munchkin farmer declared to his friend, "I bet you he'll scare the crows fast enough. He looks just like a man."

"Why, he *is* a man," the other farmer said, laughing. At the time, Scarecrow happily agreed, though he didn't grasp how to speak yet.

Now he understood why the farmer laughed.

Perhaps if he'd spoken up then, the terrified Munchkins would've tossed him into a fire and he'd never have gone through all the rest. Never met Dorothy. She would eventually have run into Nick and Lion along the road of yellow brick. They were strong, capable people. She would've been fine. His foolish company amounted to nothing.

The rustle of the corn all around him was almost soothing. He could just stay here. Tell Theo to go home. Dorothy had said nothing of how she was able to return to Oz, only that a storm brought her there again. If it were that simple, Oz would be overrun with visitors from the Outside World. No answers. No way back. Certainly he possessed the patience to stand here for four more nights until the full moon rose and robbed him of all sentience. Not as if there was much of it for him to lose anyway. By the Unseelie Court, maybe he'd even frighten a crow or two finally. He choked out a laugh that was half sob.

A whining giggle replied.

A cackle.

Squeaking sounds, growing louder, closing in.

Scarecrow turned.

Scarred, grinning muzzles emerged from the rows of corn. Three of them. How many survived the battle song? Blast and blight, he should've counted them when they left the golf course! What if more of them were sneaking up on Theo right now? He'd staggered out here too full of his own misery to recall he'd vowed not to let her out of his sight.

The biggest Wheeler snarled at him. "Hay man comezzz. No more fight."

Scarecrow tensed, ready to leap aside if it charged at him. "Go to the Nome furnaces," he spat. He filled his chest with air to give strength to his voice, opened his mouth wide for the song to burst forth—

A lean, powerful body slammed into his midsection, sharp wheels raking through his tunic. Air fled. He gasped, tried to sing as he flailed in the dirt between the stalks. The Wheeler cackled madly and brought a forewheel down hard across his throat. Scarecrow wheezed, the words of the war song a mere whisper without the force of air. With a shriek the monster raked him again. He suddenly couldn't sense his limbs. His head rolled.

A Wheeler kicked him. His nose bounced on the hard ground, dirt filling his eyes. Sputtering, he blinked fiercely, tried again to sing.

They howled with horrible laughter. "No more bad zzzongzzzz! No more hurtzzzz uzzz!"

They kicked his head back and forth, cackling, leaping and prancing as if they'd invented a wonderful game. Scarecrow spat out dirt, dizzy, struggling to retain equilibrium. Again he tried to sing. Without a chest attached to capture and funnel the air, the best he could do was a weak wheeze which had no effect on the Wheelers. A particularly hard blow against his head cut the burlap. He could feel something trickling out. No. No! Not his brains!

"Stop," he gasped, "stop!"

As he rolled over again, a flash of orange spun in his vision. He squinted. *Oh crows and blight no, please no.* Theo crouched between the dead leaves of the dry corn, her mouth open and eyes wide. With effort he wriggled himself so she could see his lips. "Run," he gasped. His voice had no strength, no volume. "Theo, run!"

The cackling Wheelers closed in on him again. He could feel the trickle of his brains turning to a steady pour. "Run," he whispered, hoping she'd hear him and take to her heels.

"No more play," the biggest Wheeler snarled, "muzzzt take him."

The night seemed darker than before. He was fairly sure his eyes were open, but he couldn't see past the row of corn standing nearest to him. The sound of the Wheelers was muffled as though dirt filled his ears. A prickling sensation spread from the side of his head, where his brains continued to leak out, to his nose and lips, then numbness.

How very odd. I wonder if this is what dying is like?

A snarling muzzle thrust up against his nose. Fetid breath in his face. "Hay man comezzz wiz uzzzz now," the Wheeler growled.

Theo would have the right words for this situation. One last brief spark of inspiration went off in his head. He smiled at the Wheeler. "Screw you," he whispered.

Blackness swallowed him.

• • • •

THEO PANTED, HER FEET thudding so hard against the packed earth she was sure the Wheelers heard her, but when she flung herself into the RV and looked back, nothing pursued. The strong wind in the rustling corn blew toward her, the rattling of dry stalks deafening, and they hadn't smelled her.

Scarecrow, oh Goddess, Scarecrow. Dirt in his eyes, straw sticking from a cut in his lips, the fear plain on his face. Voiceless, decapitated, desperately trying to warn her away. Tears streamed down her cheeks. The Wheelers were out there right now tearing him to pieces and she'd just run away. They were too big, too fierce, what the fuck could she do?

"Something better than fucking leaving him there!" she shouted at herself, grabbing her hair. She could plow this whale of a camper right into that cornfield, run those bastards over! Sure, with enough speed it could probably mow the fence down, but the Wheelers would see it coming and they were much faster. "Fuck, fuck, fuck!" She slammed a fist against the dashboard. The glove compartment clunked open, spilling the first aid kit and a notebook labeled *Softball Stats* onto the floor. "Fuck!" She kicked the stuff out of her way. The notebook bounced off the driver's seat and back at her.

Goddamn Danny, leaving his shit in here. She kicked the notebook again, helpless, furious. Asshole Danny with his detailed notebooks for everything and his prudish wife and his stupid weekend softball games and—

Theo froze.

"Yes!" she cried, and ran for the bedroom closet.

• • • •

SNUFFLING, GROWLING sounds in his ears. The vague sense of something scraping against his cheek.

"Cantzz put it back," a harsh voice snarled. More odd thumps against the side of his head, pushing him across the ground inch by inch.

He was still alive? Guess the Wheelers couldn't figure out how to eat him. Well, all they needed to do was strike a spark with their wheels on something metal, and that would be that. It should only take them a few days to figure it out.

Scarecrow giggled.

"Enoufffff," the Wheeler leader snarled. "Doezzznt need brainzzzz. Bring the piecezzz."

The corn rustled off to his left. Wait, no, his other left. Directions were such arbitrary things. He'd never really considered it before. Being brainless again was remarkably insightful. He giggled again, unable to help it. How ridiculous all this was.

Movement over there on his other left. Orange. A pumpkin? Would a pumpkin hover above the ground? Pretty sure not. Unless it was Jack Pumpkinhead. Oh dear. The Wheelers would enjoy eating his head, the poor fellow.

A figure stepped out of the waving, creaking corn. A warrior wielding a mighty club. Arcane jewels in her ears and nose sparkled in the moonlight. Her eyes gleamed green. Fae. Angry. Goodness, she could scowl. What a beautiful, powerful warrior witch. Well, if she were here to finish him off, not much he could do about it. At least he could spend his final moments admiring the grace and stealth with which she crept up on the Wheeler currently pawing at his head. Not sure what that was all about, the pawing. Scarecrow was dizzy, but the warrior seemed familiar. He squinted up at her as she drew closer. Recognition blazed at the same instant his terror returned in a sickening rush.

"Theo no," he wheezed.

Theo planted her feet, swung her club, and yelled, "Get away from him you *bitch!*" Her arms fully extended right as the weapon slammed into the skull of the nearest Wheeler.

Thunk-ruunnncchh!

Interesting. He'd forgotten bone could crush inwards like that.

The Wheeler toppled over. The others jerked around to face Theo. With a screech, the leader leaped at her. She jumped aside, bringing the club around again with a mighty wrench to *thock* against a second Wheeler's muzzle. Blood and teeth sprayed on impact. It howled, staggering back. More loosened teeth rained down when it shook its head.

"Eatzzz you! Tear you to bitzzzz!" roared the lead Wheeler. It kicked against the ground, thrashing in the cornrow, tangled a moment in the limited space.

"Theo!" Scarecrow gasped, helpless to do anything but watch. He fought to remain conscious, though he could feel more brains spilling.

"*Unngh!* Die, fucker!"

Theo brought her club down hard again on the one she'd muzzle-bashed. It dodged, jaws snapping. Theo stumbled back. A wheel slashed her. She cried out in pain, tumbling into the corn.

No! No, why was he so useless? They'd kill her, devour her!

The leader skidded past Scarecrow, knocking him aside. He rolled sickeningly, facing the ground. No, no, no— He struggled, using his tongue and lips to turn himself enough to see what was happening. He cried out soundlessly as the third Wheeler raked at Theo's legs. She scrambled to get away, trying to regain her footing. It reared up to plunge down on her. She rolled. Its wheels thumped into the dirt, and she slapped her club against its bony elbow. The Wheeler yelped, collapsing onto its forelegs. With a shriek of fury, Theo rose and swung again, knocking its jaw so hard sideways its neck cracked. It slumped, wheels sprawled.

Dizzy, Scarecrow stared. Maybe technically Wheelers didn't have elbows. What would one call them? Fore-knees? He hadn't found much in the library on Wheeler anatomy. Someone should make a thorough study of them. Not him. He'd had enough of them.

The leader circled warily. It stared with dead, black eyes at its fallen pack. "Kill you, fat little zzzow," it hissed.

Theo straightened up, panting. A sheaf of her hair fell over her right eye. "Come try it, you mangy bitch. You're not getting him."

The Wheeler sneered at Scarecrow. He stared back.

The Wheeler lunged at him. Theo burst into a run, whipping the club over her shoulder for another hit. The Wheeler braked, reversed, and threw itself right at her. She couldn't bring her arms down fast enough and it slashed at her as it leaped past. Crying out, Theo fell to one knee, nearly dropping the club.

"No!" Scarecrow gasped.

The Wheeler cackled, piercing high crazy laughter. It whirled, jaws wide, teeth gleaming, charged at her. It would run her right over. As its head dropped to bite, Theo grabbed one of Scarecrow's arms and jammed it right down the Wheeler's throat. The Wheeler stumbled, gagged, pawed at the arm wedged between its jaws. As it struggled, choking, Theo staggered to unsteady feet, raised her club high, and brought it down with all her might between the Wheeler's stony eyes.

It made a harsh, gurgling sound, dropping hard on its knees. Theo bashed it again with a grunt. It shook its head, fighting to rise, still gagged with a straw arm.

"You are *not*," Theo slammed the club down, "taking," *whack!* "him!" *Crunnnnchh.*

All three Wheelers lay motionless, lanky limbs splayed in all directions. The wind blew through the dry corn, rattling stalks and rustling leaves. Nothing else stirred.

Scarecrow blinked. Tears cleared the dirt from his eyes.

Theo stumbled to him, dropping the club as she fell to her knees beside him. "Scarecrow, oh Goddess Scarecrow, I'm so sorry," she sobbed. She gathered his head into her lap, pressing her palm to his temple where brains dribbled from the gash.

"Theo, you're hurt," he whispered. Red cuts slashed up and down her left arm, scratches on her cheek and neck from the dry cornstalks. He'd seen a gash on her leg as well. Not good. "Poison," he said, trying to force strength into his voice.

"Oh sweet Goddess, Scarecrow, what did they do to you?" Tears flowed down her face, smearing the dirt and spattered Wheeler blood. She stroked his forehead tenderly.

"Brains," he said. Her face seemed out of focus. At least she was alive. "Please, go."

"I'll fix you." She sniffled. "Those fuckers. I'm so sorry, Scarecrow."

"It's all right," he murmured. She was alive. She should put some stinging nettle juice on the wounds, though. He tried to tell her this but forgot how to speak the words. "Nettle," was all he could manage.

"I'll fix you up. I should've been faster, should've saved you before they tore you up." She wiped her face with the back of one hand, which just smeared everything more. Lucky her features weren't painted on. She scooped something from the ground. "These—these are your brains?" She held her cupped hand so he could see brown grains intermixed with silvery pins and needles.

"Magic," he agreed. The Wizard was a powerful sorcerer, so what looked like ordinary bran and pins certainly must be more than that. Why, Scarecrow was a fool before the Wizard stuffed his head with magic brains. He could tell the difference from before he gained his brains and after, even if Dorothy couldn't.

That brought a stab of pain. "Dorothy," he whispered. Memories jumbled, fighting each other. Her warm hugs. The harsh words in the diary. Her hand in his as they walked in the sunshine. Her grimace when he thanked her for restuffing him after the witch's henchmonkeys tore him apart.

Theo scowled. "That bitch was wrong. Don't you think about what she said. She was totally wrong. You are a real man, Scarecrow. Just as you are."

He tried to roll his head from side to side. "No. Just a fool. Straw."

"So what if you're made of straw? You're wonderful!"

His eyes closed and he couldn't recall how to open them. "Straw," he breathed. Her hands on him were so warm, so soft.

"You hang on. I'll fix you. Just hang on, please!"

He felt her fingers tucking more of his brains back into his head. What a mess. And what horrors he'd dragged her into. Wheelers. The dead thing invading her home. All his fault. "Sorry, Theo."

"I'm getting you out of here. Don't you dare fucking die on me."

He tried to nod. Her touch was so warm. He didn't deserve to be put back together. The rustling of the corn blended with the scrape of brains being tucked back into his head. He must be losing consciousness. How novel. Best just to relax and focus on the new experience.

"Don't you die on me. I love you."

Scarecrow smiled, drifting. What a nice thing to hear before he died, even if it wasn't true. Dorothy didn't love him. Nobody could. Just a silly stuffed thing, with no real brains at all.

• • • •

THEO SCOOPED ALL THE grains of bran and pins she could back into his head, the sharp ends pricking her again and again. Her fingers were half-numb anyway, didn't matter. Too dark out here to see much. He'd rolled all over, spilling brains. Dead Wheelers sprawled every way she turned. His loose arm was still wedged down the biggest Wheeler's throat. His torso and legs lay on the ground, straw bursting from the collar of the tunic, the torn shoulder, slashed all over.

His eyes closed. "Don't you die on me," she repeated, shaking him gently. "Scarecrow!"

His lips moved, but no sound emerged.

Dammit, no. Just because he'd survived being unstuffed and ripped apart in the books didn't mean he couldn't die in the real world. She hugged his head tight, retrieved the metal bat from the ground, and ran toward the lights of the RV.

His eyes remained shut, but when she told him to stay put on the bed, he tried to nod. She found a flashlight and ran back through the corn, panicking when she didn't see the spot right away. She tripped on a Wheeler's leg, jerking away in fear, but it was very dead. All of them lay motionless where they'd fallen. Where she'd killed them.

Her hands shook. She kept the bat tucked under one arm as she retrieved each piece of Scarecrow's body and brought all of him back to the camper, laying him out on the bed in the right order. He seemed woozy, disoriented, mumbling when she shook him to be sure he was still alive. Hard to tell if he was in shock or if these stupid bits of metal and cereal made a difference. *I mean, this is Oz we're talking about, who knows. Maybe this stuff really is magic brains for him.*

She went out once more with a paper cup and a whisk broom to find the rest of his brains. The wind tore some of the bran from her as she tried to scoop it into the cup, but she found each and every pin with the flashlight, hunting for several minutes until she was sure she'd retrieved all of them and every remaining grain of bran on the hard-packed earth. She shoved the cup into her jacket pocket. Turning, she faced the dead Wheeler with bulging, jet-black eyes. Its muzzle was dry and hard when she gingerly pried it up enough to tug Scarecrow's arm out. The sharp teeth raked along the fabric of the sleeve, ripping it more. Straw fluffed free and whisked away in the wind. At this rate there wouldn't be enough left to stuff him with even if she could repair all the rips in his clothing. She yanked loose what was left of his sleeve and glove and took it with her.

Pausing at the edge of the cut and trampled patch of dead corn, she looked back at the bodies. Desert creatures, Scarecrow said, things which hunted along the edge of the poisonous sand which ringed Oz. As she stared, breath puffing in the chilly night, the smallest of the pack crumpled. She trained the flashlight on it. Bits of its face flaked off. The wind whipped the crumbs away into the rustling corn. They were dry, dead things and if the wind kept up all night there would be little left by morning. Maybe only their wheels would remain. Some farmer's tractor would crunch over them soon.

Shuddering, she ran back to the RV. Safe inside at last, she laid Scarecrow's arm next to his body. He murmured wordlessly when she positioned his head to pour the rest of the bran and pins back in. "Shhhh, it's all right," she whispered. She stroked his brow, and a smile touched his lips.

Goddess, so horrible to see him like this. The gash in his burlap skull was ugly. She hadn't seen his hat anywhere. *Not going back out again.* He needed to be sewn up. His kit, did he still have his kit? She felt around in his pants pockets and found the small leather sewing kit, the pink stone he'd used to talk to the Tin Woodman, and a tiny wooden hinged box. Curious, she opened it. Inside nestled a silver ring set with an enormous clear green emerald.

He'd wanted to propose to Dorothy? Anger flared again. After all he'd gone through with her in Oz, all the times he'd put himself in harm's way to protect her, Dorothy saw him as no more than an animated doll. Just as well she'd died a hundred years ago. If Theo ever ran into that thankless wench, she'd slap her senseless.

Setting aside the gemstones, Theo took a deep breath. Her hands shook. She massaged them a minute until the tremors subsided. From his kit, she picked a spool of coarse tan thread matching the shade of his burlap and a needle. It took her four tries to thread the damned thing. She stuck the needle into his head just past the rip.

His eyelids fluttered but didn't open. "Just straw," he whispered. "Not real."

"Hush. Yes you are. I hope this doesn't hurt. I'm sewing up this rip, okay?"

He grimaced.

"Does that hurt?"

"Sorry I came here." His voice was barely a breath. "Hurt you. So sorry, Theo."

"I'm not. Shhhh now. Gonna sew you up."

She simmered inside as she made careful stitches, repairing the jagged gash as well as she could. It would still leave a scar, but keep his brains inside his head at least.

How dare those bastards do this to him. How dare Dorothy reject him. *Not a real man.* Theo huffed, heat rising. She steadied her fingers, tracing the edges of the wound with needle and thread. Scarecrow was every bit a man. So what if he was made of straw? He thought, he felt, he was a hell of a sight better than most men she'd met. Considerate. Kind. Smart. Great nose.

Her vision wavered. She paused, rubbing her eyes. Tiny glowing threads trailed from her fingers to Scarecrow's head.

Magic threads. Could she do this? Fix him. *Heal* him. "You're gonna be okay, Scarecrow. Better than okay. You are real, no matter what anyone says. You're every bit as good as a meat person. Hell, the only difference is you don't feel things as physically as we do."

Maybe she could change that.

Magic gleamed from her fingers, seeping into his burlap as she sewed. He sighed, eyes opening, gazing up at her. She swallowed and made herself finish the repair to his head. "I'm going to fix you up. You just rest."

"Theo?"

"What?"

"Thank you."

She caressed his forehead, ran a finger down his nose. "I need to find more straw for you. More clothes. They ripped you up really bad. You sleep, okay?"

He frowned lightly. "I feel strange."

"Shhhh." She closed his eyes gently, the magic threads still flowing from her fingertips because she wanted them to. "Rest now."

With a gentle sigh, he relaxed.

She rose to unsteady legs and made her way to the driver's seat. The engine idled. Still half a tank of gas. Just past midnight. Opening the first aid kit, she wiped antiseptic on every cut and scratch, hissing when it stung her nerves back into awareness. She chunked the RV into gear and eased it forward, centering the bulky camper on the narrow road. She offered a thank-you to the Goddess that stopping here with the engine running and lights on for over an hour hadn't caused the RV to die again, and that no one had found them.

Other than the Wheelers. She glanced at the bat laying on the floor beside the seat. Dark red coated its business end. With a shudder, she pressed the gas pedal and drove.

Once across the river into Missouri, she figured it was safe enough to get back on the interstate. Though she tensed whenever she saw a highway patrol car along the route, they didn't seem interested in her. Maybe the Oz historian guy hadn't asked for an all-points bulletin. Or else the cops didn't want to stop every beat-up RV they saw to check if it was carrying a stolen diary. She kept the camper exactly at the speed limit, going north.

Driving through the night was eerie and lonely without Scarecrow's company. Theo stopped before sunrise for a breakfast burrito and coffee at a fast food joint in Des Moines, and checked on Scarecrow while parked there to eat. His eyes were closed, but when she touched his cheek he smiled. "You hang on," she whispered to him. "Halfway home."

It was unnerving seeing him asleep, knowing this was the first time he'd ever done so. Did he dream? No nightmares, Goddess bless. Her eye fell on the diary as she walked from the bed back to the driver's seat. Theo couldn't muster any sympathy for Dorothy at this point. She could've at least told Scarecrow back in Oz that he wasn't her type, saved him this disastrous trip. Spared him the nasty comments. Then he would never have come here searching for her. Never met Theo.

She'd never have known she could do any magic at all.

Her guts twisted and soured as she drove on. She'd get him to those ancient mounds on Halloween. Get him safely home. Out of her life. She grimaced, stomach clenching. His friends needed him. And he'd die if he stayed here, anyway. But before that, she needed to remake him. Convince him he was just as good as any meat person.

The rest of the drive home was hour after hour of gray road and passing traffic. Stops at identical gas stations for the same terrible snacks and energy drinks. People stared at her until she realized blood was still spattered all over her, and washed her face in a burger stop's bathroom. More antacids chewed, gas pumped, bathroom breaks. Everything normal, uneventful, the road dragging her consciousness down as she pushed herself to stay awake. Her body was one dull ache all over.

Scarecrow slept through it all, reacting sleepily to her touch whenever she checked on him.

At last they reached the chain stores lining the interstate through Oshkosh. A fabric store sign stood above a strip mall. Theo turned onto the off ramp. Before they reached home, she needed a few supplies. Normally she'd browse a craft store for an hour and walk out with more than she needed. Today she clung to the shopping cart like a life raft, skating along the aisles with determination, leery of leaving Scarecrow alone. She bought yards of tightly woven tan burlap matching the shade of his head, soft brushed cotton in forest green, and reams of thread. Next door was a Halloween costume and prop store. The clerk helped her haul two bales of straw back to the RV. Another bag held a fine new peaked hat of black felt and gray suede gloves.

Exhausted, Theo pulled the camper into her driveway mid-afternoon. The whale barely fit, its end sticking into the street. She didn't have time to worry about it yet. She hauled everything inside and shut the blinds against the sunny, clear blue sky.

A pot of coffee brewed. She swept all her doll projects off her longest crafting table, lay Scarecrow's head gently on a flat pillow, and removed the straw from his open tunic by the fistful. Studying the pieces of his tunic confirmed it wouldn't be hard to make a copy, if she didn't go crazy on the trim. She slurped coffee, washed the grime from under her fingernails, and set to work with the burlap.

Making a full-grown body proved less difficult than her tiny dolls. The fabric flew through her sewing machine. Theo bent over it, concentrating. Glowing threads spun like spider silk from her fingertips as she worked, stitching magic into every seam. She muttered as she sewed together a torso, legs, arms, willing a spell into the making. "Scarecrow, you are every inch a real man. You will walk and touch and feel just like any meat person. You will smell and taste and use every single sense. You're just as good as a meat person and you deserve to feel everything."

When the new skin was all sewn together, she turned her attention to the tunic, making the brushed green cotton follow the same long lines as the one he'd worn before the Wheelers slashed it beyond repair. This didn't need the magical threads. She wasn't sure she had much energy left, and she instinctively knew she'd need it to attach his head.

Standing at last, she nearly collapsed, clinging to the sewing table. Not good. Not finished. Dark outside. No, she couldn't stop yet.

Unbuttoning his torn pants to remove the straw gave her a shock. She stared, blushed, gulped. Oh. Right. He *had* mentioned that. She'd forgotten. Not what she expected, but he'd said he designed it himself. She giggled nervously, took a breath. "Okay. Focus. It's just a body part. You can do this."

The organ didn't want to come away from the straw, magically attached somehow. Definitely awkward. Tugging on it was out of the question. She ended up transferring it to the new body in one scooped armful of crackly stuffing, then cut and restitched the crotch of the burlap body to accommodate it. Golden threads flowed from her fingertips and she stitched delicately, murmuring her spell all the while. "You are real, Scarecrow. You are every inch real and alive." The whole process felt surreal, but then what about any of this was normal?

Wheeler fangs were embedded in his loose arm and in some of his body's straw. She put on thick rubber gloves to pick out each of them, dumping them into a glass jar. She tossed out any of the material which had touched the teeth. When she ran out of his original straw, she cut open a fresh bale and dug in. Golden, flaxen fluff coated the table, the floor, her arms, lodged in her hair. She could barely keep her eyes open, stuffing his new body. This had to work. Had to restore life to him, give him new energy, maybe even new purpose. If she could make him experience every sense just like a meat person, maybe that would atone for having let him be ripped apart.

Goddess, please let this work.

A pair of men's dark dress pants were in the box of clothing she'd promised to hem for someone and never got around to. They were slender and suited for a taller man, so probably Adam's. They'd work. She tucked the pink stone, his leather sewing kit, and the wooden ringbox in his pockets. Tugging the newly stuffed burlap feet through the pants, she avoided looking at the part between the legs as she fastened the fly. His suede boots slipped onto the feet. Buttoning the tunic, she left the high collar open for now. She wrangled arms ending in stuffed gloves through the finished cuffs of the tunic sleeves. Finally, she took a deep breath and placed Scarecrow's head against the new body's neck.

"You can do this," she told herself. "It's just sewing."

Well, sewing with magic, but still sewing. Nothing she hadn't done a million times before. Except her friend's life depended on her getting it right.

She stared at the thread in her hand, thought about how it felt commanding her dolls to fight, the rush of connection to them. She drew the thread through the ragged base of his head, through the top of the neck where straw poked out, and as she tied the first knot she whispered, "You are a man. You're the one and only living Scarecrow, and you will move and think and feel just like anyone else. Just like a meat person."

The tiny glowing threads spread slowly from her fingertips and wove themselves into each stitch. "You are a man. You are real, Scarecrow," she murmured, her hands rising and falling, rocking gently forward and back, pushing whatever magic she possessed into every thrust of her needle. "You are real and I need you to live. Live, and think, and feel. You are real and I love you."

Not careful enough. Too tired. She startled when she pricked her thumb. A drop of blood fell. Wincing, she tried to rub it off the burlap of his chest, but it quickly soaked in. At least it wouldn't be noticeable with the collar buttoned up.

"Ow," said Scarecrow. He blinked, focused, frowned up at her. "Is that the right word? Ow?"

"Hold still, I'm not done."

When her needle plunged into his fabric skin again, he flinched. "Ow. Yes. That is the right word. I've heard Tip use it. What are you doing?"

"Sewing your head on, what's it look like?"

"I can't tell. Ouch! Theo!" He lifted a hand, weakly flapping it at her.

She pushed it down. "Nope. Hold still." Willing the glowing thread to continue, she kept going, murmuring her spell over and over. "You are real. You are real." It felt like something was being pulled out of her, unraveling from her chest through her fingers. Any second now she'd pass out. Blackness pushed at the edges of her mind, peripheral vision gone. Just a few more stitches. Nearly there.

"I feel strange."

She giggled. "Nope, same stuffed guy you were. I just added another layer for you. Better protection."

"You did what?" He fell silent, still frowning.

When he twitched, a stitch went awry. Theo cursed. "Would you please hold still? Just a couple more, almost done."

"My feet feel odd."

"That's 'cause now you actually have them." She completed the last small stitches, tied off and cut the end of the thread. The glowing magic faded from her fingertips. With a sigh, she slumped over the table. "Done. You all right?"

"I think so. Was that pain?"

Her eyes were closed. Forcing them open, she patted his arm. "Brains okay?"

"A little dizzy, but everything seems to be working." He sat up slowly. When his right glove touched the table, he flinched. "What the crows is that?"

"The table."

"It's—hard. Smooth." He lifted his hand to stare at it. "Not just solid. It has..." His eyebrows nearly met in the middle as he frowned. Theo heard a pop from under his new hat. "Texture?"

"Yep." She yawned, staggered toward the door. So tired. "If you're all good then I'm gonna sleep now."

"We're back at your home? Theo, what happened? I remember the Wheelers, you carried me to the wagon, and then nothing until just now."

"You slept. Bet that felt nice. I need to lie down."

"But that would've taken a day to journey back! Are you saying I—"

She nodded. Or thought she did. Too far to the bed upstairs. Sofa worked. Her numb feet tripped over each other. She lurched across the hall to the living room. Flopping onto the sofa was the best decision she ever made. She was asleep before her feet left the rug.

• • • •

SCARECROW SAT STILL a long moment, taking stock. He'd been sewn back together before. This was the first time it felt like—well, anything, really. Like prickles along his neck. He touched a hesitant finger to the seam. Theo did an excellent job. He could barely feel the bump where the thread worked back and forth between the bottom of his head and the neck of—wait.

A *neck*?

The tunic was open at the collar. Not sewn directly to his head. Buttons went all the way up, just as on his previous court tunic, but now straw didn't stick out of the opening. A light tan burlap continued from his head down a neck and a chest. He unbuttoned the tunic with shaking hands. Yes. All the way down. When he slowly eased down from the table, he felt the clothing rubbing against him as well as the more familiar crunkling of his straw. What in the name of all the fae was this?

The answer was impossible. Also blindingly obvious.

Theo made him a true body.

A skin of fabric under his clothing. Skin rubbing against his tunic, cradling the organ between his legs which was no longer simply tucked into his straw. Skin that sensed the air brushing against it, felt the touch of his glove when he shivered and buttoned his new tunic up to the formal collar at the top. His fingers against the cloth of the tunic was yet another new and frightening sensation.

Crows and blight, he could feel *everything*. How could meat people stand this?

Trembling at every step, he walked across the darkened studio. "Theo?" How had she done this?

Witchcraft. Obviously. The image of her standing on that very table on which he'd just awakened, strands of bright magic running from her fingers to her poppets, swam into his dizzied brains. He stumbled. Oh dear no. She'd remade him. Just like Locasta the witch tried to do, working spells into his straw, ripping him apart over and over just so she could restuff him, trying to control him, trying to discover what kept him alive. Fear rose inside him like icy water. "Theo, what did you do to me?" he demanded, running the last few steps into the parlor.

A young woman with a shock of orange hair and pale skin was half-curled on the sofa, her face smushed against a pillow, dead asleep. Her curves wedged against one another. So soft. Bits of straw stuck out of her hair. One hand dangled off the cushions. Ugly red gashes across her legs, bare forearms, and collarbone stood out in the moonlight through the open curtains. She hadn't taken her boots off. They were caked with mud and something darker.

Fuzzy memories rearranged themselves in his brains, sharpening into focus, like images in Glinda's magic picture. The Wheelers had cut her. The slash on her leg in particular was bad. Oh, no.

He knelt by her side. Lifting her leg for a closer examination sent shivers of awareness from his fingers right into his chest. Her skin was even softer than he'd perceived before. She'd cleaned the dirt from her flesh around the wounds, though spatters of blood and straw dust covered her all over. "Oh, Theo," he murmured, "you shouldn't have come back for me. You could've been killed." He'd been helpless to save her, to defend her. She'd charged into a vicious fight with no armor, no battle magic, only a metal club and her own fury, and managed to singlehandedly kill three Wheelers to save his life.

Here, now, was a hero braver than Dorothy. The Kansas girl murdering two powerful witches by sheer accident couldn't compare to this lovely witch's feats tonight.

Last night. Whenever that was. Which reminded him he didn't have much time left. Theo not only saved his life, she'd put all her energy into a new body for him. Exhausted herself. He'd be dead in a few days anyway when the full moon rose. He didn't deserve this. Why would she waste so much time and trouble on a stuffed fool? He would never have asked for this. He took her hand gently. "Thank you, Theo, but you shouldn't have."

She squeezed his fingers in return, sending a jolt of heat up his arm. "You're good's any man," she mumbled, slurring. She stirred, grimacing, and for an instant it reminded him of Dorothy turning away, Dorothy only pretending to be his friend. Then Theo muttered, "Scarecrow, don' die, stay with me, stay here Scarecrow, please," and he trembled all over so badly he needed to sit on the carpet next to the sofa, her strong fingers still gripping his. He saw tiny red wounds all over her hands. Remembered her scooping his brains back into his head.

It took effort to summon his voice, but by the third note he recovered and put all these strange, swirling, trembly emotions into the song. He sang of Death denied, of a spirit unconquerable. Theo sank into deep, healing sleep. For good measure he sang the autumn harvest race song as well, relieved when she smiled, breath calm and steady.

Scarecrow sat by her, holding her hand, bewildered, warm, whole, overwhelmed. He stayed in the same pose all night and listened to her breathing with newly attuned ears, felt the heat of her skin against his now frighteningly sensitive glove-fingers. Why had she done this to him? His brains rustled and popped under his hat, but he couldn't make sense of it. Any of it. So he sat, and listened, and felt, and at last the sun came up again.

26

No one had seen the Wogglebug since their hasty escape from the forbidden library two days ago. Now, Nick sought out Philemon, son of the Earl of Gillikin, hoping to wheedle the location of Professor Wogglebug out of the bug's fae lover.

Nick stepped aside for a procession of fae lordlings, bowing his head. Of course they noticed him. Some days he regretted having Ku-Klip the tinsmith craft him new body parts. As a man of flesh and bone, he'd been ordinary. Homely, even. The tinsmith had seen fit to "improve" his features and form when making him new bits for everything his cursed ax lopped off.

Not to mention, a tall figure of shining nickel-plated tin stood out anywhere.

"What have we here?" One of the lordlings, a minor duke with puffy sleeves on his jacket and frippery on his hat, stopped to examine Nick. "One of old Smith and Tinker's automatons?" He snapped his fingers in Nick's face. "Speak, metal man!"

"I beg your lordship's pardon. I am not a mechanical thing."

The fae laughed, all of them now staring at Nick. The duke raised one perfectly groomed eyebrow. "Oh? Are you placed here to entertain us on our way to the dining hall, then?"

Nick's face heated. He tried to keep his tone inoffensive. "No, your lordship."

"Entertain us anyway," another of the fae commanded. "Do you sing? Dance?" He pushed his elaborate cape off one shoulder in order to strike a pose with his hand on his hip.

"Alistair, read a book sometime," chirped another, smirking. "Do you not recognize this man?"

The one who'd demanded a show sniffed, eyeing Nick coldly. "Should I?"

"This is the famous man of tin who accompanied the Witchslayer girl."

"Really." The caped lord's eyes roved up and down Nick's body. "Kill any witches lately, tin man?"

"Certainly not, your lordship." Nick tried to back away. "Begging your pardons, my lords, but I am expected elsewhere."

"They say he was a man of flesh once, but chopped all his limbs off to make himself a prettier body of metal," declared an earl. That wasn't at all how his tin body had come about, but Nick knew better than to correct a lord.

"He is rather pretty," mused the duke. "Did you replace *all* your parts, then, metal man? Even your cock?"

Nick's cheeks must be glowing red by now. "Excuse me, sirs, I really must be off."

"Oh leave him be, Fennel," yawned the one who'd recognized Nick as the legendary Tin Woodman. "I'm thirsty, and the wine is that way. If we don't hurry, you know the damned witches will drink it all first."

They all tittered. "Especially if Locasta and Langwidere have arrived," the caped one quipped, to further amusement.

Nick gave them the most courtly bow he could. "Sirs, a good evening to you." He took only one step away when a hand on his shoulder pulled him back. He fixed his expression into one of bland politeness.

The duke smiled at him. "Very pretty. Come to my quarters tonight. East wing. Ask for Duke Fennel of Ev. And bring oil." Long white fingers with sharp nails raked down Nick's arm. "Lots of it."

Nick said nothing. The duke eyed him from head to foot again, lingering a moment longer at the metal plate which covered Nick's crotch, then sauntered off after his companions.

Picking his pace up, Nick swore under his breath. Rust and lightning, damned if he'd ever sleep with one of the fae. All other people were nothing but toys to their kind. Which brought fresh to mind his current mission.

Ozma Tip had recovered somewhat and insisted on attending court business today. Glinda was at court this morning as well. She hadn't spoken to Nick other than a casual comment about how nice his brand-new waistcoat appeared, which could mean she suspected he had something to do with the broken inkwell in the magical library, or it could mean nothing at all. There were dozens of fae, witches, earls and princes and queens everywhere Nick turned. More arriving by the hour from all corners of the Empire. Trying to act pleasant around them made his heart thump with restrained fury.

But no Wogglebug.

It took Nick all day just to track down the fae lordling. He must've checked every den of pleasure and disreputable alehouse in the city, only to find the smug bastard at court. Unfortunately Philemon brushed off Nick's casual questions about the Professor, saying only he'd developed an interest in fat, well-endowed Munchkins and so had no more use for "an ugly insect." Nothing to show for his inquiries all damned day. No trace of the Wogglebug anywhere. Not even head maid Jellia Jamb knew any gossip on his whereabouts. This was not good.

Darkness crept over the Palace gardens. Nick went outside to clear off the stench of fae perfume. No doubt many of them crafted spells into the scents. Nick was immune to any such tricks, but he didn't want anyone to come in contact with trace magic on his metal skin and suffer ill effects. He stood in the welcome shadow of an arbor and tried to think.

Where else might the Wogglebug be? Not in his quarters or any of the classrooms at the University. The docent wanted to be helpful, but hadn't seen him for a couple of days. He hadn't been at court according to the Tiger, who had time only for a quick whisper with Nick in the few minutes the cat took to mark his territory outside. Tiger and Lion stayed close by Ozma Tip, one on either side of the throne, while the Queen received an endless stream of nobles. All the Seelie Court seemed to be here. So far only the witch Mombi hadn't made an appearance. No sign yet of the horrible Unseelies either, which suited Nick just fine.

In the magic picture, the shambling, crooked, hideous creatures of the Unseelie Court were in tunnels underground. If they really were headed for the city, they might be coming up through the secret passages far underneath the University building. The ancient temple-turned-school concealed levels so deep, the monsters could be under it already, and no one would know.

For that matter, the deeper tunnels might go under the Palace. Scarecrow had found a secret passageway. Tip knew of a few, including a tun-

nel from the Palace to the first cellar of the University. The Wogglebug
said there were more. The longer Nick thought about it, the more strategically likely an invasion by tunnel seemed. What better way to start a
coup than for the hordes of the Unseelie Court to suddenly burst like
roaches up from the drains? The fae all camped in the Palace now would
mop up any survivors after the darker creatures killed the guards.

Tip should spend the next few nights in Scarecrow's library. Except
that would make her ill again.

Nick groaned, raising his eyes to the moon. Nearly full, it floated
above the trees, climbing into the violet sky. Two days and nights remained until Winter's Eve, and all of the city buzzed with excitement.
Rumors ran rampant concerning the gathering of the Seelie Court. It was
a feast day of the ancient religion, one old washerwoman insisted. It was
a surprise birthday party for Queen Ozma, a dressmaker was sure. None
of them suspected this festival would end the sweet young ruler's reign,
if Glinda's plan succeeded. And Nick still had only the vaguest idea what
the plan *was,* much less how to stop it.

Heading for the hills still sounded like the best option.

No safe access to the magic picture or infernally scribbling quill. No
chance to speak with Tip yet to see if she'd heard anything from the gos-
sipy fae. No idea where the Professor's wind-up bug could be or how to
use it. Nick touched the Evstone, cold in his waistcoat pocket. No word
from Scarecrow.

He was on his own, and time was running out.

If the Unseelie Court really were creeping through the sublevels beneath the University, it would be good to know exactly where the tunnels exited. Maybe if he found all the ones leading to the Palace he could
block them somehow. He could wield a hammer as well as an axe. The
walls of the cellar looked fragile. Must be in even worse repair farther below. At the very least, perhaps he'd confirm the invasion was heading this
way and be able to warn the Palace staff. Set traps. If anything could hurt
undying creatures of fire and rock.

It seemed risky, but standing around here doing nothing, with no
more information than they'd known two days ago, was driving him
mad.

He snuck through the shadows to the gardener's supply shed, a building of gleaming green marble roofed in tiles of malachite. Even the humble parts of the Palace grounds were overly fancy. The lock broke with one blow of his axe. Inside he found what he was searching for: a huge iron mallet. It was enchanted to break apart emeralds. Nick was pretty sure it could handle the hard head of a rock troll.

Or take down a support column, deep under the city.

As expected, the University was deserted. All the students had abandoned the dormitory floors to go celebrate. Even the docent was absent.

Nick descended the stairs to the cellar slowly, listening for any sound over the echo of his footsteps on the stone. A hooded lantern in one hand cast a faint light ahead of him. His trusty axe hung at his hip. The weighty handle of the mallet felt good in his grip.

This could do some damage.

The cellar was unchanged from a few days ago when the Wogglebug demonstrated his mechanical insect for them. Rough niches in the walls yawned emptily. Dripping water sounded from deep below. He followed the echoes to stone steps leading farther down.

Suddenly he wished he'd asked Lion to come with him. Cowardly though the cat still might be, he was a loyal friend. Blast and rust, he'd even accept Tiger if it meant he didn't have to venture down here all by himself. He'd heard stories about what lay below the ancient temple. The old Ozians revered the fae as gods, especially the Elementals of the Unseelie Court, and legends were still whispered of sacrifices, blood offerings, first-born babies given over to unhallowed things that ruled the night. The Pastorian kings and queens who'd ruled Oz before the Wizard came outlawed the old religion, banned the Unseelies from the walled capital city, but everyone knew worship continued in the far corners of the Empire. Might still continue in the deepest levels of the catacombs below. Really, Tip should've blocked those off already. Nick would ask her to order it done. Assuming he returned from this insane venture in one piece.

Nick started down the rough-hewn stone steps. They were smooth in the center. Many feet had traversed these stairs through the centuries, lending some unhappy evidence to the old stories. All of the bodies of the royal family which had lain in the uppermost crypt were respectfully reburied in the level below, in order for wine and other perishables to be stored in the cool cellar under the University. Nick didn't believe in spooks, but he still gripped the hammer and lantern tightly as he went down.

Might be something worse than old ghosts down here.

The catacomb walls were thick, the low ceiling arched. In growing dismay he swung the lantern in all directions. Nothing here appeared weak enough to destroy without a lot of work and noise. Was he far enough below street level that the thud of the hammer would go unnoticed? Probably, but that didn't guarantee *something* wouldn't hear the sound, and come to investigate. Long niches carved into the walls held bony remains wrapped in moldering velvet and silk. Here and there a crumbling skull wore a tiara or greened copper torc to show their former royal rank. No thieves would dare plunder these grave halls.

Spiderwebs covered the remains nearest to a dripping wall, where tiny insects crawled over the moss and slime. Seeing a round-shelled one with a long nose reminded him of the Wogglebug. The Professor was once as tiny, as ignorant as these crawling things, before becoming thoroughly educated and highly magnified in a schoolroom by an unwitting teacher with a magical projector. If he hadn't safely gone to ground somewhere, Nick shuddered to imagine what the witches would do to him. The scribbling quill of Glinda's Book of Records must've recorded at least the last second or two of their misadventure in the forbidden library. Would it have recognized the Professor under his priest disguise?

Four hallways ran from this central spoke toward the cardinal directions. Nick turned the lantern toward each, listening carefully, peering into the darkness. The faintest shuffling sound carried to him over the dribbling water. Like heavy footsteps over the echoing stone. As he advanced a few steps into the northern corridor, the sound grew louder. Rock trolls? They lived underground, deeper and colder than the Nomes, tunneling through the earth far from sunlight...

Raising the hammer, he went cautiously down the chilly corridor to another staircase, narrower than the last. A rivulet of cold water trickled down the wall, down the steps, moisture coating them in slime. He adjusted the lantern's hood down to a thin sliver of light. Though it still might give his presence away, he wasn't about to allow something to sneak up on him in total darkness. He squinted at the staircase, unable to see anything besides dark stone blocks going down, hesitating.

However, that sound was definitely something moving where nothing ought to be.

Ducking, he took slow, careful steps down. No room to swing the mallet. The stairway curved sharply, circling deeper underground. No way to fight if something loomed in his way. Tamping down panic, he forced his feet forward. Worst case, his body could block the tunnel. Prevent the Unseelies from coming up. Trapping him down here forever with them until he rusted away. They'd hammer at him with their massive fists, pounding and pounding as he rusted until at last they crashed right through his chest and—

Shuddering, he stopped. His heart beat frantically. Horrible though that scenario was, he could imagine Scarecrow nodding grimly. It was logical. Without knowing exactly how the fae planned to usurp the throne, any delaying tactic could be useful, give the rest of them time to figure out something. Nick grimaced. "Yes, but you're not the one down here, Scarecrow. I am. And it truly sucks Winkie goat teats."

The crudeness of that made him feel a little braver. Scarecrow hardly ever cursed, was so innocent about carnal things. If he'd been here, his straw friend would probably have cheered them both with a song. Damn, Nick missed his warm voice. What was the one he'd sung in the dungeons? The one that healed Lion's wounds and even mended some of the acid damage to Nick's tin. Quietly, trying to recall the words as he went, Nick sang. He wasn't sure of the Old Ozian words, but as he continued downward the tune came back to him easily enough. The gloomy lament echoed off the close rock walls. Maybe he shouldn't be singing. The stairway opened into a cavern.

A hundred glowing eyes turned to look at him in the darkness.

Nick froze, voice dying. The eyes remained fixed on him. Slowly he raised the lantern. A pile of rocks in the rough shape of a large man stood not ten feet away, massive hands empty at its sides. Its eye sockets were mere holes in its stony head, filled with glowing fungi.

Rock trolls.

Nick stood very still, hammer at the ready. After a second or so, all the trolls returned their gaze to the cavern floor. They were far too big to fit up the staircase. He turned and edged sideways into the room, prepared to flee up the steps. Again the rock trolls' heads swung up to view him, but otherwise they didn't move.

What were they waiting for?

He took a careful step away from the stairs. Another. Yet another. The trolls didn't attack. Somewhere off to his left, a voice mumbled. The glowing eyes of the trolls provided just enough illumination when he slid the hood closed over the lantern.

Someone must've summoned the trolls here, ordered them to wait until Winter's Eve to come charging up the stairs. Except they wouldn't fit, broad-shouldered and massive to a fault. Was there some other way to the surface?

Nick tiptoed toward the mumbling. Blackness yawned between two of the trolls. He slid the lantern hood open enough to verify another tunnel led off from this cavern. Just as he reached its entrance, a shuffling sound grew behind him. He whirled, hammer lifted high, bracing his feet. More trolls waddled into the cavern, emerging from a wide passageway he hadn't noticed before behind the wall of rocky monsters. The rock trolls shifted aside to let the newcomers in. Light blazed, and Nick shrank into the tunnel behind him. Spindly, tall things with heads of flame bowed into the cavern after the rock trolls, bent almost in half to fit under the craggy ceiling. Fire-walkers!

The monsters they'd seen in Glinda's magic painting were converging on this very room. No Wheelers in sight, but these dark things, formed centuries before men arrived in this realm, were threatening enough. Nick's body gleamed in the fierce orange light of the blazing Elementals. No way they wouldn't spot him. The rock trolls shuffled in front of the staircase opening. Blast and rust, no escape that way now. He slipped farther into the passage just as another troll stepped in front of the opening, effectively sealing him out of the cavern. Well, he didn't want to go back in there anyway. At least none of them pursued him. They must've seen him, but didn't seem to care. All under a spell of some kind.

The list of witches who could possibly command such ancient creatures was very, very short. Nick could think of only a couple of names on
it. Glinda and Mombi.

"What was that?" a harsh voice squawked.

Nick cringed, turning to face whatever was at the other end of this
passage. Stalagmites jutted here and there, making an obstacle
course—and cover. He crept up in the shadow of a large pillar of cave
onyx. A room beyond was lit with a red, flickering glow.

"Are you nodding off on me, you disrespectful old hag?" trilled a familiar voice. Glinda.

"Thought I heard singing for a moment," croaked a harsher voice. It
took Nick a minute to place it. The name popped into his head at the
same moment he finally saw the old witch bent over an Evstone in her
palm. Mombi.

This was the witch who'd turned Tip from an infant girl into a baby
boy, and back again on Glinda's demand. Who'd kept the boy as her
bound-slave for years while the Wizard holed up in the Emerald City
and let the rest of Oz fall into misery. Mombi tried to keep Tip, Scarecrow, Nick, and the rest of their little adventuring party away from the
city with illusions so realistic they'd never have ventured ahead on their
own. Only with the sharp nose of the Queen of the Field Mice leading
them had they penetrated the spells and reached their goal, following her
through girl-faced poppies Nick was loathe to chop down, and a field of
flames that made Scarecrow flee for dear life. All illusions, but the old
witch knew other magic as well.

Glinda's image in the Evstone shook her head and scoffed. "Well pay
better attention! Yes, there's singing, it's a grand party here day and night
right now." She waved her wand at something out of sight, and a dull
hubbub behind her faded to silence. "There, is that better?"

Mombi nodded. "I suppose they have reason enough to celebrate.
Only two more nights to go." She cackled. "You should see the Unseelie
Court gathering here. I've never beheld so many of them in one place."

"Good. The spell holds, then."

"Did you doubt my ability?" Mombi demanded. "You know of all of
us, I have the most sway with Elemental magic."

"Almost all of us," Glinda corrected with a smile.

Mombi bowed her head. "Of course."

"And how fares the anchor?"

"It's ready on this end, but not in place yet on the other side. I thought you had that under control."

Nick tried to see past the pillar without exposing himself. The anchor of straw bound in red ribbon hung in midair above a painted archway on one stone wall. All the walls were of gleaming black stone, arcane symbols carved into them and painted with a dull rust. A color which might've been dried blood.

The fresh paint around the archway glistened in the light of five red candles spaced in a circle on the floor. More candles hung on a drying rack above a cauldron. Possibly the same cauldron which they'd seen Locasta toss a living baby into.

Nick suddenly remembered tales of fae using babies' fat as tallow for candles. Heat rose in his chest and he had to force himself to stay still.

"It will be in place at the right time, I assure you," Glinda said.

None of this made sense. What was the anchor for? Why all this dark magic, and why wait 'til Winter's Eve when the witches had their army assembled already?

"It better be," grumbled Mombi. "You know the gateway won't open if the anchors aren't aligned."

"And you know perfectly well like cleaves to like. The straw remembers where it came from. The anchor will hold no matter where it is in the Other World, and the doorway will open regardless at the right time. The moons are almost in perfect harmony."

"I just would rather not step out before the Unseelies have cleared the way," Mombi complained. "You said you'd make sure the other anchor was in the heart of the old doorway, even though the mortals built some nonsense atop it." She snorted. "Wooden horses and make-believe faeries. You'd think even those half-wits would realize they built a temple to us."

Glinda giggled, sending a chill down Nick's spine. "Oh, I've seen it in the magic painting. My dear, it is truly a temple fit for our return, full of wonderments. Instruments which play music on their own. Magical creatures endlessly parading in a circle, in the reddest hall you've ever seen. Plenty of room for the Unseelies to play. Ah, how the mortals will bow and tremble." She giggled again. "The survivors, at least. And all glory again will shine from us as we resume our rightful—"

"Yes, yes, fine, I already bought into the speech," Mombi growled. Glinda frowned, but the haggard witch continued in a dismissive tone. "All of that's lovely, but you know damned well if the door doesn't open in the right place, the Unseelies will be compromised, and everything could go badly wrong. Your stupid Wheelers didn't do a very good job. Told you they were too crude. And Xixi's idiot necromancy idea went nowhere, just as I said it would."

Glinda scowled, her serpentine hair thrashing above her black eyes. Nick crouched further behind the pillar. "And I have told you, several times, I will see to it the anchor in the Outside World is in the holy place when the full moon rises. Even if he has to be dragged there in pieces and reassembled. There are yet other agents at my disposal, and I have already contacted them." She smirked. "Such easy creatures to command. Such petty desires they have."

"What about the Outside World witch?"

"What about her?" Glinda's face smoothed into a placid smile more unnerving than her scowl. She batted long pink eyelashes. "She is nothing. A pretender. You know very well all magic has faded from that land since we've been gone. This little child may call herself one of us, but I assure you she's not our kind of witch." A smile parted her thin lips. Nick shuddered at the sight of needle-sharp teeth. "In the centuries we've been imprisoned here, the mortals have forgotten all magic, while we have only grown stronger."

"Hope you're right, or this will be a very short trip." Mombi sighed. "Why aren't you down here helping with preparations? Too busy living it up with all the party people, I suppose."

Glinda's tone was icy. "Am I not speaking to you now? My presence would be missed. I will remain in the Palace until the ceremony begins. Now finish the doorway. I can see you've much to do still, and the moon ripens." With a gesture, she ended the spell, and the Evstone went dark.

"Pretentious old cow," Mombi grumbled. "She knows damned well I hate talking through the stone. Anyone could be listening in." She set aside the Evstone, stretching her back. Nick heard far more spine-bones crackling than humans possessed. "Who does she think she is, lording it over the celebrations while the rest of us slave away? Bogtrolls and curses! I deserve some cake too." She nodded, muttering to herself as she gathered her cobwebby shawls around her. "Cold down here. Could do with some hot tea and a slice of cake. Never should've let her take Tippetarius from me. No one to fetch for me. Queen, indeed! Well, let's see how much Tip likes being queen when Glinda's not here to protect her anymore." She snorted, picking her broom up. "To the Nomes with Glinda and her fancy courtiers. I'm going to get some damned cake. Let's just see her try and stop me."

With a mad cackle, she mounted the broom and gestured at the archway. The wall vanished, revealing a dark room beyond. Something moaned.

"Oh shut up. I'm done with you," Mombi snarled. "Unless I get hungry again later. You'll make a fine mock-turtle soup. *Eee hee hee heeee!*" She kicked her heels together and the broom shot through the opening. In the guttering candlelight, Nick glimpsed her flying up a set of stairs, quickly out of sight.

That opening was the only exit now. He ran through it, heart slamming inside his chest. Fearing more monsters in the dark, he yanked open the lantern. The light fell upon faceted black eyes, and a frightened groan again came from the far wall.

Nick stopped. "Oh dear heavens. Professor?"

The Wogglebug dangled from a chain fixed to the ceiling, unclothed. His armored breastplate was gone, exposing the joints of his arms and legs and what might be lumps of exoskeleton over internal organs. Two of his arms were missing the forearms and hands. One of his antennae was crimped and torn. His voice was hollow and faint. "N-Nick?"

At once Nick went to him, horrified. "Let's get you out of here." When he turned the Wogglebug to see how he was chained, the Professor screamed. Nick dropped the hammer with a clang, clapping his fingers as gently as he could over the bug's mouth. "Shhhhh!"

Tears flowed from the bug's eyes. "I'm sorry, so sorry, Nick it hurts," the Wogglebug moaned. The chain ended in a large meathook, gouged straight into the Professor's back. The hook could've pierced vital organs. Lifting him off it might cause blood to come rushing out, ending the Professor's life. However, leaving him here for the witch to throw into a stew was not an option.

Nick cupped his friend's hard cheek in his metal hand. "Can you stand?"

The Professor shook his head weakly. "I don't know. I don't know. Hurts. Nick, she—I didn't tell her anything. She pulled my arms off but I wouldn't tell her. They think I was snooping and found the library by accident. I didn't tell her anything."

Sweet sunlight, how horrible. Tears heated Nick's eyes. Blinking his vision clear, he braced his feet, set down the lantern. "My friend, I'm going to get you off that hook. It's probably going to hurt a lot. Take a deep breath."

The Wogglebug nodded, inhaled. Moving fast, Nick grabbed the top of the Professor's shelled back and lifted him. The Wogglebug keened. Carefully Nick freed him from the hook and set him on the cold stone floor. The Professor collapsed against Nick's chest.

"Can you stand? Can you walk?"

The Wogglebug shook his head. "I'm sorry, Nick. Hurts..."

"All right." Nick gathered the Professor into his arms, managed to retrieve the hammer and the lantern again. The stairs were too narrow for any of the Unseelies to use. At least they didn't have to worry about being followed. "Any idea where this goes?" Silence. Hard to tell if the Wogglebug had passed out. "Professor?"

"Cold," whispered the Professor.

Nick felt something wet trickling over his fingers, down his arms. Oh, no.

He mounted the stairs, carrying the fading Wogglebug, fear and anger rising, his thumping heart about to burst. If these stairs emerged in the middle of the fae they were done for. Nowhere else to go. With every lurching step upward, the Wogglebug sagged in his arms. The stairs went on forever, who knew where the witch might be, if he didn't get the Professor to a healer soon—

The song. Scarecrow's song from their time in the dungeons. Nick was no witch, could perform no magic, but then neither was Scarecrow and the magic song worked for him. How did it go, how did it go? Nick coughed, began singing, hesitant at first, raising his voice as the words dredged from his memory. Night after awful night, Scarecrow sang that mournful lament to get them through another round of injuries. Nick's voice echoed off the stone walls as he climbed, willing the magic to work, to heal, to help. The steps ended at a level corridor. Carven stone walls stretched off to his left and right. The lantern's weak light revealed burial niches, some full of only dust. Hard to tell if this was the same sublevel he'd passed through before.

Reminding himself to keep singing, he picked the path to his right and carried the Wogglebug along. To his relief, the Professor stirred. Not dead yet.

"Faeries of the rainbow," the Wogglebug murmured. "Music from Heaven."

"I'm not that good," Nick said.

"Do you hear them, Nick?" the Professor whispered. "They're singing us home. To the clouds."

Faint music floated from the end of the corridor. Laughter. Cheers. Nick was headed right into a roaring party. Probably where Mombi had gone for some cake.

He did an about-face and jogged the other direction, looking over his shoulder every few steps, his feet clanging against the stone. The lantern showed him only the next few steps dimly ahead. He passed the downward stairs and kept going. Where were they? Was this still below the University? His sense of direction was overwhelmed by panic, unable to feel magnetic north. Running straight, trying not to jostle the Wogglebug, he ended up in a circular room. Three other tunnels opened from it. Thank the stars, yes! He recognized some of the royal corpses from his trip through this very room not an hour ago. Nick mounted the stairs going up from the circular crypt, slowing his pace to avoid sending them both tumbling painfully.

"I didn't tell them, Nick," the Wogglebug muttered, his head rolling from side to side. "Didn't tell them anything. Not a blasted thing."

"I know. I know you didn't. You're a good man, Professor. Hang on."

Once in the University cellar, he felt safe enough to resume the song. It took him a couple of tries to recall the next verse after the chorus, but he kept at it doggedly until the right words surfaced in his memory. If only he had sharp brains like Scarecrow. Nick had tried hard to forget all the weeks spent in the Palace dungeons. He was glad they'd been walled off. That would make it harder for any rock trolls to come up that way.

Sneaking the Wogglebug back into his own quarters in the University seemed safer than lugging him over the Palace walls to Nick's rooms. The University was deserted. If Mombi was preoccupied with festivities it might take her some time to discover her prisoner missing. Nick hoped.

He lay the Wogglebug belly-down into the nest of blankets in his bed, then checked out the window before bolting the shutters closed. Down the cobbled street, every window of the Palace was lit, and fiddle music soared on the night breeze. A group of fae ladies was at the wall, arguing loudly with the guardian of the gates. Nick shook his head. Only a fool would deny them. Merely by arguing, the guardian was risking transformation into a block of wood or something equally senseless. Nothing he could do to help from here.

The party would likely go on until dawn, when the fae's powers weakened and they'd all topple into bed, drunk and sated. Nick might be able then to bring the Wogglebug to the iron-caged library. He could safely recover in there. Assuming he lived through the rest of the night. His unprotected chest rose and fell steadily against the soft blankets.

Nick's legs felt weak. He used a washrag in the Professor's washroom to wipe the tear-tracks from his face and the crypt slime from his feet, then toweled off all over. He'd need a good polishing as soon as possible to counter any ill effects from walking through the chilly damp. Returning to the bedchamber, he found a seat and took up the prisoner's song again from the beginning. As the magic swirled through the room, the hole in the Professor's back shrank and finally smoothed over into hard shell. Nick would have done anything to know if it was also healing whatever injuries the Wogglebug suffered inside.

With the song finished and the Wogglebug fast asleep, Nick used the last bit of flaming oil in his lantern to light a fire in the small hearth of the bedchamber. The Wogglebug sighed and snuggled deeper into the blankets. Nick gently covered him with another for good measure.

Nick sat in the slowly warming room, his heart calming at last in the relative safety of this cozy chamber, and tried to remember everything he'd overheard the two powerful witches saying. A lot of it sounded important, though baffling.

They'd talked about an anchor. No, two anchors. And the Unseelies. And some kind of temple, but it didn't sound at all like the cold, cavernous place rumored to be down in the crypts.

His mind kept circling back to the anchors. The obvious one, which Mombi crafted from straw, and another which needed to be at some particular place at the full moon. Somewhere in the Outside World.

The place Dorothy had come from and gone back to.

Where Scarecrow was now.

Dear heavens above. The fae weren't taking over the throne. This wasn't about a coup. Not in Oz anyway. Mombi's words came back to him in a cold rush: *"Let's see how much Tip likes being queen when Glinda's not here to protect her anymore."* And something about mortals forgetting magic, which would never happen in Oz, not with spells and fae around no matter what part of the country you went to.

"They're going to the Outside World," he gasped, rising from his seat. "This isn't about Ozma at all. They're opening a doorway to the Outside World and sending the Unseelie Court through first to kill everyone!" That army of Elementals was surely enough to slay every man, woman, and child in Kansas. He envisioned the fire-walkers setting fields ablaze. Rock trolls smashing houses, shoving screaming humans down their jagged gullets. Horrible!

With shaking hands he brought out his Evstone, spoke Scarecrow's name again and again, but the rock remained cold and unresponsive. He closed a fist around it, wanting to throw it against the wall. Blast and rust, lightning and agony! How was he supposed to warn his friend, warn everyone in the Outside World, if Scarecrow couldn't even keep the stone charged?

Nick needed magic. Needed a witch. Unfortunately, the only one he knew he could trust here was probably trapped in the middle of a wild party in the throne room, if she hadn't been locked in her bedroom already for the night. She didn't even have her full faerie powers. No one knew if she ever would, being part mortal.

How could Ozma Tip possibly stop Glinda and the other witches? How could any of them prevent any of this?

Nick slammed his fist into the wall, toppling books off shelves. A heavy tome shattered a teacup on a nearby table. Immediately regretting his anger, Nick bent to pick up the pieces. It was dainty, patterned in blue and gold flowers. Possibly it had sentimental value to the Professor.

His heart chilled. Scarecrow was the only one smart enough to work out a solution to all this, and he was unreachable, off on a trip to find Dorothy's diary. Dorothy was dead. Much as Nick sympathized, a sentimental journey gained them nothing here.

He swept the teacup pieces into a midden can. The witches had an army. Whether he or Ozma or anyone else were ready for it, this was war.

He was done being sentimental.

27

S moke filled her nostrils. Coughing, Theo pushed herself up from the bed, floundered an instant when the world went sideways, thudded hard onto the floor. "Fuck! Ow!"

A shrill beeping assaulted her ears. The smoke alarm.

Loud rustling came from somewhere over her shoulder as she struggled to orient herself. Not bed. Sofa. Living room. Home. With the smoke alarm trilling from the other end of the house.

"Theo, are you hurt?" A gentle glove touched her shoulder.

"Scarecrow!" The image flashed through her mind of his decapitated head, leaking bran and pins. The Wheelers. Hitting them over and over with everything she had, arms sore, cuts on her legs burning. His body ripped apart in the dirt. She rolled over quickly, jerked her gaze up and there he was. Whole. Worried. Kneeling on the rug in front of her, reaching to help her up.

Theo threw herself into his arms and hugged so tight his straw crunched. He nearly toppled over, throwing one hand back to brace himself. His other arm encircled her gently. The soft-scratchy burlap of his cheek was wonderful against hers.

"Oh sweet Goddess, you're alive, I thought they were gonna kill you!"

"Almost did," he rasped, and she realized she was squeezing all the air out of him.

She sat back, breathless, tears blurring her vision. "I thought they'd destroyed you. I'm so, so sorry, Scarecrow."

He prodded and fluffed his chest, undoing the squished stuffing. "You apologize a great deal for things that aren't your fault. Why is that?"

Her cheeks heated. "I'm Midwestern, duh."

"Local custom demands you think poorly of yourself all the time?"

"I—what? No. And it is my fault you were ripped apart. I should've grabbed you and run soon as I saw those bastards."

"Don't be sorry. You saved me, but Theo, you shouldn't have attacked them. You could've been killed." He took her hands in his, shaking his head, voice regaining strength. "They hurt you and there was nothing I could do to stop them. No way to keep you safe." His eyes glistened, his expression pained. "You shouldn't have done that."

She coughed, wiped her sleeve across her eyes and nose. Straw fluff everywhere. "I should've hit them before they tore you up. You were all in pieces before I thought to grab the stupid bat."

"Better me than you. Let me see the cuts, please."

She stretched her left leg out. Now that she wasn't gripped with panic, everything was sore. Dirty. Though she wasn't as exhausted as she'd expected.

"Hm. A little better. Do you feel ill at all?"

"I'm okay. Scarecrow, is my house on fire?"

"No..." He pulled away from her, fiddling his fingers together.

"Is the kitchen on fire?"

"Not all of it, no. I did open the windows. Sorry about the smoke." He winced. "And the noise. I couldn't make it stop."

On cue, the smoke alarm finally silenced. With a sheepish smile, Scarecrow stood and went to the front window. Reaching around the boards, he threw open the sash. A crow cawed, branches rustled and creaked. Sunlight painted the faded rug of the living room. "Sorry about that," he murmured, returning to sit crosslegged in front of her.

"Now who's apologizing too much?"

He gave her a frown and a half-smile at the same time, making her grin.

"Okay, so what did you burn?"

His face drooped. "Breakfast."

A giggle bubbled up from her chest. Scarecrow was alive, in one piece again, and he'd set off the damned smoke alarm trying to make food for her. Picturing him trying to reach the ceiling-mounted detector in the kitchen, floppy arms waving desperately, only made her giddier. She snickered. "What were you trying to make?"

"Oh. I found some ingredients for pan-cakes in your cupboards. I remembered you seemed to enjoy those at the waystation." He shook his head again, mouth sharply downturned. "The instructions seemed so simple!"

Alive, and failing at breakfast, and so focused on helping her. Goddess bless. Breaking into peals of relieved laughter, Theo crushed him in another hug. "I'm so glad you're alive!"

His arms went around her, warm and gentle. His hands patted her shoulders. "I feel the same, my dear friend," he murmured into her ear. "I'm worried about your injuries. Wheelers can inflict terrible wounds. All of that was my fault."

Theo released him, sniffling. Tears streaked down his face as well. In the sunlight she could see smudges of dirt on his chin and cheek. She hadn't done a fantastic job cleaning him up last night. Have to get a soapy washcloth, fix that. "The hell you mean, your fault? They ambushed you!"

"I should never have gone outside. I gave this a lot of thought last night. All these monsters seem to be drawn to me. Trying to prevent me returning to Oz, perhaps. Theo, you're not safe around me."

"Bullshit. Whatever their deal is, so far we've dealt with 'em. You and me, Scarecrow." She clasped his fingers in hers. "Nothing can stop us." His lips pursed in a frown. No. Let her enjoy this moment, this feeling that together they could overcome anything. He'd have to return to Oz in a couple days. Let her just enjoy this one moment. She embraced him again, more gently, careful not to compact his straw. "We make a good team."

"I suppose you're right." She felt him sigh and shiver, his arms holding her. "I just worry for your safety."

She inhaled his scent, fresh straw in warm sunlight. The slight mustiness of burlap. If only he didn't have to go back.

"Theo," he asked, releasing her in order to stare into her eyes, "what exactly did you do to me last night?"

Blood rushed to her face. "Put you back together, duh."

"You wove a spell into me."

She couldn't meet his searching gaze. "Yeah. I'm sorry. Probably should've asked you first." Oh hell. He'd told her evil witches took him apart and put him back together many times, casting spells on him. He had every right to be unhappy with her. "I—I just thought you should be able to feel everything like a meat person does. After what *she* said about you, I was so angry, I just—" She brushed one hand through the mess of hair over her forehead. "You're as good a man as anyone, Scarecrow. Thought maybe if you could feel things just like a human, you wouldn't be so down on yourself. It seemed like a good idea at the time." She forced herself to look into his painted blue eyes. No judgement there, just bewilderment. She swallowed. "I'm really sorry. I was trying to help. If you want, I can see if I can undo it. I'll figure out something." Not sure how. She'd probably need to make him another entire body.

He shook his head. "No, it's all right. It's merely very strange. I could feel the heat coming off the magic burner without having to touch it. Everything I touch has *texture*. Is this how you experience the world all the time?"

His senses must've been so dull before, if this was such a revelation to him. "Uh, yeah. Everyone does, pretty much." Yet again, she hadn't considered the consequences before doing what she thought was right. "I'm sorry, Scarecrow."

"Don't be. This is amazing." He chuckled. "A little overwhelming, but amazing."

"You're not mad?"

"You mean angry with you? No. Theo, no, I could never be angry with you."

"Okay. Um. Can we do breakfast now?"

Immediately he turned glum again. "I'm afraid I very much failed at that."

Theo giggled, struggling to her feet. Scarecrow braced his knees on the floor and put his shoulder under her arm to help. "It's okay. I am starving, though. Can't decide if I want food first or shower first. Need to clean you off too. You still have dirt on your face."

"Please take extra care in cleaning your wounds," he cautioned, rising as well. "I think the song magic helped with the poison, however."

"You sang to me?" All she remembered was sewing for hours and then heading for a soft surface to collapse.

"Yes. I was worried about you. You really shouldn't have attacked the Wheelers. They easily could have—"

"No. Do not tell me again I shouldn't have saved you. I'd do it again. I'll wade into a hundred ugly hyenas on wheels, naked with a butter knife, if they try to mess with you ever again."

He eyes widened. "Well. That's an unusual image."

Theo's face burned. "Yeah. Okay. Gonna grab a shower now."

As she headed upstairs, she could've sworn she heard him add, "I didn't say it was an unpleasant image..."

The hot water helped soothe every ache all over her body. She scrubbed dirt and dried blood out of her hair, tried not to think about how much of the mess on her skin was her blood and how much might be Wheelers'. She applied witch hazel to all the cuts and scars, hissing in pain at each splash of astringent. Staring into her closet, she thought about what they still needed to do.

Shit. They should ditch the RV. Return it to the storage lot right away. It had sat in her driveway too long, and if that Oz historian had reported the license plate, only a matter of time before the cops came looking. No idea if the title was in Danny's name or her parents' still, but at any rate the last thing she needed was getting dragged into an investigation. Scarecrow hadn't mentioned the diary yet. Had he found any means of returning home in its pages? It couldn't be as easy as singing "Somewhere Over the Rainbow."

Which reminded her, she hadn't checked on Gramma Hildy. She should at least call her later and say hi. After they'd figured out how to send Scarecrow home.

Miserable, she rinsed her mouth in the shower stream, but the sour taste remained.

Theo chose a black skirt and a dark green peasant blouse with long sleeves to mask the cuts on her arms, along with knee-high socks to hide the wounds on her shins. They displayed a bright scarecrow-and-pumpkin fall design printed all over. Oversized pentagram earrings and a spiked choker made her feel a little more secure. Her second-favorite pair of combat boots finished the outfit. Her favorite pair sat in a corner, covered in disturbingly rust-colored mud.

When she tromped downstairs, Scarecrow stared at her. She tugged nervously at her sleeves. "What?"

It took him a moment to speak. "Those colors are lovely on you."

"What, black and green?"

He glanced down at his new forest-green tunic over the black pants. "It sets off your hair and eyes rather nicely."

Might not go as well with the pink in her cheeks, but whatever. "Cool. Thanks. Hey, we have a lot to do today, so we better get going."

He nodded. He'd cleaned the dirt from his face, and his dark red nose and tan burlap appeared fresh. His eyes seemed brighter too. "I forgot to tell you earlier, thank you for the new tunic. You're the equal of any royal seamstress."

"Nah. You're welcome. Didn't have the energy for all the fancy trim, but I put gussets in the arms so you can move easier. In case we run into any other assholes who want to take you apart."

"Thank you, Theo." He took both her hands in his. His glove fingers were so soft. She felt guilty for not making him burlap hands too, but fingers were difficult to make right and she'd been so tired. Gloves were the easy out. "You're so thoughtful. I've never had a body like this before."

"Yeah, of course. Like I said, I just wanted to—after reading what Dorothy—" *Stupid, shut up, don't even mention her!* Theo took a breath, tried to be more coherent. "You're just as good a man as any, and better than most."

He was silent, standing there, his hands warming in hers. Embarrassed, Theo dropped her arms to her sides. "So hey, you okay if we stop for breakfast after getting rid of the RV? Then we can figure out how to get you home. I still think we should check out those mounds at High Cliff."

"Home. Yes." He sighed. "Of course. We should get you whatever you need first. I'm happy to go along with anything you wish." He sounded regretful.

Theo snapped, "Oh for fucks' sake, don't just go along with everyone else. Do what's right for you, be who you are, not who anyone else wants you to be."

He stared at her, clearly shocked.

"Scarecrow, I mean, don't go with me like you have no choice in it. Not like how you just went along with whatever Dorothy wanted. You have a life, you have stuff you want and need, right? Don't be afraid to chase your own happiness. I spent way too long trying to be someone I wasn't. For my parents, for school, for Mark. Screw that. If people don't want to be with me for me, as I am, they're not worth my time, and not worth yours either if they can't accept you as you are. Straw and all." She stopped, heated, breathless.

Wow. Way to make things intense before breakfast. I really need caffeine.

Scarecrow nodded slowly. "Thank you, Theo. For thinking so well of me."

"Of course I think well of you." She forced a smile. "Sorry. I'm bitchy before I get coffee."

"That's all right," he murmured. His voice strengthened. "And yes. I would like to accompany you for breakfast. Coffee does sound like an excellent idea." He smiled at her.

Relieved, Theo relaxed, returning the smile more easily.

She drove the camper back to the storage yard, where the front gate poles appeared to have been freshly replaced. Maybe she'd done more than nudge them trying to navigate the whale out of the exit. Oops. As she parked the RV out of casual sight among a row of similar ones, her eye fell on Danny's softball bat, its business end still stained and caked with clotted...stuff. Stuff she didn't want to think about. She hesitated, then grabbed the bat. Knocking it against the enormous tires took most of the dried gunk off. The camper itself had telltale scrapes and rusty stains on the front bumper, scratches in the metal hood. If Danny asked, she'd claim they hit a deer. She tossed the bat onto the back-seat floor mats of her car.

Though tempted to dump Dorothy's diary in the trash, she took a deep breath and held it toward Scarecrow. "You read the whole thing?"

He nodded, silent. He made no move to accept it from her.

"No clue how she went back to Oz the second time?"

He grimaced. "She went looking for storms, and wished herself back in Oz. It took her several tries. Perhaps she had some fae blood, or perhaps other forces were at work. If I ventured into a rainstorm I'd be soaked in minutes. Helpless."

"I'm sure tons of kids have tried to wish themselves over the rainbow. Guessing Oz doesn't have people from this world just popping in all the time."

"Hardly ever, unless the fae kidnapped them, as the old histories claim." He shook his head. "The Seelie Court certainly aren't going to extend any magic to help me home."

Goddess, she wished they'd never discovered this diary existed. After a moment's consideration, Theo tossed it into the backseat as well. Leaving it here with the camper would only drag her family into the theft. She'd never hear the end of it if her dad was questioned by the cops for possessing a stolen historical artifact. She'd mail it back to the museum soon as she had time. Let that lecturer coo over its historically significant contents. Theo was fucking done with Dorothy.

Scarecrow's gaze followed her movements, but he said nothing.

A short while later, shoveling amazing apple-stuffed French toast and chicken-maple sausages into her face at her favorite brunch restaurant, all thoughts of Wheelers or blood were purged from her brain. She stuck her nose into her wide mug of fresh-brewed chai. "Oh Goddess, I needed this so bad."

Scarecrow smiled. "Thank you for the coffee." He held a large mug of black coffee flavored with pumpkin spice between his hands, now and then leaning over to inhale the steam.

Theo paused, still chewing. "You should try tasting it."

"I can't drink. I don't have—"

"Who said anything about drinking? You have a tongue, right?"

He eyed the mug as though expecting it to leap at his face. "Did you enchant that as well?"

"I might've mentioned something about tasting in the spell." Theo shrugged. "Try it."

Hesitantly, he brought it to his lips. It took him a ridiculously long time to finally touch his tongue to the surface of the liquid. He jumped, spilling some of it, hastily setting it back on the table. "Hot!"

Theo giggled.

His face contorted through several expressions from startled to horrified to disgusted. "You didn't warn me it was terrible!"

She snorted so hard chai went up her nose. Coughing, laughing, she fumbled with her napkin, helping him pat his gloves dry. He glared at the coffee with an air of utter betrayal.

"It's really good coffee. Trust me," she laughed.

"It's..." He scowled. She was pretty sure if the conversational din weren't so loud in here, she'd hear his brain pins popping through the top of his head as he searched for the right words. "Bitter. Strong."

"No, *burnt* coffee is bitter, the stuff they brew here is smooth as hell. You're just not used to tasting anything."

He dipped the corner of his napkin into Theo's untouched glass of water and wiped his tongue, making her laugh harder. He shot her a hurt look, which calmed her down.

"Sorry. I'm sorry. Your face though. That was priceless."

He quirked a smile. "I suppose it must've been comical. Scarecrows aren't meant to taste things."

"But you could taste it," she pointed out.

A thoughtful expression smoothed his features. "That's true. This is assuredly a new experience."

"Sorry your first taste of anything was so disappointing."

"Just unexpected. All of this is new to me. I am glad to have someone to share it all with." He smiled, parking his nose back over the cup. "It does still smell wonderful. And my brains feel very sharp. Thank you for introducing me to this." He sighed with a rueful shake of his head. "In Oz, hardly anyone offered me food or drink since I can't consume it. I never thought before of experiencing it in any other way."

Maybe when he returned, he'd seek out more sensory experiences. *I wish I could be there to see it.*

What would living in Oz be like? Monsters all over the place. Magic a fact of life. Evil witches. Who probably wouldn't be happy about Theo not being one of them. "The flying monkeys are real, right?"

Scarecrow shuddered, gripping his coffee cup tightly. "Very much so. Filthy, crude, vicious beasts."

"In the book, they were slaves to a magic cap. The Wicked Witch of the West commanded them to attack, and later Glinda used the same cap to have them fly you and your friends back to the Emerald City."

"Oh, no, they enjoyed being horrible. I don't know if the old fae Empress of the Western Reach used a spell to call them to her in the first place, but the monkeys delight in harassing travelers. They ripped all my straw out and left me in a tree to moulder away. They dropped Nick into a deep crevasse where he lay broken for weeks. I think Lion still has scars from their dirty claws." He shook his head. "No, Glinda used some sort of doorway spell to transport me back to the city, when Dorothy was sent home. For Lion she opened a portal to the deep forest, and for Nick, the Western Reach, since his fighting skill impressed the Winkies enough for him to claim their land."

"Oh." Theo sipped the last of her chai. Hard to remember most of what she'd read about Oz was probably whitewashed for children. "As a kid, the flying monkeys scared me."

"They should. I wouldn't tangle with them again without some powerful spells to defend myself."

"Is all of Oz dangerous?"

He laid a hand over hers. "Mortal life tends to be short and unhappy under the rule of the fae. The nobles squabble amongst themselves all the time. Many savage creatures roam the dark places that wouldn't hesitate to snap up a lovely young woman for a midnight meal." He curled his fingers around hers. "Theo, magic rules everything. And I fear it's becoming darker still. Please don't even think about going there. Whatever you've read in those children's tales, I promise you things are far deadlier, nastier, and bloodier in Oz than they are here."

"We have wars here, ya know. Murders. Horrible people doing horrible things. Oz doesn't have a monopoly on evil."

"All the same, I don't want you hurt. Watching the Wheelers cut you, when there was nothing I could do—" He sucked in a breath audibly. Theo was pretty sure her spell didn't grow him lungs, but when he reacted like that it was easy to forget he was made of straw. "I've become fond of you, you know." His voice was so quiet she had to lean forward. "Please don't put yourself in danger again."

All protest died on her tongue when she looked into his eyes.

"Okay," she gulped.

He nodded, smiled, gave her hand a squeeze. Suddenly the restaurant was far too warm. She wiped her mouth, tossed her napkin down and waved at the server for the bill.

They remained quiet during the hour-long drive down to High Cliff State Park, on the eastern shore of Lake Winnebago. Theo selected more cheerful tunes, but didn't feel like singing along today. If she could figure out how to open a doorway between worlds in the ancient effigy mounds, Scarecrow would go home and she'd never see him again.

If she failed, he'd be dead in two days when the full moon rose.

Both options pretty much sucked.

Not much other traffic in the park on a weekday. An older couple sat under a pavilion, gazing out at the lake. Tall oaks and birches glowed golden in the sunlight. Squirrels hustled everywhere, burying nuts, chattering and chasing each other. Theo coaxed her grumbling car up the granite cliff road to the trailhead. Her boots crunched through a thick carpet of fallen leaves as they started into the woods along the marked trail. The scent of dead leaves in her nose was the very essence of autumn. Normally it was a smell she loved. It meant Halloween was just around the corner.

Today, that wasn't a happy thought.

Scarecrow fell into step beside her. She'd been warm enough in town she hadn't brought a jacket, just a loosely-woven long cardigan over her blouse. The wind was much colder up here. With a shiver, she curled her elbow around Scarecrow's arm, pressing up against him before she even realized what she was doing. He wrapped her arm around his waist and put his across her shoulders. When their eyes met, he smiled. A wistful smile, but a smile.

Theo snuggled against his side and matched her steps to his longer strides. Fine. He had to go back to Oz. Whatever. She was going to take all of him she could get before then, as long as he was good with this too.

They reached a wooden sign. The words PANTHER MOUND were carved and painted into it. A slight, bumpy rise, covered in fallen leaves, lay just past the sign. She'd forgotten how small the ancient effigy mounds were. If the park staff didn't keep them clear of vegetation, they'd be unnoticeable, worn down over centuries. Not so much *mounds* as *very*

small lumps that stretched a few yards. In her head they'd been much bigger. Taller. Actually capable of having doorways open in them on a magical night.

"Oh. Damn." She turned, checking out one labeled CONICAL
MOUND on the other side of the trail. More signs farther along marked
the placement of others. The conical ones were tallest, but still didn't
come up to Theo's thighs. "Not as big as I remembered."

Scarecrow leaned forward to read a placard which gave some of the
history and symbolism of the mounds. "A water panther? Do they still
live in the lake?"

"Not that I've ever seen, and I've been out on it lots of times." Grand-
pa Orville tried to interest Danny and Theo in fishing for walleye when
they were kids. Danny went along with it cheerfully. Theo hated sitting
still in the boat for hours. Hated sticking worms on hooks. Hated cleaning the fish if they caught any.

"I don't much like lakes or rivers either," Scarecrow said.

"I bet. Wet straw doesn't sound fun."

"It absolutely is not. Why don't you like the lake?"

Had her distaste been so obvious? Again, she saw no judgement in
those dark blue eyes, merely curiosity. "Too many summers pushed into
going fishing or boating or swimming. I don't like fishing, there's nothing
to do on a boat except drink, and I look like a beached whale in a swimsuit."

"A suit of clothes for swimming? Wouldn't they become soaked?"

"Not like that. Swimsuits are made of fabric that dries quickly, more
like underwear."

"Ah. So closer in appearance to the breast supporters and tiny pants
you wore the day the corpse attacked us."

How the hell did she end up in this conversation? Theo nodded, fixing her eyes on the park sign. She was still pressed against his warm body.
Pulling away right now would be even more awkward, so she stood still.

"You didn't look anything like a whale. If the ones here are anything
like Ozian whales, they'd have too many fins to ever wear something like
that."

Too much talk about bodies and whales here. "Do you get any kind of magical vibe from any of these?" Theo asked, gesturing at the leaf-covered earthen mounds.

He frowned, turning to peer intently at each of the ones within sight. "No, but I'm not a witch. Do you?"

"No."

They stood there, studying the mounds. Trees rustled, sending down more dry leaves, their colors faded to dull brown and brick-red.

Theo let go of Scarecrow, walking past the path boundary until she stood atop the nearest panther mound. She held her hands out over the earth, palms down, eyes shut. Nothing. Except now she was cold. "Goddamn it. There has to be a way. In Ireland people are always getting swallowed up by faery mounds. Farmers won't plant on them. They're supposed to open wide at Beltane and Samhain."

"This sign says the mounds were made by a tribe of people who lived here centuries ago, not by the fae," Scarecrow pointed out.

"This has to work," Theo argued. "This is the closest thing we have to faery mounds. What about a song? Do you know any songs about faery doorways or hills?"

"Let me think." Scarecrow settled himself on the ground, frowning mildly at one of the conical mounds. He removed his hat, massaging his head with one hand.

The gash Theo had sewn shut on his temple was a thin line of stitches now. It looked much worse when she sewed him up. Did her spell actually heal him? She wanted to take a closer look at it, but disturbing his concentration wouldn't help.

She paced a few yards up the trail, wrapping her arms around herself, tugging the cardigan closed. The wind swept up the high granite cliffside, blowing through the trees along the escarpment where the trail turned back north. Poplars rattled. Oaks creaked. A squirrel stood up to scold her intrusion before darting away.

There had to be something she was missing. Hell, even Mark claimed the fae were real, and once he'd taken his coven to make an offering out in the woods in a ring of mushrooms. Just stepping into that circle of fungus made Theo's hair prickle. Mark had stood in the center of it and made a long speech about the Fair Folk being guardians of great power. Offered an open jar of honey and a wooden knife he'd carved. Crows gathered in the trees, staring at them, not even cawing. The whole thing creeped Theo out. She'd had nightmares of the crows' beady eyes, of something disturbing the earth in the circle as it dug upward from far below.

Maybe that was what they needed, though. How could she find a mushroom circle? No rain in the last week. Not likely to be any fungus sprouting as the nights began to freeze.

A strong, warm tenor called her back to her surroundings. She found Scarecrow seated in the scattered dry leaves, hat on his head, arms outstretched, singing in that old language again. The tune was mournful, his voice dipping into his lowest register. Theo shivered, clutching the thin wool sweater tighter around her arms. When the last note died away, before she could make up her mind whether to say anything, he took a breath and began again in English.

"Farewell, this land of beauty
and your windswept rocks,
When I am far away in the mountains dark
Will you ever remember me?
I go tonight to the land of the fae
Where jagged coast and ragged peaks
Have claimed all ships from the sea.

"The moon is gleaming in the trees
The owl hoots and weasels creep
But I've many a mile to travel
No time for rest or sleep.

"Farewell, this land of beauty
and your windswept rocks,
When I am far away in the mountains dark
Will you ever remember me?
I go tonight to the land of the fae
Where jagged coast and ragged peaks

Have claimed all ships from the sea.

"I'll miss your quiet nights the most
When far from here I am.
Think of my name, and call to me,
Wherever I must roam."

As he sang the chorus a final time, tears trickled down Theo's face. Every nerve trembled. Oh Goddess, what if this was the right spell, and he vanished? What if the door opened right now and she never saw him again? She rushed to him, dropping to her knees painfully on the hard-packed trail, threw her arms around him. "No, wait! Don't go yet, wait, please!"

Startled, he fell backwards, and she ended up on top of him. "Scarecrow, don't go yet, please, wait," she sobbed, hugging him tight. If he went, she was going with him. Evil faeries be damned.

"Theo? What—"

"I'm not ready for you to leave," she gulped. Her heart slammed frantically against her ribs.

His arms enfolded her. "I don't want to go either."

She opened her eyes long enough to see the pain in his face. Stroked her palm against his scratchy-soft cheek and pressed her lips to his, kissing him hard.

His entire body tensed, straw rustling. His mouth remained shut, his hands frozen in place on her back, his straw crumpling under her weight. Except for one spot which resisted. With a start, she realized he wasn't responding to her, except for the one embarrassing part growing hard above where her thighs met his.

Theo backed off, cheeks on fire. "Oh Goddess. I'm sorry! I'm so sorry."

He blinked, eyes wide, not moving, sprawled in the dry leaves.

She scrambled to her feet, stumbling away, fighting tears. *Stupid, stupid, stupid!* After reading how Dorothy used him, how incredibly thoughtless to force herself on him. He clearly didn't feel that way.

She wiped her face with the long hem of the cardigan. "I thought maybe that was it. You know, like the song would open a door and you'd just go. Sorry for jumping on you."

"No harm done." He sounded confused. "The song doesn't seem to have done anything else. It was the only one I could remember about journeying to a fae land, so I thought perhaps it would work. Clearly the effects have more to do with, er, emotional responses."

Theo made herself breathe, tried to stop the tears, kept her back to him. "Would you promise me something, though? Promise you won't leave without saying goodbye?"

"I promise," he replied quietly.

Theo nodded. She brushed moisture from her eyes. The breeze was so cold. Hugging herself, she shuffled back toward the trail head. She must seem desperate as hell. Dragging him up here when these weren't even faery mounds, asking him to try a song, then freaking out and jumping on him when he did what she asked. *Good job, way to look sane and stable.*

When they reached the car, she kept her eyes averted. No idea what to do next. How to help him. How to pretend she hadn't just embarrassed the fuck out of them both. Absolutely typical, she embarrassed everyone else, might as well add the Scarecrow of Oz to the list.

"Are you all right?" he asked.

"Fine. I'm fine. Except I have no idea how to fix anything. How to get you home before you run out of magic." She choked on a laugh. "Some witch, right?"

"Theo, you're the best witch I've ever met. The only good witch."

She started the car but sat there, directionless. She pulled her phone from her purse just to have something to look at that wasn't a confused, live scarecrow. "Maybe we can find a ring of mushrooms. Don't know where they'd be this time of year. If we have to drive further south, though, so be it." Waking the screen up, she saw a text from Danny. Several texts. He was pissed. "Oh, great, exactly what I needed right now."

"Hey thanks for not bothering to let anyone know you were back in town, Mom was asking since you haven't answered your phone," the first text read.

She'd set her phone on silent mode days ago and never changed it during the road trip. There were missed calls and texts from her mother. *Oh fucking well. Sorry Mom, been busy fighting off nasty hyenas on roller skates.*

"Did you hit a deer? Now I have to go wash it before I can use it this weekend. Thanks so much sis."

"Jesus, Danny, you sound eighty," Theo growled. "I'm keeping your damned bat. I need it more than you do." She was about to shut off the screen in disgust when the word *Hildy* caught her eye. She read the rest of the texts.

"Grandma Hildy is back home in case you care. Mom talked to her last night. Also you might want to let Mom know you're not dead after your wild road trip with your pagan friends. She keeps texting me, like I would know. Call her please."

The last thing Theo wanted was to get roped into an hour-long guilt-trip-filled phone call with her mother. Mom would pester her until she agreed to join the next family church outing, ever hopeful her daughter would come back to the stifling, placid religion Mom treasured so much. Gramma Hildy, though. "Crap," Theo muttered, rubbing her free hand through her hair.

"What's wrong?"

"Gramma Hildy. I promised to come see her when she got home from the hospital. She came home yesterday."

"You were a little busy," Scarecrow pointed out. "Forgive me for keeping you away from your family."

"Stop apologizing." Theo sighed. "No, I can go see her Sunday as usual. After..." After Halloween. By then Scarecrow would either have found a way back to Oz, or he'd be dead.

He touched her arm. "I appreciate all your efforts, Theo."

"We don't know how to get you home yet!"

"I don't think there's a way back."

"There must be! A doorway, a faery ring, a tornado, something. No. No, we can't give up. I won't let you die."

He sighed. "I can't think of any songs to conjure a whirlwind or open a door in a mound of dirt. The one I just tried clearly only affected your emotions, which was not at all my intent. I'm sorry it made you do any-thing you didn't mean to do."

"What? No, I've been wanting to do that for—" Theo stopped, shame flushing through her. "I mean, I read Dorothy's diary, what she did to you. I shouldn't have made you uncomfortable." She dared a glance up.

He quirked one brow. "But if that wasn't caused by the song—why would you ever—" He faltered, touched his chest. Straw rustled. "I'm just a scarecrow. Why would you—?"

Heat flared in her breast. "You are not *just* a scarecrow. You are The Scarecrow. And yeah, I have feelings about that. About you. I get it that this makes everything awkward, I'm sorry, I can't keep pretending I'm not upset you're gonna leave, or if I can't find a way to stop it you're gonna die!"

His eyes were wide, dark brows high and arched.

Breathless, tears brimming, she wiped her face furiously. "I get it. I'm always too emotional. I'm just a stupid firecracker in a fat body."

His hand closed gently over hers. "Theo, you're far from stupid, and I see no reason why your body should be a source of embarrassment to you. At least you're strong flesh and blood, with lovely curves. Not flop-py, weak straw."

Too hot in here. She lowered the driver's side window. "You're not weak. And I like the floppy. And the crinkly straw."

He chuckled uncertainly. "That's kind of you to say, but I know I'll never be a real man. Not like this."

"Fuck that. You're perfect exactly how you are." Theo glared at him.

"So are you," he said softly.

She swallowed a lump in her throat, stomach churning. "I'm not. I'm hotheaded and stubborn and I charge into things without thinking. When I try to help other people I always end up screwing it up some-how." She sniffled. "Doing what I think is right and it turns out to be not what they wanted at all."

"I never expected to be able to feel anything, but your spell has awak-ened me to amazing new experiences, Theo. I'm still not happy you at-tacked the Wheelers, but if you hadn't, I'd be dead." He paused, lips pursed a moment. Quietly he went on, "You said people should accept you as you are, or they were a waste of your time. Those qualities you list as negative things are exactly what saved my life. You've given me senses I didn't know existed." He was sad and serious. "I'm very much aware I'm just a stuffed thing. I hope, however, you will accept my deepest admiration for you. My gratitude."

It took her a minute to find any words. "You're not just a stuffed thing and I'm gonna smack you if you keep saying shit like that. I take it back. I'm not sorry I jumped you. I've been wanting to do that for days. You're better than any guy I've ever dated."

"But I'm made of straw and fabric."

"Gee, didn't notice *at all* when I was sewing you a new body."

He frowned. "Dorothy thought I was silly and ugly."

"To hell with Dorothy. You're adorkable."

A half-smile. "Interpreter?"

"Interpret this," Theo growled, leaned toward him and grabbed the back of his head to pull his mouth to hers. His lips were dry, a little scratchy, but he accepted her kiss. His lips parted, his tongue met hers. His fingers threaded through her hair, stroking gently. She kissed him, and slowly he kissed her in return. He crinkled when she squeezed his shoulder. His movements were gentle but met hers like for like, his hands in her hair, stroking down her back.

When finally she pulled away, needing a breath, he sat there with his mouth open, eyes wide. Theo wiped the remaining tears from her cheeks, panting. "Should I not have done that?"

He gulped, shook his head. "No, I mean yes, that is, I mean, thank you."

"You don't have to thank me. I wanted to. And I'm not sorry." She glared fiercely at him. Let him try to insist he was nothing after that. She'd keep kissing him until he stopped saying he was just a scarecrow.

He nodded, voice very low. "Thank you, Theo."

They sat there, cool air whisking away the heat between them. Theo wasn't sure what to say or do next. Everything she could think of seemed small and pointless after what just happened. Fortunately, Scarecrow saved her from having to say anything by changing the subject. His voice was raspy at first.

"I need to talk to Nick. And we should check on your grandmother. See how her bones are healing."

Theo laughed. "Really? I mean, that's what you want to do right now?"

"I did promise her I'd sing for her again, after I found Dorothy, and—well. Not much time left. I should fulfill my promise to her, and try to contact Nick. Any assistance I can give him from here is the best I can do."

He was going to spend his remaining days of life trying to help others. Shame crept through her. She should run down any possible lead to help him. Gwyn had a lot more experience with magic. Despite Gwyn's disapproval, Theo should reach out to her, see if she knew where to find a faery ring, or any other possible solutions. Gwyn would almost certainly help the straw man go back to Oz if she thought his presence here was dangerous.

Theo nodded, resolve firming. "Yeah. Okay. I'll talk to Gwyn and you talk to Nick."

Scarecrow raised an eyebrow. "Aren't you still angry with Lady Gwyn?"

"Didn't say I wasn't angry, but if she wants you gone, maybe she knows of a way to help you get home." She sniffled, wiped her nose. "I'd rather you go home than die."

"You're a true friend, Theo."

"All good." She poked his shoulder. "Go ahead. I'd like to say hi to Nick again too."

With a nod, he pulled out the pink stone and once more sang the song about the stones of his homeland. However, calling Nick's name as he held the stone only made the stone glow a moment, then fade.

"Didn't the song work?"

"It worked," Scarecrow muttered, frowning. "Perhaps his Evstone hasn't been recharged. How inconvenient."

"Keep trying."

Another invocation of the Tin Woodman's name had no effect. Scarecrow shook his head, tucking the rock back into a pants pocket. "I wish I knew what's happened, but there's nothing I can do until Nick recharges his end. I'll try again in a little while." He gave Theo a wistful half-smile that made her want to kiss him again. "Shall we pay a visit to your grandmother?"

As they drove the country roads back to town, Theo held his hand. He entwined his fingers in hers, warm and crinkling, the suede so soft. Maybe when he returned to Oz he'd think more of himself. Feel more, experience more. Fall in love with someone who treated him better than Dorothy.

She knew she should be happy for him, but her guts crimped and roiled and it was all she could do to keep the bile down as she drove.

28

For once in his life, Scarecrow had no words. Nothing which could express the conflicting emotions whipping through his brains like a cyclone. If this sort of thing was what Nick navigated through all the time so cheerfully, his hat was off to the Tin Woodman. He sat silently while Theo drove the carriage, trying his best to separate out the various feelings. Categorize it all.

What a kiss! Alike to what Dorothy gave him only in that both women possessed soft, wet lips. All he'd done with Dorothy was tainted, now he understood she'd merely been testing his suitability as a convenient husband, and felt no deeper affection for him. Theo's kiss...

He wasn't sure what to think of Theo's motives. Perhaps there weren't any. She was an impulsive hugger, which he didn't mind one bit. Possibly the gloomy song he sang played on her emotions more than she perceived. Certainly no way she could prefer kissing him to a flesh-and-blood person, no matter how fond of him she'd grown.

A vague memory surfaced. Theo, tearful, saying she loved him as she stuffed brains back in his battered head.

That had to've been a dream. He'd never lost consciousness before, but certainly if the loss and jumbled return of his brains caused him to sleep, it must've also caused him to mishear things. Imagine things. No woman of flesh would want a scarecrow lover. Dorothy's diary made that starkly clear.

His new body's reaction to having Theo's bountiful person suddenly atop him was puzzling. A little frightening, to be honest. When he'd picked out his organ of lovemaking for Dorothy, it never occurred to him he'd *sense* anything with it. All the books proclaimed a man wanting to please his lover was supposed to have such a shaft, which could enter another's body to give them pleasure. Not really sure how that worked, but all the romantic texts agreed a man ought to have a goodly one. Last night, upon waking in this new-sewn form, he'd been uncomfortably aware of its existence again. While Theo showered this morning, he'd tried to adjust his trousers better so it wasn't so distracting. Clearly he should've asked Nick more penetrating questions, despite his friend's embarrassment. No one warned Scarecrow this thing would do *that* if a lovely woman of his acquaintance happened to lay on top of him. Which must explain Theo's reddened face and sudden dismount. Having a hard thing poking her stomach couldn't have been very comfortable. Crows and blight, he'd have to take care not to allow the thing to be provoked again.

So why had she kissed him? She was a wonderful friend, to be sure. She'd saved him from the Wheelers, created this new body for him, woven in a spell to let him feel and even taste. He was nearly overpowered by new sensations. Her argument for doing so mired him in confusion as well. No one else had ever declared he should consider himself the equal of a meat person. Well, the Wizard said he was smart enough for a stuffed man, but upon Scarecrow's insistence, gave him his superlative brains. Without those, he'd never have figured a way out of the palace when Jinjur's army besieged them, or thought to throw eggs at the Nome King. Theo understood how important his brains were. She'd scooped them off the ground in the cornfield, safely tucked them back in his head. Therefore, she certainly also knew he was nothing without them.

This line of thought wasn't productive. Frowning, he rubbed his chin, still unnerved he could feel his own burlap with his fingertips now. Scratchy and dry. Not at all like Theo's soft, pliant skin. Why, he failed at even the most basic standard of being a meat person, without actual flesh. She couldn't possibly want to press her pink, lovely curves up against this rough fabric, except for warmth when the wind blew cold.

Suddenly he imagined her doing just that, atop him, not clothed as she'd been on the cliffside but wearing only the skimpy underthings which revealed the beautiful, full curves of her breasts and hips and—oh dear.

He froze, staring straight out the window of the carriage. He hoped they were a distance still from Theo's grandmother's home because he needed a minute or three to deal with this unruly organ.

When he spoke to Nick, if they had time, Scarecrow had a few choice words of rebuke for his friend. Nick was a meat person once. He at least could've *warned* him.

Lady Van Baum's home was a lovely manor perched next to a steep ravine, not far from a river. Strong timbers and a tall peaked roof reminded him of the hunting lodges of the fae in the well-forested Gillikin countryside. The house was surrounded by tall trees. Though many had lost their leaves already, a few branches of fluttering gold and red contrasted pleasantly with the dark green and brown walls.

Theo shook her head at the house. "This place is really too big for her. Mom hired a cleaning service but Gramma Hildy won't let them come more than once every couple of weeks."

"Has she no servants?"

Theo laughed. "I know, right? There's even a butler's pantry, but no." She sighed. "She and Grampa Horace lived here their whole lives, pretty much. Married over fifty years 'til he died."

"Did they marry for her fortune or his title?" Scarecrow asked as they walked toward the door. "Or to produce an heir?"

"What? No," Theo replied. "They were in love."

In Oz, the only people who could afford a dwelling such as this would be fae and haughty. "I've never seen any of the fae marry for anything less than a better social position."

"We're not fae," Theo said, but her eyes were both green and brown in the afternoon sunlight. "Don't peasants marry?"

"Of course. Some countries require it, to ensure a steady population of mortals. The fae need people to serve them, after all."

Theo scowled. "How did humans even wind up in Oz if the fae rule everything?"

"Some of the Old Ozian scrolls I found mention the faeries brought mortals along with them, when they created the fertile lands out of the middle of the desert."

She snorted. "Probably kidnapped 'em from our world and made 'em breed. Gross."

"Breeding is unpleasant?" This was not what he'd been led to assume.

Theo turned bright pink from her cheeks to the collar of her blouse. He found himself following the color down and yanked his eyes back up to hers. He was suddenly very curious to see just how far the pink went.

"Uh, no. Slavery is horrible though."

Scarecrow nodded. If Lady Van Baum lived in such a magnificent palace as this, yet kept no slaves or servants, she was the most freethinking noble he'd ever encountered. What song might best please her? Perhaps the autumn race song? He glanced at Theo as she rapped on the front door. Though he'd sung that tune several times prior to meeting Theo, now it felt inextricably associated with her in his mind. Singing it for anyone else just seemed wrong.

Theo called out as she opened the door, "Gramma Hildy? It's me."

Scarecrow entered behind her, taking in the wood-paneled hall, a grand staircase opposite the entry, open doorways to either side revealing formal furnishings in dark walnut. Plush woven carpets padded the floors, and portraits hung on several walls. It was much larger and more imposing than Theo's house, with all the windows cloaked in draperies. A bit dark for his taste. He always preferred to be in sunlight.

"Theo?"

They turned to see Lady Van Baum tottering through the dining room. She paused to rearrange some bright pink flowers in a vase on the table. "There's my favorite granddaughter. I see you brought your young man as well. Come in, come in, let me get you both some cookies."

"Gramma, how are you?" Theo embraced the elderly lady. "You're not supposed to be walking around yet! Don't you have a walker? Where's the home care nurse?"

Lady Van Baum laughed, hugging Theo tightly. "Nonsense, don't need 'em. I sent the nurse away this morning. I feel fine." She smiled at Scarecrow. "How is your play research going, young man?"

He swept his hat off in a low bow. "Lady Van Baum. It's good to see you again."

Her eyes twinkled as she came closer. Theo hung onto her in obvious worry the old woman could topple over at any second, but Lady Van Baum seemed fit, if not especially fast-moving. "Are you going to sing for me today?"

"Of course, if you like. What sort of song would you prefer?"

Theo was making cutting motions across her throat with her hand and shaking her head at him. He frowned at her. Was she referring to the Wheeler attack? Certainly he wouldn't bring that up.

Lady Van Baum chuckled. "I'm sure you can guess. But first let's have some cookies and coffee."

"I'll help," Theo offered, tugging Lady Van Baum toward a door in the other end of the dining room. Her grandmother planted her feet and would not be budged, smiling at Scarecrow.

"I think your song helped me a good deal, but such a sad tune. I can tell by your accent you're from New England somewhere. Are your folks Irish?"

Why did people keep assuming he came from some sort of angry country? Perhaps the word ire meant something different here. "I have no family to speak of, Lady Van Baum, only friends."

"Well," she said, giving a satisfied nod, "now you have. Come along. You like cookies, don't you? 'Course you do." She took his hand in hers and pulled him with her in an abrupt about-face, heading for the other doorway. Her hand strength was surprising. He shot Theo a plaintive, silent plea for help.

"Scarecrow's on a really strict diet, Gramma Hildy. He has lots of food allergies," Theo said. They accompanied the elderly woman through the dining room to a large kitchen easily twice the size of Theo's. Lady Van Baum swung Scarecrow toward a table set with tatted lace doilies and a vase sporting sprigs of maple leaves. The elderly lady brushed off Theo's fussing hands.

Baffled, he stood beside the table while Theo and her grandmother chatted about hospital food, other relatives, and how much better the old woman was feeling. Theo kept darting in front of her grandmother to fetch things from cupboards and the ice chest until, with a hearty laugh, Lady Van Baum shooed Theo out of her way. The three of them settled in woven cane chairs around the table, with cups of fragrant coffee and a plateful of several kinds of baked treats.

"Surely you can afford a few bites even on your diet." Lady Van Baum beamed at Scarecrow.

Though he was curious how the various delectables would taste, he foresaw a lot of crumbs and no easy way to clean his tongue should anything stain it.

"I did mention the food allergies, right Gramma? Like really seriously allergic." Theo moved the plate away from Scarecrow.

He gave her a nod of thanks, but eyed the cookies wistfully. In Oz, spiced baked treats were sought after and gobbled down at any special occasion. It would be interesting to discover what all the fuss was about. Ah, well. He put his nose over his coffee cup to inhale the deceptively wonderful scent.

"So, your mother tells me you went on a trip to Kansas," Lady Van Baum said brightly, stirring cream into her coffee. "I want to hear all about it."

"Oh. Um."

"Did you sell any of your dolls?" Lady Van Baum prodded.

"Not this time," Theo said.

"We visited a very strange museum," Scarecrow offered.

"Oh?"

Theo shoved an entire cookie in her mouth. "We went to the Oz Museum," she mumbled around it.

Something knocked against a window over the kitchen sink. The golden, opaque curtains showed only a shadow wobbling outside, blocking the sunlight. Lady Van Baum turned to frown at it. "That reminds me, I need your brother to come by this weekend to trim all the bushes and the raspberry canes. They're growing feral again. And the trellis back there is about to come loose. I hear it knocking against the house there whenever the wind blows." She smiled at Scarecrow. "Coffee good for ya there, dear?"

He nodded, curling one hand around his cup.

"Tell me all about this museum. I'm sure Theo's told you it's my favorite movie." Lady Van Baum tutted and rose from her seat. "Forgot the pumpkin butter Theo brought over last time. So where's this museum?"

Theo grabbed Scarecrow's cup and drank half of it before he could protest. She set it back in front of him and sipped hers casually as the old lady returned to the table with a jar of golden-brown pumpkin butter. "It's in Wamego," Theo explained. "Tiny town out on the prairie."

"Oh, just like Dorothy's home, I betcha." Lady Van Baum poured more coffee into Scarecrow's cup, and fragrant bitterness wafted up at him.

"Yep, pretty flat out there. Didn't see any twisters though," Theo said.

"Well, I'm certainly glad for that!" Lady Van Baum laughed. "Do you remember the time you tried to go outside during a tornado warning at school? Danny and one of the teachers had to go looking for her," she explained to Scarecrow.

Theo turned pink again. She ducked her head so her hair fell over her face.

"That sounds dangerous," Scarecrow ventured. The trellis outside banged against the kitchen wall. It sounded closer to the corner. Sunlight glowed through the curtain of the window, no shadow blocking it.

"Oh, she was always a little firecracker," Lady Van Baum laughed, patting Theo's hand. "Always getting into something or other. Went running out to see if the twister would take her to Oz! Uff da. Only six years old, and wouldn't listen to anyone who told her no. Danny had to drag her back in kicking and wailing."

"I was not wailing! Danny exaggerates."

Scarecrow tried to smile, but now the knocking came from a different wall. A few feet away was a large glass door, covered only in gauzy sheer curtains. He'd noticed earlier it overlooked a wide deck of wooden planks, with a garden beyond. Though a few trees with scarlet and deep ruby leaves dotted the garden, none were close to the wooden deck.

"You've always loved faerytales and Oz as much as your old gramma. And now you've brought one of the Oz folks home."

"Gramma," Theo groaned, "stop."

The knocking ceased. Something scratched against the wooden deck. Scarecrow rose, staring at the glass door. "Theo..."

Her head was still down, her hands over her eyes. "Gramma, do you want to hear about the museum or would you rather keep reminding me what a stupid kid I was?"

"Oh now hon, you know I love you. Here, have another chocolate chip cookie. I made them with extra big chocolate chips."

"I beg your pardon, Lady Van Baum," Scarecrow interrupted. "You should get out of here. Now."

"What's that now, hon?" She frowned.

Theo's head jerked up. Seeing him staring at the glass door, she shoved back from the table. "What is it?"

The door exploded as a massive beast with striped fur and broad shoulders crashed through it. Its roar rattled everything in the room. Scarecrow leapt between it and Theo. It snarled, shaking shards of glass off its body, rising on its hindpaws. Blood began to stain its white-and-gray face where the glass cut it. Larger shards dropped off, clinking all over the floor. Scarecrow spread his arms wide, trying to shield Theo immediately behind him.

"The fuck is that?" she yelled.

He glanced back a moment, saw her snatch a butter knife from the table. Lady Van Baum sat frozen, jaw agape. "Khalidah," he said. "Cover your ears!" The words of the battle song sprang to mind. He opened his mouth to give them voice.

The khalidah roared, one massive paw slapping Scarecrow aside. He slammed into a wood hutch, bouncing to the floor. Not the first time he'd been thrown around by something much bigger, but this time a shock arced along his back and side. Stunned, it took him too many precious seconds to recover his wits and his footing. Pain was truly inconvenient.

Theo brandished the knife, shoving her grandmother up from her chair. "Run, Gramma!"

The khalidah's enormous head swung from side to side, nostrils flaring. When its eyes caught the light, Scarecrow realized the beast was blind. It pawed the air, snuffling, tongue lolling and licking. Its small, bearish ears were torn, the fur matted and stained brown. Something hurt it badly even before it smashed its face through the glass. He was suddenly reminded of the beast that nearly ran into Theo's carriage on their way to her home. How could a living thing breach the veil from Oz? Perhaps its innate tenacity helped it survive. If only he'd insisted on turning around that night. If this monster had been roaming the Outside World for days, no telling how many people it had already attacked.

This one was bigger than the pair which attacked their party on the way to see the Wizard, older, its thick body plump with powerful muscles, a crimp in its long, striped tail from an old injury. Its head nearly touched the ceiling. When it dropped to all fours again, its nose hit the chair where Theo had sat, startling it. Roaring again, it slung the chair out of its way. Scarecrow jumped aside and the chair smashed against the hutch. Fine ceramic plates crashed on the floor.

"Theo, get back, it's blind," he called. "Stay clear of it! Get your grandmother out of here."

Lady Van Baum stood a few steps away, eyes wide. Suddenly she went for the cupboards by the sink. "Oh no you don't, not my china set, you ugly thing!" She yanked open a drawer and produced a marble rolling pin. "My mother saved that entire set for me!"

Theo grabbed the rolling pin as well, wrestling with the old woman to keep her from charging the monster. "Gramma, run, dammit!"

"I didn't run from those muggers last year and I am not running from this...this *thing*!"

Scarecrow moved in front of the arguing women struggling for possession of the rolling pin. He waved his arms nearly in the khalidah's face. It didn't react. Definitely blind. If he could lure it away from Theo and her grandmother, perhaps he could sing loudly enough to penetrate its damaged ears. "Both of you, a kitchen implement won't crack that beast's skull! Would you please just—"

The heavy muzzle whuffed at him. With a lunge it grabbed him in its enormous jaws, turned, and leaped through the broken door.

Theo screamed *"No!"*

The beast bounded across Lady Van Baum's tidy garden, jaws clamped around Scarecrow's waist, huffing and snorting. It crashed through the woods. Branches snagged Scarecrow's hat off him, whacked his shoulders and legs. Gasping, he tried to protect his head with his arms, pain shooting through his entire midsection. Dimly he realized if he struggled, the sharp teeth holding him fast would rip him apart like candy-fluff at a fair. The khalidah surged forward, plowing aside smaller saplings, banging into larger trees, snarling each time but never slowing. It staggered down a wooded ravine at top speed, leaves scattering, sliding and slamming into trunks, but wouldn't let him go. Couldn't it tell he was straw and wouldn't make a good meal?

Scarecrow forced himself to think past the really quite startling, stabbing pain where the khalidah's teeth pierced his burlap and straw. By now they were far enough away, the khalidah running so fast, Theo and Lady Van Baum would be out of hearing range. Still ducking his head, both arms blocking the branches which continued to smack hard into him as the monster charged through the woods, he launched into the Battle Song of Red Mountain. He sucked as much air in as he could and sang loudly.

Unlike the Wheelers, the khalidah gave no sign it heard him. Its ears must've been too badly damaged. It burst from the trees, stumbling as it crossed a road, then regained speed as it charged into more forest. Scarecrow set his hands against its upper jaw and pushed, trying to draw his knees up on the other side for better leverage. Useless.

The trees cleared. The beast ran right for a broad river. No! Surely it would smell the water and veer off? Did khalidahs swim? He definitely couldn't. The stupid thing was running full speed, nothing between it and the water. If he became soaked he'd be even more helpless than he was now. Crows and blight, why weren't his brains sharp enough to—

"Sharp," he gasped, squeezed his eyes shut and concentrated with all his might. The instant he heard the pop of one of the magic brain pins through the top of his head, he yanked it out *(Owch!)* and jabbed it hard into the Khalidah's pink gums.

The monster roared, staggered, reared back. Scarecrow tumbled from its open jaws, straw scattering from the holes its teeth had torn. He scrambled away as the khalidah pawed at its mouth and shook its head. It turned, whuffing, trying to reorient on him by smell.

The water behind Scarecrow was dark, hard to tell how deep it went. As the khalidah dropped to all fours and started right for him, Scarecrow backed toward the river. Spotting stones and debris along the bank, he snatched up the biggest rock he could fit in his palm, took a terrifying few seconds to carefully aim as the monster approached, and threw. The stone bounced off the khalidah's head just below its eye.

With a roar of outrage, the khalidah charged. Scarecrow waited until the last possible second and threw himself to one side.

The beast clawed air, soaring over the bank and splashing into the river. In case it could swim, Scarecrow hastily clambered up the steep embankment. Its paws moved against the current, but the water seemed to have disoriented it. It turned south, struggling against the steady flow of the river. Scarecrow watched warily as the khalidah was pushed inexorably downstream, still fighting against the current, struggling to keep its head above water. If it kept swimming the wrong way, even its powerful legs would soon tire. Down it would go to the cold river bottom.

Scarecrow shivered. What a horrible fate, even for a vicious monster. He dreaded rivers and lakes for good reason. Waterlogged straw robbed him of all movement, gummed up his brains. Fire was terrifying, but a death by flame would take mere seconds. Death by water for him could take months.

He hurried away from the riverbank. No sign of the brain-pin. *Hope that one didn't contain any especially important memory.*

Retracing the path the khalidah had torn through the woods was easy enough, though his injuries sent jolts of unhappiness through his midsection with every step, forcing him to slow. He pressed one hand to his side where the largest rip shed straw. Blight and mold, Theo only just made him all this. Now his new burlap was torn, along with the lovely new tunic. At this rate he'd need a tailor following him around full-time, like the obsequious Munchkins trailing after Locasta to hold up the hem of her ridiculous fancy dresses.

Where the road bisected the woods, Theo came rushing toward him, his hat in one hand and relief in her eyes. Thank the sweet sunlight, at least the beast grabbed him instead of her. The thought of those fangs piercing her flesh—

He braced himself against a tree, ready for her attack hug this time. He wrapped his arms around her, inhaling her scent of flowers and dark spices, deeply relieved. She squeezed too tightly and he felt straw sifting out through the holes. Didn't matter. She was safe.

"Are you all right?" he murmured, just to be sure.

She choked on a laugh. "I'm not the one who just got used as a chew toy!" She examined him. "Oh no. Okay, you need more stitches."

"That would be nice." All his chest-straw was compacted. Theo immediately tried to help him fluff it into shape. He winced.

"Oh Goddess, you're hurt? Oh crap. Scarecrow, I'm so sorry, I shouldn't have woven that spell into you, I wasn't thinking, I—"

No, no. He wasn't going to stand for her berating herself again for this gift. Impulsively, he pulled her in close and pressed his lips to hers.

The heat of the sun cascaded from her body into his. She squeaked in surprise, making Scarecrow fear that he wasn't thinking right, his brains had been shaken around too much by the khalidah. This was taking liberties. Why, even Dorothy hugged him in sheer relief when they'd escaped some danger along the road of yellow bricks, Theo was far more expressive, he shouldn't assume she wanted—

Her tongue thrust into his mouth and he forgot how to think.

He was vaguely aware of popping sounds, caught up in the feel of her breasts pushing against his chest, the incredible heat contained in her body. He'd been wrong.

Death by fire was much slower than he'd thought.

It spread through him inch by inch and he was powerless to stop it. Didn't want to stop it. Her tongue tasted sweet, with undertones of coffee. Her dizzying scent filled his nose. She was soft and firm all over. His brains couldn't fix on any one thing, he was overwhelmed by her taste, her scent, her warmth. Sweet sunlight, what astonishing fire she contained! Like the Nome King's furnaces in a delightfully embraceable person. She moved her hips against him. Heat raced down his belly and suddenly that inconvenient organ was very much awake.

He broke the kiss, mortified, about to apologize. She stared into his eyes, panting lightly, then to his shock shoved herself fully against his entire body and caught his mouth with hers again.

More popping sounds. He shuddered all over and clung to her, drowning in fire. Wait, no, mixed metaphor, surely he could choose one or the other to describe this amazing feeling. She licked his lips, his entire head filled with her luscious spices and night-blooming flowers, and he gave up all hope. Kissing her, holding her, Theo's fire made him somehow more alive. This was all that mattered. All that could ever matter.

She broke away abruptly, leaving him stunned. Dimly he heard leaves crunching, the slide of something down the ravine.

"Gramma! What are you doing, you were supposed to stay in the house!" Theo yelled.

Lady Van Baum struggled down the ravine toward them, wobbling from tree to tree to brace herself in the uncertain footing of fallen leaves. She clutched a long, gleaming polearm of some sort, and didn't acknowledge Theo's admonishment.

"Shit," Theo muttered. Turning back to Scarecrow, she giggled. "You look like a porcupine."

That explained the popping sounds. Dazed, Scarecrow began patting the sharp brains back inside his head. Theo thrust his hat at him. "Put this back on. Cover up the straw if you can." As he obeyed, still dizzy, she strode over to her grandmother, who'd reached the bottom of the slope. "Gramma, seriously, you shouldn't have come out here! What if you'd slipped?"

Scarecrow attempted to regain some shred of dignity. He was used to having to refluff his straw, adjust his hat after some misadventure. Needing to readjust his trousers was new and uncomfortable. Fortunately Lady Van Baum didn't seem to notice, intercepted by her granddaughter and arguing over the sense of chasing after them.

"No ugly bear is going to make a mess of my kitchen and live to tell about it if I have anything to say! If your Grampa was alive he'd already be skinning it for a rug!"

"Your hip. Was. Broken," Theo scolded, pausing for emphasis between each word. "You shouldn't be wandering around without a walker, much less running through the woods!"

"You think I'd allow my granddaughter to go after a monster like that and sit home and do nothing?" Tears gleamed in Lady Van Baum's eyes.

Theo enfolded the old woman in a hug. "Oh, Gramma. I'm just worried about you."

"Back atcha, sweetie." Spotting Scarecrow, Lady Van Baum broke into a wide smile. "You're safe! Uff da, I thought that thing would kill you. Where is it?"

"In the river. Hopefully that's the last we'll see of it."

"Never seen a bear that size, they don't get big around here. Must've escaped from the zoo or something. I'll call animal control when we get back to the house," Lady Van Baum declared. She came closer to Scarecrow, sharp blue eyes raking him from hat to boots. "How bad did it hurt ya?"

"He's gonna need stitches," Theo said. "But let's get you home first, Gramma."

Lady Van Baum sighed. "I don't think I can climb all that way."

Theo guided her to a fallen log near the road. "Here, Gramma Hildy, just sit for a minute."

"Why don't you go get your car, and I'll stay here. Don't want to slow you down, with the hip and all." Lady Van Baum settling herself on the log seat. She patted the bark beside her. "Your young man can keep me company." She winked at Scarecrow.

Scarecrow exchanged an uncertain look with Theo. He shrugged and gingerly lowered himself to the log, holding his hand over the worst hole in his side.

"Oh yah, I think you'd better sit down there, hon. Theo can drive us up to the house and I'll get you some peroxide and bandages."

"Peroxide?"

"For your cuts. How bad are they? Oh, come on, let me see. I raised one son of my own and half the time my sister's boys as well, someone always getting into a scrape or falling out of a tree."

"I'm well enough." Scarecrow edged away from her reaching hands.

"You two play nice," Theo ordered, frowning. "Wait right here. If that—bear—comes back, you—"

"Got Horace's shotgun right here." Lady Van Baum thunked the butt of the odd polearm down next to her feet. She beamed at Theo. "I never was much of a hunter, but I'll sure as heck teach that bear a lesson if it tries to tangle with me again."

Theo bit her lip, hesitating.

"Go on, Theo, we'll be fine. Won't we, Scarecrow?"

"I will guard her," he promised Theo.

"Be back as fast as I can." Theo grabbed the nearest sturdy tree at the bottom of the ravine, used it to pull herself up as she took a long step, and continued hiking upward. He watched her, concerned. She seemed to be puffing and grunting a lot. A dull ache continued to annoy him, where the monster had torn his side. Human pain made much more sense suddenly. No doubt Theo's legs would be very sore after all this.

Maybe the autumn race song would be even more effective if he also rubbed her strong, soft thighs while singing it. Worth trying, at least. In the name of research.

"Good, that gives us a minute or three," Lady Van Baum said, settling herself more comfortably on the log.

He turned back to her. "Are you injured at all, Lady Van Baum? Did any of the glass cut you?"

"No, no. Looked like you took on most of it. You're such a brave young man. Cripes, my kitchen looks worse than the last time I let the grand-nieces make cookie dough." She smiled, and he returned it. She leaned closer, peering intently at his face. "I thought so."

"Beg pardon?"

"That isn't make-up, is it, young man? And you aren't wearing a costume."

Panic rose. "Of course it is, T-Theo made it for me," he stammered.

Lady Van Baum nodded. "I'll bet she did, but you're not an actor."

"What makes you think so?"

"I know what song you can sing for me. How about just a simple chorus, I'll sing it with you. 'Follow the Yellow Brick Road?'"

Blight and drought, though he racked his brains more swiftly than ever, not a single song came to mind about the road of yellow bricks. "Forgive me, dear Lady. I seem to have forgotten that one. How does it go again?"

Calmly, she lifted the brim of his hat. Scarecrow jammed it firmly back over his ears. "I beg your pardon!"

"Pins. Well, my goodness."

At a loss, Scarecrow stood, but more straw fell from his wounds when he moved. He covered the holes with spread fingers, mindful of Theo's warnings about appearing normal.

Lady Van Baum shook her head. "Sit down, you're going to keep losing your stuffing if you jump around like that." When he faltered, uncertain, she patted the log again. "Come on. Sit."

He did, curling one arm around his waist to keep the biggest holes covered. Theo's grandmother gave him a long, appraising stare. He shifted nervously. No idea what to say in this situation.

"I thought something strange was going on, when you came with Theo to the hospital," she said. "Your glove didn't feel right. Like something was off about your hands. Not wrong, exactly, just not real."

There was that word again. He really hated that word.

"I'm as real as you," he snapped. "With all possible respect, Lady Van Baum."

"I can see that." She studied him. For an instant he felt again as though he were trapped in Locasta's restraints, taken apart on a table in the dungeon for her to examine every helpless strand of his straw. Then Lady Van Baum smiled. "I'm so glad."

"I beg your pardon?"

"I'm so glad you're real. You are him, aren't you? The actual Scarecrow."

Pretense seemed useless at this point. He sagged. "Yes."

She chuckled, giggled, threw back her head and gave a delighted belly laugh which belied her small, frail body. "Wonderful! I wasn't kidding, you know. '*The Wizard of Oz*' really is my favorite movie."

He thought of the strange cavorting people who looked disconcertingly like and unlike himself and his friends, in the magic picture hanging in the museum. "Theo says I'm not that Scarecrow."

"Oh? Coulda fooled me, with that nose," Lady Van Baum laughed.

Why did everyone keep remarking on his nose? He should've left his face as it was. He touched it, spirits sinking.

Lady Van Baum took his hand in hers and patted it. "All crinkly. Heck, I should've suspected something like this would happen one day. All that wishing Theo did as a child, ya know. Her witchcraft or whatever it is she does now, spells, candles, I don't know. So how did she do it? Did she make you with a spell, or bring you here from Oz?"

Scarecrow sighed. Haltingly, he told her the barest sketch of why he'd wanted to come here, what had happened since Glinda's spell thrust him through the veil between worlds. When he reached the part about Dorothy's diary, words refused to come. "It was all for nothing. She didn't—she never felt the same."

"Oh," murmured Lady Van Baum. "Oh you poor thing."

Theo's carriage rumbled up. She waved from behind the wheel.

"It's all right," he said, feeling lighter upon seeing her sheaf of orange hair and lovely, worried eyes.

Lady Van Baum nodded. "I see that." She squeezed his arm. She'd been holding it while he talked. "And I saw how you put yourself in front of Theo. Don't you ever let anyone tell you you're not good enough, you hear me?"

"Thank you, my Lady," he replied, not taking his eyes off Theo. He hadn't mentioned the Wheelers at all, not wanting to upset this charming grandmother, but right now all he could think was how fortunate they all were. How horrible it would've been had Theo or her grandmother been seriously hurt. Or worse.

The most vicious creatures in Oz all seemed to turn up wherever he went. As if they were drawn straight to him. Anyone near him was likely to be attacked. He didn't think the khalidah grabbed him by accident. It surely smelled Theo and Lady Van Baum in the room, yet took him instead. It hadn't been after a meal.

It wanted *him*.

And he had fuzzy memories of the Wheelers saying something about taking him with them.

He hugged Theo the moment she stepped out of the carriage. Over his shoulder, Lady Van Baum chuckled, "Well, I'm glad you found my Theo. She's a wonder with a needle and thread. I'm sure she'll fix you up again in no time. And you're welcome to come sniff coffee and stare longingly at cookies in my kitchen any time you like. You just consider yourself family now, young man. And learn some more songs so you can sing them to me. You have a lovely voice." She patted his shoulder, then brushed past Theo, who was staring at her. "Dorothea Theodora, your car is a pig sty! How on earth can you stand riding around in this junk? Why don't you take it to the car wash over by the mall, the one where they'll vacuum the mats. I can give you some money for it."

"Gramma, no. Just get in the front seat, okay? Scarecrow can sit in the back."

Lady Van Baum wagged a finger at her granddaughter. "You take good care of this one, Theo. Take him right home after you drop me off and sew up those awful holes, he's losing straw left and right."

Theo's eyes widened. "What?"

"You heard me." Primly, the old lady opened the passenger door of the carriage and lowered herself into the seat, tucking her long weapon in the back.

Scarecrow murmured in Theo's ear, "I tried. She caught me off-guard asking about a song I've never heard of."

"Of course she did," Theo sighed. "So she knows?"

"Let's hurry along now, I eat dinner earlier than you young people, dear," called Lady Van Baum.

"She knows. I'm sorry."

"It's okay." Theo took his hand in hers, rubbing the fabric against her palm. Her warmth seeped into his fingers. "How bad are you hurt?"

"Nothing your expert needle can't fix." Just touching her hand, seeing her smile, made something twist in his stuffing. There was no more room for doubt. He was the monsters' target. Every second in his company, Theo was in danger. "I need to talk to Nick. We should try the Evstone again."

Theo's smile faltered. "Oh. Right. Yeah. And I should talk to Gwyn."

He nodded. "Theo, I—you mean a great deal to me. These creatures—I think they're stalking me. Tracking me somehow. Putting you at risk too."

"We'll figure it out," she said firmly, staring up into his eyes. Hers gleamed green in the sunlight. Fae eyes, witch eyes. Mysterious and beautiful.

He didn't get the chance to simply stand there, hand in hand, lost in those lovely moss-green pools. Lady Van Baum beeped the carriage horn, startling them both. "All right, you two. Save it for later." She beamed at them.

They saw Theo's grandmother safely home and helped clean up the broken glass and porcelain. Theo called someone to come fix the glass door, and failed to convince Lady Van Baum to stay at Theo's house tonight. She at least agreed to lock her bedroom door, and declared any robber would be a fool to go up against an old woman with jittery hands and a loaded shotgun.

Finally Scarecrow and Theo returned to her house. He stole glances at her as she drove, memorizing the adorable curve of her nose, the color of her eyelashes, the way her hair swept down and she kept having to brush it out of her face. Memorizing her. After tonight, he wouldn't see her again. Still two nights and days before the full moon rose, but how many more attacks would happen between now and then? How much more danger could he stand to expose her to?

None. None at all. His path was clear. He should get as far away from her as possible. Whether there was a way for him to return to Oz or not, risking her safety further was unthinkable.

He snuck looks at her lovely face, imagined the heat of her kisses on his lips, and tried to convince himself this was his only choice. He'd once told the mechanical man TikTok that Scarecrow's own brains were considered very fine, and his conscience quite active. If that were true, then there really was no argument to be made here.

No matter how much his straw heart insisted otherwise.

29

It was well after midnight, but carousing continued throughout the Emerald Palace. Nick added a fresh log to the fireplace in Scarecrow's library. Drunken revelers tried earlier to open the door, but he'd locked it. The heavy iron key now rested safely in one pocket of his waistcoat. As far as he was concerned, the door would stay shut and locked from now on.

Professor Wogglebug mumbled in his sleep, wrapped in quilts and furs on the sagging old sofa in front of the fireplace. Nick smuggled him from his quarters into the Palace, hidden in a wagon of provisions. Jellia Jamb snuck Nick and the Wogglebug from the guarded cellar storeroom to the back kitchen door, and he carried the unconscious Professor up to the second floor library. Though every wing of the Palace swarmed with nobles from all corners of the Empire, by dawn this morning most of them had passed out. Nick's heavy steps failed to wake the ones snoozing on the floor right outside the library, so full of wine and rich food were they. Jellia brought up willow bark tea, extra quilts, and a cold compress with ice.

All day, Nick tended the Wogglebug. Impossible to tell if he had a fever. The hole in his back was gone, though a depression remained in his carapace. His front remained unprotected. If they could seek out old Ku-Klip the metalsmith at some point, perhaps the craftsman could fashion a breastplate to cover the Wogglebug's exposed arm and leg joints. Nick sang the Prisoner's Lament again, but couldn't tell if it made any difference.

By now Glinda had surely noticed Nick wasn't at court all day, and Mombi must've discovered her captive missing. Nick wavered between wanting to sneak down to the throne room balcony to check on Ozma Tip, and fearing as soon as he stepped from the safety of the library, the guards would arrest him. As day wore into night and no one save a couple of rowdy courtiers knocked on the door, his anxiety grew. Was Glinda hunting for him? Had Mombi found a trace of oil, perhaps, in the crypt tunnels, and begun crafting a spell to harm him? Their continued inaction worried him.

Jellia promised to return with more provisions for the Professor sometime before dawn. Now he feared she'd be caught. She was only flesh and blood. The fae perfected a whole host of torture techniques against mortals. He shouldn't have involved her at all. Then again, guilt or innocence rarely made a difference to a witch bent on making an example of someone.

Nick paced, angry with himself. He shouldn't be locked safely away here while his Queen was trapped right in the middle of hundreds of faery nobles. The Lion, Tiger, and faithful TikTok were no real defense if things turned ugly. He should go check on her. The Wogglebug would be safe enough here.

A quiet sound came from the door. Nick slipped his axe from its holder and tiptoed over as quietly as he could. The latch jiggled. He raised his axe, watching the bolt. If one of Glinda's guards thought to catch him sleeping, they had a hard lesson coming.

"Nick? Are you in there?"

"Tip!" He threw back the bolt and opened the door. The young Queen crouched on the threshold, her delicate pointed nose poking out of an elaborate head-wrap. Her green eyes, though shadowed, were immediately recognizable. "Quick, inside!"

As he ushered her over the threshold, he suddenly thought of Mombi and her transformative illusions. No full-blooded fae could enter this room. But what if the witches sent some hapless mortal servant in disguise?

"Don't shut it yet," Lion growled, bounding on silent paws from the dark corridor. He shouldered past Nick.

"Just a second." Nick kept his axe raised. "Lion, what's the first thing I said to you?"

"What, ever?" Lion snorted. "You screamed like a girl, as I recall, when I jumped out of the woods at you. I think you were more frightened than I was."

Nick relaxed. "Just checking."

Tip unwrapped her scarves but kept her heavy robes on, heading straight to the fireplace. The Palace was chilly on a late fall evening. "It's us. Don't worry, Mombi's too busy to cook up any illusions right now." She startled when the Professor shifted a bit on the sofa. "Sweet sunlight, is that the Wogglebug?"

"Shhh." Nick bolted the door again. "He needs rest. Mombi had him—well, it wasn't good."

"What? What did she do?" Tip peered at the blanket-shrouded form. "Oh trolls' asses, he's missing an arm!"

"Two," Nick corrected, easing her away from the sofa.

Lion snarled. "That witch. When I get through with her—"

"I sympathize, but don't be ridiculous," Nick said. "Where's Tiger? What are you two doing here?"

"Looking for you, of course," said Lion.

Tip kept staring at the Wogglebug. "Will he grow them back?"

"I don't know. I've sung the magic healing song to him three times now. It sealed up the hole in his back, but I don't know if his internal injuries are any better."

"The hole in his back?" Tip's voice rose.

Wincing, Nick motioned for her to quiet down. "Mombi hung him on a meat hook in the tunnels below the University." As Tip and Lion snarled, he motioned for quiet again and continued, "That's not the worst of it though. The witches have an army down there. The Unseelies."

"That's it, you're staying in here," Lion growled, one enormous paw pushing Tip toward a chair.

She resisted. "Go get Tiger. We left him guarding a snoring lump of pillows in my chambers," she explained to Nick. "Tiger distracted the guard and we slipped out. At least all the time I spent with Mombi as a child taught me a few tricks. Guards think I'm locked in my bedroom."

"You're still quite young, Your Highness," came a faint voice from the sofa, "but I'm thankful you did learn something useful."

"Professor!" Tip clasped the spindly hand of the Wogglebug. "What did they do to you?"

He shook his head weakly. "Hideous things which I shall add to the roster of crimes the fae have committed against the citizens of Oz, if ever we escape this mess. However..." He trailed off, wracked by coughs. Nick helped him sit up and offered him a cup of water. The bug shivered, wrapping blankets closer around his exposed midsection. "Your Highness, I have ill news to report. The witches are planning an invasion with the Unseelie Court!"

"We know." Tip's brow furrowed. "Don't you remember the magic picture?"

"They sucked out his brain," Lion murmured, eyes wide. "Like that time Locasta took Scarecrow's brains out and put moths in to see what would happen."

"I have not lost my mind, you overgrown housecat," the Professor snapped. He wheezed, gulped water, and waved one arm at the fireplace. "Rock and fire! The oldest fae, the Elementals, are gathering below us for an assault, but not on your Empire, my dearest liege."

"They're planning to attack the Outside World," Nick chimed in.

"I was going to say that," the Wogglebug grumbled. "Is there still willow-bark tea? My skull is overheated and all this fur in the room isn't helping my allergies."

Nick set the kettle back on the hearth. It was a relief to hear the Professor's complaints. That at least meant he was fully conscious and not consumed with searing pain.

Lion stared at him. "The Outside World? Dorothy's world?"

"Nobody can get to the Outside World," Tip argued.

"Scarecrow did."

Tip glared at the Lion. "Yeah, fine, but that was a special deal. Nothing living can get through the veil. No flesh. Every basic spellbook says so. Didn't you ever hear how King Mo the Mage was ripped apart screaming in front of his entire court when he tried to go through the veil between worlds? Why do you think they call him Mo the Multitude? They say you can still see shards of him baked into the floor in the palace there."

Nick shuddered. Lion's ears flattened and his whiskers stood straight out. The Wogglebug only nodded.

"I'm glad to see someone here remembers their history lessons. The witches are making some sort of portal. I saw it being constructed, in the caverns below the city." He drew the blankets tighter. "That's what they needed infants' blood for. I fear a census will show quite a number of mothers are missing children in your Empire today, Your Highness."

"I overheard the Pink Lady talking to Mombi," Nick said quietly. "They're planning on leaving Oz. All of them. Leaving you behind to deal with whatever monsters they aren't taking with them to conquer the Outside World. Tomorrow night." He removed the steaming kettle from the fire and poured it over willow shavings in a stoneware mug. Even if all Nomedom was breaking loose, they still had an injured friend to heal. "We need to get out of here. You'll get sick again, and the Palace isn't safe."

Tip glared at him, arms crossed. "I'm fine. We're staying. Where's this portal exactly?"

Gently, Nick held her arms, bent to stare into her bright eyes. "Tip, right now the Good Witch doesn't seem to care what happens to you when they go. She and Mombi are preoccupied with their plans. If you try something, they will kill you." He squeezed her shoulders lightly. "Do you understand? As your Royal General, I am telling you, don't get in their way. Safer if we just head for the forest. Tonight. Soon as the fae all pass out."

She shrugged off his touch. "So you think we should just leave Jellia? And Jack and the Sawhorse? And what about the staff? Just leave them here to face an army of nasty lords and ladies and who knows what else?"

"We'll warn them," Nick suggested.

Lion snorted. "Half of 'em would tattle to the fae to save their own skins before we made it out the front gate."

Nick handed the tea mug to the Wogglebug, who gave him a grateful nod and sipped slowly. "There isn't anything we can do, Tip! I'm hoping the fae will be too busy with their grand adventure to bother with the staff or anyone else on their way out."

"So we just let 'em march into Dorothy's world and kill everyone in Kansas? That's your big plan?" Lion demanded.

"I don't have a plan!" Nick yelled. "I don't know what else to do. We're talking about the most powerful witches in Oz casting a spell way beyond anything you can do, Tip, and you know more about magic than any of us!" He struggled to lower his voice, feeling his metal heating all over. "I don't know of any way to stop them. All I can think of is to get you someplace safe. Far from here."

The Wogglebug pointed at him. "Friend Nick—"

"No! No more arguments. We need to get the Queen to safety." He was so heated he could feel a thrumming in his metal belly.

Lion and Tip stared at him. The Wogglebug coughed. "Nick, I believe your waistcoat is vibrating."

The Evstone! Jellia had sent it out to be recharged, given it back to him when she dropped off the willow bark. He'd forgotten about it, busy tending to the Wogglebug. He pulled it out. It jumped in his palm. A distant, familiar voice called, "Nick? Can you hear me? Nick Chopper?"

"Scarecrow!" Cupping the stone, he shed tears of joy upon seeing the face of his friend appear in the pink glow above the magical rock. Tip and Lion immediately crowded him. So everyone could see, Nick moved closer to the sofa and knelt. "Are you all right?"

"Nick!" Scarecrow's smile faded. "I'm afraid I'm all wrong, my friend. I have made an unhappy discovery. Terrible creatures from Oz keep turning up wherever I go. They tried to kill me, and hurt Theo."

"Theo?" Tip asked.

Scarecrow's face brightened. "Ozma Tip! I'm very glad to see you're with Nick. Good heavens, is that Lion as well? How fare you all?"

"I am also here," said the Wogglebug.

Scarecrow barely glanced at him. The two men never really accepted each other. Scarecrow was insecure about his brains, and the Wogglebug often bragged how Thoroughly Educated he was. "I see that. Are all of you safe?"

"We're in your library," Tip said. "The Pink Witch can't get in here. We need to get Tiger though. And then we need a plan. We need your brains."

"At your service," Scarecrow agreed at once. "What has the Good Witch done?"

Nick wanted to cry. Scarecrow was alive and he'd surely come up with a plan. Some way to ensure nothing awful happened to Tip. He brushed moisture from his eyes with his handkerchief. "Oh, goodness, what *hasn't* she done? The old fae are plotting horrible things. They've murdered babies, summoned the Unseelie Court as their army, tortured the Professor—"

"What?"

"I gave them nothing, but by now Mombi knows some of us are wise to their dreadful plans," the Wogglebug said. His voice was still weak, but he sat upright and clutched his mug of healing tea with dignity.

"Tell me everything," Scarecrow demanded.

Nick explained it all quickly. The rock trolls and fire-walkers amassing below the old temple, the secret tunnels, the portal painted with arcane symbols in fresh blood. "The Good Witch plans to invade at a temple in the Outside World. They're sending the Unseelies through their magic portal first to clear the way, and then I think the entire Seelie Court will march through. Every single fae for leagues around is here in the city right now. I'm betting all of them will follow the Pink Lady and Mombi." He shuddered. "Scarecrow, I don't know how to stop them."

The straw man frowned, rubbing his chin. "I don't know anything which could harm a rock troll. The furnaces of the Nome King, possibly, if you could force them into it. Less is known about the fire Elementals. Legend refers to them all as the Undying."

"Do you know any songs that might work?" Tip asked.

Scarecrow shook his head. "I'll give it some thought, but nothing comes to mind."

"We don't have time," Nick urged. "The full moon of Winter's Eve is tomorrow night."

"I still have two nights here," Scarecrow said. "So the worlds aren't aligned yet. Good. What else? Did they say where this Outside World temple is located?"

Nick tried to recall all Glinda had said. "Something about it being in a holy place. Creatures parading endlessly in a red room and instruments playing themselves? A temple fit for the return of faerykind to that world. Mombi mentioned something about it being an old site mortals built on top of, without knowing it—"

"Crows and blight," Scarecrow gasped, "I know where they're going! Right where the Pink Witch sent me, when I arrived here. Where Theo found me."

"Can your witch friend do anything? Perhaps the two of you could block the gateway on that side." Hope flickered in Nick's velvet heart.

"She's not that kind of witch. Her powers are more..." Scarecrow paused, looking over his shoulder a moment. He lowered his voice. "She saved my life, Nick. Wheelers tore me apart. She attacked them with a metal club, killed three of them without using any magic at all."

"I like her already," Tip muttered.

"We saw the Wheelers in the magic picture," Nick exclaimed. He strained to view Scarecrow's image in the Evstone more closely, but it wavered and fluttered. "Are you back together?"

"Yes. Theo made me a new body. A magic body." Scarecrow raised a hand, curling and uncurling his fingers as if they puzzled him. "She sewed spells into me. It feels very strange."

"Oh dear. Are you very sure she didn't make you—"

"She's not that kind of witch," Scarecrow said firmly, frowning. "I trust her. She's a good person, Nick. A rather wonderful person, actually. She's given me an astonishing gift. Her talents are unique, yet she doesn't understand how amazing she truly is." He gazed off into the distance a moment, then snapped back in focus. "Which is why whatever happens, I can't have her involved. The Wheelers cut her in our fight. She used some sort of healing potion and seems well enough now, but I can't. I can't risk her being hurt. Her magic isn't strong enough to stand against the Oz witches. I'll go myself."

Lion and Nick exchanged a look. Did Scarecrow have feelings for a witch? This was unexpected, to say the least.

"Do you remember anything else the witches said about this portal?"

"Oh! There's an anchor. They have one anchor in front of the portal on this side, that requires another in the Outside World. Mombi seemed very concerned the Good Witch didn't have the other one in place yet. Said if it's not at the right place at the right time, it could mess up their plans." If only Nick possessed Scarecrow's sharp brains, to remember every word exactly. He was pretty sure that was the gist of it, though. He turned to the Wogglebug. "Professor? Anything else you overheard?"

"It was rather difficult to concentrate, what with the constant agony and so on."

"I'm sorry. I wish I'd found you sooner," Nick apologized.

The Wogglebug sighed. "Friend Nicholas, I am in your debt. No apologies needed. Perhaps, in a twisted way, it's fortunate you only found me after Mombi was finished with me and could return her attention to her cabal."

"So how do we stop them, Scarecrow?" Tip asked. "You must have a plan. How do we stop them from sending an army into Kansas?"

A smile quirked the straw man's lips. A pang went through Nick's heart. Scarecrow had been adorable with his painted sack head, but this new one was far more expressive, and he'd clearly practiced looking more human.

"This isn't Kansas, Your Highness, but another country a great many miles from it. If this fae temple is where I think it is, where the whirlwind dumped me, it's nearer to me than that. I should be able to get there before the moon rises on Winter's Eve, find this anchor, and destroy it. This should prevent anything from crossing through. If so, however, it'll mean more trouble for all of you. I'd recommend flight." He tapped a finger to his lips, thinking. "You could put the Gump back together. Theoretically, the Powder of Life is still latent within its separate parts, and I know the head is still alive, so reassembling it might work for a hasty exit." He pointed toward the Wogglebug. "I see one of the sofas from it right there."

"Theoretically that could work," the Professor agreed. He'd accompanied them on their flight from the Palace, back when General Jinjur and her army of women staged a coup, believing Scarecrow and his friends were merely tools of the fae. Scarecrow directed the building of a flying machine out of whatever they could find in the palace, with the trophy head of a wild gump, and Tip brought the assembled creature to life with magic powder stolen from Mombi. If that magic still worked, and all they needed to do was find and reassemble its parts, they could fly anywhere.

"I need to know what the anchor looks like," Scarecrow said.

Nick shrugged. "Like an anchor. Made of straw and bound up in red ribbons, but otherwise exactly like what fishermen use to keep their boats in one spot in the rivers, only smaller."

"Hmm. It may take me some time to find it, in that strange temple. The whole place is full of oddities."

If he could find it, even Scarecrow should be able to destroy something so fragile. Prevent the portal from opening. But that would mean... "Scarecrow, can't you try to get through this portal first? You could ask your witch friend to destroy the anchor on that side as soon as you're through."

"No," Scarecrow snapped. "I won't put her in any more danger. I've hurt her enough just being in this world. I'll find the anchor and ensure it won't work. No more monsters will come through. I'm not sure how the Wheelers or the khalidah even made it over here."

"We saw the Pink Lady summoning the Wheelers. Maybe she has something set up in her Ruby Palace to force through a few creatures at a time," Tip mused. "Maybe the veil between worlds is thinner right now."

"Wait. You mentioned seeing those in the magic picture. How did you get hold of that?"

"We snuck into the forbidden library, through the fireplace," Lion spoke up. "Which was a terrible idea, just so you know. You're not always as bright as you think you are. You didn't mention that stupid Book of Records was in there."

"I didn't know," Scarecrow replied, eyes wide. "Oh dear. It wasn't there the last time I was actually in the room. The Good Witch must've installed it."

"What's done is done." The Wogglebug waved one hand dismissively. "Let us concentrate our efforts on stopping this invasion before it starts."

"He'll be trapped over there," Nick protested. "He'll die!"

"Nick," Scarecrow said gently.

"No, this isn't right!" Nick wrung his hands. "Scarecrow, if your witch friend can help, we need as much as we can get. I'll go down under the tunnels again and when the full moon rises, we'll pull you through somehow before the witches have a chance to use the portal, your friend can destroy the anchor on her side, and we'll all run like the flying monkeys are after us! We'll use the Gump, we'll get far away from here, all of us, and—"

"Nick, stop."

"You have to get home! Just jump through the instant it opens, and—"

"Nick, I'm not coming home. It won't work."

"But—"

Scarecrow sighed, shaking his head. "If an army of the Unseelies will be lined up and waiting to step through the moment the portal opens, I haven't a chance of surviving them. Nor have you. Asking Theo to come along for any of that..." His throat worked silently, as if swallowing a lump of straw. "No. I will go alone, find the anchor, and rip it apart if it's the last thing I do."

"But it will be," Nick said.

Scarecrow shrugged, smiled sadly.

"No," Ozma Tip announced loudly, startling them all. "Glinda and her horrible army aren't going to the Outside World, and I won't let them stay in Oz." Nick cringed at the mention of the witch's name, but Tip was determined. "We'll get you back, Scarecrow. If she can sling around dark magic then so can I. I need spells! The book I took from the forbidden library has a few tricks but not enough. Don't you know any songs? Battle songs powerful enough to rip apart the Unseelies, end them for good?" When Scarecrow shook his head, she stomped a foot. "Nome bollocks! I have to get back into the forbidden library, get more books. Or those old scrolls, there has to be something good in them or Glinda wouldn't hide them away!"

Lion growled. "No way. You're not going back in there. I'll do it."

"You don't need to." Scarecrow's image in the Evstone wavered. The stones were losing power. "I brought the song scrolls to my library years ago. Seemed safer, once I found out how powerful the songs could be." The image flickered out, then returned, fuzzy. "Sorry Nick. I'll recharge the stone and get to the temple, find the—" The stone went dark.

Nick cursed. Recharging his stone meant leaving the safety of the library. "No! No, he can't do this, he'll die, we cannot let this happen! Tip, please," he begged, turning to the young ruler. Her face was pale, knuckles white where she held her robes tightly around herself. The room felt colder than before.

"The scrolls. We have to find the scrolls. There has to be a way," Tip said.

"I'll help," Lion agreed.

Shelves from floor to high ceiling nearly covered every wall. Tucked among the dusty books were scrolls upon scrolls. And all of them, Nick realized, would be written in Old Ozian.

"Tip, will you be able to read them?"

"I can help," the Professor said. "Bring me the dictionary from the table over there."

They spread out, yanking scrolls from shelves, piling them on the sofa, the reading tables, the floor. Tip unrolled one and it began to crumble.

"Careful!" barked the Wogglebug. "These are ancient records, not a note passed around in class!"

Lion snorted. "Wish Scarecrow bothered organizing any of this mess."

"He did, but it only made sense to him," Nick groaned. "Tip, do you know how to recharge an Evstone?"

She shook her head. "Maybe there's a spell for it in all this mess somewhere."

Nick redoubled his efforts to fetch every single scroll in the hope some of them, *one* of them, would provide the spell to solve everything.

As minutes crept into hours, he could see Tip's eyes dulling, her breath becoming shallow. His heart sank. If the spell existed, if they could locate and translate it in time, if Glinda didn't send the guards to break down the door and drag them all out, then maybe they'd come out of this alive and well. Maybe there was some magic which could save Scarecrow from turning into a pile of clothes and straw at the full moon. What if he died before he could destroy the Outside World anchor? What if Glinda marched through and conquered the Outside World, ruled it the way the fae did Oz? If Glinda succeeded, Tip and he and the rest of them would be left here defenseless against the monsters of Oz, the dark things which kept out of the cities only from fear of the fae. Thousands of people would die in both worlds. And if somehow they prevented the witch from going through the portal, she'd turn her wrath on the young Queen for sure.

Either way, the straw man would be dead, and Nick didn't think much of their chances here.

He pulled another armful of scrolls from a high shelf. There had to be a solution. If the worst came to pass, if he could save only their young Queen, he'd go down swinging his axe gladly.

30

S carecrow tried twice more to contact Nick at Theo's house. Each time, the Evstone glowed, he called to Nick, and after a moment the stone faded. He was about to try a third time when Theo cursed loudly.

Fearing the worst, he shoved the stone into a pocket and ran to the kitchen, summoning the words to the battle song. "What happened?"

Theo cradled her left hand in her right. Blood seeped through her fingers. "Cut myself with this stupid dull knife trying to peel this god-damn rutabaga."

Scarecrow grabbed a towel from the counter and wrapped it around her hand, pressing tight to staunch the bleeding. "Oh dear. Why are you peeling a root? Is this for a spell?"

She coughed a laugh. "No, I was trying to make dinner."

Various vegetables clumped on the counter. He recognized carrots and cabbage along with other things less familiar. A large pan waited atop the magic heating cube, and a tall glass jar of oil and various dried herbs in small containers cluttered another counter nearby.

He checked the blood. Still going. Nudging her toward a stool, he remarked, "I didn't know you could cook."

"Not my strong suit. I usually just order out. But this stuff'll go bad if I don't eat it soon. My friend Cassie gave me the veggies. You'd like her. She's a greenwitch, does farming spells mostly." Theo sat, shoulders slumping. "I wanted to make something that would smell really good, so you could enjoy it a little too. I might even be able to get it to taste right."

"You're still tired," he judged, noting the paleness of her skin in contrast to the darker circles around her eyes. "Your sleep has been erratic all week, based on what I've observed with other meat people."

"Yeah, well, what else is new."

He continued to press her hand into the towel. The white fibers were turning red. He swallowed down fear. "How do you feel?"

Her eyes turned up to him, full of such weariness he wanted to sing her well, sing until he had no voice left if it made her better even for

420

an hour. "Just tired. Not hurt bad, don't worry. Fingers bleed more, you know."

Scarecrow slid onto a stool next to her, keeping pressure on the wound. "You seem to avoid sleep often. You were fighting someone in your nightmare, that night during our journey. What do you dream?"

She shook her head. "Just the usual bullshit everyone has. Being late for class and failing school. Trapped underwater unable to find the surface. Stuff about my—Normal nightmare crap, I guess."

"If you say so. I can't sleep, so I can't dream. It seems to me, though, not all dreaming is terrible. Don't artists use dreams for inspiration?"

"Not mine," Theo said. "My dreams always suck. Except for when you've sung me to sleep." She turned pink.

He checked the towel, satisfied to see the bleeding had stopped. "Those don't convey the same sucking sensation?"

She giggled. "Nope."

"I wish I could capture the Autumn Harvest song for you, so you could hear it every night." He imagined sitting with her head in his lap, singing her to restful sleep with pleasant dreams. Her warmth filling his body and a smile on her lips. Content he'd done something useful for her. Perhaps she'd allow him to do so tonight.

Once she was asleep, it would be easier for him to slip away.

What a disloyal, terrible thought. What choice did he have? A vicious corpse, Wheelers, the khalidah. He hadn't thought it possible for anything living to get through the veil, much less that dark magic and monsters would come after him, endanger anyone near him. Clearly they all targeted him. Which meant Glinda wasn't satisfied simply to cast him out of Oz, she wanted him destroyed. Why send him here at all, then? She could've burned him, shredded him, any number of horrible deaths while still in Oz.

"We could record you on my phone. That way I'd have..." Theo paused. "Something to remember you, after you go back."

No point in saying again he couldn't come up with a way home, saw no means to extend the spell keeping him alive on this side of the veil. If anything of his consciousness survived the end of his existence at the full moon, he would dearly love to remember her as well. Her kindness, her delicate touch each time she'd sewed him back up. She'd repaired him again as soon as they arrived at her home this evening, and her touch upon his burlap skin was almost more than he could quietly bear.

"I'd be happy to sing for you again, Theo."

The pain in her eyes made his chest hurt. He forced a smile. "First, however, you need food. I may recall some Ozian recipes, if you don't mind me trying them in your kitchen."

Her mouth fell open. "You can cook?"

"In theory, why not?" He surveyed the items arrayed on the countertops. Yes. Fairly sure he could make something edible from this. The ingredients weren't unlike Munchkin fare. He'd asked to read the recipe of the main dish after the last harvest festival he'd attended, curious what made so many of the guests praise the food and the cook. Though still unenlightened after reading it, it hadn't appeared difficult to make, and required no magic. It had to be easier than those dratted pan-cakes.

"In theory." Theo stared at him, expression unreadable.

At least she no longer seemed as though she were about to pull him into another embrace. He wouldn't be able to bear that again. Not after realizing she meant a great deal more to him than an ally. Not after realizing he put her in danger just by being here.

Yet he couldn't leave immediately. Tend to her needs first, that was best. The responsible thing to do. Once he was sure she was well and safe, he could depart with a clear conscience.

"In theory, yes."

She snorted. "Okay. Sure. Go for it. Try not to set off the smoke alarm again. And be careful with the oven, it's really hot." She wobbled as she stood.

Worried, he held her arms. "Are you sure you're all right?"

"I'm fine. Promise. I'll go put a bandage on this cut." She straightened her back, brushed her hair out of her eyes. "Then I'll try Gwyn again. She hasn't replied to my texts. I'll try and track her down online. Or maybe just see where the nearest faery mushroom ring might be. Someone has to've posted about it in one of the online witchy groups, if there's any around here."

He was going to tease her about an interpreter again, but the memory of her lips on his when last he spoke that word stopped him cold. How could pain fill his chest when he wasn't physically injured? He merely nodded, releasing her reluctantly. "Nick still isn't answering, but perhaps he's keeping away from all witches, including the stone-crafters who could recharge his Evstone. I can't fault that plan. I'll simply keep trying."

"What, while you're cooking? You think that's a good idea? I mean, um, you're very smart, but—"

"Do both at once? Why, what a marvelous idea. That would be more efficient. You're right. Thank you, Theo." How brilliant she was! He always concentrated on one thing at a time to give it the full force of his magic brains. He absolutely should be accomplishing as much as possible with so little time left.

She shook her head. "Okay. Um. I'll check on you in a few, see if you need any help."

"Thank you, but I believe this task is simple enough. May I use the pumpkin by your hearth, or is it consecrated for a spell?"

Theo leaned on the doorjamb. "It's just a pumpkin. Sure, you can use it." She pointed to knobs on the top of the magic cooking box. "Oven controls are there, be careful, that gets really hot."

"Thank you. And these ingredients? Are any of them dangerous?"

"Uh, no. Just regular herbs and spices."

"Good." He turned to the small tins of spices, examining each to see what it held. He opened one labeled *oregano* to sniff and decided it was more of a Gillikin sort of herb.

Suddenly the room felt colder, as if the sun had gone behind the clouds. He turned back to the doorway, but Theo had vanished. He heard her tread upon the squeaky wooden stairs. Why did her absence make him feel cold, dampen his spirits as thoroughly as a rain shower?

He picked up the kitchen knife and busied himself, carefully peeling the hard skin off the root she'd left on the cutting board. Much as he tried to focus on the recipe for the stuffed baked pumpkin, all he could think of was the warmth of her arms around him, and how absolutely unfair it was he couldn't simply spend his remaining time in this world wrapped up with her, exploring this whole kissing thing. Thoroughly.

Once the vegetables were chopped and the pumpkin hollowed out, spices rubbed into its orange flesh and the pan carefully placed into the strange metal box of an oven, he realized Theo hadn't stopped back in. "Theo?" he called softly, walking down the hall. He heard her voice in her crafting studio. Leaning in through the open doorway, he found her sitting with her back to him, her phone pressed to one ear.

"I didn't say that," she argued. "No, he is not, and would you just shut up and listen for a sec?"

He rapped on the doorframe, startling her. Theo swung around, lowering the phone.

"What? Everything okay?" Her body was tensed, her tone worried and urgent.

Scarecrow raised a hand. "Nothing is wrong. Just making sure you're feeling better."

"I'm good." She flashed him a smile, then grimaced, returning her attention to the magic phone. "No, everything is fine. Nothing is crashing through the window, no monsters, all good here. It's quiet."

Which served as a reminder he should contact Nick and then get as far away from Theo as he could before something else tried to hurt her.

"Gwyn, no. I'm asking for help, so peace, okay? For five minutes?" Theo pleaded.

This sounded like an emotional conversation. He should give her some privacy. Scarecrow walked back to the kitchen, taking the Evstone from his pocket. He cupped the stone in his hands and called, "Nick? Nick Chopper, can you hear me?" The stone glowed.

"Scarecrow! Are you all right?"

Relief flowed through him upon seeing his friend's face, followed by a heaviness as if someone were piling rocks atop him, compressing his straw. "Nick! I'm afraid I'm all wrong, my friend." He related his theory about the Ozian monsters targeting him.

He listened grimly to what his friends had been through in the past few days of Ozian time, gave them a few details of his own misadventures. Learning Glinda, Mombi, and the rest of the Seelie Court planned to force their way into this world on Winter's Eve was less of a shock than he would've expected. Nothing he'd put past them at this point. Realizing where their temple must be on this side of the veil surprised him, but upon reflection, it made sense that he would've emerged in some location already attuned to the fae. A weak spot in this world. Perhaps Glinda sent him there specifically to test whether the veil was thin enough for the witches' terrible portal to succeed. As he listened, argued, considered how dangerous it would be to bring Theo along on this last unpleasant adventure, his thoughts dragged as though someone poured molasses into his head. He could think of nothing to stop the Unseelies, no way to get home. A sick sinking dread filled his straw at the very idea of leaving this world. Leaving Theo.

Bringing her to the portal was out of the question. "No. I will go alone, find the anchor, and rip it apart if it's the last thing I do."

"But it will be," Nick pleaded, silver eyes shining with tears.

Scarecrow shrugged, smiled sadly. If his final act was to keep the fae out of Theo's life, he'd pronounce himself content. Assuming he still had the brains by then to pronounce anything.

He told them all the Old Ozian song-scrolls were in his library, dismayed that Tip's insistence on finding the hidden magical library had resulted in such torment for his friends. Though he didn't particularly like the Wogglebug, neither did he wish such horrors upon the Professor who was so devoted to their Queen. A song must exist which could hide his friends from the fae, or give them a means to escape the Unseelies.

The stone's glow faded, the faces of his friends melting disconcertingly in the image above it. "Sorry Nick. I'll recharge the stone and get to the temple, find the anchor, and keep those hags out of this world. Whatever it takes," he promised, but the stone was dark. Not sure if Nick heard him, but he knew Scarecrow well enough to predict what he'd do.

"Oh crap, did I miss the call?" Theo asked.

Scarecrow's head jerked up. "Oh! Yes. The stone's lost power again. I'll recharge it. What did Lady Gwyn say?" Better by far if Theo hadn't heard any of that.

Theo plopped onto a stool, leaning on the counter. She looked careworn and discouraged. "She doesn't know of any faery rings around here, or any spells to open a portal to Oz. And she still thinks you're dangerous, so we had some words."

He winced. "She has a point."

"No she does not. Don't you start." She glared at him, then sniffed the air. "She's out of town tonight, but she'll come over first thing tomorrow and help research spells to reach the land of the fae, which has to be Oz. What on earth did you put in that, it smells amazing!"

He blinked, caught off guard again by her mercurial turn of mood. "Well, you didn't seem to have any ground gillienuts, so I used this. It smells similar, so I'm hoping the taste will be comparable."

She bounded off the stool, pushing past him to open the oven for a better whiff. "Cinnamon and pepper?"

She stood almost touching him. Certainly the warmth he felt was the heat from the oven, not her. He remained perfectly still. Hard to say whether touching her or not touching her was causing him more distress. "Yes. I hope the meal turns out acceptable for you."

"It's great. I can't believe you actually cooked. Thank you."

He shrugged. "I hoped it would relieve you of some trouble, when you're clearly worn down, and no wonder, after all—"

He didn't get a chance to finish this thought. Her arms wrapped around him and she stood on tiptoes to brush her lips against his.

Oh sweet sunlight. So warm, so incredible! He embraced her, leaning in so she wouldn't have to strain to reach him. She tasted of spices and fire. Her softness pressed against him everywhere, she clung to him as if afraid to ever let go. Scarecrow welcomed her breath on his cheek, the thump of her heart against his chest. He explored her mouth with his tongue, felt her returning the attention. He shut away the part of his brains insisting there was no way he could feel pleasant to her, all scratchy dry burlap and crinkling straw, and gave himself over to the moment. To her mouth on his, her hands gripping his back, her living heat flickering into every inch of his body. To the kiss.

When she let go, taking a deep, shuddering breath, reality crashed back into his awareness. Her bare arms bore ugly red scars from the Wheelers. Her eyes were closed and she appeared about to drop. All this pain and weariness because she'd protected him, revived him.

She clung to his arms. Scarecrow eased her onto a kitchen stool, ignoring her murmured protests. "Sit down, please. I can't carry you if you collapse."

"Yeah, the floor in here wouldn't make a good bed. I have slept on it before, but we won't talk about those nights." Eyes opening, she stood again. He put a hand on her shoulder, but there was no stopping Theo when she had an idea. "I know what we should do. How long 'til dinner's ready?"

He glanced at the clock on the wall. The number markings were foreign to him, but after watching it awhile earlier he'd confirmed the minutes roughly corresponded to more familiar Ozian timekeeping. "Perhaps another twenty minutes? I may have lost track of the time while speaking with Nick."

"Oh! What did Nick say?"

Scarecrow swallowed to clear his throat of compacted straw. Her taste remained on his tongue. "Nothing terribly hopeful, I'm afraid." No point in telling her anything more troubling. He didn't want her involved in any of it.

"Oh." Glumly, she took his hands in hers, stroking his fingers. "Scarecrow, I'm sorry. Are your friends safe?"

"Good enough for now, yes." He nodded at the oven. "We should focus on making you well, my dear friend. Food, then rest." He gave her a strained smile. "If Lady Gwyn is coming back to berate me some more, I should prepare myself." She chewed her lower lip, which by now he knew was a precursor to her launching into some worrisome subject. To distract her, he asked, "You seemed as though you had some brilliant idea a moment ago. What was it?"

"Oh, yeah, well, not brilliant. Just something I thought maybe we could do together. Something I do every fall, I thought maybe you'd like too."

"A surprise?"

"Yes! I'll go fix it all up while you get dinner ready." She let go, hurrying to the doorway, but turned back. "Hey Scarecrow?"

"Yes?"

"We'll get you home. I promise."

She was so determined. He nodded, silent.

Her departure from the room felt again as though the sun had abandoned him. Shoving the feeling away, he hunted through the cupboards for plates and tableware. This was a harvest feast dish, and he ought to present it to her with every flourish found at Queen Ozma's table.

When at last the stuffed pumpkin was artfully arranged upon a platter, it was almost too heavy for him to carry. Dratted straw arms. He struggled into the dining room with it, but Theo wasn't there. "Theo?"

"In here," she called from the parlor.

He carried the fragrantly steaming dish a little farther. A fire crackled in the hearth of the parlor behind a screen of metal wires. Alarmed, he stopped and nearly dropped the platter. Theo leapt up from a pile of pillows on the floor to take it from his hands. "I got it, I got it, wow, that smells amazing!"

She set the food upon the low table before the fire. The sofa was pushed aside, the rug in front of the fireplace piled with fluffy blankets and pillows. A bottle of dark red wine and two goblets waited on the table. Theo smoothed down her gown. The gesture drew his attention from the dangerous flames. She'd changed into a long shift which clung to her curves. It was dark crimson with orange and yellow pumpkins painted all over it. Stockings of orange and yellow stripes covered her feet.

She crossed her arms, blushing. "I don't have any sexy nighties. So I went for comfy fall stuff."

"You look wonderful," he murmured.

Her blush deepened. "Thanks. What is this food? It smells amazing. Do we need plates or do we just dig in with fingers? What do people do in Oz?"

"Just a moment." He fetched the rest of the tableware from the kitchen. Arranging a formal place setting on the low table, he tried to ignore the frightening crackling of logs in the flames. He poured her a goblet of the wine and stood back. "There. Lady Theo, please accept the best Ozian food I know how to make. Normally a harvest feast has several courses, but I fear that's beyond my skills."

She sat on the blankets and poured a little wine into the second goblet. "Thank you, so much. Please, have a seat." She patted the pillows next to her.

Reluctantly he knelt, somewhat farther from the hearth than she'd indicated. When a knot of sap popped, he cringed.

Theo's eyes widened. "Oh Goddess, the fire. I'm so stupid. I'm sorry! I'll put it out." She scrambled toward the hearth.

"No, if the fire makes you more comfortable, please don't put it out for my sake."

She hesitated. "Are you sure? I wasn't thinking, Scarecrow. You seem much more human without your straw poking out. Almost forgot for a minute."

He relaxed a bit, noting the screen prevented any sparks from leaving the fireplace. Most of the hearths in Oz had no such protection. "It appears safe enough. And I want you to be comfortable."

She scooted closer to him and smiled, taking a sip of wine. "I always loved dinner and sleeping in front of the fire on a cold fall night. Sometimes when I was little, our parents used to let us do this on Halloween. We'd roast marshmallows and have hot mulled cider and fall asleep still in our costumes."

"Costumes?"

"Oh man, you don't even know about Halloween." Her eyes brightened, the flames' reflection turning them emerald. "It's my favorite holiday ever. It comes from the Celts, who—"

A bell rang in the hallway, followed by rapping at the front door.

"Perhaps Lady Gwyn arrived back tonight?"

Theo frowned. "No. Not expecting anyone. I bet it's Danny. I've been ignoring his texts."

Scarecrow sighed. "Perhaps you should reconcile with your brother. He doesn't seem a bad fellow. I could tell he worries about your safety."

She scowled, standing up. "I don't need anyone worrying about me. I can take care of myself, been doing it for years." She stomped into the hallway. Scarecrow trailed after, though he wasn't sure what assurances he could give an angry brother at this point that Theo was safe with him.

Especially as he knew this was false.

A young man stood squinting in the porch lamplight. He held out a large, flat pouch. A dark wagon was parked across the street by the cemetery. "Pepperoni with anchovies, right?"

"I didn't order a pizza, and I sure as hell wouldn't order that," Theo said. "Wrong house."

"Oh. This isn't—" The young man pulled a piece of paper from a pocket and peered at it closely. "Ten-o-five north Owaissa?"

"Next door. The ones with no Halloween decorations up. Figures they'd like anchovies."

"Oh." The young man stared at Scarecrow, but then Theo shut the door and relocked it.

"Seriously, kid, get GPS, or learn to read house numbers. Not hard." She sighed. "Who the hell eats anchovies? Eww. Come on, I want to try this fantastic food you made." Tugging Scarecrow by the hand, she returned to the parlor, sliding shut the door to the hall behind them. "If anyone else interrupts, I'm ignoring them."

Scarecrow resettled himself on the pile of blankets beside the table. He hoped the food would be to Theo's taste. Fairly sure he hadn't used any anchovies, whatever those were.

She removed the top from the steaming baked pumpkin stuffed with savory spiced vegetables and barley. The scent of it filled the room, pleasant and not unlike the spices Theo herself wore. He waited tensely until she tried a mouthful.

"Oh holy hell this is amazing. This is really the first meal you've ever cooked?" She stared at him as though he'd performed astonishing magic.

Pleased, he nodded. "Do you approve, then?"

"Do I approve. Fuck yes, this is the best fall stew I've ever tasted." She chewed, swallowed, stuffed another hearty forkful into her mouth. "Did you seriously make this from memory? On your first try?"

"I did need to substitute a few ingredients, so I judged them by scent. It's close to the harvest stuffed pumpkin I recall."

"Taste it," Theo urged, offering him a few veggies on her fork.

"I'm not sure that's—"

"If you don't like it, I'll help you clean your tongue off." She giggled.

Hesitantly he touched the food with the tip of his tongue. Flavors crowded his brain, unidentifiable, strange, interesting.

Theo shoved the mouthful between her own lips. "Try it with the wine."

For a moment he was reminded of the drunken fae women pouring dandelion wine over his head, laughing at his protests, on a vastly different Winter's Eve. Theo simply waited, watching him, a happy smile brightening her face. He grasped the fragile wine goblet carefully and brought it to his lips. A small taste did, in fact, complement the food. He nodded. "Not bad."

She beamed, and he smiled back. If only he had time to explore all of this with her. New smells, tastes, experiences. "You were saying something about Halloween?"

"Oh, right." He listened for the next half-hour while Theo ate and drank heartily and told him about a yearly festival held here, wherein children mimicked the fae by dressing in fanciful disguises, going house to house demanding sweets. It all sounded rather too like the games and parties the Seelie Court held to celebrate the end of autumn and start of winter every year. He'd never fared well at those parties. How odd that scarecrows and witches were considered traditional costumes here.

"Of course, for witches, it's a more serious time of year. Samhain is the night when we honor the dead. I've done that a couple times, but honestly I prefer Halloween stuff. It's more fun."

"Witches here honor the dead?"

"Yeah. It's what Samhain was originally about, at least as far as Celtic historians can tell. A time when the dead could visit their loved ones here, and when the boundary between this world and the faerie lands was thin." She nodded fiercely. "And we're gonna get you home then. Just need to find the right place to do it. Maybe the old mounds at High Cliff could still work, even if the fae didn't make them."

He knew exactly where the portal was going to be, after speaking to Nick. No. Best if Theo didn't hear of it. If things went very wrong, as they well might, he didn't want her anywhere near the place.

"Are there songs about Winter's Eve?" she asked.

"There are. Would you like to hear one?"

"What does it do?"

He chuckled. "Nothing magical. The one I recall best is simply a folk song celebrating the turning season."

Theo yawned, pulling a smaller blanket from the pile to drape over her shoulders. "Would you sing it for me?"

"Certainly."

She touched his arm. "Could I, maybe, just sit closer to you? You're really warm. Would that be okay?"

She'd read the diary, at least in part. She knew what Dorothy had done. And this lovely, sweet witch was asking his permission to be close to him. Not demanding—asking. Something in his chest warmed, suffusing him with a bittersweet happiness.

"Of course." He shifted around so he was facing the fireplace, far enough from it to feel relatively safe. Theo yawned again, trying to hide it behind a hand. He reached for a pillow. "If this would be more comfortable?"

She grinned. "Nah. You're already a pillow." She snuggled against him, her body curled against his legs. "This is nice," she whispered. The fire crackled gently. Heady spices filled the room and his nose. Her warmth seeped into his straw, already heated by the reflected flames. What he wouldn't give to stay just like this forever.

"Oh! Wait." She stumbled up and out of the room, chilly air sweeping in and making the fire dance. Dismayed, he was about to go after her when she returned, tapping at her phone. "Almost forgot. I wanted to record you, if that's still all right."

"Record me?"

With a grin, she tapped the phone again and his own voice leapt out: *"Record me?"*

"Astonishing." He peered at the glass. All he saw was a line and a red button at its end, with some blocky arcane symbols showing underneath. Presumably this was some magical language Theo learned as part of her witchery.

"Not as good as the real thing." Theo settled back on the blankets, her voice soft. "But at least this way, after you go home, I'll still be able to hear your voice." She blushed. "I really like your accent."

"At court they make fun of me. The Munchkin country accent isn't considered cultured."

"Fuck 'em." She snuggled into the blankets, resting her head on his leg. She didn't seem bothered by the crinkling of his straw, her cheek against his trousers. She tapped the phone and set it on the table. "Ready."

Nervously he cleared his throat, casting his memory in search of the right key.

"As the leaves turn to gold and the fields all to frost,
Do you hear the wind whistling down from Trotter's Peak?
Gather ye grain 'fore the green life is lost,
Give thanks to the guardians for life small and meek.

"Oh come Winter's Even, the music is reelin',
On and on, on and on, into the night!
On and on, on and on, all of us singing,
All of us dancing, bring up the lights!
Come Winter's Even, we'll go on a-reelin'
On and on, on and on, into the night!

"See the bright apples a-fillin' the table,
Feel the bright fire a-keepin' us warm.
Raise your glass high and give thanks if you're able,
Safe in the tavern we'll come to no harm.

"Oh come Winter's Even, the music is reelin',
On and on, on and on, into the night!
On and on, on and on, all of us singing,
All of us dancing, bring up the lights!
Come Winter's Even, we'll go on a-reelin'
On and on, on and on, into the night!"

Theo pressed against him, all soft curves and heated flesh. Her leg slid over his, and warmth shot up to his midsection. Doing his best to ignore the growing tension in a certain spot, he continued singing.

"Now we all toast to the gods who watch over
Valleys and villages, making all right.
Bless the sweet sunshine that soon will return here
Bringing us everything good in its light."

He repeated the chorus, and Theo stirred gently against him, her arm wrapping around his thigh. Her breath came evenly, steadily, falling asleep. He lowered his voice for the last verse.

"As the leaves turn to gold and the fields all to frost,
Do you hear the wind whistling cold out in the streets?
Hold to me, lassie, we'll give thanks together
First at the table and then in the sheets!

"Oh come Winter's Even, the music is reelin',
On and on, on and on, into the night!
On and on, on and on, all of us singing,
All of us dancing, bring up the lights!
Come Winter's Even, we'll go on a-reelin'
On and on, on and on, into the night!"

Quietly, he sang the chorus once more, a bit embarrassed. It occurred to him now this was a rather lusty song, but then again, the Munchkins were a lusty people. How they managed to keep their spirits up under the yoke of the fae was beyond him. Then again, few of them suffered direct contact with any of the ruling class. As long as tribute continued to the Seelie Court, they permitted the common folk to largely do as they pleased. Until they had a whim to go torment a mortal peasant. Perhaps being mostly ignored by the fae was reason enough to celebrate.

Theo mumbled indistinctly, snuggling more tightly against him. Her face was innocent, untroubled. He stroked one hand over her head. "Theo?"

"Mmn?"

"May I sing you to sleep? You need a good rest."

"Mmm hmm." She shifted against his leg, nuzzled her cheek on his tunic.

Sunlight and golden fields, if she kept doing that he wouldn't be able to move at all soon. He needed to sit stiffly as it was just to avoid her head brushing against the organ between his legs, which right now seemed intent on pushing its way through his trousers. He took a moment to compose himself, took a deep breath, and sang the autumn race song as quietly as he could. His fingers played with her hair, tracing lines through it. She was warm and wonderful and falling asleep on him.

At the end of the song, her breast rose and fell in a slow, deep rhythm. Good. He sat there in growing anxiety. Every minute he lingered was a threat to her safety. Even with boards on the downstairs windows and a fire burning in the hearth, he could imagine flying monkeys breaking in upstairs. Giant spiders enclosing the porch in a web. He shuddered. Theo sighed again, but didn't waken.

He stroked her hair once more. She was fast asleep. Carefully, moving as quickly as he dared, he eased pillows under her head, into her arms, sliding away from her. He should make all haste to the place where animals paraded in a red room, the strange temple Theo called the House on the Rock.

He found the road atlas in her studio, among the things they'd brought inside from her carriage this afternoon. Dorothy's diary sat on a table. He stared at it a moment, then looked back through the partly open door across the hall. Such a stark contrast, now he knew what Dorothy really thought.

Knowing he'd never have Theo's kiss again hurt. Quite a bit.

Blast and blight, he'd promised not to leave without saying goodbye.

A hasty hunt through her craft materials produced a pen and a bound notebook of thin white paper. He stained his fingers with ink while dipping the pen. Crows and blight, would he always be clumsy? He snorted. *I suppose I will for another two days, at least.* He scratched out a note, for once not taking minutes to consider every single word. There was no time. The more distance he put between himself and Theo right now, the safer she'd be.

His eyes fell upon her keyring as he wrote, and a wild idea sprang into his brains. Surely he was intelligent enough to operate her carriage. He'd watched her for days. How difficult could it be?

He separated the correct key from the pile of them, amended his goodbye note, and tiptoed into the parlor. Theo slept peacefully, hugging a large pillow. His chest constricted around a straw heart. In a better world, that should be him in her embrace.

He set the note on the table, propped against the wine glasses.

No. He couldn't simply leave like this.

Scarecrow knelt next to the sleeping witch, the only good witch he'd ever known, and bent to place a kiss upon her forehead. "Goodbye, Theo," he whispered. "Thank you for everything. May your life be long and free from pain." He hesitated. The words fluttered in his head like yearning moths, demanding to be spoken. "Goodbye, my dear friend. I love you."

Quietly, he closed the parlor door behind him. Unlocked the front entry and let himself out. Walked from the porch to Theo's carriage and opened the driver's door. Every step felt as though his straw were soaking wet, weighing him down.

Footsteps sounded behind him. Scarecrow turned and a person hooded in black slammed him against the carriage. He struggled. "Unhand me!"

Two others rushed forward from the darkness, garbed all in black, their faces hidden. The one holding him pinned his arms. He lashed out with both feet only to have someone else catch them, wrapping twine swiftly around his ankles. Theo, no, he'd left the door unlocked, they would go right in and—no!

He managed the first two words of the Battle Song of Redtop Mountain before one of them slapped something sticky and tough across his lips.

"Shut up! Grab its feet, I got the head."

Panicking, Scarecrow twisted, fought with all his strength, but straw was no match for several meat people. They tied his hands behind his back, hefted him bodily across the street and tossed him in the back of the same dark wagon he'd noticed earlier. As he strained to pull free of his bonds, one of the people pushed their hood back and studied him coldly.

"So you thought you could horn in on my girl and I wouldn't notice, hm? Nice try." The man's voice was theatrically deep. He stroked a dark goatee on his chin as the others piled into the wagon and shut a sliding metal door. Unlike Theo's friend Arturo, this man's eyes were gray and cold.

"You didn't say it was a person," one of the others said, eyeballing Scarecrow. "Mark, man, this is kidnapping. I thought we were just gonna scare your ex and grab whatever magic thing she—"

"Not my ex," the goateed man interrupted. "She's just acting out. Wanting attention."

Was this the same Mark who'd assaulted Theo? Scarecrow had never wished harm so badly on a living creature as he did right now.

"And this isn't a person. Take a closer look," Mark commanded.

Another face, younger and rounder, thrust into Scarecrow's. His protest was muffled by the sticky plaster over his mouth. The round-faced young man stared closely at him, shining a light in Scarecrow's eyes. Wincing, he tried to turn his head, but the one called Mark clamped a hand painfully on Scarecrow's ear.

"This is the anchor. Straw, just as the faery guide foretold."

"Holy shit," exclaimed another person. The delivery boy who'd asked about anchovies. "His eyes are painted. How can they move if they're painted on?"

"Do you believe me now?" Mark demanded.

Round-face nodded. "Yeah. Hell yeah. I mean, ya know, I already did, but this is wild."

These men had waited across from Theo's home for hours. The confused delivery boy earlier had been no accident.

"We have the anchor," Mark announced loudly, his voice ringing inside the metal wagon's walls. "Just as the faery guide foretold. Drive, Nightcat. I want us at the temple with plenty of time to spare. Once we're there, we'll consult the guide again."

As he felt the wagon lurch into motion, a sick dread filled Scarecrow. Two anchors. Nick even told him the one in Oz was made of straw. How stupid he was not to catch on right away. Anchors to create a bond be-tween the witches' portal in Oz and one they planned to open in Theo's world. He'd allowed Glinda to open his body, to attach the ridiculous or-gan in his straw because he'd been fool enough to think Dorothy might want him if he were more like a living man. Clear enough where the witches procured the straw for the anchor on their side.

All too horribly clear now what the anchor was here.

These people must be in service to Glinda. They would do with him whatever she ordered. And as the wagon bumped over the roads, one thought kept him from utter despair: *At least they hadn't gone after Theo. At least she slept peacefully, free of harm. For now.*

His heart sank. Until the fae came through the portal. Then all storms would break loose.

31

S lowly the sunlight creeping around the boards in the windows filtered into Theo's awareness. She sighed, snuggling closer to Scarecrow. But he felt wrong. Too squishy, no crinkling.

Opening her eyes was a mistake. Far better if she'd stayed in the lovely dream. She'd been skipping, actually skipping, along the road of yellow
brick, arm in arm with Scarecrow, laughing, the sun shining on swirling
autumn leaves and fat pumpkins lining the road.

Instead, she found her arms and legs wrapped around pillows, the fire
long extinguished and cold, and a note propped on the table.

"No," she groaned. "Please tell me you didn't do this."

His handwriting was a little shaky, in an elaborate script which took
her way too long to decipher. Her guts churned.

"My dearest Theo,

*"You have come to mean far more to me than I thought I could
ever feel. It seems I have a heart after all, and it's ripping apart
because of what I must do. Every minute you spend with me
puts you in terrible danger, so I must go. Nick told me where the
witches plan to force their way into your world and I will not allow that. I'll do whatever I can to stop them, to close their door to
this world before it even opens. To keep you safe.*

*"Apologies, my friend, but I must borrow your carriage, and I
fear I won't be able to return it to you. You should be able to retrieve it from the place you found me in two days' time.*

*"Please do not come looking any sooner, and if your witchy senses
perceive anything out of place on Winter's Eve, run. Run for the
most remote countryside and hide. Nick and Ozma and I will do
what we can to keep Glinda and her hideous army out of your
world, but should we fail, the fae will certainly kill any witch-*

es here who won't swear allegiance to them. Please warn Lady Gwyn and your other friends as well.

"Whatever happens, I won't be back. I'm so very sorry. I hope you will think fondly of me, and always know me to have been,

Your devoted,

Scarecrow."

"Son of a fucking whore!" Theo yelled. She ran to the front door, yanked it open, and stared at her car still sitting in the driveway. The driver's door was half-open.

The wind whisked all warmth from her body. Barefoot, in nothing but her nightgown, she stumbled to the car. Bits of straw were lodged under the tire. The key lay on the pavement. Frantic, she checked the grass, the dirt, found no Wheeler tracks or paw prints. No trace of him in the street.

She pounded on the front door of her neighbors, the Singers. No answer. Hugging herself against the cold, she ran to the Reeves' on the other side of her house and knocked. Mrs. Reeves peered suspiciously out of a front window.

"Please! It's an emergency!" Theo shouted.

The door unlocked and reluctantly Mrs. Reeves peered out. "What's wrong?"

"Last night, did you hear anything outside? In my yard? See anything, anyone?"

"Just those loud friends of yours slamming their doors and driving off like a buncha crazy people," Mrs. Reeves snapped. "You really ought to think of your neighbors before you invite guests over at midnight. And put some clothes on, for heaven's sake."

"I didn't have any friends over," Theo protested. "Only Scarecrow."

Mrs. Reeves' nose poked high in the air. "Oh, I heard him too. Yelling. Not much like the one in the movie, if he's living in sin with you,

I hafta say. Buncha young hooligans fighting in the street! It was a nice quiet neighborhood before you moved in."

Theo choked, suddenly overheated despite the chilly day. Her fists clenched as she struggled not to tell this self-righteous bitch which orifices she could stuff her opinions up. "Fighting. Who was fighting?"

"Well, I didn't see 'em, just heard 'em." Mrs. Reeves wagged a finger at Theo. "Young lady, you better get yourself straight with the Lord, and stop hanging around with these heathen people. If you catch pneumonia from being out here in only your nightie and end up meeting your maker tomorrow, I imagine he'll have some terrible news for you about where you're going."

"Fuck off," Theo snarled. "She'll have some shit to say to you about judging others."

"Oh!" Mrs. Reeves slammed the door.

Theo hurried back inside her house. Fighting in the street? Scarecrow yelling, doors slamming. Whatever happened, she'd slept through it all. Completely oblivious while someone took him and drove off. She grabbed her phone. Who to call first? The cops? Gwyn? She barely had any battery charge left. Racing to the studio, she plugged the phone in. The audio recording app showed an error: DEVICE STORAGE FULL. It kept going until it ran out of room. The file was huge. What the hell good was having a recording of his voice if something horrible happened to him? Panicked, she hit Gwyn's number.

Voicemail. "Gwyn, it's me, I need your help, someone took Scarecrow and they're probably going to kill him and I don't know where to start looking, please come over soon as you get this. Bring your pendulum or a dowsing rod or something, I don't know, I have to find him, it's been hours, he could already—" She choked on a sob. "Could already be dead. Please." She stood there shaking, lost, hearing the message tone beep again.

No point in calling the cops. They wouldn't believe any of it, would no doubt tell her that her boyfriend would probably turn up in a day or two. She could just imagine their tired faces while she pleaded with them. Her brother would say much the same, and likely scold her for letting a man she barely knew into her house, into the RV. Yeah, he'd be more upset about the RV.

Cassie. Her greenwitch friend dealt with crops and water and stuff, maybe she knew a way to track down a man made of straw. Theo called her. The phone rang and rang. That woman really needed to get a goddamn cell phone.

She texted Gwyn, unable to type right, eyes blurry. Tears streamed down her face. "Fuck, fuck, *fuck!*" she screamed, slamming the phone down on the desk. Her Mac woke up. The open browser still showed the route of the Kansas trip. Crying, Theo sank onto a work stool. *Scarecrow, I'm so sorry, I shouldn't have let you sing to me.* As restlessly as she usually slept, any noise in the street would've woken her for sure. If she hadn't agreed to hear his lovely voice singing her to sleep, happily snuggled against him. "No," she moaned, burying her face in her hands. *Fuck, I'm so stupid. Should never have relaxed for a minute, and now he's probably—* Unable to finish the thought, she broke down bawling onto her desk, stomach clenched, fighting the urge to throw up.

She was still slumped there, eyes wet and puffy, nose completely clogged, when the doorbell rang. She forced herself to get up and answer the door. She half expected Mrs. Reeves to have called the cops on her.

Gwyn filled the doorway. She swept Theo into a bear hug.

Fresh tears filled Theo's eyes. She clung there, sobbing.

Somehow she ended up back in the living room. Arturo and Adam came over as well, and one of them started a new fire in the hearth while the other made tea for everyone. They murmured comfort, hugged her, made sure she was wrapped in blankets and fetched a box of tissues from the bathroom. When at last Theo quieted, Gwyn was right there beside her.

"All right, girl. Think you can talk now?" Gwyn asked.

Theo sniffled, nodded, drank the soothing herbal tea. "They took him. I slept through the whole fucking thing. I don't know who. But things have been attacking us since—"

"What kinda things?" Arturo asked.

She shook her head helplessly. "Things. Monsters from Oz keep trying to kill him." She glared at Gwyn. "I'm not the one in danger, he is."

"Wait. Monsters from Oz?" Arturo gave an uncertain laugh.

Theo whirled on him. "Yes. From actual Oz. As in over the Yellow Brick Road, okay? Ask Gwyn, she knows."

The boys turned to Gwyn. She sighed. "Hon, not to say I told you so, but he really didn't belong in this world."

"He belonged. *Belongs.* He belongs here. And I don't want to hear another goddamn word about it."

Adam picked the note up from the table. "Can I read this?"

Theo nodded.

Adam frowned at it. "Wow. Wish my penmanship was this pretty." He read the note aloud. When he reached the end, Adam added, "Oh, man. I'm so sorry, Theo."

Theo sat there, nose over her teacup, thinking of Scarecrow at her kitchen counter sniffing coffee for the first time. How betrayed he looked when it didn't taste as good as it smelled to him. His smile when he declared the brew helped him think.

Gwyn frowned. "So he left. Any idea what time?"

"I don't know. I fell asleep. The bitch next door said she heard yelling outside at midnight. And a car door slamming."

Arturo nodded thoughtfully. "We saw your car in the driveway, so clearly he didn't get far before whoever it was pounced on him." He shook his head. "Still trying to wrap my head around the idea that a faery land in a kids' book is a real place."

"I see someone wasn't paying attention the day we talked about faery rings and avoiding anything in the forest that looks too tempting," Gwyn remarked.

"I thought you were speaking metaphorically."

"Guys, please," Adam muttered.

"Help me find him. Please. Someone grabbed him to stop him from going to the House on the Rock. That's where I found him. Where the portal will be, tomorrow night. He has until moonrise tomorrow before his magic runs out and he dies. If they haven't killed him already." Theo grasped Gwyn's arm. "You have to know some way we can track him. Straw! I have some of his straw. Can you use your pendulum or something?"

"He's really stuffed with straw, not just a costume?" Arturo asked. Adam shushed him.

"If all of this is true," Gwyn said, "then—"

"Of course it's true!" Theo shouted. Tea spilled over her blankets. Angrily she slammed the mug onto the coffee table.

Gwyn sighed. "Theo. He is a fae being. From some other world, and none of the stories about the faery lands end well for mortals. He does seem to care for you, but you can never trust the faeries. How do you know anything he told you is true?"

Theo shot to her feet, furious. "Because he's the Scarecrow of Oz and he's not fae at all! He hates the fae! They run Oz, they're evil as shit, they *tortured* him for fucks' sake! Glinda sent monsters to kill him and they nearly did, if I hadn't beat the hell out of them with a baseball bat they would've completely ripped him to pieces!" She sucked in a breath to yell louder. "I had to sew him a new body and put his brains back in his head after what they did to him so do not *ever* tell me he's one of those bastards, because you are absofuckinglutely *wrong!*"

Everyone stared at her.

Adam stepped forward and hugged her. Theo heaved for breath, hugging back, ashamed of her tears. Pissed off anyone would make her feel ashamed about anything.

"Okay," Adam soothed her, rubbing her shoulders. "It's okay, girlfriend. Breathe. We'll help."

Arturo nodded. "If the noise your neighbor heard was someone abducting your boyfriend, then that means someone was waiting outside your house, which is frankly creepy. You didn't see anyone outside last night?"

Theo sank onto the sofa. "No. Well, some idiot pizza guy knocked on the door while we were having dinner. Wrong house." She grimaced. "I should've asked the prissy old bat next door if she ordered a pizza. With anchovies. Who the hell eats that shit?" Suddenly recalling the van parked across the street, a chill swept through her veins. The van. The pizza guy. Her stingy, judgey neighbors had never ordered pizza, not in the five years Theo had lived here. "A van. There was a van parked out front. All black. Fuck!" She rubbed her eyes harshly. "I wish I'd heard anything.

I was stupid, I asked Scarecrow to sing me to sleep so I could record him, shoulda stayed up instead."

"Wait," Arturo asked, "you recorded it?"

Theo nodded. "Yeah. He can sing magic. That's how he put me to sleep. Long story."

"So he knows more spells than the protection song," Gwyn mused. "I'd like to hear them."

"Where's your phone?" Arturo asked.

"Studio, charging." The instant he went after it, Theo understood. "Oh damn. You think some of that got recorded?"

"Worth a listen," Arturo agreed, returning to the living room. He handed Theo the phone.

Quickly she brought up the audio file and played it. The tenderness in Scarecrow's voice when he asked if he could sing her to sleep brought fresh tears to her eyes. As the autumn race song began, she started upright. "Oh! Plug your ears, guys, sorry." She fast forwarded a couple minutes. Gwyn blinked, shook her head as if dazed. Even Arturo glazed over a bit. Theo chuckled nervously. "That one's magic. Puts me right to sleep." Allowing the file to play once more, they heard a long silence. "Crap. Maybe I missed it." She was about to backtrack when she heard the gentle rustle of his straw, his voice hushed.

"Goodbye, Theo. Thank you for everything. May your life be long and free from pain."

Dammit, she didn't want to bawl again. Not even in front of her friends. Adam appeared stricken. Arturo frowned. Gwyn sat passively, expressionless.

"Goodbye, my dear friend. I love you."

A knot traveled up her throat from her stomach. She clapped one hand over her mouth.

Adam rubbed her shoulder gently. The recording kept going. The scrape of the living room door being closed, the creak of the front door opening and closing. Theo turned the playback volume up loud as it could go. They heard a thump, then Scarecrow shouting *"Unhand me!"*

The next voice sent a shock of fury through Theo. She knew that voice all too well.

"Shut up! Grab its feet, I got the head."

"Oh shit," Adam muttered.

Theo shot to her feet, slinging the blanket from her shoulders, pounding toward the stairs.

"Theo, wait," Gwyn called. "Where are you going?"

"Damned if I'm gonna kick that motherfucker's ass wearing anything he can ogle me in," Theo snarled, taking the stairs two at a time.

She yanked on loose sweats and an oversized tee, her wrist braces and her heavy boots. The bloodstains on them were right and good for this job. Back downstairs, she grabbed the baseball bat from the studio.

Gwyn's impressive form blocked the door. "Theo, no."

"Move, Gwyn."

"This isn't the right way."

Theo propped the bat on one shoulder. "Oh yes it fucking is. You know who that was. We all know who that was. Mark took Scarecrow. If he's hurt one little straw, I am gonna kick his teeth in."

"So that was Mark," Arturo said, somewhere behind Gwyn in the hallway. "I wasn't one hundred per cent sure, only met the guy a couple times."

"Yes that was Mark. Goddess knows what fucked-up scheme is in his head, but if he's hurt Scarecrow, I'll—"

"We'll go with you," Adam said.

Gwyn put a hand on Theo's arm, gently. "We will all go over there and see what's happened. And if we have to, we will handle it. Peacefully, but firmly." She stared down Theo. "You are not hurting anyone."

Arturo peered over Gwyn's shoulder at the bat. "Is that blood?"

Theo grimaced. "Wheelers."

"Do I want to know?"

"You really don't. Gwyn, if Mark's hurt him..." Theo repeated, but the words backed up in her throat, refused to come out.

Gwyn sighed. "We will deal with Mark. Together. No bashing heads."

Theo reluctantly agreed, but refused to give up the bat. At the very least, Mark's car could stand some artistic redesign.

They piled into Arturo's old van and drove over to Mark's parents' home. Last Theo heard, he was still living in their basement. They'd seemed Midwestern-polite but distant to Theo before, and clearly disapproved of Mark's coven activities. Hard to tell whether they suspected their son was a narcissistic douchebag.

She replayed the recording again, hearing other voices indistinctly, the roll and slam of a van door, the screech of tires. Mark and his coven buddies. Jeremy and David, if she had to guess. Jeremy was barely eighteen and in awe of the more sophisticated Mark. He'd go along with anything Mark said or did. David was the type of self-styled witch who kept suggesting they perform all rituals sky-clad and hold orgies to increase their sex magic prowess, while eyeballing Theo like a flank steak. Theo flatly ignored him. Didn't matter who Mark had roped into kidnapping Scarecrow. She'd dole out some rough payback to every one of them.

Mark's parents' home was an eighties ranch in one of the most boring subdivisions in town. The lawn was freshly mowed despite the dying grass, leaves raked, cutesy Halloween decorations outside. Gwyn led the procession up to the front door and rang the bell. Mark's muscle car wasn't in the driveway.

Mrs. Meier opened the storm door only a crack, eyeing the group uncertainly. "Yes? Can I help you?" She recognized Theo. "Oh, hello there. If you're here to see Mark, he'll be back Sunday."

"Oh? We didn't realize he was out of town," Gwyn said.

Theo butted in front of her. "Where is he?" she demanded. When Mrs. Meier leaned away from her, Theo grabbed the edge of the door. "Was he here last night? Did he bring anyone over?"

Mrs. Meier shook her head. "No, he left yesterday afternoon. Is something wrong?"

"I just really need to talk to him. In person. Right away."

Mrs. Meier's eyebrows shot up. "Oh sweetie, are you expecting?"

Goddess forbid. "No, it's—"

"We just want Mark to do the right thing," Arturo spoke up. "For both of them."

Theo bit her tongue, fuming.

Mrs. Meier rubbed her forehead. "Oh my. Well. I think he said he was going to Spring Green for the weekend. Some Halloween thing over there. He went with some friends. I could call him if you—"

"It's all right. We'll track him down. Thanks." Gwyn steered Theo firmly away from the door. "Happy Halloween!"

Theo glared at Arturo as the door closed. "Really?"

He shrugged. "Fastest way to get hold of a straight guy. Or send him running for the hills."

They piled into the van. Adam asked, "So, we heading to Spring Green? We could check the parking lots of all the motels there, I guess. It's not that big a town."

"I know where he's heading, but it doesn't make sense. Unless he's already..." No reason Mark would take Scarecrow to the House on the Rock. Scarecrow might already be ripped apart, straw flung to the winds along the side of the highway. Or burned to ash. Tears stung her eyes.

Gwyn touched her hand. "Where is Mark going?"

"Has to be the House on the Rock. The only other thing in Spring Green is the Frank Lloyd Wright house, and I'm pretty sure they don't do anything for Halloween." Theo struggled to keep her voice steady. She'd rather scream, burst into the Meiers' house, trash the basement looking for any trace of her sweet straw man. Destroy anything of Mark's she could get her hands on. She gulped air. "But he wouldn't have taken Scarecrow there. All these things attacking us, they all—"

Wait. The Wheeler. The meanest one who'd commanded the others. Hadn't it said something about taking Scarecrow with them? Even after they ripped him apart. *Bring the piecezzz.* The doomed clerk at the gas station, nervously asking if they were heading to the House, while a squeaky-wheeled assassin waited behind the door. The khalidah had carried Scarecrow off. It could've simply destroyed him on the spot. Goddess only knew what the zombie's mission was, but it had seemed to be warning them of something before it disintegrated.

"Theo?"

She blinked at Adam, swallowed thickly. "Or maybe they were *trying* to take him there. Not keep him away from it."

Gwyn frowned. "Tell me more about this doorway."

Theo dredged up every bit of information she could recall. Everything Scarecrow had told her about the conditions of his visit here, all she knew about what was going on in Oz. Scarecrow hadn't said anything to her about the witches of Oz coming here before his note. Which meant he'd held things back from her.

That hurt.

Arturo drove them back to Theo's house. By the time he pulled up to the curb, all of them were quiet, thinking.

Gwyn broke the silence first. "This is serious. Very, very serious. Why didn't you tell me any of this before?"

Theo glared. "Oh, you mean the night you were calling him unnatural and bad for me?"

"Theo, this is extremely dangerous. You should listen to Scarecrow's warning and stay away from there."

"I do not fucking believe you," Theo exploded. "How dare you! If you'd rather hide at home while all fucking hell breaks loose, be my guest, but I'm going after him. If I have to bash my way through Mark and his stupid little coven, I am going!" She shoved open the van door, snatched up the bat, and stomped toward her house.

"I'm not saying I believe a portal to another dimension is going to open in a place where they charge money to see fake antiques that haven't been dusted since nineteen seventy-nine," Arturo remarked, puffing after her, "but Adam and I will go with you. You can't take on Mark's whole group by yourself."

"Fucking watch me."

What would Scarecrow do? He'd plan. He'd gather spells, weapons, read books. As satisfying as it'd be to just wade in there and start swinging for the fences, realistically, she'd need more. Even though it meant spending precious time here before she went after him.

She began packing all her faery dolls, even the ones not yet finished. If only she had something bigger, something fiercer. It might take every one of her tiny faelings to bring down even one Wheeler or khalidah or whatever the evil witches were bringing with them, and then what?

Gwyn caught up with her, echoing her thoughts. "What do you intend to do with all these?"

Theo straightened, wiping her eyes. "Make them attack. I made them, I control them. Scarecrow showed me I could."

"For reals?" Adam asked.

Arturo stared deadpan at her. "You're shitting me."

Theo shoved more dolls into a plastic carrying tub. "I shit thee not. Scarecrow showed me I can do real magic. With these, anyway. With anything I sew."

"Damn, now I want to make dolls too. Or at least a giant stuffed attack bunny or something," Adam said, looking excitedly around the studio.

Arturo rolled his eyes, but that sparked a thought for Theo. She opened the closet where she'd thrown her larger projects. Digging through a pile of stuffed animals in need of repair, she pulled out her first, her favorite, Vernor. "Aha!"

Gwyn shook her head. "Poppets? You can make actual poppets that can walk around and do your bidding?" Theo shrugged angrily, stroking the stuffed hippo's head. Gwyn blinked at her. "Really. You know we were burned at the stake just for having those a few hundred years ago."

"My dolls took down a zombie. If a dangerous doorway is opening and all the worst parts of Oz are coming through, I'll take whatever weapons I have," Theo snapped. She plopped the stuffie onto a work table, frowning critically at him. The animal's lopsided eyes and goofy open mouth didn't look capable of stopping anything. Unless she threw it at someone and tripped them. Turning to the collection of buttons and beads to see if she had anything sharp, her eye fell upon the small jar full of Wheeler fangs she'd cautiously plucked from Scarecrow's torn body.

Poisonous, he'd said. Very old, Elemental magic from the Ozian desert.

Might as well see if she could fight fire with fire. "Can someone bring me some more rubber gloves?"

Gwyn settled herself on a stool with a heavy sigh. "You know I can't let you children run off to a dangerous and probably suicidal confrontation with dark magick."

"I am twenty-goddamn-six and I will do what—"

Gwyn waved a dismissive hand. "Adam, you shouldn't be in here, with your allergies." Straw fluff coated the tables and floor still. "Go brew us a pot of gingko and ginger tea. And then please gas up the van."

Theo stopped. "Wait. You're not going to argue with me?"

"There is no arguing with you when your heart's involved, Theo." Gwyn smiled. "I wouldn't be a very good friend if I let you charge ahead without me. Adam. Tea. Now, please. Arturo, fetch those gloves." She peered at the jar of teeth. "What exactly did those come from?"

They may as well hear all of it. Theo forced herself to take a breath, give thanks for her friends, and offer a silent prayer to the Goddess that Scarecrow might still be alive. "Okay, so, we were on the road, and I really needed to pee."

"Classic," Arturo quipped. "Isn't that how 'Sleeping Beauty' starts?"

Theo talked, drank the energizing tea, and drilled, sewed, and glued as quickly as she could, weaving glowing threads into her creation as she went. She willed fierceness into it, protectiveness, vengeance. It was all the magic she knew how to do.

It would have to be enough.

32

Scarecrow listened to the footsteps of people on the brick path just outside the niche where he lay. The first few times he'd cried out, but his voice was muffled by the strong, sticky material still holding his mouth shut. Mark's coven of fae worshipers enclosed him in a suffocating sack too strong for him to break through. Hands and feet bound, they'd carried him into this cold place and wedged him inside a dark crevice. He felt cold rock against his back. He heard their voices as they stuffed him into the hiding place.

"This should do until tonight. We'll come back at five when the place closes for the Darkside set up," Mark said.

"So it's really happening tonight?" asked the delivery boy.

Their voices faded as they walked away, but Scarecrow caught a few more words. "It is. Let's go find a stand to hang it from."

A chuckle. "This is gonna be so lit."

Once they were gone, he struggled, but the bonds held firm. Good thing he didn't need to breathe. The sack sucked against his face, unpleasantly slick and smelling of mechanical oil, so opaque he couldn't see a thing. Organ music played distantly. No idea what time it was, how long until moonrise.

Mark and his coven drove Scarecrow in their wagon for hours yesterday, stopping several times for mysterious side trips without him, left him alone in it through a very long night when they slept at an inn. He tried to separate his wrist from his sleeve. Perhaps scratching at the binding over his mouth long enough with rough straw might wear through it, allow him to speak. To sing. But Theo's craftsmanship proved too strong. He strained to rip his right arm free of his wrist for some time, well past the point of surprising pain, but her stitches refused to come loose.

He caught a glimpse of sunlight this morning when the wagon door opened and the dark coven piled in, only for them to strawhandle him into this giant black sack. Helpless, he cursed them incoherently, but only the round-faced one called Jeremy seemed at all perturbed. Mark and the two other young men folded him into the sack as though he were a floppy doll, carried him into wherever this was, and stuffed him in a hiding spot to await the night.

He lay there consumed with worry for hours as feet clomped past him, distant voices laughed and talked, people passing unaware of his plight.

If Ozma Tip could find the song scrolls in his library, she'd have a fighting chance, assuming she could surprise Glinda. Assuming the Ozian witches didn't have some sort of horrible fate already in motion for the young Queen.

Praise the sweet sunlight, let Theo stay away. Amazing though her magic was, she was no match for Mombi, Locasta, or Glinda. Bound and silenced, he was no help at all. Whatever Mark's crew planned for him tonight, it was clear he wouldn't have a chance to fight. Couldn't protect Theo or his Ozian friends. Whatever being an anchor entailed, with his new physical sensitivity he was certain it would be highly unpleasant.

At least he'd be dead in a few hours, but the fae could torment his friends for years. No way to stop them. Fervently he willed Ozma Tip to use whatever magic she found in the library to keep herself, Nick, and the others safe.

"Spread out, keep in touch, he has to be here somewhere. And if you run into Mark let me know right away. That asshole is mine."

Theo!

Oh no, no, she couldn't be here, it wasn't safe! Her voice, the heavy tread of her boots passed right outside the niche where he was concealed. Scarecrow thrashed in panic, yelled against closed lips, slammed himself against the narrow walls of his confinement.

She didn't hear him. Several people tromped past. He heard Lady Gwyn's voice: "No beating anyone up, Theo. I mean it."

"At least not until we find Scarecrow," Arturo remarked.

More voices, fading, indecipherable. He struggled, kicked, thrashed side to side. The sack stretched but didn't burst. The hard ties around his wrists and ankles clamped firmly. He couldn't rip loose any of his stitches.

Tears soaked into Scarecrow's cheeks. No. Please, no. She couldn't be here. He never should've mentioned where she could find her carriage, hinted where the doorway from Oz would open. No doubt in his mind now. He was imprisoned at the strange temple called the House on the Rock. He remembered well how dark and confusing a maze it was. Mark and his coven could be costumed, and no one would be the wiser—until the moon rose, the door opened, and the horrors of the Unseelie Court invaded this world. The ancient Elementals. The Undying, things which were never born and never died. Blight and ruin, that's what the walking corpse had been trying to tell them! *'Ware the not-dead of Oz.* No sword or axe could kill them, and only ancient spells might affect them at all. If Theo were here when they invaded...

He moaned, slamming his shoulder uselessly against his prison. The ache that brought was nothing compared to the chill in his heart.

All of this, because he'd foolishly hoped Dorothy might somehow find him appealing. Might actually want a floppy straw creature as a lover, a partner. All this because he'd begged Glinda for a way to come here.

The fiery young witch he loved would probably die tonight. His friends were in terrible danger. The fae would return here, to again rule the world from which they'd been banished centuries ago. And all of this was his fault.

Overwhelmed, his brains shut down. He wept.

• • • •

BY NOW, THE GUARDS outside Ozma Tip's royal chambers must've reported to Glinda that the Queen was not in her rooms. Glinda would send out a search party for all of them. Nick paced, checking the sharpness of his axe for the twentieth time. As long as the door held, they'd be safe here in Scarecrow's library. If the witch sent armed guards to batter the door down, Nick and Lion could make a bottleneck out of the guards' bodies. Though he wouldn't put it past them to bring arrows and oil and set fire to the library, force everyone in the room out. He eyed the remaining covered buckets of water standing in corners. Scarecrow worried about witches and fire, but never planned for a prolonged siege of the room. Nick hadn't considered every way the guards might try to get at them until now.

Tip's eyes were red. Her head nodded over the desk. She roused herself, tossed another scroll aside, and spread the next one out, peering closely at it. On the sofa, the Wogglebug had passed out, old Ozian lexicon in one hand. Nick felt badly for him, but they had no time for rest. Gently, he shook the Professor's shoulder.

"Professor. Wake up. Nap time's over. I'm sorry."

The Wogglebug's head lifted, faceted eyes darkening, orienting on Nick. "Oh. Forgive me. I must've fallen asleep." He rustled through a pile of scrolls. "Where was I?"

Nick checked on Tip. She barely glanced at him, mumbling acknowledgement when he asked how she felt. "Find anything?" he asked.

"This one," she raised one scroll set apart from the others, "might help. It mentions a rainy swamp. Might bog down the rock trolls or turn them to mud, if we're lucky." She rubbed her eyes. "I remember Scarecrow said once that the words or the intent of the song might trigger the magic. I really wish he'd written down what they all do."

"He doesn't know what they all do," Nick sighed.

She nodded tiredly. "I'll keep reading. I want lightning, or a hole to open in the earth and suck them all down forever. Or for them all to drop dead on the spot."

As long as it only affected the fae and the monsters, Nick had no issue with any of that. He checked on Lion, who'd been feeding logs into the fireplace all night, both for warmth and to ensure nothing could surprise them through the secret tunnel.

Lion's whiskers twitched. "We should've heard from Tiger by now. I'm worried."

"Tiger can take care of himself."

"He's not all that bright," Lion said.

"Then I hope he's bright enough to run," Nick snapped. Lion recoiled. Nick took a breath to compose himself. "I like Tiger, he's a loyal fellow. But we cannot spare anyone to go check on him. Glinda will send someone to search for Tip and we have to be ready to defend her. Here. However we can."

"So we're waiting on magic," Lion muttered, glancing at Tip and the Wogglebug.

"Yes."

Lion shifted around, stretched his forepaws so all his claws showed. "All right."

Nick bent to clap him on the shoulder. "Good."

Tip sat up straighter. "Wait a second. This is it."

"Are you sure?"

"Yeah. I think so." She handed the scroll to the Wogglebug. "Am I right?"

The Wogglebug peered at the scribbles on the scroll. He hummed a bar of the music noted upon it. "Possibly."

"Look what it says, the third verse," Tip insisted. "The bit about the wind between worlds. That's what that says, right?"

A wind between worlds? Like the cyclone which blew Dorothy to Oz! "Wait. The goal is to *stop* the fae from going to Dorothy's world."

"What if it brings Scarecrow back?" Tip argued. "He knows more about this magic than we do. He memorized a whole bunch of these songs."

The Wogglebug frowned. "Your Highness, read the first verse. It speaks of a terrible silence, a place without life or hope. I don't think we want to—"

"So we skip that part!"

"Your Highness, this might not be wise."

Tip stood, wavering unsteadily. She slammed a fist on the desk. "I am sending all of those bitches to the Nome furnaces or wherever that spell takes them!"

Another thump sounded. Tip's hands were still. The pounding came again from the door. "Open up! Open up in the name of the Emerald Guards!"

"How about no," Lion snarled, padding to the door. He crouched, ready to attack.

"Open up, you criminals!"

Something about the gruff voice sounded familiar. Nick went to the door, axe raised, exchanging a look with Lion. "Wait. Is that—"

A growling giggle came from the other side of the door. "C'mon, open up, you ugly Nomes! In the name of the stupid guards and stuff."

Lion rolled his eyes, easing from his crouch. "Damn that idiot."

Nick sighed and unbolted the door. The Hungry Tiger grinned at him. "Ha ha ha! Had you going, huh? You really thought I was the guards."

"Be quiet," Nick hissed at him, checking the hallway. No one else around. "How did you get past them?"

The Tiger grinned wider, showing a number of sharp teeth. His muzzle stained red. "Howd'ya think?"

Nick stepped back, holding the door open. "Get in here."

The Tiger pranced, tail swishing, clearly delighted with himself. "Took forever to peel off all that armor, but they were almost as tasty as I bet fat little babies would be. There's two guards who can't report anything to Glin—*raaaaawwwwrrrrr!*" He snarled in pain, jerking, a bolt sticking from his back right leg. Another crossbow bolt thwacked into his flank and he collapsed, blocking the door open.

Nick grabbed his forelegs to drag him inside. A bolt slammed into Nick's shoulder, knocking him backwards, and the guards rushed the door from their hiding spots behind the marble pillars. Nick staggered, swung his axe, chopped into a guard's arm. Lion sprang forward, bearing one of them to the floor, teeth and claws ripping at the man's neck. Nick heard commotion behind him but was too busy fighting off two heavily armored guards with halberds. "Tip, run!" he shouted.

Another guard aimed past him. Nick leaped but the bolt was faster. He heard Tip's cry of pain, whirled, saw her fall. The Wogglebug struggled free of the pile of books and blankets, blocking Tip, his skinny arms spread wide.

Nick chopped into a guard's neck. The man gurgled, sinking. Nick wrenched the blade away and swung again, his axe clanging off the breastplate of another. Palace guards swarmed the room, pushing him back, stepping over the motionless Tiger. Lion's swatting paws and enraged roar emerged from under a moving pile of armor. Halberds and swords stabbed.

"Stop," Ozma Tip shouted, "I command you all to stop!"

One of the guards paused. "Your Majesty, Glinda ordered us to capture these traitors!"

"Nick, stop!" Tip yelled, trying to push the Wogglebug out of her way. A bolt protruded from her right shoulder, her arm limp, blood reddening her gown. "All of you, stop! Guards, if you kill them, I will kill all of you!"

She raised her royal scepter and a brilliant green light flashed, blinding Nick for a moment. "I will not warn you again! Everyone stop right this minute!" she shouted. Her voice rumbled the ceiling. Dust shook down.

The nearest guard let go of him. Nick blinked his vision clear, ears ringing, raised his axe. "Nick, no!" Again her powerful voice made his joints clang, his chest rattle. He stared back at her.

"Tip?"

She shoved the dazed Wogglebug out of her way and staggered to the door. Her eyes were bright emeralds, full of light. "I am your Queen and I say all of you must stop fighting immediately, or I shall put you to death." Her voice hurt Nick's ears.

Lion cringed, panting. Tiger wheezed, shuffling out of the way, his back right leg dragging. The guards let go. One of them knelt, beads of sweat standing out on his forehead. The others followed suit, laying their weapons on the cold, blood-spattered floor.

"Forgive us, Your Majesty," said the one who'd spoken before. His epaulettes marked him as a captain. "We were told these villains enspelled you. They mean to execute you and rule in your place." When Ozma didn't reply, staring coldly at him, he gasped, "We came to rescue you."

"You shot her," Nick snapped, raising his axe again, taking a step toward the captain.

The captain shook his head. "No, no, not to hurt her, the bolt was to break the grip of the dark magic upon her!"

"Do I appear as though I am under a dark spell?" Ozma Tip demanded, standing right in front of the captain.

He groveled all the way to the floor. "Your Highness, I'm sorry. I don't know. Glinda the Good told us—"

"To the Nomes with Glinda!" Tip shrieked, slamming the butt of the scepter upon the floor. "How dare you attack my friends!"

"Glinda is good," the captain murmured. The other soldiers repeated the words, including the ones Nick had thought were dead. "Glinda is good."

"She is far from it," Nick snapped. He went to the trembling Tip. Blood streaked from her shoulder to her hip, dripped from her garments.

"Nick, the bolt is iron," the Wogglebug exclaimed. "Get it out of her!"

Alarmed, he wrapped one arm around her, hooked his axe to his belt, and checked the wound. "Give me something to stop the bleeding," he ordered. The Wogglebug grabbed a quilt and stumbled toward him. The green glow was gone from Tip's eyes. Her eyelids fluttered and she sagged in his grip. He took firm hold of the crossbow bolt, offered a quick prayer, and was roughly jerked back by strong hands before he could remove the bolt.

The guards took his axe, held him down, their eyes all glazed. "Glinda is good," they muttered, "Glinda is good."

"She's got them under a spell!" Nick yelled, thrashing, but more of them pressed onto his arms, his legs, sat on his chest. "Tip!"

She sank to the floor. The Wogglebug dove in time to prevent her head from hitting the marble.

Lion snarled, but the guards piled atop him. One produced a large fishing net and they wrapped him in it. The more he fought, the worse he became tangled. Tiger managed to stand and took a swipe at them but a guard stuck his halberd under the great cat and flipped him off balance. Another swung a battle hammer into his skull. Tiger collapsed.

"No!" Nick screamed, unable to rise under the weight of five guards in full plate armor.

The guards swarmed Ozma Tip, accosted the Wogglebug, carried both of them from the library. "Glinda is good. Glinda is good."

"Stop this, wake up, snap out of it!" Nick pleaded. They wrestled manacles onto his arms, chained his legs together, forced him up and through the doorway. It took six of them to drag Lion. They left the motionless Tiger where he lay, blood pooling under his head and hip. No way to tell if he was dead or merely unconscious. Three guards also hadn't moved since Nick and Lion took them down. The chanting guards ignored the fallen, leaving them behind.

"They won't listen," the Professor groaned. His limp body swung between two guards as they carried him and Ozma Tip toward the central staircase of the Emerald Palace.

"Professor, sing something!" Nick called. Desperate to keep Tip in sight, he stopped resisting and let them push him forward in jerking steps.

"That song could kill us all," the Wogglebug shouted back, "including Her Highness."

Robbed of a choice, Nick went with the chanting, dazed guards down the main stairs. Standing in the grand throne room, her hair dancing wildly above her ruby tiara, Glinda waited in dark red robes, with Locasta and Mombi watching from one side. A few other high-ranking fae clustered in the shadows.

"*There* she is," Glinda trilled. "I thought Her Majesty would never join us! Shame on you, Nick Chopper, for delaying her arrival to her own party."

"Your idiots shot her," Nick spat. "She'll die if you don't get her a healer immediately."

"Already arranged," Glinda said, still smiling. She pointed at one of the guards holding the unconscious Queen. "You. Remove the bolt."

The glassy-eyed guard yanked the bolt from Tip's shoulder, standing stiffly with it. Fresh blood welled from the wound. Nick struggled against the chains. "You'll kill her!"

"I have no intention of killing her," Glinda replied. "Oz needs their Queen. Mombi, see to it."

The grizzled old witch clucked, shuffling forward to receive Ozma in her bony grip. "Tsk, such a mess. He's right, you know. Your stupid tin cans nearly killed the girl."

Glinda flicked a dismissive hand at her. "Get her cleaned up. She needs to be on the throne at moonrise so all the people can see her."

"I still don't see why we don't just cast an illusion in her place."

"Because," Glinda purred, gliding closer to Mombi, "I. Said. So."

"What about these fools?" Locasta asked, gesturing at the rest of the party.

"They should be in the throne room as well. Sweet little Ozma and her loyal friends. Where is the Tiger?" She snapped her fingers, and the captain blinked. "You. I told you to bring all of them. Where is the Tiger?"

"Dead," said the captain, slowly looking around him. "The Queen! What happened?"

"An assassination attempt, bravely foiled by you and your men, Captain. Don't you remember?" The man nodded slowly, eyebrows knit. Glinda turned to Nick. "Pity. I always thought the two cats made nice bookends for the throne. Such a pretty image of power. And you and the straw man sitting beside her as well. Ah, well. We work with what we have."

"I think Mombi has the right idea for once." Locasta's cold gray eyes flicked from Nick to the Wogglebug to Lion. "Kill them. Set illusions on some pacified guards in their place."

"The people know these fools too well. No, they shall be at the side of their beloved ruler for her Winter's Eve party tonight. All her citizens may come celebrate in the Palace." Glinda slid closer to Nick, silent across the gleaming floor. Her gown and robes rippled although no wind blew indoors. Her smile widened, her coal-black eyes bore into his. "Here is what you are going to do, friend Chopper. You will be mended and polished, and this evening you will stand by the throne, and you will greet the guests and enjoy the festivities."

"You can enspell me all you want," he muttered. "Someone will notice the difference."

Her long eyelashes fluttered like moths. "Why, I don't need to enchant you at all. Any of you. Because if any of you make a wrong move, or speak a word against me or the Seelie Court, all these nice boys in their shiny armor will fill your metal skull with bolts and cut that heart from your chest, and then they will kill the Queen. So you will smile, you will bow, you will behave as if tonight is like any other court feast."

Behind her, the captain of the guard paled and took a step back. Without turning, Glinda gestured and whispered, and the man stiffened again, staring straight ahead.

Glinda's breath in Nick's face reminded him of carrion a week dead in the forest, picked over by vultures. "Do we have an understanding, Nick Chopper?"

"This is monstrous," exclaimed the Wogglebug. "Your Highness! Your Highness, wake up!"

"Shut up before I pull your mouth-parts off," Locasta snarled.

Glinda turned slowly, fixing the lesser witch with a bright smile. Locasta scowled, but said nothing else.

"She's weak, but she'll live," Mombi announced. "Bring her to my quarters. I'll stitch up the wound and put a poultice on it. You, go and fetch me her emerald gown." She pointed at one of the fae courtiers watching from the alcove. Same duke who'd wanted to make a bed plaything out of Nick.

"I'm not a servant," the nobleman huffed.

Glinda turned her smile on him. "I believe you were asked to do a small favor by my sister, dear Duke."

The Duke paused, nodded, hurried off. Two of the courtiers volunteered to take the unconscious Queen from Mombi and followed her as she hobbled away. "Pah! *Sister,* my dry womb," Mombi growled.

Glinda tittered. "She's so grouchy before midnight. Come, the rest of you. See to these fine gentlemen's needs. Ready them for the celebrations, then ready yourselves. We want to make a good impression on the mortals tonight." She giggled louder. "Especially the ones who aren't expecting us to come home."

Nick watched his friends be dragged away. The sun shone through the stained glass high above. Hours to go before nightfall, but split up and guarded as they were, how could they possibly accomplish anything? The guards marched him to the smithery.

Sitting in manacles while the frightened blacksmith pounded the dents from his body and the apprentice buffed his plated tin to a high shine, Nick thought about the last scroll Tip discovered. What if singing it brought about the death of everyone within hearing? Could even Tip survive the effects, weak and wounded?

It might be their only hope of stopping Glinda. He was willing to die, if it meant the Seelie Court would be no more. He couldn't ask the rest of them to sacrifice themselves. If Tip sang it, she at least could control the spell. He had to get her down to the tunnels. If the song could close the gateway, kill the witches, destroy the powerful Unseelie Court, certainly that was worth dying for.

If he could get her past the guards without getting them both killed. All of them killed.

He stared glumly at his shiny chest as the blacksmith rebuttoned his waistcoat over it. The Evstone was still there, a lump in his pocket. Scarecrow would figure out something. Destroy the anchor. Foul this dark plot. As smart as his straw friend was, surely he'd already succeeded. Then all Nick needed to worry about was keeping Tip alive, when Glinda discovered her magic doorway didn't work and took out her fury on them.

Tip had to sing the spell if the gate opened. Had to sing it if it didn't. Either way, Nick and his friends would likely die, but at least Oz would go on with its Queen and without the manipulations of the Seelie Court. This thought, finally, made him smile.

"Could you dry my eyes, please?" he asked the smith's apprentice. "Can't have anything rusting before the big night."

· · · ·

THEO CROUCHED AMONG the mannikins in the bathroom. Her knees hurt. She checked her phone. Eight minutes had passed since the House on the Rock officially closed. She'd ducked in here when she saw one of the staff coming, but didn't want to crouch on top of a toilet. Plus they might open the stall doors to check. In keeping with the rest of the bizarre attraction, even the restrooms were done up weird. This one boasted green shag carpet on the walls and ceiling, faux rocks built around the sinks, and a ledge seven feet off the floor displaying flower-headed mannequins in bright sequined dresses among fake greenery.

Boosting herself from the fake rocks to the ledge had been difficult enough. Crouching behind one of the wider mannequins, waiting silently, was driving her insane.

Last night, she'd ducked outside the area of the Darkside tour, risking permanent expulsion from the House if she were caught. Arturo, Adam, and Gwyn searched the Doll Room, the Carousel Room, the Organ Room and the gardens. No sign of Scarecrow or Mark and his sad little minions anywhere. She didn't sleep all last night, pacing outside a motel room after the staff ushered everyone out. Again today, soon as the House opened, they all spread out and hunted without success.

The moon would rise in an hour. Her stomach churned. Theo pressed both hands to her guts, controlling her breathing.

Then the bathroom door swung open, and a female staff member walked in. She looked around briefly, pushed open the toilet stalls, and walked out, shutting the lights off as she went.

Crap. Climbing up here with the lights on sucked. Getting down was going to be an absolute bitch.

Scarecrow had to be here somewhere. Had to be. If she was wrong, if Mark took him somewhere else, or if he were already ripped to shreds—

No. Not an option. She would not accept that.

She waited a couple more minutes. Texted the rest of the group, *"I think we're clear. Can you bring the dolls?"*

"Saw the service entrance. We'll head that way," Gwyn replied.

"I'm in the music room. Lights still on here but no one is around," Adam texted.

"Where the hell did you hide in the music room?" Arturo asked.

"Behind grand piano in Blue Danube." Several displays in the convoluted Music of Yesterday hall featured room-sized setups of instruments which appeared to play themselves. The Blue Danube display had practically a whole chamber orchestra.

Good, so Adam was also still inside the House, though a long walk from her own hiding spot. The House didn't reopen for the Darkside tour until six-thirty, after the moon had risen. No way was Theo waiting around. *"If you can get the dolls to the service entrance by the organ room, I think I can make them come to me from there. I'll open the door when you have them right outside.*" A couple dolls were tucked in her pockets right now, but with time running out and the staff setting up the Halloween props for the night's show, might as well go all in.

"*That'll set off the fire alarm,*" Arturo noted.

"*So text me when you have everything right there exactly! And don't touch the teeth!*" Theo shoved her phone in her purse.

She slowly lowered herself from the display ledge, feet kicking until she located the rock surround of the sinks. She damned near lost her balance upon landing, her arm banging against the fake rocks, feet slamming hard onto the tiled floor. Panting, she eased the bathroom door open.

The glass-walled café just outside was dark, the dull glow of the setting sun through the trees enough light for her to navigate. She pressed against the wall, peering around the curved hallway into the red-lit Organ Room. Her view of the opposite end of the room was obstructed by the immense chandeliers of red globe lights, the "trees" of kettledrums stacked one atop the other floor to ceiling, and an entire copper distillery. Though the Carousel Room was more famous, she'd always preferred the absolutely overwhelming scale of this room. It felt like a temple to some obscure god, with drums and organs any way she turned, all bathed in red lights.

From this vantage point above much of the warehouse-sized room, she could see a couple of staff members setting animatronics into place, turning on strobes, and posing skeletons on organ benches as if playing.

She crept to the railing of this elevated walkway and peered below until she located the emergency exit sign. All too easy to get turned around in this wild maze of a place, especially in the surreal lighting, but pretty sure that was the right door. She just needed to get down to it without the staff spotting her. Fortunately they were all focused on their spooky set-up duties. The ones she'd noticed a minute ago were moving away, adjusting lights and laying pressure sensors out in front of pop-up ghosts and ghouls. A group of four black-clad people in matching masquerade-style masks brought a body bag and a wooden crossbeam on a metal stand out in front of the biggest organ on the lowest level, where the yellow brick path down from the Carousel Room ended and the red carpet of the slanted walkways began. Framed by bare birch trees, the organ pipes rose like a church at least two stories high. Nothing stood in that spot last night when Theo came through. Impatiently she waited for the costumed staff to finish their set-up. If she tried to cross down to the door now, they'd see her.

They cut open the body bag and hefted a green-clad form out.

It moved.

No. Oh Goddess no.

When the masked people cut the ties binding his hands and lifted the Scarecrow onto the crossbeam, he struggled weakly. The masked kidnappers held him up and lashed his wrists to the pole. His head turned toward her, and Theo saw the duct tape over his mouth, the fear in his wide eyes.

"You motherfucking cunts!" she cried, and burst into a run down the ramp.

33

A battle cry drew Scarecrow's attention to the ceiling. In the disorienting red flashing lights, he saw someone running down a series of slanted walkways, a tattered skirt billowing behind her, heard the pounding of heavy boots under the loud organ music and unnerving shrieks and groans.

Oh no.

Mark laughed. "Perfect! Just as the guide prophesied. I knew she'd come back, and now she'll see just how powerful I am."

"Holy shit, is that Theo?" asked Jeremy.

"Finish the ties," Mark ordered, pointing at Scarecrow's feet hanging against the pole. His coven obeyed, securing the bonds which held Scarecrow's hands to the crossbar and lashing his ankles to the upright pole.

Scarecrow strained. No way to see the sky down here, but it must be close to moonrise—since he was losing his ability to move.

Theo reached the bottom level of the room, her breast heaving, eyes narrowed, fists clenched. She halted a few steps away from them.

Mark spread his arms. "Milady! What a pleasant surprise."

"Let him go."

"Or what?" Another of the coven sneered.

"Fuck you, David. You'll see 'or what.'"

"I don't go by that anymore. It's Nightcat now."

"It's Douchebag Number Two, for all I care. Mark, let Scarecrow down, or I will put you in the fucking morgue. And you, you pizza-guy motherfucker, if you touch my Scarecrow again I'll shove your fucking anchovies up your dick."

Scarecrow shook his head weakly. She couldn't be here when the gateway opened. If he were free to sing, he could injure these disciples of Glinda enough for Theo to escape unscathed. Give her a head start.

Mark's tone chilled. "Theo, you have no idea what you've stumbled into. There are forces at work well beyond your capacity to comprehend. I have been in direct contact with ethereal—"

"Let me guess, she calls herself a goddess and she's promised you a place at her side or some shit. Reality check, Mark, the witches of Oz are trying to bust into our world tonight and they aren't going to give a rat's ass about you or your sad little LaVey wannabes." Theo flipped her hair out of her eyes. They gleamed green in the pulsing lights. "Let him go right now."

"Were you really trying to make me jealous with this floppy thing?" Mark asked, advancing toward her. Theo's fists raised, legs braced apart. "Creating a sex doll doesn't make me jealous, Theo, it just makes you pathetic."

Scarecrow tugged at the hard ties holding his wrists up but couldn't budge an inch.

Mark's coven fanned out, watchful, though they remained behind their leader. Four against one, and this time Theo didn't have a weapon.

She thrust both hands into hidden pockets and pulled forth tiny things with several limbs. Her dolls! Theo grinned and spread her palms, and the two dolls stood slowly as if just waking up. Glowing threads ran from her fingertips to their backs. "Hey kids, see that douchebag pretending to be a cult leader? Go tear his face up."

The dolls launched into the air, dragonfly wings whirring right at Mark. Startled, he raised his hands too late. One faery doll smacked into his forehead, grabbed his hair, began yanking fistfuls of it. Mark cursed, batting it away. The second hovered a moment, then dove at his open mouth. His scream turned to a choking gurgle.

Jeremy stood slack-jawed next to Scarecrow, hands empty. The pizza delivery boy retreated, looking around frantically. Nightcat reached into the bag they'd brought and pulled out a hammer.

Scarecrow shook his head, desperately trying to yell at Theo. *No, don't do this, just get out of here, please!*

"Hey, what's going on here?" A woman clad all in clack with a badge on her shirt strode toward them, climbing over one of the metal railings blocking the organ pipes from a different walkway. "Miss, what are you doing?"

"Don't kill him, just hurt him a lot," Theo commanded her poppets, backing away from the advancing official. The faeries buzzed around

Mark's face, jabbing with sharp claws. He snarled, yelped, swung his hands at them, but they were incredibly fast. Blood ran from the corner of his mouth and trickled down his forehead.

"Holy cripes, what are those?" the official gasped, finally seeing the dolls.

"This crazy bitch attacked us!" yelled the delivery boy, pointing at Theo. "We were just setting this prop up and she came outta nowhere!"

"He is not a prop! They kidnapped him!" Theo shouted.

"Get it off me! Get it off!" Mark howled, batting at his tormentors.

Theo's friend Adam called down from a higher catwalk. "Theo!"

She turned. "Door's over there! Open it so I can get the other dolls in here!"

He stared a moment, no doubt seeing the poppets in action for the first time. To his credit, he recovered his wits and ran toward an EXIT sign.

"What in the hell," the official murmured, stock-still, eyes fixed upon the buzzing faeries.

Nightcat lunged at Theo, swinging the hammer. Scarecrow yelled, muffled. She didn't turn in time, saw the blow coming too late, tried to block. She cried out when it hit her forearm. Nightcat sidestepped her wild kick, swung the hammer again, landed another hit against her elbow. Theo cradled her injured arm, backing away. "Faeries! Attack him!" She pointed at Nightcat.

Immediately the dolls abandoned Mark and swooped at Nightcat. Theo planted a kick in his stomach the moment the dolls distracted him, sending him tumbling. She shoved past the bewildered official. "Scarecrow!"

The delivery boy leapt forward to grab her by her injured arm. She gave a furious, wordless shriek, swinging a fist which caught his jaw, staggering him, but he didn't let go. Mark stumbled, bloody, but grabbed her other arm.

"Stop that!" cried the official, "Hey, knock it off! Security!" She yanked a rectangular object from her belt and shouted at it. "Security, there's a fight going on in the Organ Room lower level, get down here immediately!"

Scarecrow shook his head helplessly. More mortals right where the gateway would open. Theo was trapped. He strained against his bonds. Useless.

An alarm blared. A gust of air blew through as a door swung open. Struggling, Theo gestured toward it. "Faeries! Vernor! Here!"

"Security!"

"You stupid bitch," Mark snarled, wrenching Theo closer to him, "I was going to make you my serving wench in the New Order, but now you die."

Theo spat in his face and stomped her boot hard on his foot. Mark jerked backward, pulling her with him. Nightcat successfully smacked one of the dolls to the ground and crushed it underfoot. The other one dove at his right eye. Screaming, he grabbed the doll and flung it away, blood pouring out of his eye socket.

Jeremy shouted, "Jesus, Mark, let's get out of here!"

Mark slapped Theo hard across the face, sending her to her knees. Scarecrow jerked in place, screaming curses inside.

Suddenly buzzing wings filled the air. Dolls with insect faces, bird beaks, tiny horns and claws all swarmed Mark, his coven, and the official. With a frightened squeak, the official fled. Jeremy fell to his knees, covering his face with both hands, sobbing. The other three men quickly had their hands full, swinging, swatting, jerking in pain. A battalion of tiny knights mounted on furry wolves and wooden unicorns charged across the floor. In their midst gallumped an awkward, floppy thing the size of a very fat lamb, made of purple calico, thick feet slipping and sliding when it hit the smooth brick floor. Its wide mouth opened for an impressive roar, revealing rows of yellowed fangs.

"Fuck this!" The delivery boy leaped one of the metal fences and ran, chased by a couple of faeries pecking at him like sparrows after an intruding crow.

Nightcat and Mark kicked knights into the base of the pipe organ, tore flying faeries from their hair. They let go of Theo, too busy fending off attacks to deal with her. She levered herself upright against a fence rail, panting, her face red.

Mark's mask was gone, pulled off in the struggle, his eyes full of hate. "You fucking bitch," he yelled, "I'm the real witch here, not you!"

Theo yanked back on a thread, tugging a faery doll away from Nightcat. He keened, both hands over his injured eye. She pointed at the strange stuffed beast, now crouched at her side. Her voice shook. "This is Vernor. His teeth are poisonous. Get the fuck out now or I'll order him to bite you."

"My eye," moaned Nightcat. "It stabbed my fucking eye!"

"Holy shit!"

Theo's witch friends Adam, Arturo, and Lady Gwyn were lined up at a railing, staring at the fight. Arturo clambered over the rail, which broke the stunned motionlessness of the others. Adam hopped over and ran towards them. Lady Gwyn headed down the ramp, too dignified to climb over.

Mark ripped the wings off a doll, slamming it to the floor. Seeing the other witches coming, he abandoned the fight, grabbing Nightcat by one shoulder and hauling him with him. "You'll be fucking sorry, bitch!" he yelled, disappearing through a dark doorway. Jeremy remained curled on the floor. Theo snapped her fingers and all the dolls which could still move clustered around her.

"Well," Arturo remarked, slowing as he reached her, "that was definitely a thing."

"I didn't mean for them to hurt his eye," Theo gasped. She was shaking, holding her hurt arm close to her chest. Thank the sweet sunlight, she didn't seem to be fatally injured. "I'm so sorry, I didn't think it would go that far, those assholes just wouldn't back off!"

Adam stared at the dolls, hesitating. Theo pointed shakily at her friends, addressing the dolls. "Friends. Protect them."

Gwyn caught up, huffing and puffing. "Theo, what did you do?"

"What she had to," Arturo said.

Theo hurried to Scarecrow, standing on tiptoes to pull the sticky patch off his mouth. He winced. "Scarecrow!" she exclaimed, "Oh Goddess I'm sorry. I'm so sorry these assholes kidnapped you and I slept right through it. We've been looking for you since yesterday! Are you hurt?" She tugged at the tie binding his left hand to the crossbeam.

He'd give anything to embrace her once more. "Theo, you shouldn't be here," he whispered.

She strained to hear him. "Did they hurt you? Hang on, we'll get you down."

He shook his head. His vision swam, the flashing lights and eerie sounds all around disorienting. "Theo, you have to get out of here, the moon is rising."

She grabbed his tunic in both hands, glaring up at him. "I'm not leaving you."

"I'll be dead in a few minutes and the entire court, Seelie and Unseelie both, will enter this world," he argued. Hard to force strength into his voice. She had to listen, had to leave immediately. "You can't win against them, Theo. Your dolls are no match for this. Take your friends and flee as far as you can. Please."

"Sing the war song," she argued back. "We'll cover our ears!"

"I won't get the chance when the doorway opens," he protested.

"No! It can't end this way! There has to be something we can do."

Moisture blurred his eyes. He didn't bother to blink them clear. So tired. This must be how she felt, all the time, so weary and yet pushing herself to speak, to act. "Theo, Glinda said I will die at the full moon. I can already feel it happening."

"What exactly did she say? Spells have specific conditions." Theo raised her voice, giving his clothing a shake, rousing him from a growing stupor. "Scarecrow! Tell me exactly what she told you."

It took effort to dredge the words from his memory. His brains seemed mushy. "She said the spell would only last until the next full moon, and then, if my heart's desire accepts me truly, her love will sustain me. If she doesn't, at the full moon my magic fails. I'll be like any other scarecrow in this world. Lifeless." He sighed. "We know how that turned out."

Theo stroked a hand down his chest. "She didn't specifically say Dorothy?"

He frowned. "Well, no, but..."

"Scarecrow," Theo snapped, shaking him fully awake again. "Stay with me. What is your heart's desire?" Tears filled her eyes, lovely pools shifting between dark brown and dark green as the lights played over her face. "Who is your heart's desire?"

He gazed down at her sadly. She was beautiful, so full of heart and courage and intelligence. So much more wonderful than he could ever hope for.

"In a perfect world, you are," he murmured.

"Scarecrow, I love you."

He frowned, trying to grasp what she was saying. Something prickled inside his head.

"Do you hear me? I love you. I want you. Stay with me. Please."

Sharp consciousness returned to him in a rush. His chest felt warm, the bonds at his wrists hurt. He blinked down at her, hope fluttering wildly in his straw. "You what?"

She hugged his legs, tears flowing down her cheeks. "You are my heart's desire, and if you want me to be, I'm yours."

"You want me like this?" He tried to nod at himself. After being roughly handled, straw stuck out of his body in spots, poking between two of his tunic buttons. He felt shaken, jumbled, astonished.

Theo coughed a laugh. "If that's what you're into, I can go with it." She beamed at him. "Yes, Scarecrow. I love you just as you are. You don't ever have to change anything for me."

"I love you, Theo," he said, voice regaining strength. A thousand thoughts crowded his brains, shoving each other, dizzying. "You need to get out of here. Now."

"Getting you down first. Little help?" she called to her friends.

Arturo came over, opening a pocket knife, with Adam right behind him. "That is the sweetest thing I've ever seen."

Gwyn shook her head. "Hurry up. He's right, we need to get out of here. Moon's rising right now. Can't you feel it?"

"Hey!" Two large men dressed in black with badges on their chests headed for them, scowling. "You all need to leave."

"Trying to," Arturo muttered. He reached up and cut through the manacle binding Scarecrow's left hand to the pole.

"Thank you," Scarecrow said. Gwyn was right, he could feel something strange, like movement in his straw.

From a great distance, he heard Glinda's voice: *"It is time."*

Fear chilled his entire body. "Theo, no, it's too late, get *ouuuuaaaaah-hh!"*

Searing pain ripped down his chest and stomach. Buttons popped, flying off his tunic, the garment flapping open as a heavy claw thrust through his body. Scarecrow shrieked, back arching.

The arm of a rock troll shoved out of his stomach, then a second arm, then it pushed him open from the center and stuck its head out.

The last thing Scarecrow saw before agony overwhelmed him was the shock on his beloved's face.

• • • •

NICK STOOD STIFFLY beside the throne. Lion lay opposite. The Professor was ensconced in a comfortable chair a step down from the throne on Ozma's left. All of them tense, smiles pasted on, as the Great Hall filled with chattering, laughing, dancing commoners. From the balcony ringing the room, the Seelie Court watched the festivities. Dozens of nobles here Nick didn't recognize. Some were masked. Some, he felt sure, only pretended to wear masks. Flowers arranged like faces, winking at him. Antennae and antlers. Every member of the Seelie Court gathered above them, watching, waiting, while the setting sun bathed the room in red light.

Ozma Tip slumped in the throne, barely conscious, dressed in a gown and robes of spun emeralds. Guards stood on either side of her, their swords drawn, eyes glassy. They didn't move but their purpose was clear. Nick spotted several marksmen in the balcony as well, crossbows at the ready, still as statues. How many of the guards were under Glinda's spell, compelled to act in ways they might not ordinarily? He grieved for the guards he and Lion killed. Those men might not've had a choice.

Glinda's majordomo, a tall and especially broad-shouldered Winkie Elite, stood in front of the throne dais. The man's cold, clear eyes registered every guest who wandered too close. He raised his spear slightly every time, making sure everyone got the message. Some mortals willingly served the fae, no matter how evil things turned.

The Emerald City townspeople mingled on the marble floor with Munchkins, Gillikins, Quadlings, Winkies. Everyone in their finest outfits, proudly displaying the traditional styles and colors of their home countries. All here to praise Queen Ozma, give thanks to the Seelie Court for a prosperous year, and party all night while the fae upstairs held their own celebrations for different reasons. The fae were more subdued than they'd been all week. No drunken carousing, no orgies out in the open. They glided among each other, talking in hushed voices, smiling down. Their tension was like an oppressive storm gathering overhead.

Nick leaned toward the throne. "Your Highness?" he asked, careful to keep his tone formal and light. "How are you feeling?"

Tip coughed. Her hand rested over the spot where she'd been wounded. "Nick, get me down there. Show me where the gate is."

The glassy-eyed guards gave no sign they heard. Lion's ears twitched. The brushing-out he'd received didn't quite hide the red scars all over his body where the netting had cut him, the poultice-wrapped wound on his back from a guard's halberd.

"Your Highness, quite a party, don't you think?" Nick asked, noting the Winkie guard's stare upon him. Nick smiled at the soldier. "How wonderful to see people here from all corners of the Empire."

"Nick, can you kill him?" Tip whispered.

Nick paused, smile frozen.

Lion muttered low, "I can."

"I don't see that pink bitch anywhere," Tip said.

The Wogglebug approached the throne, stopping just shy of the scowling soldier. He made a low bow. "Your Majesty. I trust your illness has improved somewhat?"

Tip grunted. "Sure."

"How delightful to see so many high-ranking witches of the Seelie Court with us tonight," remarked the Wogglebug, nodding at the grand stairs. Glinda stood halfway up them, in private conference with Mombi and Locasta. Langwidere hovered a step away as well. Hooray, the gang was all here. "It is an honor indeed to tread the same floors as they."

"Lovely," Nick said, his smile strained.

The Wogglebug straightened, pain crossing his face. He was dressed in a silk waistcoat, tailcoat, and trousers, with waxed antennae. His movements all evening were careful and deliberate. Clearly if a fight broke out, he'd be in no condition to participate. "I wonder if perhaps Her Majesty would grace us with a song?"

Tip tried to sit more upright. Her face was white as chalk, eyes bright emerald, like a living, jeweled statue. "I wouldn't dream of entertaining only a few of the court, Professor. We must be sure everyone can enjoy it."

The Wogglebug nodded. "Perhaps at some point the festivities may change venue. As you say, Your Highness, we must be sure not to leave anyone out."

How in blazes they were going to get to the tunnels and unleash any spells upon the massed Unseelie monsters, Nick had no idea.

Glinda clapped her hands, and the musicians ceased playing. Conversation hushed. The Good Witch of the South, garbed all in red with sparkling rubies in her tiara, floated down the stairs. "Good evening all! Dear friends, gathered guests, and of course, Your Most Benevolent Majesty," she trilled, "it is the very cusp of Winter's Eve, on a night like no other for centuries. I propose a toast!"

Around the hall, servants flowed through the crowd bearing trays of wine goblets. Were they poisoned? The courtiers upstairs were also being served. No way of knowing if it was all from the same casks. Nick didn't eat or drink anymore, so the servers didn't offer him any, but they handed a glass to the Wogglebug and set a dish in front of the Lion. Ozma Tip accepted a goblet, but set it upon the wide arm of the throne.

Glinda lifted her glass high. The witches beside her did the same, eyes gleaming in the amber glow of the magic lamps around the hall. "To the true ruler of the Seelie Court!"

Murmurs around the room echoed her. Hundreds of glasses upended over thirsty mouths. The Wogglebug mimed a sip and then held onto his glass. Mombi chugged her entire gobletful and smacked her lips. Glinda drank, then set her goblet upon a servant's tray. In the balcony, the fae drank theirs. Lion sniffed his dish but didn't touch it.

"And now, why don't we start off this party with a game?" Glinda suggested. She elbowed Locasta.

"How marvelous," the rust-haired witch growled. Glinda shot a glare at her, and Locasta pulled a face but then raised her voice. "Yes, how marvelous. I love a good party game."

As if on cue, Langwidere chimed in. "I want to play Find the Rabbit!"

A traditional children's game. A group would run and hide, as rabbits do, and one child would play the hunter and try to find them all.

Mombi chuckled. "Why don't we make it interesting? Let's have Her Highness be the hunter, and all of us can be the rabbits. And the last person to be found gets a prize from the Royal Treasury!"

Whispers spread through the crowd of commoners. Upstairs, the fae giggled. What in all rust and storms were the witches playing at?

Glinda swept across the hall, people shuffling out of her way. She curtsied before Ozma Tip, a smile widening her face. "What do you say, Your Majesty?" Before Tip could even reply, Glinda whirled and threw her arms in the air. "She loves it! Huzzah for our wonderful Queen!"

The crowd erupted in cheers. Several of them beckoned to the servants for more wine, all smiling, anticipating the game and the prize. "All of you, hide only in the Palace, to make things fair for our fair Ozma." She tittered. "Ready? Rabbits, rabbits, run for your holes!" She gestured at the lamps.

The hall plunged into darkness. Squeals, laughter, and then the commotion of people scrambling to go find a hiding place in the dark filled the air.

Now or never.

Nick charged the Winkie soldier. The instant he clashed against the soldier's spear, he heard the *thwip* and *thunk* of crossbow bolts. Oh heavens no! "Tip!" he shouted over the din, but then the soldier grunted and shoved him back. Nick's axe was gone, but he still remembered how to throw a punch. As the soldier stabbed at Nick, Nick sidestepped and landed a metal fist on the man's jaw, sending him sprawling. More crossbow sounds and the clang of swords against stone from the throne. Faint light shone through the stained glass ceiling from lamps on the Palace grounds.

"I got her," Lion growled. "Finish that bastard and let's go!"

The soldier shook his head roughly, reaching for his dropped spear. Nick stepped on it and punched the man again. This time the soldier stayed down, knocked cold. Nick's knuckles were dented from the metal chinstrap of the soldier's helmet. He bent them more or less into shape. "Professor?"

The Wogglebug emerged from behind a tapestry in an alcove. "They're still shooting!" He ducked back when a bolt bounced off the marble floor a foot from him.

The enspelled palace guards kept loading their crossbows and shooting at the empty throne, at the spots where Nick and Lion had been. One of them ran out of ammunition but kept pulling back and triggering his crossbow, heedless. All of the fae upstairs had vanished, along with the witches. "They're going to the tunnels! Tip, we have to go after them."

Lion padded silently from behind the dais, bearing Tip on his back. She clung to his mane, her eyes wide and bright. "Be careful. Mombi may have set traps in case we follow."

Good point. "Professor? Are you coming?" Nick called, then jogged a few steps to the right before one of the guards shot at the spot where his voice had been.

"Get out of here, I'll take care of the guards and catch up if I'm able," the Wogglebug called back.

"Are you sure?"

"Quite sure. I was reminded recently of a rather gloomy little ditty about Death, and I believe these boys deserve a nice rest."

Ah. "Take care." Nick ran for the exit. Lion's gait was awkward, undoubtedly pained at every step, but he loped ahead. As they traversed the corridor leading from the throne room to the main palace doors, Nick heard the Wogglebug begin singing in a lovely baritone. He clamped his hands over his ears and ran. Lion and Tip were far enough ahead they kept going, unaffected.

As he passed one of the reception parlors, someone knocked over a vase inside. People hiding, still convinced this was all a game. Plenty of sofas and furniture in that parlor. Plenty of antique bric-a-brac they'd probably stumble over, old armor and—

He skidded to a halt.

And an impressive sword over the mantel, if he recalled right. The sword of the legendary General Fyter of Oz, a hero of the war against Ev long ago. Nick kicked the door fully open, sending a Munchkin squealing and scurrying.

"Hey! Don't scare us like that! This room is full, go find your own place to hide, tin man!"

Nick wrenched the old sword with its elaborate hilt and grip from over the fireplace, testing its weight in his hand. Not as balanced as his axe, but a quick slash against a sofa cushion confirmed the blade was sharp. "I don't hide," he said, striding back out of the room.

Lion waited in the shadows of the courtyard. "Where'd you go?"

Nick brandished the sword. "Needed this."

"Good idea." Lion panted, whiskers bristling. "No sign of any of 'em."

"The tunnels," Tip said. "They must've gone through the secret tunnels from the palace."

"Can we beat them to the gateway?" Lion asked.

"Maybe. Hurry!"

No guards stood at the gate. They ran along the brick street toward the University. As they neared the stone wall marking the grounds of the former temple, a sparkling mist arose. Tiny lights crackled within it, dazzling, dizzying, like miniature bolts of lightning. Nick slowed, hesitant. He'd seen Locasta throw a jolt of stormfire at a servant who'd displeased her once and never had the chance to provoke her again.

"Illusion," Tip announced, waving her scepter at it.

Something heavy shook the ground, made Nick's joints rattle. A figure loomed from the mist, ticking. Gears whirred as the round ball of a head rotated to fix them in its glowing eyes.

"That's not..." Nick gasped.

Tip grinned at the massive brass figure as it placed one foot forward, angling its body to block their way. "TikTok! I wondered where you went."

Its voice grated like metal scraping metal. "You. May. Not. Pass. It. Is. Dan-ger-ous."

"I know," Tip said. "We'll be fine. Move, TikTok."

When Lion started forward again, the mechanical man bent lower and put its hands in the way, barring the entrance to the University. "It. Is. Dan-ger-ous. Your. Ma-jes-ty. Glin-da. Set. Me. To. Keep. You. Safe."

"Nome bollocks," Tip swore. "TikTok, I don't want to hurt you. I order you to step aside."

The thing's head swiveled side to side. "It. Is. Dan-ger-ous."

"I don't know if any songs will make him move," Tip said. "I could try the rainy swamp one, maybe."

Light glimmered off the brass man's round body. The moon, creeping up over the trees, huge and golden. "We don't have time!" Nick shouted. He raised his sword, trying to judge where best to strike on the nearly impervious mechanical servant.

A blur of orange slammed into TikTok's left leg from the side. Knocked off balance, the mechanical man swung its other leg wide to compensate, too late. The huge round body tilted, thudded onto the bricks, and began to roll. It grabbed at a shop awning, ripping it away as it picked up speed. The crash and clang as it bounced downhill toward the city gate echoed loudly between the buildings.

Problem solved.

Nick turned to see Tiger lying in the sparse grass inside the gateway to the University grounds, panting. Jellia Jamb ran over. "I told you this was a stupid idea!" she cried, falling to her knees beside the beast. Fresh blood flowed from his flank.

Lion went to him at once. "Tiger, you're alive!"

Tiger nodded at the maid spreading a bandage on his wounds. "Thanks to her. I always thought she just brought food. Turns out she knows other stuff too. Neat, huh?"

"You're an idiot," Lion snarled, cuffing Tiger's nose, but there was no force behind the gesture. They nuzzled each other.

"Thank you," Nick told the Tiger. He looked at Jellia. "And thank you. Is he going to recover?"

"If he goes back to bed where I had him and stops trying to be a hero," she muttered.

"We need to move fast," Nick pointed out. "The moon's coming up."

Lion nodded at the University door. "Lead the way."

"One of these songs has to work," Nick muttered, raising the sword once more and heading for the old stone doorway.

"Wait!" Jellia offered a handful of bandage cloths to Nick. "You might need these." When he stared at her, uncomprehending, she thrust them at him again. "You're going to sing spells? Like Scarecrow's songs? You'll need to stuff your ears then."

Nick nodded, handing some of the cloths to Tip. She tucked them inside her bodice. Nick shoved a few in his waistcoat pocket. "Thank you. Jellia, get out of here, both of you, fast as you can."

"Don't have to tell me twice," she agreed, shoving the Tiger. "Come on, get up, just a little farther, Stripey."

As Nick strode into the old temple, he heard the big cat rumble a laugh. "Stripey! 'Cause I have stripes. I get it."

Lion snorted. "I love that big dope."

Nick hurried to the cellar stairs. No sound save for the quiet drip of water somewhere. "Any magical traps?" he asked.

Tip leaned forward unsteadily, left hand gripping Lion's mane tight, and waved her scepter in her right. She could barely hold onto it. "Clear. I think."

Nick picked up a lantern and shook it. A little oil left. He found a match and lit it, closed the lantern hood to a sliver, and they started down. "Once we see them all, you sing," Nick whispered over his shoulder. "The one you found about a wind. We'll plug our ears and you sing as loud as you can."

"Yeah, I know how magic works, Nick."

He hoped she recalled it well after only a minute or two reading it. Part fae she might be, but she didn't have Scarecrow's perfect memory. If even one word was wrong, the spell might not work. At least, that was his friend's theory. Nick wished again he'd listened more closely to Scarecrow's overly enthusiastic proclamations about the Outside World and magic and Old Ozian. All of it seemed academic at the time, not something which could mean life or death.

Nick descended the slimy, treacherous stairs to the lower crypt level. Laughter and music echoed eerily in the circular hub where four rough-hewn halls met. He glanced back at Tip, raising the lantern to see her face. Shadows ringed her eyes. Her emerald crown hung askew, tangled in her hair. She looked frail as a street urchin. Blast and rust, she shouldn't even be here. If she died, Oz would be plunged into chaos. Again.

He wanted to tell her how sorry he was. How willing he was to take the brunt of any killing blow, any dark magic cast at her.

She blinked at him. "What are we stopping for?"

"They beat us to it," he said. "They're all down there celebrating. And they have an army of Elemental Unseelies with them, to clear their way. I'm hoping it'll just be the courtiers at the back when we charge in, but they might have posted a few of those horrible things as guards."

"Everyone in that room is dead," Tip whispered, clutching Lion's hair tighter. "They just don't know it yet."

Nick had no reply.

They found the old stone stairs to the caverns. A babble of noise, laughter, shouts carried up. If they were very lucky, the witches down there were too focused on opening their gateway to notice any party crashers. The moon must be above the trees by now. With all the cheer he could hear below, the witches' spell must be starting. Two moons rising as one, here and in Dorothy's world.

Dorothy. Impetuous, demanding, bold, and dead an age ago. Which meant, Nick realized with a shudder, Scarecrow was probably dead as well. No heart's desire found. If he hadn't managed to destroy the anchor in the other world, the fae would pierce the veil and go through. No one left to stop them, unless Tip really could sing them all to the endlessly burning furnaces of the Nomes.

His heart thumped slowly, chilled. "Get ready," he said, stuffing bandage cloths in his ears. He helped Lion do the same. Tip refused.

"Down we go, then." Nick took a deep breath, steeled his spine. He started down the last set of narrow, twisting stairs.

They opened into the same cavern he'd found before. This time, a crowd of fae nobles filled the room, passing bottles of wine around, laughing, falling all over each other. Rock trolls alternating with fire-walkers ringed the walls, motionless. The fae nearest the stairs noticed Nick. They pointed, laughed, said things he couldn't hear.

He raised the sword high. "Get away!" Too many of them between here and the passageway to the room where he'd seen Mombi creating the gateway. He didn't see her or the other more powerful witches, but hacking his way across the room would certainly get Glinda's attention fast.

Suddenly the fae nearest Nick stumbled. Nick's footing wobbled. The cave rock churned. Rain burst from overhead, slamming down cold and fierce. The fae shouted, jostled each other, fine velvet slippers caught in the muck underfoot.

Tip clung to Lion, singing.

Lion nudged Nick from behind, pushing him forward. Nick staggered through the crowd, the harsh rain soaking into his joints. He'd be lucky to see daylight again. Strength alone kept him moving, the swamp sucking at his every step. He slapped the flat of his blade against a doe-headed duchess in his way. Brought the butt of the sword down hard on the skull of a duke who drew a rapier and lunged at him. Nick got Lion's attention, jerked his head toward the cave wall. Lion slid against it, protected on that side, so Nick could stride alongside him and Tip, deflecting angry noblemen with his sword and his metal body. They struggled toward the passageway.

Tip kept singing. Nick couldn't make out the words, only saw her mouth open wide, her eyes shut, her scepter glowing green.

Thunder rumbled the room, vibrations coming up through the ground.

Oh no. If this magical storm included lightning, Nick was sure to be struck senseless. He saw no flashes yet, just the curtain of rain and fae screaming, staggering and slipping, continually getting in the way. The rumbling continued, growing worse as he neared the passageway entrance. Where Locasta appeared, surprise on her wrinkled face.

Nick didn't have time to hesitate. He swung the blade as she brought both hands up to cast a spell, bracing his shoulders for the impact. The witch's mouth turned into a wide circle as the sword sliced through both her wrists. Her hands flew into the wall and dropped to the muddy floor. Blood spurted on the rough ceiling.

The witch waved her arms wildly, shrieking. Nick flinched, blood spattering his face. He shoved her aside, forging into the passageway, but someone grabbed his waist. He whirled, sword ready.

It was Tip. She shouted something, pointing back at Lion. Several courtiers crowded the entrance, waving swords, and behind them a minor witch gestured, her mouth moving, casting a spell. The rain stopped. Lion faced the crowd, snarling. He swiped at the nearest fae with claws outstretched.

Tip pushed at Nick's waist. Nodding, a dull roar growing in his ears and his feet unsteady on the still-shaking ground, he strode forward, ready to cut down anything in their way. Tip's hand clung to the hook on his hip where his axe normally rested. He pulled her along, hastening around the stalactites in the corridor.

The room where he'd seen Mombi before was now lined with Unseelies. Slowly they advanced, all walking toward the gateway painted on the wall. The glyphs traced in blood around it burned red. A shimmering haze filled the gateway. Each rock troll and fire-walker that stepped inside vanished. Glinda and Mombi stood in the center of the room, arms raised, chanting. Feeling Tip let go, Nick lowered his shoulder and charged, bringing the sword up.

Suddenly the witches disappeared.

Nick staggered, barely stopping himself from falling into the gateway. Heavy stone arms crushed him in a hug from behind. He fought, arms pinned. Mombi appeared behind Tip, grabbing her scepter away, slapping her face so hard the young Queen reeled into a wall. The spindly hands of a fire-walker closed over her shoulders. Tip cried out, struggling, and a branchlike arm wedged into her mouth, muffling her, dragging her against its wooden body. Its burning head tilted as if it was curious what sort of creature it had trapped.

Glinda was suddenly right in front of Nick, grinning. Black eyes and sharp teeth, red hair thrashing with a life of its own. She plucked the cloth from his ears. "Since you insist on seeing us off, I will allow you to watch until the last of us goes through, and then this delicate stone flower will crush you into scrap metal and leave you to rust."

"What about her?" Nick jerked his head toward Tip.

Glinda sighed. "Terrible about the Queen. She ought to have known better than to come down here on Winter's Eve to worship the old gods. Sometimes the sacrifice they demand is rather dear." She giggled.

"He cut Locasta's hands off," Mombi said. Locasta staggered in, her wrists wrapped in scarves, eyes blazing. When she saw Nick she screamed with renewed fury. Mombi clucked. "There, there, he'll be dead soon, and we'll find you some new hands. I'm sure Langwidere can help."

"Get back in place. Send the army through," Glinda ordered.

"I want to go now," Locasta hissed. "I want to go *now*! You've sent enough of these monsters already. Why should they enjoy the Outside World before we do?"

"We've been over this," Glinda snapped, frowning.

"No! It's time! I want to go!" Locasta howled, her voice rising in pitch until Nick winced. "The full moon is up! The veil is torn! I am sick of this tiny world and its horrible, stupid creatures! I want to go home! Now, Glinda! The time is now!"

"Very well," Glinda sighed, "Very well, Locasta."

"Do you think that's wise?" Mombi asked.

Glinda's head lifted, her eyes reflecting the fiery red of the arcane symbols surrounding the gateway. "The anchors hold. Several of the Elementals have gone through without any problem. I can hear the screams of the mortals." Her teeth glittered. "I don't see why not."

Nick strained against the rocky arms holding him fast. Unable to move, he did the only other thing he could think of. Forcing strength into his voice, he sang a mournful tune, the voice of Death trying to persuade a prisoner to give up all hope.

Tip's eyes rolled up and she went limp.

Glinda stared at him a moment, then began laughing. Nick faltered, recovered the words, kept going as loud as he could. Mombi looked from him to Glinda, a smile spreading her chapped lips. Nick sang of despair and hope. The Unseelie holding Tip held her out at arms' length, seemingly puzzled by her sudden limpness. It dropped her to the floor like a sack of potatoes, turning toward the portal once more.

Glinda's laughter rang painfully in Nick's ears. She cupped his cheek in one cold hand, grinning at him. "You silly boy. That's a song for healing pain." She caressed his face. He shuddered, stammering to a stop. "Witches know no pain, you ignorant tin can. Only fury and power."

Locasta's wrist stumps soaked her clothing with blood, yet she wasn't affected by the song at all. Shouts came from the passageway. A fae duke, his finery ripped and hair undone from its ribbons, stumbled into the room. "Whatever you did, the Lion's no trouble anymore. Keeled right over," he announced. His eyes darted to the gateway. "Is it time yet?"

Glinda laughed. "Yes. Yes! It is time." She smoothed down her hair, her robes rippling around her. "Let us reclaim our rightful home. It is time!" She gestured toward the passageway to the larger cavern. "Langwidere, darling, attend."

The summoned witch came in, a frown wrinkling her delicate brows. The head she'd chosen to wear tonight sported blond hair done up in curly ringlets and startling violet eyes. Langwidere collected heads and traded them at whim. Nick was willing to bet there was a servant lugging suitcases full of them somewhere in the next room. She cast a curious glance at Nick, then demanded of Glinda, "Are we going now?"

Glinda smiled. "*We* are. You need to remain here for now. Once the rest of the Seelie Court has gone through, send the other Elementals and then you may join us."

Langwidere stomped a foot, sending a ringing tone through the room. "Why can't I go now?"

"Because someone has to command the Unseelies." Glinda waved dismissively at the rock troll holding Nick. "They're docile enough under my spell, even you should be able to handle them."

"But—"

"Stay, Langwidere." Glinda's smile was cold. The lesser witch shut up.

Mombi shoved the royal scepter at Langwidere. "You might need this. Just remember—you don't get to keep it."

Langwidere pouted, crossing her arms.

Without a second glance at Nick, Glinda glided forward and vanished into the portal. Mombi hurried after her, Locasta striding past with furious purpose. The haze swallowed them up, leaving the Unseelie Court standing in place dumbly.

The fae duke crowed. "Yes! Off we go! Everyone, hurry!"

A rushing crowd of faerie nobles pushed into the room, jostling the Unseelies, the unconscious Tip buried beneath a throng of gathered skirts and velvet slippers. Nick struggled in the arms of the rock troll. "Tip! Tip, wake up!"

The fae shoved each other, eager to go through the portal before their neighbors, a noisy, perfumed mob. None of them gave him a passing glance. Witches and dukes, earls and ladies, all vanished one after another through the red-lined gate on the wall. All headed for the Outside World, to wreak havoc upon a place with no magic. No defenses. A world with no more Dorothy and no more Scarecrow.

Nick began to cry. No point in holding the tears back anymore.

34

"**S**carecrow!" Theo screamed. She slapped the rocky head shoving its way out of his chest. Her hand stung. The monster was oblivious.

Arturo grabbed her around the waist, hauling her back. "Theo, no!"

"Don't you fucking 'no' me! It's killing him!"

Arturo held her firmly. Adam grabbed Jeremy's arm, dragging the cowering boy away from the monster.

"Let go of me!" Theo shouted, struggling, but her brawny friend wouldn't let go, slowly backing up. The rock-thing, looking like Ben Grimm's cousin on meth, reached to the floor, pulled one sturdy leg out, then the other. As it stood with a grinding sound, Theo called to her attack stuffed animal. "Vernor! *Sicc'em!*"

Her calico hippo stuffie bounced absurdly over the yellow bricks. The monster's stone head tilted to observe the roaring hippo. Vernor chomped. *Crack!* The stone thing lifted its foot. Vernor held on, growling. The monster shook its foot but the hippo wouldn't be dislodged.

Oh Goddess, please, let this work!

The two security guys stood gaping up at the eight-foot thing. Then one of them charged at it, brandishing a taser. "Enough of this crap!"

The darts bounced off the rocky chest of the monster. Its head turned, followed by a swing of its heavy arm. The guard didn't dodge in time. The monster simply backhanded the guy as though his easily two hundred and fifty pounds weighed nothing. Hitting his head on the metal railing, the security guard crumpled to the floor.

His partner fled.

"Yes!"

Theo's head jerked up. Mark stood on one of the catwalks, arms raised, a manic grin on his bloody face. "Yes! This is it! The New Order of magic begins now!"

"Mark, you asshole!" Theo screamed, "You stupid, selfish asshole! This is all your fault!"

"The faery queen will make me her consort for this," he called down. "Not seeing a downside here, sorry."

Gwyn's eyes were wide. "He really is worse than I thought."

"Gwyn, help me!" Theo yelled, renewing her struggle. She freed one arm, the injured one, as Arturo didn't have that one held as tightly. Thank the Goddess for friends who didn't want to hurt her. She flung her hand toward the stone monster. "Babies! Take that thing down!"

Her dolls swarmed the monster, jabbing at the dull green lights in its eyesockets, buzzing in its face, crawling up its body. The stone thing's movements were slow, and the flying dolls easily dodged its punches. The ones trying to climb up it weren't as lucky. Several were brushed loose and crunched underfoot. "No," Theo sobbed, "No!"

Suddenly the monster stopped. A purplish ink spread between its rocks, shooting up from its foot. When it reached the head, its eyesockets turned purple, then gray, then the entire thing fell apart. Rocks smashed across the floor. Arturo stumbled back and Theo wrenched free of his arms.

Whimpering, Vernor scrambled out of the pile and came to Theo. She crouched to pet him. "Good boy. Very good boy, Vernor!" The little hippo's ears wiggled happily, mouth falling open to reveal most of the Wheeler teeth she'd fastened in him had broken off. They were buried under the lifeless rocks somewhere. At least the poison worked.

The surviving faerie dolls returned to her. Quite a few less than before, but the job was done. "When I'm done here, I am going to kick your balls up your throat!" she yelled at Mark. He scowled down at her.

Scarecrow groaned. Theo rushed to him, touching his cheek. "Oh Goddess, hold on, we'll get you down! Hold on!"

"More," he whispered, shaking his head weakly. "More...coming..."

Theo squeaked, startling back, as a ball of flames thrust through Scarecrow's stomach. He cried out, unable to move. Straw crackled and sizzled, then a wave of cold dew formed where the flame-headed creature's hands touched, putting out the licking flames on Scarecrow's clothing. The flame-headed thing braced spindly fingers on either side of the hole in Scarecrow's body and pulled itself out. Its body was a crooked tree, long-limbed and creaking, its head impossibly burning without consuming the rest of it.

"Bite it!" Theo shouted, flinging the hippo at the monster.

The flame-headed walking bush caught the stuffie in both branch-fingered hands and ripped it in two.

Theo gasped. Her dolls attacked the fiery monster, but it was much faster than the stone thing, whirling, swatting, catching dolls in its long claws and dropping them into the flames of its head. She flinched as one burned to ash when it hit the roiling ball of fire.

The security guard moaned. Arturo ran to him, checked his head. "Lay still, buddy, you're gonna be okay. Where's the fire extinguisher?" The man mumbled, and Arturo gave him a gentle shake. "Hey. Focus. Place is gonna be on fire any second. Where's the extinguisher?"

The guard looked around dazedly, pointed at one of the pipe organs. Adam leaped a railing, found the extinguisher tucked behind the display, and turned it on the flame-headed creature. It shrieked, clawing at its face. Adam advanced, streaming foam right into the thing's coal-black eyes. Suffocated, the fire flicked out, and the headless thing clattered to the floor. It didn't move again.

Another rock thing was already thrusting its way through the narrow portal in Scarecrow's midsection. He stirred with a low moan. Oh Goddess, he could feel pain now, and this must be agony. Theo snatched up poor Vernor's front end and slapped his open mouth against the rock monster's face. It grunted, pushing the lifeless hippo away, bringing its legs out and standing upright. Ignoring Theo, it took a few steps out of the area before the great pipe organ, stone head swiveling slowly to take in its surroundings. Massive hands clenched into fists as it strode toward Gwyn. She scrambled away, putting a railing between herself and the monster. It lifted a leg to kick, then stumbled. With a groan, the monster dropped to its knees. A small lamp overhead jolted loose and crashed over its shoulders. It brought one hand to its face, seeming disoriented. The poison was working! Might not've been enough left to kill it, though.

Adam *fooshed* the extinguisher at another fire monster clawing its way out of Scarecrow, killing it stuck halfway through. Scarecrow's head drooped, unconscious, with this crazy awful thing sticking out of him. Adam helped her haul the dead monster out. She tried to push straw back in. A shimmering curtain of mist swirled inside Scarecrow's body. Unwilling to touch it, Theo stroked his cheek.

"Scarecrow? Wake up, please, say something," she pleaded.

"Theo, get away from him, restuffing him won't close the gateway," Gwyn said, picking her way past the stone creature. It ignored her, clutching its head.

"Then tell me what will!"

"I don't know," Gwyn admitted. "This is way past anything I've seen before."

"It is only beginning!" crowed Mark. "Just wait until the faery queen arrives!"

"Shut the fuck up Mark!" everyone chorused.

Scarecrow's eyelids fluttered. "Theo?"

"I'm here. I'm right here. Let's get you down and close this awful thing."

He grimaced. "Not...sure...you can." His voice was faint. "Stand...back, please."

"Why?" A chill shot through her heart.

His deep blue eyes opened, gazing into hers. "I'm going to end this. Don't want you hurt."

"No, stop, what do you mean?"

He chuckled softly. "Time to fight fire with fire. I love you, Theo. Goodbye."

"Don't you dare!" Theo shrieked, trying to climb the pole, trying to pull him down, but he lifted his head and began to sing.

• • • •

ONE OF THE SONGS HE'D memorized, he'd never dared to sing once he knew the old Ozian words held powerful magic. Scarecrow brought those frightening words to mind and began singing them in the ancient language. He knew it was going to hurt, but only for a few seconds. If he was the gateway's mouth as well as its anchor to this world, destroying both was the only way to keep his love safe.

He sang of the need-fire, the cleansing flame, a bonfire raised at harvest's end to thank the gods and bless the fields. Flames which demanded sacrifice. The modern Ozians tossed inanimate scarecrows into bonfires as a remnant of the original ceremony. This song was from the old times, the real thing.

The fire started in his chest, searing up his shoulders, flames licking into his straw.

Blight and mold, this hurt so much worse than he'd feared!

His voice faltered. No. No, this must be done! Smoke trickled into his nostrils, stung his eyes. He drew whatever energy he could from sheer will and sang louder. Theo screamed, but he shut his eyes, forced himself to keep going, the flames greedily eating through his chest.

He hoped he did have a soul, and that it would remember her.

• • • •

"I HATE THEM," LANGWIDERE muttered, glaring as the last of the courtiers stepped into the shimmering gateway with a cheery wave.

"Nobody cares." Nick kept struggling. The rock troll stood impassively, its arms in an unbreakable grip around him.

"Maybe I'll take your head with me," Langwidere mused, one long finger on her pursed lips, studying him. "Of course I'd never wear it, but it might make an amusing ash-tray. After I hollow it out." She came closer. "Or is there anything even in there? Oh, right, you're not the one with the brains. Silly me."

"Pretty sure the only empty-headed person here is you."

"You dare mock me?" She thrust her face up to his, nostrils flaring, blond curls jiggling, shaking the emerald-tipped scepter at him. "I have heads smarter than your whole body, you worthless chunk of metal!"

"That doesn't even make sense," he argued. Maybe if he could keep her talking, keep her distracted, the Prisoner's Lament spell would wear off and Tip or Lion could free him. He spotted the sword on the ground, just out of reach.

A lump of emerald-green cloth stirred near the feet of a rock troll. Tip! She was alive! He'd feared the fae had trampled the unconscious Queen in their mad rush.

The movement caught Langwidere's attention too. She turned in a swirl of lace and gauze. "Well! Look who's still with us. Now there's a pretty head, if it hasn't been stomped on too badly. Oh yes. I think I'll take her head. No one will make me wait at the end of the line again, wearing that sweet face!" She set down the scepter, confirming Nick's suspicion she didn't know how to use it, but then magic sparked between her hands.

"Tip!" Nick shouted, kicking, held fast.

A thin arm darted from behind the witch, grabbing the scepter. Ozma Tip gripped it tightly in both hands and swung at the back of Langwidere's head as though Tip was still a boy and this was the Oz-ball hit that would make his reputation on the playground. *Thock* to the back of her pretty skull.

Langwidere fell face-first in the dirt. Breathless, trembling, Tip stood there in only her under-things, staring with bright, haunted eyes at Nick.

He nodded, impressed. "Good hit."

"Thanks." Her thin arms dropped. "Told you I picked up a few tricks from living with Mombi all those years."

"All the fae went through."

"I saw. Been hiding behind a stack of rocks since that thing dropped me, with my ears stuffed. Good thing the witches didn't bother to check my illusion. Too eager to get where they're going." She indicated one of the silent trolls. "And good thing these're all enspelled to just stand around 'til someone tells them to move." She waved the scepter at the one holding Nick, speaking a single word of Old Ozian. It released him. Nick hugged his Queen gently. When she hugged back, he felt her trembling. All this took so much out of her.

"How do we stop them? They already left," he pointed out. The gateway shimmered, the red runes glowing.

Tip frowned, reaching one hand toward it. "It's not completely lined up yet with the Outside World. There's a delay. Minutes, seconds maybe, but still a delay 'til both worlds are completely in harmony. I can feel it."

"So what do we do?"

"Destroy the gate!"

"That leaves all the witches and the Unseelies who already went through in the Outside World," Nick protested. "They don't know anything about magic over there! The witches will run amok!"

His words echoed faintly in the gateway. *Amok...amok...amok...* Shivering, he backed away from it.

"I'm gonna try the wind song." Tip took a stance in front of the gateway. "Maybe it'll rip 'em apart while they're still in between the worlds."

"Or blow them all straight to the Outside World, which is where we *don't* want them," Nick argued.

"You got a better idea?" she snapped, glaring up at him.

"No!"

"Then we're doing this. Get ready in case it works the other way and they start coming back."

Nick stood just beside the gateway, sword raised to chop down anything poking its ugly head back through. This felt wrong, but Tip had a point. They had no idea how to shut down the gate, or if this song would even work the way they wanted it to. What if hundreds of fae and the Unseelies came rushing back here all at once? What if Nick himself was sucked in? He dug his metal feet into the dirt floor as much as he could.

Tip raised the scepter, her wounded arm trembling, and inhaled.

Nick cried out, "Wait!"

"Why?"

"I hear singing."

• • • •

THEO SNATCHED THE EXTINGUISHER from Adam, aiming it at Scarecrow. Foam splattered his chest, his shoulders, suffocated the flames.

Scarecrow sputtered at her. "No, what are you doing?"

"The fuck are *you* doing?" she retorted, tossing the canister aside and grabbing his tunic in both hands. "You are not the goddamned Hanged Man!"

He spat out foam. "Are you seriously going to make me ask for an interpreter right now?"

She wanted to laugh and cry all at once. "You are not doing this! We will find another way."

Gwyn gestured at the metal railings enclosing the space. "Wish these were iron, we could maybe pry one up and use it to block the portal. They look like aluminum though."

"Look around," Theo agreed. "Something in all this has to be cold iron!"

"Iron, yes" Scarecrow said slowly, "The protection song. Irene and the faery."

Gwyn frowned. "I don't know—"

"It could work," Theo argued. The hole in Scarecrow was ugly, a hazy glow framed by charred straw and blackened, burned clothing. Goddess, he must be in so much pain. She met his frown, her vision blurred with tears. "It has to work. Sing it. I'm not letting you go."

"Theo," he murmured.

"Sing for me. Please."

A nasty, leering voice boomed theatrically from overhead, setting Theo's teeth on edge. "Oh dear, was it too much to see him on fire? I'll be sure to let you watch him burn once the New Order is secure. You can't stop it."

"Fuck you, Mark." Theo took Scarecrow's free hand. She squeezed his fingers, encouraged by the faint pressure he returned. "You can do this. Sing so the fae can't come through."

His expression was full of worry, but he nodded. "Theo, promise me, if this doesn't work, you'll run." He grimaced again. "I can feel them coming. The fae. Glinda."

"I'm not—"

"Blight and crows, Theo, promise me!"

She pressed his hand to her cheek, kissed it. "Okay."

He nodded, raised his head and his voice, holding her hand.

"Come in, ye travelers, in from the cold
The wind is blowing out fierce and bold

I've iron and ale and I'll tell you a tale
Of a wicked fae queen and a maiden of old."

She sang with him, some of the words returning to her. She jumped when Arturo took her left hand. He began singing as well, stumbling over the words at first, then growing more confident.

"Irene had a cow and a sheep and a man,
The fae grabbed them all and off she ran.
Irene cursed the night, and wished a mean blight
On the crooked old faery who ruled all the land."

Adam's thin tenor joined them. He took Arturo's left hand and dragged Jeremy forward as well, though Mark's acolyte was clearly confused. Gwyn's left hand closed firmly over Theo's right, clasping both her fingers and Scarecrow's. She reached behind him and took Jeremy's hand, forming a circle with Scarecrow at the center. The witches sang, voices rising together, swaying.

"Away to dark fortress Irene had to go
She took only her salt and her iron hoe
To fetch back her man was her desperate plan
As she walked alone in the bitter snow.

"Now the queen was a crafty old fae, it is true
The chill in her hands would turn a man blue
Her gate was unlocked, all mortals she mocked
For killing her was a feat no mortal could do."

The haze inside Scarecrow rippled. He flinched, faltering. Theo gripped his hand tightly and sang louder, willing her love into him. Warmth kindled in her chest, spreading down her arms into her hands. He picked up the tune once more, regaining strength.

"Irene caught her sleeping and struck her a blow
Straight over the head with her iron hoe.

With husband she fled back to their homestead
And the queen chased them screaming of blood and woe.

"Now Irene knew well no fae could she kill,
She hoed swiftly round them and with it salt filled.
The queen struck in all might but to her great fright
The iron and salt her very blood chilled."

Shouts and cries sounded faintly from the glimmering surface of the portal. Staring straight into it, Theo saw figures moving, faces distorted. A red-haired woman with black eyes loomed suddenly, mouth opening to reveal needle-sharp teeth. A clawed hand reached for Theo, about to break through the portal.

The circle of witches glowed. The light grew brighter still, heat filling her breasts, her stomach, her core. Theo braced her entire body, focused her contempt on that face, willed all of her energy right at it. She shouted the last verse.

"So gather ye close by the fire, my dears,
Drink to Irene and forget all your fears.
That snowy cold howl is the old faery's yowl—
Let her scream all she likes, she won't get in here!"

The ring of light slammed into Scarecrow, a forcible wave shaking them all. Theo held tight, eyes squinted against the brightness. Screams echoed as if inside a tunnel, followed by a low howl building to a screech. Scarecrow cried out, back arching. Theo gripped his hand tightly, felt her boots skidding. "Keep hold!" she yelled.

The howl grew to a roar. The chandeliers shook. One crashed to the floor in a shower of sparks and glass. Jeremy screamed, letting go, cringing.

Loose straw whipped through the air, disappearing into the hole in Scarecrow's chest. Staring in, Theo saw figures flailing, screaming, whirling. A cyclone. A *fucking cyclone* inside the portal. Inside Scarecrow. And he was only straw.

• • • •

TIP LEANED TOWARD THE gateway, peering inside, scepter raised. Its green light penetrated the haze a short distance, but Nick could see nothing useful. For lack of any better support, he took hold of her brassiere strap to keep her from falling in. "Not so close!"

"I'm fine." Tip squinted, then suddenly straightened. "Dirty Nome arses! It's blocking them!"

"What is?"

"That song! It's blocking their way through!" Tip rubbed her eyes, bit her lip. "Won't stop Glinda long, but they're all held up. The whole ugly crowd of them."

"Scarecrow?" Nick asked, hope springing back to life in his heart. Its beat quickened.

"Yeah! And what sounds like a bunch of witches. Can't you feel the magic?" She spread one palm toward the gateway.

All Nick felt was relief. "He's alive! He must have his witch friend with him."

"There's more than two voices, and whoever it is, they know what they're doing." Tip braced her legs apart, eyes narrowing. "Now's our chance."

"What?"

She smiled grimly. "Gonna blow them all to the winds. They can't go forward. This'll keep 'em from coming back."

She began singing. Nick hastily pulled more of the cloth bandages from his waistcoat and stuffed his ears. A wind kicked up from Ozma Tip's raised hands. As her voice rose, ancient notes ringing from her mouth, a wave of circling air plunged from her hands into the gateway, sending wild ripples through the haze. He wrapped his arms around her waist, leaning backward, bracing his feet as everything in the room was tugged toward the gateway.

And then, despite the cloth in his ears, he heard the screams begin.

• • • •

"NO!" THEO YELLED, HER voice whipped away by the wind. Arturo held tighter to Adam as the force of it staggered them both.

The wind jerked Scarecrow off the pole, tearing his hand from his wrist. The zip ties binding his feet to the pole held. His body whipped back and forth. Straw scattered. Theo leaped forward, wrapped her arms around his midsection, fell hard on the floor still hugging him. His feet tore. His cry of pain ripped something in her chest. "No, no, stay with me, I got you!" she shouted. The wind howled inside the portal, sucking his straw in, a cyclone pulling everything away. Theo's arms and legs wrapped around him, trying to press his sides closed, but she felt herself drawn toward the sucking gateway. "No!"

Suddenly strong arms gripped her in a bear hug. Gwyn, eyes shut, on the floor with her, pressing her own body over Theo's. Arturo joined her, then Adam. All of them holding Scarecrow, keeping him from being sucked entirely in on himself. They had to close it, had to stop this, this would kill him!

If only she were a real witch! If only she knew real magic like Oz witches, not just stupid sewing tricks with stupid glowing magic—

Thread. Magic thread. Magic thread which she somehow wove from her fingertips.

"Be whole," she gasped, working her fingers back and forth as though she held a needle, finding the burnt edges of his burlap skin, drawing them together. Her fingertips glowed. Yes. Yes! "Be whole, be well, be healed, Scarecrow," she cried, unable to hear herself, but the thread formed between her fingers. She kept sewing. The burlap came together, stitches glowing. Squinting her eyes against the wind, she chanted the spell over and over, stitch after stitch from his belly up his chest. He groaned, but the wind lessened.

"Be whole, be well, be healed, Scarecrow," she begged, working her fingers fast as she could. The burned edges began fading to tan.

Arturo took up the chant with her. "Be whole, be well, be healed, Scarecrow." Then Gwyn, then Adam, all their voices added to the spell. Heat flooded her spine, spread through her veins, poured out her fingertips. The damage began undoing faster, burlap sweeping up the edges and covering the hole right behind her nimble hands as though it never existed. The swirling wind stuttered.

She kept at it, working the glowing thread back and forth with an invisible needle, their voices all as one. "Be whole, be well, be healed, Scarecrow!" Stitch after stitch, the wind lessened. As she tied off the final knot, the breeze died completely. The eerie mist vanished.

The remaining rock monster toppled over and didn't move again.

Theo lay on the floor, her body curled around Scarecrow, crying in relief.

He stirred, eyes opening. "Theo?"

With a choked laugh, she stroked his cheek. "Hey."

He frowned mildly. "Straw. Didn't we discuss this already?"

Arturo chortled, shaking his head. "Okay, that's it, I'm done." He let go of them, standing with a groan. Adam helped Gwyn up, then held out a hand to Theo.

She shook her head. "I'm good right here." She lay still, exhausted, gazing into Scarecrow's eyes. Dark blue paint, yet full of life and wit.

He pressed his nose against hers. Such a great nose. His voice was gentle. "Theo, you're wonderful."

"Not too shabby yourself." She caught his lips in a kiss. His cheek and nose brushed hers, scratchy-soft, warm, comforting. She hugged him tight. He grunted in pain. "Oh! Sorry."

"I'm not." He smiled. Tears trickled down his face. She wiped his cheek with a finger. He bent his head to kiss her hand.

The surroundings sank in. Fire alarm clanging still. Very hard bricks under her. Arm hurt like a bitch from that asshole with the hammer. The portal was closed. Scarecrow was still alive. His gaze was full of wonder, studying her face.

"So. Um," she began.

"Yes, my dear?" That mild, adorable accent. He pronounced it *deah*. Warmth shot down her belly. Oh, he could call her that forever.

"The gateway is absolutely closed?"

He considered it, frowning, then nodded. "It's closed. Gone. Can't feel it at all now." He chuckled softly. "You *are* that kind of witch."

She snickered, but this was serious. "Okay. Good. But now you're stuck here. I don't know any way to get you back to Oz. Are you okay with that?"

"May I stay with you?"

"Hell yes!"

"Thank you." He smiled. "May I have my hand back now? I want to hold you, and this would be too scratchy." He held up one wrist, straw sticking out. Guess her spell couldn't regrow appendages. She'd been more focused on closing the portal.

Theo sat up, blood rushing to her feet dizzily. "Oh shit, I forgot. Does it hurt?"

He nodded, slowly sitting up, brows knit. "Very much so."

"Guys, get his hand please?" Theo asked. The zip ties held the stuffed glove to the crossbeam. His boots were still fastened to the pole as well. She never wanted to see a traditional scarecrow on a pole ever again. "And his feet?" They'd ripped off at the ankles, boots and all. Arturo cut free the glove, then the boots.

Gwyn shook her head, hands on her hips, and laughed. "Well. Guess we have a new coven initiate."

Adam grinned. "I see a handfasting in the near future."

Theo blushed. "Guys. Stop."

"Noooooo!"

Theo looked up, startled, at the dark thing dropping straight down.

• • • •

SCARECROW SHOVED THEO, rolling her sprawling out of the way, centering himself under Mark a split second before the man landed. Scarecrow had served as a soft landing for friends many times. He didn't mind. Bones could break—straw only compacted. He wasn't prepared for it to hurt this time, and the dagger through his shoulder sent an additional jolt of fire along his arm. Screeching incoherently, Mark raised the dagger to stab again.

Scarecrow grabbed the man's collar in his good hand and shoved the rough straw of his open wrist into Mark's nose. Mark choked, struggled, coughed. "I've had about enough of you," Scarecrow snapped. "You're just a flying monkey without wings. If you ever bother Theo again, I will feed you my straw 'til you choke on it. Understand?"

Theo kicked Mark's head from the side. The man slumped over, eyes rolling up.

"And if you ever touch my Scarecrow again, I'll sew your balls under your nose so everyone can see what a dickhead you are!" she yelled.

Scarecrow blinked at her. "I wasn't done."

"I am. With this jackass, anyway."

"Guys, that was super cool and all, but we gotta go," Arturo said. He hooked a thumb over his shoulder. "Van's parked right out there, assuming no one's towed it yet."

"Arturo, you go check. Adam, see if these children brought any more zip ties and take care of this trash," Gwyn commanded, pointing at Mark. "I see security peeking their heads out now all the fun's over. I'll deal with them."

She lumbered purposefully toward a man with a badge who was running down the slanting pathways toward them.

"Are you all right?" Theo touched Scarecrow's shoulder.

"I will be." He smiled for her. Everything hurt. Experiencing all of the physical world would take a great deal of adjustment.

"Here's your feet. I'll stitch 'em back on real quick." Theo knelt, her magic thread appearing. She tugged his torn burlap feet from his boots and deftly began sewing them back on his legs. As she worked the glowing thread back and forth, her body moving up and down, her generous breasts strained the open collar of her blouse.

Then again, some physical experiences were absolutely extraordinary, and he felt eager to experiment in more detail.

Perhaps a bit too eager. Theo glanced up. "Okay, how's that feel?" She noticed the effect she was having.

Embarrassed, he adjusted his position, tried to smooth his tunic down.

She ducked her head, face reddening, giggling. "Never mind. I see how it feels."

"Sorry," he mumbled. His lack of control was mortifying. How did meat men deal with this?

"I'm not." She grinned at him.

The guard tried to peer around Gwyn. "Ma'am, I need all of you to come with me now. We'll sort this all out up front." He spoke into a rectangular box. "Base, I have a scarecrow with a hurt leg down here, and another guy looks unconscious." He paused, listening to garbled words Scarecrow didn't quite hear. "That's what I said, a scarecrow with a hurt leg."

"Shit," Theo giggled, hastening her stitches on the other foot. She thrust his own hand at him. "Hold this." He shoved it in a pocket.

The guard scowled. "Hey. Hey, you! Scarecrow! And you, miss. Weren't you here last week with this same stunt?"

"Time to go," muttered Theo, pulling Scarecrow to his feet. He stumbled into a run with her, heading for the exit. Adam waited there, holding the door open, beckoning wildly. Theo laughed, her hand over Scarecrow's, pulling him along as he tried to regain his balance. Feeling returned to his feet as he went.

His eyes met hers. They shared a grin. "You *are* that kind of witch, and by all crows, I believe you're fae to boot," he told her.

She laughed. "Be fae, do crimes. Come on!"

They ran for the open door. Moonlight shone through the trees outside. He stumbled again and she hauled him upright. He was light on his feet, a stuffed thing, held together by her magic, yanked along by this wonderful madwoman witch.

Why, she could strawhandle him all she liked. He didn't mind anymore. She was, after all, his heart's true desire.

35

Everyone was too exhausted to drive home after they finally retrieved Gwyn from the local police station. She hadn't given the cops anything useful, arguing loud and long about religious freedom and a witch's need to be in a sacred spot on Halloween night and just how reliable were these witnesses who claimed to have seen tiny flying faeries and a giant made of moving rocks, anyway? Theo waited down the street with the others at a fast-food place for two hours before the cops grudgingly allowed Gwyn to walk out uncharged, but permanently banned from the House on the Rock. The clean-up back at the House was no doubt a pain in the ass for the staff.

Theo felt a little guilty, but not remorseful enough to confess to any involvement. Maybe next month she could send them some funds anonymously for repairs. At least the Unseelies only trashed part of one room.

They dropped the shellshocked Jeremy by his car to return to Appleton, with a warning to steer clear of Mark thereafter. Mark remained at the police station. Theo frankly didn't care what they decided to do with him. If the cops came by to question her back home, she'd refer them to the Van Baum family lawyers. Make her family ties useful for once.

She called around and finally found a single room at a motel a short drive out of Spring Green. Despite Theo's worry that an angry Ozian witch would bang on the door, or a gang of Wheelers would roll into the parking lot, she found her eyelids drooping while she sewed Scarecrow's other hand back on and helped wipe the extinguisher foam from his chest. *Gonna have to make him a new tunic. Again.*

"You should rest," he urged.

"What if—"

Gwyn relaxed on one of the two queen beds in the motel room, sighing deeply as she laid her glasses on the side table. "The gateway is closed. There won't be anything else bothering us from Oz."

"How can you be sure?" Theo demanded.

"Can't you feel it?"

"Like getting out of the pool after a long swim," Adam said. "Feels like we all got soaked but now everything is warm and dry again."

Theo was too anxious to lie down. Adam and Arturo stripped off their outer clothes and crawled into the second bed. Gwyn yawned. "Get some sleep, Theo. Everything's peaceful now. Blessed Samhain."

Scarecrow settled on a small loveseat by the window. "I'll keep watch," he promised. With the room lights out, only dim illumination outlined the edges of the curtains. Theo sat next to him. He shifted over to make room.

"Okay if I just sit up with you?"

He smiled. "Whatever you wish."

Soon the only sounds were the rattle of the heater and the quiet breathing of her friends. Theo snuggled closer to Scarecrow, shivering. Now that the giddiness of their mad dash to the van was long gone, the horrors of the night kept replaying in her head.

His arms enfolded her gently. "Are you all right?" he whispered.

She tucked her head against his chest. "You nearly died."

"This is true. But I didn't, thanks to you."

"That horrible thing I saw trying to come through the portal at the end. Was that Glinda?"

His hand stroked down her hair. "Probably. She'd want to be the first of the fae to step through, I'm sure."

"Horrible." Fresh tears heated her eyes. "How could the books be so far off from the real Oz?"

"Perhaps your author wanted only to paint a delightful picture of a magic land for young children, not attest to a bloody and violent history."

"Are there kids' stories in Oz?"

He chuckled, a low sound rustling the straw in his chest and throat. "Of course. Mothers tell their little ones fanciful tales of a land where the fae cannot go. Where mortals live their entire lives without seeing a single witch, and even the noblemen are mortals like King Pastoria."

"So this world is a faery tale to Oz?"

"I suppose that's one way to view it."

She snuggled into his arms, curling her feet up on the loveseat. They were silent a long time. His warmth calmed her. Maybe everything really was over. Maybe they were actually safe now.

"Scarecrow?"

"Yes, my dear?"

My deah. Heat suffused her. Yeah, he could call her that forever. "Are you sure you're okay with this?"

"Well, it's rather strange actually feeling pressure on my straw, but yes, I'm comfortable if you are."

She shifted so she could see his eyes. "No, I mean, are you okay never going back to Oz? Being in this world?"

He studied her a moment. "You're asking if I'm content to remain with you?"

"Yes."

"Theo," he whispered, "you are my heart's desire. I've been praising whatever goddess you worship for this. For the chance to give you everything I can, do everything I know how to make you happy. I know I'm not as pleasant as a flesh man would be—"

"Stop that," she growled. "I want you just as you are." She raised her head to kiss his lips. A long, soft, sweet kiss.

"Even though my mouth is burlap?"

"I like it."

"And even though my body is crinkly straw?"

"You give the best hugs." She squeezed him for emphasis.

"And the nose?"

She stroked a finger down it. "I definitely stan the nose."

He chuckled. "Interpreter."

She planted a kiss on his nose.

He sighed, nuzzling her hair. "I am inexpressibly happy, Theo. I hope you are too."

"I am." Drowsily, she realized she was falling asleep in his arms.

Scarecrow noticed. "We should get you to bed. You've been through a lot."

"You're the one who got ripped open!"

"I've always said it's not so bad being a scarecrow, when one has friends around to help if anything happens."

"Would you two please shut up and go to bed," Adam mumbled.

"Not moving," Theo grumped. She snuggled tighter against Scarecrow, stroking one hand over his chest to reassure herself he was whole and safe.

He rested his chin lightly atop her head. "Sleep, my love. I'll keep watch."

"You won't go anywhere?"

His arms tightened around her. "Never again. I'm yours, little witch."

She snorted. "I'm not little."

"You're perfect. Just as you are."

She intended to debate him, but it turned out she'd already fallen asleep.

• • • •

WHEN THEY ARRIVED AT her home sometime after noon, Theo darted from one room to another, asking Scarecrow a thousand questions about what he preferred. Patiently, amused, he assured her he really didn't need much in the way of comforts. No, the pumpkins and corn arrangements on her porch didn't make him think of the cornfield where the Wheelers attacked. No, he didn't need her to move any of the furniture, and liked the reading lamp next to the armchair in the parlor. Whatever she had on hand to eat or drink suited him fine, since he couldn't consume any of it.

At last he took hold of her arms, laughing. "Theo. I don't need anything. You don't have to change anything about how you live."

She peered up at him through a wild sheaf of pumpkin-orange hair. "You sure? You'll tell me if you don't like something, okay?"

"I will." He hadn't seen the upper floor yet. Where did she sleep? The idea of perhaps being welcomed into her private chambers finally sent a happy shiver down his straw spine. "May I see any of the upper level? If that's not too much of a secret."

"Oh. Oh, Goddess. I didn't mean to make you feel like you couldn't come upstairs." She blushed. "In fact, um, if you want, I'd love you to sleep with me tonight. In my bed. I mean, be there when I sleep. Since you don't sleep. If you want to."

The idea of holding her all night, his arms around her, filled him with happiness. "I'd dearly love to stay with you. Awake or asleep."

She led him by the hand upstairs and showed him a comfortable chamber with a wide bed. A window set at an angle in the ceiling, as well as others tucked under eaves in the walls, let in abundant sunlight. Pillows and blankets were tossed aside, clothing strewn everywhere. A small bookshelf near the bed held volumes labeled OZ. Perhaps he could finally learn what all this children's story nonsense was about.

"Ugh, it's a mess." She quickly scooped up a pile of clothes, tossing them into a hamper in the open closet.

"Perhaps I can help."

She stared at him. "You want to clean up my room?"

"Oh." This must be a rude suggestion, given her shock. "I'll need you to teach me what is and isn't acceptable here." Just when he'd mastered all the intricacies of court manners, now he'd need to start all over.

"No, I've just never had a boyfriend who wanted to help with chores at all." She fussed with her blouse and skirt. "I've been wearing this like three days now. I must stink. Didn't feel like showering at the motel since I didn't bring anything to change into. You mind if I wash up?"

"Do whatever pleases you." He trailed behind her, curious, when she went into a bathroom next to her bedchamber. A large tub was inset in one wall, a curtain drawn over it.

She paused, arms crossed over her chest. "Okay, I'm gonna get a shower. You might want to leave the room. I splash a lot, and the room will steam up."

This sounded wise. Wet straw was never pleasant, and he feared with this new bodily awareness, a good soaking would feel even worse. How often did it rain in the Outside World? He'd have to ask. So many new things to learn. With a nod, he retreated.

Scarecrow sat on the carpet in the upstairs hallway, in a bright shaft of light through a stained-glass window above the staircase. His straw warmed comfortably. Golden trees languidly swayed outside another window. The sound of running water indoors was strange but not unpleasant, like a waterfall. He cradled the Evstone in one palm, sang the Stone Song again, and as soon as it glowed, called to his friend. "Nick? Nick Chopper, are you there?"

Nick's worried face appeared above the stone. "Scarecrow! You're alive!"

Scarecrow chuckled. "We seem to be having this same conversation too often, my friend."

Nick wiped a tear away. "I wanted to contact you, but then I thought, what if you were...and that was too horrible to face. I'm so sorry."

"Everything is well here," Scarecrow assured him.

"Is that Scarecrow?" Ozma Tip shoved Nick aside, relief plain in her face. "I was so worried the wind caught you too when I saw bits of straw whirling around!"

"Did you cause that?"

"Good heavens, is that the Scarecrow?" The elegantly waxed antennae of Professor H.M. Wogglebug, T.E., appeared over Tip's shoulder. "Here I was concerned perhaps Her Highness' wild spellcasting had finally exasperated you as well as the rest of us, and that cyclone song would prove to be," he paused for effect, "the final straw."

Scarecrow glared at him. "What did we agree about puns?"

Nick pushed the Professor aside. "Don't mind him, he's been strutting around for days since the witches vanished. We all have." His smile was marred by a tear creeping down from his left eye. "It's so good to see you."

"What happened?"

Nick blew out a breath. "Well, everything!"

Scarecrow listened in growing concern as Nick told him of an ambush which wounded the Tiger and captured Lion, the witches' cruel party game on Winter's Eve, how Tip sang and Nick hacked their way through a crowd of fae underground, only to watch helplessly as Glinda sent monsters of the Unseelie Court through a gateway built of dark magic and blood. "We thought all was lost, but then we heard you singing! Was that your witch friend with you?"

"Theo, yes. And several other witches."

"Oh my." The Wogglebug adjusted his spectacles, an affectation which always annoyed Scarecrow, but at least his smugness meant he was recovered. "Well, of course. I'm sure they had no wish for their rule to be usurped by the Oz witches. A matter of territory, assuredly."

"No, they're not like that here," Scarecrow said. "Theo isn't at all like that. They sang with me to keep evil out of their world. That's all."

"If you say so," the Wogglebug said.

"I most certainly do," Scarecrow snapped.

Nick held up both hands in a calming gesture. "We're very glad you survived. Did the spell do much damage on your side?"

"The gateway ripped a hole through me. Glinda meant me to serve as their doorway to this world as well as the material to anchor it. I don't think the wind song added much, as I was already in terrible pain. Oh, it did rip one hand and both feet off. I was tied to a pole at the time."

He recited all this matter-of-factly, but Nick's eyes grew wide and Tip paled. "I'm so sorry, we didn't know!"

"How could you have? Happily, Theo saved me. Nick, she truly is an amazing witch. She closed the portal herself. The other witches gave her their energy, but she was the one who stitched me up, kept the wind from pulling me in."

Nick shuddered. "Please thank her for me."

Tip clasped her hands together. "Scarecrow, I didn't mean for you to get hurt. When I saw your song stopped them all from going through to the Outside World, I realized it might be our only chance to get rid of all of them for good!"

Curious, Scarecrow asked, "Did none of them return to Oz?"

"Not one!" Nick shook his head.

Tip smiled grimly. "Not one single nasty fae. We waited and watched after the wind died down. I sang until I almost passed out, and Nick made me stop. Lion and Nick waited all night in case anything poked its head back out, but nothing did."

"I went back down with a mallet and destroyed that horrible gate," Nick added. "So they'll never be able to use it again. The Unseelies were gone. No sign of them at all. Looked like they dragged off Langwidere's body, too. Good riddance. They went back to whatever deeper caverns they came from."

"How many days has it been since Winter's Eve?"

"Three glorious days," the Wogglebug announced, with a twirl of his mustache.

"And no sign at all of the fae?"

"They're gone," Tip said quietly. "They're not in Oz at all. Don't know where the spell blew them to, don't care. No more fae in Oz."

Scarecrow was sure if they'd ended up in the Outside World, one or more of the witches would've tracked him down right away to express their displeasure. "Oz without any Fair Folk." All of the implications sank into his brains. "Heavens, Tip, you'll need to send envoys to the countries at once! Appoint someone right away to the Ruby Palace, the Quadling villages are so sparsely settled as it is, you'll need to—"

"We have," Nick assured him. His smile was sad. "Wish you were here to take one of the thrones."

"Ruling ill-suited me, my friend."

"Are you coming back?" Tip asked.

Behind the closed door to the bathroom, Theo was singing. Scarecrow couldn't make out the words, but the tune was cheerful. "Nick, do you remember what Glinda said, when she sent me here? The conditions of the magic to keep me living on this side?"

Nick frowned. "You could only live past the full moon if your heart's desire accepted you."

"Yes." He smiled at his friends, at a loss to put into words what he felt.

Nick swallowed, dabbed his eyes with a handkerchief. "I'm happy for you, Scarecrow. I truly am."

"Wait, so is he coming back or not?" Tip demanded.

The Professor laid a spindly hand on her shoulder. "Your Highness, what Scarecrow is saying is he has found his heart's desire, and she loves him as he is."

The Evstone image flickered. "I'll continue to advise you, as often as I'm able,"

Scarecrow promised.

Tip squared up her shoulders and gave him a firm nod. "You better. As your Queen I order you to check in whenever you can." Her clear green gaze softened. "And you must present your wife to me next time, so I can thank her personally."

"Wife!" Crows and blight, he hadn't even considered such an arrangement. Would Theo want that?

Nick's next words were muffled, distorted, as the Evstone's magic sputtered out. "I miss you," Nick said, "but I understand."

Before Scarecrow could respond, the stone went dark.

He sat there, peace disturbed. His wife. Could he ask Theo to make such a sacrifice? Loving him was one thing. Dorothy's harsh words barged into his brains again. How absolutely unsuitable he was for a husband. Silly, floppy, stupid, useless.

No, he couldn't possibly ask Theo to marry him. Surely that was a step too far.

"Scarecrow?"

He stood quickly, nearly falling down the stairs. Didn't matter how much he practiced walking, his boneless limbs meant he'd never be graceful. He'd need to be more careful, now that he could feel pain. A tumble wasn't a careless matter anymore.

"Coming!" He pushed open the bathroom door, steam wafting out.

As Theo drew the curtain away from the tub, he stared. Clear rivulets dripped from her hair down her round shoulders, her generous breasts, the curve of her stomach. Everything revealed.

He wanted to trace her body with his fingertips, explore all her curves and secret places. It took his brains a moment to remind him he was standing there staring at her.

She blushed. "Is this okay?"

"You're beautiful," he murmured.

She ducked her head. "Bullshit. I'm fat, I know it, it's fine."

"You're going to have to explain to me how the shape of your body correlates to standards of beauty. You look wonderful to me."

Her eyes searched his, full of doubt. "You seriously don't see this?"

"I see you're trembling."

"Little cold. Can you get me a towel from the closet there?"

At once he went to her, wrapping a towel around her, pulling her close. Theo giggled, pushing him away, though she kept the towel. "No, you'll get wet!"

"You can always pull my straw out and dry it in the sun."

"There's other things I want to do with you. Can't do them if you're all spread out drying."

A hundred possibilities flitted through his head, dizzying. "Other things?"

Her eyes searched his. "Would you—I mean, I know you've had some bad experiences, but—do you think you might want to, um, explore some things in bed?"

Realization dawned. "Theo, are you saying you want to have physical congress with me?"

If anything, she turned redder, laughing. "Physical—oh Goddess!" She clasped one hand to her mouth, towel wrapped tightly around herself, turning redder.

Dismay dragged his heart to his feet. How foolish to assume she'd want to engage with him in that way. It wasn't as though he'd ever been anyone's lover, not really. His one night with Dorothy was bewildering, dismaying. Such a fool he was still. Well, he could ask Theo to remove this inconvenient organ. He'd be happy just embracing her, kissing her, lying quietly beside her through the night and spending his days in her company. Why, if he hadn't asked Glinda for this absurd alteration to begin with, she wouldn't have had the opportunity to take his straw to make the anchor.

"I am gonna have to teach you some other words. Maybe some dirty ones."

He frowned. "How do you determine which words are clean or dirty?"

"We'll talk about social standards another time." Theo's cheeks were still red. She touched his chest. "And yes, I'd like to have congress with you." He froze, stunned, unprepared for her next question. "So, um, does that actually work?" She nodded at his trousers.

"My legs?" he muttered, his brains utterly jumbled.

"No, your, um..."

"Oh. Er. It's been acting rather oddly."

"What kind of oddly?"

"Well, when you kiss me, or press against me, it turns all hard and hot." Hadn't she noticed? She'd been wedged against him at least twice now when this thing proved embarrassing. "Ever since you enchanted this new body."

She dropped the towel. "You mean like this?"

Her arms drew him in, her warm, soft, wonderful body rubbed right up against his, and Scarecrow gasped at the immediate warmth in his belly and lower down. Never had he imagined being aflame would feel so marvelous, so sublime, and she did it somehow without ever lighting a match.

Didn't matter if she wanted to marry him or not. She judged him good enough to let him explore all these wild new sensations with her. More than he'd hoped for.

He pressed his lips to hers and happily went under her spell.

• • • •

THEO BROKE THE KISS only long enough to lead him to her bed. He held her shoulders, a dazed smile on his face, while she loosened his belt, unbuttoned his tunic. Scarecrow tried to free his arms while she was undoing the buttons and ended up tangled in the tunic sleeves, making her laugh.

He stumbled in the trousers, falling, wincing. "I've never had clothing before which I could take off without coming unstuffed."

"All good." She helped him out of his boots and pants, blushing at the shaft that sprang up immediately once freed. Half of her wanted to just throw him down and mount him. But he was so clearly distressed, so fumbling, he needed a gentle approach.

She coaxed him onto the bed, her heart racing. Sweet Goddess, such an innocent. He wasn't acting like she should feel privileged to be with him, wasn't pushing her down to take what he wanted. What was sex like in Oz? Did fae do things differently?

Oh! Oz. Here she was, selfishly focused on sex, when his friends might still need help. "Hey, we should call Nick, make sure he's all right."

"I did, while you were washing. He's safe. Everyone is." Scarecrow told her Ozma Tip had sung up the cyclone that nearly took him with it, but which swept the Oz witches and all their haughty fae brethren to parts unknown. As he talked, she sank into the bed, and obligingly he lay down with her. Theo held his hands, stroking his fingers, listening in growing amazement.

"Holy crap. So no more witches in Oz at all?"

"Except Tip."

She stared up at the skylight. "Wow."

"It's almost unthinkable, isn't it?"

"Your friends gonna be okay?"

Scarecrow shrugged. "I hope so. I promised to keep checking in with the Evstone. I still have a duty as Royal Advisor which I intend to keep."

"Yeah, no, of course." Theo remembered his farewell note. "Hey. Next time you receive bad news from Oz, or really anything, don't hide it from me, please."

Somber, he brought her hand to his lips, kissing gently. "I am sorry, my dear. That all could have gone very differently, and you..." He shook his head. "I couldn't bear for you to be hurt. No more things withheld, if that's what you prefer."

"That is absolutely what I prefer." She curled her fingers over his, searching his eyes. "Scarecrow, you know I am going to get hurt sometimes. And I'll get old. And one day I'll die. You know that, right?"

He nodded. "I take some comfort in the probability that when that day comes, my magic will die with you."

He clearly meant it. That was the sweetest goddamn thing she'd ever heard.

She stroked a hand over his chest. He crinkled and rustled, the straw yielding to her touch, his burlap skin soft and textured. She wanted to feel him all over her. Trembling, she placed his hand on her breast.

He froze.

"What's wrong?"

"Forgive me, this is—Dorothy made me do that."

"Oh." She stroked his cheek gently. "How about you touch me wherever you want, and I can do the same?"

He nodded. She kissed him. He returned the kiss, embracing her. His fine burlap rubbed deliciously against her breasts, his body holding her warmth. Her fingers roved over his face, his chest, down his sides. Tentatively he stroked one hand over her breast, lingering at the nipple. Theo sighed, pushing up into his palm, encouraging him. She slid one leg over his, pulled him closer. Unusual though his cock was, it felt as hard and ready as any man's pressing against her belly. He groaned, lips still caught in hers.

She let go to ask, "That all right?"

"I think so. Theo, you feel so wonderful. So soft and warm."

She chuckled. "I was going to say the same thing. You're going to be perfect on cold nights."

His voice sounded thick. "Happy to be your pillow, your comforter, anything you want."

She swallowed down the lump in her throat. "You're more than that, Scarecrow." His eyes met hers, worried, searching. How could painted eyes convey so much emotion? She kissed his cheek, his nose. "You're so much more than that."

"Oh Theo." He embraced her tightly, tears beading in his eyes.

Dammit, now she was going to cry too. "Shhh. I love you."

"I love you." He gave a choked-sounding laugh. "How strange that those words should have so much significance. They're so simple."

"Too many people use them without meaning it." She brushed the moisture from his face.

He searched her eyes. "I believe you truly do."

"Scarecrow, I've been looking for a partner who's happy with me just like I am my whole life."

He frowned. "You were with partners who didn't want you?"

"Guess I was there, and convenient. Like you with Dorothy." She kept brushing her fingertips across his face. His eyes closed.

"I was a fool then. Clumsy. Ignorant." His voice was quiet. "I fear I still am. At least when it comes to this sort of thing."

Theo ran her hand over the surprisingly sleek straw poking out of his head. She swallowed, trembling. "You want to learn some new things?"

His eyes opened, deep blue and earnest. "Always."

Her mouth met his. Theo's hand brushed down his body and closed over the hard shaft between his legs. He gasped, embraced her closer, kissed her deeply. Suddenly he broke away. "Theo, stop, I'm on fire!"

She couldn't help it. Giggles bubbled up. "No, you're not."

"Are you sure?" He pulled back worriedly.

"You're not on fire. Promise."

He hugged her again. "This is very strange. It's going to take me some time to become used to your magic."

"That's not magic." Though his body rubbing against her was making her wonderfully hot as well.

"It must be." He stared at her, eyes full of wonder. "Who but a witch could love a scarecrow?"

"Dammit, I am going to make you see how sexy you are." She couldn't take this any longer. Theo pushed him onto his back and straddled his thighs, rubbing herself against him. He groaned, soft hands clasping her hips, stroking down her buttocks, then up again to her breasts. She leaned back with a happy sigh as his fingers explored her. His suede over her nipples felt amazing. All of him felt amazing, all scratchy-soft against her bare skin. If she didn't have a fabric fetish before, she sure as hell did now.

"Theo," he whispered, stroking her sides, "Beautiful Theo. My dearest. I want—I think I want to go further. May we?"

Goddess yes! The feel of him rubbing her in all the right places was driving her crazy. She wasn't sure she could take all of him, but she was wet enough to try. "Yes. I want that. I want you."

"Show me what to do."

"Let me ride you."

"Oh." Confusion spread across his face. "I don't think I'm strong enough to carry you on my back."

Theo broke down laughing, kissing his face, his nose, his mouth.

He returned the kisses, embracing her. "Did I say something amusing?"

"You," she kissed his nose again, "are adorable."

"All right," he murmured. "Theo, are you positive I'm not burning?"

She grinned. "Guess we'd better do something about that." Raising herself up, breathless, she took hold of his shaft, guided him slowly inside.

"Oh!" His back arched, hands gripping her hips tightly. "Theo!"

"Oh my Goddess, Scarecrow," she gasped, easing onto him. So hard, almost too thick for her to handle, but she wanted him. Wanted him filling her. When his cock finally slid all the way into her, she stopped, shuddering, thighs tensed over his, holding his shoulders tight. "Oh fuck yes!"

"Is it all right?" His eyes were full of concern. Far more worried about her than his own pleasure.

"Perfect," she sighed, and started slowly moving. "Oh yes, oh Goddess, so perfect."

Scarecrow moaned, rising off the bed to capture her right nipple in his mouth. His soft burlap and softer tongue swirling around the sensitive flesh sent a shock through her. She jolted atop him, crying out. When he paused, she gasped, "Don't stop, please don't stop, *ahhhhh!*"

She rode him harder, faster, loving his groans, his heat, his touch all over her body. "Sing to me," she begged. "I want to hear your voice."

"Not sure I can right now," he gasped. "Oh! Oh Theo, my sweet witch, my dear one," he cried as she bore down on him again.

Theo's hands braced on his shoulders, loving how he filled her, his heat making her feel she was the one about to burst into flames.

He broke into song.

"O will you race with me, chase with me, dance with me?
Will you harvest the light and keep safe the sun?
Oh yes, I will race you and chase you and dance with you
From the rise of the moon to the set of the sun,
Forever in autumn 'til winter has come.
Forever, my dear one, my light of the sun!"

Instead of making her sleepy, an amber light pulsed from him up into her, filling her, filling the room with warmth and love. "I love you, Scarecrow, my sweet Scarecrow," she panted, delighted at how he thrust up into her, matching her rhythm. His hands roved from her breasts down to their joining. Suddenly his questing thumb pressed into her pearl. Theo screamed, bucking. *"Yes!"*

"Sweet sunlight, Theo," he gasped, "something is—feels like—*ohhh!*"

Beautiful fire filled her, tremors rippling throughout her, every nerve prickling. Shrieking joyously, she bore down hard onto him again, again, felt him shuddering as well, holding her tightly. Breathless, overcome, she collapsed onto him, felt him pulsing inside her. He was wonderful and warm and loved her as just she was and she never wanted to let go of him.

She lay there panting, overcome. Her tears dripped onto him.

With shaking fingers he brushed them from her face. "My dearest one," he whispered. "You are astonishing. Thank you."

She'd crumpled his straw. Rolling off him, she tried to fluff him back into shape with a breathless chuckle. "Ope, sorry about that."

"I'm not." His voice was weak, but he beamed at her. "That was wonderful!"

"Yes, it was." She curled up beside him, his arm around her waist. As her heart gradually slowed, the dizzy waves calmed and she could breathe deeply again. He was staring wide-eyed at the ceiling. "You okay?"

He was quiet a moment, as if taking internal stock. "I believe so. Is this sort of explosion normal?"

She hadn't been sure he'd achieve that, but he could cry, so what the hell. Magic. "It is for meat guys, yeah. You seriously never felt any of this before?"

His fingers traced through her hair. "I couldn't feel much at all before you wove your spells into this body. This is a little overwhelming, to be honest."

"We can go slower. Do more foreplay next time. I kinda got carried away." She nuzzled his nose, kissed his lips. Cuddling next to him felt right, felt perfect.

He blinked. "There's more?"

"Uh, yeah. Lots more." She thought about him kissing his way down her thighs, growing warm all over again. Imagined taking his cock into her mouth. What would he taste like? Struck by the improbability of what he'd just achieved, she said, "So hang on. You said you designed that yourself."

"Yes. Is it not correct?"

"It's a little intimidating. And how the hell is corn not hard all the time?"

"That would be uncomfortable and make wearing trousers difficult." He was ridiculously matter-of-fact about this. "I picked it from the best crop, and had it enchanted. How else should I have made it?"

"If that's actually—how did you even—I mean, I felt you. When you, um. It felt just like it should."

His puzzled frown smoothed out, eyebrows going up. "Oh, you mean the slippery part? Ozian corn is self-buttering."

Theo burst into helpless laughter, clutching him tightly. "Oh no. Oh Goddess. Wow. Oh man, oh no, you're fine, it's fine, it's just I never thought I'd be into cornography."

"Interpreter, please."

She kissed him, slow, deep, and lovingly.

He sighed. "If you don't care for it, perhaps you can make me a better one."

"You'd be okay with that?" Holy crap, a guy who wasn't hung up on his manhood. "You really don't have any ego about this."

"Its entire purpose is to please my heart's desire. And at any rate, I know my brains are my best feature, not my form."

Theo chuckled, stroking his face. His smile stoked the fire in her breast. "No. I love you just as you are. Don't change anything. You are amazing."

He shook his head, still smiling. "I'm just a scarecrow. You're wondrous."

"No, you are."

"Why are we arguing about this? You're clearly far more skilled at love magic."

"Scarecrow, it's not magic. It's practice. Though you are one remarkably good beginner."

"Well, I did read a few books on the subject of love." His smile faded. "I see now how inadequate they all were. Even the one which detailed a husband's duties." He stilled, then sighed and gave her a half-smile. "Foolish of me, I know."

She remembered the emerald ring in its delicate wooden box. "Were you going to propose to Dorothy?"

He grimaced. "As I said, I realize I am still very foolish. I understand now no real woman would want a straw man for a husband."

Theo hiked herself up on an elbow. "I am going to burn that fucking diary. Screw what she thought."

He frowned. "Theo—"

"No! No." She sat up, taking his hands in hers. "I am not letting you do this."

"Do what? If—if you no longer wish to have me as your lover, I can—"

She grabbed his shoulders, pulling him close. Alarm flitted across his features but he didn't resist. "Yes, I want you! And yes you are good enough to be a husband!"

"I am?"

"Yes. You are." She glared at him. He seemed unsure whether to be frightened or relieved. "What did you think my heart's desire meant, anyway?"

"Well, for me, it means I never want to be without you." He gulped. "I would dearly love to spend all my days with you, Theo. In whatever role you'll have me."

"You are my Scarecrow, I am your witch, and if you want me to," she sucked in a breath and spoke the most dangerous words, the most vulnerable words, "I'll be your wife."

She held her breath, waiting. She'd never asked that of Mark, or the boys before him. Never asked because deep down she knew they'd laugh. Though Scarecrow wouldn't mock her, no idea how he'd take it. *Please let him stay, please let him not be like them, he can't be like them, not him—*

"You would have me as your husband? Even though I'm not," he paused, fear in his eyes, "not a real man?"

"Yes you fucking are, and I thought you hated that word!"

"I do."

"Then why would you use it again?"

"Theo, no," he murmured, a smile finally touching his lips again. "I mean, *I do.* If you would truly have me, just as I am."

Heat shot from her heart to her stomach. "You—yes. Fuck yes! Scarecrow, you're exactly what I want. What I need. As long as I'm what you want too."

He chuckled. "I never thought I'd marry a witch, but here we are, and I feel as though I'm going to fly right out your ceiling window."

She laughed, happy tears burning her eyes, and gathered him into an embrace. He hugged back strongly, lovely burlap brushing against her skin. Good Goddess, she'd need to buy more gentle laundry soap at this rate, because she planned to get him wet and dirty a lot. Their mouths sealed in a fierce kiss, his hands stroked from her breasts down her hips, and she fell back, pulling him onto her.

He broke the kiss, head turning toward the window. "Is that your door chime?"

"Who the fuck," Theo growled, clambering across the bed to peer out the window. The bedroom overlooked the porch roof so she couldn't see who was at the door, but she didn't recognize the car in the driveway. It wasn't a cop car, thank the Goddess. The doorbell rang again, followed by knocking.

Theo snatched a baby wipe from her bedside table to clean up and tossed another at Scarecrow. Baffled at first, he caught on and copied her. She grabbed a nightshirt from a pile of clean laundry and stuck her feet into slippers. Brushing her hair roughly with her fingers, she decided, *Screw it, whoever's interrupting is gonna damned well see what they're interrupting.*

Scarecrow hurriedly cleaned up and dressed as well, putting the pants on backwards, tangling his arms somehow in his tunic. Theo pulled it all off and helped him do it right. The bell kept ringing. Scarecrow scowled. "How annoying. Would it be rude to simply ignore whoever it is?"

"Maybe. But I want them to know they're being rude for interrupting us. Nothing like making someone seriously uncomfortable to ensure it never happens again." She stomped downstairs. The house was darker than normal. She should pry all the boards off the windows, and get the plate glass replaced in the studio. Let light back into the place. Winter would arrive any day, and she'd want all the sunlight she could get.

Of course, staying in bed with Scarecrow as much as possible sounded good too, and her bedroom windows let in enough light.

Scarecrow ducked into the parlor as she approached the front door. He emerged wielding a fireplace poker. Theo exchanged a determined glance with him, braced her shoulders, and unlatched the door.

Standing on her porch, eyes wide as a deer in headlights, was the Oz historian who'd given the lecture at the museum.

"Oh shit," Theo muttered.

"Hello," said the historian. He looked over her shoulder, where she could hear Scarecrow rustling, then back at her. "Ah. You're Dorothea, right?"

"Nobody calls me that," she growled, then realized she'd just confirmed her identity. This guy must've tracked down the plates on the RV, got her address from her parents or Danny. "Crap."

"Sir, you are interrupting," Scarecrow announced, moving closer to Theo.

The historian turned red. "I, ah, see that. I'm sorry. But I need to talk to you. Do you still have the diary?"

"Yeah. Was gonna mail it back. You can take it if you want." Theo glanced at Scarecrow, who nodded. "We don't need it anymore."

The historian adjusted his glasses, his gaze fixed on Scarecrow. "What happened back at the Museum—your song. That was a spell, right? You're real. Oz is real?"

Scarecrow exchanged another look with Theo, raising an eyebrow.

She sighed. "Yeah. Let me guess, you want to know all about it."

"I very much do. If that would be all right?"

"Depends. You turning us in for stealing the diary?"

"No, if you're willing to give it back."

Scarecrow sighed. "I no longer need it."

"You're real," the historian murmured, staring at him. "The actual living Scarecrow of Oz."

Theo knew a true fan when she saw one. Well, what the hell. She stepped back. "You wanna come in?"

"May I? Yes, thank you. Hi. Jim Thicke." He offered a handshake. Theo accepted.

She didn't want to share her Scarecrow with the world, but maybe an hour or two with someone who'd studied all the books would be allowable. "I'll make some coffee. Or do you want tea instead?"

"Oh, whatever you have is fine. I really just want to talk to you both." The man's eyes shone with hope. "I want to hear about Oz." Though he was clearly an older gent, right now he was a kid again, caught up in faery stories about a magic land of tin men and Munchkins.

Boy, did he have some hard truth coming.

Theo gestured to the living room. "Come on in, have a seat. I'll start some tea." She stretched up to give Scarecrow a kiss. He kissed her back eagerly, smiling when she released him. Theo smiled at the astonished historian, then headed for the kitchen.

"Coffee for me, please," Scarecrow called after her.

The historian asked, "You drink coffee?"

"No, I can't drink. The scent helps sharpen my brains." His tone was calm, contented, and Theo could picture the smile on his face.

Snickering, she pushed through the kitchen door and started the coffee pot and the kettle. Sunlight dappled the floor, though the room was a little chilly. Tonight would be freezing, and any day now snow could arrive with a vengeance. She imagined curling up with Scarecrow under the blankets, and grinned.

Down the hall, she heard the warm tenor of her love's voice, speaking in that adorable not-quite-Boston accent, telling the historian the truth about Oz. She'd let the man stay the afternoon, send him home with a lot to think about. Then she'd take Scarecrow back upstairs. Or maybe not, maybe they'd stay in the pile of blankets in the living room. She wouldn't need a fire to be warm in his arms. He'd sing to her, his beautiful voice giving her sweet dreams, safety, comfort.

This time, she knew when she awoke, he'd be there. Smiling at her. Adorkably crinkly all over and happy to be with her, just as she was. Her Scarecrow. Her *husband*. Warmth spread throughout her body. Her perfect partner. Screw that stuff about not looking any further than her own backyard. Sometimes your heart's desire could only come from some-place very far away.

Damn. At some point they'd have to break the news to her family. They could wait, all except Gramma Hildy. She'd get around to telling the rest of them eventually. Maybe after the wedding.

Like in twenty years or so.

Theo made the coffee extra strong. Who knew what wonderful things those magic brains might come up with, given the proper provo-cation? Carrying mugs into the living room, she felt warm and happy anew when Scarecrow smiled again and thanked her.

She wrapped a throw blanket around them both, leaned into him, sipped her tea, and contemplated teasing him under the blanket while he tried to focus on the historian.

Scarecrow smiled at her. Still hard to believe he was all burlap. So ex-pressive.

"Don't even think about it, my dear," he murmured in her ear.

The historian was going on about how much he'd loved the books as a child.

Surprised, she replied, "About what?"

"Performing some mischief on me right now."

"Or else what?"

"Or else," he whispered, as the historian stammered to a halt, "I will remove a single straw from my body and tickle you mercilessly with it."

She sucked in a breath.

Scarecrow turned back to the historian. "Excuse us. You were say-ing?"

Theo choked back a mad giggle, gulping hot tea.

He was her Scarecrow. He belonged here. And she was over the rain-bow to be his dear little witch.

the end

Author's Note and Acknowledgements

This book crept into my head during rewrites for my previous novel, *Straw Man*, which also involves a witch and (sort of) a scarecrow. Theo was created as a friend for greenwitch Cassie, and she stomped into every scene she was in and took it over, so I knew she needed her own book. The image of a witch kissing a scarecrow which finished out *Straw Man* stuck with me and took on a life of its own.

I rewatched the classic MGM *Wizard of Oz*. I re-read the first few Oz books by L. Frank Baum and sought out more. Books. Comics. Dark Oz and alt-Oz. Though I hadn't delved into Oz since childhood, the characters came to life again for me immediately, and as an adult I more thoroughly appreciate the Wogglebug's smugness and awful puns, Scarecrow's insecurity over his intelligence, Nick Chopper's sensitivity, the undercurrent themes of identity and acceptance. I love these characters. I wanted to do something with them.

Then while driving back from Windigo Fest in Manitowoc, Wisconsin, on a dark and rainy October night along a rural road, I thought *What if Scarecrow went on a road trip with a witch* and the bones of this story fell into place.

Nearly a year of researching, writing, rewriting, and taking a deep dive into the wonderful and welcoming online Oz community followed. I decided to use the first three books as my starting point *(The Wonderful Wizard of Oz, The Marvelous Land of Oz,* and *Ozma of Oz)* and ran wild from there into darker, more adult territory.

No matter how much I love Scarecrow and Theo, this book wouldn't have happened without the support and encouragement of my friends, and the wonderful skills of the pros who agreed to take on this project with me.

Deepest gratitude goes to:

My partner Scott, who yet again suffered months of being an author partner while I threw myself into writing as often as I could. You are always my model for a perfect partner, love.

My friend and publisher Sue London, who agreed to jump into a 120-year-old fandom with me, and who makes an excellent sounding board for all romance ideas. (Also, she writes killer adventure Regencies and you should read her books. bysuelondon.com)

My editor Julie Hutchings, for making the transition from longtime online friend to challenging and encouraging editrix so smoothly. She took a decent lump of rock here and made it into an emerald. (Also, she writes fierce dark fantasies and you should read her books. juliehutchings.net)

Artist Sandra Chang-Adair, for bringing Theo and Scarecrow so vividly to life with her cover illustration, and for doing such beautiful work on such a short deadline. She took my verbal descriptions of the characters and of the action and painted a cover I can't stop grinning over. (Also, she has a gorgeous portfolio at sandrachang.net and you should go look.)

Thanks also to my beta readers Erin, Erica, Suren, and Scott, for their honest and thoughtful reactions to this story, and suggestions for improving it for both Ozian readers and folks unfamiliar with Baum's books. Each one of you enriched this tale, and by turns delighted me and made my brains work harder. (As you know, it's all about the brains.)

Thanks to Jane Albright, head of the International Wizard of Oz Club, for taking the time to virtually walk me through the layout of the Oz Museum in Wamego, Kansas for the heist chapters. (Check out ozclub.org, ozis.us, and ozmuseum.com for a ton of great Ozian stuff!)

Thanks also to John Fricke for his entertaining and informative blog posts about all things Oz (allthingsoz.org/blog); to Christianna Rickard for her written reminisces about Oz and her Uncle Ray; to Erica and Colin for inviting me to speak during OzCon International 2021 and for being generally awesome people (ozconinternational.com); and to the entire online Oz community on Facebook for being so welcoming, knowledgeable, and entertaining!

A special thank you to Zoe and Sean of the "Spirit of Oz" troupe. I happened to befriend these lovely people during the writing of the most emotional chapters of *Straw Song,* and came to recognize important things about myself with their unwitting influence. Realizing deeper connections of identity between myself and Scarecrow, as I wrote him, has been wonderfully life-changing, and I don't think any of it would've struck me without reading Zoe's experiences. Also, Zoe's portrayal of Scarecrow is absolutely wonderful, and she makes a deliciously wicked witch as well! (thespiritofoz.com)

As always, much gratitude is due my friends and family who've tolerated me going on about Oz for a year now. I love all of you, so I'll warn you now: *there will be more books.* I'm sorry. I can't help it. Talk to my damned muses who won't shut up.

Thank you to every reader. You make this adventure possible!

{{{clawhugs}}}

K.

also by K.A. Silva:
WENDIGOGO
STRAW MAN